Indiana Historical Society

Indiana Historical Society Publications

Diary of William Owen

Indiana Historical Society

Indiana Historical Society Publications
Diary of William Owen

ISBN/EAN: 9783741186769

Manufactured in Europe, USA, Canada, Australia, Japa

Cover: Foto ©Andreas Hilbeck / pixelio.de

Manufactured and distributed by brebook publishing software
(www.brebook.com)

Indiana Historical Society

Indiana Historical Society Publications

Indiana Historical Society

PUBLICATIONS.

Volume 4.

INDIANAPOLIS:
THE BOBBS-MERRILL COMPANY.
1895.

CONTENTS OF VOL. IV.

INDIANA HISTORICAL SOCIETY PUBLICATIONS.

VOLUME IV.   NUMBER 1.

DIARY

OF

WILLIAM OWEN

From November 10, 1824, to
April 20, 1825

EDITED BY

JOEL W. HIATT

INDIANAPOLIS:
THE BOBBS-MERRILL COMPANY.
1906.

PREFACE.

The manuscript of this diary of William Owen has remained in the hands of his only daughter—formerly Mary Francis Owen, now Mrs. Joel W. Hiatt—for many years and its existence, save to a few, has been unknown. It is fragmentary in form. It is possibly the close of a journal which had been kept for years before. Its first sentence in the original is an incomplete one, showing that there was an antecedent portion. The picture of the times is so graphic than the Indiana Historical Society publishes it, on account of its historical value. Mr. Owen was 22 years old at the time of its composition. 106850

William Owen was the second of four sons born to Robert and Ann Caroline Owen, of Scotland. Their names were Robert Dale, William, David Dale, and Richard. Three of them, Robert Dale, David Dale and Richard are known where ever the sun shines on the world of literature or science. William, who, because of habit or for his own amusement, wrote this diary is not known to fame. He was the second son, Robert Dale being his senior by one year. He was born in Scotland in 1802. His father, Robert Owen, was one of the most successful cotton manufacturers of the United Kingdom. His last factory was situated in New Lanark, on the Clyde, in Scotland. It had been built by David Dale, the maternal grandfather of William Owen, and had been purchased of him by Robert Owen and associated capitalists.

David Dale had occupied an exalted position in the business portion of Scotland by reason of his sagacity, his wealth and his high moral qualities. His factory operatives were distinctly better off morally and physically than the most of those in the United Kingdom.

When Robert Owen bought this establishment it was his ambition to make it the model in all the world as regards the physical, moral and intellectual condition of its operatives. To this end he bent all the energies of his great executive abilities. New Lanark became the place to which the feet of philanthropists of the world were turned. The number of visitors from 1815 to 1825, the year in which Robert Owen bought the village and lands of New Harmony, Ind., according to the register at New Lanark, was nearly 20,000. It was in such an atmosphere that the first years of William Owen's life were spent. The spirit of the place was one of intense business activity, rigid system and all pervading benevolence. His education up to the age of 15 years was conducted by private instructors.

At the age of 15 he, with his brother Robert Dale, was sent to one of the most unique institutions of learning in the world, the college of M. deFellenberg, at Hofwyl, in Switzerland. The instruction was under the most eminent professors and embraced all the branches of learning, but its great peculiarity lay in the spirit which pervaded the place and its mode of regulating the entire student life. The professors exercised no authority outside the class room. The discipline was committed to the student body who chose from their number their own rulers and who made all laws for their government, subject only to the veto of Von Fellenberg, a power which he rarely exercised.

Princes and impecunious students stood on terms of perfect equality. Those became rulers in the student body who were thought to be best fitted for such positions, regardless of the rank of their parents. The ideal which this body placed before itself was perfect manlines and uprightness of character, coupled with strict attention to their duties. What a fine training for a citizen of a republic !

William Owen completed the course here in three years, when it is supposed he returned to New Lanark to engage in its activities. Nothing is known of his life between his graduation at Hofwyl and the commencement of this diary in 1824.

His father was coming to this country to inspect the property of Rappites at Harmony, Ind., with a view to its purchase and to the establishment of a community there in which he hoped not only to duplicate the great good that he had accomplished at New Lanark, but to greatly improve on the happy conditions which he had established there. He chose William Owen to accompany him and it is an account of that journey which is given in the accompanying narrative. This is not the place to discuss the philosophy of Robert Owen or the reasons for his failure to realize his cherished ideals. They were noble; and his sons having been reared amid the benign influences of New Lanark, and having witnessed the great good that he accomplished there were in hearty sympathy with his plans. It may not be amiss to invite the attention of the reader to the reflections of Mr. Owen on the subject of a community in the latter portion of his journal. They evince rare wisdom in one so young.

When Robert Owen arrived in New Harmony, after having returned to England, William Owen assumed for a short time the editorial care of the New Harmony Gazette, a paper which they established in 1825. Soon, however, he relinquished that to take charge of the busines interests of the family. He superintended the conduct of a general store which had been acquired from the Rapps. From that time on his life was given to business. He helped to establish the Posey County Agricultural Society. It was designed to stimulate by competition the production of the best in that line. He organized the Thespian Society for the production of plays. His activities were incessant and unwearied in all directions that promised to promote the happiness and welfare of the people. In 1835 he was an incorporator of a proposed Manual Labor College. In 1834 he was chosen by the Evansville Branch as Director of the State Bank of Indiana. Dr. Schneck says of him in this connection: "And, indeed, he was always selected to make out the yearly exhibit of their financial condition."

His activities were not confined to the humdrum of personal business but he extended his investigations to the domain of national finance. As showing his erudition in this field I produce an autograph letter addressed to him by James Buchanan, of Pennsylvania, then a leading member of the U. S. Senate.

Washington, 22 February, 1842.

"Dear Sir:

I have been honored by the receipt of your letter of the 27 ultimo accompanied by your plan of an Exchequer. You will perceive from the reports of the Committees of the Senate and the House that they have adopted some of its principal features. What may be the result, it is not possible for me to predict; but for myself I feel strongly disinclined to authorize this Government to issue any paper currency intended for circulation or to deal in the exchanges of individuals, no matter what restrictions may be imposed by law to prevent the abuse of the power. I entertain strong doubts both of the constitutionality and expediency of any such measures.

Whilst I say this, however, I must do you the justice to declare that in my humble judgment, your plan evinces a thorough acquaintance with the subject and it is developed with clearness and force."   Yours respectfully,

JAMES BUCHANAN.

WILLIAM OWEN, ESQ.

From the editorial writings in the Gazette, from fugitive scraps of poetry which he left, and from two Fourth of July orations which he delivered in New Harmony it may be justly concluded that his literary abilities were of a high order and that, had he chosen that sphere of life, he would have shone with as much brilliancy as did his brother Robert Dale Owen. His oration on the Fourth of July, 1835, is especially rich in exalted, generous sentiment expressed in noble and commanding diction.

Mr. Owen died in New Harmony in 1842, at the age of 40 years.

JOEL W. HIATT.

New Harmony, Ind., January 16, 1896.

DIARY OF WILLIAM OWEN.

Wednesday 10th November, 1824.

We sailed from one of the wharfs on the North River. Opposite to us was Hoboken, a small village. Having the tide in our favor, we sailed on at 10 or 12 knots per hour. The banks of the Hudson are at first rather flat, with small heights on which houses are prettily scattered.

After some time we passed the spot where the river divides, forming the north and east branch of the Hudson River, thereby enclosing Manhattan Island on which New York is situated and which constitutes the county of the same name.

In ascending the river, the hills gradually increase in height, forming, after some hours sail, the Palisades, which are a range of perpendicular rocks rising from a sloping bank on the west side of the river to a height varying from 200 to 550 feet. . About one o'clock the day became rather gloomy, but it soon cleared off and turned out a fine evening. At 2 we went to dinner. My Father got a ticket to the Ladies Cabin, but Capt. McDonald and myself dined with the men. We had scarcely ventured down before, as they kept the room very warm and close. We got enclosed among farmers, some of whom if anything caught their eye, would pull their fork out of their mouths and stretching over, would plunge it into the favored dish. I tasted for the first time, but did not much relish, the sweet potatoe.

After dinner, we entered upon what is called the Highlands. This is really very beautiful scenery, quite as fine as any to be seen on the Scotch lakes. We walked the deck almost the whole day till dark. The hills are almost uniformly covered with wood, which generally retiring a

(7)

little from the river, leaves a plane below, which, elevated 80 or 100 feet above the river, finishes with an abrupt descent. Many of the hills were 13, 14 and 1500 feet high. The highest are Anthony's Nose, the Sugarloaf and Butter Hill. The turnings of the river are often sudden so as to present to view the appearance of a lake enclosed by finely wooded mountains on all sides. On the top of an eminence above West Point lies a fort, further down a military Academy and close upon the river a village, occupied by persons connected with the military.

During the whole day, we passed sloops and other small vessels, passing up and down the river. Indeed on leaving New York the view of the bay and the numerous vessels sailing to and fro presented a very lively appearance. A little before dark, a most beautiful scene presented itself. Several of the most lofty Mountains projected themselves in to the river, as a fine and bold foreground, while the river opening into a large bay presented a long continued range of romantic hills in the distance, with the town of Newburgh and several other villages on its banks. During the day we passed continually log houses and landings. Many of the houses were painted a bright pink. We passed a low flat on which were a number of hay stacks. This was a swamp but as soon as frost sets in they are then are enabled to bring horses upon it and so carry home the hay. Even after dark, continued walking up and down under an awning spread over the after part of the vessel, as the night continued mild. The awning had been riddled by the sparks of fire which, issuing from the engine chimney, occasionally fell upon it and burned round holes in it. We obtained berths in the Ladies Cabin and retired between 9 and 10. Not much sound sleeping.

Thursday, 11th, November.

At 6 we were called by the Steward, having arrived at. Albany, after passing Athens, Hudson etc., some hours before. We went to the Eagle and after getting washed, breakfasted about 8. The inn or tavern is a large house with good rooms. They have a drawing room to retire into till the bell sounds. Perhaps 50 persons sat down to breakfast. As the Legislature is sitting here at present, going on with the elections, the city being the seat of government for New York, the Inn is more than usually crowded.

After breakfast, we sat down to write, My Father going out to call on DeWit Clinton: He soon returned and said we should go immediately to the Shaker settlement near Wiskeyana, about 7 miles distant. We set out in a light carriage, calling in passing by, on Lieut. Gen'l, the Honorable Stephen Van Rensselaer, called the Patrone, being a very extensive landed proprietor and possessing the only entailed estate in the Union. He invited us to dinner next day and gave us several ppublications, issuings of the neighboring counties. We then proceed over a very rough road, either deep in mud or sand, through forests of low oaks and white and yellow pine. In driving along we were much pleased with the scenery, bounded in the distance by the Katskill Mountains.

At half past 11 we arrived at Waterwhich, 7 miles N. W. of Albany, Shaker Settlement, founded by Ann Lee, and were shown into a house where we were received by a woman to whom we gave a letter we brought from DeWit Clinton, and who at first, was very stiff and formal, though ready to communicate anything in her power. Soon after, a man named Seth Young Wells, who appears to be a leading man amongst them, came in and we then proceeded with him to view their settlement, having then a glass of Metheglia, made from honey. It consists of 3 or 4 good brick buildings and a number of substantial loghouses.

We first entered a large building which is the workshop of the men. We found here whip-makers, joiners, shoemakers, tailors, etc. They make a number of whips for

sale, but said they made them too light because they
sell better.   We saw several articles in joining very
nicely made, particularly some screws made from hickory.
They appear to make their working utensils themselves.
There were pieces of white and yellow (the common) pine,
of cedar, ash etc. laying about. We found several young
people learning the tailor and shoemaker trades. The shoemakers did not appear healthy. The women wear rather
high heeled shoes, because by keeping the heel warm it pre-
vents them catching cold. We saw both boots and shoes in
progress. They showed us some silver pens of their own
making which slide upon black handles, and some of which
are in silver cases with a pencil at one end, like wise some
very neat pipes, the heads of clay, the handles of a kind
of osier. My father showed them a Rhodium pen. Sometime afterwards, a brother came in when they asked that
it might be shown to him, which was done. I suppose it is
he who makes them. We saw but few men, perhaps 10 or
a dozen. They had uniformly, reddish brown trousers, a
gray or brownish gray frock coat, with a folding over
collar, peaked in the center behind, either with hooks and
eyes or buttons, or a weggoners frock or gray cloth, a large
old fashioned waistcoat of the same, with glazed colored
metal buttons, boots or shoes, a colored neckcloth and a
large broad brimmed, brown gray cloth or straw hat, some
even bound around the edge.

From the workshop, we proceeded to the blacksmith's
shop, where we found no one at work but saw two little
boys who are learning the business. They have two forges.
We were then summoned to dinner about 10 o'clock. We
were shown into a middle sized room, where we found dinner laid out for four, having been joined soon after we arrived by a whaler from Massachusetts. They told us to be
quite at our ease as the room was our own. We found a
large pewter basin of milk-warm water, in which we
washed our hands before sitting down. We were waited

upon by two females, the males having all retired. The females were dressed in brown worsted gowns, white quaker shaped caps and silk handkerchiefs, every thing put on very neatly. All we had was cooked very nicely. They gave us stewed veal, boiled beef, pork and potatoes, kedney potatoes and turnips and mashed squashes, a fruit that grows like a gourd and dried apple pies,—a plate of each apiece—besides common and sage cheese, excellent butter, bread made from corn and rye and wheat and rye, and cider. Such a dinner that though we were anxious to taste every thing it was almost impossible. During dinner, we had each of us a table napkin, besides each a napkin to lay bread on. After dinner, we again washed our hands. We then viewed the kitchen and cooking apparatus which was very complete indeed. Two women cooked for the whole number, at present 99. They are in all about 250, within a few miles of each other, but divided into three families, each family having everything in common. They had dined at 12 o'clock. They dine in two separate parties, the women at a different table from the men on account of greater convenience. Two females wait at table. Each female is in her turn cook and waiting maid for a month or sometimes for two months at a time. These dine after the others. They said they found not the least difficulty in arranging these matters, every one being quite disposed to take her turn. We talked a long while with a number of females in the dining room. They were dressed as those formerly described, with the exception of cotton instead of silk handkerchiefs. Those whom we saw out of doors had gray silk, quaker shaped bonnets.

From the dinning room we proceeded to the bed rooms, where we found two beds for two persons each with a gray woolen coverlet, turned down at top showing two beautifully white pillows. The rooms were uncommonly neat and clean. Floors well fitted of stained pine very glossy, the walls white washed, a little mirror and drawers and

other conveniences in the sides of the room. The floors
covered with gray worsted cloth. In each we found an
iron stove, well contrived, with a ventilator at the floor,
to create a draft and ventilate the apartment. We afterwards entered a sitting room where the females assemble
in the evenings for sewing, knitting etc. By means of folding doors or using springs, they can throw this and the
adjoining room and passage into one, to form a place for
meeting in the evening for worship. Two buildings are
appropriated for dwellings. The women sleep on the one
side of the house and the men at the other but they have
continual opportunities of talking to one another, meeting
very often with each other. We now proceeded to the
women's workshops. On the road, the church and school
houses and washing house were pointed out. All the other
buildings are connected with the farm. We found seven
or eight females weaving and reeling. They were making
cottons or linens: not very fine but stout. They buy the cotton thread. We talked a good while with the women who
did not appear at all too bashful but quite at their ease, as
if they were talking to one another.. Some of them had
graceful manners and many, particularly of the elderly ones,
were good looking enough. By this time they had lost
all their reserve and seemed quite pleased, particularly as
my Father explained many things he meant to do on their
plans, and often said very right, quite right, when they explained many things they did. The only peculiarity in
their conversation is yea and nea instead of yes and no.

After this, we visited their tannery and curriery etc. We
saw some very well dressed skins. On asking if they
found any difficulty in finding persons willing to undertake
the more unpleasant occupations, they replied none. Some
chose some particular trade, others made no choice. Blacksmith's work they found very severe; but few of them able
to support it. We saw some very large hogs. They feed
them on ground corn mixed with very hot water and al-

lowed to stand 24 to 48 hours. They have 20 or 30 cows and 150 sheep, some of them merinos. They have large sheep folds covered, with open pens close by. We saw a threshing mill in one barn and a machine for making cider, as well as one for grinding the apples first.

A cart drives in above and pours them into a hopper. We then saw the school house scarcely fitted up as yet. In summer and winter they have a day school. None just now, but a little instruction at night. We saw them making cheese; and in a barn a large quantity of corn. They have a washing machine like an inverted fulling machine. After this we visited their cellar. There we found a large quantity of cider. We observed also at a distance a large orchard of apple trees. We then returned to the house we called at first, and bought two silver pens, on account of the society, and a large whip of their manufacture, for which we paid two dollars. They had previously given us two pipes each. Three or four elders and deacons govern them. Whatever they determine, the rest follow.

After being in the carriage they asked us our names; we gave them our cards and came away very much gratified. They too, seemed pleased with us though when we came away and shook hands, they did not seem quite to understand it. I dare say, they had not met with such visitors before. I do not know when I have spent a day so agreeably before. Even this sample made us all in love with a community.

One man whom I asked what he did when he wanted a coat, said, he asked for one and that they often wished him to take more coats than he required. They have no private property. Some of them are usually traveling for pleasure or visiting relatives. This is done at the expense of the society. One woman said she was at Jersey this year and had travelled 600 or 700 miles. They have about 1,000 acres rented from Gen'l. Rensselaer. This land was originally poor but they have improved it much. They consider the situation, being now drained and worked, very healthy. They have but little snow. They have a surgeon who was absent this day at New York, but in difficult cases they call in another from Albany. We did not see any agricultural occupations, this not being the season for it, but I observed a number of bee hives from which the metheglia is made. They must have some very ingenious fellows amongst them, for we found a number of admirable little contrivances and conveniences. They showed us a spinning jenny made in Lebanon, another establishment about 25 miles from Albany but they do not use it. If one society makes what another does not, they make fair exchanges of labor and do not use any money in the exchange. We found some very neat carriage wheels made at Lebanon, of oak. The end of the axles were boxed in. They made their own looms, which were very neat.

All the society, from their contenance, appeared happy and contented. They labor as much as they feel inclined to and no more. They said they would be unhappy if they did not labor. Of course as they get old, they do less. The women who weave every thing are only employed in that department perhaps one-half day; the remainder, they employ in household work etc. The men too, have often a change of employment; indeed, one man can sometimes follow several trades. They appear quite aware of the advantage of union, but seem to consider their principles or similar ones, as the only bond of union that can keep them united. When my father talked of establishing communities, they asked: of Quakers? or Jews? or what ? and shook their heads when they found it was for all sects. They were at first, very poor but seem now very comfortable. For those who wish to join the society, there is a house of probation, where they dwell till they determine upon conforming in all respects to the Shaker views and habits. They often take children from common society and bring them up amongst them, thus keeping up their numbers, for they account celibacy one of the Christian virtues.

We left them about four, quite delighted even with this approach to a community and return to Albany, instead of going to a cotton mill 5 or 6 miles off, as we had intended. We passed several houses on the road with a few acres cultivated around them; not so comfortable looking nearly as the Shaker's.

While walking down a hill which commands a beautiful view of Albany and the river, we met two shakers returning with goods in a couple of carts. We told them we were much pleased with what we had seen, upon which one asked if we would like to remain with them. We said we would make some communities still better than theirs and that they would come to us. He asked if we forbid marriage. We said no. He replied then you can't agree; there will be continual quarrels. These men were a fair sample of the settlement; they were good looking,—more intelligent than common laborers, as, indeed, all, both men and women appeared and were even cheerful. At 5 we returned to Albany and as we had still an hour before dark, we looked about us a little. We observed the streets very ill-paved, though some of them were broad, the houses being irregularly built, having brick and wood buildings of all shapes and sizes. It lies on the right bank of the river on a gentle slope. On an elevated position we saw the State House, a handsome building of stone. We entered and a member of assembly politely showed us what was worth seeing. The Assembly Room is handsome and conveniently arranged, with a portrait of Washington in the centre. The Senate room is smaller, with Jefferson's portrait. We saw the State Library, which is open to the public. After we had viewed all these the member of the Assembly who had accompanied us, asked us sit down in the Assembly Room, attentions which in England, are rare in the House of Commons. Indeed, altho' all the

Americans seem to consider themselves your equal (the tavern keeper often mixing in conversation) yet, we have as yet found them always civil and obliging, quite as much if not more so than people are in England.

The day throughout was remarkably fine. In the morning, the thermometer stood at 36 degrees and we had a very slight sprinkling of snow, just perceptible towards evening.

Capt. McDonald and myself were very busy all evening bringing up our journals, We found the Eagle an excellent house. We had roasted apples at tea and fried potatoes at breakfast in addition to the usual appendages to an American table, and as it is customary to pour the tea into the saucer, we had each a little plate on which to place our cups.

Friday, 12th November.

Beautiful morning. Thermometer at 7 o'clock 26 degrees. My Father called on Governor Yates after breakfast and left us writing. Gov. Yates invited my Father to dinner tomorrow which he was obliged to decline, as he intended leaving Albany tomorrow morning. At ten we all went to DeWit Clinton's house in Pearl Street. He is a gentlemanly looking man, with an intelligent contenance. Capt. McDonald and I staid but a short time and we promised to send the drawing to my Father. We did so and then called on Gen. Rensselaer, with a letter we had forgotten to deliver before. Afterwards, we walked to the Grand Canal which joins the Hudson at Albany to Lake Erie at Buffalo. It is 332 miles long, 4 feet deep, 35 feet broad on top, and 25 at bottom. We walked up thesecond lock and saw a boat passing up in it. It raised it 16 feet. The side of the lock are well built of limestone. We were told that there are three divisions of the canal. One of these which is to Utica, (130 miles?) has 53 locks. We then returned along the canal to the basin by which it joins the Hudson. Saw several canal boats going backward and forward. This canal was planned by DeWit Clinton and executed by the State of New York alone. They received now from very low tolls upon it nearly $400,000 per annum. Lake Erie is upward of 330 feet above the Hudson here. After returning to the Inn, Gen. Rensselaer called to apologize for not accompanying us to Wiskeyana. My Father returned from Gen. Clinton's very much pleased with him, thinking him a sensible, practical man. We went about 2 to the State House and were there introduced to two members of the Assembly, Messrs Kolius and Wheaton, two representatives from New York. The debate was concerning the choice of electors for President and Vice President. Lists of electors who favor the different candidates had been proposed. Adams stood highest and Crawford, next; but neither had a sufficient majority to be chosen. The Senate have declared for Crawford. The Crawford party talked today of voting for Adams, as neither wished to yield. In that case, the other candidates being thrown out, as the two houses would fix upon different men, they must meet together and vote either for Crawford or Adams, till one or other has the majority. The Crawford men hoped then to get the Clay party to vote for their man and thus secure their point. Nothing was decided today.

At four, we went to dine at Gen. Rensselaer's. Met his wife and daughter, DeWit Clinton, young Rensselaer, Mr. King, a senator from New York, etc. After dinner there was good deal of discussion regarding communities. Those who were strangers seemed to regard the whole as visionary at first; indeed they were inclined to make game of it, but altho' there was too little time to make it clear to them, they were set right in many respects. Saw at supper in the Eagle Tavern, Mr. Koolius. Cold day throughout.

Saturday, 13th, November.

Another beautiful clear day. Thermometer at 7 o'clock stood at 22 degrees. Met at breakfast, Mr. Hammond who is from New York and who had been at Lanark two years ago. At 9 we went on board the Firefly steamboat, which conveyed us three miles down the river to the Keat Steamboat which could not get up farther on account of a bar which there runs across. Several vessels were lying upon it in expectation of high water. As there was rather less wind than yesterday (tho even then scarcely perceptible) we found it less cold than we expected. Indeed during the day it was pleasant enough, as we could always change the temperature by approaching the engine chimnies. In going down the river we saw a good deal of ice and on board I observed some full an inch thick. The Keat is very large double-decked steamboat. The ladies have two cabins astern, a private one above deck and dining one below. The gentlemen's is in front and below. All the machinery is above the lower deck. The cabins are fitted up very conveniently, with sliding tables. The curtains sliding out from the berths, form a kind of small state room. The ladies dining cabin can be divided into two or three rooms as required. It contains thirty-two beds. The fare is much superior to that of the Hudson, indeed nearly as good as in the best taverns, but as the passage money is only three dollars, it must be an unprofitable business. The Captain, pilot and engineer, have all cabins, besides two baggage houses. Above both decks is a fine open promenade. She has two engines of 60 horse-power each. I believe she is the finest boat on the rivers of the States. The company was much more respectable than that of the Hudson. We met Mr. Hill, of Hoboken, Cashier of the Bank there, and a friend, who had gone up with us. We were introduced to Mr. Bird of Philadelphia. The Hudson followed upon us just part of the way, but never shot a head, tho, we being larger were obliged to take larger sweeps. We took up all the passengers from them. These boats land and take in passengers, usually without stopping. A little plank is lowered to the required place. Then the rope is allowed to run till they are ready, when they are lowered back again. In this way, we put passengers on board the Richmond which passed us two hours sail from Albany with out either of us stopping for an instant. We passed several vessels which had sunk in the river. One lay all on one side with her mast peeping out. After passing Hudson, a considerable town, we saw the Katskill mountains in great beauty about seven or eight miles off; sometimes with a richly variegate foreground both of which were charmingly reflected in the water of the Hudson. For many miles the east bank which commands these delightful scenes, is the property of the Livingston family. One in particular, reminded me much of some ancient English Manor. We dined in the Ladies cabin and landed about 8 o'clock at NewBurg, opposite to which is Katskill, where Mr. DeWint resides, on whom we propose calling tomorrow, for which purpose we remain here. We put up at the Orange Hotel, a large, pretty good tavern. Conversed for an hour with three young ladies and gentlemen in the public room. One lady advised us to see the military academy, below, superintended by Col. Face. It is said to be well conducted.

Sunday, 14, November.

Thermometer at 7 o'clock stood at 34 degrees. Another very beautifully clear day. After breakfasting with the party of the foregoing evening, we crossed the Hudson in a teamboat drawn by seven horses and capable of containing several wagons and horses, to Fishgill, from whence we had to walk about one-half a mile to Mr. DeWint's house, which is finely situated on an eminence north of the village and commands an extensive prospect. We found them preparing for church and accompanied them to a small building in which the Dutch reformed service is performed, differing from the Scotch church in having printed form for ordination, Baptism, etc. The service consisted in prayer, singing, reading, prayer, sermon, prayer, and singing. The congregation appear much like what you would find in Lanark church, if we except one of two of the leading and one or two of the poorest families. They had a band of singers, to lead the congregation. After church, we walked a mile inland to view the little village and cotton spinning establishment at Matewan, belonging to Messrs. Schenck. We walked through some of the rooms. The machinery seemed in good order. We returned to dinner and by the way, invited a neighoring proprietor, Mr. R————. We found on our return, Mr. DeWint, from Denmark, cousin to the proprietor. The weather about mid-day was remarkably fine, quite like an England June or even July day. In the evening, Mr. Schenck called and My Father explained his plans to them. They appeared to receive them very well, on the whole, particularly Mr. Schenck, whom, we were told, when he returned home continued to explain them to his family till 1 o'clock A. M. We were pressed to remain all night, to which we complied, and sent a note for R. Watson to Newburgh, that he might bring our bags to us. He had not arrived at 11. We therefore went to bed without, I sleeping in the same bed as my father, notwithstanding which, we did pretty well.

Monday, 15th November.

We had of course no shaving or other apparatus in the morning, nor clean linen of any kind. We managed comme cela, my Father borrowing razors. About 10 we drove in a Jersey Wagon, which is a long cart upon four wheels, with seats fixed inside, which have a slight spring, (tho' by the by, two of us had only chairs.) to Watleawan, where we met two of the proprietors, Mr. Schank and Mr. Lenraid.

They conducted us first thro an extensive workshop where we found machinery of all sorts in progress, made with a great deal of skill and ingenuity. I particularly remarked turning lathes for iron in which the chisel was moved by the machine. The teeth of those small wheels which required a very regular and equal motion were oblique instead of being perpendicular to the sides of the wheel. They appeared to answer the purpose for which they were intended. They plated the rollers themselves and used soft leather to cover them with instead of hard. This they fastened entirely by cement, both in the roller and at the edges. They kept it down till dry by means of a hollow tube which they passed over it In turning the bobins, there was a sort of plane which was so fastened as to plane them of itself to a proper size. We afterwards visited their cotton spinning building. Below, we saw a shaft connected with the waterwheel which is put in gear every night and which works a fire engine close by, which is so placed as to command the public building; likewise, one connected with a regulator which opened and shut the sluice as required. The cotton passes thro' two sets of cards. It is weighed and spread behind the card; when the weight is all carded a bell is rung, when another child takes this off and carries it to the next card. It is then drawn 25 times. Afterwards it is put into round cases which turning round give it a twist before it enters the rollers. After passing through them it is as fine as the stretchers make it with us and is wound round bobbins by the machine. It is in fact a roving and stretching frame united. It works beautifully. It then passes to the spinning frames where it is wound either on bobbins or immediately on shuttles. There was very little breakage and the thread was very strong. The coarser numbers are made from Bows the best from Sea Island. They have no mixtures at all. We saw two mules worked by a man and a boy. They appeared to go slow. They had together 512 spindles. The man earned for himself

about $10.00 a week. In the room were beading mach-
ines which worked by themselves and one for preparing
them for this, which stopped of itself whenever a thread
broke. We visited their store which contains all sorts of
articles and bought a pair of warm mittens.

We then passed to the foundry which is small. The
bellows worked by the Waterwheel. We then drove to
Glenham, a woolen factory belonging to the same proprietor. There they spin, weave, dress, pull etc. They
showed us some very excellent looking cloth indeed, made
both from saxon and Merino wool. They expect to gain
a premium for it in New York, where on Wednesday, there
is to be a competition. They will sell it for $10 or $11.00;
We saw very fine black cloth which sells for $5.00. They
have a German dyer who seems to understand the business
well. I spoke a little German to him. They have an excellent machine for cutting the nap made by a farmer near
them called White. He is making a fortune by his patent.
The people were at dinner when we arrived. They soon
returned and were all very neat and tidy indeed. better
dressed than most of our young women, and many of them
had a good deal of manner. Their hair was remarkably neat.
This applies to both establishments. The dwelling houses
are frame buildings, very neat tho' small. We entered one
and found it very comfortable. They are all painted white
or red outside with a shingle roof, which painted gray, very
much resembles slate. 100 square feet of this roofing of
the best wood (white pine) costs four or five dollars and is
calculated to last thirty, forty, and sixty years. The shingles are·two feet long, 6 inches broad, and 1 inch thick.
They are laid on so thickly that only three of four inches
of each are left outside. The situation of both villages is
very romantic. Both are driven by water, of which there
is sufficient even in summer. There is a night school. The
population very orderly and quiet.

We returned to Mr. De Wint's, about three o'clock to

dinner. The day had been very wet, but we were fortunate during the whole in always being under cover when it rained. The day continued pretty warm with a smart south west wind. About dusk, we got down to a dock built into the river several 100 ft. by Mr. DeWint from which boats start. As it was so late, we got a sailing boat and soon got over safely. We went to the Orange Hotel and paid our bill. We were accompanied by Mr. Schank and his friend Mr. Ulrich, a German, who went with us also about 9 o'clock on board the Chancellor Livingstone, which then arrived from Albany, on its way to New York. We found De Wit Clinton on board. Capt. McDonald met a brother officer. My Father was introduced to several people. We found an after cabin under the ladies cabin, which is on deck, and a small cabin in which we got three berths. All the cabins were very hot and close from the number of people on board; she is a fine vessel with two steam engines. We soon went to bed and I slept pretty well.

Tuesday, 16 November.

Another wet, close, disagreeable day. We were called at Daybreak having arrived at New York about four o'clock, and got soon to the City Hotel. We had no time to wash or dress, but commenced immediately to prepare dispatches for the ship Canada which sails this morning for Liverpool at 10 o'clock. I wrote to Mrs. Owen and Robert. Received a letter from Leipsig dated Sala Bei Parma, 20th Sept. We were very much hurried in writing and got wet taking them to Mr. Day's counting house where we called with them. Between 11 and 12, Judge Ogden called and found with us Messrs. Schenck and Mr. Wilkins, Schenck's son-in-law, who promised to take us tomorrow to the exhibition of woollens etc. Judge Ogden talked of his estate on the St. Lawrence which he thought the very place for a community. He left a plan of it and description. We went below with him and he introduced us to his sister

Mrs. Waddington and to Mr. and Miss Waddington. His sister is rather a pleasing woman. A pretty quaker called to offer lands for sale on the Ohio. Mr. Owen called on Mr. W. Bayard and engaged us to dine with him tomorrow at 5 o'clock, a late hour here. I received a letter from Hunton.

After dinner we called on Jeremiah Thompson and Mr. Thomas who was preparing to sail for New Orleans tomorrow. There we staid a couple of hours and then returned to Mr. Ogdens in Greenwich street, along with Ludlow whom we met at Mr. Thompson's. At Mr. Ogden's, we met Mrs. Ogden and Mr. Ogden Jr., likewise Mrs. Judge Ogden a very pleasing enthusiastic woman. We then returned home, supped and wrote journal. Towards evening, the rain ceased and the clouds began to disperse, tho' still hot, but not so oppressive as before. We sat all day with the window open. Our motions seemed to be noticed. This evening's Post mentioned our return from Albany.

Wednesday 17th November.

After breakfast, My Father and I went to Prof. Griscom's in Grand Street. On our way, we met Mr. and Mr. Thomas; Mr. Thomas was preparing to set out for New Orleans. While at Griscom's, Mr. Eddy called. A long discussion in which both seemed very friendly and inclined to go a long way with us. They had heard reported that W. Allen or Joseph Foster had left N. Lanark Establishment and that my Father was no longer manager. Of course, we set them right in these respects. Returning I met Mr. Schenck who promised that his brother would call at 1 o'clock to take us to the fair. My Father went to Dr. Hosack's where De Wit Clinton is residing. About 12 he returned. Mr. Day had called in the meantime. Mr. Owen called on Mr. Buchanan who read to him a well written report on the Indians. We at the same time called on Mr. Ogden and left the addresses there as no one was at home. As Mr. Bolton, Capt. McDonald's friend, sails in a few days for Europe, and said he would take anything for us, we looked about for some curiosities, but could hit upon nothing that pleased us. At 1 o'clock we went to the exhibition of goods for a premium with Mr. Schenck and were shown a variety of articles, which do credit to the manufactures of the states. Amongst other things were some beautiful blue, black and claret colored broad clothes made by Mr. Schenck and at Shepherd's bush, Duchess Co etc. some beautiful bonnets made from spear grass, very stout cotton sail cloth, excellent hats, and improved power loom for broad clothes and improved Balance, some articles of plane and cut glass, besides cotton and other goods of various descriptions. On the whole we were satisfied that they would soon equal us in'most branches. The exhibition, was in the ground floor of the armory. We went up stairs to view them and found 10,000 stands of arms in excellent order. We then called on Dr. Mc Neven, lecturer on Chemistry in Col. College, a very pleasant kindhearted and sensible Irishman, and afterwards left our cards at Mr. McVickar's whom we found at dinner. We returned to the Inn a good deal fatigued and in want of luncheon as it was half past three o'clock. Four letters to Mr. Owen from Hunter and Flower. Hunter is getting better. and Flower has had the gout. Both very impatient for our arrival. James Banks, Katskill; called; he wished to know how Motherwell is going on. He advised to settle in the state, north or west, instead of in Indiana. Judge Irwin called and we were thus detained so long, that after dressing, we found ourselves very late for dinner. We took a coach and got to Mr. Bayard's which is quite out of town about half past five. We found there Gen. DeAlvear from South America, with whom my Father talked a good deal tho he speaks little English, Mr. Clibborn, Ogden's brother and a nephew to the Judge, Mr. Bayard, Mrs. Clibborn and a Frenchman. It was

rather a stiff dinner party. Returned and wrote journal.
Carlos De Alvear, said he was born in one of 31 communities now conducted on the system of public property.
They are the remains of what was established by the
Jesuits and contain about 9000 inhabitants each.   His
father was commissioned, to determine the boundaries of
their possessions and was residing in one of these cities
in Paraguay. at the time of his birth.   Paraguay lies in the
fork of the Rio De La Plata.

Thursday 18th November.

Engaged in packing up all the morning. Judge Ogden
called at 10 and gave Mr. Owen a letter to President
Monroe.   Before 11 we went down to the steamboat
Bellona and met on the wharf Harvey and Ludlow. Mr.
Schenck also met us there and introduced us to Mr.
Wilkins, his daughter, and to Miss Schenck his niece.
Mr. and Mrs. Waddington proceded with us to Philadelphia. We descended the Hudson a short distance and
then entered Staten Island Sound lying between New
Jersey and Staten Island. We raised an immense flock of
ducks in the bay, certainly many thousands. The shores
both of Jersey and Staten Island here are low and wooded;
Now and then a small eminence sloping down to the
water's edge. Both banks have numerous cottages scattered up and down, which enliven the scene. We passed
10 or a dozen fishing boats who were pulling up oysters by
means of two small or 1 large rake with great iron teeth.
At two o'clock we dined and were introduced to Mr. and
Mrs. Loyd and her mother. Mr. Loyd is a senator; rather
clever man. Soon after dinner we entered the Ranton
River and met several steamboats going up and down.
We stopped at two villages for passengers. One of these
boats, the Thistle, intends racing, I was told, against the
Pioneer, a small ferry boat, next week. · Betting even.
The Thistle is said to be one of the fastest boats in the

States. She does the distance from New York to New Brunswick in three hours, 45 miles. This costs to those who do not dine or board 12½ cents.

About four o'clock we arrived at New Brunswick, where we landed and stept into four coaches which were awaiting our arrival. We were obliged to leave a great part of our luggage behind, which they promised should join us in the morning at the Steamboat at Trenton. In our coach were eight passengers. These stages hold nine passengers having a seat without a back in the middle. The baggage is stowed away behind and a little before. No outside passengers at all. R. Watson sat with the driver. The upper part of the coaches is merely leather buttoned on to frame work which doos not defend well from cold. We therefore wrapped ourselves well up. We had four very good black horses, much better than I had expected, indeed they would not have disgraced our English stage coach even near London. We passed over a level country partly cleared, partly oak forest, which gave us some idea of the difficulty attendant on clearing land. The soil was sandy and the road to me appeared very bad although we sat on patent spring seats, whose motions by the bye, I did not prefer to the common stuffed seats. It soon became dark so that we saw but little of the country. We passed Princeton, where there is a large academy and arrived at Trenton, prettily shaken, about half past 8 o'clock. The distance is 28 miles divided nearly equally into two stages. We supped and soon went to bed. We got a room with three excellent beds. Clear frosty day throughout. Pleasantly cold.

Friday 19th November.

We were called at half past three as my Father desired that we should be awake a quarter of an hour before the other passengers. Waited full half of an hour after we were ready. At five, we set out in the stages again and

met the steamboat on the Delaware about 7 miles down
the river whither she dropped down the previous night, as
the tide was low this morning. On the road, one of the
carriage poles broke, which detained us after we arrived at
the boat a half hour till they came. No baggage came,
owing we suppose to our starting an hour earlier than
usual, on account of the low tide. At 7 a good breakfast.
On board we had the mother and sister of Joseph Bonnaparte's present mistress, who resides a few miles from
Trenton. J. Bonnaparte gave to the mother $10,000 when
this girl came to live with him. A passenger seeing her,
as she is stout, asked the captain how much she weighed?
10,000 was the immediate reply. J. Bonnaparte after losing the kingdom of Spain, purchased an estate here. His
mistress is said to be uncommonly beautiful; her sister is
very pretty. He is liked here. The banks of the Delaware
which we passed are usually quite flat, with wood a little
back from the river. A number of beautiful country seats
are thickly scattered particularly on the Pennsylvania
shore. At Macleans Hook & Chester, we took in passengers. At the latter place several quakers came on board
and a very pretty lady, who however squinted.

We arrived at Philadelphia about 11 o'clock and went
to the Mansion House, having first shaken Hunter by the
hand. At 2 we dined at Mr. Austin's with Mr. Flower,
who gave us a letter from his son regarding Harmony,
which stated that Rapp would sell at New Year if my
Father did not buy before. Saw Mr. and Mrs. Bleak from
Edinburgh there. After dinner I walked with Mr. Bleak
thro' the city. Found a number of handsome houses a
great many marble staircases, some fine public buildings
and one marble house. The foot pavement is usually brick;
a small part I saw of white marble. Some houses are built
of very beautiful brick. The streets are all right angles and
often very regularly built. Cleaner than at New York.
Some pretty squares. Walked to the Schuylkill which

bounds the city to the west. Saw a handsome wooden
bridge of one arch and an eminence to which the water is
throw which supplies the city. The streets which run north
and south are called first, second, third streets, etc. More
blacks than at New York. A good many quakers. A
clear cold day. In the middle of the city east and west,
runs Market Street, north and south Broad street. In
Market street I saw an immense number of wagons standing with the horses before them. I was told that these
horses are never put into a stable, but are left out in the
street both winter and summer. Some of them come
several hundred miles with goods. Some wagons have four
horses, one before the other. But those from a distance
have usually five, two and two abreast, and one in
front. The cart horses are rather light and are usually
trotted when the cart is empty. Ash and Walnut are the
fashionable streets. They have usually handsome houses
in them. Almost all the doors, windows, etc., are painted
white, which is well as the white marble contrasts well
with the brick houses.

Saturday 20 November.

Breakfasted at the public table at half past eight and
afterwards sat down to write letters for a Liverpool packet
which sails this day. Wrote to my mother, regarding our
tour hither. While writing we were often interrupted by
visitors. Mr. Rush first called and before he was gone,
Mr. Warder introduced himself. Then Hunter called and
introduced Col. Clarke an eminent civil engineer. We
were thus detained so long that when we went to Hunter's
to give them to Mr. Ganaty, a friend of his, who meant
to go by the packet, the Algonquin, he had already departed
for the boat. We therefore proceeded there and after a
little time found him on the boat and gave him the letters.

We then returned and found Flower, who had a carriage
waiting to take us about. Mr. Warder returned and intro-

duced a Mr. Brown. My Father said he would walk to the houses he meant to call at. We got in and after stopping with Mr. Flower at two or three shops, we drove up Market street and proceeded to Fairmount on the Schuykill. On the way, stopping in Market Street, we met Mr. Bird whom we had met on the Kent. Here we found a building with three undershot water wheels 16½ ft. broad and 16½ ft. in diameter, two of which worked a piston 4½ ft. long and one a piston 4 ft. long. These work in double pumps and raise 42 barrels per minute, 105 ft. high.

Two of the waterwheels are 50 and the other is 40 horse power. The water thrown up supplies the town. The view to the opposite side of the Schuykill is pleasing; meadows and woods prettily interspersed, with villages and spires at a little distance. A great part of the town at this end is neatly laid out, but no buildings at all erected. Here and there you see a sign post with the name of the intended street. After returning to the inn, as my Father was not there, we went to a watchmaker in order to get my watch repaired. At three we all went to Hunter's to dinner.

We met there Messrs. Page, Lewis, Vance, Dr. Wairing etc. The party was not quite so stiff as that of yesterday, but still it made us like our inn better than even such a boarding house. A little conversation after dinner with Dr. Wairing who is a physiologist and who contended strongly for individual character and temperament in the formation of man. After dinner, my Father called at Flower's and settled finally on setting out on Tuesday. Mr. Flower said he had written to his son to buy Harmony for himself if he did not arrive before a fixed day, I think the 20th December. Mr. Stuckman, a druggist, called and said he knew several individuals ready to join a community both here and at Pittsburgh. It seems that he had tried to establish one already, but somehow or other, the scheme was given up. At half past seven, we called at

Hunter's and Messrs. Wan and Wairing went with us to the Athenaeum, where Mr. Vaughan to whom my Father brought a letter, had a literary soiree. We were introduced to a number of individuals; to the Swedish charge d'affairs, Col. Long, who published a very celebrated travels in America, etc., a great many names we did not hear distinctly. We saw Dr. Brown from Lexington who had just returned from Europe and who proceeds to-morrow west. He seems inclined to go a great way. We amused ourselves with talking and looking at books or prints, besides having tea and supper. Returned and wrote journal. A most beautifully clear and delightful day throughout. The thermometer stood at 8:00 A. M. at 32 degrees and during the greater part of the day, the temperature was quite as one could desire it if we had the power of choosing for ourselves.

The principal public buildings are the United States and Pennsylvania banks both of white marble. Most of the houses are narrow as the ground is paid for by the number of feet fronting the street; the purchaser being allowed to extend his house as far back as he pleases.

Sunday 21 November.

Breakfasted at the ordinary time. About half past 9 Mr. Longstreth called to go with my Father to Madame Fretageot's, who lives three miles out of town. About the same time, Hunter came in with a friend called Mr. Cusen; a clever young man. My Father promised to go with him at 10 to-morrow to the Waterworks. We went with them as far as the Quaker Meeting house in Ash St. the largest in the city, being desirous of seeing them here, being the first quaker city in the world. We found a great number of individuals there, men on the right hand, women on the left. A large proportion of males had cast off the quaker garb either in whole or in part but the greater number of females were in Quaker costume. The

most common dress was a grey silk gown, a white or
French gray shawl or scarf and a french white silk quaker
shaped bonnet. The bonnets were all shades from a dark
brownish grey to the lightest french white. We heard one
male, an elder, and two female friends speak. None of
them were very eloquent, indeed, the male seemed to
ponder over every word he uttered pausing usually for a
very long space, time after time, every three words. About
half past 11 we were all moved by the spirit to depart. We
walked a little about and saw several churches dimiss
which gave us an opportunity of seeing the people to advantage. Quaker fashions amongst the ladies, certainly
prevail to a great extent. Capt. McDonald and I called
on Mr. W. Meredith to whom young Ogden gave us a
letter. Not at home.

We therefore returned to the inn and prepared to go to
Mr. Loyd's to dinner, where we were to go at half past one
o'clock. Found my Father already there. Met Mr. and
Miss Loyd and Mr. Hess, a Savannah gentleman, who had
been at the Ohio this summer. He was very much pleased
with Cincinnati; and talked of settling there. Mr. Loyd
after dinner returned to the Mansion House with us and
we read to him the proposals for a socialist community.
He objected to the shares being sold to resident members
at the original price. He thought that they should be sold
at what they would fetch at any given time when the sale
might happen to take place. We went all together to call
on Mr. W. T. Warder and on Mr. Chapman. Both from
home. Returned back to the inn and called on Hunter.
Promised to return at half past eight to show the drawings
to Col. Clark. Went at 6 to Mr. Longstreth's house in
Ash Street. Met there a large party at tea. After tea all
set in a circle and My Father explained his views in as far
as regarded first principles. Mr. Price's sister is a little
lively woman. She was quite delighted with the account
of the children at New Lanark. On the whole a very pleas-

ant party. Returned at half past 9 to Hunter's. Showed
the drawings to Col. Clark, who approved of them much.

The whole day was beautifully clear. Perhaps about
midday fully warm for exercise. Thermometer at 8:00
o'clock A. M. stood at 36 degrees.

Monday, 22 November.

Another fine day. Beautifully clear, that is, the sun
shines brightly all day with seldom if ever even the smallest cloud to be seen. Thermometer about 12 o'clock 55
degrees. Say from 50 to 55 degrees has been the temperature in the shade during the day, for many day past, perhaps since our return from Albany, where we found it
somewhat colder.

We breakfasted at 8 with Mr. Sparkman. Met there Mr.
Wilson and a young man, his son. We called on Mrs.
Holmes wife of Mr. Holmes, who promised to advance
$30,000 and Mr. Holmes, wishing my Father to lecture
at the Franklin Institution tonight, He promised to come
and converse with them. Mr. C———— came wishing him
to meet a society of Commonwealth. We could not attend
as we leave town before the day of the proposed meeting.

My Father called on the British Consul. Capt. McDonald and myself returned to the Hotel after seeing Hunter
for a minute and found there Mr. Creson and Mr. Eli
Pierce. When my Father came, he went out with Mr. Creson to see the Waterworks. Just before he went, Capt.
Maxwell called and at the same time, I received a note from
Bailey for him saying that the parties who had brought
some luggage hither which we had left at New Brunswick,
meant to summon him today as he had refused payment,
because when we left the baggage, it was promised to be
delivered here free of expense. My Father called there
and paid it.

Capt. McDonald, when Capt. Maxwell was gone, went
out to see Meredith with young Price. They found him

not at home. I sat down to write journal, but at 12 Mr.
Chew and friend, and afterwards Mr. Redwood Fisher called by appointment. Soon after my Father and Creson and
Capt. McDonald and Price returned. My Father showed
them the drawings. While doing so, John W. Condy called and soon after Mr. Washington Smith, who had been
at Lanark introducing Mr. Turner Camae, and Mr. Thos.
Say along with Mons. Leseur. About 2 they all went. A
man brought a letter of introduction to Lang the book-
seller from Clibborne, and Mr. Vaughan looked in for an
instant. My Father went out with Mr. Fischer to see Mr.
Walsh. Having promised to call on Fisher tomorrow at
9 o'clock.

At 3 Mr. Vaughan called and we went with him to Dr.
Rush's to dinner. We met there Mrs. Rush and her father,
Mr. Ridgeway and Mr. Kuhn, Mr. and Mrs. W. Meredith,
Mr. Beckel, two of Mr. Rush's brothers and several others.
A splendid entertainment. Mrs. Rush is a pleasing lady
and both she and her husband were anxious to make the
party as agreeable as possible. Soon after six, we were
obliged to leave the dining room; we went with Mr.
Vaughan to Mr. Foster's, a man of color, who had a large
sailmaking establishment. We found there Mr. Foster
and family, Mr. Greenville, agent from St. Domingo and
two others. Mr. Foster seemed much pleased to see us.
We were shown some very good writting of his son's a
boy between 11 and 12 years of age. The Misses Foster
are rather pleasing girls. On account of their color they
are not visited. I am told they are very accomplished.
After drinking tea there we were obliged to run off soon
after 7 to attend the meeting at the Franklin Institution.
On our way thither we called at the Mansion House and
found there Mr. Creson and Mr. Eli Pierce who went along
with us. When we entered the room, we with difficulty
made our way through the crowd, as the room was more
than filled. Mr. Browne opened the meeting and my Father

explained that he had not come to lecture having had no
time to think of what he should say, but that he would be
happy to talk over the subject with them. He began by
stating the principles upon which he proceeded and afterwards gave a general outline of what he proposed to effect
He did not enter into detail. He then, at the request of one
of the gentlemen, related some few particulars regarding
New Lanark. He afterwards declared that he was so exhausted when he commenced that he never felt himself
less equal to the task. No other person spoke. About half
past eight, we adjourned and at the proposal of Mr. W.
Meredith, who was present, Capt. McDonald and I went
along with him to an evening party in Chesnut street, at
the house of Mr. Marcoe. We were introduced to Mrs.
Marcoe, to her sister Mrs. Cork, to Miss Marcoe, to Miss
Seaton, etc. Mr. Smith, Mr. Page etc., were present. We
having had no time to change our dress, did not dance.
Nothing was danced except quadrilles, here called cotilions
and a black played on the violin. It resembled an evening
party, in the old world, almost in every respect. The ladies
appeared to me to have rather less reserve than those
whom I have met with at home, and were on the whole
better looking, tho' the clear British complexion usually
failed. A very pleasant party. Mrs. Marcoe said she was
very sorry my Father had not come this evening and that
she would be happy to see us more particularly any Monday Evening. We got home about 12. Paid some very
extravagant bills.   106880

Tuesday 23rd, November

My Father went at 7 to Carey's where he breakfasted.
He met there a young man who had been at New Lanark,
and who spoke very well of it, whereever he went. He
afterwards called on several individuals, who names we
did not hear. He gave Thomson's work to Walsh, editor
of the National Gazette. I got my watch from Mr. Droz.

Mr. Vischen came, sent by Mr. Flower. He is a Swiss who has been at Harmony. He seemed to think the Harmonists knew little of their pecuniary affairs.

We got all our baggage ready and went a little before 12 to the Baltimore boat, our party now consisting of Mr. Owen, Capt. McDonald, Mr. Hunter, Mr. Fowler, Miss Ronalds, and myself. We met on board several friends who had come to take leave of us and others. We set sail at 12, sailing down the Delaware to Newcastle, 33 miles. On board there sailed with us Mr. and Mrs. Everett (brother of the professor) Mr. and Mrs. Tucknor and Emma, her sister, Miss Seaton, Dr. Mease, Mr. Obersteufer, a young man who had been in the Bureau at Hofwyl, etc. The day was delightful indeed. Pleasantly warm, even on the river. My Father talked a good deal to the ladies. The shores were very flat all the way. I observed now and then a small village and a good deal of good pasture land, banked out of the river. At New Castle about 4 o'clock, our party got into a stage after, with great difficulty, stowing away all our baggage. Our fellow travellers, filled, with ourselves, eight stages. We travelled 16 miles over a very tolerable road to a small village called Frenchtown. We arrived at half past eight having been for some hours in the dark. We got on board a fine steamboat, after having much difficulty with our baggage in the dark. We supped and drew lots for our beds. Mr. Owen, Capt. McDonald and I were lucky enough to get berths in the after cabin. We went to bed early. In the night, a man, whom we could not awaken at all, snored terribly.

Wednesday 24th November.

After sailing down the Chesapeake Bay, we found ourselves in the morning at Baltimore, having arrived there about three. We procured a cart and proceeded to the Indian Queen. Here with great difficulty obtained rooms. We got a sitting room below. After washing, in an ap-

paratus prepared under a corridor, beside which over a
door we observed written up "shaving and hair dressing,"
"Razors set in an elegant style," etc., we breakfasted at
the public table about 8. Here as in all the hotels, where we
have yet been, we find it to be the custom to ring a bell one-
half or one-quarter of an hour before breakfast. When we
arrived, the landlord, Mr. Barnum, who appeared quite
a gentleman, being introduced to us, shook hands all
around. In coming up the principle street, Market St., to
the hotel. I was pleased with it, from contrasting it with
the somber and regular streets of Philedelphia which tire
from being so much alike. It is a broad handsome street
with a good deal of bustle and show in it. Tartans made a
conspicuous figure in it.. Soon after our arrival, Mr. Liernan called, to whom my Father gave a letter of introduction
from a gentleman in Philadelphia. Mr. Owen went out
with him and visited Mr. Murphy, Editor of American, Gen.
Harper, introduced by Mr. Thomas, Mr. Meredith, coun-
celler at law, by Judge Ogden. Mr. Liernan introduced
him to Mr. Oliver one of the richest and most benevolent
men in the city. Mr. Owen gave Mr. Liernan letters for
Mr. Gwiren and Mr. Maher, whose addresses were unknown
to him. In the meantime, Capt. McDonald and I wrote our
journals. When my Father returned, we went upstairs and
saw Mr. and Mrs. Ticknor, Emma, and Mr. and Mrs. Everett. Soon after Gen. Harper called and invited us to come
to his house in the evening. We heard that Miss Seaton is
his adopted daughter. We were informed that a fair was
holding about three miles from town. We therefore engaged two hacks at $2.00 each and proceeded thither. The
appearance of the country was very pleasing; gently undulating, with many cottages interspersed among small oak
woods, scattered up and down. The road was very tolerable. We found an enclosure on one side of the road
where the fair was held. After paying $1.00 each admit-
tance money, we found that almost all the cattle had been

taken away the previous day. We saw a good bull or two,
and a few Barbary sheep with immense tails. Likewise,
some good swine. There were specimens of domestic manufacture which we were not allowed to inspect, as the examination of premiums was about taking place. In another
part of the ground, were several agricultural instruments;
ploughs, horseshoes, cornshellers, straw cutters, a threshing mill, a machine for raising coals, etc. Some of them
were ingenious enough. The chairman invited my Father
to dine to morrow which he was obliged to decline. We
returned about 2 to the inn. The day was remarkably hot,
like a summer's day in England, where the sky in clear. We
are now in the Indian Summer, a series of 15 or 20 days
which are much hotter than the period before and after,
and which occur nearly every fall sooner or later. I have
not heard it accounted for.

After dinner we walked to the exchange, a large handsome stone building; when we got there it was too dark to
see anything at all. At 7 we went to Gen. Harper's where
we found Miss Seaton, Mr. Hunter's nephew, Mr. Ticknor,
and some others. I walked back to the inn for the dresses.
We returned before 9. Capt. McDonald was unwell with
a cold. He staid at home. Heard that Gen. Lafayette had
arrived. Warm even in the evening, but a little hazy,
which oftentimes happens at this season.

Thursday 25th November.

Prepared to leave the city. Thermometer at half past 8
A. M. 51 degrees. A beautifully clear morning. Mr. Owen
paid a few visits. We met Mr. Lewis at the Hotel. In
the public room, we observed a large square machine containing three or four shelves, on which the dishes are conveyed down to the kitchen. Mr. Barnum presides at table,
but as it seemed, rather to see that every thing goes right.

He said that with some others, he had at one time offered $100,000 for old Harmony. He seemed to think New Harmony likely to be unhealthy. We engaged the stage to ourselves for $28.00 and having nearly filled it with baggage, we set out about 9 o'clock. About 12 miles off we stopped and walked to Williamson's factory. He is a pleasant man. He showed us a cotton spinning, weaving and bleaching establishment: which are now in progress, only a small part being yet filled with machinery. He has also a grist and saw mill and makes his own machinery. The factory was founded two and one-half years ago. All of it, as well as a small neighboring village, is built of brick. The machinery seemed to work well.

We passed through a country which was for the most part sandy. Oak was the prevailing tree but we saw hickory, black walnut, the tulip tree etc. Alternate hills and dales presented to us a pleasing view. Cottages were scattered here and there, a little cleared land lay usually on each side of the road and we passed several extensive farms with good houses; also a few little villages. We made three stages of the 38 miles. We dined about 5, remaining perhaps one-half hour, and arrived in Washington a little after seven. The road was sometimes very good, but often deep in sand or gravel. Of this latter substance, in those places which had been hollowed out by the rain, we observed a great' thickness. In entering the city, we observed the Capitol, a large building, a little elevated, by moonlight. The city appeared to be very straggling but the streets broad. Messrs. Flower and Hunter and Miss Ronald remained at the Indian Queen. We went to Godsby's Hotel, where we supped on Canvassback, a kind of duck found only in the Chesapeake etc. We had good accomodations as we had written forward yesterday evening. Thermometer at 1 o'clock 70 degrees. A beautiful day. Cooler and clearer than yesterday.

Friday 26th November.

After breakfasting at the public table, we went out in a hackney coach and left my Father at Mr. Adams. We proceeded to the Indian Queen where we found Hunter who walked with us to the Capitol. This is a fine stone building, with mixed architecture, which stands on an eminence commanding a fine view of the city and surrounding country. We went up to the bottom of the dome and wandered all over the building. We met a man there who said he had resided in Indiana 40 miles from Cincinnati. He came to town to take out some patent rights. He had invented a number of machines. One which broke and hulled hemp and which was also a threshing machine for wheat etc. He had a bell worth $14.00 which could he heard three miles off. We met Mr. Flower and Miss Ronald and accompanied them to the Chamber of the Senate and House of Respresentatives, both fine rooms. The library was not open. We were shown two paintings, one of the first sitting of Congress, in which the declaration of independence was made, the other of an English officer delivering his sword to Gen. Lincoln. In one of the halls, niches are being prepared for these. There are a great many committee and clerk rooms. The front is not yet finished; but it will certainly be a noble building when completed. We observed some pillars of beautiful potomac marble like pudding stone and a new order, made of stalks of Indian corn.

We afterwards returned to the hotel. The city appeared to be built in an inconvenient manner. Scarcely a fitted up street in it; a house often one-fourth or one-half of a mile from its nearest neighbor, and the intervening ground an irregular barren waste. Of course, the streets cannot be lighted or a good police kept up. It contains between eight and ten thousand inhabitants; There is no merchantile business going on. A number of hackney coaches and carriages are on the streets, which become necessary on account of the great distance from one place to another. I observed a number of horses standing waiting for their riders, and many riding up and down. I have seen here a good many fine looking horses; they are small and showed a good deal of blood.

The principal street is Pennsylvania avenue planted on both sides with poplars. At one end stands the capitol and at the other the president's, a handsome stone palace, between four large brick buildings, containing the public offices. Neither of these front down the street. The President's house commands the Potomac, a fine river which bounds the city on one side. There is little wood around the city, but the distant hills on both sides of the Potomac appear to be wooded, tho at present they appear to be very bare. A few miles down the river, lies Alexandria.

My Father returned at 1 having visited the Honorable J. Q. Adams, Secretary of State, and seen at his house Dr. Watkinson, under secretary. From there he proceeded to the President, who was engaged, but hoped to see him tomorrow at 11; then to Mr. Crawford's, the Secretary of the Treasury. Afterwards he went to Mr. Calhoun, secretary of War, with whom he promised to take tea tomorrow. He now went with us to Mr. Adington, British charge D' Affairs, who was from home, and had afterwards a long conversation with Mr. Wirt, the Attorney General, who appeared very much interested. He called on Mr. Taylor who was at dinner. In the meantime, I wrote to Mr. Applegate. At half past three we dined at the public table. We then went to the Indian Queen and took Miss Ronald with us to view a wooden bridge over the Potomac. It is one and one-fourth miles long and thirty or forty ft. broad. We took tea with Mr. Flower and met there Mr. Biddle and Dr. Watkins and son who called on Mr. Hunter. We returned to the inn (Franklin's Hotel) and my Father called on Mr. Reynold's, a friend of Price's and on Gen. Wingate, who was from home.

Thermometer at 10 was 56 in the shade. The whole day gloomy and in the evening a smart shower.

Saturday 27th November.

During the night some rain. In the morning cloudy, but between 9 and 10 the clouds dispersed, and the day continued clear and warm. Thermometer between 9 and 10, 66 degrees in the shade.

At 7 o'clock, Mr. Speakman called and talked some time with Mr. Owen. My Father settled that he had better go in the stage tomorrow at three A. M. whether we go or not. Mr. Owen went at half past eight to breakfast with Mr. Reynold's. At 10 he went to Mr. Adams' and about 11 to the President. We remained writing and about 12 o'clock went out towards the president's house. We met Mr. Owen coming out and went with him to see Mr. Wirt, the Attorney General. While he remained there, Capt. McDonald and I went to look for Hunter. We found him just returned from a dentist, where he had got three teeth drawn, which had pained him. He thought he had better remain at the Indian Queen at the present, as the Doctor advised him not to go out. We returned to the Attorney General's and then drove with Mr. Owen to Mrs. Blake's where we found Mr. Reynold, who accompanied us to Dennison Hotel, to visit some Choctaw and Chickesaw chiefs who are now there, transacting business with the United States Government. We were shown into a room where we found some gentlemen from the South western states and some half breeds, who we supposed, were the indians we had come to see. After waiting some little time we were conducted to another room where we found nine or ten Indians and an interpreter "sitting in Council" as they called it. When we went in, we were introduced to them by their Indian names, and we shook hands with them all round and then sat down so as to form with them a circle round the room. In the middle, of them, sat one dressed in Military uniform with gold epaulets, and red sash, and hat, and feathers, called Gen. Push-a-mat-a-ha. He began the conference by saying with a good deal of gestures that he was happy to see us and to shake hands ith his white brethren Mr. Owen said that he was anxious to see the Indians united and that many individuals in England were very solicitious for the welfare of the Indians. After a few sentences, which were all explained by a mutual interpreter who sat near the chief, the latter asked my Father's name and said he was Gen. Pushama-taha. Another chief appeared to be a shrewd fellow, said he would talk a little. He then said that they were sur-rounded by French, Spaniards, English and now by Amer-icans, and that he was very friendly to them all.

Mr. Owen replied he wished to see all united, both white and red, and that he thought the Indians were superior to the whites in many respects; in sincerity, friendship, and honest dealings, tho' the whites certainly possessed many advantages over them. He was desirous of knowing whether the Indians would prefer amalgamating with the whites, or forming a separate body quite distinct from them. The Indian replied that he was aware that the whites were so superior to them that they could only cope with them by imitating them, which they were endeavor-ing to do as well as possible, tho' still a great way behind. That they had schools established in several places and were commencing the fabrication of cloths. The inter-preter added that two who were there were proofs of what might be made of them. (These were so like Americans that I should never have supposed they were Indians, as they talked English well. One in particular, was quite a polite gentleman.) Mr. Owen cautioned them against adopting what had been found injurious in civilized life, and said that he had come more than three thousand miles to promote plans, by which he hoped to make the red brethren superior to the whites. He said Indians taken when young amongst white, would become like whites, and vice-versa and he concluded that it would be possible to unite the good in the Indian and in the civilized lives, so as to make a being superior to both. He further said it would be possible to bring all knowledge of the world together to one place so that each might enjoy the benefit of it. The Indian replied that he agreed with him. that he was strengthening his former ideas and thanked him for his advice. He several times said he was much pleased with his "talk." While this was going on, the general before mentioned, (who we were told has become very dissipated and was then a little intoxicated) fell fast asleep, his hat fell off and he began to talk in his sleep. All this they took no notice of. They told Hunter afterwards that this man had acquired dissipated habits and that they were very sorry that he had been present. They were quite ashamed of him. They told him they had been much pleased with the "talks" we had had, and Hunter was so much affected by meeting them that he longed to hasten westward. He said, turning to the interpreter, you can understand my feelings. He did not undertand their language at all.

The language spoken, seemed to require many words to express our ideas and each word to be pronounced apart from every other one, almost as a sentence by itself. There were some stout, fine looking fellows among them. They were all dressed in English costume, which however did not appear to sit well upon them. It seemed to confine them much. They usually sat with one leg laid horizontally across the other. Two of the oddest had very withered complextions, like some of the old highland women I have remarked at New Lanark. At the end of a almost every sentence, my Father said they cried out "say, sa" or "na, na say sa, " which implied that they agreed and were pleased. The intrepreter who has been with them 50 years, says he prefers their mode of life to that of the whites. In coming out, we met Hunter, Mr. Flower and Miss Ronald going to see them. We proceeded to call on Gen. Wingate, who had left his card in the morning. We met there his wife, and daughter and father and mother. While we were there Mrs. and the Misses Adams called upon them. We dined at half past three at the hotel, and then called on Jules De Wallenstein, sec. of the Russian legation. He was from home. By mistake, we went to the Russian Ambassadors. My father left his card with Wallenstein's servant and promised to see him when he returned in a few weeks. We then called at Williamson's Hotel on Mr. Ticknor who was at dinner. We proceeded to the Indian Queen and talked with Flower about our journey. We then went to Dr. Watkins and leaving my Father there, we went to the Marine Corps Depot to deliver a letter given to Capt. McDonald by young Ogden for Mr. Auchmaty there. He was dining with his colonel. Returned for my Father and calling on Hunter, settled we could not start tomorrow at three A. M.

We then drove to Williamson's Hotel to see Mr. Ticknor and friends, where we were introduced to Mr. Wallenstein, and then went to call on Mr. Talhoe. Returned to the inn and drank tea, and I dispatched letters to Robert and Mr. Applegate. Journalized.

The coach cost us $5.00 per day. Both the Hackney coachs and horses are here very good. A great many nice riding horses, I observe about. They are much used here, indeed the distance makes them necessary, and they are mostly taught to amble and canter. Most of them show a good deal of blood. Messrs. Wingate, Wallenstein, Talhoe, Watkins, Addington, Raggles, Ticknor, Dr. Staughton, Col. Col left cards today. Thermometer at 10 P. M. 51 degrees.

Sunday, 28th November.

A very beautiful day. Thermometer between 9 and 10 A. M. stood at 56 degrees. We arose betimes and packed, to prepare for our journey. We found that the stage started this morning at 4 A. M. and that we could not get ready for it at that time. We therefore determined upon going by a private conveyance. We breakfasted at our inn at 7. We were waited upon during our stay here by a black slave, who, upon being questioned, said he was a native of Maryland, belonging to a gentleman residing in the state of New York, who had no right to sell him to any one but himself. He said he should be here four years, when he would probably go to St. Domingo. He at present pays his master $100.00 per annum and he is allowed to do what he likes to do and to hire himself to whom he pleases. He said he was happy and comfortable. This was the first black I had seen whom I knew to be a slave, but I am informed that nine-tenths of all the blacks in Maryland are slaves. After packing we went to Brown's Inn to Mr. Flower. At the stage office, next door we found that no stage could be had and that if we meant to get on we must take one of the hacks that ply in the street. We spoke to two men who offered to take us to Hagertown for $6.00 per diem, each, including all expenses to us of tolls etc. We expected to get some cheaper at our inn. We returned and soon after Mr. Flower followed us, when we found no one willing to take us for $6.00. We hauled about thro' a number of different offices and at last we found two drivers who agreed to take us for the above mentioned sum of $6.00 per diem, each at four days, equalling $24.00, for two days to Hagerstown and two days returning.

About half past one we were ready to go, having lost all morning by these arrangements, but we found that notwithstanding we left everything behing except a portmanteau each, the little light hack could not stow all away. We were therefore obliged to hire a third one. We therefore started with our party in one, Mr. Flower's party in another, and R. W. with the greater part of the baggage in the third. We proceeded pretty well without stopping except to give the horses water thro' Georgetown, and Rockville to Clarksburgh, where we arrived about half past eight. The distance from Washington is 27 miles. After passing Georgetown, a village on the Potomac, a short distance from Washington, containing between seven and eight thousand inhabitants, we ascended a considerable hill, from which we had an extended prospect of the city, river and surrounding country. We passed through a country pleasingly undulated, of a light soil, cleared in many places to a considerable distance on each side of the road, varied by forests of oak, and occasionally hickory, walnut, sycamore etc. The road as far as Rockville, fourteen miles, is pretty good tho rather hilly. From thence to Clarksburgh, it becomes rough and uneven. We put up at Mrs. Shelley's inn, where we were comfortably accommodated. We got a good supper, having taken nothing but a little cold meat and bread at Rockville since we breakfasted, and went to bed.

Monday, 29th November.

We started by daybreak about half past 5 and went to Fredricktown, 15 miles to breakfast, over a very rough and hilly road, through a romantic country, where we arrived about half past 11. On the road I discovered that I had left my watch behind. I therefore wrote a note at Fredricktown to Mrs. Shelley, requesting her that it might be sent to Godby's Hotel, Washington. We stopped at Talbott's who gave us a good breakfast. While there several droves of hogs passed: they were proceeding to Baltimore, coming from Ohio and Kentucky. The morning was wet and during greater part of the day, the fog continued to hide the prospect from us. We started about 1 o'clock and arrived between seven and eight at Boonsboro, 15 miles distant, having crossed the South mountain, the first of the range of Blue mountains. We passed thro a romantic hilly

country in which lay some fine farms. I particularly remarked a little village beautifully situated in a small cultivated valley, surrounded by finely wooded hills, which reminded me much of Swiss·scenery.

Capt. McDonald, Hunter and I who were together in one
carriage, had a very interesting conversation regarding the
Indians, and past recollections, and future anticipations,
more particularly regarding a new state of society.

We supped at the Hotel at Boonsboro, which appeared to
be very comfortable. One of our horses was knocked up,
but having obtained another, we proceeded 12 miles further
to Hagerstown, on the Antietam creek. We traveled in
the dark and arrived about 11 o'clock. We sent to the
Stage Office, where we found a host rather nonchalant. We
were told that we could have no other conveyance than the
stage which should start next morning at 4 o'clock. Tho'
a great deal fatigued, it was determined to go on by it
in order to cross the mountains as long as we had fine
weather.

Tuesday 30 November.

Having been awoke at half past three, we started at
four and proceeded 27 miles to Hancocktown to breakfast.
We arrived about half past 10 and found that they had
give us up for the day. We however soon got a good
breakfast. Hancock is a small village prettily situated.
On starting we had an excellent driver who carried us on
fast. We passed through a most romantic country, continually ascending and descending hills, one, two and three
miles in height, which gave us a varied prospect of hills
and dales partly cultivated but mostly wooded with oak,
interspread with black and white hickory, black and white
walnut, the tulip tree, sycamore etc. Several mountain
tops are covered with white pines, but of course, forests
are at present bare, only the faded oak leaves still left here
and there to point out what is wanting to the scene.

We met on the road the proprietor of the stage, who

drove us the following stage, partly with six horses. We supped about 6 at Slicers and arrived at Cumberland at ½ p. 10, very much tired, indeed. This day we crossed Sidling hill and Tower hill, which is 112 miles from Baltimore, and afterwards Nicholas mount. These mountains are part of the chain of the Allegheny's which separate the Mississippi rivers from the east coast. On the road between Fredricktown and Washington, Pa. we met continually droves of hogs, often 600 together, being driven, usually from Ohio and even Indiana, to Baltimore. They traveled 8 and 10 miles a day and of course must repay the expenses of even such a journey or no one would undertake it. We also passed and overtook a great number of wagons with 4, 5, or 6 horses always in good condition and high spirits, of good breed and well fed. Got to bed about ½ p. 11. A most delightful day. We walked up several hills but found the weather rather too hot for such exercise. The stage is a long body on springs and can contain 14 persons on the inside. It has a wooden covering and back and leather sides. These we found it very pleasant to have rolled up on both sides in the day, during the whole journey. Fine clear moonlight. We were accompanied by two gentlemen, Mr. Card and Mr. Barbee.

Wednesday, 1st Dec.

Started per stage, as being the only conveyance, at ½ p. 5. We went 14 miles to breakfast and arrived about ½ p. 10 at Allegheny, having crossed the Savage Mount. The whole of the scenery was very romantic and beautiful, especially from the tops of the heights to which we ascended. The view was fine, alternate hill and dale, often enlivened by clear meandering streams and by large cleared and fertile tracts of land or sometimes by neat little villages, one of which in particular reminded me of Swiss scenery, being composed of rustic log houses with rough wooden roofs, lying in a finely wooded valley in the

Blue Mountains. We proceeded from Allegheny with
6 horses, to a beautiful valley in Pa., in which lies
Smithfield, a nice little village whose situation struck me
more than any I had yet seen. Here we met General
Jackson, who had just arrived. He is a fine looking old
man and widower. We overtook several parties of emigrants, all bound for the Ohio. They had usually a wagon
with their utensils, and often a horse or two for some of
the party to ride. They traveled 18 or 20 miles per day.
The greater part of the road was encompassed by trees and
from the top of the different ridges of the Allegheny's
which we traversed this day we had wide extended prospects, less romantic than those of the Blue Mountains.
We were advised to proceed immediately. We therefore
this time supped and started, because an hour's sleep would
make us swear when awoke, the host said. We reached
Brownville about ½ p. 4 and were told we must
wait for daylight. "We laid down on the floor, feet to the
fire, and slept till 6, when we breakfasted and proceeded
at 7 to cross the Monongahela river in a ferry. We passed
a finely undulated country and reached Washington, Pa.
at 2 o'clock. The day had been cloudy and now it
commenced raining pretty smartly. On the road we
never got washed till we stopped for breakfast and then we
had no conveniences for it. We now got dressed and
washed, and while we were undressed and thus employed,
a stage arrived. The parties were shown into the same
room as we possessed. A young lady, daughter of a General and Senator (Beecher) came in while we were thus
employed, and with great nonchalance sat by the fire and
dressed her hair. We dined and slept till 9, supped and
went to bed.

Friday, 3rd Dec.

Started at 5 per mail for Pittsburg. It rained pretty
heavily, though it ceased after some time. The road, as we
now left the National turn-pike, was very hilly and

muddy, but we had good cattle and an excellent coachman, called Waugh. We breakfasted at his house, 12 miles, and he then drove us to Pittsburg, 14 miles further. We arrived at 2 o'clock. We had the stage to ourselves, as the two gentlemen had proceeded yesterday to Wheeling to take steam for New Orleans. Pittsburg lies between the Monongahela and Allyghana rivers, and it is a smoky, dirty looking, manufacturing town with 9 to 10 thousand inhabitants. A good covered wooden bridge crosses each river. On the opposite Monongahela bank is found coal, sand stone, lime stone, a good soil and below, a river to float all produce away. We called on Messrs.Baldwin, Ross and McDonald. Stayed with the former all evening. Mr. Owen saw Mr. Speakman and Mr. Bakewell, a glass manufacturer.

Saturday, 4th Dec.

Mr. Owen breakfasted with Mr. Backwell, we at the hotel. The hotel is a good one. Mr. Craig, a young man, seemed to have the principal charge. Here, as well as in all the principal hotels I saw, the landlord is quite a gentleman, shaking hands on our arrival and departure. Hunter and I called on Messrs. McDonald, Fowler and Baldwin, Mr. B. came back to the hotel with us. We found there Messrs. Rapp, Ross, Sutton and Weig, Rapp's friends. We determined to go to Economy tonight. We set out about 2 with a sharp cold air. Messrs Rapp, Watman and Owen, in Rapp's carriage; Sutton and Wm. Owen in Sutton's gig; Hunter and McD. riding Messrs. Rapp and Baldwin's horses; Mr. Flower, Miss Ronalds and Mrs. Sutton in a hired carriage. On leaving Pittsburg we crossed the Allyghany river by a handsome wooden bridge and proceeded along the right bank of the Ohio, over a rough and often muddy road, in which hill and dale are very frequent. The road is cut in the side of a sloping bank, which in many parts is very abrupt and in one place, called the narrows, there is only room for one vehicle. When two meet there they must find great difficulty in passing, indeed in many places it would be utterly impossible.

We passed a new steamboat, which was being towed up the river in order to get its engines at Pittsburg. It belonged to Rapp and company and is called the Wm. Penn. He means to bring his people up in it in the spring. It is 70 or 80 tons burden. We traveled without stopping about 18 miles and arrived about an hour after dark on a fine bottom perhaps ½ mile in width, where the road, turning abruptly to the left, led us through a wood to Economy, which at present consists of several good frame houses finished and with others now in progress. Mr. Sutton, with whom I went, said that when Mr. Rapp first came over, he had advanced him a good many articles on credit; since then he had been very kind to him. He told me that men and women who are married sleep together; yet Rapp's power is so great as to conquer nature. One man had, contrary to agreement, got a son by his wife. He expected to be turned off, but Rapp said "he might have done much worse." We stopped at a new frame house in which Mr. Rapp and some others lived. We were introduced to his daughter and to Mr. L. Baker, the latter of whom speaks English well and acted usually as interpreter. Not expecting such a large party, we had to wait about an hour for supper, which when served proved to be very good, consisting of Turkey fowl, buckwheat cakes, honey etc. While supper was preparing very good Harmonie wine was handed round and we were shown by a map of Posey county, in which Harmonie was shown by being painted green. Mr. Owen had also a good deal of interesting conversation with Mr. Rapp. After supper 10 or 12 came in and were introduced to us. After a little conversation Mr. Owen showed them some of the drawings he had brought with him. Mr. Rapp said he had had it, at one time, in contemplation to build in a very similar manner, but that he had yielded to Frederick Rapp's advice, he being a more experienced architect. He jokingly said that he must not look any longer, else he would be tempted to commence building a 4th establishment.

About ½ p. 10 we retired. Mr. Flower, Mr. Owen and I slept in two rooms adjoining each other. We found our beds rather short.

Sunday, 5th Dec.

We awoke about 7 o'clock and found that yesterday evening's cold had produced snow, which lay an inch or one and a half inches thick on the ground. On proceeding to the breakfast room we found Mr. Baker there. Shortly after Mr. Rapp came in. Both said they had been thinking so much about what they had heard that they had slept but little all night. About 8 we breakfasted. We were waited on by a young woman named Rachel, who spoke a little English and has a very interesting appearence. Mr. Owen conversed a long time with Mr. Rapp. He explained the formation of character and many of the results deduced from it. Mr. Rapp appeared to agree to all of it. Indeed, he said he had long thought so too. He seemed much pleased to find an individual with whom he had so many ideas in common. He said he had often exclaimed to himself "My God! is there no man on Gods's earth who has the same opinions as myself and can help me in my plans? I am now lucky to have come in contact with such an one" He anticipated already the pleasure we should have in frequent intercourse with each other, by means of the numerous steamboats which are continually plying the river, should my father be induced to purchase Harmonie. On being asked why he left the Wabash, he said the climate did not agree with the Germans; although the English and Americans found it quite healthy; and then he said something about having done there as much as he could both for himself and the neighborhood and the necessity of therefore commencing a new settlement.

About 11 we were summoned to meeting by a psalm tune played on a keyed bugle and a French horn. It had a fine effect. The members we soon saw assembling, and on entering a frame building opposite Rapp's house, we found in the upper story about 100 persons assembled, the women on one side and the men on the other. They sang in chorus a hymn on Friendship remarkably well, and after a short prayer, Mr. Rapp spoke from the 169th psalm. He and all his associates speak a patois, resembling Swiss German, which made it very difficult for me to follow him. He spoke in an easy, familiar manner, apparently without preparation and with great fluency. He remarked among other things that when we found that which we hold to be our duty and our natural feeling to be in unison then we were sure we had found the truth and that we always found ourselves compelled to act accordingly; however much we might try to do so we could not get rid of it. He also said that whoever does wrong disturbs the harmony of the Universe and in order to restore it again we must either do something, or if that was not possible, we must suffer something. He asked them if he had spoken well. They answered him "Yes, it is the truth." If he meant that no one could do wrong without producing misery to himself and others, he was right. He said "as often as we do wrong, if we are conscious of it, whatever one might suppose, we were always getting nearer perfection; meaning, I suppose, that the more knowledge we gain from experience-that is from doing wrong and being conscious of it-the nearer we approach to happiness. On the whole as a sermon it was good and practical, with comparatively little fanaticism about it. Afterwards another ode to Friendship was sung and the whole was concluded within an hour. After the meeting, the two musicians played several tunes at Capt. McD's request and my Father showed all the drawings to Mr. Rapp, and to 12 or 14 members who understood a little English, and who seemed very

much pleased with the plans. Mr. Rapp seemed quite con-
vienced of the immense advantage to be derived from
union of interests. He said $1,000 were to them as $10. to
an individual. Mr. Rapp thought that my Father was the
individual who had the means to realize these ideas, having both the capital and plenty of hands. My father said
that Economy would suit very well and that the houses
now built would serve as temporary residences for those
employed.

Mr. Owen promised to let Mr. Rapp have a full set of
the drawings as soon as they arrived from England. We
walked out as far as the river before dinner. It is a couple
of hundred yards off and the ground is elevated very con-
siderably above it. The embryo streets are laid out at
right angles and are 60 feet broad. We dined before 12.
Mr. Rapp gave us a letter to Fredrick Rapp and we left
him, apparently sorry to part with us, about 1 o'clock.
The members appeared to pay a great deal of respect to
Mr. Rapp; indeed to do just as he desired. We saw none
under 18 years of age. Their countenances showed con-
tentment and absence of anxiety; but they seemed not to
have much knowledge of the world or of what was going
on around them. They seemed to be quite friendly and
disposed to talk but they said little before Mr. Rapp. Mr.
Waterman drove Mr. Owen and me in Mr. Rapp's carriage
Hunter and Sutton went in the gig, Capt, McD. rode and
Mr. Flower and Miss Ronalds were in a hackney coach.
It had not snowed since morning but it continued dull all
day, the snow still covering the ground. In the evening it
cleared up to frost. My Father told Mr. W. to tell Mr.
Rapp that the world did them injustice and that he was
better pleased with what he had seen than he expected to
be. Mr. W. is rather intelligent and seems to be very fond
of Rapp. He said he was sure Rapp was pleased by our
visit. He is a Dutchman. Both Germans and Dutch are
here called Dutch. He spoke a little English; indeed al-

most all of them appeared to know a little, more or less. We reached Pittsburg before dark and were told that the river had risen a little and that the Pennsylvania, a tried Steamboat, would sail next morning at 9 o'clock. Mr. Owen called on Mr. Bakewell, who promised to take berths for us in the above mentioned Steamboat. After he returned Mr. Speakman called to take leave of us, as he returns tomorrow to Philadelphia, and to introduce a man who had resided some years in Harmonie. He considered it unhealthy; indeed this opinion provailed whereever we have been as yet. Shortly after Messrs. Bakewell and Page, partners in an extensive glass manufactory, called; also Mr. Baldwin, a lawyer, one of the principal people here, who was for some time in Congress but has now so much to do that he has been obliged to decline being elected for two years past. A baker, named McNiven, called and gave my father a very good paper regarding human nature as it appeared to him. Mr. Sutton came in soon after and introduced a young man named Albers, a German, who has been some time in the states and who intends proceeding per the Penna. on his way to Harmonie and thence to New Orleans.

Monday, 6th Dec.

A clear frosty morning. We awoke about daylight and after breakfasting at the hotel and packing up we arrived at the steamboat exactly in proper time. Miss. Ronalds, who staid with Mr. Flower at Dair's hotel, was not ready, but Mr. Bakewell detained the boat for half an hour. At ½ p. 9 we set sail, leaving the LaFayette Steam Boat preparing to start at 10. This is a new boat that has never yet been tried. It draws from 6 to 12 inches more more than the Pennsylvania, which draws from 3 feet to 3½ ft. of water. It is propelled by a steam engine on the high pressure principle, of 70 or 80 horse power. The cabin contains 16 beds and the ladies cabin 2 single and two

double beds. The cabins are above the level of the water
and the deck above them is covered with a roof from
which stout canvas hangs down on all sides. Here the
steerage, or as they are called deck passengers, sit, eat and
sleep. As they had a stove upon deck it was very comfortable. The fare to Louisville is $15.00 including board
The deck passengers, who board themselves, pay $6.00.
We started with as many passengers as the boat could
contain comfortably. Amongst others, besides our own
party, which consisted of Miss. Ronalds, Mr Flower,
Messrs. Owen, McDonald, Hunter, Wm. Owen and R.
Watson, we had on board Mr. Albers, the German, and a
friend, Mr. and Mrs. Drake and Tom. Macks, actors, etc.
and on deck a man with his wife—a very pretty, agreeable
woman—and children. Mr. Hunt, the owner of the boat
accompanied us and acted as commander. The Captain's
name is Cunningham, both very pleasant people. During
the night the Ohio had risen a little, the Monongahela
falling but the Allyghana rising more rapidly. On the
whole the hight of the river was such that we expected to
be enabled to get on with little water to spare. We went
down the river cautiously at the rate of 9 or 10 knots an
hour. We had excellent pilots on board, so that we
always kept in the deepest channel. Once or twice during
the day we grazed the bottom in making rather sharp
turns in the river. Soon after starting it became cloudy,
which ended in a regular fall of snow which continued
during the evening. We were thus prevented from enjoying the beautiful scenery on the banks of the river, which
an occasional peep told us we were loosing. We passed
several little towns and villages and a little before
Georgetown we passed the boundary line of Penn., having
thence Ohio on the right and Virginia on the left, and
reached Steubenville about 4 o'clock. This is a flourishing
settlement in the state of Ohio, situated on the right side
of the river and on the second bank. It is 73 miles from

Pittsburg. After dark we reached Wheeling, distance 96 miles form Pittsburg. It lies in Virginia on the left bank of the Ohio river and extends a good ways along the shore, having only one good street. It is in a flourishing state. Owing to the state of the weather we did not land. We remained here some hours and started soon after the moon rose. As the LaFayette did not overtake us here we concluded that she had not been able to set sail, as she had intended. Between 9 and 10 we retired to our berths. During the whole evening the cabin was remarkably close and warm, from the number of occupants and a large stove in which a roasting fire was always kept up. The Americans in general delight in large fires and heated rooms, to which we find it difficult to accustom ourselves.

Before retiring for the night we went above stairs and found that a man. his wife, and child had laid on a matress before the fire, although a number of men were standing around. It surprised us a little, but, situated as they were, they could not do otherwise.

Tuesday, 7th Dec.

We arose at daybreak. I found my head rather inclined to ache from yesterday's heat and also from the steam which escaped at intervals from different parts of the engine and often filled the whole vessel. The morning was damp and dull.; it continued so all day; now and then a little sprinkle of snow. We continued to sail through a beautiful country, having the state of Ohio on the right and Virginia on the left. The banks, except when cleared for settlement, were finely wooded; sometimes the hills rose abruptly form the waters edge, at other times receding, they would leave extensive bottoms of the finest land extending many miles between them and the river. The sycamore appeared to flourish most. It was everywhere seen in great abundance and of the largest growth. Elms,

oaks, cotton-woods, sugar trees and wild grape vines were
also discernable. The Missletoe is also seen hanging on
numerous trees all along the river. The plant is never found
on the ground. Its seeds appear to be carried by the birds
from one tree to another. Some time after breakfast we
passed the Congress steamboat aground in the river where
the channel is very narrow. We passed it with difficulty,
the captain having gone before and taken soundings. The
Congress passengers were anxious to go with us, but the
Captain thought it would be unfair, as it was expected to
get off soon. Soon after we reached Marietta, very neat and
pleasant looking town, situated in the state of Ohio, between the forks of the Great Muskingum and the Ohio. It
lies on an extensive bottom. In the Ohio lay the
Mechanics steamboat and I observed on the shores of the
Muskingum two in progress. I was very much pleased
with this place as far as could be seen from the steamboat,
which did not remain there. Marietta is 188 miles from
Pittsburg. In the afternoon we passed a very narrow channel opposite Ambersons island, where we two times
grounded for an instant. We soon after reached Letarts
falls which, though dangerous to small craft, are so insig-
nificant that I could only see a small ripple on each side
and R. Watson, who had been looking for them, asked soon
after we passed whether we should come to them soon.
After dark we lay to for an hour or two till the moon arose.
During the night we passed the rock of antiquity, on which
a number of figures have been engraved. In the evening
Mr. Drake played a little on the violin. He plays with
taste and tollerable execution. He and F. Mark also gave
us a comic song or two. About 10 o'clock we overtook a
flat boat which hailed us. Its passengers had already gone
to bed, but they soon appeared and proved to be the rest
of Mr. Drake's party; Mr. and Mrs. A and Miss. Drake,
with 3 children, came in quité dishabille. They appeared quite at ease and Mrs. Drake performed the duties of a

mother to her little infant before the whole party, while little Drake tumbled head over heels to amuse us. Several passengers who were asleep were awakened by the noise of the children, and had we not been amused by the novelty of the scene we should not have been pleased at being detained till 12 o'clock from bed, as we could not retire till the ladies left the cabin.

They had been out of Pittsburg 9 days in this boat.

Wednesday, 8th Dec.

A little before breakfast we made for the Ohio shore in order to take in wood. We found a boat with four or five cords in it. These cost $1.25 and $1.50 each. While this was being taken on board, we went to a small cottage standing on a high bank, surrounded by a little cleared land, with fine sycamore trees in front. We found there 3 females in a very neat house. One in particular seemed to catch my Father's fancy. They said they liked the situation but that it was lonely and access to it by land difficult. We soon returned and found breakfast ready. Our party was now much so increased that the breakfast table could not contain us all at one time. The morning was pleasant and it appeared that no snow had fallen here. The banks of the river and the numerous islands which we had passed presented a fine and rich appearance. The land up to the top of the hills, I was informed, was a fine, deep soil. During the greater part of the day we sailed between the states of Ohio and Kentucky. About 12 we again halted for wood, and, visiting a neighboring cottage in Ohio, found two men and several women and children at dinner, which consisted of meat, vegetables, milk, cider, cornbread etc. The dwelling was a log house. It seemed quite snug and weather tight. About an hour before dark we landed at Mayesville, Ky., 441 miles from Pittsburg. Here Wm Bakewell, Jr. left us intending to proceed to Lexington Ky. He said he had been in expectation of sailing for more than a month, but as he remains at Lexington all winter,

he was in no great hurry. The Drakes likewise left us as
they were bound for Frankfort, Ky. Drake, senior, came
very poor, 14 years ago, from England. He now owns the
theatres at Frankfort, Lexington, Cincinnatti and Louisville. Mrs. Drake is said to be the best actress in the
United States. She has a fine figure and is a beautiful,
interesting woman. The government of Kentucky, sitting
now at Frankfort, they meant to perform there, but had
been detained some weeks beyond their time by the low
stage of the river. We walked through the town—Mayesville—and found a good front and tolerable second street.
Hunter and my Father bought mits and Mr. Owen had a
bantering conversation with the storekeeper regarding money and labor notes. He told us that a gallon of whisky,
which will make 12 individuals quite drunk, can be bought
for 12½ cents. After the moon rose we set sail, having
taken several passengers and a carriage and couple of
horses on board. While sailing down the river the
thought struck me very forcibly that mankind could never
be happy so long as they continued philosophers and acted
from reflection; that a natural, happy character could only
be produced when mankind shall have been so trained that
his feelings, habits and impulses shall always lead to do the
best without the aid of reflection. It is thus that those
actions which appear to be the result of reflection are denominated affected. Before retiring for the night I went on
deck. It was a clear frosty night; the moon shone beautifully and her bright reflection in the clear water of the river
and the finely wooded banks, seen dimly by her pale light,
presented a lovely prospect, as if to tempt us to steal a
little from the night.

Tuesday, 9th Dec.

After having been awakened by strange noises in the
night, we found ourselves at daybreak at Cincinnati, 515
miles from Pittsburg, where we had arrived between 3 and

4 in the morning. We walked out to view the town. It
was a clear, cold morning. The city is finely situated on a
high bank, over which the river has never been known to
rise. It presents a very neat and clean appearance. Like
other American towns, it is laid in a regular manner. It
has a number of fine streets. Almost all the houses are
built of brick, and many of them present a handsome appearance. On the whole it seems more desirable as a
residence than any we have seen. We were told that the
society is excellent. It is growing very fast. Twenty
one years ago there was scarcely a house standing. Now
it contains about 13.000 inhabitants. The city stands on
the side of a gentle slope rising from the top of a high,
abrupt bank and many of its streets extend to a great distance both parallel and at right angles with the river. We
returned to breakfast and I afterwards walked out with
Miss. Ronalds. After vewing the city, we walked to the
eastern outskirts, about 1 and ½ miles, where we found a
celebrated mound of earth, perhaps 40 ft. high, supposed
to have been raised by ancient Indians, of a race now
not known, for religious purposes. A little after 10 we
again set sail leaving behind us a small steamboat, the
Ohio, which had advertised to start at 2 o'clock. We proceeded quickly and passed some beautiful scenery, which
looked more beautiful from being viewed through the medi-
um of a clear, calm, delightful morning. I had a long conversation with Turner, who at one time had met for 18
months together, with 30 families, all anxious to emigrate
on the principle of united property. The scheme dropped
through as they had no leader with sufficient practical experience. He said he would join the first community established. I likewise talked for some time with a Swiss, one
of the first settlers of Vevay, Indiana. He came 20 years
ago from Switzerland. He said the vine did not produce so
much as was expected. They grow Cape and Madiera
vines. All the production is consumed near them. About

60 Swiss families are there now. All do not grow the vine. We had on board several Ohio Navigators, which we found useful and amusing. Twice during the day we took in wood on the Indiana shore. We visited two families and found them only tolerably comfortable. They did not much like their residence. One woman said it was lonely and unhealthy. She seemed to prefer Ohio. In the evening it rained heavily. After tea we collected amicably around the stove on deck, along with 10 or a dozen deck passengers, amongst whom were 3 or 4 females. By degrees we obtained one song after another, both from them and others. I remained there a couple of hours. I believe it was kept up till 12 o'clock. Messrs. Turner, Hart, McDonald, Albers etc. sang, as well as the ladies.

Friday, 10th Dec.

On awakening we found ourselves at Louisville, nearly 680 miles from Pittsburg, having completed the voyage in 3 days and 16 hours, including all stoppages; a very happy voyage considering the stage of the river.

We went through deep mud, the rain having continued all night and still continuing, to Washington Hall, W. Allen. Here we obtained a room with 3 beds. Hunter went immediately to Shippingport to transact some business. Mr. Turner called after breakfast and introduced his partner. Mr. Owen received a note from Hunter regarding a steamboat in which to proceed and taking a hack drove down to inquire about it. He found that the Favorite sails for New Orleans on Sunday, water permitting, but that all the berths and accommodations in the cabin are already taken. Messrs. Stanley and friends are going by her. We dined in a private parlor with the ladies and Drs. at 2 o'clock. We found the party so stiff that Capt. McDonald and I agreed upon preferring the public table. It continued raining all morning or rather a Scotch mist; for the continued rains that we have so far witnessed are very fine, yet penetrating easily, wet as much as much heavier rain usually does. In the afternoon it ceased, and was still and cloudy and the streets very muddy. After dinner we called on Messrs. Turner and Reeder. Found them engaged in business and Mr. Turner preparing to return back the same evening to Pittsburg by the Pennsylvania. We drank tea at the public table and afterwards, at Dr. Lindsay's request, Mr. Owen showed the drawings to him and Dr. and Mrs. Chase. They all seemed very much interested and no one offered any objection of moment. Dr. Chase remarked that this was the only feasible plan he had ever seen, by which emancipation could be carried into effect; adding that no one ever attempted to justify slavery as an abstract principle, but merely on the ground of emancipation being at present impracticable without hurting both master and slave. There were many parts of the country at present unoccupied; the government might grant this to the negroes to construct a settlement on this plan. While this was going on Mr. Flowers, who had been dining out, returned with Miss. Ronalds and told us he had met with the English M P's who are travelling this country. He made some objections to Mr. Owen's plans but the rest of the party seemed to dissent from him. We talked a little with the slave who waits on us. He was bought by Mr. Allan 7 years ago for $900, has since refused $1500. for him. He said he liked this place very much. He is a native of Virginia. I drew a little in the evening.

Saturday, 11th Dec.

A fine morning. Capt. McD. and I breakfasted at the public table, Mr. Owen with the Drs. At 8 o'clock the therm. stood at 55 degrees. Mr. Owen proposed writing a short expose of his system, Capt. McD. and I, therefore, strolled out to view the town. Capt. McD. called on the English M. Ps. They were out; gone to Mr. Ormsby's. We are told that they are here considered proud, that they have not much communication with the inhabitants. Louisville has one good street parallel with the river; the others are short, soon leading to fields of woods. It contains about 4000 inhabitants and has a hospital and four churches. It likewise supports a theater during some months of the year. A number of hackney coaches ply the streets. These are the first we have seen west of the Allyghana mountains. We walked south to the outskirts of the city, through numerous muddy crossings and puddles, owing to the late rain. As far as the city has been laid out, the ground, as yet unoccupied by buildings, is covered with grass and the streets marked off by palings; further on still is surrounded by woods. We ascended a gentle slope which extended our prospect a little. The city seemed to be situated on an extensive bottom of good, though sandy, soil. The whole bottom is supposed to have been deposited by the river, whose course at this point has been gradually thrown more to the northward. It is surrounded by a great many pools and marshes, which render the situation unhealthy. We met an inhabitant who seemed to be conversant with the foibles of the place. He told us that at the point where we stood the magistrate had drawn a line, beyond which the gamblers and loose characters were not permitted to reside. He said that a good many individuals came here who ruined their health much more by their disoluteness than by the climate. He gave us a very poor idea of the morality of the place. On returning we found Mr. Jacobs with my Father, to whom he had been introduced by letter. We dined at the private table and afterwards Mr. Owen, Capt. McD., Miss. Ronalds, young Lindsly and I walked down towards Shipping port. We met Hunter who showed us a silk plant, senna, honey locust, etc. We found near the river some fine old sycamores and honey locusts with very long spikes. It was a very beautiful evening; almost too warm for walking. At 5 o'clock we saw plainly the hour by the watch. The even-

ings are evidently longer than in Scotland; but there is
almost no twilight. Darkness comes on very soon after
sunset. We drank tea at the public table and were introduced to Messrs. Warburton and Shade. Capt. McD. went
with Hunter to Shipping port and drank tea there. After
tea Mr. Owen went with Mr. Flower to be introduced to a
Mr. Tom and I wrote to Mrs. Owen, (his mother.)

Sunday, 12th Dec.

We breakfasted at the private table. Afterwards Mr
Owen explained his plan to Mr. Allan, our host, Mrs
Allan and family and General Breckenridge. He said the
arrangements were intended to perform all the objects of
society; that therefore to understand them it was necessary to understand the material to be worked upon viz—
human nature. He would therefore state his ideas on the
subject. He then stated what human nature was and the
effect of circumstances upon it, therefore how necessary it
became to introduce a system excluding all vicious and
including all virtuous circumstances, in as far as our experience went. He then explained the drawings. All parties
said but little in reply. But they appeared pleased, though
doubtful of the practicability of the proposed arrangements
McD. and I went to the Presbyterian church and heard Dr.
Chase preach a good, practical sermon, to a small but
decent congregation. Mr. Owen wrote an outline of his
system. We dined at the public, Mr. Owen at the private
table. It rained all day and a strong fog arose off the river.
The therm. which remained nearly stationary all day stood
at 12 o'clock at 61 degrees. In the afternoon we were engaged writing.

A black, who cut my Father's hair this morning, said he
had been free for 4 years. He had paid $150. per annum
to his master, till he was able to save $1,000. which he paid
for his freedom. Since then he has given $900. for his wife
and one child. He must have worked very hard to accom-

plish all this; indeed he told us he had worked nearly night and day for years.

Monday, 13th Dec.

Got up at daylight to prepare to set out per steamer Favorite. Fine morning. Therm. at 8 o'clock 41 degrees. We have found Washington Hall, Allen proprietor, a good inn and attentive servants. Milk is put on the table at breakfast and supper. We drove down to Shippingport, a little village below the falls, about 2½ miles from Louisville. We arrived about 10 o'clock and found the Favorite, a large steamboat of 320 tons, in which we meant to start, not yet finished loading. She had been delayed some time by having left open some port holes, by which she became full of water as soon as her lading sank her so far. We did not start till about 2 o'clock. This being the first boat that had sailed for some time, she was very full of passengers and freight. Owing to the number of passengers on board and the delay in sailing we did not dine till near 5 o'clock. A little before dark we landed on the Indiana side to take in wood, having sailed about 25 miles down the river. We visited a family near the river and found them tolerably comfortable. Wood here sells for $1.37½ per cord. We took in 9 cords which feed 6 boilers, required for one piston. The power of the engine of 70 or 80 horse power. They consume about a cord an hour. In the Favorite the paddles are quite behind the boat and the machinery aft of the cabin. This is convenient except as regards a sharp turn, in which case the side paddles are more effective. The cabin is small, containing only 16 berths, but we had 35 cabin passengers. The ladies cabin had 4 berths. We had 6 ladies besides 3 children, including 2 who came on board when we stopped to take on wood. We remained where we took in wood, the river being too low for night sailing. Amongst the passengers were, besides our old party, Messrs. Stanly, Wortley, Dennison and Labrouchet,

(4 English gentlemen, M Ps) Mr. Beebee—whom we had left at Washington Pa and had passed at Marietta—Mr. Briggs—who was left behind at Liverpool when we sailed for New York, but who afterwards came over in the Pantheon—Dr. and Mrs. Chase and Mr Albers and some others who came with us in the Pennsylvania, several New Orleans gentlemen, etc. The deck is covered in and contains several bed steads. Great part was filled with cargo, but besides other deck passengers, they contrived to stow away 47 slaves, going down to be sold. About 10 o'clock mattresses began to be laid down for those who had no berths. We, going so short a distance, came in for last places. Hunter gave up his berth to my Father. Mr. Flower got a mattress and McDonald Hunter and myself got a little corner close by the stove, the whole free space in the cabin being quite full. I, at last, as the mattresses seemed to be exhausted, laid myself down on a few cloaks and covered myself with my great coat. A cold clear evening.

Tuesday, 14th Dec.

We started between 4 and 5 o'clock. About 7 we got up and breakfasted about ½ p. 10. I was rather sleepy and stiff with my night's position, being pent up in a very small space between Mr. Flower and Mr Hunter. We washed in the open air, as is the custom in the steamboats and most of the small taverns. A beautiful, clear, frosty morning. We raised from the river a large flock of wild geese which flew away, making a loud noise. We made this day 150 miles. As it grew dark we landed on the Kentucky side at a wood yard. We visited a house belonging to one Sam Davis, who had no wife, but 2 slaves. About ½ p. 9 I went on shore and found 8 or 10 passengers collected around a fire, at the foot of a maple, about 100 yards from shore. We soon increased the fire by large, dry, old logs lying about in all directions and by weeds which grew near and which burnt with a beautiful flame. On looking round we found a tree hollow inside for 10 or 12 feet up. About 11 we set fire to this and the hollow part, serving as a tunnel, it soon raised a great flame. Mr. Bartlett, the clerk of the boat, came to tell us our couches were prepared. He sent the steward with some brandy to us. We asked for some beef to roast and he soon brought us some beef and pork etc. We continued to ply the fire well and the tree wasted away fast. Hunter was quite in his element. Three of the English gentlemen who were present seemed to enjoy it very much. Besides 'these were Messrs. Albers, Briggs, McDonald and myself. Hunter cut some 3 pronged forks with which we roasted the beef and on trial it proved very good. We proposed a racoon hunt, which is always at night, but for lack of dogs we gave it up. We continued plying the fire well and waited anxiously for the fall of the tree, occasionally raised the war whoop led on by Hunter. At last, about 2 o'clock, it fell to our great joy, carrying with it several others in its fall; which was very grand, well worth waiting for. We set up a loud yell and came away leaving the proprietor two immense piles of ashes. He was with us all the time and very glad of our frolic, as the ashes we left and the ground we cleared were well worth $10. On coming away Hunter proposed ducking him, upon which he took the alarm and kept clear of the water. We returned to the cabin and crept very quietly into our corners.

Wednesday, 15th Dec.

We started some time before daylight. We were awoke at 6, having had 4 hours sleep. A beautiful morning, very cold. About 12 o'clock—having about 8 passed a little village called Owensboro—we reached Evansville, a county town, 264 miles from Louisville, in Indiana. It contains between 30 and 40 houses. We visited one or two. One

woman was quite astonished to see us. She did not seem
to know what to make of our visit. But she received us
politely, as indeed all the women do whom we have visited.
We took in a large quantity of pork until about 2 o'clock
and reached Mt Vernon a little after dark. A most lovely
sunset. A clear sky except one or two clouds in the west,
which came of a fiery red, soon changing into a beautiful
neutral tint, and that again into a dull pink. During the
whole of our voyage from Louisville the wooded bank,
with its immense sycamores presented nearly the same
appearance as higher up the river except that the bank
became less high and the hills more distant. On the whole,
considering the confined accomodations, the party was very
agreeable and disposed to be accomodating. The English
gentlemen suited themselves quite to the circumstances by
which they were surrounded; they appeared to have come
to this country with a proper spirit, being inclined to
accomodate themselves to what they should find and not to
rail at everything they saw different from what they had
been accustomed to. They were a fine specimen of their
countrymen. A little before we left the vessel my Father
showed his drawings to them. The boat got close up to
the shore with difficulty. We waited on the shore for
nearly ¾ of an hour for a cart to convey the luggage to
the inn. We proceeded to Mr. James' hotel where we got
supper—no milk to be had here—Our party was Messrs.
Owen, McDonald, Flower, Albers, Miss. Ronalds and myself. Messrs. Owen McD. Albers and I slept in two rooms
adjoining each other. In the morning we found our door
opening into the outer air quite open. We supposed a dog
who was seen in the room opened it.

Thursday 16th Dec.

We rose at daybreak and after breakfasting we loaded
2 wagons, with 4 horses each, and having placed ½ the baggage in each so as to form seats, we sat in them ourselves.

Capt. McD. and Albers walked on before. We passed over a track called a county road, at first pretty good. About ½ way for some miles there were many very step though small hills. It was with great difficulty that the horses could get up and down; indeed once I thought they could not have accomplished it, their feet slipped out so much. We passed a few log houses and a few acres of cleared land around each. We saw some beautiful tulip trees, very large indeed; also some fine black and white walnut, beech hickory, dog wood, etc.

We walked several miles and my Father accompanied a woman on horseback some distance and had a good deal of conversation with her. She said she got many things from Harmony, but did not like the place because marriage was prohibited. He also talked to two women who were washing by the roadside, called Polly and Sallie French. We saw a flock of turtle doves, some beautiful woodpeckers with red heads, etc. and a number of gray squirrels in the woods. We were some time in Harmonie lands before we were aware of it. During the whole distance the land was rolling, as it is called, and presented a fine appearance. A few miles before we reached the town the soil became dryer, more sandy and lighter and the character of the woods also changed. The beech, ironwood, etc. disappeared, giving place to more white and other oak. After travelling about 15 miles, we came about 2 o'clock in sight of the town, lying below us about a mile off, on an extensive bottom cleared to a good distance, which ended near where we stood in undulating hills, on which the vineyards stood. The morning had been beautiful, frost in the night, but about 7 the therm. stood at 34. The sky had gradually become covered with clouds and it began to rain a little as we entered the town. We stopped at a house on which "Private Entertainment" was written up; this we were told enabled them to turn any one away who might happen to misbehave himself. We washed and dressed, which we

much needed, and between 3 and 4 we sat down to dinner
without McDonald and Albers, who had not yet arrived.
We had a pretty good dinner of veal—which the driver said
was a standard dish—etc. After dinner Mr. Fredrick Rapp
called upon us and Mr Owen and I walked out with him.
We walked through the town and observed the brick and
wooden churches, Mr. Rapp's large brick house and opposite to it another, fully as large, in which he told us about
40 persons reside as one family. We walked down a gentle
declivity outside the town to the bottom on which the river
rises usually once a year, but above which the Wabash
never rises; from this a road, raised above the neighboring
surface, so as to be passable during floods, leads to the river
about, ¼ or 1-3 a mile from the town. The Wabash, which
is at present low, appears to flow very slowly. A steep bank
encloses it on the Indiana side, perhaps 20 feet above its
present level and a creek enters it near the road, which we
were told sometimes overflows. Fredrick Rapp said the
first thing they did when they arrived, was to drain all the
pools, etc, so that now as soon as the river falls the water
runs off again. He says the river rises usually very regularly and slowly perhaps from 3 or 4 weeks in the spring
and falls again for 2 or 3 into its regular banks again. Only
once in the Autumn has it over flown since the Harmonites
have been here. In the fork between the creek and the
river we saw a flat boat in the stocks, nearly finished, for
taking goods to New Orleans, in the river 4 keel boats for
taking produce up and down the river. Besides these were
several other flat boats loading produce from Harmonie,
bought by other proprietors from Rapp. In returning we
met McDonald and Albers just arrived, who had ordered a
dinner for us at Springfield, expecting us to come that way.
They told us they had talked to a number of persons on the
road, among others they had met a Major General carrying
the mail bags. We walked to Mr. Rapp's house and got out
on the balcony at top to view the village. It is built on the

whole in the shape of a square, divided by two streets crossing each other at right angles, running north and south and
east and west, the latter leading from Shawneetown to
Vincennes and the former from Mount Vernon to Saint
Louis on the Mississippi; each of these squares into four
smaller squares, which are again intersected by other
smaller streets, crossing each other at right angles. Near
the middle of the village, on the south western square
stands the two churches. The wooden one is oblong with
a spire at the east end, the other is of brick in the
shape of a cross, directly west of the wooden one and almost touching it. In the front of this—the wooden one—
is a small open square with a fountain in the center, termin-
ating in the fork of the two streets. Mr. Rapp's large brick
house stands in the S. E. corner of the N. W. square and on
the opposite side of the street which runs N. and S. is a
large brick dwelling in which about forty persons reside as
one family. The village presents a motly appearance,
no two houses being built together and large and small,
brick, frame, and log houses being intermixed all through
the place, though all built so as to preserve the straight
lines of the streets. In the south east quarter stands the
store on the street which runs north and south, and further
back a cotton spinning establishment, driven by a horse
and cow, walking on an inclined plane, a green for dying
and bleaching, a dying house, a cotton and woolen mill,
the former with power looms and the latter with a patent
machine for cutting the nap. These are driven by a steam
engine, which also sets an adjoining flour mill in operation. Besides this there is a large brick granary. Behind
Mr. Rapp's house there is another built partly of brick and
partly of stone. Near this is a green house, a small store
house and Mr. Rapp's garden, with a mound in the
middle. North of the town about 1-3 of a mile off runs the
Wabash river nearly from e. to w. and s. w. To the south
of the western squares lie some orchards and adjoining

them on the same line the labyrinth, with a house in the middle. To the south of the eastern part, but on some hills about ½ or ¾ of a mile distant, are the vinyards on the south and southwest exposures. Between them are also orchards. Further on are sheep tracks and to the east of the village is a large quantity of cleared land. After viewing the town from the top of Mr. Rapp's house, we returned home to tea. Mr. Vissman, the inn keeper and Mr. Stewart, a lawyer from Springfield, supped with us this evening. They told us Mount Vernon and Springfield are at variance regarding the county town, both being desirous of that honor. In the evening it commenced raining.

Friday, 17th Dec.

During the night it rained very much and this morning when we awoke we found that it still continued and that the streets were very wet. The therm. at 7 o'clock stood at 54. We went out to view the churches and ascended to the top of the new one from whence we had a fine view of the village, etc. The inside of the new church is not yet finished but, as the pillars and woodwork inside are of black walnut, which admits of a fine polish, I have no doubt that when completed it will present a handsome appearance. We then proceeded to a green house, behind Mr. Rapp's house, in which we found fine orange and lemon trees, etc. The oranges were all plucked, but the lemons were very fine and were to be found in all stages, from the blossom to the ripe fruit. The house is so constructed that it can be rolled away in the summer time, leaving the trees in the open air. Near this green house we viewed a small house with dried apples, etc., and then proceeded to a large granary close by, built of stone with the top story of brick. Here we found flour, rye, corn, etc., in very neat order and good preservation. It is free from rats. It is 4 or 5 stories high. In a neighboring building we found some men weaving by hand. We then viewed their wine and cider press, to which by means of a screw almost any power may be applied. As they dine at 11, we returned to Mr. Rapp's house and dined with him and his granddaughter, Gertrude, a very pretty, innocent young girl of 15 or 16, who after dinner played some airs tollerably on the piano-forte and sang a few German songs, along with 3 other girls, also very good looking, whom Mr. Rapp sent for, and afterwards we again proceeded with Mr. Rapp. In the southeast part of the town we found in a log house the distillery, which appeared of a simple construction. The water required is pumped by two dogs, who moved alternately a tread wheel. Each dog pumps for an hour. They make 2nd and 3rd spirits without any trouble. As the machine performs the whole process, the whisky runs out quite ready for use. They make a large quantity for sale. We then came to a small enclosure in which are some young deer and close by in a shed we found a fine elk, 4 years old, with beautiful branching antlers. He was tame and allowed us to pat him. In a neighboring hut we found 6 large bulls, very fat indeed. A short distance off we passed through a tannery and curriery, where we saw some good leather and a small bleaching ground, near which is a dying house. They showed us some very good madder grown here, much superior to what they had imported. From this we passed to another building in which is a steam engine of horse power, made by themselves. It appears to work well. In an adjoining building is a cotton spinning and weaving establishment. We found two double cards and one throssel and one mule with other machines in proportion. They put about 90 threads to compose one and they had no stretching frames. Their spindles revolve about 900 times a minute and a great part of their machinery is of wood. Above we saw three or four power looms working very well. In a neighboring building we were shown the woolen manufacturing. Here we found two double cards and one spinning frame for warp and one for weft, both driven by the hand, of a complicated construction, performing but few different movements. We also saw a machine for cutting the nap and another for preparing homespun cloth without cutting the nap. Near this is the fulling house. We were then shown the flour mill with 3 pair of stones, 2 for flower and 1 for corn. I saw some very beautifully fine flour. From thence we proceeded to another building where a new cotton mill has been erected, about the same size as the other one. My Father showed some of the workpeople how to do their work with greater correctness and expedition. It had rained a good deal all day and while here a very heavy shower came on. The mill is driven by oxen walking on an incline plane. The mill stopped to let them rest and while we waited till the shower was over, the women in the room formed a circle and sang several songs to us of their own accord. The words are usually about friendship and harmony and the music is their own. Those who work together learn to sing with each other, thus forming a number of small singing parties. After the shower we returned to the inn. Mr George Flower arrived just before dark. He had set out from Albion about ½p. 2. The streets this day were very deep in mud. In returning the sky presented a very singular appearance, being of a bright green color near the horizon.

Saturday, 18th Dec.

The rain having continued through a great part of the night, we were surprised this morning to find the ground quite hard owing to a cold west wind which had risen. We walked out to see the labyrinth, which is now not so beautiful as in summer, owing to the want of foliage, flowers, etc. In the center of it is a house, not locked, yet no one can get into it. From thence we proceeded to the vinyards which are planted on the west side of several hills south of the village. The therm. stood at 7 o'clock at 30 degrees, but the wind was nevertheless so piercing as to make a cloak absolutely necessary. The day was dull and occasionally a little snow. The vinyards are interspersed among orchards, and we were told that last year the peaches were so abundant that the hogs had been fed upon them for a month. We returned to the village and saw the brick house, where a quantity of finished brick were stowed up. Mr. Rapp said they were very good. We then visited some cellars under the new church and under Mr. Rapp's house, which were all well filled with wine, cider, etc., also a small garden behind Mr. Rapp's house, which Gertrude Rapp is fond of cultivating. In the center stands a mound covered with petrefactions formed by a spring on the property. In a back yard we saw a stone with the mark of two feet upon it, with a ring in front, supposed to have been made by an Indian before the stone was hardened. Mr. Rapp found it upon the Mississippi and sent some men to hew it from the rock. Mr. Rapp returned with us to the inn and dined with us. We afterwards rode out with him to view a grist mill about 4 miles off, on a branch of the Wabash called the Cut Off. We rode through the woods without much regard to the roads and ascended and descended some very steep hills, Mr. Albers, who staid behind for a few minutes, lost us and did not again rejoin us till we returned. The grist or merchant mill has 3 stones, 2 for flour and one for corn. When going night and day, the 2 flour stones grind 56 barrels in 24 hours. In returning through the woods we saw some fine sights for building and near the mill a sandstone quarry.

Mr. Hugh Ronalds arrived at breakfast and accompanied his sister on her rambles. We met them as we returned home. In the evening a little discussion.

Sunday, 19th Dec.

At 9 we went to church, where Mr. Frederick Rapp discoursed for an hour. He spoke from Isaiah regarding the

Millenium, which he considered to have commenced 30 odd years ago; that they were the commencement and that it consisted in men living together as brothers, each for all, all for each. We dined at 11 and at ½ p. 12 we were summoned to church by the band playing different airs. When we were all seated different parties of men and women sang hymns etc. for an hour and ½, the band assisting occasionally. Mr. Rapp said good or not so good, as the case might be, when each finished. They sang tollerably, but almost all the females with a nasal twang. Afterwards we walked and rode while the bretheren returned again to church. It was a beautiful evening. In the morning there had been a little snow, the therm. at 26 degrees, but it soon cleared up and the sun set with a fine clear sky. At 5 o'clock evening it was still light. We returned to tea with Mr. Rapp, or rather to an elegant supper, composed of all sorts of meats, cakes, etc. Afterwards, in an adjoining room, music commenced and we had a concert of vocal and instrumental music till 9 o'clock. There were 12 or 14 singers and a piano forte, 2 violins and 2 flutes and a bass. Gertrude Rapp, George Rapp's grand daughter, sang and played. She is a very natural and pretty girl of 15 or 16. During the concert wine, fruit, etc. were passed about.

Monday, 20th Dec.

A beautiful, clear, cold, calm morning. therm. at 7 o'clock 17 degrees. Miss. Ronalds went with us to see the manufactures, which detained us till ½ p. 10, when Mr and Miss Ronalds, Capt. McD. and I set out on horseback to proceed to Albion. My Father remained behind with Mr. Rapp—the Messrs. Flower had returned on Sunday—. We crossed the Wabash in a ferry and then proceeded over a deep and muddy road, which runs through a flat, which is a large island in the Wabash, covered with canes, which are good food for cattle in winter. After traveling five or six miles we crossed the Fox river, a branch of the Wabash river. We then got to higher ground and proceeded through a country covered with small timber, chiefly oak. We rode at a slow jog trot and passed a few farms. After traveling about twenty miles we came out of the woods and were much gratified at beholding a large open country, extending several miles, and including perhaps 4000 acres bounded by wood. We crossed one end of this prairie and arrived at ½p. 4 at Mr Flowers, called Parkhouse, a square building at the edge of the prairie, in a good situation. It seemed very comfortable. The day was very beautiful and with great coats on was too warm for exercise. About six we supped with Mr R. Flower.

Tuesday, 21st Dec.

A cool pleasant morning. Mr G. Flower, Cap. McD. and I walked to a number of cottages on the prairie. We saw Mr. Cold, Mr. Cave and a black woman called Sally, who was nearly kidnapped some time ago. We dined with Mr G Flower. His cottage or log house is near Mr R Flower's and was the first cabin built in this neighborhood. He contrived to make himself very comfortable—comparatively—in it. Mrs. G. Flower is a very pretty, lively woman. She has 3 children. She came out with Mr. Birkbeck, who was to marry her, but Mr. F. won the day. This caused a rupture between the families. Mr. George Flower has 2 sons by a former wife, Richard and George. We had a long discussion in the evening. Mr. and Mrs G. Flower seem both much inclined to a community.

Wednesday, 22nd Dec.

A dull cold day. Therm. at 10 o'clock 35 degrees. We walked to Albion and saw Mr. Pickering, Mr. Flower's son in law, who showed us a plan he had made out of Harmonie. We delivered a letter to Dr. Spring, a surgeon, and to Mr Beckett, a West India planter. We saw Mr

Orange, who has a small inn, Washington Hall and Mr. Lewis, a scientific gentleman from England, whom we found with one of his sons, hunting a rabbit with an axe, as it had taken refuge in a hollow tree. Albion presents the appearance of a small American town, 2 or 3 brick buildings, including the public buildings, and perhaps 20 log houses. Saw Mr. Flower's cotton gin, which consists of a number of circular saws, which draw the cotton through openings too small to admit the cotton seeds. It is turned by cattle walking on an inclined plane. Dined with Mr G. Flower and afterwards walked with Miss Ronalds to her home and stayed there playing chess with Mr Ronalds and talking till near eleven. I had left a horse outside. This got off and we had first to catch him and find his bridle, which being done, he carried me in the dark ½ mile through the woods of Mr Flower's. There is very little comfort here. Everything is done in an inferior manner. No one dresses tidily, but dirty coats, shoes, etc. Mr Ronalds tans and works very hard but to little purpose. He has 2 children. Mr Flower usually visits his daughter and son every day and so passes his time. He is a very warm hearted man and very fond of his descendants. Mrs. Flower is a nice woman but lamed by a fall.

Thursday, 23rd Dec.

A very beautiful day; a little frost. After getting Miss Ronalds mounted and riding with her to Mr. Pickering's, to get another side saddle, I was obliged to walk back a mile as my horse, which I had fastened to a paling, got his head out of the bridle and ran home before me. I and a party of ten or a dozen persons started on horseback, with about an equal number of dogs of all kinds, greyhounds, halfbreeds, bulldogs, pointers, etc., to course for deer on the prairies. After starting 2 deer, we called on Mr Orange whose farm is at the s. w. extremity of the prairie, before Mr Flower's house, here named the Boltinghouse prairie, but commonly called the English prairie. We found here Mrs Orange and Mrs Jolly, cousin of Mr Beckett, a very pretty, lively woman. Our party consisted of Miss Ronalds and Messrs. Flower-2, Orange-2, Beckett, Ronalds, Dr. Spring, Capt. McD. and myself. After leaving Mr. Orange's and riding through a great deal of brush and underwood, in doing which we saw a rabbit or hare and squirrel and killed an opposum, we returned to Boltinghouse prairies and had some capital runs after 8 or 9 deer—which we started at two different times—for several miles. We got home about ½p. 4 without catching any deer, as the grass on the prairie was so long that the greyhounds never got sight of the deer, although we from our horses could see their backs above the grass. Mr D. Orange nearly rode over one of the deer. Mr. Flower has invited his children to dine with him at 4, hoping that Father would arrive this day, but we at 5 dined without him as he did not arrive.

Friday, 24th Dec.

Very beautiful day. Therm. at 7 o'clock 32; in the afternoon it stood at 56 in the shade. Miss Ronalds, Capt. McD. and I walked to Albion, with Mr. G. Flower. We called on a working blacksmith, J. D. Johnston, Esq., Justice of the peace and deputy sheriff of the county—Edwards —, who talked about a bill for the admission of the county having been laid on the table. We proceeded then to Mr Warrington's school, in a small room in a stone building, where we found him instructing about 15 boys and girls. He showed us some good specimens of writing and told us he made the children take places. We then called on Mr Beckett, but his wife being in deshabille would not appear, though Miss Ronalds asked if she could not be seen. Afterwards we called on Mrs Carter, with whom I wished to barter a deers horn, but could get nothing for it. Mr. Carter was not at home, being now on a visit to some Kickapoos, which are supposed to be now about 40 or 50 mile off. They are now hunting, intending going down in the Spring to attack the Osages, who killed a number of their tribe some time ago. We then walked through a fine wood about 2 miles to Wanbro—Mr Birkbeck's settlement —and called on Mr Brown, a shoemaker, with whom we and Mr G Flower engaged to dine on Tuesday next. From thence we returned through the Boltinghouse prairie, about 2 miles, home. We found the heat quite oppressive; very pleasant sitting in the open air in the shade. We got in about ½ p. 4, dined with Mr G Flower. We had scarsely finished when we were informed my Father had just arrived with a Harmonite called Joe Healey. They had left Harmonie about ½ p. 9 and my Father had guided himself by a map of the Illinois, which he had with him. About ½ a mile from here he to took the Albion road instead of the one which leads directly to Mr G. Flower's house, but he had been set right by Mr Cave who met him just in time and who knew him by his resemblance to me. In the evening we had supper and musical party at Mr Flower's, attended, besides his family and ourselves, by Mr and Mrs Carter, Mr and Mrs Lewis, who all sang, and by Messrs Cave, Spring and Ronalds, who played the violin, flute and violincello. All the pieces sung and played in chorus were hymn tunes. The two principal performers, we were told, were absent, JudgeB and Mrs Pickering. The former is leader and the latter presides at the piano forte, which was left out this evening altogether.

Saturday, 25th Dec

Christmas day A most beautiful day, not a cloud to be seen for two days. Therm. at 10 o'clock 56, afternoon 62 in shade, after sunset 52. Mr. Flower Mr Owen and I rode to Mrs Ronald's and sat down in the shade as being the pleasantest place we could find. Mrs Ronalds is a quiet, pleasant lady and has two children, Kate and Hugh, 4 and 2 years old. We then rode on to the prairie and rode twice

through the prairie fire, which, owing to there being no
wind, moved very slowly. It certainly would be terrific
enough to see a fire like this coming up to your log cabin.
They then fight it, as it is termed, endeavoring to overcome it by striking it with clapboards, which are about
2 or 2½ feet long and are used to cover log houses. The
fire we saw was at least ½ mile long and we were told that
it had been known to proceed so rapidly as to overtake a
man on horseback, even though he were galloping at full
speed to escape from it. It is usually stopped by a road
or a fence. We rode slowly over Boltinghouse's prairie
and viewed several beautiful sites for communities; indeed
we all agreed that Duke Hamilton Park was not at all de-
graded by being compared with it; yet we were told by
everyone that no one could form any idea of its beauty in
the spring when gazing on it in its present faded and dried
up appearance, surrounded by and studded with black leaf-
less trees. My Father told us that he had been riding
about in the woods every day since we left him, dining on
cold meat and Harmony wine, in old trees which were
lying on the ground and enjoying this life very much. The
capabilities of Harmony seem to please him more and
more. He settled nothing with Mr Rapp but expects him
on Monday with his daughter here. Though moving very
slowly we found the heat of the sun quite relaxing and the
thought occurred to me, how insupportable the heat must
be when the thermometer stands 40 degrees higher, which
we were told is sometimes the case. I was told by one
man that he had seen the thermometer at 106—I think at
109—but this very rare indeed. The therm. rises usually to
96 or 98 but the average greatest heat is 80 or 90 degrees.
After leaving the prairie Miss R. Mr. O. and I rode to
Albion and met on the road a large party going to dine at
Dan. Orange's. We saw then for the first time Mrs Beckett. She is rather a pretty woman. From Albion we proceeded to Wanbro' and called on Mr. Birkbeck, when we

saw Mrs Pell—a very pretty but dejected looking woman—
and Mrs Hanks, both Mr Birkbeck's daughters, Mr Birkbeck is now at Vandalia, having been appointed Secretary
of State and his sons my Father met at Harmony, on
their road to New Orleans with a cargo´ for that market.
Produce sent from here has 9 mile carriage to Bompas,
whence the Wabash conveys it further. We returned
home about two miles over the prairie. We dined at 5 at
Mr. Flower's, whither his children had been invited to eat
Christmas dinner, of which roast beef and plum pudding
formed a conspicuous part.

Sunday, 26th Dec.

A very fine day. A very little hazy. Therm. in the
morning 52 in the afternoon 57 degrees. I wrote till one.
My Father and the rest of the party went to chapel, where
Mr. Ronalds read a sermon to them. At one I walked to
town, called on MrPickerings and at two went to a meeting where Mr. Owen intended speaking, which had been
notified the day before. As the room was too small for
those present, we adjourned to the open air, and after the
benches had been removed and filled, members stood or
occupied fallen trees. Mr. Owen spoke for about two and a
half hours to about 200 persons, who were very quiet and
apparently interested. I observed a great many ladies
both old and young, many with infants in their arms, and
almost all English emigrants, as almost all the settlers of
Albion and neighborhood are from Britain. My Father
explained his principles and showed how they must naturally produce union and good feeling and banish anger and
irritation from society. He told them that this and only
this was true religion and that we might be sure that when-
even this was wanting, whatever might be the individual
belief, there was no true religion. He then read the rules
and regulations of a community and showed his drawings.
All parties seemed much pleased. Although the day after

Christmas, we found ourselves quite warm and comfortably seated in the open air, till the sun went down,
about which time the meeting broke up. In the evening
my Father showed the drawings to Mr. Pickering.

Monday, 27th Dec.

A fine day but hazy; therm. at 9 a. m. 52. It reminded
me much of an English summer's day. Mr O ,Dr Spring
and myself rode to Albion and afterwards proceeded to
Wanbro'. G. Flower rode with us but when we came there
he left us, as he does not visit the parties there. We called
on Mrs Pritchard, whose husband is dead, and who has 4
daughters and sons. They appeared a nice family. While
here my horse, which was hitched to a paling before the
door, broke loose by pulling down the fence. We then called
on Mrs Pell and Mrs Hanks and left a book given us by Mr
W.L. Fisher for Mr Birkbeck. From thence we proceeded
to call on Mr Hall who lives on the prairie. He seemed an
intelligent man and to understand what he was about. He
told us that out of 250 persons living within 5 miles around
him, his house forming the center, only one adult had died
within 3 years, the time he had been there. In the same
time 5 infants have died, all born within the year. He considered the situation remarkably healthy. He told us that
peaches grown at his house about 60 feet above the lowest
part of the prairie had done very well; those about 30 feet
above it had not succeeded: he supposed owing to the
damp arising from the low ground. His house was built
in the wood. He and his sons and one man had brought
in 3 years 85 acres under cultivation, all woodland and
covered with brush. He had a very comfortable house, a
log house, with a brick chimney and glass windows. The
houses in this part of the country form the following gra-
dations.

1st, a log house, of round unsmoothed logs, sometimes
with the interstices filled up with clay and having a wooden

chimney and no glass windows. The roof made of clapboards. 2nd, a log house with smoothed logs, all openings filled up with clay, having glass windows and a stone or brick chimney and clapboard or shingle roof.

3rd, a frame house, weatherboarded, with good windows and doors, a brick chimney, shingled roof.

4th, a substantial stone or brick building, with good doors, windows, chimney, etc.

Of this latter kind there are but few here. No 2 is the most common, but all as well as combinations of one or more of these Nos. are to be found. Almost every house has a balcony, for very hot or very wet weather. The barns, stables, etc. are seldom other than open loghouses of unsmoothed logs. Now and then you see a frame or brick building, for instance at Harmony. Mrs. Hall showed us some chiccory which she uses for coffee. When roasted and ground it smells and tastes very much like coffee and she considered it much superior to Hunt's mixture. She uses red root for tea and sassafras buds, blossoms and leaves, which she considers much superior to the sassafras root which is usually made use of. From Mr Hall's we rode to the burnt Prairie where we called on Mr Clark, who lives in a large brick house, built for coolness in summer. We then returned through Wanbro' and arrived about ½ p. 4 or 5. By the way we passed the remains of a camp meeting, where the pulpit, benches and the remains of some log cabins were still visible. We were told that these meetings some times last several days, during which time some one or other is speaking all the time, both day and night. In front of the pulpit is an open space, where those who become converted fall down and rage. When we returned we found Mr and Miss Rapp just arrived. About 6 we dined at Mr G. Flower's, where 25 persons sat down to dinner, amongst whom were Mr and Mrs Flower, Mr and Mrs Ronalds, Mr and Mrs Lewis, Mr and Mrs Carter, Mr and Mrs D. Orange, Mrs Jolly, Mr and Mrs Berkett, Miss Ross,

Miss Ronalds, Mr Pickering, Dr Spring, Mr and Miss Rapp, our party and their own family. As the table could not contain the whole party, we dined at two different times; one set finishing one course, then making room for the other, and so on. Afterwards we had a long and very interesting discussion regarding responsibility, praise, blame and rewards and punishments. Mr Flower, Mr Pickering and Mr Ronalds were violently opposed, declaring that if these were given up there could be no Christian religion, no God, no resurrection. Mr Owen contended that doing away with praise and blame, and all artificial rewards and punishments did not interfere with the necessary consequences which follow from good or a bad action, which originate with the power which regulates the Universe. Messrs. Carter and Lewis favored my Father and Mr Rapp agreed with Mr Flower and the ladies seemed to take great interest in the discussion which seemed quite new to them. G. Flower put on the boy's (Scotch?-) dress and his sister the girls. They were much admired, but the boys dress seemed to be considered too void of shame. About 11 o'clock Mr and Mrs Carter and Lewis sang some very pretty songs and about 12 the party broke up. During the day G Flower and R Watson were out shooting. They saw nothing worth shooting at. But there are plenty of deer, racoon, oposum, muskrat, squirels, turkeys, to be found in different places near this; besides a few bears, wild cats, catamounts, now and then a panther, plenty of foxes, rabbits or hares—both these and foxes when hard pressed take to and ascend hollow trees—quails, turtle doves, etc. The wood peckers of all sorts are considered too plentiful to be counted game; as well as turkey buzzards, which resemble large hawks and are of great use. There are many kinds of snakes but wherever many hogs are about snakes disappear, as hogs are very fond of them as food.

Tuesday, 28th Dec.

A rainy wet day. Thr. about 48. Mr Rapp and my Father had a good deal of conversation together and after breakfast Messrs. Ronalds and Pinkey came in and seemed very much inclined to oppose Mr Owen's principles with great warmth. Capt. Mc D. talked to them. Mr. T. Brown called on my Father and had some conversation with him. He seemed an intelligent man, was quite aware of the impossibiltity of controlling one's belief. He said he left England because he was not independent from the want of the necessaries of life; here he found himself still less so, though from other causes. The individual system, he thought, opposed man against man; what one gains one day his neighbor loses; and what his neighbor gains at another time is obtained from him again and thus both are dissatisfied. Mr Rapp told me that his average crops are: wheat 25 bu. per acre, Rye 25 bu., corn 75 bu. for last three years. In 1822 his wheat averaged 30 bu. per acre and one field 36 bu. Wheat in Illinois averages 15 bu. but is under very bad cultivation. One man near this raised 154 bu. of corn per acre.; but 40 bu. corn is considered a good crop. Mr Rapp get as much much cotton in Indiana as he requires for 10 cents in goods, the cotton laid down. He has a cotton gin driven by oxen which has 40 saws. He receives ⅛ th of all cotton he gins for ginning it. He considers 800 lbs per acre an average and 1000 lbs a good crop. Three fourths is lost in ginning, including the ⅛ paid for ginning; but the cultivation is very trifling, plowing, sowing, hoeing, breaking the tops, and picking it when ripe. Here in Illinois they grow from 500 to 600 lbs. per acre; but they seem to have little trouble and to take little care of it. Mr Flower gets at Louisville 15 cents for cotton.

In the evening Messrs Lewis and Carter called as a deputation from a party of a dozen or more who had signed a paper offering to join a community. They said they had got the names in a great hurry. They could get

very many more in a short time. Some of the names were
Messrs. Lewis, Carter, Orange, Spring, Young, Birkbeck,
Beckett, etc Mr Owen agreed to meet as many as chose
to attend on Thursday at 1 o'clock at Albion. Miss Rapp
spent the day with Miss Ronalds. Miss Rapp is pretty,
unaffected, good humored and with great simplicity of
character. She is a good specimen of Harmony training;
but her chief want is knowledge of every kind. ⟨She sang
a few simple air tunes without any awkward bashfulness
or false modesty, common in society. She was on the
whole certainly too passive a being.   .

Wednesday, 29th Dec.

A dull day, but no rain of any consequence. Therm. at
midday 50 degrees. Mr and Miss Rapp returned to Harmony. They set out soon after 9. My Father seems much
inclined to the purchase of Harmony, including the stock
on the farm and about 7000 acres of land in Indiana and
Illinois. We wrote a great part of the day and read newspapers, which had just arrived in great numbers. Mr F.
had letters from Edward dated Oct. 21st. All well at
home. He complained of dull rainy weather. Rain every
day since his arrival. We dined at Mr G. Flower's, as Mr
and Mrs Flower were with Mrs Pickering all day. They
had set up with her all the previous night as she was very
feeverish.

Thursday, 30th Dec.

A dull day, but no rain of any consequence. Therm. at
12 o'clock 42. I sketched Messrs Flower's houses and a
little before 12 o'clock we all—Mr Owen, Miss Ronalds
and myself—walked up to Albion to attend a meeting which
had been appointed for that hour. We went to Mr F's brick
tavern and after waiting for some time, my Father opened
the meeting by showing his drawings. There were upwards of 100 persons present, who were very quiet and orderly. During the meeting a tipsy man came in, but no

one seemed to notice him and he departed. My Father said the meeting had been called to endeavor to discover any means of bettering the condition of the inhabitants of Albion. He told them he knew no way by which they could be enabled to do it themselves, or any means by which it could be accomplished, so long as they remained in their present situations. He said if he completed the purchase of Harmonie, he thought he could promise them comfortable lodging, the most wholesome food, the most useful clothing and a good education for their children, but that to accomplish this it would be necessary to exert something of the same labor and diligence, as was at present necessary for their support, for some years and to allow themselves to be guided by one who had long been conversant with the, principles and practices necessary to such an undertaking. He added that as belief was in no respect under the control of the individual it was necessary that each one should be allowed perfect liberty of conscience. He told them also that it had occurred to him only this morning, that, perhaps, if he purchased Harmonie, the community might rent the houses and land from him and cultivate the land in common. Mr Brown thought they could not do it by themselves. Mr Clark wished to know what become of their present property. Mr Owen thought if the soil was wet it might be laid down in grass, if dry in cotton or farmed for the private benefit of the individuals of the society. Mr. Warrington asked why a community might not be established nearer so that the present houses should remain of value. Mr O said if any one could form a community near them he would give it all the assistance in his power. The meeting lasted about an hour and a half and we then, in compliance with a previous invitation from the ladies of Albion, went to Judge Wattle's where, after waiting about an hour, supper was served up. There were present nearly the same party as on Monday at Mr G Flower's, Mr and Mrs Cave and Mr and Miss Rapp excepted and Mrs Wattle added.

We were waited on by Mrs Wattle, Carter, Lewis, Jolly and Miss Ross, who seemed already to have commenced the community system. Soon after 6 we took leave, greatly to their disappointment, as they said they had counted on our company until 12 o'clock, but my Father was tired and as we proposed leaving Albion tomorrow we wished to spend the evening with Mr Flower. On returing home, we found tea laid out for us at Mr G Flower's and Mr Warrington awaiting our arrival. We talked to him about the management of children and this led us to the attributes and properties of God. Mr. W. agreed that man's actions were the result of necessity, but he was puzzled, because in that case he must throw the blame of all the misery in the world on his Creator. When returned home we prepared for next day's journey and went to bed.

Friday, 31st Dec.

A dull but pleasant morning. therm. at 8 o'clock 33. and occasional glimpses of the sun during the day. Miss Ronalds, Messrs Owen, Flower, McDonald and myself started on horseback for Harmonie, at ½ p. 9. We rode on a jog trot over the prairie and along a rising ground, thickly covered with oak, called the barrens. We passed some fine sights on this ridge. About 3 miles from Bompas we joined the Shawneetown road, which we again left 6 miles from Harmonie and, crossing the Fox river, passed over a low island covered with evergreen canes. We reached the ferry about ½ p. 2, where we left our horses. The evening Mr Rapp spent with us. We tasted some wine made from wild grape. It seemed strong and was made without sugar. These vines when pruned produce no grapes at all. Mr Rapp told us that ground could be cleared for $6 per acre and mentioned in what way he had been cheated by clearers when he first came viz: cutting the rails outside the fence cutting the trees too high up, instead of all above 2 feet thick 2 feet above the ground and leaving all under 2 feet as high as their diameters.

Saturday, 1st Jan. 1825.

The day was cloudy and rather cold. My Father spent the greater part of the day with Mr Rapp. Mr Ronalds arrived from Albion about ½ p. 10. Mr. G Flower, Capt. McD and I visited the sheep pens and saw nearly 800 very fine merinos of all ages. Mr. Rapp intended taking from 100 to 150 of these with him to Economy. The sheep were in a very good state and appeared to have been well taken care of. Mr G Flower said that he had perhaps 6 or 8 whose wool was finer than that of any of these, but that the great bulk of these were better than his. He did not like the idea of any of the sheep being taken away, as he said that in a flock there are always 3 or 4 superior to any of the rest and that Mr Rapp would certainly take these with him. As the day presented the appearance of snow, Miss and Mr Ronalds and Mr G Flower set out at 3 o'clock to return home, fearing a detension if they remained another day. After they were gone McD. and I walked out and ascended one of the hills near the Cut Off from which we had an extensive prospect. Toward the river the hill is steep and romantic, being elevated above the river about 250 feet.

My Father mentioned in the evning that he had decided on the purchase.

Sunday, 2nd Jan.

A beautiful clear day. Therm. at 7 o'clock 22. I went at 9 to hear Mr Rapp preach. His sermon was concerning the millenium. Mr Owen and Mr Rapp spent a great part of the day together, settling the particulars of the purchase. Mr Schnee, innkeeper at Springfield, called on us this morning. At Mr Rapp's recommendation Mr Owen engaged him to take charge of the coarse woolen carding, fulling, dyeing, etc., which situation he had formally held in a mill in Pennsylvania. In the afternoon Mr Owen, Capt. McD. and I walked along the banks of the Cut Off and ascended several hills there with whose romatic appearance we were

much pleased. One, of a conical form, seemed well calculated for holding large meetingsfor any purpose, being flat
at the top. We contemplated with pleasure the prospect
of seeing a large number of our friends and associates
winding around its base, accompanied by bands of music,
and raising their voices in joyful shouts or in melodious
strains. At 6 we went by invitation to Mr Rapp's; where
we supped and afterwards assisted at a concert, composed
of the same performers as that we attended a fortnight
ago. Mr Rapp talked of the taxes payable on the estate.
The State tax is $.01 (1 cent) per acre and the county tax
is ½ cent per acre. Besides this every man is liable to be
called out 5 days per annum on militia dutyand 5 days for
the roads, in default of which, each man from 18 to 50 must
pay 75 cents per day.

Monday, 3rd Jan.

A beautiful clear day. Therm. at sunrise 20 degrees.
This afternoon Mr Owen and Mr Rapp signed each a paper
with the particulars of the sale of Harmonie.

Mr Clark an Englishman, who has been much with the
Indians brought a letter from Mr Birkbeck. He advised
Mr Owen to see the country west. He said that the prairies
on the Illinois river were much finer land than that of this
place. Mr Clark was on the Rocky Mountains 3 years ago,
on a trading expedition with the Indians. He had not been
a gainer by it, as the party was robbed of their property
while returning. They had left Missouri, in their route, to
the south and proceeded to a northern ridge of the mountains. He said that the Indians were much superior to
those in the neighborhood of the whites. He considers the
————, a tribe which range up and down between the
headwaters of the Arkansas and Mexico and who raise
great numbers of fine horses and mules, to be most advanced in knowledge amongst the Indian tribe. He thought
the Indians on the Rocky Mountains the happiest beings
in the world.

They could shoot in a half a day enough meat to last them for a week and then they did nothing, as the women brought the game home, cooked it and did everything. He had on some leather trousers, prepared by them. He said that they tanned it in 24 hours with a decoction of the brains of the animal whose skin they prepared.

About 3 o'clock we set sail in a keel boat, manned by six rowers and a captain. This was the first time we had been in one. It is a large open boat with a long square box about 4 feet high and broad placed in it. It reminded me much of Byron's description of a Gondola. "Just like a coffin, clapt in a canoe, where none can make out what you say or do." The rowers were under shelter, with merely an open space for the helmsman behind, and sufficient on both sides and in front to enable you to walk round. We proceeded down the river at perhaps the rate of 4 miles an hour, talking of various matters relative to our future proceedings. We continued sailing all night. Soon after dark all the sailors went below to supper and left the boat in our care. My Father and Capt. McD rowed and I was left alone to steer, which I then tried for the first time in my life, in the dark, down an unknown river, with whose soundings I was quite unacquainted and with whose windings I was unfamiliar. However, we sailed down very nicely without any accident or detention, except on one sandbar for ½ an hour during the night. A little before dark we passed a flat boat aground. Mr. Rapp had provided everything very comfortably for us. A plank laid across the boat served as a table and we had pewter plates and tin mugs, with plenty of cold meat, bread, butter, tea, coffee, milk, sugar, etc. We slept on Buffalo hides, wrapt in a blanket; as it froze during the night, we felt rather cold, but notwithstanding had a pretty comfortable nap.

Tuesday, 4th Jan.

Very beautiful day but cold in the morning; indeed we found it comfortable to keep on greatcoats during the day, as long as we continued in the boat. As we had left our thermometer at Harmonie we could not ascertain the precise temperature. We passed a great many geese and duck on the river, which we endeavored to shoot, having a rifle and fowling piece on board; but they were too wild for us; the geese in particular keeping at a respectable distance. We also saw a number of turkey buzzards and some large whiteheaded eagles. We visited a cottage, where we stopped for wood, and found in it a large family. They seemed pretty healthy, although the bank is occasionally overflown. The Father complained of pleuresy. Ten miles above Shawneetown, and about 65 from Harmonie we entered Ohio, where its stream is divided by the Wabash island. We arrived at Shawneetown—75 miles— at ½ p. 3 o'clock afternoon. We went to the Columbia inn, kept, by Squire Rawlins, a fat good natured gentleman. We met here a Kentucky captain and some others with whom my Father conversed in the evening. Shawneetown is built on rather an elevated bank on the right side of the Ohio; it is however sometimes, during floods completely inundated. It is composed of one street, running parrallel to the river and contained about 800 persons. We observed a frame house that had been removed upon rollers, from the place where it had formerly stood.

Wednesday 5th Jan.

Another beautiful clear cold morning. When we awoke, we found that a steamboat, the Indiana, had just arrived from Louisville, and that it intended proceeding up the Wabash if possible, having been engaged by Mr. Rapp to take some Harmonians up the river. We were introduced to Mr. ———— one of the editors of the Illinois Gazette, a weekly Shawnee paper, for which we subscribed and he offered to put in any advertisements or other communications which we might require. We also saw Mr. Caldwell, a plain business man, agent for Mr. Rapp here, and also storekeeper. About 2 o'clock, we started in the Indiana and proceeded up the river; we entered the Wabash and as the river became shallow and the pilots on board were unacquainted with the channel, we cast anchor about two miles above its mouth.

We towed the keelboat in which we had come down along side of us, and in the evening, we invited the crew on board to sing for us, which they willingly complied with. We had on board besides Captain Clark, a smart little fellow, and two pilots, etc., Mrs. Clark and Mrs. Fitch from Vincennes, two very nice, intelligent ladies.

Thursday 6th Jan.

A very beautiful morning. Captain Clark had set a young man on shore at Mt. Vernon to inform Mr. Rapp of his arrival, we therefore lay by waiting their coming. We amused ourselves, some by setting fire to or cutting down trees, others by hunting. Some fine deer and squirrels and paroquets were killed . We had some squirrel at dinner. It was very good. I wrote a long letter to Robert informing him of the purchase of Harmony and of all our proceedings and intentions. One of the pilots told me, that every stranger was almost sure of being taken ill with the yellow fever at Orleans, if he remained there during the unhealthy season. He knew a ship's crew which arrived there quite well, who were all dead, except one, in three days. About two, Mr. Rawlins came on board, intending to wait for Mr. Rapp and between four and five, three keelboats arrived with goods and informed us that Mr. Rapp and the party would meet us at Mount Vernon, when we arrived there. We ran down to the mouth of the river, before dark, and after having reloaded three keelboats, we started at half past ten, nearly four hours sooner than the Captain had calculated upon. So much for Harmony alertness. We then went to bed.

Friday 7th Jan.

About half past two, we were awoke, by being told we were very near Mount Vernon. About four we arrived and soon Mr. Rapp and a great many females came on board. They had been at James Inn all night. They soon got under weigh and we took leave of my Father, who proceeded with them, while Capt. McDonald and I went to James'. We breakfasted after seven with the sherriff of the County, and a man who had been taken up for murder and who was being taken to Tennesee; also with Mr. Schnee and Mr. Rawlins. We then rode to Harmonie on two of Mr. Rawlin's horses, which had been brought thither by him the previous evening. We arrived about 11. A clear cold morning but during the day it has become. cloudy.

In the evening, Mr. Burton and Mr. Wood from Albion came in. Capt. McDonald not very well.

Saturday 8th January.

After breakfast we called on Mrs. Rapp and Miss Gertrude, and talked of their friends. We then returned home and wrote our journals. After dinner we took a long walk and talked to several farmers we met with who seemed favorably disposed towards our establishment.

Sunday 9th January.

A dull cloudy day, with every appearance of rain in the afternoon. Capt. McDonald and I employed ourselves in composing a systematic advertising regarding the reception of families into Harmonie. In the afternoon we took a walk in south easterly direction. When we returned, we found at the Inn a large party, amongst whom were Gen. and Mrs. Evans, Gen. Willy, Mr. Brown, Mr. Daniel, Mr. and Mrs. Neil, eac. We spent the evening in conversation. Indeed from the little experience of solitude which we have lately had, we have begun to be aware how necessary society is to the happiness of man. The two generals appear

to be sensible men as well as Mr. Brown, Mr. Hall, a lawyer and Arbuthnot, sadler, all from Princeton.   In the

Monday. 10th January.

A clear frosty morning. Thermometer 21 degrees. A
very beautiful day. We visited without a guide, the cowhouses, barns, barnyards, and stables. The cowhouses are
capable of containing 40 to 50 cows, calves, etc, and the
stables contain 40 stalls. The barns were full of various
kinds of straw. Besides the cows in the stalls we visited,
each family has a certain number of milk cows, one of
which we looked in upon, and found 10 cows to a family of
perhaps thirty persons. After dinner we went to the new
cotton mill erected in April last. We found the gin at
work. It gins from 800 to a 1000 ℔s. per day, and works
twice a week Mondays and Tuesdays. We staid some time,
in the spinning room, and Capt. McDonald explained some
of the leading principles of the new system to the work
people, who appeared very happy and to have very light
labor. In this mill there are 11 girls, a man who gins and
looks after the cattle on the wheel and occasionally an
overseer. Afterwards we walked up the Wabash as far
as the Black River. In the evening, there was a concert in
the church. We had a great deal of conversation with the
Princeton gentlemen. Amongst other things, they explained
to us the manner in which land is divided. A line is run
from north to south thro the east end of each state, called
the first meridian and lines are drawn parrellel to this
at the distance of six miles from each other. One of these
near the center of the state is called the second meridian
and the land between the lines parallel to these merid-
ians, is designated according to its position east of these
lines, first, second, third, etc., range from the first or second
meridian. Near the center of the state, a line is run from
east to west, called a base line and parrallel to it, distant
six miles from each other, are lines drawn which, crossing

the ranges, divide them into townships six miles square, designated according to their position first or second township north of south of the base line.

These townships of 36 square miles are again subdivided by lines running east and west and north and south into sections of 1 square mile, which are designated by calling the section at the north-east corner, No. 1, the one below No. 2, and so on to 6; 7 is west of 6; 13 west of 12 etc. 36 is the north-west corner. these sections are subdivided into quarter sections, called n. e.., n. w., s. e., and s. w. each containing 160 acres. This is the smallest portion sold by the state and costs $1.25 per acre, money down.

I received a letter from Mr. Flower regarding some families in Vincennes who, he thought would join us. Wrote to My Father enclosing a letter to Jacob Call from Gen. Evans.

Tuesday 11th January.

We were anxious to ride over to Albion but could not get any horse Gen. Evans offered us one for $100.00. A very beautiful morning and lovely day. Thermometer at 24 degrees. We visited today the engine house, the dyehouse and bleachfield and the cotton and woolen factories. The engine appears to be very well attended to and we were told is now in good order. We also saw the barn with the threshing mill and the large frame built granary close by. In the cotton and woolen factory, there are women and girls and three men.

The Princeton gentlemen left us this morning, and shortly after, Mrs. and Mr. Beckel arrived from Albion. This evening, Mr. Alexander Stewart, a scotsman, a veterinary surgeon, who studied in London and Edinburg and was 14 years surgeon to the Perth Agricultural Society, and who now resides about 15 miles from Albion, arrived here with a letter from Mr. R. Flower. He is anxious to join the community and wishes my Father to bring out four

daughters, along with the rest of the Scotch emigrants.
We showed him the paper which we had drawn up. A
very beautiful day.

Wednesday, 12th January.

Thermometer in the morning 24 degrees. Wind changed
in the evening to east when it became warmer, than for
some days back. Looked again at some horses, but none
pleased us. In the afternoon we rode out, with George to
the Oil and Saw mills. Neither was at work. We then
proceeded to the prarie east of the town, and returning saw
a trap for wild pigs. We then called on Miss Gertrude,
and when we returned to the Inn, we found there two
shakers from Berea, O, who said if Mr. Rapp was expected in two or three days, they would wait his arrival
here. They showed us some silk made by themselves.
They drank rye coffee, which they like very well. Mr.
Steel from Albion arrived here this evening. He proposes
sending two son-in-law here to school.

Thursday—13th January.

A fine morning, but rather hazy. Thermometer 36 degrees in the morning. Wind north-east. The day continued cloudy and lowering and in the evening, it began to
rain, which continued all night. About half past 10 we
started on two of Mr. Rapp's wagon horses for Albion,
having first called on the ladies at Mr. Rapp's house, who
told us they expected Mr. Rapp to return on Saturday, as
he promised not to go farther than Louisville. We were
accompanied a great part of the way by Mr. Steel, who
told us he had been bred an apothecary in London, but
had not been able to find employment in that way here.
I am informed that he has married a wife twice his age
and that he has a farm near Albion. We rode but slowly,
as our horses were not much accustomed to riding and we

arrived about half past three. We found Mr. Flower confined with the gout in the stomach; but he saw us for a few minutes in the evening. Miss Ronald drank tea with us at Mr. Flower's she having just returned from assisting Mrs. Washington, in teaching her girls how to make their frocks.

Friday 14th January.

The rain still continued this morning, tho it ceased soon after breakfast; but throughout the day, it continued still very dull and cloudy and very wet under foot. We walked over after breakfast to Mr. George Flower's. He told us that Mr. McIntosh, an intelligent Scotsman, living at the grand Rapids, had informed him, that about thirty families of French living at Casinet, near Vincennes, meant to emigrate in a body and talked of settling at the mouth of the Wabash. They are mostly farmers, industrious, and docile in character, and he thought they might be induced to settle with us. We talked of riding over to see Mr. McIntosh and Vincennes, but as we were not prepared for such an expedition, and as Mr. George Flower, could not go with us, we gave up the idea. Mr. I. Brissenden, a would-be-communicant, called on us, desirous of more particular information, which we could not give him. While we were at dinner, Judge Wattle, (who has just been appointed an Illinois Judge with $1000 per annum) He seemed an intelligent man; he was sorry he had not seen Mr. Owen. He is an Albino; his eyes we could not see, as he wore large spectacles, but his hair was quite white. In the evening, we received a letter from John Wood, inquiring many particulars about our terms of admittance. Capt. McDonald returned for answer, we could not tell him till Mr. Owen returned. A good deal of ennui from having nothing to occupy the body or to interest the mind. A game of chess, before going to bed.

Saturday 15th January.

A fine morning, a pleasant south wind and a few clouds. Themometer stood at 38 degrees. Mr. Flower was a little better this morning. Mr. Pickering has been very ill ever since our last visit, but he is supposed to be getting better. We mounted our horses at Mr. Ronalds. Mrs. Ronalds had been confined three days before; she is getting better very quickly. We then proceeded to Judge Wattle's where no one was at home. At the door we met Dr. Pugley who introduced himself. He said he would be at Harmony next day. Afetrwards, we looked in upon Mrs. Carter and, crossing the prarie, we called Mr. D. Orange, where we joked some time with Mrs. Orange and Jolly. We thence proceeded towards Harmonic. After riding about an hour the sky overcast, and we experienced a heavy shower of rain; which however, soon cleared off. We met Mr. and Mrs. Beckel and Mr. Carter, who had remained at Philip's all night, and we arrived at the ferry at half past three. After putting up our horses, we called on Mr. Rapp. We found that Mr. Rapp had not yet returned. At the tavern, we met the shakers, we had left there, when we started. We saw Baker, Mr. Miller etc. In the evening, Capt McDonald talked to the shakers and I journalized. The weather changed alternately cloudy and clear.

Sunday 16th Jaunary.

A fine morning. Themometer at 7 o'clock 34 degrees. A pleasant breeze during the day from South-west, changing to west, carrying light clouds occasionally over the sky, which remained however, usually clear. We employed ourselves in remodeling the prospectus relative to those anxious to join our society, which we had drawn up some time ago. No sermon in the church, owing to Mr. Rapp's absence. The principal observable occupation of the Harmonians was music, which they carried on in small parties in different parts of the village. After dinner, we walked out in a southwesterly direction over some very high hills, which overlook the Wabash, and near which is a plain suitable for a village, from which we had some fine views and regarding which, we indulged in some grand speculations. We returned about five and found at the tavern, Messrs. Hale and Clark, and Dr. Pugsley from Albion. We spent the evening in conversation with them. Mr. Hale mentioned many necessary particulars regarding our projected society. He seems to be a good practical farmer.

We find it uncommonly dull and stupid having so little to interest the mind ; the body may be exercised by walking but the mind gets dissatisfied under idle speculations or a dull routine of doing nothing.

Monday 17th January.

A beautiful day. After breakfast, we started out with Messrs. Clark and Hale and Dr. Pugley to Community Hill and the surrounding eminences which they admired much. We then decended to the Mill on the Cutt Off and crossed the dam to the Island. The mill is superintended by two brothers. In has two pair of stones for wheat and one pair for corn, which can only be worked to advantage in pretty water. The two wheat stones grind 56 barrels on an average in 24 hours, each barrel weighing 196 ℔s. net weight. From the mill we ascended another hill which commands the town and returned round the back of the orchards which surround the town, entering it from the North side.

D. Pugley expressed a wish to join us. He said he was very sorry for the differences existing at Albion and he wished he had yielded to Mr. Flower ; but he opposed him, because he wished to be the great man and he could not brook that.

We returned to dinner about three. Afterwards, we conversed a good deal. Capt. McDonald explained his views, which appeared to interest them a good deal. In the even-

ing, Mr. Barton arrived with a letter from Mr. George
Flower offering us horses. We declined, afraid of offending the Harmonians.

Tuesday 18th January.

A dull morning. We walked out after breakfast and
passing over the farm, we proceeded to the oil mill, when
we found two men at work. They were engaged making
linseed oil, by grinding linseed under large stones and
then pressing it. They made oil from Hemp, walnuts,
peachstones, etc. We then viewed the saw mill. On the
way, we experienced a little rain. After dinner we visited
the steam engine, barns, stabling, the flour mill, the elk,
the distillery and a piggery containing 520 hogs.

Wednesday 19th January.

Messrs. Hall, Clark, and Pugley left us after breakfast
and we visited Mr. Rapp and Dr. Muller. After dinner,
we walked into some weaving shops, to the tanners shop,
the tannery, the tallow chandler's ,and the hatter's. In
the evening, we conversed with Mr. [Webb?] from Carmi,
vho is erecting a building for cotton spinning there. We
; fterwards noted down a few Scotish airs.

Thursday 20th January.

After breakfast, we saw Dr. Muller and then proceeded
to Springfield on two of Mr. Rapp's horses. The ride
thither is very pleasant; a good many farms lying on each
side the road. We then rode with Mr. Schnee about four
and a half miles further and visited Mr. Philips, a land
surveyor, who was then teaching about twenty or thirty
children. The children looked rather pale. Mr. Philips
seemed a slow but thinking man. We explained to him
a few of my father's ideas. We then returned to Schnee's
and dined with him and Mr. Stewart. Mr. Schnee would

take no payment. In the evening when we returned at
our inn, we found there Messrs. Hornbrook and Medlow,
both settled at Sandersville, 28 miles from this and 10 miles
from Evansville. They are settled on the barrens, but are
getting pretty good crops. Mr. Hornbrook was an iron
founder in England and had a woolen mill. Mr. Medlow
was a Hamphire farmer. They seemed inclined to propose joining us. A letter from Mr. Owen from Louisville
dated 10th inst.

Friday 21st. January.

A beautiful clear morning. We visited with Messrs.
Meadlow and Hornbeck, the woolen department. with
which they seemed pleased. About 12 o'clock, they returned home. We then walked out and after dinner we
called on Mrs. Rapp and Miss Gertrude, who sang Auld
Lang Syne to us. Dr. Muller came in and assisted.

We then visited the chandler's whom we found engaged
in making candles. He had nearly finished 1000 during the
day. We then proceeded to the ropemakers, where three
men are employed, who heckle hemp and flax and make,
during the summer, about 6000 ℔s. of rope. They have
an extensive rope-walk through an orchard. In the evening, I wrote to R. Brenckley of Albion and Capt. McDonald
studied astronomy with Dr. Muller, for whom, I also corrected a sheet of an english publication written by Mr.
Rapp.

Saturday 22nd January.

A very beautiful day. After dinner we visited the southwest cow houses and afterwards the smithy, with six
forges and the brick kilns, where we found a number of
excellent brick and looked for but could not find, a furnace which we were told is there. In the evening, I wrote
to Mr. Pelham, Zanesville, Ohio and we had a little music.

Sunday 23rd January.

A very beautiful day. We corrected this morning a publication for Dr. Muller and in the afternoon, took a walk with him and talked over the subject of education and of the formation of character. In the evening, wrote and read some astronomy.

Monday 24th January.

A most beautiful day. During the day, we all agreed it was almost like summer and it was certainly more agreeable than most summer days in Scotland. We proposed going to the Island, but being advised to defer it, we walked about the town and look into several uninhabited log cabins, which were in a bad state. We then proceeded to the brewery, where about 500 gallons of beer is brewed every other day and then to the distillery in which 36 gallons of whiskey is produced daily. One run producing about 12 gallons in six hours, including all the necessary preparations.

After dinner, we obtained a string 100 ft. long, with which we measured the outline of the town. We also visited a small still, which makes daily about 20 gallons whiskey, and observed a carpenter drying wood in a log house. The wood had only been cut a few weeks. He said the thick logs would take a fortnight to dry. In the evening, made music, and astronomised and wrote.

Tuesday 25th January.

A fine day but a little hazy. After breakfast, we rode over the island along with George H. Plackhammer and Mr. Richard. Near the landing place, we arrived at some extensive meadows, where a number of cattle and a few young colts were feeding. We then proceeded to ride round the island. We raised a few deer near the enclosure. To the northeast of the Island another small one lies cut off by a branch of the cut off. We proceeded along the north bank and found several other enclosures, and a small prairie. A great part of the island seems capable of affording excellent pasturage for cattle. We shot one turkey and saw a great many but only got in shot of one other. We stopped at one of the farms and tried a few shots at one of the trees. We returned back about four o'clock and paid Miss Rapp a visit. In the evening, we proceeded in laying down the town from our yesterday's notes.

Wednesday 26th January.

The morning we employed in writing, I to Dale and Richard and Capt. McDonald to Mrs. H. After dinner, Mr. Brockwell of Evansville and two other gentlemen called to inform themselves of our intentions. They appeared very favorably disposed. We afterwards received a visit from Mr. Morris of Carmi, who is anxious to be tavern-keeper. When they left us we continued our measurements of the town and in the evening, we astronomised with Dr. Muller and Miss Rapp, at which time, we observed three of Jupiter's moons and two belts and afterwards sketched in part of the town. A most beautiful day througout.

Thursday 27th January.

A most delightful day. Our town measurements we continued this morning, and also called on Dr. Muller. After dinner, Mr. Matthew arrived from beyond Bonpas, enquiring our intentions regarding settlers. Mr. Matthew is an englishman who arrived here some time after Mr. Birkbeck. We then rode with G. Plackhammer to the old saw mill, where we found the dam out of repair, but a great of it nearly new. In going thither, we passed several enclosures, whose inhabitants, Mr. Rapp had brought out. We returned by Dennis's ferry whose farm, which contains mostly 1000 acres, lies on the Illinois shore. He rents from Harmony. On this side is also an improvement. We passed in returning, Community Hill. In the evening we had a long conversation with Dr. Muller.

Friday 28th January.

A beautiful day without a cloud. We visited the pottery where no one was at work. Also a carpenter's shop and the cooperage. They told us there were nine coopers. Each makes about two barrels per day, sometimes three. The wood they use is usually two years old but sometimes they lay it in water for a month, which seasons it nearly as well. We then saw the tinman, who is in a shop alone. He is nearly self-taught. He never saw a tinman at work. We continued our survey of the town. An Irishman, named McGuire a saddler, near Princeton, applied to us about adoption into the community We told him, we could settle nothing till Mr. Owen returned. We afterwards saw him quite tipsey. Stewart, the farrier, with his son and neighbor Mr. Alexander came for the same purpose. Stewart is an inferior talker. Mr. Lewis arrived about two o'clock and we had a great deal of conversation with him. He offered his service as assistant tallow chandler.

Saturday 29th January.

A beautiful day with a cloudless sky. Mr. Lewis staid all day. We continued our survey and in the evening, I wrote to my Mother.

Sunday 30th January.

A beautiful day. In the morning we employed ourselves in writing and in the afternoon Mr. Clark's sons arrived, two fine stout young men, and a Mr. Owen who resided in the northern part of the state at Bloomington, fifty miles south of Indianapolis. There was a concert in the barroom in the evening.

Monday 31st January.

A cloudy, dull day. We endeavored to bargain for some horses today but the backwood men think we ought to pay for everything three times double!!! We visited the stocking weaver. We found there four looms. One weaver weaves four pairs of coarse stockings in one day, which one woman would require four days to. Fine stockings, he weaves one and one-half pair per day. We likewise visited the sheep and orchard etc. In the evening we had a long and interesting talk with Messrs. Clarks and Owens, who seemed to agree in a great measure with what we advanced. Mr. Owens said he had never heard the doctrine of necessity so clearly laid down as by Capt. McDonald this evening.

Tuesday 1st of February.

A dull morning. The Messrs. Clark left us after breakfast. Dr. Muller having printed a notice for us. I was employed this morning in correcting the press. It occupied me almost all day. Beautiful evening. Mr. Lewis arrived.

Wednesday 2nd of February

Clear, cold day. Went with Mr. Lewis to visit the chandler's shop. Called on Mrs. Rapp and visited Hood, who keeps the ferry.

Thursday 3rd. of February.

Clear, cold day. Mr. Lewis left us. Continued surveying. In the evening went to Mrs. Rapp's where there was music. Recived a letter from Robert dated Oct. 17th. Wrote to American Farmer and to Mr. Pelham of Zanesville, Ohio.

Friday 4th February.

Fine morning. At five we went out with all the men in the town armed with clubs, into the corn fields to knock down the corn stalks. This is easily done on a clear frosty morning as they are then very brittle. The morning was not cold enough, for we found them a little tough. Before breakfast all the stalks on the farm were laid low. After breakfast, we started on horseback with Mr. Owens and rode to Princeton, distant 28 miles. The day was mild and cold and the road hard and part sandy crossing a barren ridge. A number of improvements on the road. We arrived about four o'clock at Princeton. It is situated well, on high rolling ground with good farms in and around and many of the houses are finished with some taste. We remained at Mr. Daniel's Tavern and saw Mr. Daniel, Messrs Brown, Hall, Arthbuthnot, Gen. Evans and Woddsworth, who is a good axemaker, talked of joining us here. We were afraid of snow in the evening. In the evening, a large circle gathered around the tavern fire.

Saturday 5th of February.

A beautiful clear day. We called on Mr. Philips, formerly mail coach contractor, in Scotland, who has a fine, well cleared farm on a beautiful rising ground near the town. His house is small. But he paid very (high) for his land, $16.00 and $20.00 per acre. We also called on Evans, Messrs. Arbuthnot and Hale, and visited the spot where it is proposed to build a seminary.

The town appears stationary and little is doing. When it was first settled, many English settlers staid there, which made the town thrive, but latterly it has been thrown on its own resources. Mr. Owens proceeded to Vincennes. Spent the evening with Gen. Evan's family. The mail from Evansville arrived this evening.

Sunday 6th February.

A beautiful morning. We started with Mr. Philips after Breakfast for Vincennes. The road is good the greater part of the way. We crossed White River at the upper ferry at ten miles from Princeton. Soon after we passed

Major Robbs. Before arriving at Vincennes, we crossed
a pretty extensive prairie ar common, to the right of which
are several artificial mounds supposed to have been raised
by the indians, for watchtowers, and got in about half past
four. The evening had become dull. We called on Mr.
Hay and were introduced to Mr. Masey, an Englishman,
and to Judge Blackford, Supreme Judge of the State. We
put up at Mr. Jones' Spent the evening at Mr. Hays'
where we found Messrs. Hay and Elston, an Irishman in
the land office, and Mrs. Hay and Elston. It rained a little
as we returned home.

Monday 7th of February.

Dull morning and rain the greater part of the day. Mr.
Philips returned home after breakfast. We walked with
Mr. Hay round the town and visited a saw and grist mill,
which appeared to be conducted with little order. The
town appears not to be in a flourishing condition.

Vincennes was settled the same year as Philadelphia, by
Canadian French who traded with the Indians. On account
of the friendly feeling between both parties, the French
were suspected of favoring them during the Indian war.
which prevented their amalgamation with the Canadians
now settled there. These families were almost all very
poor and illiterate and many have now left town and gone
to St. Louis, Kaskaskia, and other places to the westward.
It contained formerly 1500 inhabitants but now the number does not amount to 1000. Most of the houses are frame
and many appear to be unoccupied at present. There are
but few stores but a good many doctors. It is situated on
the left bank of the Wabash, close to the river and is
surrounded on all sides by a prairie on which races are
occasionally ridden. We walked with Mr. Masey to the
receiver's office, a large brick building, where was held a
general meeting of subscribers to the library there. They
conducted their business pretty regularly and remained

together till two o'clock. We were here introduced to Dr.
McNamie and Kuykendoll, and to Mr. Badolet of the land
office, to Mr. Harrison, receiver, son of Gen. Harrison,
and to Messrs, Smith, Scott, etc. In the evening, we took
tea with Mr. Hay and met Mrs. Smith, the Misses Mc-
Namie and Kuykendoll, and Judge Blackford.

Wrote to Mr. Owen enclosing notice.

Tuesday 8th February.

Left Vincennes at 11 with Mr. Hay and Elston, after having a good deal of talk with Mr. Badolet, who promised to
visit us at Harmonie. We rode across the prairie, passing
through the west end of the town, inhabited by French,
most of them in wretched cabins, and I observed a large
common field belonging to them planted with Indian Corn.
About two miles from Vincennes, we rode past the Village
of Casinet, an assemblage of little poor cabins, almost all
frame built, inhabited by French, with small fields around
them. The situation is very flat indeed and unhealthy.
Messrs. Hay and Elston rode with us eight or ten miles
and then left us, directing us how we should proceed.
We rode on through the woods and having taken the wrong
road, we missed the proper ferry and keeping on the Indiana side, we rode on till we reached the rapids at Beadle's
Mill. Supposing this to be the way to Mr. McIntosh's
house, whither we were bound. We were shown a path
through a little slash, and after some difficulty found out
Mr. McIntosh's house. It had commenced raining some
hours before we had arrived, and we were therefore glad
of having arrived. After conversing some time, we found
that we had mistaken our man and had found Mr. J. Mc-
Intosh. We explained the mistake to him and we determined as it had happened, to remain with him all night.
He entertained us very hospitably and we found him an
intelligent Scotsman, a turner by trade, and a baptist
preacher We had a crack with him regarding Auld Lang

Syne. He has been in this country 40 years. It continued raining all evening. We gave him one of the notices and had some conversation with his son.

Wednesday 9th February.

Capt. McDonald and I slept together. It continued raining in the morning, but after breakfast it ceased and we started accompanied by Mr. J. McIntosh. He gave us directions how to proceed after riding three or four miles with us. We proceeded through very muddy roads and after riding six or seven miles, reached Palmyra, once a county seat, located on the river in a good situation, but now containing only one family, all the other houses being shut up. From thence we left the straight road, and crossed a creek by a bridge, as we feared it might be too deep for the horses. We then endeavored to regain the road, but choosing the wrong one, ,we crossed another creek, in which the water rose as high as half way up the flaps of our saddles and found that the road led us through a wild prairie. We then concluded that we had made some mistake and turning to the left, at last found a house, which we supposed might be Mr. McIntosh's as it was surrounded by a fine farm. However, we found we were mistaken. We were then directed to a house at some distance, and near this we were shown a foot path, which led us through a low bottom and at last Mr. McIntosh's house. The roads were extremely deep and muddy. We found him at home. We found a fine old man. His house is pretty large, but only partly finished in side. It is situated on a bank near the river opposite the rapids and in floods is quite surrounded by water. We were introduced to a black woman as his housekeeper but who seems to answer all the purposes of a wife, as he has three black children by her. Two of them are fine children. Mrs. J. McIntosh who is from New Jersey, had informed us of them before, saying she would go often to see him, were it not that he had a black woman and that he fondled the little black things as if they were as white as snow. Mr. McIntosh showed us a number of papers relative to a meeting held at Vincennes by the French in order to reply to some insinuations made against their fidelity by Gen. Harrison. We had a good deal of conversation with him and he seemed much inclined to go all together with us. He appeared to be a deist. It rained in the evening. After we had supped the black woman and the children and a negro man sat down with us. They also remained in the room during the evening.

Thursday 10 of February.

Rain all day, almost without interruption. We found we could not leave Mr. McIntosh's that day. We therefore remained talking to him all day. Of course it was very dull.

Friday 11 of February.

It still rained in the morning. After breakfast it was fair. We started with Mr. McIntosh and rode to Mount Carmel, which is about two miles off on a fine situation on a high bank, near the Wabash.

In going thither, we had passed another little slash. We were introduced to Squire Stewart, who keeps a nice little store, and then we got ferried across the river and landed below the mouth of Patoka. The ferryman showed us how to proceed and we went along a footpath, often uncertain whether we were right or wrong. We reached a house, where we again got directions. We proceeded and soon came to a slash about a mile long through which merely a cow path directed us. We found it very difficult to know whether we were right or wrong, but at last we found our way through. The slash was always half way up the horses legs and often deeper. About midway my hat was knocked off by a branch and as I must dismount into the water, I felt reluctant to do so. While I hesitated, my hat filled with water. At last I got it, but not till it was quite soaked by the water. After getting out of our way, we came to Judge Montgomery's, seven or eight miles from the ferry, who directed us how to proceed. We mounted some rising ground and rode perhaps 10 miles across the barrens occasionally getting a little out of the right road. At last we reached the Princeton road about half past four o'clock. We still had about 10 miles to ride. The road was very deep and our horses began to fag. The evening came on apace, and the twilight was almost quite gone, before we came to a very steep part of the road, three or four miles from Harmony. As the horses were well acquainted with this part of the road, we managed to get through and at last reached Harmony about half past seven. The night was very dark and cloudy, ,but we had one little shower during the ride. We were very tired and worn out. We were well entertained by Mr. Ecksenberger, and soon went to bed.

Saturday 12th of February.

Fair. We called on Mrs. and Miss Gertrude Rapp and likewise conversed a considerable time with Mr. George Rapp who had returned Saturday last. He gave us an account of my Father's voyage and of his meeting at Pittsburgh, and he said he started from Pittsburg on Wednesday 23rd. ult. In the afternoon we walked out and found the roads pretty dry. A beautiful evening.

Sunday 13th of February.

A dull day. rather cool. I journalized. John Ayers, a miller ,arived with a letter from Mr. Owen.

Monday 14th February.

A dull morning. North wind. Thermometer at 7 o'clock 40 degrees. Mr. Rapp called to ask about a postmaster. After dinner we called on Miss Gertrude Rapp and also on Dr. Smith, visited the carpenter's shop etc. Mr. Ranken

called, desirous of joining the society. In the afternoon
Mr. Orange arrived from Albion and John Ayres left us.
A beautiful evening. We practiced music a little.

Tuesday 15th of February.

A beautiful day. In the morning rather hazy and during
the day a few light clouds. Before dinner engaged in writing and conversing with Mr. Orange, who was formerly
a brass founder. Sewer from Springfield and several neighbors called. Sewer an applicant as a farmer. Mr. Orange
left us at four o'clock. After dinner we walked through
the orchards which are very extensive and I gave a geography lesson to some of Dr. Muller's pupils. I bought a
horse for $60.00.

Wednesday 16th of February.

A beautiful day. We visited the saddler's shop and Mr.
Schreiber. Ordered a saddle and bridle. We were visited
by three neighbors, one Downie, a carpenter, wishes to
join the society. Visited the rope walk. In the evening
very heavy rain. We practiced music and learnt German
and wrote.

Thursday 17th of February.

A beautiful, pleasant day. This day the Harmonians
celebrated the anniversary of their union into a society.
They began with music between five and six o'clock and at
9 they went to church; at 12 they dined and remained together with a short interval until near five o'clock; and at 6
they supped and remained together till after 9 o'clock.

What they were engaged in we did not learn as they kept
it to themselves, but they seemed to think they had passed
the day agreeably, and from many expressions which they
made use of, I should conclude that the meeting, from
some cause or other, had tended to strengthen the bond of
Union subsisting among them. Part of the day was prob-

ably employed in getting a knowledge of the state of their affairs. They have now been united 20 years. They transacted no business at the store but many persons arrived on business and were disappointed as they had not given any notice of the intended holiday before. This the Americans thought they should have done. But they seemed to wish to throw a veil of secrecy over all their proceedings. Before breaking up at 5 o'clock, they marched out of the church in closed ranks preceded by their music, all singing. They halted before Mr. Rapp's house and sang a piece of music and then dispersed. While they were so engaged, Capt. McDonald and I kept the tavern and we were visited by several people. In the evening, we practiced music and germanized.

Friday 18th February.

A beautiful day. In the afternoon, Mr. Rapp had another long meeting of his people in the church. Mr. Kell, a Cameronian preacher who had studied in Glasgow, ,called to make a proposal from a Princeton lady, Miss Eliza Parvin, who is anxious to join the society. Mr. Philips, land surveyor, called also.

Saturday 19th of February.

A fine day. We received a letter from George Flower, and an invitation to a ball on Tuesday at Albion. We returned answers by Mr. Burton. Having received a map from Mr. Rapp, which we colored, we proceeded to inspect all the houses, in order to give my Father an idea of them on his return. Visited by several neighbors.

Sunday 20th of February.

Engaged in describing the houses. Walked and rode a little. In the evening we were invited by Mr. Rapp to take tea with him. We met there Mrs. and Miss Gertrude Rapp, Mrs. George Rapp (Gertrude's mother) Caroline Beiser,

the housemaid, and George, the hostler. After tea, Dr.
Muller came in, also several performers on different instruments and a number of female singers, whereupon, a concert commenced which lasted untill half past nine.

Monday 21st of February.

The day cloudy, with some rain. We continued our inspection of the houses, several of which were inhabited.
We found all the inhabitants except one woman very
willing to let us see everything we wished. Saw today in
a cornfield near the river two wolves for the first time. In
the evening two gentlemen from Carmi arrived, and two
Englishmen settled near here called, Messrs. Shepherd and
Nottingham, a gardner. Shepherd managed to get a little
tipsy.

Tuesday 22nd of February.

A dull morning. I started about 10 o'clock on horseback
for Albion. Soon after crossing the ferry, it commenced
raining and continued with very little intermission till I
arrived within one-half mile of Mr. Flower's house. I continually was in hope that the rain would soon cease and
therefore did not feel inclined to return back, and my Kentucky boots and cloak kept me tolerably dry. It must not,
however, be denied that a ride over an uncultivated woodland country, where for many miles not a habitation or
improvement is to be seen, without a single companion,
particularly over a deep muddy road, while the rain descended in torrents, is certainly a situation not to be
greatly desired. The prairie, I found particularly soft and
wet. On my arrival, I immediately changed my clothes
and after dining, about 7 o'clock, drove in Mr. Flower's
wagon with Mr. and Miss Ronalds, to Albion, Mr. George
Flower following on horseback. The night was now beautiful, but owing to the darkness, we were guided by a boy
who walked with a lantern before the horses head. When
we arrived, we found but few persons, owing to the wet-

ness of the day, However, after waiting some time, we entered into the ball room and found that we formed a considerable party. Among those present were: Mrs. Judge Wattle, Charter, Beckett, Orange, Brown, Cave, R. Birkbeck; the Misses Ronalds, two Browns, Ross, Scott, Johnson; Messrs. Judge Wattle, G. Flower, H. Ronalds, Dr. Spring, Beckett, Brown, Cave, Cone, Jesse Brown, Pritchard, two Bartons, and Wood.

I led off with Mrs. Carter in a country dance. Afterwards in the course of the evening, we danced a Kentucky reel, but except that, only country dances. I saw no one in the room at all intoxicated, which they said was often the case. On the contrary, though several stood usually near the whiskey, the greatest decorum was observed. About half past twelve, we all went below to supper, which was laid out on two tables and about half past one, we returned home as we came. But some stayed until five in the morning. One man below stairs, I observed tipsy, but he did not belong to the company. What happened after we left, I can't say. I was a good deal tired with the day'r exercise. .

Wednesday 23rd of February.

A beautiful morning. I talked with Mrs. and Mr. George Flower, called on Mr. Flower who is somewhat better. Saw Mrs. Pickering, a pleasing women. After dinner Messrs. Brisenden and Stewart called. Stewart had just returned from Natches. He was questioned as to the prices of stock, corn etc. Amongst other questions that were put, were the following: How are horses selling? How are slaves selling? I saw one sold for $400.00.

A male or female?

Female. She was a very likely slave.

I reckon the common field slaves are much lower?

Yes.

Is the market overstocked with that kind of stock or is there a brisk demand?

It is overstocked.

Which is more sought after, male or females?

Females. I saw one female who was so nearly white, that one could scarcely have known that there was any black blood in her. The slaves belong to the owners of the mother; thus if she be pretty white, the children may become almost entirely so, but being born of a slave they are slaves too.

In the evening, I went to Mr. Flower's, when Messrs. Wood called and we had a long discussion about selfishness and disinterestedness, Mr. Flower contending that selfishness would govern a community as it has governed individuals heretofore.

Thursday 24th of February.

A very beautiful morning. Very pleasant. I talked over matters with George Flower and then prepared to start. Two men called just as I was about to proceed. I spoke a few words with them and then started. George Flower accompanied me a little way across the Prairie. I found the traveling pretty good, and about midday, the sun very warm. The horse performed his journey very well. I met some few travellers on the road with whom I had some conversation. I arrived before five and called upon Miss Gertrude Rapp and gave her an account of the ball. A letter arrived from my Father dated Pittsburg, the 25the ult. Judge Blackford arrived this evening.

Friday 25th of February.

Soon after breakfast, it commenced raining and rained very much all day. Employed in writing the police report. In the evening, Mr. Lewis arrived.

Saturday 26th of February.

Fine day. Visited the houses to get acquainted with their condition. Conversed with Mr. Rapp and Mr. Lewis. River rising fast.

Sunday 27th of February.

Very delightful day. Engaged in writing in the morning. After dinner the Harmonians assembled to the call of the bugle and at Mr. Rapp's invitation, we joined them. We walked, preceded by music and occasionally singing, to the vineyards, into one of which we entered. In the center of one is an open space, from which leads an alley overhung by vines. Here we remained for some time listening to the Harmonian's band. We then proceeded to a hill whence we had a fine view of the town, which appeared to be situated in a fine valley between two hills. We here seated ourselves in a ring and Mr. Rapp seated on an old stump, read for an hour an account of the Moravians. After some music and singing, we proceeded on our return. We reached the top of the hill which overlooks the road; here M. Rapp stopped and said "follow me ye young and you old can go round." With that he began running down the hill and all the young part of the population both males and females, (and who likes to be thought old?) followed him as they might. The others came more leisurely. Afterwards we returned with music as we had come. It was very pleasant out of doors, being neither too hot or too cold and the whole population appeared to enjoy the walk. While reading concerning an establishment, which had been ruined through extravagance, he took occasion to remark that they would beware of luxury, which would be their ruin, in which they seemed to acquiesce.

I rode out in the afternoon. River rising quickly.

Monday 28th of February.

A fine day with some clouds. We continued our inspection of the houses and called on Mrs. Rapp. The river falling.

Tuesday first of March.

Very rainy. all day. Occupied in writing all day, the police report. River rising fast. In the evening, not-so much rain. Gave a lesson on geography. Judge Blackford, who went on Monday to the court at Springfield, returned today.

Wednesday 2nd of March.

Little rain but dull day. Continued visiting the houses. Capt. McDonald not very well. We visited Mrs. Rapp. Rode out in the evening. Visited by neighbors.

Thursday 3rd of March.

Pleasant day but cloudy. No rain. Capt. McDonald still not well. Engaged in writing. In the morning Mr. Hood came desirous of selling some corn. In the afternoon I went to the vineyard and assisted in pruning the vines. In the evening Messrs. Wood and two farmers from Albion arrived to talk over matters.

Friday 4th of March.

Morning cloudy. The clouds soon dispersed and it became a beautiful pleasant day with a few light clouds. Continued to visit the houses. A man from Vincennes called this morning and offered corn for sale. His boat had struck on a snag about seven or eight miles below this and sunk one-half way so as to damage a great part of it. I could not venture to purchase it, as I did not know how much we might require.

The Phoenix Steamboat having arrived during the night, in order to take away some of the Harmonians, they were employed all morning in loading her. After dinner we walked down to the river. We found there almost all the Harmonians assembled, occupied in various way, some loading the boat, other unloading the wagons, which were continually arriving, some preparing themselves to go, other taking leave of their friends, on which occasion not a few tears were shed.

One peculiarity I remarked, which originated in their peculiar notions and German habits, was that all the kissing that took place, was from man to man, instead of as is customary in England, passing among man and wife, and between females amongst themselves. There were also a considerable number of backwoodsmen and their ladies, who contributed to enliven the scene. Altogether, it was the most lively and busy scene, I have witnessed in the Western states. About three o'clock she started, taking with her about forty Harmonians. Dr. Embry settled at StLouis, enquired concerning Dr. Price, who, he said, was his cousin and a "fine man." Afterwards, I visited the tanners and soap boilers in order to inquire what it was necessary to get, to carry on these businesses. They were very communicative. Talked also to the miller. In the evening, conversed with Messrs. Blackford, Battell and Dr. Smith about Free Agency in Man. George Eaton called in the morning and said that a meeting would be held in Squire McRonald's, his uncle's, house, on Tuesday week to debate the subject of a community.

Saturday 5th of March.

A most beautiful day. This day and yesterday reminded me much of two summer days, the sky presenting very much the same appearance as often in England. Having purchased some corn from Hood, the ferryman, we went to see it measured. Afterwards, we were engaged all day in our visitation of the town. We find the women usually very willing to show their houses to us. In the evening, I wrote to my sisters and we had a long conversation with Judge Blackford, who is very friendly. River rising.

Sunday 6th of March.

A good deal of rain throughout the day. Engaged in writing police report. River began to fall today, an inch. Judge Blackford left us today and returned to Vincennes.

Monday 7th of March.

In the afternoon showery. Engaged in writing. Conversed with several of the tradesmen. Called on Mrs. Rapp. River fell an inch.

Tuesday 8th of March.

Fine day with some clouds. Beautiful evening. Capt. McDonald having been unwell for some days past, took salts this morning. Visited the tanners, hatters, wagoners, smiths, and potters, etc. In the afternoon rode out. Mr. Williams from Carmi arrived. Astronomy.

Wednesday 9th of March.

Looked over some of the store accounts. Visited tinman, brewer, miller etc., and rode out in the afternoon with Mr. Rapp for four hours. Went to the vineyard. River rising slowly.

Thursday 10th of March.

A few showers. Wrote police report. Visited Mrs. Rapp; found Gertrude and her mother ironing, without their jackets. In the afternoon visited brass foundry and vineyard. In the evening, Mr. Elliott from Evansville arrived, offering himself as a brewer; also James from Mt. Vernon and Steel from Albion. River rising slowly. Letter from Mr. Pelham.

Friday 11th of March.

A beautiful day. In the morning cloudy. Mr. Williams left us. Purchased for $50.00 a horse from Mr. James. Mr. Orange and Dr. Spring arrived from Albion, having been detained at Hood's all night. Visited Dyehouse, granaries, etc., also vineyard. In the afternoon, rode out. Capt. McDonald, and Dr. Muller and talked with Mr. Rapp. Four gentlemen arrived from Kentucky. A man passed through town, endeavoring to track a stolen horse. River rose two and one-half inches.

Saturday 12th of March.

A fine morning. Walked through the town taking notes. A man brought this morning a stud horse which he intended keeping about 15 miles from this. Talked with Mr. Rapp. In the afternoon talked with Messrs. Grady, Pennypacker, Litchenberger, etc. who are anxious to join the community. Visited the cotton mills etc.

Sunday 13th of March.

A beautiful day almost without a cloud; The most pleasant I think we have yet experienced. Engaged with the police report. The Harmonians walked out towards the river and Mr. Rapp afterwards read to them. As we had no invitation to join them, we walked to the cut off hill and after remaining there for some time, we walked into the orchard and discovered for the first time, what we supposed was the burying ground of the Harmonians. Rode in the afternoon to the little prairie and so thro the wood home again. Between eight and nine o'clock, walked through the town and found the young people collected in small parties in different houses, singing together. Called on Dr. Muller and also he on us. Spring is now beginning quite to make its appearance. During last week plowing for oats has been going on and today I plucked up a stalk of wheat by chance from a spot that appeared particularly fine and found it upwards of 15 inches long. The sheep have been pasturing upon it for some days. The peach blossoms are making their appearances every where and in some instances a solitary blossom had been seen for 14 days past. The weeping willows have looked for some time quite green, and the green grass is making its appearance on the hills. The woods are now alive with birds of different kinds, which were all gone till now. Large flocks of doves are to be seen every where also yellow paroquets (These remained during winter) blackbirds, who chirp like the note of a rusty Wheelborrow, great quantities of partridges, winter birds, and a variety of others besides. The frogs also have long since begun their croaking, which altho it has been compared to a concert, I have found by no means very harmonious. Every one agrees that this has been the mildest winter and the earliest spring they have ever known and I understand it is general remarked throughout all the states. Indeed even as far north as Pittsburg, there has been scarcely any snow at all. A good many butterflies are also to be seen. Mr. Rapp engaged two ploughs for us.

Monday 14th of March.

A very beautiful day. After breakfast, I visited the vineyards and afterwards assisted in digging and sowing the tavern garden. Found it very hot and in the house it was quite pleasant, with the windows up, without a fire, which however we got lighted, inthe evening. After dinner, I walked with Mr. Rapp through his garden and the orchards. Wind south east and River fell same as yesterday.

Tuesday 15th March.

Day showery. River fell since yesterday five or six inches. Pruned some trees in the garden. After dinner called on Mrs. Rapp and talked for a long time with Mr. Rapp. Yesterday and today, Mr. Schnee has been bringing some of his effects here. Lieut. Col. Drake called. We talked to him about forming a regiment here. Mr. Rapp expected this evening the William Penn, his steamboat. Dr. Muller rode to Vincennes and Capt. McDonald accompanied him seven or eight miles. Mr. George Flower arrived in the evening.

Wednesday 16th of March.

Dull morning. Some very heavy showers. Walked about with George Flower and called on Mr. Rapp. Talked a long while with some neighbors who talked of joining us. The peach and apricot and plum trees are now mostly in blossom.

Thursday 17th day of March.

Dull day with some rain. Mr. Flower, Mr. Rapp and I rode over to the island, and made the tour of it. As we found plenty of grass, we ordered on our return the young cattle to be turned out of the enclosure they were in. We found but a very small part of the island under water. The highest points are five and six feet lower than the situation of the town. We returned about half past one and found some ladies and gentlemen of the backwoods engaged conversing with Capt. McDonald. Between two ond three o'clock, the William Penn arrived. She is a fine boat, of perhaps 150 tons burthen. Her arrival produced a great sensation in the town. All the male part of the population turned out immediately; the females for some reason or other hung back. John Ayers arrived.

Friday 18th of March.

Dull morning; the clouds dispersing in the afternoon. Between twelve and one o'clock, the steamboat set sail with fifty of sixty Harmonians having fired a salute in answer to the musical band, which being collected on the shore, played several pieces. Capt. McDonald took horse, when we returned and going down to the cut off, met them there

again, and was saluted by them. It is said that they
reached the mouth of the cut off, nearly 12 miles by water,
in thirty minutes. I think there must have been some mistake. It passed Mt. Vernon at 11 o'clock the same night.
John Ayers who had come to see the mill here returned
home as Mr. Rapp was too busy to be talked to on the subject and he had said before he would have no one in the
town till my Father's arrival. River falling.

Saturday 19th of March.

A beautiful clear day. Mr. Rapp rode out with Mr.
Flower over the farm. Afterwards Smith and I rode out
with him likewise. In the evening the Misses Wright, who
were on their way to New Orleans, to meet the Marquis
De LaFayette, arrived. They brought us news of my
Father's proceedings in Washington. Miss Wright is a
very learned and a fine woman, and though her manners are
free and unusual in a female, yet they are pleasing and
graceful and she improves upon acquaintance. Mr. Rogers
from Vincennes arrived, also; He wishes to join a community.

Sunday the 20th of March.

We walked with the ladies to the vineyard and hills, from
which we had a fine view. At one o'clock we attended a
musical meeting in the church and afterwards walked
through the house and garden af Mr. Rapp. In the evening, we supped there with Mr. and Mrs. and Miss Gertrude
Rapp. Afterwards, a good deal of music. A very fine day.
River stationary.

Monday 21 of March.

A dull morning; a slight shower, but soon clearing off
and becoming a fine day. After visiting the cotton mill,
the Misses Wright set out on their palfreys, with Mr.
Flower for Albion. After dinner, we employed ourselves in

the garden and orchard. Mr. James from whom we had bought a horse some days ago, having called on Saturday and appearing disposed to cancel his bargain, it was this morning cancelled and he took it with him. River falling.

Tuesday 22nd of March.

A fine day and warm. Engaged in writing to Applegate and in pruning the orchard. River falling.

Wednesday 23rd of March.

Wet day. Rain all day. Called on Mrs. Rapp. Mr. Rapp sent us a basket of apples, which had been kept all winter in the ground. They were quite fresh and good. Judge Emerson, called on us. We called on Dr. Muller Finished writing to Applegate. River slowly falling.

Thursday 24th of March.

Rain great part of the day. Mr. Rapp called today. Visited the cotton mill. Rode out in the afternoon. The hills looked very well at present, all the peach trees being in full blossom. In the town itself, wherever one looks, the peach trees catch the eye; indeed it now presents the appearance of nothing but peach blossoms and houses. There is an appearance of so many peaches that I have been told, were three-fourths of them killed, there would be still too many for the trees. I find the rainy weather particularly dull. I am tempted to think that it is very difficult to get over one's old habits, even at the age of 22, and that those are the happiest who, having had one mode of life chalked out for them, continue to pursue it through life. The enjoyment of a reformer, I should say, is much more in contemplation, than in reality. For surely one who thinks all around him equal or superior to himself in intellect must receive more pleasure from associating with them than one who thinks all with whom he converses less intelligent and less correct in their views of human nature

than himself. Did I not expect that those who were
brought up in a community, shall continue to live in that
manner, will enjoy more happiness than I anticipated for
myself, and more than they can experience when brought
up and living under the old mode of society, I should not be
disposed to promote the formation of a society, as I at
present am inclined to doubt whether the happiness of the
present generation will be increased. Perhaps this feeling
may have arisen in my mind from my present situation and
prospects, more particularly as some months ago my
anticipations of happiness and enjoyment were very flatter-
ing.

I doubt whether those who have been comfortable and
contented in their old mode of life, will find an increase of
enjoyment when they come here. How long it will require
to accustom themselves to their new mode of living, I am
unable to determine. This post day again, and we have
not received any letter yet from my Father since he, left
Louisville. We hear he has had two public meetings at
Washington which were well attended by all the first
people.

Friday 25th of March.   '

Another dull day. A good many showers. During the
night the river rose two and one-half inches. We are now
in hourly expectation of my Father's arrival and Mr. Rapp
expects a steamboat every day. We find it very tiresome
riding alone through a thick forest. In the evening, Mr.
George Flower arrived from Albion. Miss Wright he left
going on to Shawneetown. Miss Wright, he says, is very
much interested in the system.

Saturday 26th of March.

Dull day but clearing up a little. Called on Dr. Muller in
the evening. River rose in the night five inches. The
woods are becoming rather more lively. The wild peach

and plum blossoms are now to be seen and the sugar and elmtree are pretty green. The meadows are also becoming green. The peach blossoms are just beginning to fall.

Sunday 27th of March.

Dull morning. Towards evening the clouds dispersed and it became beautifully clear. The stars shone particularly bright.

About two o'clock the Steamboat, Plowboy, arrived on her way to Terre Haute. She staid her about an hour. We talked about going up in her but feared that my Father might arrive before her return. About ten at night, the William Penn arrived in 35 hours from Louisville. My Father had not arrived in Louisville when these boats started.

Monday 28th of March.

A dull day but the clouds dispersed about sunset. Engaged in pruning the orchard. Began a letter to Hippolyte. The William Penn set out with about 130 Harmonians soon after 12 o'clock. We hear that on their last trip a child fell overboard and was drowned. Messrs. Schnee, Lichtenberger, and Collins called, as they expected my Father had arrived. Also a clock maker from Montrose, who now resides in Shawnetown. Mr. Elliott from Evansville, who arrived last evening, was anxious that I should advance some money to rescue a farm etc. of his, which had lately been sold for a debt. I could do nothing for him. In the evening called on Dr. Muller, and corrected the press for him.

Tuesday 29th of March.

A fine morning. In the evening, a thunderstorm, but not very violent, from the west with rain. River rising fast. Engaged in the orchard.

Wednesday 30th of March.

Showery. Talked with Mr. Rapp. Called on Mrs. Rapp, and Dr. Muller who is preparing to set out for Economy. He told us today that marriage is not forbidden amongst them, but that, as they expect Christ to reappear soon, they wish to be prepared to meet him in a fit state, which could not be if they were taken up by sensual pleasures. In the evening, Mr. Steel arrived form Albion. River rising fast.

Thursday 31st of March.

A fine day with some clouds. Messrs. Pickering and Loftus arrived. They started again at two for Albion. We were visited by two men who, having rented and sold their farms and having no where to go, have brought their families up the river till within five miles of this. As we have not got possession of the property, we could do nothing for them. Mr. Rapp promised to rent them a house on Tuesday if my Father did not arrive sooner. Messrs. Jessman and Pennypacker talked to us also. River rising fast. Mr. Pearsham arrived from Albion.

Friday first of April.

Fine morning without a cloud. The Ploughboy arrived at seven o'clock. This is Good Friday, a day kept by the Harmonians very holy. Very delightful day. River rising very fast. The steamboat started again. Two men from Farifield, Illinois arrived. They wished to join us here. One had sold and the other rented his farm and had brought their families till within six miles of this place. Mr. Rapp told them that as Mr. Owen had not arrived he would rent some houses to themonTuesday next. Messrs. Steele and Bearsham returned home. Very beautiful and delightful day.

Saturday 2nd of April.

Called on Mrs. Rapp. In the evening, Mr. Sorgenfice and Mr. and Mrs. Ridgeway arrived from Albion. They had been obliged to swim in Fox Island several times. River rising.

Sunday third of April.

Very beautiful day. Talked to Mr. Sorgenfice etc. Capt. McDonald set out with Mr. Rapp for Vincennes.

Monday 4th of April.

Very beautiful day. River rising. Messrs. Sorgenfice and Ridgeway returned home. Mr. Hood took them around Fox Island in the boat. Heard that my father was at Cincinnatti, some days ago. Mr. Schnee removed his family to day to this town.

Tuesday 5th of April.

Mr. Hood, and Gaston and Haleman, a cooper, and tanner rented to day a house in town. River rising.

Wednesday 6th of April.

Close day. River rising slowly. A little drizzling rain during the day. Sheep sheering. Went to see it and found 25 young women sitting on the ground, each with a sheep in her lap. Each woman sheers from 8 to 14 sheep per day. The fleeces weigh from three to nine pounds average above 4 pounds.

Thursday 7th of April.

Dull morning. River standing. Engaged in orchard.

Friday 8th of April.

Fine day with some clouds. Messrs. Rapp and McDonald returned from Vincennes. They had proceeded as far as Buseron. Visited Mrs. Rapp and the new settlers. River falling fast.

Saturday 9th of April.

The Steamboat Ploughboy arrived at 6 o'clock, going up the river. River falling fast. Visited the new settlers. Got them removed to better houses. Received a letter from My Father by Mr. Clark.

Sunday 10th of April.

Fine day. Wind northerly. River falling very much. Now within its banks.

Monday 11th of April.

Fine day. Engaged all day in taking an inventory of the store.

Tuesday 12th of April.

Fine day. Engaged in the the store all day.

Wednesday 13th of April.

Fine day. Engaged in the store. At 1 o'clock my Father arrived by a wagon. He came down the Ohio in the William Penn and was accompanied by two Cincinnatti gentlemen, and a Mr. Borne from Baltimore. He was very well. Wrote in the evening notices and letters to different gentlemen giving notice of a meeting to be held this day week.

Thursday 15th of April. to Saturday 17th.

Beautiful weather. Saturday dull and in the evening some rain. Engaged in continuing the store inventory. This week James Struck, Greenwood, and Coats, removed into the town. My Father was much occupied with visitors.

Sunday 18th, Monday 19th and Tuesday 20th of April.

Fine weather. Messrs. Sorgenfice, Grant, and Ridgeway called on us. On Tuesday evening many persons arrived from Albion etc. River low.

INDIANA HISTORICAL SOCIETY PUBLICATIONS
VOLUME IV · NUMBER 2

THE WORD HOOSIER

By JACOB PIATT DUNN

AND

JOHN FINLEY

By MRS. SARAH A. WRIGLEY
(His Daughter)

INDIANAPOLIS
THE BOBBS-MERRILL COMPANY .
1907

THE WORD "HOOSIER."

During the period of about three-quarters of a century in which the State of Indiana and its people have been designated by the word "Hoosier," there has been a large amount of discussion of the origin and meaning of the term, but with a notable lack of any satisfactory result. Some of these discussions have been almost wholly conjectural in character, but others have been more methodical, and of the latter the latest and most exhaustive—that of Mr. Meredith Nicholson[1] —sums up the results in the statement "The origin of the term 'Hoosier' is not known with certainty." Indeed the statement might properly have been made much broader, for a consideration of the various theories offered leaves the unprejudiced investigator with the feeling that the real solution of the problem has not even been suggested. This lack of satisfactory conclusions, however, may be of some value, for it strongly suggests the probability that the various theorists have made some false assumption of fact, and have thus been thrown on a false scent, at the very beginning of their investigations.

As is natural in such a case, there has been much of assertion of what was merely conjectural, often accompanied by the pioneer's effort to make evidence of his theory by the statement that he was "in Indiana at the time and knows the facts." The acceptance of all such testimony would necessarily lead to the adoption of several conflicting conclusions. In addition to this cause of error, there have crept into the discussion several misstatements of fact that have been commonly adopted, and it is evident that in order to reach any reliable conclusion now, it will be necessary to examine the facts critically and ascertain what are tenable.

The traditional belief in Indiana is that the word was first put in print by John Finley, in his poem "The Hoosiers Nest,"

1 "The Hoosiers," pp. 20-30.

and this is noted by Berry Sulgrove, who was certainly as well acquainted with Indiana tradition as any man of his time.[1] This belief is at least probably well founded, for up to the present time no prior use of the word in print has been discovered. This poem attracted much attention at the time, and was unquestionably the chief cause of the widespread adoption of the word in its application to Indiana, for which reasons it becomes a natural starting-point in the inquiry.

It is stated by Oliver H. Smith that this poem originally appeared as a New Year's "carriers' address" of the Indianapolis Journal in 1830,[2] and this statement has commonly been followed by other writers, but this is clearly erroneous, as any one may see by inspection of the files of the Journal, for it printed its address in the body of the paper in 1830, and it is a totally different production. After that year it discontinued this practice and issued its addresses on separate sheets, as is commonly done at present. No printed copy of the original publication is in existence, so far as known, but Mr. Finley's daughter—Mrs. Sarah Wrigley, former librarian of the Morrison Library, at Richmond, Indiana—has a manuscript copy, in the author's handwriting, which fixes the date of publication as Jan. 1, 1833. There is no reason to question this date, although Mr. Finley states in his little volume of poems printed in 1860, that this poem was written in 1830. The poem as it originally appeared was never reprinted in full, so far as is known, and in that form it is entirely unknown to the present generation, although it has been reproduced in several forms, and in two of them by direct authority of the author.[3] The author used his privilege of revising his work, and while he may have improved his poetry, he seriously marred its historical value.

As the manuscript copy is presumably a literal transcript of

---

1 History of Indianapolis and Marion County, p. 72.
2 "Early Indiana Trials and Sketches," p. 211.
3 Coggeshall's "The Poets and Poetry of the West," and Finley's "The Hoosier's Nest and Other Poems" published in 1860.

the original publication, with possibly the exception that the title may have been added at a later date, I reproduce it here in full:

·ADDRESS

Of the Carrier of the Indianapolis Journal,
January 1, 1833.

THE HOOSIER'S NEST.

Compelled to seek the Muse's aid,
Your carrier feels almost dismay'd
When he attempts in nothing less
Than verse his patrons to address,
Aware how very few excel
In the fair art he loves so well,
And that the wight who would pursue it
Must give his whole attention to it;
But, ever as his mind delights
To follow fancy's airy flights
Some object of terrestrial mien
Uncourteously obtrudes between
And rudely scatters to the winds
The tangled threads of thought he spins;
His wayward, wild imagination
Seeks objects of its own creation
Where Joy and Pleasure, hand in hand,
Escort him over "Fairyland,"
Till some imperious earth-born care
Will give the order, "As you were!"
From this the captious may infer
That I am but a groveling cur
Who would essay to pass for more
Than other people take me for,
So, lest my friends be led to doubt it,
I think I'll say no more about it,
But hope that on this noted day
My annual tribute of a lay
In dogg'rel numbers will suffice
For such as are not over nice.

The great events which have occur'd
(And all have seen, or read or heard)
Within a year, are quite too many
For me to tarry long on any—
Then let not retrospection roam
But be confined to things at home.
A four years' wordy war just o'er
Has left us where we were before
Old Hick'ry triumphs,—we submit

(Although we thought another fit)
For all of Jeffersonian school
Wish the majority to rule—
Elected for another term
We hope his measures will be firm
But peaceful, as the case requires
To nullify the nullifiers—
And if executive constructions
, By inf'rence prove the sage deductions
That Uncle Sam's "old Mother Bank"
Is managed by a foreign crank
And constituted by adoption
The "heir apparent" of corruption—
No matter if the facts will show
That such assertions are not so,
His Veto vengeance must pursue her
And all that are appended to her—
But tho' hard times may sorely press us,
And want, and debts, and duns distress us,
We'll share a part of Mammon's manna
By chart'ring Banks in Indiana.

Blest Indiana! In whose soil
Men seek the sure rewards of toil,
And honest poverty and worth
Find here the best retreat on earth,
While hosts of Preachers, Doctors, Lawyers,
All independent as wood-sawyers,
With men of every hue and fashion,
Flock to this rising "Hoosher" nation.
Men who can legislate or plow,
Wage politics or milk a cow—
So plastic are their various parts,
Within the circle of their arts,
With equal tact the "Hoosher" loons,
Hunt offices or hunt raccoons.
A captain, colonel, or a 'squire,
Who would ascend a little higher,
Must court the people, honest souls,
He bows, caresses and cajoles,
Till they conceive he has more merit
Than nature willed he should inherit,
And, running counter to his nature,
He runs into the Legislature;
Where if he pass for wise and mute,
Or chance to steer the proper chute,
In half a dozen years or more
He's qualified for Congress floor.

I would not have the world suppose
Our public men are all like those,
For even in this infant State
Some may be wise', and good, and great.

But, having gone so far, 'twould seem
(Since "Hoosher" manners is the theme)
That I, lest strangers take exception,
Should give a more minute description,
And if my strains be not seraphic
I trust you'll find them somewhat graphic.

Suppose in riding somewhere West
A stranger found a "Hoosher's" nest,
In other words, a buckeye cabin
Just big enough to hold Queen Mab in,
Its situation low but airy
Was on the borders of a prairie,
And fearing he might be benighted
He hailed the house and then alighted
The "Hoosher" met him at the door,
Their salutations soon were o'er;
He took the stranger's horse aside
And to a sturdy sapling tied;
Then, having stripped the saddle off,
He fed him in a sugar trough.
The stranger stooped to enter in,
The entrance closing with a pin,
And manifested strong desire
To seat him by the log heap fire,
Where half a dozen Hoosheroons,
With mush and milk, tincups and spoons,
White heads, bare feet and dirty faces,
Seemed much inclined to keep their places,
But Madam, anxious to display
Her rough and undisputed sway,
Her offspring to the ladder led
And cuffed the youngsters up to bed.
Invited shortly to partake
Of venison, milk and johnny-cake
The stranger made a hearty meal
And glances round the room would steal;
One side was lined with skins of "varments"
The other spread with divers garments,
Dried pumpkins overhead were strung
Where venison hams in plenty hung,
Two rifles placed above the door,
Three dogs lay stretched upon the floor,
In short, the domicile was rife,
With specimens of "Hoosher" life.

The host who centered his affections,
On game, and range, and quarter sections
Discoursed his weary guest for hours,
Till Somnus' ever potent powers
Of sublunary cares bereft them
And then I came away and left them.
No matter how the story ended

> The application I intended
> Is from the famous Scottish poet
> Who seemed to feel as well as know it
> "That buirdly chiels and clever hizzies
> Are bred in sic a way. as this is."
> One more subject I'll barely mention
> To which I ask your kind attention
> My pockets are so shrunk of late
> I can not nibble "Hoosher bait."

It will be noted that throughout the manuscript the word is spelled "Hoosher" and is always put in quotation marks. Mrs. Wrigley informs me that her father had no knowledge of the origin of the word, but found it in verbal use when he wrote. She is confident, however, that he coined the word "hoosheroon," and the probability of this is increased by the fact that he did not quote it in his manuscript. In later editions of the poem he used the form "Hoosier." His original spelling shows that the word was not common in print, and several years passed before the spelling became fixed in its present form.

Although the word "Hoosier" has not been found in print earlier than January 1, 1833, it became common enough immediately afterwards. In fact the term seems to have met general approval, and to have been accepted by everybody. On January 8, 1833, at the Jackson dinner at Indianapolis, John W. Davis gave the toast, "The Hooshier State of Indiana."[1] On August 3, 1833, the Indiana Democrat published the following prospectus of a new paper to be established by ex-Gov. Ray and partner:

PROSPECTUS
FOR PUBLISHING
THE HOOSIER
AT GREENCASTLE, INDIANA,
BY J. B. RAY & W. M. TANNEHILL.

We intend publishing a real *Newspaper*. To this promise, (though comprehensive enough) we would add, that it is in-

1 Indiana Democrat, Jan. 12, 1833.

tended to make the *moral* and political world contribute their full share, in enriching its columns.

The arts and sciences, and agriculture and commerce, and literature shall all receive a due portion of our care.

Left to our choice we might refrain from remark on presidential matters; but supposing, that you may require an intimation, suffice it to say, that our past preference has been for General Jackson and his administration; and we deem it premature to decide as to the future without knowing who are to be the candidates. Those men who shall sustain *Western measures*, shall be our men. Believing that there is but *one* interest in the *West*, and but little occasion for partyism beyond the investigation of principles and the conduct of functionaries, we would rather encourage *union* than excite *division*. We shall constantly keep in view the happiness, interest and prosperity of *all*. To the *good*, this paper will be as a shield; to the *bad*, a terror.

The Hoosier will be published weekly, at $2 in advance and 25 cents for every three months delay of payment, per annum, on a good sheet of paper of superroyal size, to be enlarged to an imperial as the subscription will justify it.

This paper shall do honor to the people of Putnam county; and we expect to see them patronize us. The press is now at Greencastle. Let subscription papers be returned by the 1st of Sept. when the first number will appear.

On Oct. 26, 1833 the Indiana Democrat republished from the Cincinnati Republican a discussion of the origin and making of the word "Hoosier," which will be quoted in full hereafter, which shows that the term had then obtained general adoption. C. F. Hoffman, a traveler who passed through the northern part of the state, says, under date of Dec. 29, 1833:

I am now in the land of the *Hooshiers*, and find that long-haired race much more civilized than some of their Western neighbors are willing to represent them. The term "Hooshier," like that of Yankee, or Buckeye, first applied contemptuously, · has now become a *soubriquet* that bears nothing invidious with it to the ear of an Indianian.[1]

On Jan. 4, 1834, the Indiana Democrat quoted from the Maysville, Ky., Monitor, "The *Hoosier* State like true democrats have taken the lead in appointing delegates to a National Convention etc." On May 10, 1834, the Indianapolis Journal printed the following editorial paragraph:

The Hooshier, started some time ago by Messrs. Ray and Tannehill, at Greencastle, has sunk into repose; and a new paper

1 "A Winter in the West," p. 226.

entitled the "Greencastle Advertiser," published by James M. Grooms, has taken its place.

It is quite possible that this statement was made with the mischievous intent of stirring up Gov. Ray, for he was rather sensitive, and the Whigs seemed to delight in starting stories that called forth indignant denials from him. If this was the purpose it was successful, for on May 31 the Journal said:

We understand that another No. of the Hooshier has been recently received in town, and that it contains quite a bitter complaint about our remark a week or two ago, that it had "sunk into repose." We assure the Editor that we made the remark as a mere matter of news, without any intention to rejoice at the suspension of the paper. Several weeks had passed over without any paper being received, and it was currently reported that it had "blowed out" and therefore, as a mere passing remark, we stated that it had "sunk into repose." We have no objection that it should live a thousand years.

The new paper, however, did not last as long as that. It was sold in the fall of 1834 to J. W. Osborn who continued the publication, but changed the name, in the following spring, to the "Western Plough Boy." On Sept. 19, 1834, the Indiana Democrat had the following reference to Mr. Finley:

The poet *laureat* of Hoosierland and editor of the Richmond Palladium has threatened to "cut acquaintance with B. of the Democrat!! The gentleman alluded to is the same individual that was unceremoniously robbed, by the Cincinnati Chronicle, of the credit of immortalizing our State in verse, by that justly celebrated epic of the "Hoosier's Nest."

On Nov. 29, 1834, the Vincennes Sun used the caption, "Hoosier and Mammoth Pumpkins," over an article reprinted from the Cincinnati Mirror concerning a load of big pumpkins from Indiana.

These extracts sufficiently demonstrate the general acceptation of the name in the two years following the publication of Finley's poem. The diversified spelling of the word at this period shows that it was new in print, and indeed some. years elapsed before the now accepted spelling became universal. On Jan. 6, 1838 the Ft. Wayne Sentinel, republished the portion of the poem beginning with the words, "Blest

Indiana, in her soil." It was very probable that this publication was made directly from an original copy of the carrier's
address, for Thomas Tigar, one of the founders and editors
of the Ft. Wayne Sentinel, had been connected with the Indianapolis press in January 1833, and the old-fashioned news-
paperman was accustomed to preserve articles that struck his
fancy, and reproduce them. In this publication the poem is
given as in the Finley manuscript, except that the first two
times the word occurs it is spelled "hoosier" and once afterward "hoosheer," the latter evidently a typograpical error.
At the other points it is spelled "hoosher." This original form
of the word also indicates that there has been some change in ·
the pronunciation, and this is confirmed from another source.
For many years there have been perodical discussions of the
origin of the word in the newspapers of the State, and in one
of these, which occurred in the Indianapolis Journal, in 1860,
when numerous contemporaries of Finley were still living,
Hon. Jere Smith, a prominent citizen of ·Winchester, made
this statement:

My recollection is that the word began to be used in this
country in the fall of 1824, but it might have been as late as
1826 or 1827, when the Louisville & Portland canal was being
made. I first heard it at a corn-husking. It was used in the
sense of "rip-roaring," "half horse" and "half alligator," and
such like backwoods coinages. It was then, and for some years
afterwards, spoken as if spelled "husher," the "u" having the
sound it has in "bush," "push," etc. In 1829, 1830 and 1831 its
sound glided into "hoosher," till finally Mr. Finley's "Hoosier's
Nest" made the present orthography and pronunciation classical,
and it has remained so since.[1]

Of course, this is not conclusive evidence that there was a
change in pronunciation, for Mr. Smith's observation may
have extended to one neighborhood only, and it may have
taken on a variant pronunciation at the start, but his testimony, in connection with the changed spelling, is certainly very plausible.

There have been offered a number of explanations of the

[1] Indianapolis Journal, January 20, 1860.

origin of the word, and naturally those most commonly
heard are those that have been most extensively presented
in print. Of the "authorities" on the subject perhaps the
best known is Bartlett "Dictionary of Americanism's" which
was originally published in 1838 and was widely circulated
in that and the subsequent edition, besides being frequently
quoted. Its statement is as follows:

Hoosier. A nickname given at the West, to natives of Indiana.

A correspondent of the Providence Journal, writing from
Indiana, gives the following account of the origin of this term:
"Throughout all the early Western settlements were men who re-
joiced in their physical strength, and on numerous occasions,
at log-rollings and house-raisings, demonstrated this to their
entire satisfaction. They were styled by their fellow-citizens,
hushers, from their primary capacity to still their opponents.
It was a common term for a bully throughout the West. The
boatmen of Indiana were formerly as rude and primitive a set
as could well belong to a civilized country, and they were often
in the habit of displaying their pugilistic accomplishments upon
the levee at New Orleans. Upon a certain occasion there one
of these rustic professors of the "noble art" very adroitly and
successfully practiced the "fancy" upon several individuals at one
time. Being himself not a native of the Western world, in the
exuberance of his exultation he sprang up, exclaiming, in a
foreign accent, "I'm a hoosier, I'm a hoosier." Some of the New
Orleans papers reported the case, and afterwards transferred the
corruption of the word "husher" (hoosier) to all the boatmen
from Indiana, and from thence to all her citizens. The Kentuckians, on the contrary, maintained that the nickname expresses
the gruff exclamation of their neighbors, when one knocks at a
door, etc., "Who's yere?"

Both of these theories have had adherents, and especially
the latter, though nobody has ever found any basis for their
historical features beyond the assertion of this newspaper
correspondent. Nobody has ever produced any evidence of
the use of the word "husher" as here indicated. It is not found
in any dictionary of any kind—not even in Bartlett's. I have
never found any indication of its former use or its present
survival. And there is no greater evidence of the use of the
expression , "Who's yere?" when approaching a house. As a
matter of fact, the common custom when coming to a house
and desiring communication with the residents was to call,

"Hallo the house!" And this custom is referred to in Finley's line:
He hailed the house, and then alighted.

. Furthermore, if a person who came to a house called "Who's yere?" what cause would there be for calling the people who lived in the house "who's yeres?" There is neither evidence nor reason to support it. But there is still a stronger reason for discarding these theories, and most others. To produce the change of a word or term by corruption, there must be practical identity of sound and accent. It was natural enough for the Indiana pioneers to convert "au poste" into "Opost." It was natural enough for the New Mexican settlers to change "Jicarilla" to "Hickory." It was natural enough for the Colorado cowboys to transform "Purgatoire river " to "Picketwire river." But there is scant possibility of changing "husher," or "who's yere"—as it would probably be spoken—into "hoosh-er." This consideration has led to the suggestion that the expression from which the word came was "who is yer?" but there is nothing to support this. The early settlers did not use "is" for "are" but usually pronounced the latter "air." And they did not say "yer" for "you," though they often used it for "your."

Another theory, almost as popular as these, derives the word from "hussar," and this theory, in its various forms, harks back to a Col. John Jacob Lehmanowsky, who served under Napoleon, and afterwards settled in Indiana, where he became widely known as a lecturer on the Napoleonic wars. The tradition preserved in his family is that once while in Kentucky he became engaged in a dispute with some natives, and sought to settle the matter by announcing that he was a hussar. They understood him to say that he was a "hoosier," and thereafter applied that name to everybody from Indiana. This theory has several shapes, one being presented by the Rev. Aaron Wood, the pioneer preacher, thus:

The name "hoosier" originated as follows: When the young men of the Indiana side of the Ohio river went to Louisville,

the Kentucky men boasted over them, calling them "New Purchase Greenies," claiming to be a superior race, composed of
half horse, half alligator, and tipped off with snapping turtle.
These taunts produced fights in the market house and streets of
Louisville. On one occasion a stout bully from Indiana was
victor in a fist fight, and having heard Colonel Lehmanowsky
lecture on the "Wars of Europe," who always gave martial prow-
ess to the German Hussars in a fight, pronouncing hussars
"hoosiers" the Indianian, when the Kentuckian cried "enough,"
jumped up and said: "I am a Hoosier," and hence the Indianians
were called by that name. This was its true origin. I was in
the State when it occured. [1]

Unfortunately, others are equally positive as to their "true
origins." The chief objection that has been urged to this
theory is that Lehmanowsky was not in the State when the
term began to be used, and the evidence on this point is not
very satisfactory. His son, M. L. Lehmanowsky, of DePauw,
Ind., informs me that his father came to this country in 1815,
but he is unable to fix the date of his removal to Indiana.
Published sketches of his life[2] state that he was with Napoleon at Waterloo; that he was afterwards imprisoned at
Paris; that he escaped and made his way to New York; that
he remained for several years at New York and Philadelphia
where he taught school; that he came to Rush county, Indiana, and there married and bought a farm; that after bearing
him seven children his wife died; that he then removed to
Harrison county, arriving there in 1837. These data would
indicate that he came to Indiana sometime before 1830. The
date of the deed to his farm, as shown by the Rush county
records, is April 30, 1835. Aside from the question of date,
it is not credible that a Polish officer pronounced "hussar"
"hoosier," or that from the use of that word by a known
foreigner a new term could spring into existence, and so
quickly be applied to the natives of the State where he
chanced to live.

To these theories of the origin of the word may be added
one communicated to me by James Whitcomb Riley, whose

1 Sketches, p. 45.
2 Salem Democrat, October 25, 1899; March 28, 1900.

acquaintance with dialect makes him an authority on the subject. It is evidently of later origin than the others, and not so well known to the public. A casual conversation happening to turn to this subject, he said: "These stories commonly told about the origin of the word 'Hoosier' are all nonsense. The real origin is found in the pugnacious habits of the early settlers. They were very vicious fighters, and not only gouged and scratched, but frequently bit off noses and ears. This was so ordinary an affair that a settler coming into a bar room on a morning after a fight, and seeing an ear on the floor, would merely push it aside with his foot and carelessly ask, 'Who's year'?" I feel safe in venturing the opinion that this theory is quite as plausible, and almost as well sustained by historical evidence, as any of the others.

In this connection it is of interest to note the earliest known discussion of the meaning of the word, which has been referred to as republished in the Indiana Democrat of Oct. 26, 1833. It is as follows:

HOOSHIER.

The appellation of Hooshier has been used in many of the Western States, for several years, to designate, in a good natural way, an inhabitant of our sister state of Indiana. Ex-Governor Ray has lately started a newspaper in Indiana, which he names "The Hoshier" (sic). Many of our ingenious native philologists have attempted, though very unsatisfactorily, to explain this somewhat singular term. Mordecai M. Noah, in the late number of his Evening Star, undertakes to account for it upon the faith of a rather apocryphal story of a recruiting officer, who was engaged during the last war, in enlisting a company of HUSSARS, whom by mistake he unfortunately denominated Hooshiers. Another etymologist tells us that when the state of Indiana was being surveyed, the surveyors, on finding the residence of a squatter, would exclaim "*Who's here,*"—that this exclamation, abbreviated to *Hooshier* was, in process of time, applied as a distinctive appellation to the original settlers of that state, and, finally to its inhabitants generally. Neither of these hypotheses are deserving any attention. The word Hooshier is indebted for its existence to that once numerous and unique, but now extinct class of mortals called the Ohio Boatmen.—In its original acceptation it was equivalent to "Ripstaver," "Scrouger," "Screamer," "Bulger," "Ring-tailroarer," and a hundred others, equally expressive, but

which have never attained to such a respectable standing as itself. By some caprice which can never be explained, the appellation Hooshier became confined solely to such boatmen as had
their homes upon the Indiana shore, and from them it was
gradually applied to all the Indianians, who acknowledge it as
good naturedly as the appellation of Yankee—Whatever may have
been the original acceptation of Hooshier this we know, that the
people to whom it is now applied, are amongst the bravest,
most intelligent, most enterprising, most magnanimous, and
most democratic of the Great West, and should we ever feel
disposed to quit the state in which we are now sojourning, our
own noble Ohio, it will be to enroll ourselves as adopted citizens
in the land of the "HOOSHIER."—Cincinnati Republican.

Here is a presentation of the question, ten months after
Finley's publication, covering most of the ground that has
since been occupied. The "hussar" theory is carried back to
the war of 1812, long before Col. Lehmanowsky was in this
country. The "who's here" theory is carried back to the
government surveys, although it is certain that there were
few, if any, "squatters" on government lands in Indiana before the surveys were made. The "husher" theory, in embryo, is presented in the writers theory, which is apparently
conjectural, except perhaps as evidence that the word was
applied to the rather rough-looking class of .flat-boatmen
who made their trips down the Ohio and Mississippi.

There has been notable tendency to locate these stories
at Louisville, and to connect them with the building of the
Louisville and Portland canal which was under construction
from 1826 to1831, inclusive. The "husher" story is located
there by several of its advocates. Another story, of recent
origin, coming from one Vanblaricum, was recounted by
Mr. George Cottman in the Indianapolis Press of February
6, 1901. Vanblaricum claimed that while passing through
southern Tennessee he met a man named Hoosier, and this
man said that a member of his family had a contract on the
construction of the Louisville and Portland canal; that he
employed his laborers from the Indiana side, and the neighbors got to calling them "Hoosier's men," from which the
name "Hoosier" came to be applied to Indiana men gener-

ally. Vanblaricum could not give the address of his informant, or any information tending to confirm the story. At my request Mr. Louis Ludlow, Washington correspondent of the Indianapolis Sentinel, made inquiry of the representatives from the southern districts of Tennessee, and learned that none of them had ever heard of such a story, or knew of the name "Hoosier" in his district. An examination of the directories of Atlanta, Augusta, Baltimore, Chattanooga, Cincinnati, Kansas City, Little Rock, Louisville, Memphis, Nashville, New Orleans, Philadelphia, Richmond, St. Louis, St. Joseph, Savannah, Wheeling, Wilmington, the District of Columbia, and the state of Tennessee, failed to reveal any such name as Hoosier. As it is hardly possible for a family name to disappear completely, we may reasonably drop the Vanblaricum story from consideration. The same conclusion will also apply to the story of a Louisville baker, named Hoosier, from whom the term is sometimes said to have come. It is now known that the occurrence of "Hoosier" as a Christian name in the minutes of an early Methodist conference in Indiana, was the result of misspelling. The members name was "Ho-si-er (accent on the second syllable) J. Durbin," and the secretary in writing it put in an extra "o." It may be mentioned in this connection that "Hooser" is a rather common family name in the South, and that "Hoos" is occasionally found.

One of the most interesting wild-goose chases I ever indulged in was occasioned by a passage in the narrative of Francis and Theresa Pulszky, entitled "White, Red and Black." The Pulskys accompanied Kossuth on his trip through the States and visited Indianapolis·in 1852. In the account of this visit Mrs. Pulszky says:

Governor Wright is a type of the Hoosiers, and justly proud to be one of them. I asked him wherefrom his people had got this name. He told me that "Hoosa" is the Indian name for maize, the principal produce of the State.

This opened a new vista. The names "Coosa" and "Tallapoosa" came to memory. How simple! The Indiana flatboatmen taking their loads of corn down the river were called "Hoosa men" by the Southern Indians, and so the name originated. But a search of Indian vocabularies showed no such name for maize or for anything else. The nearest approaches to it are "Hoosac" and "Housatonic,," which are both probably corruptions from the same stem, "awass," meaning beyond or further. The latter word is supposed to be the Indian "wassatinak," which is the New England form of the Algonquin "awassadinang," meaning beyond the mountains.

In 1854 Amelia M. Murray visited Indianapolis, and was for a time the guest of Governor Wright. In her book entitled "Letters from the United States, Cuba and Canada" (page 324), she says:

Madame Pfeiffer (she evidently meant Mrs. Pulszky, for Madame Pfeiffer did not come here and does not mention the subject) mistook Governor Wright, when she gave from his authority another derivation for the word "Hoosier." It originated in a settler's exclaiming "Huzza," upon gaining the victory over a marauding party from a neighboring State.

With these conflicting statements, I called on Mr. John C. Wright, son of Governor Wright. He remembered the visits of the Pulszkys and Miss Murray, but knew nothing of Madame Pfeiffer. He said: "I often heard my father discuss this subject. His theory was that the Indiana flatboatmen were athletic and pugnacious, and were accustomed, when on the levees of the Southern cities, to 'jump up and crack their heels together' and shout 'Huzza,' whence the name of 'huzza fellows.' We have the same idea now in 'hoorah people,' or 'a hoorah time.' "

It will be noted that all these theories practically carry three features in common:

1. They are alike in the idea that the word was first applied to a rough, boisterous, uncouth, illiterate class of people, and that the word originally implied this character.

2. They are alike in the idea that the word came from the South, or was first applied by Southern people.

3. They are alike in the idea that the word was coined for

the purpose of designating Indiana people, and was not in existence before it was applied to them.

If our primary suspicion be correct, that all the investigators and theorists have followed some false lead from the beginning, it will presumably be found in one of these three common features. Of the three, the one that would more probably have been derived from assumption than from observation is the third. If we adopt the hypothesis that it is erroneous, we have left the proposition that the word "hoosier," was in use at the South, signifying a rough or uncouth person, before it was applied to Indiana; and if this were true it would presumably continue to be used there in that sense. Now this condition actually exists, as appears from the following evidence.

In her recent novel, "In Connection with the De Willoughby Claim," Mrs. Frances Hodgson Burnett refers several times to one of her characters—a boy from North Carolina—as a "hoosier." In reply to an inquiry she writes to me:

The word "hoosier" in Tennessee and North Carolina seems to imply, as you suggest, an uncouth sort of rustic. In the days when I first heard it my idea was also that—in agreement with you again—it was a slang term. I think a Tennesseean or Carolinian of the class given to colloquialisms would have applied the term "hoosier" to any rustic person without reference to his belonging to any locality in particular. But when I lived in Tennessee I was very young and did not inquire closely into the matter.

Mrs. C. W. Bean, of Washington, Ind., furnishes me this statement:

In the year 1888, as a child, I visited Nashville, Tenn. One day I was walking down the street with two of my aunts, and our attention was attracted by a large number of mountaineers on the streets, mostly from northern Georgia, who had come in to some sort of society meeting. One of my aunts said, "What a lot of hoosiers there are in town. In surprise I said, "Why I am a Hoosier." A horrified look came over my aunt's face and she exclaimed, "For the Lord's sake, child, don't let any one here know you're a hoosier." . I did not make the claim again for on inspection the visitors proved a wild-looking lot who might be suspected of never having seen civilization before.

Miss Mary E. Johnson, of Nashville, Tenn., gives the following statement:

I have been familiar with the use of the word "hoosier" all my life, and always as meaning a rough class of country people. The idea attached to it, as I understand it, is not so much that they are from the country, as that they are green and gawky. I think the sense is much the same as in "hayseed," "jay" or "yahoo."

Hon. Thetus W. Sims, Representative in Congress from the Tenth Tennessee district, says:

I have heard all my life of the word "hoosier" as applied to an ignorant, rough, unpolished fellow.

Mrs. Samuel M. Deal (formerly Miss Mary L. Davis of Indianapolis) gives me this statement:

While visiting Columbia, S. C., I was walking one day with a young gentleman, and we passed a rough looking countryman, "My! what a hoosier," exclaimed my escort. "That is a very noble term to apply to such an object," I said. "Why so," he inquired. "Why I am a Hoosier—all Indiana people are," I answered. "Oh! we do not use it in that sense here," he rejoined. "With us a hoosier means a jay."

The following three statements were furnished to me by Mr. Meredith Nicholson, who collected them some months since:

•John Bell Henneman, of the department of English, University of Tennessee, Knoxville, writes:

The word "hoosier" is generally used in Virginia, South Carolina, Tennessee as an equivalent for "a country hoodlum," "a rough, uncouth countryman," etc. The idea of "country" is always attached to it in my mind, with a degree of "uncouthness" added. I simply speak from my general understanding of the term as heard used in the States mentioned above.

Mr. Raymond Weeks, of Columbia, Mo., writes:

Pardon my delay in answering your question concerning the word "hoosier" in this section. The word means a native of Indiana, and has a rare popular sense of a backwoodsman, a rustic. One hears: "He is a regular hoosier."

Mrs. John M. Judah, of Memphis, writes:

About the word "Hoosier"—one hears it in Tennessee often. It always means rough, uncouth, countrified. "I am a Hoosier," I have said, and my friends answer bewilderingly, "But all

Indiana-born are Hoosiers," I declare, "What nonsense!" is the answer generally, but one old politician responded with a little more intelligence on the subject: "You Indianians should forget that. It has been untrue for many years." In one of Mrs. Evans's novels—"St. Elmo," I think—a noble philanthropic young Southern woman is reproached by her haughty father for teaching the poor children in the neighborhood—"a lot of hoosiers," he calls them. I have seen it in other books, too, but I can not recall them. In newspapers the word is common enough, in the sense I referred to.

It is scarcely possible that this widespread use of the word in this general sense could have resulted if the word had been coined to signify a native of Indiana, but it would have been natural enough, if the word were in common use as slang in the South, to apply it to the people of Indiana. Many of the early settlers were of a rough and ready character, and doubtless most of them looked it in their long and toilsome emigration, but, more than that, it is an historical fact that about the time of the publication of Finley's poem there was a great fad of nicknaming in the West, and especially as to the several States. It was a feature of the humor of the day, and all genial spirits "pushed it along." A good illustration of this is seen in the following passage from Hoffman's "Winter in the West"[1] referred to above:

There was a long-haired "hooshier" from Indiana, a couple of smart-looking "suckers" from the southern part of Illinois, a keen-eyed, leather-belted "badger" from the mines of Ouisconsin, and a sturdy, yeomanlike fellow, whose white capot, Indian moccasins and red sash proclaimed, while he boasted a three years' residence, the genuine "wolverine," or naturalized Michiganian. Could one refuse to drink with such a company? The spokesman was evidently a "red horse" from Kentucky, and nothing was wanting but a "buckeye" from Ohio to render the assemblage as complete as it was select.

This same frontier jocularity furnishes an explanation for the origin of several of the theories of the derivation of the name. If an assuming sort of person, in a crowd accustomed to the use of "hoosier" in its general slang sense, should pretentiously announce that he was a "husher," or a

1 Published in 1835, Vol. 1, Page 210.

"hussar," nothing would be more characteristically American than for somebody to observe, "He is a hoosier, sure enough." And the victim of the little pleasantry would naturally suppose that the joker had made a mistake in the term. But the significance of the word must have been quite generally understood, for the testimony is uniform that it carried its slurring significance from the start. Still it was not materially more objectionable than the names applied to the people of other States, and it was commonly accepted in the spirit of humor. As Mr. Finley put it, in later forms of his poem:

> With feelings proud we contemplate
> The rising glory of our State;
> Nor take offense by application
> Of its good-natured appellation.

It appears that the word was not generally known throughout the State until after the publication of "The Hoosiers' Nest," though it was known earlier in some localities, and these localities were points of contact with the Southern people. And this was true as to Mr. Finley's locality, for the upper part of the Whitewater valley was largely settled by Southerners, and from the Tennessee-Carolina mountain region, where the word was especially in use. Such settlements had a certain individuality. In his "Sketches" (page 38) the Rev. Aaron Wood says:

Previous to 1830 society was not homogeneous, but in scraps, made so by the electic affinity of race, tastes, sects and interest. There was a wide difference in the domestic habits of the families peculiar to the provincial gossip, dialect and tastes of the older States from which they had emigrated.

The tradition in my own family, which was located in the lower part of the Whitewater valley, is that the word was not heard there until "along in the thirties." In that region it always carried the idea of roughness or uncouthness, and it developed a derivative—"hoosiery"—which was used as an adjective or adverb to indicate something that was rough, awkward or shiftless. Testimony as to a similar condition in

the middle part of the Whitewater valley is furnished in the
following statement, given me by the Rev. T. A. Goodwin:

In the summer of 1830 I went with my father, Samuel Goodwin, from our home at Brookville to Cincinnati. We traveled
in an old-fashioned one-horse Dearborn wagon. I was a boy
of twelve years and it was a great occasion for me. At Cincinnati I had a fip for a treat, and at that time there was nothing
I relished so much as one of those big pieces of gingerbread
that were served as refreshment on muster days, Fourth of July
and other gala occasions, in connection with cider. I went into
a baker's shop and asked for "a fip's worth of gingerbread." The
man said, "I guess you want hoosier-bait," and when he produced it I found that he had the right idea. That was the first
time I ever heard the word "hoosier," but in a few years it became quite commonly applied to Indiana people. The gingerbread referred to was cooked in square pans—about fifteen
inches across, I should think—and with furrows marked across
the top, dividing it into quarter-sections. A quarter-section sold
for a fip, which was 6¼ cents. It is an odd fact that when
Hosier J. Durbin joined the Indiana Methodist Conference, in
1835, his name was misspelled "Hoosier" in the minutes, and
was so printed. The word "Hoosier" always had the sense of
roughness or uncouthness in its early use.

At the time this statement was made, neither Mr. Goodwin
nor I knew of the existence of the last four lines of Finley's
poem, in which this same term "hoosier-bait" occurs, they
being omitted in all the ordinary forms of the poem. The
derivation of this term is obvious, whether "bait" be taken
in its sense of a lure or its sense of food. It was simply
something that "hoosiers" were fond of, and its application
was natural at a time when the ideal of happiness was "a
country-boy with a hunk of gingerbread."

After the word had been applied to Indiana, and had entered on its double-sense stage, writers who were familiar
with both uses distinguished between them by making it a
proper noun when Indiana was referred to. An illustration
of this is seen in the writings of J. S. Robb, author of "The
Swamp Doctor in the Southwest" and other humorous
sketches, published in 1843. He refers to Indiana as "the
Hoosier state," but in a sketch of an eccentric St. Louis character he writes thus:

One day, opposite the Planter's House, during a military parade, George was engaged in selling his edition of the Advocate

of Truth, when a tall hoosier, who had been gazing at him with
astonishment for some time, roared out in an immoderate fit
of laughter.

"What do you see so funny in me to laugh at?" inquired
George.

"Why, boss," said the hoosier, "I wur jest a thinkin' ef I'd
seed you out in the woods, with all that har on, they would a
been the d—dest runnin' done by this 'coon ever seen in them
diggins—you're ekill to the elephant! and a leetle the haryest
small man I've seen scart up lately."

Unfortunately, however, not many writers were familiar
with the double use of the word, and the distinction has gradually died out, while persistent assertions that the word was
coined to designate Indiana people have loaded on them all
the odium for the significance that the word has anywhere.

The real problem of the derivation of the word "hoosier,"
is not a question of the origin of a word formed to designate
the State of Indiana and its people, but of the origin of a
slang term widely in use in the South, signifying an uncouth
rustic. There seems never to have been any attempt at a
rational philological derivation, unless we may so account Mr.
Charles G. Leland's remarks in Barriere and Leland's
"Dictonary of Slang, Jargon and Cant," which are as follows:

Hoosier (American). A nickname given to natives of Indiana.
Bartlett cites from the Providence Journal a story which has
the appearance of being an after-manufacture to suit the name,
deriving hoosier from "husher—from their primary capacity to
still their opponents." He also asserts that the Kentuckians maintained that the nickname expresses the exclamation of an Indianian when he knocks at a door and exclaims "Who's yere?" However, the word originally was not hoosier at all, but hoosieroon,
or hoosheroon, hoosier being an abbreviation of this. I can
remember that in 1834, having read of hoosiers, and spoken of
them a boy from the West corrected me, and said that the
word was properly hoosieroon. This would indicate a Spanish
origin.

The source of Mr. Leland's error is plain. "Hoosieroon"
was undoubtedly coined by Mr. Finley to designate a Hoosier
child, and what the boy probably told Mr. Leland was that
the name to apply properly to him would be Hoosieroon. But
that alone would not dispose wholly of the Spanish sugges-

tion, for "oon" or "on" is not only a Spanish ending, but is a Spanish diminutive indicating blood relation. In reality, however, Mr. Finley did not understand Spanish, and the ending was probably suggested to him by quadroon and octoron, which, of course, were in general use. There is no Spanish word that would give any suggestion of "hoosier." The only other language of continental Europe that could be looked to for its origin would be French, but there is no French word approaching it except, perhaps, "huche," which means a kneading trough, and there is no probability of derivation from that.

In fact, "hoosier" carries Anglo-Saxon credentials. It is Anglo-Saxon in form and Anglo-Saxon in ring. If it came from any foreign language, it has been thoroughly anglicized. And in considering its derivation it is to be remembered that the Southerners have always had a remarkable faculty for creating new words and modifying old ones. Anyone who has noted the advent of "snollygoster" in the present generation, or has read Longstreet's elucidation of "fescue," "abisselfa," and "anpersant"[1] will readily concede that. And in this connection it is to be observed that the word "yahoo" has long been in use in Southern slang, in almost exactly the same sense as "hoosier," and the latter word may possibly have developed from its last syllable. We have a very common slang word in the North—"yap"—with the same signification, which may have come from the same source, though more probably from the provincial English "yap," to yelp or bark. "Yahoo" is commonly said to have been coined by Swift, but there is a possibility that it was in slang use in his day.

It is very probable that the chief cause of the absence of conjectures of the derivation of "Hoosier" from an English stem was the lack in our dictionaries of any word from which it could be supposed to come, and it is a singular fact that in our latest dictionaries—the Standard and the Century—there

---

1 Georgia Scenes, page 73.

appears the word "hoose," which has been in use for centuries in England. It is used now to denote a disease common to calves, similar to the gapes in chickens, caused by the lodgement of worms in the throat. The symptons of this disease include staring eyes, rough coat with hair turned backward, and hoarse wheezing. So forlorn an aspect might readily suggest giving the name "hooser" or "hoosier" to an uncouth, rough-looking person. In this country, for some reason, this disease has been known only by the name of the worm that causes it—"strongylus micrurus"—it sounds very much like "strangle us marcus" as the veterinarians pronounce it—but in England "hoose" is the common name. This word is from a very strong old stem. Halliwell, in his "Dictionary of Archaic and Provincial Words," gives "hooze" and "hoors," and states that "hoos" occurs in the "Promptorium Parvulorum," and "hoozy" in the "Cornwall Glossary," the latter being used also in Devonshire. Palmer, in his "Folk-Etymology," says that "hoarst—a Lincolnshire word for a cold on the chest, as if that which makes one hoarse," is a corruption of the Old English "host," a cough, Danish "hoste," Dutch "hoeste," Anglo-Saxon "hweost," a wheeziness; and refers to Old English "hoose," to cough, and Cleveland "hooze," to wheeze. Descriptions of the effect of hoose on the appearance of animals will be found in Armatage's "Cattle Doctor," and in the "Transactions of the Highland Society of Scotland," fourth series, Vol. 10, at page 206.

There is also a possibility of a geographical origin for the word, for there is a coast parish of Cheshire, England, about seven miles west of Liverpool, named Hoose. The name probably refers to the cliffs in the vicinity, for "hoo," which occurs both in composition and independently in old English names of places, is a Saxon word signifying high. However, this is an obscure parish, and no especial peculiarity of

the people is known that would probably give rise to a distinctive name for them.

There is one other possibility that is worthy of mention—
that the word may come to us through England from
the Hindoo. In India there is in general use a word commonly written "huzur," which is a respectful form of address
to persons of rank or superiority. In "The Potter's Thumb"
Mrs. Steel writes it "hoozur." Akin to it is "housha," the title
of a village authority in Bengal. It may seem impossible that "hoosier" could come from so far off a source, and
yet it is almost certain that our slang word "fakir," and its
derivative verb "fake," came from the Hindoo through England, whither for many years people of all classes have been
returning from Indian service. It is even more certain that
the word "khaki" was introduced from India, and passed
into general use in English and American nurseries long before khaki-cloth was known to us.

As a matter of fact, words pass from one language to another in slang very readily. For example, throughout England and America a kidnapper is said in thieves' slang to
be "on the kinchin lay," and it can scarcely be questioned
that this word is direct from the German "kindchen." The
change in meaning from "huzur" to "hoosier" would be ex-
plicable by the outlandish dress and looks of the Indian
grandees from a native English standpoint, and one might
naturally say of an uncouth person, "He looks like a huzur."

It is not my purpose to urge that any one of these suggested possibilities of derivation is preferable to the other,
or to assert that there may not be other and more rational
ones. It is sufficient to have pointed out that there are abundant sources from which the word may have been derived.
The essential point is that Indiana and her people had nothing whatever to do with its origin or its signification. It was
applied to us in raillery, and our only connection with it is
that we have meekly borne it for some three score years and

ten, and have made it widely recognized as a badge of honor, rather than a term or reproach.

————

Addendum, February, 1907. The greater part of the preceding was published in the Indianapolis News of Aug. 23 and 30, 1902. Afterwards I rewrote and enlarged it. Since then there have appeared two publications which threw some additional light on the subject. One of these is an account of Col. Lehmanowsky, purporting to be autobiographical, published under the title, "Under Two Captains," by Rev. W. A. Sadtler, Ph. D., of Philadelphia. This demonstrates that Lehmanowsky believed he originated the word, for he gives the following account of it:

In this connection I may mention an amusing incident that occured somewhat later in a town in Kentucky, where I happened for a day or two. There was a drunken brawl in progress on the street, and as quite a number were involved in it, the people with whom I was speaking began to be alarmed. I remarked just then that a few hussars would soon quiet them. My remark was caught up by some bystander, and the word hussar construed to mean the men of the State of Indiana (from which I had just come), and thus the word "Hoosier". came into existence. Such is the irony of fate! Learned men have labored long to introduce some favored word of the most approved classic derivation, and as a rule have failed. Here a chance word of mine, miscalled by an ignorant loafer, catches the popular fancy and passes into Literature.[1]

At the same time he furnishes conclusive evidence that he did not originate it, for he says that he did not leave Washington for the West until the spring of 1833; that he went as far as Ohio with his family and passed the winter of 1833-4 in the state,[2] reaching Indiana the next spring, or more than a year after "The Hoosier's Nest" had appeared in print. His story, as given above, locates the incident at a still later date.

The other publication is the third volume of The English Dialect Dictionary, in which appears the following:

————

1 Pages 188-9.
2 Pages 182-5.

"Hoozer, Cum. 4 (hu-zer) said of anything unusually large."

The "Cum 4" is a reference to "A Glossary of the Words and Phrases pertaining to the Dialect of Cumberland;" edition of 1899.

Although I had long been convinced that "hoosier," or some word closely resembling it, must be an old English dialect or slang word, I had never found any trace of a similar substantive with this ending until in this publication, and, in my opinion, this word "hoozer" is the original form of our "hoosier." It evidently harks back to the Anglo-Saxon "hoo" for its derivation. It might naturally signify a hill-dweller or highlander as well as something large, but either would easily give rise to the derivative idea of uncouthness and rusticity.

There is a suggestiveness in the fact that it is Cumberland dialect. The very center of hoosierdom in the South is the Cumberland Plateau with its associated Cumberland Mountains, Cumberland River, Cumberland Gap, and Cumberland Presbyterianism. The name Cumberland in these, however, is honorary in origin, the river and mountains having been named for that Duke of Cumberland who is known to the Scotch as "The Butcher of Culloden." But many of the settlers of this region, or their immediate forebears, were from Cumberland county, England, and so "hoozer" was a natural importation to the region. Thence it was probably brought to us by their migratory descendants, many of whom settled in the upper Whitewater Valley—the home of John Finley.

JOHN FINLEY.

For many years Mr. Finley was known as "The Hoosier Poet," an appellation since transferred to James Whitcomb Riley, who wrote of him:

"The voice that sang the Hoosier's Nest—
Of Western singers first and best—"

Readers are always interested in the development of an author. They naturally inquire of his ancestry, early environment and education: how much was due to native talent, how much acquired by association with kindred spirits.

Mr. Finley's ancestors were Scotch-Irish Presbyterians; the family was driven from Scotland to Ireland by religious persecution, and failing to find the religious and political freedom they sought the seven brothers emigrated to America, in 1724. Samuel Finley became president of Princeton College; John explored the western wilds with Daniel Boone, and the youngest brother, William, settled on a farm in Western Pennsylvania. His son, Andrew, married and removed to Brownsburg, Rockridge county, Virginia, where John Finley was born, January 11, 1797.

Andrew Finley was a merchant in the village, but the family occupied a farm in a beautiful valley near the Blue Ridge Mountains. This mountain range could not fail to impress a child of poetic temperament—the blue haze veiling its summit, the drifting clouds that clung to its side, the rising sun dispersing the mists in the valley, or, the shadows creeping over valley and mountain as the setting sun disappeared beyond the western horizon, all left lasting pictures in his memory and influenced his after life.

His school days were cut short by his father's financial reverses, following the capture of a cargo of flour by the British during the war of 1812. This misfortune threw the boy of sixteen on his own resources, and, as nothing better offered he accepted a position with a relative who was conducting a tanning and currying business in Greenbrier county. This was a most humiliating alternative for a young Virginian whose surroundings led him to look upon manual labor as only fit for slaves, but it was part of the discipline of life which resulted in marked regard for all practical workmen, and an abhorence of the institution of slavery.

In 1816 he joined an emigrant company and with fifty dollars in his pocket, a saddle-horse and rifle and a pair of saddle-bags, turned his face towards the "Eldorado of the West." His first stopping place was Cincinnati, Ohio, but in 1820, we find him in Richmond, Ind., where he lived to see a small village develop into a thriving city.

Taking an active part in its growth, he was rewarded by the confidence and esteem of his fellow citizens who elected him to various offices of trust and responsibility. His official career began in 1822, as Justice of the Peace. He represented Wayne county in the Legislature, 1828-31, and then was Enrolling Clerk of the Senate for three years. During this time he met the leading men of the State and formed many lasting friendships. 1833-37, he edited and held a controlling interest in the principal newspaper of the county, the Richmond Palladium, and in 1837, was elected clerk of the Wayne County Courts, with a term of seven years; this necessitated a removal to the county seat, Centerville, but on the expiration of the term (1845) he returned to Richmond, having always considered it his home. Elected mayor of the city in the spring of 1852, he retained the office, by re-election, until his death, December 23, 1866, having almost continuous public service for more than forty years.

He was a man of sterling integrity; none who knew him ever doubted his word; an oath could not make it more binding. As a member of the Masonic fraternity he was active in the relief of the poor and needy; his sympathy and assistance were freely given to the ignorant negroes seeking refuge in Indiana: he looked upon them as children that had been deprived of their birthright.

A self-educated man, his reading covered a wide field; he was familiar with standard English authors and was a constant reader of the best current periodicals and newspapers, especially those containing the opinions of leading statesmen on political questions and internal improvements.

He was twice married, and had six children, one son, Maj. John H. Finley, gave his life for his country in the war for the Union—from this blow the father never recovered. A widow and three daughters survived him. Robert Burns was his favorite poet, the humor convulsed him with silent laughter, and "Highland Mary," or "The Cotter's Saturday Night" brought the quick tears to his eyes.

Mr. Finley's reputation as a poet was established when the Indiana Journal published "The Hoosier's Nest," January 1. 1833. It was the first "Carrier's Address" written by the author, and was followed by an "address" to the Journal for eight or nine years in succession. The Palladium also had an annual "address." These were rhyming reviews of State and National questions or humorous references to peculiarities of candidates for public office. They were of local interest but did not arrest general attention as the graphic description of Hoosier life had done. After a lapse of seventy-five years "The Hoosier's Nest" is still in demand at Old Settlers' Picnics, and at the reunions of the many "Hoosier Clubs" springing up wherever Indiana's sons have become prominent in the Great West. The following extract is conceded to be the best description of pioneer life to be found in print:

> "I'm told in riding somewhere West
> A stranger found a *Hoosier's Nest*—
> In other words a Buckeye cabin,
> Just big enough to hold Queen *Mab* in;
> Its situation, low but airy,
> Was on the borders of a prairie;
> And fearing he might be benighted,
> He hailed the house, and then alighted.
> The Hoosier met him at the door—

Their salutations soon were o'er.
He took the stranger's horse aside,
And to a sturdy sapling tied;
Then having stripped the saddle off,
He fed him in a sugar trough.
    The stranger stooped to enter in—
The entrance closing with a pin—
And manifested strong desire
To seat him by the log-heap fire,
Where half a dozen *Hoosieroons*,
With mush and milk, tin cups and spoons,
White heads, bare feet, and dirty faces,
Seemed much inclined to keep their places,
But Madame, anxious to display
·Her rough but undisputed sway,
Her offsprings to the ladder led,
And cuffed the youngsters up to bed.
    Invited shortly to partake
Of venison, milk, and *johnny cake,*
The stranger made a hearty meal,
And glances round the room would steal.
    One side was lined with divers' garments,
The other spread with skins of *varmints;*
Dried pumpkins overhead were strung,
Where venison hams in plenty hung;
Two rifles placed above the door;
Three dogs lay stretched upon the floor—
In short, the domicile was rife
With specimens of Hoosier life.

The word *Hoosieroon* was coined for the poem, and
"*Hoosier*" no longer designated a rough, uncouth backwoodsman but a self-reliant man who was able to subdue
the wilderness, defend his home, and command the respect
of his neighbors:

"He is, (and not the little-great)
The bone and sinew of the State."

"Bachelor's Hall" was published anonymously, and was
immediately credited to the Irish poet, Thomas Moore; it was
reproduced in England and Ireland many times before the
authorship was established. It was set to music for "Miss
Leslie's Magazine," and was sung at a banquet given for the
members of the Indiana Legislature:

"Bachelor's Hall! What a quare-looking place it is!
Kape me from sich all the days of my life!
Sure, but I think what a burnin' disgrace it is,

Niver at all to be gettin' a wife.
See the ould bachelor, gloomy and sad enough,
    Placing his tay-kittle over the fire;
Soon it tips over—St. Patrick! he's mad enough
    (If he were present) to fight with the Squire.

Pots, dishes, pans, and sich grasy commodities,
    Ashes and praty-skins kiver the floor;
His cupboard's a storehouse of comical oddities,
    Things that had niver been neighbors before.
Late in the night then he goes to bed shiverin';
    Niver the bit is the bed made at all;
He crapes like a terrapin under the kiverin':
    Bad luck to the picture of Bachelor's Hall!"

His poem entitled, Our Home's Fireside, expresses his appreciation of domestic life. He felt that the homes of a country are the fountain of all true happiness, and the bulwark of civil and religious liberty:

"There's not a place on earth so dear
    As our Home's Fireside,
When parents, children all draw near
    To our Home's Fireside;
When the toil-spent day is past,
And loud roars the wintry blast,
Then how sweet to get at last
    By our Home's Fireside!

'Tis wedded love's peculiar seat,
    At our Home's Fireside,
Where happiness and virtue meet
    At our Home's Fireside;
When each prattler, loth to miss,
Climbs to claim the wonted kiss,
'Tis the sum of human bliss,
    At our Home's Fireside."

He was ambitious to write a National Hymn which should voice the patriotism of the people, but this wish was never gratified. The "Ode for the Fourth of July" was an effort in that direction—constant attention to business prevented the cultivation of his poetical talent:

"ODE FOR THE FOURTH OF JULY."

Tune—"Hail to the Chief."

Hail to the day that gave birth to a nation!
And hail each remembrance it annu'lly brings!
Hail Independence! Thy stern declaration

Gave Freedom a home in defiance of Kings.
　　Britain's despotic sway
　　Trammeled thy early day.
Infant America, "child of the skies."
　　Till with a daring hand
　　Freedom's immortal band
Severed thy shakles and bid thee arise!

Then was the standard of Liberty planted—
　The star-spangled banner proud floated on high;
Columbia's sons met the foeman undaunted,
　With firm resolution to conquer or die.
　　Precious the prize they sought,
　　Dearly that prize they bought:
Freedom and peace cost the blood of the brave.
　　Heaven befriended them,
　　Fortune attended them—
Liberty triumphed o'er tyranny's grave!

Peace to those patriots, heroes, and sages,
　Whose glorious legacy now we enjoy!
May it descend to the world's latest ages,
　Like primitive gold, without any alloy!
　　Then let our motto be,
　　"Union and Liberty,"
High on our national banner enshrined,
　　Like a bright morning star,
　　Glittering from afar,
Casting its beams o'er the world of mankind.

When urged by friends to make a collection of poems for publication; he found, (in 1866), that many had been lost beyond recovery, his hope of writing something more worthy of preservation made him careless of that which had been published; there is, however, considerable variety in the collection, ranging from "grave to gay." These are some of the titles; "Lines," written on opening a mound on the bank of Whitewater near Richmond, Ind. containing a human skeleton. "What is Life," "What is Faith," "A Prayer," "My Loves and Hates." This was the first poem written for publication. "Valedictory, on closing my term as Clerk of the Wayne County Courts."

In lighter vein are, "Advertisment for a Wife," "The Last of the Family," "To My Old Coat," and "The Miller."

Mr. Finley was not a church member but his creed is embraced in the following sentence—"The Fatherhood of God and the Brotherhood of Man."

An unpublished fragment, found after death in the pocket-book he carried, shows his truly devotional spirit:—

> "My Heav'nly Father! deign to hear
> The supplications of a child,
> Who would before thy throne appear,
> With spirit meek, and undefiled.
>
> Let not the vanities of earth
> Forbid that I should come to Thee,
> Of such as I, (by Heav'nly birth)
> Thy Kingdom, Thou hast said, shall be."

TO JOHN FINLEY.

By Benjamin S. Parker.

> "Hail thou poet occidental,
> First in Indiana's Clime—
> Whose true passions sentimental,
> Outward flowed in living rhyme.
>
> Let no more thy harp, forsaken,
> Hang upon the willow tree,
> But again its chords awaken
> To thy songs blithe melody,
>
> As thou didst in time now olden,
> When our Hoosier state was young,
> 'Ere the praises of these golden
> Days of progress yet were sung."

Strickland W. Gillilan, wrote a "Versified Tribute."

> He nursed the Infant Hoosier muse
> When she could scarcely lisp her name;
> Forerunner of the world's great lights
> That since have added to her fame,
> He blazed the way to greater things,
> With "Hoosier's Nest," and "Bachelor's Hall;"
> And, while the grand world-chorus rings
> With songs our Hoosier choir sings,
> Let not the stream forget the springs,—
> Let Finley's name before them all."

INDIANA HISTORICAL SOCIETY PUBLICATIONS
VOLUME IV   NUMBER 3

WILLIAM HENRY HARRISON'S

ADMINISTRATION OF

INDIANA TERRITORY

BY

HOMER J. WEBSTER, A. M., Ph. M.

INDIANAPOLIS:
Sentinel Printing Co., Printers and Binders
1907

INDIANA IN 1811.

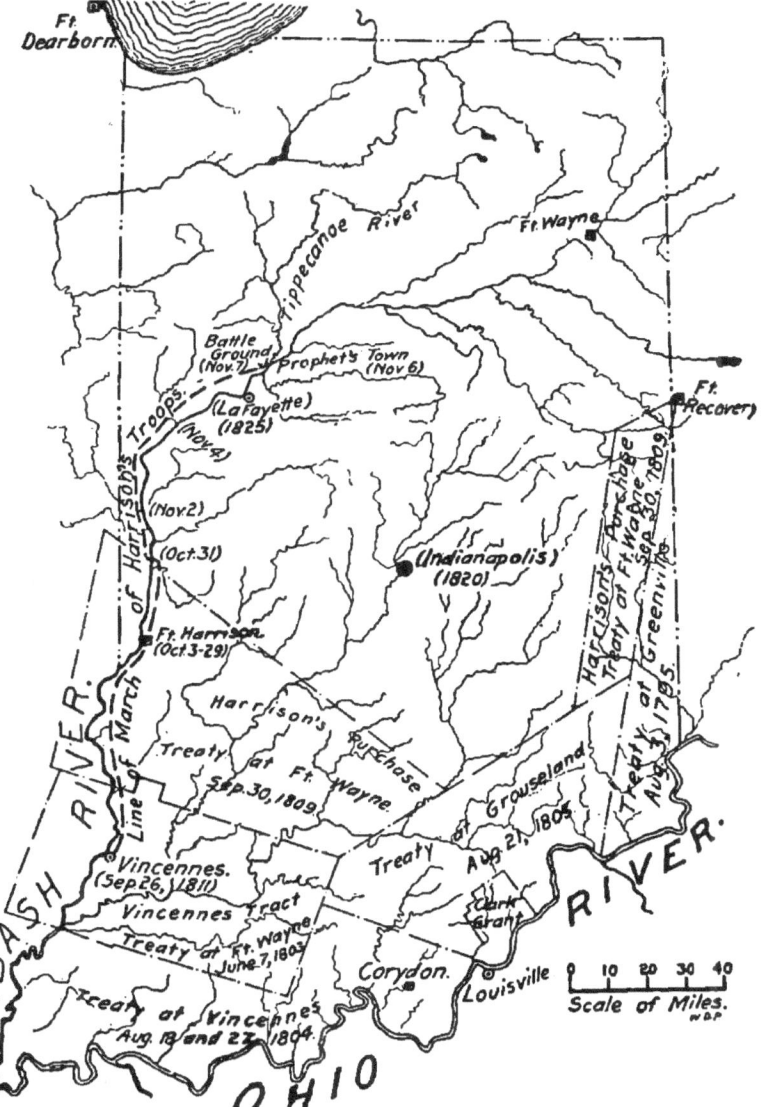

PREFACE.

Most of the sources of information upon which the following work is based, are indicated in the footnotes in connection with the text. It has been my aim, where conciseness would permit, to quote these sources freely and thus let them tell their own story and eliminate my personal opinions as much as possible. This plan brings the reader one step nearer to the truth and gives him a more accurate knowledge than any paraphrasing or summarizing could do. Especially have I endeavored to have Governor Harrison, the central figure of this study, to speak for himself. As to slavery in the territory, the excellent treatment of this subject by J. P. Dunn, in his "Indiana," published in the American Commonwealths' Series, seems to have left nothing to be desired. To secure material it was necessary to visit Chicago, Madison, Indianapolis, Louisville, Cincinnati and Washington.

To Professor W. D. Pence and to Mr. George S. Cottman, I am under obligations for the map of Indiana in 1811.

My thanks are due to W. E. Henry, State Librarian at Indianapolis; Reuben G. Thwaites, Secretary of the State Historical Society of Wisconsin; Miss Catharine Lord, Secretary of the Ohio Historical and Philosophical Society, Cincinnati, for their kindness in giving me access to materials; and to Mr. Waldo G. Leland of the Carnegie Institution of Washington, for assistance in finding ma-

terial in the government archives in that city. To the
Hon. Reuben T. Durrett, President of the Filson Club,
Louisville, Ky., my thanks are due, not only for access to
his great library, the best private collection in the west,
but also for his kind hospitality during my stay in Louisville. To Mr. J. P. Dunn, Secretary of the Indiana Historical Society and author of Dunn's "Indiana," my
thanks are due for several valuable suggestions. I should
also be ungrateful were I not here to express my thanks
to Dr. Hubbard Madison Smith of Vincennes, who
pointed out to me all the old landmarks of that historic
place, and especially the spot where Harrison had his
famous interview with Tecumseh, and the fine brick house
there, which Harrison had built in 1804 and occupied
during the remainder of his stay in the territory. My
gratitude is also due for further inspiration given by the
hospitality of Mrs. George Eaton, one of the Harrison
family, who occupies the old homestead at North Bend,
Ohio, to which Harrison repaired after the war of 1812.
Here he made his home the remainder of his life, and here
also, on a bare and isolated summit, overlooking the
graceful and silvery windings of the beautiful Ohio, his
tomb bearing the simple inscription—"Harrison," he is
laid to rest.

H. J. W.

Alliance, Ohio, November, 1907.

INDIANA TERRITORY

CHAPTER I.

THE TERRITORY AND THE GOVERNOR—PRELIMINARY VIEW.

On May 7, 1800, President Adams approved an Act of Congress, "to divide the territory of the United States northwest of the river Ohio, into two separate governments." This act went into effect July 4, 1800, and thus constituted the Indiana Territory, which was separated from the remainder of the Northwest Territory by a line from the Ohio river opposite the mouth of the Kentucky river to Ft. Recovery, until it intersected a line north from the mouth of the Big Miami, thence straight north to the Canadian boundary. It thus embraced all of the present State of Indiana except a triangular area in the southeastern portion, based upon the Ohio river and extending about half way up the eastern border, the western half of Michigan, all of Illinois, Wisconsin and that part of Minnesota east of the Mississippi river, and a line drawn north from its source to Canada, this latter area embracing about 26,000 square miles.[1] A little later when the State

---

1. Donaldson's Public Domain, p. 101.

(179)

of Ohio was carved out, its western boundary was formed
by a line drawn north from the mouth of the Miami, and
thus the triangular strip remaining between Ohio and
Indiana was added to Indiana. At the same time all the
eastern half of Michigan, which was cut off from Ohio
upon the admission of the latter State (1803), was made
a part of Indiana Territory and continued to be so until
the separate organization of Michigan Territory in 1805.
This Act of May 7th also provided that the form of government to be established in Indiana should be "similar in
all respects" to that provided by the Ordinance of Congress of July 13, 1787, for the Northwest Territory; and
the inhabitants were to enjoy all the rights and privileges
granted to the people by the said Ordinance. First, the
territory was to be governed by a Governor, and three
Judges to be appointed by the President by and with the
advice and consent of the Senate. The Governor and
Judges were to constitute the only officers of government
—legislative, executive and judicial—and in making laws
their discretion was limited to a choice from the laws already adopted by the original States, and these laws were
also subject to approval by Congress. Unless disapproved
by Congress, the laws were to remain in force until the
organization of a General Assembly in the Territory,
after which time the Assembly might alter them as it
might see fit. Whenever "satisfactory evidence" should
be given the Governor that such was the desire of a majority of the freeholders, even if the prescribed number of
five thousand free male inhabitants of twenty-one years,
as prescribed in the Northwest Ordinance, should not be
attained, the Territory was to have a General Assembly,
Legislative Council and a Representative in Congress. In
other words, it was to pass to the second grade. It was

further provided that the General Assembly should consist of from seven to nine members, who were to be elected for two years; while the Legislative Council was to consist of five members and to be appointed for five years. By a law of Congress, August 7, 1789, a change was made whereby the Legislative Council of the Northwest Territory was to be appointed by the President and not by Congress, as had been required by the Ordinance of 1787. The five members were to be chosen by him from a list of ten selected by the Territorial House of Representatives. Also by this law the Territorial Governor was to make his reports to the President. These changes in the provisions of the Ordinance were applied to Indiana Territory. By the Act of May 7, 1800, also, the seat of government of Indiana Territory was to be located at Vincennes, on the Wabash.

The man to whose influence and efforts this division of the Northwest Territory was largely due, was William Henry Harrison, who was at this time the first delegate to Congress from the Northwest Territory. In the life of Nathaniel Massie, by his son, we find a letter of Harrison to Massie, dated January 17, 1800, in which he contemplates moving in Congress for this division. On May 13, 1800, six days after the passage of the Act constituting the Territory, William Henry Harrison was appointed by President Adams as its Governor.

Harrison was born in Berkely, Charles City County, Va., twenty-five miles below Richmond, February 9, 1773, and was the youngest son of Benjamin Harrison, Governor of Virginia, who was a member of the Continental Congress, and one of the signers of the Declaration of Independence. His father, who was descended from one of Cromwell's veterans named Harrison, had tied with

John Hancock for the speakership of the Continental Congress, and in 1775 was a member of a committee in that body whose report formed the basis of our Militia System, with which his illustrious son was to have so much to do.[1]

Having received a classical education at Hampden-Sidney College, he began the study of medicine in Richmond in 1790. In April, 1791, he was sent to Philadelphia to continue his studies under Dr. Benjamin Rush and was placed under the guardianship of his father's intimate friend, Robert Morris, the financier of the Revolution. His father died when William Henry was on his way to Philadelphia, and in the following summer, upon expressing his dislike for the medical profession to Governor Lee, of Virginia, the latter recommended him to enter the army. Contrary to the wishes of his guardian and friends, Harrison at once applied through Governor Lee to General Knox and President Washington for an army position and, to use his own words, within twenty-four hours from the first conception of changing his profession, he was appointed as an ensign in the Tenth United States Regiment of Infantry. He made his way on foot to Pittsburg, thence down the Ohio and reached Ft. Washington in November, 1791, just as the remnant of St. Clair's

---

1. For the main facts of Harrison's early biography given here I have drawn from various sources. I would mention above all his own autobiography, published in the "Cincinnati Daily Enquirer," November 5, 1870, taken from the "New York Express" of November 2, 1870, and written at his home in North Bend, Ohio, July 20, 1839. This clipping is preserved among the Clark Papers, Ohio Historical and Philosophical Society, Cincinnati. It was written upon request for publication and sent to Hon. James Brooks, then a correspondent in Washington, 1839, and was later presented to the New York Historical Society, and was republished in 1870. It was also published in the Zanesville (O.) "Signal," November 18, 1870, and a copy of this paper was secured by Lyman C. Draper and added to the Draper Collection of the Harrison Papers preserved at Madison, Wisconsin, by the State Historical Society.

I have drawn the biographical data also from various lives of Harrison especially those by Dawson, Hall, Todd and Drake, and Montgomery.

army, which had been defeated on November 4th, arrived
there. The village of Cincinnati was composed of twenty-
five or thirty log cabins, but the inhabitants and settlers
had an abundant supply of whisky, for which the wretched
soldiers exchanged the remainder of their scanty pay; so
that Harrison said he saw more drunken men in the two
days following his arrival there than he had seen in all
his previous life.

His reception in the army, he says, was far from cordial on the part of most of the officers and troops, who
were jealous of his promotion and they assured him that
a single march to the interior post would end his military
career by causing his voluntary resignation. But such
talk only raised his "dander," he said, and made him more
determined to hold out. His duties were very severe during the winter of 1791-2, but his constitution hardened
under privations and he withstood the temptations to intemperance which surrounded him. In the intervals of
field duty he applied himself to study. His own library,
he said, consisted of only the volume of "Cicero's Orations," which he had used at college, and the large edition
of "Blair's Lectures." But the number of professional
works in the hands of the officers was not inconsiderable,
and he gave much attention to the study of tactics. He
was prepared for this study, he says, from his previous
knowledge of history. To quote his own words, "Inferior to many of my class at college as a Latin and Greek
scholar, I was considered inferior to but one in Belles
Lettres and particularly in History. I was acquainted
with the accounts of all the battles described by ancient
authors from Homer to Julius Caesar, and I had actually
read through the ponderous work of Rollin three times
before I was seventeen years old." This partiality for

history, especially military history, on the part of Harrison is strongly impressed upon one who reads his letters and speeches. He is constantly referring to the conditions, tactics, etc., in ancient battles. This tendency to revert so often to Roman military history is well illustrated by the anecdote of Daniel Webster, who, when Secretary of State, in speaking of revising and pruning Harrison's inaugural address, said he had killed "seventeen Roman proconsuls as dead as smelts."[1]

In 1792 he was made Lieutenant, and in 1793 he joined the legion under General Wayne and was soon made an aide-de-camp to him. He won praise from this General for his faithful services, especially at the celebrated battle of Fallen Timbers, near the Maumee, August 20, 1794, which gave Wayne his great victory over the Indians and brought peace to the frontier, negotiated by the Treaty of Greenville, 1795. He was married in November, 1795, to Anne Cleves Symmes, daughter of Judge John Cleves Symmes, negotiator of the Symmes purchase.[2] Shortly after this General Wayne placed him in command of Ft. Washington. Upon the death of General Wayne in 1797, Harrison resigned his commission in the army and retired to the farm.

Soon after this he was appointed Secretary for the Northwest Territory, to succeed Winthrop Sargent, who had been appointed Governor of Mississippi Territory. While holding the office of Secretary, being ex-officio Lieutenant Governor, he performed the duties of Gover-

---

1. Harvey: Reminiscences of Webster, pp. 160-163.

2. When Harrison was wooing the daughter of Judge Symmes, he is said to have been asked by the Judge, what were his means of supporting a wife; whereupon he placed his hand on his sword and replied: "This is my means of support."

nor for a considerable time while Governor St. Clair was at his home in Pennsylvania. He says that he was indebted to General Wayne for the recommendation which brought him this appointment. When Wayne visited Philadelphia in the fall of 1795, knowing that Harrison intended to leave the army, he so strongly recommended him to President Washington that the latter promised to give him the first suitable appointment which should become vacant in the Northwest Territory. No such vacancy occurred till after Washington's term expired, but the recommendation remained, and President Adams promptly gave him the appointment as Secretary when the vacancy came.

In 1799 the Northwest Territory passed to the second grade, which gave the people the right to make their own laws and to have a Representative in Congress. Arthur St. Clair, Jr., son of the Governor, and Harrison were nominated for Congress. Of the twenty-one members of the two houses of the Territorial Legislature, eleven voted for Harrison against ten for St. Clair, and thus he was elected October 3, 1799, as the first Representative to Congress from the Territory. His competitor, St. Clair, was a Federalist while Harrison was a Republican, but he was discreetly reserved on this subject—until the Republicans came into power. The object of those who solicited him to become a candidate for Congress, he says, was to obtain an amelioration of the laws for the sale of public lands, which were very unfavorable to the settlement of the country. He took his seat in Congress in January, 1800, and was appointed chairman of a committee of seven members, which he says was the first general committee under the Constitution having charge of the subject of the public lands. Harrison proposed his

plan to the committee and it was adopted. Mr. Gallatin
was a member of this committee and assisted Harrison in
securing the adoption of his plan. The law had required
that lands should be sold only in large tracts or in complete sections, thus depriving the small farmer from
buying his land directly from the government and giving
middle men and land companies the opportunity of making money at the expense of the purchaser. Harrison secured the passage of a law, May 10, 1800, whereby half
the lands might be sold in sections and the remainder
in half sections, directly to the purchaser from the government. , Also easy terms of payment were secured
whereby but one-fourth had to be paid within forty days,
the second fourth within two years, the third within three
years, and the fourth within four years.[1]

As to his appointment to the Indiana Territory, Harrison says that he at first declined it because he thought
Governor St. Clair would soon retire from the government
of the Northwest Territory, and that he would be able to
become St. Clair's successor. But some of President
Adams' chief supporters were also desirous of succeeding
St. Clair and so through party management Harrison
was shelved into Indiana in the hope of saving the Ohio
division for the Federalists. By the advice of political
friends and relatives he accepted the appointment.

Harrison was afterward frequently charged of being a
Federalist, but the testimony of Judge Jacob Burnett on
this subject seems conclusive. In a public speech in Cincinnati in speaking of this charge, Mr. Burnett says :[2] "A
more unfounded falsehood was never invented. My personal acquaintance with him began in 1796. . The inti-

1. United States Statutes II, Law of May 10, 1800, p. 73.
2. Todd & Drake's Life of Harrison. p. 23.

macy between us was great and our intercourse was constant, and from that time until he left Cincinnati I was in the habit of arguing with him on political subjects. I was a Federalist, honestly so, from principle. I can, therefore, speak on this subject with absolute certainty, and I affirm most solemnly that, under the administrations of Washington and Adams, Harrison was a firm, consistent, unyielding Republican of the Jeffersonian school. He advocated the election of Jefferson and warmly maintained his claims against Mr. Adams."

CHAPTER II.

FIRST YEARS IN THE TERRITORY AND THE LAWS OF THE GOVERNOR AND JUDGES.

On July 4, 1800, then, the government of Indiana Territory began. The Executive Journal[1] of the Territory opens thus: "St. Vincennes, July 4, 1800.—This day the government of the Indiana Territory commenced; William Henry Harrison having been appointed Governor, John Gibson[2] Secretary, William Clark,[3] Henry Vanderburgh and John Griffin, Judges in and over said Territory."

Secretary Gibson was the only official who acted during the first six months. Harrison did not arrive till

---

1. Published in the Indiana Historical Society Publications, Vol. III.

2. John Gibson was a native of western Pennsylvania to which place he later retired. He was present with the Indian chief, Logan, when the latter delivered his famous speech in 1774 to be sent to Dunmore of Virginia. For Logan's speech and Gibson's relation thereto, see Jefferson's Notes on Virginia in his works, Vol. 8, p. 308.

3. This was not the brother of George Rogers Clark, and later Governor of Missouri Territory, as stated in Appleton's Cyc. of Amer. Biog. See English's Conquest of the Northwest, Vol. II, p. 1015.

January 10, 1801, and the territorial court did not convene till March 3, 1801. On January 10th, the very day of his arrival at Vincennes, Harrison issued a proclamation requiring the attendance of the territorial judges at Vincennes for the purpose of adopting and publishing laws for the government of Indiana Territory. They met on January 12th and continued in session two weeks when they adjourned, having adopted six laws, one Act and three resolutions. The laws of the Northwest Territory were not formally re-enacted in Indiana Territory, but those passed before the division were tacitly understood as still applying to Indiana after the division.[1] This fact was of the utmost importance in tiding the infant Territory over its early years, for having now returned to the first grade, it could legally adopt new laws only from the original States; and these laws were not usually applicable to the new conditions in Indiana, while those of the Northwest Territory passed since its advancement to the second grade were very suitable.

Chronologically, Harrison's administration of Indiana Territory divides itself into two periods—first, the period under Governor and Judges; secondly, the period under the second grade of government—that is, by Governor, Council and Assembly, with also a representative in Congress. The first period extended from July 4, 1800 to December 5, 1804, when, as the result of the election for that purpose, Harrison issued a proclamation declaring that the government did

---

1. As an extreme case of this we note that by the decision of the territorial court, 1813, a law passed in North West Territory after 1800, was held to be still in force in Wayne county after its annexation to Indiana Territory, 1802, although an entirely different law was in force in the rest of Indiana Territory. W. W. Thornton, "Bench and Bar," p. 25.

On this subject see Indiana Historical Society Publications II, article by Daniel Waite Howe on "Laws and Law Courts of Indiana Territory."

then pass to the second grade. The second period extended from December 5, 1804, to September 24, 1812, when Harrison assumed command of the army of the Northwest and left the civil administration of the territory in the hands of his veteran Secretary, John Gibson, until the arrival of the new governor, Thomas Posey, on May 25, 1813. Indeed, Harrison's civil administration practically ended in the summer of 1811, when he became occupied with Indian affairs and was preparing for the defense of the Territory which led to the campaign on the Tippecanoe.

The chief subjects of interest in Harrison's administration are: The work of the Governor and Judges; slavery; passing to the second grade; the work of the Governor and Legislature; divisions of the Territory; the public lands; Indian affairs; treaties and land cessions; and, above all, the power and policy and personal work of the Governor throughout his four successive terms, or twelve years of administration.

But first, a few observations on the condition of the Territory about 1800. From the census report prepared by Secretary Gibson for the year 1800, we find the total population of the Territory to be 5,641;[1] and the white population within the present limits of Indiana was not over 2,500. These figures included negroes and slaves, but of course not Indians. The number of Indians in the Territory was estimated at 100,000.[2] The enumeration shows a population of 135 slaves. The only important settlements were Clark's Grant on the Ohio, opposite Louisville, St. Vincennes on the Wabash and

---

1. Indiana Historical Society Publications, III, p. 83.

2. The Eastern division of the Northwest Territory, that is, Ohio and Eastern Michigan in 1800, according to Carey's Atlas, had a population of 45,365.

Kaskaskia and Kahokia on the Mississippi near St. Louis. Only three counties then existed:[1] Knox, including all of southern Indiana; St. Clair, including the northern Illinois country; and Randolph, including the southern part of Illinois. Knox County then was all that had been formed within the limits of the later State of Indiana. Knox county had but 28 slaves in 1800, while Randolph had 107. The population were chiefly French, the only English settlement being that of Clark's Grant on the Ohio. There had been but one session of court having cognizance of crimes held in the Territory of Indiana during the five years preceding its separate organization, and this was a strong argument in Congress for the division of the Territory.[2]

Further light is thrown upon the condition of the Territory in Burnett's "Notes"[3] in which he describes a journey from Cincinnati to Vincennes in December, 1799. His companion was Arthur St. Clair, Jr., son of the governor. Leaving the river at the falls of the Ohio (Louisville) and proceeding by land to Vincennes, they encountered en route a camp of four or five Indians, two panthers, eight or ten buffalo and one wild cat! Yet in a letter[4] from Harrison at Vincennes, October 15, 1801, to James Findlay of Cincinnati, he says among other things: "I am much pleased with this country. Nothing can exceed its beauty and fertility. I have purchased a farm of about three hundred acres joining the town, which is all cleared.

---

1. Indiana Historical Society Publications, III, Intro. to Exec. Jour.

2. See Amer. S. Papers Misc. I, 206, for report of committee in Congress recommending division of the territory.

3. Notes on the Northwest Territory by Jacob Burnett (Cincinnati, 1898), p. 72.

4. Harrison Family Papers No. 43, Torrence Collection, Ohio Historical and Philosophical Society, Cincinnati.

I am now engaged in fencing it, and shall begin to build next spring if I can find the means. How comes on the distillery? I wish you to send me some whisky as soon as possible.   *   *   *   *   I wish you could muster resolution enough to take to the woods and pay us a visit. I am sure you will be so much pleased with this place and the prospects that would open to you, that you would consent to move here.   *   *   *   We have here a company of troops commanded by Honest F. Johnson of the 4th. We generally spend half the day together, making war upon the partridges, grouse and fish; the latter we take in great numbers in a sein."

To consider now the work of the Governor and Judges, we note that they held four sessions for the passing of laws, as follows:[1]

First session, January 12 to January 26, 1801. (6 laws, 1 Act, 3 resolutions).

Second session, January 30 to February 3, 1802. (2 laws).

Third session, February 16 to March 24, 1803. (1 law and two resolutions).

Fourth session, September 20, 1803, to September 22, 1804. (7 laws, 1 Act, 7 resolutions).

As the fourth session continued over a year, the law makers doubtless met only at intervals. The first session began only two days after Harrison's arrival at Vincennes. The first law passed by the Governor and Judges was entitled, "A law supplemental to a law to regulate county levies," showing that the laws previously adopted in the Northwest Territory were still regarded as applying to Indiana Territory, and were assumed as a basis for

---

1. Territorial Laws 1801-1806.

further legislation. Again follows a resolution repealing certain parts of a law passed by the General Assembly of the Northwest Territory. Further illustration of this is given in the title of the sixth law passed: "An Act repealing certain laws and acts and parts of certain laws and acts" of the Northwest Territory. And again in another law of this first session: "A law in addition to a law entitled," etc. The importance of this fact has already been observed.

But besides the laws of the Northwest Territory the Governor and Judges were also allowed to adopt such laws from the original States as might be desired. Let us note then the other sources of their laws. Some of them were from other than the original States, Kentucky, for instance, and hence were not authorized by Congress, although that body seems never to have objected to such laws. Most of the laws of the Governor and Judges were taken from Virginia and Kentucky—slave States—and especially from Virginia. Only two laws were taken entire from a free State—Pennsylvania. In this respect Indiana Territory was in marked contrast with the Northwest Territory under the first grade, as Mr. Howe points out,[1] for of the thirty-eight laws of the Maxwell Code (laws of the third session of Governor and Judges, Northwest Territory, 1795), twenty-six were taken from Pennsylvania, six from Massachusetts, and only three from a slave State—Virginia.

As might be expected, the first law related to the raising of revenue. Then came a resolution repealing the provisions of a law of the Northwest Territory, whereby lawyers were required, before being licensed to practice,

---

to have studied law for four years and to have resided in the Territory one year. One of the most important laws of the first session was that establishing Courts of Judicature and was adopted from the Pennsylvania code, January 23, 1801. This law provided for a system of courts, as follows:

1. The "General *Quarter-sessions* of the Peace," to be held four times every year in every county. This court was a criminal one, to be held by three or more Justices of the Peace in each county, nominated and authorized by the Governor, and to be held for three days each session.

2. Appeals from this court and all other courts might be made to the *General Court*, the *Supreme Court of Record* which was to be held twice every year at Vincennes.

3. The *Circuit Courts.* These were to be held once a year in each county, to try such issues in fact as should be depending in the General Court in regard to cases arising in that county. They were to be presided over by one or more Judges of the General Court, who were required thus to go on the circuit. This was also a court of appeals from the Quarter-sessions and Common Pleas Courts of the respective counties in which they were held.

4. The Courts of *Common Pleas.* These were county courts and had cognizance of civil cases and were to be held in each county four times a year, and presided over by the justices of the Common Pleas, commissioned by the Governor. The sessions were to begin at the same time and place as the Quarter-sessions.

Besides these four chief classes of courts provided for in this law of the first session of Governor and Judges, others were soon established; viz., the Justices' Courts,

Courts of Chancery, Probate Courts and Orphans' Courts.

The settlement and government of the Territory rendered it necessary to have surveyors[1] appointed, and the two laws of the second session have to do with this subject. The two resolutions and the one law of the third session are of minor importance.

The laws which were most thoroughly worked out were those concerning the levying and collecting of taxes. The seventh law of the fourth session, regarding county levies, covers eighteen pages. Any one who gave in an imperfect, false or fraudulent list was subject to pay a fine of fifteen dollars and his property was subject to a triple tax. The following rates were established: on each horse, mare, mule or ass, a sum not exceeding fifty cents; on all neat cattle above three years old, a sum not exceeding ten cents; on every stud horse a sum not exceeding the rate for which he stands at the season; every bond-servant and slave, a sum not exceeding one hundred cents; on every able-bodied single man of the age of twenty-one years and over, not having taxable property to the amount of four hundred dollars, a sum not exceeding two dollars, nor less than fifty cents.

The criminal laws and punishments were chiefly those of the Northwest Territory. By a law of the fourth session bigamy and also unlawfully to take away a maid, widow or wife were capital crimes. Pillories, stocks and whipping posts were also maintained.

---

1. The indefiniteness of boundaries caused great difficulty in punishing crimes. Harrison wrote the Secretary of War (1801) expressing his anxiety that the government should speedily have the lands surveyed and the boundaries fixed. Dawson's "Harrison," p. 8.

CHAPTER III.

SLAVERY AND THE ADVANCE TO THE SECOND GRADE OF GOVERNMENT. THE DISTRICT OF LOUISIANA AND THE TERRITORY OF MICHIGAN.

Hardly had the Territory been set apart when the subject of slavery demanded attention. The sixth Article of the Northwest Ordinance prohibited slavery in the Northwest Territory, and the question was vitally connected with the settlement of the Territory. The situation is well set forth by Thomas T. Davis, Esq., of Kaskaskia, in 1803. He says:[1] "If persons migrating here are not permitted to bring their negroes with them, it will be many years before we become a State. Persons wishing to hold slaves will go on the Spanish side; those who are against it will settle in the State of Ohio, where the point is settled.   *   *   *   The former inhabitants here (the French) were all slave holders, and the adoption of the ordinance induced them to believe their negroes would be liberated and they immediately quit this place and went on the Spanish side of the Mississippi river."

As to the slaves already in the Territory, in view of the interpretation of the sixth Article by the authorities, it appears that their owners need not have been frightened; for upon appealing to Governor St. Clair as to its meaning, he held it to be prospective, not retroactive. He argued that if Congress had intended to emancipate the slaves already in the Territory, compensation would have been made to their owners.[2] And this view of the

---

1. Letter of October 18, 1803, published in "The Palladium," a Kentucky paper of that time.

2. Hinsdale's Old Northwest, p. 350. St. Clair Papers I, 205-6.

matter prevailed in the subsequent government of the
Northwest. The deed of cession of the Northwest Territory to the United States by Virginia guaranteed to the
inhabitants "Their possessions and titles" and this was
brought forth to oppose the sixth Article and support the
claim to property in slaves in Indiana Territory. As
early as 1796 the inhabitants of the Illinois country had
petitioned Congress for the repeal or alteration of the
sixth Article of the Northwest Ordinance so as to permit
the introduction of slaves into the said Territory.[1] This
petition purported to be "For and on behalf of the inhabitants of the counties of St. Clair and Randolph;" and was
signed by four names—John Edgar, William Morrison,
William St. Clair and John Dumoulin, and was dated
Kaskaskia, January 12, 1796. This petition was not
granted and was criticized by Congress as unauthorita-
tive and unrepresentative. On October 1, 1800, therefore, another was prepared and signed by 270 names and
was presented to Congress January 23, 1801, during the
first session of the Governor and Judges. This petition
was laid on the table[2] and no further action was taken
upon it. This second petition also came from Randolph
and St. Clair counties, and is noteworthy in that while
it asked that the slaves brought in should continue in
slavery during their lives, their issue born in the Territory were to be declared free—the males at thirty-one and
the females at twenty-eight years of age. But such petitions were not to be confined to the Illinois country. The
next slavery movement was the Vincennes Convention
of December 20, 1802. This was called by Governor
Harrison in response to petitions for it. Delegates to this

---

1. Amer. State Papers, Public Lands, I. 61. Indiana Hist. Soc. Pubs. II. 417
2. Annals Sixth Congress, p. 735. Ind. Hist. Soc. Pubs. II, 461.

convention were chosen as follows[1]: From Knox county,
4; Randolph, 3; St. Clair, 3; and Clark, a county formed
from the eastern part of Knox, February 3, '01, 2. Harrison was made chairman and the convention was in session seven days, when, December 28, they had agreed upon a memorial to Congress, asking the suspension of the
sixth Article for ten years. But those to be brought in
and also their progeny were to remain permanently in
bondage. It was also pointed out in this memorial that
the prohibition of slavery retarded the settlement and development of the country. The petition was referred to
a committee in the House of Representatives, of which
John Randolph was chairman. This committee reported
adversely March 2, 1803,[2] declaring "that the rapid population of the State of Ohio sufficiently evinces * * * *
that the labor of slaves is not necessary to promote the growth and settlement of colonies in that region.
* * * * In the salutary operation of this sagacious
and benevolent restraint, it is believed that the inhabitants of Indiana will, at no distant day, find ample remuneration for a temporary privation of labor and of
emigration."

The next important move for slavery in Indiana was
the passage of "A law concerning servants" by the Governor and Judges at their fourth session, September 22,
1803. This law was adopted from the Virginia code and
provides that all negroes and mulattoes who shall come
into this Territory, under contract to serve another in any
trade or occupation, shall be compelled to perform such
contract specifically during the term thereof. * * *
The benefit of the said contract of service shall be assign-

---

1. Dunn's Indiana. p. 303.
2. Amer. St. Papers Pub. Lands, I, 146. Ind. Hist. Soc. Pubs.. II. 470.

able by the master to any person being a citizen of this
Territory to whom the servant shall   *   *   *   freely
consent, etc." In all cases where free persons were punishable by fine, servants were punishable by whipping at
the rate of twenty lashes for eight dollars, unless the
servant could procure some one to pay the fine. But no
servant was to receive more than forty lashes at any one
time.

Meanwhile the inhabitants of the Illinois country had
been active in another way in trying to secure the introduction of slaves. The next move was to secure a representative assembly. so they might make their own laws,
and have a delegate in Congress; that is, to advance to
the second grade of government. Congress would not
then have a veto on their laws as it had on those of the
Governor and Judges, and they would no longer be confined, as they nominally had been, to laws taken from the
original States. As early as April 11, 1801, John Edgar
wrote to Governor St. Clair that a petition had been circulated, addressed to Governor Harrison and asking for an
assembly, and saying that about nine-tenths of the inhabitants of St. Clair and Randolph counties approved the
measure.[1] And now, at this early date in his administration, came a test of Harrison's skill in political leadership.[2] The majority of the people desired the second
grade of government in order to secure slavery. The
Territory was then Federalist while Harrison was a Republican. To grant this change would be to give the government into the hands of the legislature, which would
likely be in opposition to him and thus his political influence and soon his position might be lost. He must op-

1. St. Clair Papers, II, 583. Dunn's Indiana.
2. Dunn's Indiana.

pose the second grade, but must not offend the people. He accordingly wrote a "letter to a friend," which was published, as it was intended to be, and in which he elaborated on the *expense* and greatly increased taxation the change would involve. This argument was effective and stayed the movement for the time.

But the Illinois faction soon espoused another plan. This was brought to a head in the fall of 1803, when petitions were circulated for the annexation of the Illinois country to Louisiana. But here again they met defeat, for early the next spring, by Act of Congress approved March 26, 1804, the upper part of Louisiana, the "District of Louisiana," was attached, for the purpose of government, to Indiana. This was merely a personal union, and only provided that the Governor and Judges of Indiana were also to pass laws for the District of Louisiana. But the laws of Indiana were not to extend to this District. The law was to take effect October 1, 1804. Accordingly, the Governor and Judges held a special session October 1, 1804, and passed six laws for the government of this District. Harrison was cordially received by the people of the District of Louisiana as Governor. Upon his arrival at the town of St. Genevieve, he was received by a committee and presented with a very complimentary address, approving his appointment and expressing confidence, hope and congratulations. But a hope was also expressed that they would soon be ready for and receive a separate and representative government.[1]

During the summer of 1804 already, Harrison and President Jefferson had been in correspondence regarding the division and organization of the District and upon October 1st, the same day the laws were passed, Harri-

---

1. Nat. Intelligencer, January 9, 1805.

son issued a proclamation dividing the District into five
counties. In a letter of Harrison to Jefferson, dated June
24, 1804, he states that he has ascertained the population
of the District to be 9373; 7876 whites and 1497 blacks.
But these were all located near St. Louis. When he was
made Governor over this District in addition to the Territory of Indiana, he was entrusted with the largest domain ever committed to the charge of any one under the
President of the United States. And yet the Governor
and Judges were too far removed to administer a very
efficient government, and the necessary neglect, combined
with a fear that the people might also have to yield to
the provisions of the Northwest Ordinance in regard to
slavery, caused dissatisfaction and a petition for separate
government.[1] This was granted by Act of Congress, approved March 3, 1805. So that Harrison was actually
Governor of the District for about five months. To offset
this clamor for separate government we have, on the other
hand, the addresses, both of the citizens of St. Louis and
of the militia officers of the District, July, 1805, com-
mending the "assiduity, attention and disinterested
punctuality" which he had manifested in the temporary
administration of the District of Louisiana.[2] While Governor of this District, Harrison declined to receive the
fees to which he was entitled by law, although those for
trading licenses alone would have amounted to hundreds
of dollars.[3] In this connection it is interesting to note the
additional recompense actually received by the Governor
and Judges for their extra services in governing the
District of Louisiana. By an Act of Congress, approved

---

1. Dunn's Indiana, 318, 319.
2. Todd & Drake's Biography, p. 26. Dawson's Harrison, p. 85.
3. Todd & Drake's Sketches of Harrison, p. 223.

March 3, 1807. (just two years after the act separating
the governments) this amount was fixed at $300 for each.

It was about this time that Wayne county was detached
from Indiana and constituted as the Territory of Michigan. This county had been formed by proclamation of
the Governor January 24, 1803, after the carving out of
Ohio, which threw the eastern half of Michigan
into Indiana Territory. Its western boundary was
the north and south line through the western extremity
of Lake Michigan, and its southern boundary the east
and west line through the southern extremity of this
lake,[1] as proclaimed by Governor Harrison. But it is to
be noted that this western boundary of Wayne county
was not the same as the western boundary of Michigan
Territory formed two years later, for this latter was a
north and south line from the southern extremity of Lake
Michigan[2] and not the tangent line on the west side of
this lake which had been the boundary of Wayne county.
This separation was eagerly sought by the inhabitants of
Wayne county, or Michigan, and in the fall of 1803, November 1st, we note the adoption by the United States
Senate of the report of a committee to whom was referred
the memorial of Joseph Harrison and others, resident in
Wayne county. The report said among other things:
That it appeared from the Census of 1800 that the Territory contained 3972 free white inhabitants, and that they
are separated from the other settlements of Indiana Territory by a distance of at least 350 miles, and that the
prayer of the memorial for a separate government ought
to be granted. The next fall we have another appeal to

---

1. Exec. Jour., pp. 114, 115.
2. See Law of January 11, 1805, organizing territory of Michigan.—U. S.
Statutes at large.

Congress for relief, as follows :[1] We memorialists, citizens and inhabitants of that district of Indiana Territory situate, etc.   *   *   *   * humbly pray the interposition of Congress, giving us a separate Territory. The memoralists refer to previous petitions for the same, and say that but one sentiment prevails within this district upon the expediency and necessity of separation. They say that in September, 1803, the legislature of Indiana Territory adopted several laws, but that those laws, although adopted more than twelve months past, have never yet been seen in this place and, of course, have not come into operation in this district. By stating this fact, they say, we do not intend to attach any blame or censure upon our Governor, but to show the impracticability of communicating with the seat of government. The movement for the second grade is given as additional reason for wishing to separate, as it would increase expenses to maintain it and would tax them beyond benefit or ability to pay. The memorial was signed by James May and others—Detroit, October 24, 1804. By Act of Congress, approved January 11, 1805,[2] it was provided that after June 30, 1805, this Wayne county should be organized as the Territory of Michigan.

As we have seen, the inhabitants of Indiana Territory in 1800 were largely French. These people cared nothing for self government. They did not wish to be bothered with it. They had been schooled to monarchical forms and so naturally expected to be ruled by officials. The provisions of the Northwest Ordinance, therefore, whereby so much power was reposed in the Governor during the first grade of government, had no terrors for them.

---

1. National Intelligencer, December 12, 1804.
2. United States Statutes at Large.

During this grade, not a single official was to be elected by the people. The President appointed the Governor, Secretary and Judges, and the Governor appointed all other officials. But two forces were operating, both of which tended toward the second grade of government: First, the slowly swelling stream of English settlers who came into the Territory with their Anglo-Saxon ideas of democracy and self government. Second, the desire of the people for slavery. It was as a *means* to secure both these ends, slavery and representative government, or we might say it was as a means to secure the one end, slavery, through representative government, that the change to the second grade was effected, and that later, as we shall see, the Territory was divided in 1809.

It had now become evident that the only way to secure the admission of slaves was by advancing to the second grade. Congress had shown no disposition to permit the repeal of the sixth Article, so that if the people of the Territory were to be helped in this matter they must help themselves. A majority were as yet pro-slavery, and Harrison had fallen in with this majority for political support. But Harrison had *opposed* passing to the second grade in 1801. He must now favor it and for the same fundamental reason—to make his official position secure. He could not now desert the slavery party without losing his office.[1] The incoming anti-slavery settlers would soon become sufficiently numerous to require the government to pass to the second grade, and they would also soon be in the majority and cause Harrison's overthrow if he did not now seize the opportunity and cater to his dwindling pro-slavery majority and open the way for increasing

---

1. See Dunn's Indiana, p. 322, on Harrison's position at this time.

their numbers by removing the barriers to the admission
of slaveholders. Just as he had feared defeat from the
Federalists in 1801 if they were given a chance, so now
he feared defeat from the incoming and growing anti-
slavery party if he did not act promptly and make himself secure while he could. It was a critical time for the
slavery party, which consisted chiefly of the original
French settlers. It was clearly a case of "now or never"
with them. So the plunge was made. Harrison having opposed the second grade in 1801 kept in the background,
but his party defended the change of policy by saying that
the increased population since 1801 would sufficiently
lighten the burden of the additional tax. Harrison, on
August 4, 1804, issued a call for an election on September
11th,[1] only five weeks' notice. Only 400 votes were cast
in the whole Territory, owing to the short notice; and
Wayne county did not receive the word in time to hold an
election. It is no wonder its people were clamoring, as
we have seen, for a separate government. The returns
showed a majority of 138 in favor of the change,[2] and
on December 5, 1804. Harrison issued a proclamation
stating that "satisfactory evidence"[3] having been given
of the wish of the majority of the freeholders to pass to
the second grade of government, the Territory is and
from henceforth shall be deemed to have passed into the
second or representative grade of government, etc., and
appointed January 3d following for the election of representatives in the various counties. He apportioned the
representatives among the counties as follows:[4] Knox

---

1. Dunn's Indiana.
2. This majority resided almost entirely in the central county, Knox, including Vincennes. Taken as a whole, both the extreme eastern and western
portions of the territory, according to the small vote polled because of insufficient notice, opposed the change.
3. Executive Journal, 125.
4. Executive Journal.

county 2, St. Clair 1, Randolph 1, Dearborn 1. Clark 1, and Wayne 3, thus making 9 in all. These he directed to meet in Vincennes, February 3, 1805, to elect ten men from whom to appoint the Legislative Council. But meanwhile, January 11, 1905, Congress had passed the Act establishing the Territory of Michigan, which removed Wayne county. Since the Northwest Ordinance required a minimum of seven members for the House of Representatives, and since the assembly had declared the election of the delegates from St. Clair to be void, Harrison, by proclamation on April 18th[1] called for a new election of St. Clair county and apportioned to it two members, thus making the required number, seven in all.

By an Act of Congress of 1789, the President of the United States was to appoint the five members of the Legislative Council from a list of ten names sent to him by the Territorial House of Representatives. But Jefferson declined to make these appointments because he knew none of the nominees, and so he said. "It would be to substitute chance for choice were I to designate the five." He, therefore, sent the papers with the spaces for the names left blank, to be filled in by Harrison himself, recommending[2] him to reject (1) dishonest men, (2) Federalists, (3) Land jobbers and (4) to give due attention to geographical distribution. Harrison replied[3] "that he followed Jefferson's directions as far as possible, having chosen four 'staunch Republicans;' but both those nominated from Knox county were Federalists, and that as this was the largest county in the Territory, it was necessary to take one of them. In all our elections the

1. Executive Journal.
2. Letter Jefferson to Harrison. April 28. 1805, Jefferson Papers. Dept. of State.
3. Letter Harrison to Jefferson, June 18, 1805.

contest lay between those who were in favor of adopting the second grade of government and the admission of negroes and those who were opposed to these measures." Harrison was discreet enough not to let it be known that the selection of this council had been made by himself. Wayne county, meanwhile, having been separated from the Territory, there were seven members in the House of Representatives, representing the five counties of the Territory, Knox and St. Clair counties having two representatives each; Randolph, Clark and Dearborn counties one each.[1] Clark and Dearborn counties had been formed by proclamation of the Governor and embraced the southeastern part of the Territory. Clark was set apart February 3, 1801, and Dearborn March 7, 1803, the latter embracing all the Territory east of the Greenville Treaty line.[2]

CHAPTER IV.

THE GOVERNOR AND THE FIRST ASSEMBLY.

The Governor called the first session of the legislature for July 29, 1805, and upon their assembling July 30th, he delivered an address. In this he first congratulated them "upon entering on a grade of government which gave to the people the important right of legislating for themselves."[3] He also recommended the passage of laws along the following lines :[4]

---

1. Dunn's Indiana.

2. For the formation and boundaries of these new counties, see Exec. Jour of the Territory. Ind. Hist. Soc. Pubs. III.

3. Dillon's Indiana, p. 416.

4. Dawson's Harrison, p. 45.

1. The sale of intoxicating liquors to the Indians should be prevented.

2. The reorganization of the inferior courts of judicature was necessary. At present these Judges received little or no recompense, requiring the appointment of many of them and thus preventing uniformity of decisions. Those who pronounced the sentence were often not the same Judges who heard the pleadings.

3. The Militia law was much too complicated for the state of the society and population. A system uniting simplicity and energy was desirable.

4. The laws were not strict enough in regard to horse stealing. The population and riches must be increased before they could dispense with the present sanguinary system.

5. "From the construction which I have put on the Ordinance of Congress, the erection of new counties will rest with the legislature[1]."

6. He stated that he had aimed at impartial distribution of the representatives among the several counties, but that statistics were defective and that an enumeration must be taken.

7. But the most difficult and delicate task he said, would be to create a revenue that would be adequate, well apportioned and not too burdensome; and to appropriate with the strictest frugality and economy the sums which must be chiefly drawn from industry and improvement. "A few months," he continued, "have already produced the most favorable change in our affairs. Our possessions, circumscribed on all sides by the Indian territory, have

---

1. Dawson notes that the other governors were not so generous in construction and appropriated this power to themselves.—Dawson's Harrison p. 74, note.

been enlarged to the extent of an empire and the most fertile and contiguous parts opened for sale and settlement upon terms which give hopes of becoming a freeholder to the most indigent of our citizens. The treasurer will lay before you an account of all the receipts and expenditures from the commencement of the government. If a considerable deficit is found it will also be found that not a sixpence has been appropriated which had not for its object some public and important purpose." After encouraging the assembly to look forward to statehood, he concluded thus: "You may with confidence rely upon my co-operation in every measure which is calculated to promote the interests of the Territory, and I fervently supplicate the Supreme Ruler of the world to crown your labors with honor to yourselves and advantage to your constituents."

The replies of the houses were made separately. The House of Representatives thanked him for his address in which they discerned the solicitude for the future happiness and prosperity of the Territory which had been uniformly evinced by his past administration. "We feel the same pleasure you express for the happy change which has taken place in the form of government." * * * * and "We look forward hopefully to independent statehood." They said that subjects recommended to their consideration would receive due attention, and that they had no doubt of his cordial co-operation.[1]

The Legislative Council responded in similar vein. Speaking of statehood they said: "And we have every reason to believe from past experience that your exertions will not be wanting for the attainment of that ob-

---

1. National Intelligencer, October 16, 1805.

ject." "The confidence which our fellow citizens have uniformly had in your administration has been such that they have hitherto had no reason to be, jealous of the unlimited power which you possess over our legislative proceedings. We, however, cannot help regretting that such powers have been lodged in the hands of any one; especially when it is recollected to what dangerous lengths the exercise of those powers may be extended."[1] This warning note seems to have been effective, for we find no account of Harrison's ever provoking criticism by misusing the veto power, but once. This was in 1811 when he vetoed a bill for removing the capital from Knox county, which was complained of in Congress as an Act of tyranny.[2]

Passing to the laws of the first General Assembly, the first one enacted was in response to Harrison's first recommendation to restrict still further the sale of liquor to the Indians. In this connection we should first note the proclamation of the Governor of July 20, 1801.[3] This forbade any trader from selling or giving any spirituous liquors to any Indian within a mile of the town of Vincennes, or nearer than across the Wabash. He further requested the people to "inform against all those who violate the Sabbath by selling or bartering spirituous liquors, or who pursue any other unlawful business on the day set apart for the service of God." Then again in his address to the first assembly he said: "You have seen our towns crowded with furious and drunken savages; our streets flowing with their blood; their arms and clothing bartered for the liquor that destroys them;

---

1. Dawson's Harrison, p. 77.
2. Dunn, 383. Annals 12th Congress, p. 846.
3. Exec. Jour. Hist. Soc. Pubs. III, 102.

* * * whole villages have been swept away. It is a dreadful conflagration which spreads misery and desolation through the country and threatens the annihilation of the whole race."[1] Such a spirited appeal brought forth the Act approved August 6, 1805, by which any person was forbidden to barter or sell liquor to any Indians within thirty miles of any conference or council with the Indians, under penalty of fine from $50 to $500 or from three months to six months imprisonment.[2]

In a letter to the Secretary of War, July 15, 1801, Harrison wrote:[3] "I can at once tell upon looking at an Indian whether he belongs to a neighboring or to a more distant tribe. The latter is generally well clothed, healthy and vigorous; the former, half naked, filthy, and enfeebled by intoxication; and many of them are without arms, excepting a knife which they carry for the most villainous purposes." * * * "The chiefs of the Pottawatomies, Sacs and Kickapoos who lately visited me are sensible of this corruption and earnestly desire that the introduction of whisky among them may be prevented." Harrison says in this letter that though there are but about six hundred warriors on the Wabash, the annual distribution of liquor is about six thousand gallons.[4] Harrison wrote in the same letter that the tribes nearest Vincennes, (Piankeshaws, Weas and Eel River Miamis) were the "most depraved wretches on earth," that they

---

1. Dillon's "Oddities of Colonial Legislation," p. 548. Dillon's Indiana 416. Dawson, 73.

2. Territorial Laws.

3. Dawson, p. 11.

4. In this connection we recall the words of Henry Adams (History of the U. S., Vol. VI, p. 69): "As the line of American settlements approached, the nearest Indian tribes withered away;" and that "no acid ever worked more mechanically on a vegetable fiber than the white man acted on the Indian."

were daily in the town and frequently intoxicated to the number of thirty or forty at once, when they committed the greatest disorders, drawing their knives and stabbing every one they met; breaking open the houses, killing cattle and hogs and breaking down fences.

The first assembly, as might be expected, was not long in passing "An Act concerning the introduction of negroes and mulattoes into this Territory," approved August 26, 1805. By this Act any one owning a negro or mulatto of or above fifteen years of age might bring him into the Territory and within thirty days go before the Clerk of the Court in whose presence the owner and negro should agree as to the number of years which the negro should serve his owner; and in case the negro should refuse to serve, then at any time within sixty days thereafter, the owner, might remove him to any place where by the laws he would be permitted to hold or to sell him. Negroes under fifteen might be brought in and retained in service, males till thirty-five, females till thirty-two years of age. The offspring of such negroes owing service, born in the Territory, were to be held to service, the males till thirty, the females till twenty-eight years of age. This was the indenture law of 1805. The next year, December 3, 1806, an additional "Act concerning slaves and servants" was passed whereby they were forbidden to roam from the premises of their owners, and any person aiding or harboring an absconding servant was subject to a fine of $500.

Reference has been made to the law passed by the governor and judges for the establishment of courts of judicature. But none of these were invested with chancery jurisdiction and some of the judges as early as 1802 peti-

tioned Congress to grant such jurisdiction.[1] It was also
desired to have the right of appeal from the General
Court of the territory to the United States Supreme
Court. Thomas Terry Davis writes of a verdict being
obtained in the former court, in 1803, for $13,000 which
involved a doubtful legal question.[2] By act of Congress,
approved March 3, 1805, chancery jurisdiction was
granted to the superior territorial courts, and writs of
error and appeals were authorized to the Supreme Court
of the United States.[3] At its first session, then, the Assembly passed "An Act for organizing a court of chancery" which was given the powers usually exercised by
courts of equity. The court was to sit at Vincennes, was
to consist of one judge appointed by the Governor and
was to hold two sessions annually, besides extra sessions
when necessary.

The practice of the high court of chancery of England
was adopted. Acts regulating practice in this court were
passed in 1806 and 1807. John Badollet was first chancellor and resigned in 1806. Thomas T. Davis was then
appointed but died in 1807. The court was very slow in
getting started, owing, it seems, to lack of funds to pay
the chancellors adequately for their services.[4] So that
Harrison in his speech to the second Assembly, August
18, 1807,[5] two years after the law was passed establishing
the court, stated that no session of this court had yet been
held, and that it should be held as soon as possible. Waller

1. D. W. Howe, Laws and Courts in N. W. and I. T.—Annals Cong. 7 Cong.,
1st session 1802, p. 1131.
2. Letter in the Palladium, October 18, 1808.
3. A committee in Congress in 1803, recommended a Chancery Court: but
opposed appeal to the United States Supreme Court.—Amer. State Papers,
Misc. I, No. 169.
4. D. W. Howe, Ind. Hist. Soc. Pubs. II, 28.
5. "Western Sun." August 22, 1807.

Taylor was the third chancellor, was appointed in 1807 and continued till the court was abolished by act of March 11, 1813, when two judges of the General Court were appointed chancellors at $50 apiece, to assist in finishing the cases then on the docket. The old Circuit Court was then given chancery jurisdiction. "Thus ended the only court having chancery jurisdiction exclusively that ever sat in Indiana."[1]

Let us note here the humble beginnings of the judiciary in Indiana Territory. By referring to the dockets of the General Court[2] we see that the first session began and ended on the same day, March 3, 1801. A grand jury of nineteen "good and lawful men" were sworn in. The records for this session comprise but three pages of script. The rules for the court were adopted and four cases considered, an indictment for murder, one for assault and battery, another indictment and a recognizance. Orders were entered for the examination of four candidates for the degree of Counsellor, to be held the first Monday in September. The court then adjourned till September 1st. The second term, September, 1801, held but six days, but tried several cases involving damages of from $1,000 to $2,000, for trespass. The business of the sessions increased rapidly in 1802 and 1803, but there was a dearth of it in the spring of 1804, only two pages being required for the meager records of this session, which ended thus: "Only one judge having attended,

1. W. W. Thornton in "Bench and Bar in Indiana," art. on territorial courts.

2. The original dockets or order books of the General Court of the territory (1801-1816) are still preserved in two manuscript volumes in the Supreme Court Library at Indianapolis. The first book contains 457 pages and ends with the September term, 1810, and is in very bad condition. The second begins with the March term, 1811, and ends at the 120th page, Tuesday, September 16, 1816, and is in excellent condition.

and the court having been kept open for three days according to the law of the territory, wherefore ordered that the court do adjourn till called in course, conformably to the same law."[1]

In the September term, 1802, may be noted some ridiculously trivial penalties. For example, a dependent accused of assault and battery and false imprisonment was found guilty and fined twelve and a half cents. Others for assault and battery were fined "one cent and costs." But of course the amount of fine was of secondary importance to the principle involved. Besides, we must remember that twenty-five cents was the regular wage for a day's service as witness in court in the territory,[2] although judges received $2.50 per day.

As to the manner of holding court sessions, we are given an interesting account of one held in Wayne county in 1811.[3] The court was held in the woods with family chairs and logs for seats, and the jury retired to logs at a convenient distance for deliberation. The judges of the General Court, as we have seen, were authorized to hold the Circuit Courts, and in exercising this power Judge Parke tried his first case in Wayne county, riding all the way from Vincennes for this purpose alone. He had a log for a desk, and the case was in regard to the theft of a twenty-five-cent pocket knife. Not until December 4, 1810, was the office of Prosecuting Attorney for the territory established.

Reverting to the laws passed by the first Assembly, we note one approved August 22, 1805, for the relief, under certain prescribed conditions, of persons imprisoned for

---

1. Record Book I. p. 105.
2. See Docket of General Court, September term, 1809, for the list of claims for day's wages as witness in court.
3. D. W. Howe, account taken from Young's History of Wayne county, p. 80.

debt. Also an Act incorporating the Borough of Vincennes, approved August 24, 1805, by which a chairman and nine assistants were made a corporate body. This was the first act creating a municipal corporation in Indiana. On this same day also, August 24, 1805, was approved, "An Act to incorporate the Indiana Canal Company," for the purpose of digging a canal around the falls of the Ohio. This was the first private corporation formed by statute in Indiana, but the enterprise did not succeed. Among the names of the twelve directors appointed, were those of George Rogers Clark and Aaron Burr. The first Assembly also passed an act "respecting certain crimes and punishments" which provided, "That if any person or persons shall steal or purloin from another person or persons any horse, mare, gelding, mule or ass, he, she, or they so offending shall for the first offense pay to the owner of such horse, etc., the value thereof and receive not less than fifty nor more than two hundred stripes, and shall moreover be committed to the jail of the county until such value be paid with the costs of prosecution. Upon the second conviction, the offender shall suffer the pains of death." By another section of the same law it is provided, "That any person who shall steal any hog, shoat or pig, or mark or alter the mark of any hog, etc., with an intention of stealing the same, for every such offense, upon being thereof lawfully convicted shall be fined in any sum not exceeding $100 nor less than $50, and moreover receive on his or her bare back any number of lashes not exceeding thirty-nine nor less than twenty-five." Finally, this first Assembly elected Benjamin Parke as the first delegate to Congress from Indiana Territory.[1]

---

1. He held this office till 1808 when he resigned, having been appointed by Jefferson to a Federal judgeship in the territory.

At the second session of the first Assembly an act was approved November 29, 1806, to incorporate a University in Indiana Territory. The names of Governor Harrison and Secretary Gibson very appropriately head the list of the twenty-three trustees of this "Vincennes University." Besides the president, there were to be appointed not more than four professors "for the instruction of youth in the Latin, French and English languages, Mathematics, Natural Philosophy, Ancient and Modern History, Moral Philosophy, Logic, Rhetoric and the Law of Nature and Nations." It was further provided that a Professor of Divinity, of Law, and of "Physic" should be added whenever the trustees should deem it necessary. Provision was also made for a library for the University. It was provided that the trustees should not at any one time hold or possess more than 100,000 acres of land for the University. They were enjoined to use their utmost endeavors to induce the aborigines to send their children to the said university for education; and these were to be maintained, clothed and educated at the expense of the University. Whenever the funds of the school would permit it, all students were to be educated free of charge. An annex for ladies was to be added and also a grammar school. And finally, it was provided that for the support of the University, there should be raised a sum not exceeding $20,000 by a lottery. But lotteries were very common in those days and were not so regarded as now. In response to petition Congress had passed an act, March 26, 1804, setting apart one township of land for the benefit of an institution of learning in the Vincennes land district, and on October 10, 1806, the Secretary of the United States Treasury selected and set apart a township in what is now Gibson county for this purpose. Then

came the act of the territorial Assembly, incorporating
the University and recognizing it as the beneficiary of
these lands donated by Congress. It was not until 1811,
however, that the school was actually opened.[1] Of the
Board of Trustees Governor Harrison was elected first
President (1806) while the first President of the University (1811) was Rev. Samuel T. Scott.

Another educational act was that approved December
3, 1806, to incorporate the Vincennes Library Company.[2]
On December 6, 1806, was approved an act to prohibit
the sale or gift of liquor to Indians within forty miles
of Vincennes, under penalty of from $5 to $100 fine. The
second session also passed a resolution, approved December 4, 1806, for revising the laws of the territory, simpli-
fying and indexing them and having them published.
The result was the revision of 1807 which brought the
laws into compact form.

CHAPTER V.

THE FINAL STRUGGLE OVER SLAVERY; THE DIVISION OF THE TERRITORY AND THE REPEAL OF THE INDENTURE LAW.

Let us now return to the subject of slavery and trace
it to the division of the territory and then observe finally
the repeal of the indenture law. Although by this law of
1805 the Assembly introduced slavery into the territory,

---

1. See History of Vincennes University by Dr. H. M. Smith, of Vincennes,
who in 1897 was elected President of the Board of Trustees of the University.

2. In the "Western Sun" of March 23, 1808, is found a list of the books then
contained in the Vincennes Library. Two hundred ten are given and among
them we note the following: Vattel's Law of Nations, Adam Smith's Wealth
of Nations, Washington's Letters, Jefferson's Notes on Virginia, Tucker on
Slavery, Goldsmith's Roman History, also his "England," More's Utopia.
Military History, etc.

the time of petitions had only begun. During that same summer of 1805 three noteworthy petitions were sent from Indiana to Congress. On August 19th, just a week before the passage of the indenture law, the Assembly prepared a petition asking Congress, among other things, to permit the introduction of slavery. At the same time that Congress took up this petition of the Assembly it had also to consider the most weighty petition, perhaps, ever sent up from Indiana. This was from the Illinois country again, St. Clair and Randolph counties, and its object was to secure the separation of these counties from the part of the territory east of the Wabash, and also the free admission of slavery. The petitioners made a strong plea for separation. They referred to the great distance, one hundred eighty miles of wilderness road, between them and Vincennes. They also referred to the passage to the second grade of government against their will, pointing out that the majority both in the Illinois country and the extreme eastern part of Indiana as well (that is. Clark and Dearborn counties combined) had opposed the second grade, as shown by the election returns, which were scanty, owing to insufficient notice having been given; all of which was true. And yet they said that the executive was "satisfied that there was a majority of the freeholders in the Territory in favor" of the change. They complained bitterly of the additional expense incurred and of their inaccessibility to the seat of government. There were about three hundred fifty signatures to this petition. From 1804 until 1809, separation and slavery were constantly sought by the people of the Illinois country. On the other hand we have a similar petition to Congress in 1805 from the eastern part of the Territory—Dearborn county. It also refers to the great

distance of the people from the seat of government, and
requests that they be placed under the government of the
State of Ohio. The committee to which these petitions
were referred, reported in favor of suspending the sixth
Article for ten years, but opposed any division of the
Territory. The report, however, was never acted upon
by the House. The counties of Randolph and St. Clair
renewed their memorial early in 1806, and this was followed in 1807 by a set of resolutions passed unanimously
by the General Assembly, addressed to Congress and
strongly opposing the sixth Article. The committee in
Congress again reported favorably, but again no action
was taken. Randolph and St. Clair counties in 1807, also
presented their third annual petition to Congress.   A
counter petition from Randolph was also sent, opposing
division of the Territory. Again, September 19, 1807,
a petition was sent up to Congress from the assembly.
But about the same time, October 10, 1807, it is gratifying to note a counter petition from Springville, Clark
County. It is noteworthy for advancing the doctrine of
squatter sovereignty—forty years before Lewis Cass did.
It opposed slavery and asked Congress to defer action
until the people of Indiana themselves should form a constitution and decide the matter.[1] Dearborn county also
renewed its petition this fall, asking that the Indenture
law be revised, or that they be annexed to Ohio. This
time the petitions of the legislature and of Springville
were presented to the Senate where a committee to which
they were referred reported adversely, while in the House
no action was taken. It seemed needless to continue further this fruitless bombardment of Congress for the sus-

---

1. Dunn. 359. American State Papers Misc. I, 485.

pension of the sixth Article, and so the scene of battle
shifted largely to Indiana itself during the year 1808,
and so far as Congress was petitioned further it was for
division and not for slavery. Two petitions were sent up
from Illinois for division and presented to the House on
April 6th, but the committee to which they were referred
reported on April 11th that, owing to pressure of other
business and the expense which the division would en-
tail upon the general government, it was inexpedient at
that time to make the division.[1]

The Illinois people were dissatisfied in regard to Harrison's distribution of appointments, complaining that
they were all given to people east of the Wabash, and this
was an additional incentive to separation. At the fall
election of 1808, the opportunity came to send to the legislature men from Illinois who stood for division. A
combination[2] took place between the anti-slavery faction
east of the Wabash and the anti-Harrison, pro-slavery
faction from Illinois, with the result that the House of
Representatives stood for division of the Territory, and
against slavery for the eastern division. In other words,
the House of Representatives was anti-Harrison on both
issues, division and slavery. It was soon given opportunity to assert its position. It was besieged with fifteen
petitions, eleven anti-slavery and four pro-slavery, which
also marked a wholesome change in the attitude of the
people themselves. The petitions were referred to a
committee of which General W. Johnston was chairman,
and October 19, 1808, he delivered their report. This
masterly production was a strong argument against
slavery and was unanimously adopted by the House.

1. American State Papers Misc. I, 922.
2. Dunn, 367.

The same forenoon on which this report was adopted, the House also passed unanimously a bill to repeal the Indenture law,[1] but this bill was unanimously opposed in the Legislative Council, in which but three of the five members were present. As to Territorial division, meanwhile, on October 11th the House of Representatives had also passed by a vote of three to two, a resolution in favor of it,[2] and resolving that the Delegate to Congress be instructed to use all the means in his power to procure at the next session the said division. And here also the Legislative Council took opposite ground and passed a resolution[3] that the Delegate to Congress be instructed to oppose division. Jesse B. Thomas, however, was elected to Congress by the Assembly, by six votes of the ten cast, one of which was his own, with the understanding that he would work for the division of the Territory, although the Harrison party claimed that he was pledged not to do so. The chief hope of the Illinois faction was to have a man elected to Congress to succeed B. Parke, who had just resigned, who would work for division. So they had Thomas pledge himself under bond to work for division.[4] He did work for division of the Territory, and a law was passed providing for this, February 3, 1809, the division to take place March 1st ensuing. By this Act of Congress all that part of the Territory "lying west of the Wabash river, and a direct line drawn from the said Wabash river and Post Vincennes, due north, to the territorial line between the United States and Canada" was constituted a separate

1. Dunn, 375.
2. House Journal, Western Sun.
3. Journal Legislative Council, October 26, 1808, Western Sun.
4. Ford's History of Illinois, p. 30.

Territory and called Illinois. The Legislative Council of 1808, had also sent to Congress a resolution asking that the council and the delegate to Congress be made elective by the people, and that the term of councilmen be reduced from five years to four, and these changes were also secured by Congressional enactment. By the same Act, the Suffrage Act of February 27, 1809, the apportionment of representatives was taken from the Governor and placed in the hands of the assembly; and it further provided that until there should be six thousand free white males of twenty-one years or over, in the Territory, the number of representatives should be not less than nine, nor more than twelve.[1]

The Harrison party which had been standing for slavery and union in the Territory had thus been forced to accept the division, and we shall soon see that it was likewise compelled to yield to the increasing anti-slavery movement. The principles of democracy were also triumphing and the people were obtaining more and more power. As Mr. Dunn puts it,[2] "From a form of government in which the Governor was everything and the people nothing, the Territory had in eight years advanced to a form of government more nearly republican than anything contemplated by the Ordinance for the territorial period." In 1801 the people could vote for nothing. In 1809 they could vote for both Houses of the legislature, and also for the delegate to Congress. But the Governor still held the appointing power, the right of prorogation and the absolute veto. The division had also simplified the political situation. It took from Indiana an

---

1. A year before this, January 9, 1808, Congress had passed a similar act for the territory of Mississippi.—U. S. Statutes.

2. Dunn's Indiana, p. 383.

element strongly pro-slavery, but which was also largely opposed to Harrison, and it gave the anti-slavery party the upper hand in the Territory. The outcome was inevitable—slavery must soon go and Harrison was politician enough to discern this, and not openly to oppose it and thus lose his balance. By his shrewd diplomacy and conservatism he was enabled to retain his hold on the people and his office, and let events take their course.[1]

By this division the Territory of Indiana was reduced practically to its present territorial limits. Two slight additions were made upon its admission as a State in 1816. A ten-mile strip was added to its northern boundary. Also, owing to an ambiguous clause in the division Act of 1809, a small strip was added above Vincennes in 1816, due to the termination at the Wabash, north of Vincennes, of the north and south line of the western boundary, instead of letting it continue to Vincennes. The line was to extend "to the Wabash and Vincennes,"[2] but it crossed the Wabash due north of Vincennes and then struck the river again at this city, the river bending westward between these points; so that by the interpretation of 1809, the clause was taken literally, while by that of 1816 the line was extended only "to the Wabash."[3]

The people of Knox county had opposed the division for two reasons: First, it would increase their taxes by throwing the maintenance of the government upon a smaller population, and, secondly, it would call for a removal of the capital at no distant date to some place farther east and more centrally located.

---

1. The census of 1810 gave Illinois a population of 12,282. At the time of division it was estimated that the population east of the Wabash was 17,000, and that west of it 11,000.

2. See act dividing the territory, 1809.

3. See Enabling Act of Congress, approved April 19, 1816.

Owing to the slow means of communication, the news of the division of the Territory was several weeks in reaching Vincennes, and by the election law of 1807, representatives to the assembly were to be elected the first Monday in April, 1809. This election was held accordingly on April 3d. Harrison seems to have heard of the division before this time, but he permitted the election to take place and on the next day, April 4th, he issued a proclamation[1] stating that whereas the Territory had been divided it was necessary to make a new apportionment, which he accordingly did, and gave to each of the counties, Knox, Dearborn and Clark, one new representative, and also one representative to the new county of Harrison which had just been formed from Knox and Clark, October 11, 1808.[2] This made the House of Representatives consist of eight members—3 from Knox, 2 from Dearborn, 2 from Clark and 1 from Harrison. He also called for a new election, for these additional members, to be held on May 22d. But meanwhile also, February 27th, the Suffrage Act had been passed which gave the assembly the right of apportionment of representatives and required the minimum number to be nine. Harrison, of course, had not yet heard of this Suffrage Act. It is to be noted that it gave to the assembly the power of apportionment of representatives, but that no assembly could be formed till an apportionment was made, so that Harrison did about the only thing practicable to do, except that he had constituted the House with eight members instead of nine, as required by the new law. On April 10th he issued another proclamation, stating that in accordance with an

---

1. Executive Journal, p. 154.
2. Executive Journal.

Act of Congress at the last session, he was empowered
and directed to divide the Territory into five districts,
each of which should send one member to the Legislative
Council. He, therefore, formed Dearborn, Clark and
Harrison counties into separate districts, and divided
Knox into two districts and directed that the election of
the Council should be held on the same day as that of the
representatives. A delegate to Congress was also to be
elected on this same day, May 22d, and Jonathan Jennings was elected to this office on the platform of "No
slavery in Indiana."[1] This was another blow for the
Harrison party and their feelings were sufficiently shown
on July 4th at a public celebration at which Harrison
was chairman, when the following toast was proposed
and drunk: "Jonathan Jennings—the semblance of a
delegate—his want of abilities the only safety of the
people—three groans."[2] From this time the Harrison
party leaders became known as the "Virginia Aristo-
crats," while their opponents posed as the party of the
people.

But would this election be allowed to stand? The legislature of eight members convened at Harrison's call,
October 16, 1809. Harrison and the majority of the
members considered its organization valid, but some of
the members disputed it, and, after considering the question four or five days, Harrison dissolved the assembly,
at its own request.[3] An interesting contemporary account of this irregular assembly is given in the *Western
Sun*, the official publication at Vincennes at that time.
From this account it appears that the members did not

1. See Dunn's Indiana for account of campaign.
2. Dunn, p. 400, Western Sun, July 8, 1809.
3. Dillon, 437-8.

actually convene till the 17th, when Harrison delivered his usual message, to which we shall refer later. Two days later, the members of the House of Representatives waited on the Governor to reply to his address when he said that if there still existed doubts in their minds as to the propriety of proceeding to legislate, he wished them to pursue such a course as would remove them, but that he considered their power to legislate as complete as the United States could make it. Finally, they agreed to memorialize Congress for its decision. They also passed a joint resolution apportioning representatives just as Harrison had done, except to give one more to Dearborn county and thus make nine in all, as required, and this was approved by the Governor. Before separating, in response to numerous petitions, the assembly also recommended to the general government the re-appointment of Harrison as Governor. This was passed unanimously in the House, and three to one in the Council, although the assembly was an anti-slavery body. His third term had expired July 4, 1809, but Madison had not yet re-appointed him.

Congress supported Jennings as territorial delegate and he retained his seat. But it decided that the assembly was unauthorized by law, December 15, 1809, but authorized the Governor to re-apportion the Territory and call an election for a new assembly. Accordingly, February 21, 1810, the Governor issued a proclamation[1] re-apportioning the Territory just as the irregular assembly had done, and called an election for April 2d for the choice of delegates to the third General Assembly. In response to the Governor's call, this body

---

1. Executive Journal, p. 138.

convened at Vincennes November 12, 1810. The most
noteworthy legislation of this assembly was the repeal of
the Indenture law. Harrison approved the repeal Act
December 14, 1810, knowing that the majority of the
people of the Territory demanded it. Thus, the law admitting slavery into Indiana Territory was at last removed by
the casting vote of James Beggs, President of the Legislative Council, after staining the statute books for five
shameful years. The evil of the Indenture law cannot
be expressed by the mere fact that the number of slaves
in that part of the Territory which later formed the State
of Indiana, was increased during those five years from
twenty-eight to two hundred thirty-seven.[1]

CHAPTER VI.

HARRISON IN RELATION TO THE SECOND ASSEMBLY.

Let us now consider Harrison's relations with the
second and third General Assemblies and their work,
which will complete this part of the study; for with the
laws of the fourth assembly he was not concerned. The
sessions of the territorial assembly at which laws were
passed were held as follows :[2]

First assembly, first session began July 29, 1805.

Second session began November 3, 1806.

Second assembly, first session began August 17,[3] 1807.

Second session began September 26, 1808.

Third assembly, first session began November 12, 1810.

Second session began November 11, 1811.

---

1. Census Reports.
2. List taken from Ind. Hist. Soc. Pubs. II. p. 144 Paper by D. W. Howe.
3. See Dunn, p. 357.

Fourth assembly,[1] first session began February 1, 1813.

Second session began December 6, 1813.

Fifth assembly, first session began August 15, 1814.

Second session began December 4, 1815.

Harrison's speech at the opening of the first session of the second assembly, August 18, 1807, is suggestive.[2] He first states that the session was called earlier than had been planned in order to remedy existing difficulties in collecting taxes. The quantum and ratio of the tax, he says, should be fixed by the legislature and not by an executive officer, as the existing law provided. "However," he continues, "One consolatory circumstance has been fully established; that a revenue equal to all our necessities can be raised, and that, too, without oppression or inconvenience to the people." He then refers to the Superior Courts, saying that the organization which had been adopted was satisfactory, but that, as we have elsewhere noted, no session of the Chancery Court had yet been held, and that this should be done as soon as possible. As to marriage, he says that the existing law does not authorize clerks who issue licenses to demand security that there are no lawful impediments. "This is a glaring inconsistency, for bigamy is a capital offense in our code." "It is better to prevent crime by careful inquisitions and regulations before granting licenses, than by the infliction of punishments afterwards." As to divorce, he says that the General and Circuit Courts are authorized to grant it, but that this plan, though

---

1. The sessions of the Fourth and Fifth Assemblies are given merely to complete the territorial period, but all the laws of the first session of the Fourth Assembly were approved by Sec. John Gibson, Harrison then being occupied with the war; while those of the second session were of course approved by the new governor, Thomas Posey.

2. Western Sun, August 22, 1807. Dawson's Harrison, p. 94.

widely practiced in the United States, has been generally
condemned. He recommends that divorce power be
lodged in the legislature and that divorces be made difficult to obtain.[1] Then the militia system is discussed. This
was Harrison's hobby. He says that every one able to
possess arms should be forced to have them; and those
unable should be provided. "One of the principal characteristics which distinguishes the citizens of a free government from the subjects of a despotic one is the right
of keeping arms; and that any American should neglect
to avail himself of this valuable privilege, manifests a
supineness which is highly censurable." The necessity
for military preparations is impressed by conditions both
on the Atlantic coast and on the frontier. The English
and Indians both are hostile, and the English provoke
the Indians to hostility.

"A very strict enforcement of law against abuses of
settlers themselves against the Indians must be upheld,"
he says, "in order to give the Indians no excuse for attacks, and also because it is right." "A powerful nation

---

1. In connection with Harrison's recommendations on marriage and
divorce, it is interesting to quote the records of the General Court for April 8,
1811, on a divorce case, Mary Antis vs. Francis Antis. (Record Book II, p 15):
"And now at this day came the parties by their attorneys and the court, having
fully advised of and concerning the premises, do order, award and decree a
divorce between the parties, from bed and board; and the court do further
award and decree that the said Francis Antis do pay to the said Mary Antis on
or before the first Tuesday in September next, the sum of fifty-two dollars; and
further, that the said Francis Antis do restore to the said Mary Antis within
forty days, one bed, under bed, two pillows, one bed quilt, two sheets, two
blankets, two pillowcases, two quilts, one loom, two reeds, one dining table,
one chest, one trunk, one hackle, one pair steelyards, two 3-gallon pots, one
6-gallon pot, one oven with lid, one frying pan and one cow and calf, which it
appears were of the proper goods and chattels of the said Mary Antis; and
further, that the said Francis Antis deliver and restore within the time last
aforesaid, to the said Mary Antis her wearing apparel." Again, we find in the
records of the September term, 1811, a second divorce suit, Francis Antis vs.
Polly Antis, and this divorce was also granted, making two such suits for
Francis within six months. Whether "Polly" was so successful as "Mary" in
recovering all her goods and chattels, the records do not show.

·

rendering justice to a petty tribe of savages is a sublime
spectacle, worthy of a great republic." * * * *
"Although the agency of a foreign power in producing
the discontents among the Indians can not be questioned,
I am persuaded that their utmost efforts to induce them
to take up arms would be unavailing, if one only of the
many persons who have committed murder on their
people could be brought to punishment. While we rig-
orously exact of them the delivery of every murderer of
a white man, the neglect on our part to punish similar
offenses committed on them forms a strong and just
ground of complaint for which I can offer no excuse or
palliation." * * * * "The defect seems to be not
so much in the law as in the execution."[1]

"The sale of public lands in the district of Vincennes
since the last session and preparation for opening other
land offices, gives us a nearer prospect of the accomplish-
ment of our hopes and wishes, by the formation of a State
government. Such an event ought to be accelerated by
every means within our reach." Having concluded his
discussion of the affairs of the Territory, he closes with
a tirade on our relations with England on the sea, refers to the Chesapeake affair, and sounds the trumpet
of war. This address called forth appreciative responses
from both houses of the assembly. Referring to British
relations, Harrison, in one of his dispatches to the federal
government about this time, said,[2] "that he was in possession, on the banks of the Wabash, of a political bar-
ometer by which he could ascertain the disposition of the
British government toward the United States better than
our ambassador at London: for it appeared that when-

---

1. Western Sun, August 22, 1807.
2. Dawson, p. 93.

ever the affairs of that government either prospered or
failed in Europe, the effects were soon discovered by the
conduct of its agents among the Indians on our frontiers."

As to failure to punish the whites for crimes committed
against the Indians, an illustration[1] will show the need
of the improvement in the administration of justice which
Harrison urges. In October, 1802, a white man and an
Indian quarreled and a little later the white man
murdered the Indian in cold blood. He was brought to
trial, and, though he was proved guilty, the verdict, "not
guilty" was promptly rendered, and this though the cul-
prit was an infamous character. So great was the prejudice against the Indians that it was almost impossible
for them to obtain justice. But the case of James Red
shows that Harrison did what he could to prevent such
injustice. Red, in November, 1805, unprovoked, killed
a Delaware Indian in cold blood. Whereupon he was
apprehended and a special court was appointed for his
trial. Considering his conviction and punishment of great
importance, and the Attorney General being away, Harrison took it upon himself to have an eminent lawyer come
from St. Louis to conduct the prosecution. For this, by
the way, Harrison was severely criticized. But just before the trial was to be held, Red escaped from jail. Harrison made every effort to have him caught, and upon
hearing that he had reached the Ohio, offered three hundred dollars for his apprehension.[2]

By the Treaty of Greenville (1795) it was agreed that
murderers should be given up by both Indians and whites.
Between that time and 1801, several Indians had been

1. Dawson, p. 65.
2. Dawson, p. 85.

murdered by whites and the whites left unpunished.[1] The
Delaware chiefs enumerated six Indians who had been
killed in this time, only one of which had been done "in
a justifiable manner."[2] Many of the settlers, like the
uncle of Abraham Lincoln, thought it a virtuous act to
shoot an Indian at sight.[3] In fact, the murder of Indians
was not considered murder at all. Many of the settlers
were inclined to shoot them like animals, and Harrison
was determined to educate the whites to respect the rights
of the Indians. When such murders were committed he
offered large rewards for the apprehension of the crim-
inals. We have an account in the Western Sun, November 26, 1808, of two trials at Kahokia. The grand jury
brought in two bills of indictment for murder—one
against a Delaware Indian, the other against a white. Both
were clear cases of murder. The Indian was sentenced
to death. He said that a white man in his place would
be cleared, but that he was a dog and had no friends.
That his words in part were true appears from the fact
that the white man was released on the charge of man-
slaughter and branded in the hand with the letter "M."
Again, a letter of Harrison to Eustis, Secretary of War,
June 6, 1811, shows that such conditions still continued.
He reports that an Indian was recently killed by an inn
keeper in Vincennes; that the Indian came into the inn

1. In October, 1801, Captain Allen, an Indian chief, delivered up two In
dians for committing murder on the whites, although his own son had been
murdered by a white about a year before, and although Harrison had not succeeded in his efforts to apprehend this murderer and bring him to justice.
But even under such extenuating circumstances, and although Allen plead for
their release, Governor Harrison felt bound to have these victims executed.—
Dawson, p. 13.

2. Dawson, p. 7.

3. Henry Adams' Hist. of the United States, VI. 72.

keeper's yard drunk and perhaps was insolent, but that
he was unarmed and that there was not the least necessity for killing him.   Harrison immediately caused the
perpetrator to be apprehended and ordered a special court
for his trial.   He was acquitted by the jury almost without deliberation.   In some degree to quiet the exasperated
friends of the Indian, Harrison made them a present of
about seventy dollars' worth of goods.   "Since the
above," he continues, "two Weas were badly wounded
by a white man about twenty miles from here.   I sent
out a surgeon to their relief.   Such instances (and the
latter was if possible more unprovoked than the former)
have a great tendency to exasperate the Indians and prevent them from delivering up those who may commit
offenses against our laws."   "Such was the case," he continues, "with the Delaware tribe upon my demand of
White Turkey, an Indian who had robbed a house.   They
said they would never deliver up another man until some
of the white persons were punished who had murdered
their people."   Then follows a surprising sentence—
"They would, however, punish him themselves and did
put him to death."

Again, in the same letter[1] Harrison says: "I wish I
could say the Indians were treated with justice and propriety on all occasions by our citizens, but it is far otherwise.   They are often abused and maltreated and it is
very rare that they obtain any satisfaction for the most
unprovoked wrongs."   These statements of Harrison
near the close of his administration, show how bad these
conditions continued in spite of all he could to to amelio-
rate them.   The sweeping statement of Henry Adams

---

1. Draper Collection, Harrison Papers.

seems to be correct: that "no jury in the Territory ever convicted a white man of murdering an Indian."[1]

It is not the purpose to consider the laws of the assembly in detail, but of those passed at this session of 1807, besides the complete revision already referred to, should be mentioned one in regard to organization, authorizing and requiring the Common Pleas Courts to divide the counties into townships. Also, a law of this session inflicted imprisonment for "not exceeding forty years" and another provided for "thirty-nine lashes on the bare back, well laid on."[2]

To pass to the session of 1808, Harrison's speech to the legislature[3] contains less of interest than the one just considered. He observes that the revenue laws are inadequate, as proved by the empty treasury; but that this is due to the mode of collection, not to the rate of assessment or inability to pay. He says they should adopt a system which has been successfully employed in the States. No pains should be spared to perfect the militia. Especially should severe punishment be inflicted upon officers for neglecting to produce the required returns and reports. The County Levies are unjust—the tax on work horses and milk cows especially, for it subjects the poor to an unequal share of the public burdens; the milk cow, ox and work horse being the poor man's means of subsistence. He recommended the survey of roads to be managed by the Territory, and the surveyors to be paid from the territorial treasury. This would relieve the poor men in small counties—perhaps relieve them from the

1. History of the United States, VI, 72.

2. "An Act concerning servants," approved December 3, 1806; revised and approved September 17, 1807.

3. Western Sun, speech of September 27, 1808.

poll tax.[1] Horse stealing, he said, should be carefully
guarded against and punished. Courts of Chancery were
strongly advocated because so much property had been
transferred bona fide without due form of law, and
should be protected. As to Indian relations, his words
sounded especially optimistic: "We can challenge the
world to produce a similar instance of a great and powerful nation, respecting on all occasions the rights of its
weaker neighbors." * * * "And as all the wars
which have arisen between ourselves and the aborigines
are justly attributable to the prevalence of foreign influence among the latter, we may fairly calculate that our
Indian frontier will be free from those alarms which have
retarded settlement." Again he concluded by referring
to our relations with England. He strongly urged patient
forbearance and upheld the Embargo of Jefferson. "We
shall drain," said he, "the cup of concilation to the
dregs."

On September 29th the House of Representatives resolved itself into a committee of the whole to consider
the Governor's speech, and they agreed upon six resolutions:[2] First, that so much of the Governor's speech
as referred to the state of the revenue be referred to a
select committee. Five more similar resolutions were
adopted, referring to select committees those parts of his
speech respectively which referred to (2d) the militia,
(3d) the abolition of taxes on certain articles, (4th) punishment for horse-stealing, (5th) the Court of Chancery,
(6th) the organization of schools. Then follows the
amusing appointment of these committees, which suggests

---

1. This poll tax was especially obnoxious to the French inhabitants, and
caused them to hold an indignation meeting the previous year at Vincennes.

2. Western Sun, November 12, 1808.—Journal of the House.

how few members were available for such service at this time. The Journal reads:

Thereupon Messrs. Johnson and Jones were appointed under first resolution.

Messrs. Jones and Johnson were appointed under second resolution.

Messrs. Johnson and Jones were appointed under third resolution.

Messrs. Jones and Johnson were appointed under fourth resolution.

Messrs. Johnson and Jones were appointed under fifth resolution.

Messrs. Jones and Johnson were appointed under sixth resolution.

Johnson was from Knox county in which Vincennes was located, while Jones was from Randolph county on the Mississippi. So that these committees were appointed with due regard to geographical distribution—both the eastern and western portions of the Territory being always represented. Variety is also secured, since each committee differs from the one preceding or following. As already noted, this business was transacted on September 29th, while by referring to the entry of the Journal for September 26th, the first day of the session, we read the names of six members of the House who took their seats. It would seem then that this concentration of committee honors may have been due to about half the members, on this eventful day, being either absent or tardy, or it may have been due to the superior fitness or popularity of these two men. The House organized by appointing both a Clerk and Assistant Clerk!

A somewhat similar condition existed in regard to the attendance of the Legislative Council at this session. On

October 14, 1808, Harrison sent a message[1] to the House of Representatives regarding the resignation of Mr. Gwathmey from the Legislative Council, saying he had received his resignation, but upon learning that but three members had assembled and that one of these was likely to leave, he had endeavored to induce Gwathmey to take his seat in order to prevent a dissolution of the legislature, as there might otherwise be no quorum.

Two further special messages of Harrison to this session of the assembly deserve notice.[2] The first, dated October 20, 1808, refers to the Militia law. He says, "It appears that the Commander-in-Chief is only authorized to call the militia into service when there is an actual or threatened invasion. There are a thousand exigencies which may require a part of the militia to be called out, other than invasion; and in every State the executive is invested with this power," etc. The other message, dated October 26th, refers again to the injustice of the tax on work-horses. He says, "The average price of work-horses in the Territory is not over $40, and yet the tax is fifty cents, while an investment of $100 in lands pays only twenty cents to the Territory and ten to the county. The tax on horses in Kentucky is but nine cents, I am told. Let us imitate this wise example of our neighbors and relieve the poorer classes from the intolerable burden which oppresses them."

Although not bearing directly upon the Governor's administration, a few of the proceedings of the session of 1808 are of special interest. The governor's suggestions, of course, were always carefully considered and often carried out by the assembly. On October 17, the Council

---

1. Journal of House. Western Sun.
2. Ibid.

"Resolved that the delegate to Congress be instructed to
use his endeavors to procure a law to be passed, vesting
the power of electing the members of the Legislative
Council and also the delegate to Congress in the citizens
of the Territory entitled to vote for representatives to the
General Assembly." And as has already been seen, this
change was effected by the Suffrage Act of February 27,
1809. At this session also occurred the first contested
election case in the Territory. This was over the election
of Rice Jones, a member of the House from Randolph
county, who was finally allowed to sit. An attempt was
also made to impeach Mr. Morrison, a Judge in Randolph
county, but this also failed. Several acts were vetoed[1]
by the Governor at this session. One of these related to
the office of Attorney General, and Harrison rejected it
because he thought it encroached upon his own powers.
Finally, an explanation is given at this time why the Journals of the assembly were never printed except in the
Western Sun. In the Journal itself is found the report
of the Committee on Printing.[2] This committee had been
directed to have all the previous laws and the journals
printed. But they felt that the laws were more important
and should be printed first, and this required almost a
year. Besides, the printing cost one dollar per page, so
the journals would have cost about $400, and the com-
mittee thought it was not worth this much.

To pass to the irregular session of 1809, in his address
of October 17th, Harrison congratulated the assembly on
the happy change effected by the recent Suffrage Act
passed by Congress, and added that "it showed, too, that
the unfortunate division of the Territory could only have

1. Western Sun, November 12, 1808.
2. Ibid, November 5, 1808.

been accomplished by a misrepresentation of the wishes
of four-fifths of our citizens." He then spoke on the
legality of the call of this assembly, explaining the facts
and his views, to which I have already referred. Then
he refers to finances and taxes, saying that the *land* tax
is about the only proper one for the Territory. He refers to the brightening prospects owing to increasing sales
of public lands and the recent acquirement of a vast and
fertile tract from the Indians.[1] "The commission with
which I am honored," he says, "is independent of the
people. I am, however, so perfectly convinced that their
confidence and support are so essentially necessary to the
proper discharge of many important duties, as to be un-
alterably determined that the moment which brings a conviction that their confidence has been withdrawn shall ter-
minate my commission by a voluntary resignation." As
to military regulations, he reminded them that they
should take the military laws of the States which had been
tested, and introduce them into Indiana Territory, and
that only by following such rigid and well established
lines could they hope for success. He refers again to
selling liquors to the Indians : "To use a figure of one of
their orators, 'It resembles a mighty conflagration which
spreads death and destruction through their villages,
which none but the power which kindled is able to ex-
tinguish.' " In conclusion, he recommends the cultivation of harmony and the spirit of conciliation toward
each other and the avoidance of local prejudices.

In regard to Harrison's reference to popular support,
we have already observed the action of this assembly a
few days later in strongly recommending the renewal of
his appointment. One week after this action of the as-

---

1. Treaty of Ft. Wayne, September 30, 1809, to which I shall refer later.

sembly, October 28, 1809, at a meeting of the officers of the militia of Knox county at Vincennes, resolutions were passed unanimously, strongly urging the re-appointment of Harrison on the ground of his superior fitness and especially on account of his military knowledge and skill, and his ability to manage successfully the affairs with the Indians. It was further resolved that it was the opinion of the meeting that these were the sentiments of the whole regiment they represented.[1]

CHAPTER VII.

HARRISON AND THE THIRD ASSEMBLY.

Harrison's opening address[2] to the first session of the Third General Assembly, November 12, 1810, is devoted chiefly to Indian affairs and the threatening attitude of the Shawnee prophet and his brother Tecumseh since the Treaty of Ft. Wayne of the previous autumn, but we shall consider this subject later. He speaks of a number of new counties being in contemplation and suggests that several of them might be combined to form judicial districts for superior courts, then he concludes by recommending military discipline and education, the necessity of which is naturally impressed upon him by the attitude of the Indians. He fears the finances of the Territory would not support the camps of discipline which he had in mind, yet he feels that this is the ideal plan; and while hampered for means, he says much could be done toward keeping up the military spirit until the general government should take the matter in hand. Youth, he says, is

1. Western Sun.
2. Journals. Western Sun.

the proper period for military instruction and next in importance to teaching men their rights is teaching them the art of defending these rights. Ours is the only Republic which ever existed which neglected this part of education. In Greece and Rome it was always emphasized. Congress has provided a section of land in each township for the support of schools. Let me recommend that in the system of education to be established, the military branch be not neglected. "Let the masters of the inferior schools be obliged to instruct their pupils in the military evolutions, and let the University have a Professorship of Tactics in which all the Sciences connected with the art of war may be taught."

It is well to refer in this connection to two letters[1] written by Harrison to Governor Scott of Kentucky, dated March 10th and April 17, 1810. In the first he writes: "Professorships of Tactics should be established in all our seminaries, and even the amusements of the children should resemble those of the ancient Gymnasia, that they may grow up in the practice of those exercises which will enable them to bear with ease the duty of the camp and labors of the field." The government, he says, should pay the citizens for drilling for five or six weeks every year. In the second letter he says that the militia is the only proper body for the defense of the republic; that the term is properly applied only to citizens who are disciplined or trained for war; and that we have, indeed, no militia. "We must become a nation of warriors or a nation of Quakers—we must proscribe every attempt at military improvement or its study must become universal." "No instance can be produced of a free people preserving their liberties who suffered the military spirit

---

1. Published in the Western Sun at the time.

to decline among them—nor of any losing them as long as this spirit pervaded the body of the nation."

This first session of the Third Assembly, November 12, 1810, was the last to which Harrison could give due attention, for the next year he was occupied with Indian affairs. Sixty-three Acts were passed at this session, which continued for thirty-eight days. The repeal of the Indenture law has already been mentioned; and in connection with this was a law imposing $1,000 fine and disqualification for office upon any one for unlawfully removing a negro from the Territory. This assembly also petitioned Congress to permit a removal of the seat of government, and appointed a committee to select a new site.[1] Three new counties were formed at this session and no others were formed until 1813. These were Jefferson, Franklin and Wayne, and were all formed out of the counties of Clark and Dearborn.[2] A reapportionment of representatives was also made at this session. Finally, we must note the amendment of the militia law on behalf of the Society of Friends who had petitioned for the same at their monthly meeting held at Richmond, August 25, 1810.[3] By the law as it then stood, almost every one between the ages of eighteen and forty-five were required to serve in the militia; but in response to this petition the legislature on December 19th amended the law so that Friends were exempted in time of peace, and subjected to an extra tax instead of service in time of war. But such an exemption could not long be tolerated when war was impending and was soon repealed. After what we

---

1. Congress accordingly passed an Act approved February 25, 1811, providing that a new seat of government might be selected and purchased for the capital of Indiana Territory, embracing one section of land, and entry to be made as soon as one-twentieth of the price should be advanced.

2. Introduction to Exec. Journal. Ind. Hist. Soc. Pubs. III, 74.

3. See Dunn, pp. 408-9.

have heard from Harrison on militia service, we only wonder that he signed in the first place the amendatory law providing for their exemption.

Just a word as to Harrison's relations to the second session of this Third General Assembly which convened November 11, 1811. This was just four days after the battle of Tippecanoe and Harrison was unable to meet with the assembly until November 19th. This was Harrison's last meeting with the assembly, and his address was very brief.[1] He simply referred to the necessary delay in meeting with them, and to the recent victory, in which, he said, "our own militia behaved in a manner to do credit to themselves as well as the Territory." He also said, "If in the late action it had pleased the Almighty to seal with my life the victory which was to ensure their [the people's] safety, the sacrifice would have been cheerfully made." As to legislation, he only said that he was now too much occupied with other matters to attend to this, but referred them to his recommendations in previous addresses. This assembly not only petitioned for the renewal of Harrison's appointment,[2] but the two Houses framed and sent to him a most cordial appreciation of his services and paid the highest tribute to his merits and ability.

Harrison's powers and prerogatives were considered in 1808, both in the territorial legislature and in Congress, as well as by the Governor himself. From the Journal of the territorial House of Representatives under date of October 11, 1808, we quote: "Resolved that our delegate in Congress endeavor to procure a repeal of that

1. This address is given in the Western Sun; also in Niles' Register, Vol. 1, p. 221.

2. Western Sun, December 28, 1811.

part of the Ordinance which vests in the Governor of the
Territory an absolute negative on all acts, and also that
part which confers on him the power of proroguing and
dissolving the General Assembly, when in his opinion it
shall be expedient; and that he use his endeavors to procure a law vesting in the said Governor powers in those
respects similar to those exercised by the President of
the United States according to the Constitution." In Congress, Mr. Poindexter of Mississippi, presented a bill for
repealing these parts of the Ordinance referred to. It
was considered in the House of Representatives November 18, 1808, but was indefinitely postponed by a vote
of 57 to 52.[1]

On the other hand, a resolution was passed by both
Houses of this same territorial legislature, "That whereas, in all the States fugitives from justice may be demanded by the executive thereof, and whereas, the court
of Kentucky has recently held that this power does not
extend to territories under the Constitution, therefore,
Resolved, that the delegate to Congress be instructed to
urge that body to pass a law extending this power of demanding such fugitives to the executives of territories."

That Harrison guarded his prerogatives carefully is
shown by the following messages from him to the Houses
of this assembly. In the Journal of the Council for October 24th we note a message from Harrison in regard
to a proposed law directing that the executive should remove the clerk of any court upon the application of that
court. He said, "I cannot consent that a single judge,
or any number of judges, shall have the right to direct
the executive in any matter which is purely of an executive nature." Again, in the Journal of the House is

---

1. Annals of Congress, Vol. 20.

recorded a message of similar import, dated October 25, 1808. He says, "I can not give my consent to the bill which originated in your House, entitled 'an Act concerning the Attorney General and for other purposes,' because it violates the Ordinance which declares that the appointment of all officers is vested in the Governor of the Territory. Were it indeed otherwise, I should consider it highly improper that the officer who prosecutes the pleas of the United States should derive his appointment from any other source than the United States or their servant and agent, the governor for the time being."

As to the Governor's power of proroguing and dissolving the assembly at pleasure, we quote from his message to the irregular assembly, October 21, 1809: "I have considered your request for a dissolution of the present legislature," etc. * * * * * "It has ever been my wish to assimilate as far as possible the government of the Territory to those which prevail in the States—to cancel those rougher features of our Constitution, which are so justly offensive to republican delicacy, and which nothing but the infancy of our political State renders tolerable. Of this description is the power given to the Governor to prorogue and dissolve the legislature at pleasure. An application of the people themselves, or their representatives, forms one of the few occasions on which I would consent to us this power; and although the propriety of the measure at this time is not altogether apparent to my mind, yet in compliance with your wishes, I have thought proper to determine, and do now declare that this present legislature is, from this moment, dissolved, and the powers delegated to it by the people again revert to them."[1]

1. Dillon's Hist. of Ind., pp. 437-8.

CHAPTER VIII.

THE PUBLIC LANDS.

The acquirement and disposition of the public lands brought Harrison into relations with the settlers on the one hand and with the Indians on the other, and also with the authorities at Washington, and formed a very important part of his work in the Territory.

Upon Harrison's arrival in the Territory, the only important land cessions which had been settled in part, as we have seen, were Clark's Grant on the Ohio, that about Vincennes and that about Kaskaskia and Kahokia. By the treaty of Greenville, some patches had been ceded on the upper Wabash and about Ft. Wayne, and the old grant at Vincennes had been confirmed, though left indefinite as to its exact limits. Clark's Grant of 150,000 acres had been ceded in 1784, and confirmed at Greenville in 1795. Harrison's first difficult task was in the disposition of the tracts already acquired by making and confirming grants to settlers. This was extremely complex and difficult work owing to the fraudulent titles which were presented.

The Congress of the Confederation, August 29, 1788,[1] resolved that measures be taken for confirming in possessions and titles the French and Canadian inhabitants and other settlers at Post Vincennes, who on or before 1783 had settled there and professed to be citizens of the United States, or any of them. Four hundred acres were to be allotted to each head of a family. Next, the Congress of the new government took up the matter and confirmed this action (March 3, 1791) providing for grants

---

1. Jour. Cont. Congress IV, 858; A. S. P. Pub. Lands I, 32.

of.four hundred acres for all heads of families who dwelt
at Vincennes or in Illinois in 1783, and to those who had
since removed from there if they would return within
five years. Also, one hundred acres were given to each
militiaman. Surveys were made but no grants were issued and complaints were, therefore, made about 1800
that the government was not giving its citizens due attention in this matter. This was given in a report of a committee on the division of the Territory,[1] March 3, 1800,
and was a strong argument for the establishment of Indiana Territory, which was soon effected. When Harrison
arrived, then, he first had to attend to land grants to individuals and to fixing the hazy and indefinite boundaries of
the old cessions from the Indians. In this work he met with
almost insuperable difficulties on account of forged and
spurious claims of all kinds. None but a shrewd investigator could unravel the titles. In a letter to the Secretary
of War, February 26, 1802, he gives his views as to the
correct boundaries of the Indian grants at Vincennes and
Kaskaskia.[2]

As to individual titles, the difficulty was still greater.
In a letter to Jefferson,[3] January 19, 1802, he speaks of
the dishonesty of the members of the court which had
been established at Vincennes in 1780 under authority of
Virginia. The members absented themselves from court
in turn while the others made out land titles for them, and
by this means large tracts about Vincennes had been
claimed, and the holders were now selling them to innocent people. Speculators had bought up part of these
claims at ridiculous prices, "one thousand acres for an

---

1. Amer. St. Papers Misc. 1, 206.
2. Dawson, pp. 16-17.
3. Amer. State Papers, Public Lands 1, 123.

indifferent horse or a rifle gun." Then these lands were
sold out in smaller lots to settlers. With each grant was
given a formal deed reciting the grant of the court under
the pretended authority of the court of Virginia. Harrison wrote, "I should not be surprised to see five hundred
families settling under these titles in the course of a
year." He forbade the recorder and prothonotary to record or authenticate the purchases of the speculators.

The situation at Kaskaskia was still worse. We quote
from a letter from that place to Albert Gallatin, dated
October 18, 1803:[1] "You have no guess how the United
States are imposed on by the Spanish officers since they
have heard of the cession of Louisiana. Grants are daily
making for large tracts of land and dated back. Some
are made to men who have been dead fifteen or twenty
years and transferred down to the present holders. These
grants are made to Americans, with a reserve of interest
to the officer who makes them." Under such circumstances, there was but one thing to do—to establish land
offices and have a register and receiver of public moneys
at each office. This would relieve the Governor and
Secretary from much drudgery and clerical work in examining and confirming or rejecting titles. Accordingly,
March 26, 1804, Congress passed an Act dividing the
Territory into three land districts and establishing land
offices at Detroit, Vincennes and Kaskaskia—one in each
district. By Act of March 3, 1807, an office was also established at Jeffersonville which was opened in April,
1808, and by Act of February 21, 1812, one was established at Shawneetown, on the Ohio, just below the mouth
of the Wabash. The former task of the Governor in regard to individual claims now devolved upon the land

1. Published in Kentucky Gazette, March 13, 1804.

commissioners at these offices, and we need not follow them through their arduous and long protracted tasks. In a letter[1] from the commissioners of Kaskaskia, February 24, 1806, to Albert Gallatin, Secretary of the Treasury, they state that their office has much more business to settle by way of claims than both the other offices of the Territory. They made regular reports to the Secretary of the Treasury and impressed upon him the necessity of renewing their commissions in order to finish their work. They had at one time nearly three thousand claims to act upon and were much retarded in the work by perjuries and forgeries.[2] In their report for 1810, they said they had rejected 890 claims as illegal and fraudulent.[3] By Act of February 20, 1812, Congress provided for a revision of the land claims in the district of Kaskaskia.

But to secure a good title was only the beginning of the difficulty the settlers had to encounter in regard to their lands. The greatest burden was to meet the payments and pay the taxes. The "Western Sun" for January 27, 1808, publishes a list of over ninety farms in Knox county, varying from twenty-five to four hundred acres each, which were offered for sale by the sheriff for non-payment of taxes for 1806. Again, in the issue of July 2, 1808, is a list of about 130 farms in Randolph county which were for sale for the same reason. Moreover, these latter were all donated lands—one-hundred and four-hundred acre tracts. The territorial assembly at its session in 1810 petitioned[4] Congress for a repeal of the provision in the land law requiring back interest from

1. State Papers, Public Lands I, 285.
2. Western Sun, October 22, 1808.
3. State Papers, Public Lands II, 102.
4. Journal. Western Sun, December 22, 1810.

date of the purchase on the installments that were not
paid when due, also for two years extension of time for
payment.   They said the farmers of the Territory had
been pinched by want of money and lack of market, due
in part to the Embargo which they had supported for
their country's sake.   On March 2, 1809, Congress had
passed an act providing for an extension of time for two
years for those whose last payments were to fall due on
or before the 1st of the following January.   And again
on April 30, 1810, a similar law was passed for the relief of those who had purchased before January 1, 1806.
Both these laws, it will be observed, relieved only those
who were under immediate pressure at the time and both
required the payment of back interest on arrears.   What
was needed was a law extending the time for *all* pur-
chasers, and relieving them from back interest.   The tax
collector of Knox county under date of May 26, 1812,
advertised no less than three hundred tracts of land in
that county for sale because of failure to pay the taxes.[1]
By Act of Congress approved April 23, 1812,[2] an extension of three years' time from January 1, 1813, was
granted to those who had purchased prior to April 1,
1808, and whose lands had not already been sold.   The
payment was to be made in four equal annual installments
beginning January 1, 1813.

---

1. Western Sun.
2   Statutes of the United States, II.

CHAPTER IX.

INDIAN TREATIES AND LAND CESSIONS.

The achievement which brought Harrison most fame while Governor of Indiana Territory was his successful campaign against the Indians in the fall of 1811, ending in the famous battle of Tippecanoe. Next after this, he was best known for his successful negotiation of treaties for land cessions from the Indians, of which he made in all thirteen.[1]

In the petition of the Vincennes Convention, December 28, 1802, of which Harrison was chairman, we find the following paragraph: "Your memorialists beg leave further to represent that the quantity of lands in the Territory open for settlement is by no means sufficiently large to admit of a population adequate to the purposes of civil government. They, therefore, pray that the Indian titles to the land lying between the settled part of the Illinois country and the Ohio, between the general Indian boundary line running from the mouth of the river Kentucky and the tract commonly called Clark's Grant, and between and below the said Clark's Grant and the Ohio and Wabash rivers, may be extinguished; and as an encouragement for a speedy population of the country, that those lands and all other public lands in the Territory may be sold in smaller tracts and at a lower price than is now allowed by the existing laws," etc.

---

1. The texts of these treaties may all be found among others in the first volume of the American State Papers on Indian Affairs, and in the Senate Documents No. 4254. Also the description and maps of all the cessions are given in the eighteenth report, Part 2, of the American Bureau of Ethnology, by Royce and Thomas. Helpful maps of the cessions in that part of the territory which later constituted the State of Indiana, are also given in Smith's History of Indiana, Vol. I, and in Henry Adams' History of the U. S., Vol. VI.

In connection with Chapters IX and X, the reader will find it helpful to refer to the map preceding the preface to this study.

The authority by which Harrison negotiated the treaties of cession was quite distinct from his commission as Governor. He did not receive such authority till 1803, and the first treaty he negotiated was in the summer of this year. On February 23, 1802, however, Dearborn, Secretary of War, had written to Harrison that the various Indian agents and Factory agents in the Territories were all to be under the supervision and direction of their respective Governors.[1]   On February 3, 1803, President Jefferson sent the following message to the Senate: "I nominate William Henry Harrison, of Indiana, to be a commissioner to enter into any treaty or treaties which may be necessary with any Indian tribes northwest of the Ohio, and within the Territory of the United States, on the subject of boundary or lands." This appointment was unanimously approved by the Senate, February 8th. A few weeks after this appointment of Harrison, Jefferson wrote him a long letter which outlined the Indian policy which he wished Harrison to pursue.[2] This was a policy of peace and yet a policy of encroachment as way should open. He encouraged Harrison to obtain lands from them for the United States. "To promote this disposition to exchange lands which they have to spare and we want for necessaries which we have to spare and they want, we shall push our trading houses, and be glad to see the good and influential individuals among them in debt; because we observe that when these debts get beyond what individuals can pay they become willing to lop them off by a cession of lands." The President further explained his policy in a letter to Harrison in which he stated that Louisiana had been

1. Dawson, p. 34.
2. Jefferson's Works. Letter of February 27, 1803.

ceded to France; that the French understood the management of Indians better than any other nation; that to
guard against their intrigues it became necessary to form
strong settlements on the Mississippi, the lower part of
the Ohio, the Wabash and Illinois rivers, which could be
done only by extinguishing the Indian titles to the lands;
that this could not be done at once, but by watching occasional opportunities. "I was authorized to draw for
any money I might deem necessary," wrote Harrison,[1]
"and bestow presents and gratuities among the Indians
as I deemed proper. I held this commission during the
whole period of my governorship, and in thirteen treaties
extinguished the title to about fifty million acres."

In Harrison's letter to the Secretary of War, February
26, 1802, already noted, in speaking of the settlement of
a number of questions[2] with the Indians, he says, "I am
persuaded that nothing can be done with respect to any
of these objects but in a general assembly of the chiefs
of all the tribes. There appears to be an agreement
among them, that no proposition which relates to their
lands can be acceded to without the consent of all the
tribes; and they are extremely watchful and jealous of
each other, lest some advantage should be obtained in
which they do not all participate." But, he continued,
not merely was such an assembly desirable for adjusting
relations between the Indians and the United States, but
also among the Indians themselves. For a meeting had
long been wished for by them in order to settle some

---

1. Autobiographical Letter, 1839.

2. The principal subjects for adjustment suggested were: The establishment of roads and houses of accommodation between the settlements, and
fixing of the boundaries of the old Vincennes and Kaskaskia grants, provision
for the security of traders in the Indian country, and to extend to the Sac
nation the provisions of the treaty of Greenville.

disputes among themselves which, but for Harrison's mediation, he says, would have ended in war. "These disputes, on account of the jealousy among them, can not be amicably settled but by the mediation of the United States.[1] Accordingly, September 17, 1802, Harrison held a council with the Indians at Vincennes and arranged the basis of the Treaty of Ft. Wayne of the following summer. Owing to jealousies and disaffection engendered by a British Indian agent, McKee, Harrison had great difficulty in getting the chiefs together, and when assembled he had still more difficulty in obtaining the confirmation of the old Vincennes grant. They denied that any real cession had ever been made and said it was only to be *used* by the whites. Harrison concluded that only those chiefs who were under the influence of the French of Vincennes had agreed to the transfer. With the aid of Captain Wells, however, he succeeded in getting the chiefs to appoint four persons to represent all the tribes, who should meet the representatives of the United States at Ft. Wayne for the purpose of drawing up a treaty. Here again Harrison had difficulty in getting the chiefs together, but he finally succeeded by telling them their annuities would be distributed among those who attended. Here again also he had difficulty in coming to an agreement with them, the Delaware and Shawnee chiefs leaving in anger.[2] Finally, however, this, Harrison's first formal treaty with the Indians, was made June 7, 1803, in which his proposals at the Council of Vincennes were confirmed. The treaty of Greenville, 1795, had been made

1. This mediation of the United States, through Harrison as its agent, in preserving peace among the Indiana Indians, reminds us of the fable of the cats and the cheese, in which the monkey, as arbiter, ate most of the cheese in striking a balance between them.

2. Dawson, p. 49.

with twelve tribes. This treaty was made with nine
tribes: The Delawares, Shawnees, Putawatimies, Miamis, Eel Rivers, Weas, Kickapoos, Piankeshaws and
Kaskaskias.

By this treaty the land about Vincennes was ceded to the
United States with definite boundaries—the "Vincennes
tract." It extended along the Wabash from the mouth
of the White river to Point Coupee, about twenty-five
miles above Vincennes, and from twelve miles west of
the river to seventy-two miles east—a large parallelo-
gram. Besides this, the Salt Springs on the Saline Creek,
a tributary of the Ohio, just below the Wabash, were
ceded to the United States. It was also agreed that as
soon as the tribes occupying that Territory should consent to the measure, several tracts of land for way-
stations from Clarksville to Kaskaskia via Vincennes,
should be ceded. This consent was secured by a supple-
mentary treaty at Vincennes on August 7th.

On February 21, 1803, Secretary Dearborn had written to Harrison directing him to take the first opportunity
for negotiating with the chiefs of the nation, or nations,
who claimed the land in the vicinity of Kaskaskia, and a
tract bordering on the Mississippi and Ohio, up each
river a considerable distance from their junction, for a
cession of lands.[1] In accordance with these directions,
Harrison's next treaty was with the Kaskaskias, or Illinois Indians, which was negotiated at Vincennes, August 13, 1803. By this treaty all of Illinois south of the
Illinois river and west of the Saline Creek, except two
small tracts, was ceded to the United States. The Kaskaskias had dwindled away until only a remnant remained
and they were glad to cede their vast territory in return

---
1. State Papers, Indian Affairs I, 701.

for their maintenance and protection by the United States, for which ample provisions were made in this treaty. The annuity was to be increased to $1,000; a house was to be built for the chief and a field, not to exceed one hundred acres, was to be enclosed for the tribe. "And whereas, the greater part of the tribe have been baptised and received into the Catholic church, to which they are much attached, the United States will give annually for seven years, one hundred dollars towards the support of a priest," etc. Three hundred dollars was also promised to assist in building a church.

On June 27, 1804, the Secretary of War wrote to Harrison again, suggesting the propriety of procuring a cession of lands along the Illinois river from the Sacs. And he suggested that if any of the other chiefs should be inclined to follow the example of the old Kaskaskia chief, they should be encouraged to do so—especially the Piankeshaws, whose lands divide the Vincennes territory on the Wabash from the cessions of the Kaskaskias. It would also be desirable, he said, to obtain the tract between the southern line of the Vincennes tract and the Ohio river. We shall see that these three suggestions all bore fruit in the form of three subsequent treaties.

Next came the treaties with the Delawares and Piankeshaws[1] made at Vincennes, August 18th and 27th respectively, 1804. By the first of these the Delawares gave up their claim to all territory lying between the Ohio on the south and the Vincennes tract and Vincennes-Clarksville road on the north. Provisions were also made for

---

1. The Piankeshaws had belonged to the Miami Confederation, but had seceded from it about 1770. The Delawares soon after this had come from the east and had been given the right to occupy the lands south of Vincennes by the Piankeshaws in return for aiding the latter in their war with the Kickapoos.

teaching them agriculture and the domestic arts. But the Piankeshaws had also claimed this territory, which made it necessary to treat with them to secure a clear title. This was done a few days later by giving them an additional annuity as had been done for the Delawares, and the title was thus secured to the land to half a mile northward of the most northerly bend of the Vincennes-Clarksville road.

Harrison's next treaty was with the Sacs and Foxes of northern Illinois and beyond the Mississippi, made November 3, 1804, at St. Louis. This was when Harrison was also Governor of the district of Louisiana. By this treaty a large tract was obtained, partly west of the Mississippi river and north of the lower Missouri, and extending on the east side of the Mississippi from the Illinois to the Wisconsin river, thus embracing all of the northwestern part of the present State of Illinois, and the southern portion of Wisconsin, besides a large area in what is now the State of Missouri. For this large cession the Indians received an annuity of $1,000 in goods, and goods to the value of $2,234.50 at the time. This treaty was regarded as the most important of all those which Harrison negotiated. "It secured," says Dawson, "the largest tract of land ever ceded in one treaty by the Indians since the settlement of North America."[1] Moses Strong, in his history of Wisconsin Territory, says, in writing of this treaty, that "As it had been made and signed by only five Indians on the one side, its validity was denied by one band of the Sacs, of which Black Hawk was chief, and the settlement of lands ceded by it was the alleged cause of the outbreak known as the Black Hawk war, twenty-eight years later."

1. Life of Harrison, p. 59.

The treaties with the Delawares and Piankeshaws in 1804, by which the southern part of the Territory had been ceded, aroused bitter opposition on the part of Little Turtle, a Miami chief, and others. The Piankeshaws were a tribe of the great Miami Confederation, and Little Turtle claimed that they had no right to make the cession without the consent of the other Miami tribes.[1] Other Indians, especially some Delaware chiefs, were also fomenting ill feeling over the last cession. Thus the right of the Delawares to cede was questioned by some of their own chiefs and also by the Piankeshaws, while the right of the Piankeshaws to cede was questioned by Little Turtle representing the Miamis. Accordingly, on May 24, 1805, Secretary Dearborn wrote Harrison saying, "It is the opinion of the President that you ought with as little delay as possible, to cause a meeting of the Delaware chiefs and some of the principal chiefs of the Miamis and Putawatimies for the purpose of such an explanation of the doings, so much complained of, as will satisfy the chiefs,"[2] etc. Again in the same letter he says that if Harrison should judge it advantageous to distribute two or three hundred dollars among the Miamis, Putawatimies and others by way of quieting their minds in regard to the recent cession, he may do so.[3]

Harrison secured an assembly of these tribes together with the related tribes of Weas and Eel rivers at Grouseland, near Vincennes, August 21, 1805. Not only did he succeed in satisfying them for the time being in regard to the last cession, but he also secured a new cession of great importance. By this treaty was ceded to the United

---

1. Dawson, p. 61 et seq.
2. State Papers, Indian Affairs I, 701.
3. Letters in Dept. of State.

States all the remainder of the Indian lands of southeastern Indiana, and bounded on the north by a line drawn from the northeastern corner of the Vincennes tract to a point on the Greenville Treaty line, fifty miles from the Ohio river. It was also provided that this northern boundary should not cross the east fork of White river. For this large and valuable tract, $4,000 was paid down, besides annuities aggregating $1,600. It was also agreed that, as the Miamis, Eel rivers and Weas were formerly and still considered themselves as one nation and as they had determined not to dispose of any more of their lands except by the consent of all these tribes, the United States would respect their wishes in this matter.

Five days after the negotiation of this treaty Harrison wrote Secretary Dearborn a suggestive letter, which he mailed with a copy of the treaty.[1] The first difficulty in the recent conference, he said, was to satisfy the Indians of his right to make the treaty of the previous year with the Delawares. This was made satisfactory excepting the clause which guaranteed to the Delawares the land between the Ohio and White rivers (the land just secured by the enclosed treaty). This dispute Harrison left for the Miamis and Delawares to fight out among themselves. The Delawares were related to the Miamis in regard to this tract just as they had been to the Piankeshaws in regard to the tract ceded the previous year. The Delawares finally gave up the contest. Then the Miamis and Potawatomis asked for large annuities such as the Delawares were receiving, and Harrison told them they could secure these only by a further cession of lands, and so the treaty was made. The consideration, he said, was greater than he could have wished, but that "it was

1. State Papers, Indian Affairs I, 701.

not possible to reduce it one single cent. * * * * A knowledge of the value of land is fast gaining ground among the Indians." One of the chiefs, he added, considered part of the land worth $6.00 per acre. Harrison further wrote that he thought the present tract contained at least two million acres and embraced some of the finest land in the West. Three days later, in a letter to Jefferson, Harrison wrote that the compensation for this tract amounted to about one cent per acre, but that he hoped to get the next cession enough cheaper to bring down the average.[1] It should be noted that at this time the lands were sold to settlers by the government at $2.00 per acre. At this conference also Harrison partially cleared the way for future cessions. First, he obtained an acknowledgment, on the part of the Pottawatomies and others of the exclusive right of the Miami tribes, to sell the lands on the upper Wabash. The guarantee of those lands to the Miami tribes (Miamis, Eel Rivers and Weas), he wrote, could not then be avoided, but he hoped they might later be induced to divide their lands which they then held in common. As to the Piankeshaws, he held them aloof from the present treaty with a view of dealing separately with them, and he wrote that he could venture to promise that all their lands which lay between the Wabash and the Kaskaskias cession and below a continuation of the line running through Point Coupee, would be the property of the United States in ten days after he should receive instructions for that purpose, and for a consideration which would compensate for the high price paid for the present cession. The letter closes with an interesting statement, which bears incidentally upon Harrison's attitude toward slavery. He says: "In pursuance of the

---

1. Jefferson Papers. Dept. of State. Letter of August 29, 1805.

President's directions, I have promised the Turtle fifty dollars per annum in addition to his pension; and I have also directed Captain Wells to purchase a negro man for him in Kentucky and draw on you for the amount."

In response to this letter, Secretary Dearborn wrote Harrison October 11, 1805, expressing satisfaction and pleasure over what he had accomplished and by the direction of the President he requests him to close a bargain with the Piankeshaws for their claim to the lands between the Wabash and the Kaskaskia Cession, as proposed in Harrison's letter of August 26th. Accordingly, on December 30, 1805, Harrison negotiated a treaty with the Piankeshaws at Vincennes by which they ceded all their Territory between the Wabash on the east, and the Kaskaskia cession on the west, and between the Ohio river on the south, and the extension of the northern boundary line of the Vincennes tract to the Kaskaskia cession, on the north. The tract was from eighty to ninety miles wide east and west at its northern extremity, and about the same width north and south, while its frontage on the Ohio river was less than twelve miles, as the western boundary was between the Saline Creek and the Wabash.[1] Two square miles of land were to be reserved in this tract for the Indians and they were also to retain the right to hunt on these lands. In return the United States was to extend its protection and add $300 to their annuity, besides a payment of $1,100 in cash.

In forwarding this treaty on January 1, 1806, Harrison added in a letter[2] that he also agreed that the United States should for five years bear the expense of repairing their guns, but that he had forgotten to insert this in the

1. Kaskaskias Treaty of 1803, Art. 5; Postscript to Harrison's letter to Dearborn, January 1, 1806.
2. State Papers, Ind. Affs. I, 705.

treaty. He wrote that such service was highly appreciated by the Indians. He mentioned the necessity of prohibiting any person from trading with the Indians anywhere upon the lands of the United States without a license. He said, "The title to so large a portion of the Indian country has been extinguished, from which a great number of them still draw their support, that it is much to be feared they will fall a sacrifice to the merciless rapacity of the traders, unless they are restrained by the same penalties by which those are subjected who reside at the Indian towns." He gave confident assurances of the pacific disposition of the tribes under his superintendence, which is worthy of notice, when so much land had recently been acquired from them.

We here reach a pause in the negotiation of cessions, and no others are secured for almost four years. The lands have now been secured all along the Ohio to its junction with the Mississippi and also all along the Mississippi from the Ohio to the Wisconsin. Moreover, the overland routes from Clarksville to Vincennes and from Vincennes to St. Louis now passed entirely through ceded lands.[1]

On July 15, 1809, the Secretary of War wrote Harrison[2] that the President authorized and instructed him "to take advantage of the most favorable moment for extinguishing the Indian title to the lands lying to the east of the Wabash, and adjoining, south, on the lines of the treaties of Ft. Wayne and Grouseland." To prevent any future trouble it was further suggested that chiefs of all the tribes having any claims whatever to these lands should be present at the treaty. These directions resulted

---

1. Excellent maps of all the Indian land cessions in the United States are given in the 18th Report, Part 2, Amer. Bureau of Ethnology, by C. C. Royce.
2. Indian Affairs I, 761.

in the Treaty of Ft. Wayne, of September 30, 1809, together with two subsequent treaties negotiated the same year. This Ft. Wayne treaty was made with the Delawares, Potawatomis, Miamis, and Eel Rivers. The largest tract obtained at this time was comprehended between the old Ft. Wayne and Grouseland cessions on the south, the Wabash on the west up to Raccoon Creek, and the so-called "10 o'clock line" on the northeast, which was so drawn as to make the tract thirty miles wide at the narrowest part. The next tract in size secured at this time was a long strip twelve miles in width, extending along the Greenville Treaty line from Ft. Recovery on the north to the Grouseland cession on the south. The compensations given for these large tracts were annuities aggregating $1,750, besides goods to the amount of $5,200, to the four tribes present. The consent of the Weas was also acknowledged to be necessary for a clear title to the first cession, as already mentioned at the treaty of Grouseland.

An interesting agreement was made in this treaty by which any theft or injury committed by an Indian of one of these tribes upon one or more of another tribe, was to be reported to the United States agent charged with delivering their annuities; and then upon the determination of damages these were to be deducted from the annuity of the tribe of the criminal and given to the person injured. Lastly, it was further agreed to make an additional cession of a tract fifteen miles wide on the west side of the Wabash and also extending northward to the Raccoon Creek, for an additional annuity of $400, provided the Kickapoos should agree to it. Then a separate article was agreed to with the Miamis and Eel Rivers which was also considered a part of the main treaty. As we have

already seen by the treaty of Grouseland, these Indians
had the exclusive claim to the lands on the upper Wabash,
so that some extra concessions were felt to be due to
them. Accordingly it was agreed to provide them with
$500 worth of domestic animals each of three succeeding
springs. And should the Kickapoos agree to the last article of the treaty, further annuities should be granted of
$200 to the Miamis and $100 each to the Eel River and
Weas. Again, on October 26, 1809, Harrison made a
treaty with the Weas at Vincennes whereby they agreed
to the cessions made at Ft. Wayne and received in return
an additional annuity of $300 and a present sum of
$1,500, with the promise of the further annuity of $100,
when the Kickapoos should consent to the cession west of
the Wabash.

So lastly we have the treaty with the Kickapoos negotiated at Vincennes, December 9, 1809, by which they
agreed to the former cessions and received an additional
annuity of $400 and goods to the amount of $800. They
also ceded a new tract which extended up the west side of
the Wabash to the Vermillion River. Harrison in writing to the Secretary of War the following day said of
this cession: "This small tract of land (of about twenty
miles square) is one of the most beautiful that can be
conceived, and is, moreover, believed to contain a very
rich copper mine. I have myself frequently seen specimens of the copper"[1], etc. For this tract an annuity of
$100 and $700 in goods were given.

This completes the list of Harrison's treaties with the
Indians while Governor of Indiana Territory. If we
count every one a separate treaty, they are twelve in number. I find but one other which he negotiated, that at

---

1. State Papers, Indian Affairs I. 762.

Greenville, Ohio, July 22, 1814, which makes the thirteen he refers to in his autobiography. To recapitulate, there were three in 1803, three in 1804, two in 1805 and four in 1809. The total amount of lands thus acquired was about 75,000 square miles. Yet the greater part of this was west of the Wabash and when Illinois was separated in the spring of 1809 there remained in Indiana only a wide belt of ceded lands across the southern end of the territory, with strips extending half way up the eastern and western borders, thus presenting somewhat the form of a crescent. Todd & Drake in 1840 in writing of Harrison's business management in the purchase of these lands said: "Perhaps no individual has ever disbursed so large an amount of the public treasure as Governor Harrison and had so little difficulty in adjusting his accounts with the War Department. This arose from the simple mode in which he kept his accounts. He refused to keep any amount of the public money on hand."[1]

In his opening speech to the legislature, November 12, 1810, Harrison said: "Although much has been done toward the extinguishment of Indian titles in the territory, much still remains to be done. We have not yet a sufficient space to form a tolerable State. The eastern settlements are separated from the western by a considerable extent of Indian lands, and the most fertile tracts within our territorial bounds are still their property. Is one of the fairest portions of the globe to remain in a state of nature, the haunt of a few wretched savages, when it seems destined by the Creator to give support to a large population, and to be the seat of civilization, of science, and of true religion?"[2]

---

1. Todd and Drake, p. 27.
2. House Journal, Western Sun, December 8, 1810.

CHAPTER X.

TECUMSEH AND THE PROPHET AND TIPPECANOE.

A cloud now appeared upon the horizon, and Indiana passed under the shadow of Tecumseh and his brother, the Prophet.[1] In 1806 we hear of them settled with a number of followers on White River. In May or June, 1808, they moved to the Tippecanoe Creek and settled about a hundred and fifty miles above Vincennes, forming the "Prophet's Town." This was a strategic position, about half way between Lake Erie and the Ohio and easily accessible to both and within easy reach of all the Indians. Ft. Dearborn (Chicago), Ft. Wayne and Detroit were within easy reach. Tecumseh's aim was to form a confederation of all the tribes based upon a union not of the chiefs merely but of the warriors themselves; and this confederacy was to have control of all the lands. He wished to prevent the piecemeal cession of lands by petty tribal chiefs which had been taking place.[2]

The objects of these leaders at this time seemed peaceful, industrial and temperate. The settlers at Tippecanoe village resisted all temptation to drink and avowed themselves to be tillers of the soil. But they insisted that the whites should keep their distance, and not take any more of the Indians' land.[3] Indeed, they claimed that all past

1. This illustrious pair are said to have been born near Springfield, Ohio, sometime between 1768 and 1780, the exact date being unknown.
2. Dillon, 442-3. Henry Adams' United States, Vol. VI, p. 78-79.
3. In writing to the Secretary of War, Harrison quoted the plea of an old chief to him as follows: "You call us your children. Why do you not make us as happy as our fathers, the French, did? They never took from us our lands; indeed they were in common between us. They planted where they pleased; and they cut wood where they pleased, and so did we. But now, if a poor Indian attempts to take a little bark from a tree to cover him from the rain, up comes a white man and threatens to shoot him, claiming the tree as his own."—Dillon's Indiana, p. 424.

cessions were invalid because not sanctioned by all the Indians. In the latter part of June, 1808, a messenger from the Prophet visited Harrison at Vincennes and told him that the Prophet told his followers "not to lie, to steal, nor to drink whiskey; not to go to war, but to live in peace with all mankind. He tells us also to work and make corn."[1] Harrison replied to this deputation in part as follows:[2] "It is the determination of the President in case any of the tribes who became his children by the Treaty of Greenville should lift up the tomahawk against him, that he will never again make peace as long as there is one of that tribe remaining on this side of the lakes." * * * "The long knives (Americans) are not less brave (than the Indians) and you know their numbers be as the blades of grass on the plains, as the sands on the river shore," etc. Such threatening words could not be justified, of course, by the direct message from the Prophet. They are to be explained from the fact that Harrison mistrusted these direct messages of peace as deceptions, and it would seem that he meant to intimidate the Indians and cause them to give up any warlike purpose which they might be concealing. Following these messages, in August, 1808, the Prophet visited Harrison for two weeks at Vincennes and professed a peaceful attitude. The visit was repeated in the summer of 1809. Then the fatal die was cast in negotiating the treaty of Ft. Wayne, September 30, 1809, in which the whites encroached a hundred miles further up the Wabash. From this time, unless these last cessions should be given up, and left unsettled by the whites, war with the Indians became inevitable. For this cession was above everything

1. Dillon's Indiana, p. 428.
2. Western Sun, July 2, 1808.

else just what Tecumseh and the Prophet were determined
to prevent. In a letter to the Secretary of War, June 4,
1810, Harrison wrote: "I have received information
from various sources which has produced entire conviction on my mind that the Prophet is organizing a most
extensive combination against the United States." He
then tells of the Prophet and the Kickapoos refusing to
receive their annuity of salt, and pulling the man's hair
who was in charge of it. The Prophet also sent word to
the governor that his people should not come any nearer
to him nor settle on the Vermillion River, that he "smelt
them too strongly already."[1]

On the 12th of August, 1810, Tecumseh, attended by
about four hundred warriors, came to hold his famous
council with Harrison at Vincennes.[2] This lasted for
about ten days and it was on the 20th of August, when
Harrison was replying to the chief that the latter lost his
temper and a conflict was almost precipitated. At this
juncture Harrison withdrew and refused to speak with
him further. The next morning, however, upon the so-
licitation and apology of the chief, the conference was renewed, but all to no purpose. Tecumseh would not permit the survey and settlement of the lands lately ceded

---

1. American State Papers, Ind. Affairs I. 799; Western Sun, June 23, 1810.

2. Two interesting stories are related in regard to this meeting:

The first one following seems to be well authenticated; the second, if not
true, is certainly a good story. It is said that Harrison had a seat reserved for
Tecumseh at the council, but when the interpreter told him that his father
(Harrison) wished him to be seated, he rose to his full height and said that
the Sun was his father, and the Earth was his mother, and that he would re-
cline on her bosom. Whereupon he sat down on the ground.

The other story is that at another time during the council, Tecumseh
called for a bench, and when it was brought he and Harrison sat down on it.
Tecumseh then began to crowd Harrison, and as the latter moved over Tecumseh continued to crowd him until Harrison remonstrated. Whereupon Tecumseh asked him how he would like to be crowded clear off the bench just as the
Indians were being crowded off their lands by the whites.—Draper Collection,
Tecumseh Papers, III, pp. 69, 73.

and declared that those few who had consented to the cession must suffer for it.

The attendance of Indians at the annual council at Ft. Wayne, October 1st, following, was much larger than usual, being 1,779,[1] which was doubtless due to interest and exticement over the land situation. Yet in the Western Sun[2] for October 18th there was an editorial on the Indian situation, written after the writer had interviewed Harrison, stating that there was "not the least cause of alarm;" that there had not been for the last four years less probability of a rupture, that the party attached to the Prophet had dwindled to a contemptible number and that even these were not well united.

In his message to the Assembly, November 12, 1810,[3] Harrison discussed the Indian situation. He said that the treaty of Ft. Wayne had offered an opportunity for foreign agents and disaffected persons. The greatest difficulty in negotiating this treaty, he said, was that of ascertaining the tribes which should be admitted to it. Liberal principles had been adopted. The Miamis had owned the territory originally and held the only true title. Other tribes had since invaded their territory and secured the title of use or occupancy and in order to satisfy all, these had been admitted as parties to the treaties. That is, the Delawares, Potawatomis and Kickapoos only, in addition to the Miamis. No other tribes had any just claim. Not till eight months after the treaty was made, he said, were the claims of the Prophet made known, whereupon a furious clamor was raised by foreign agents and disaffected persons for excluding him

1. Kentucky Gazette, Nov. 6, 1810, extract of Letter from Indian Agent at Ft. Wayne.
2. The Vincennes Paper.
3. Western Sun, December 8, 1810.

from the treaty. The Prophet, he said, was not a chief,
but an outcast of his tribe and was despised by his real
chiefs, the principal of whom was present and consented
to the treaty, disclaimed any right of his tribe to be a
party to it, but encouraged the other chiefs to negotiate
party to it, and encouraged the other chiefs to negotiate
he sent to him to come to Vincennes and present his claim
and told him it would be duly considered. The Prophet
sent his brother Tecumseh, who could show no just
claim. His only plea was that *all* lands belonged to *all*
the tribes and that no tribes had a right to sell any without the consent of all. Yet Harrison said that in spite
of the attempts to keep the Indians worked up against
the government by malicious misrepresentations and
bribes on the part of British agents, the following of the
Prophet was now on the wane.

The instability and delicacy of the situation was shown
in another statement which Harrison made in this message: "A single artful or imprudent observation from a
designing or careless individual is frequently sufficient to
destroy the labor of weeks and to induce the Indians to
abandon an intention which they seemed to have adopted
after the maturest deliberation."

On the 10th of October, 1810, Harrison wrote to
Eustis, Secretary of War, asking for authority to build a
fort on the new purchase to ward off the Indians and also
to survey the lands and open them for settlement. The
Secretary consulted the President, who decided[1] that it
was not expedient to undertake this before the following
spring, partly because of the lateness of the season and
the threatening state of affairs in West Florida which
seemed likely to require the attention of all disposable

1. Letter Eustis to Harrison, October 26, 1810.

forces. In a letter of March 7, 1811, the orders were repeated, to take no aggressive action.

In June, 1811, again, the salt sent up the Wabash for the
Indians was seized at the Prophet's town and the Prophet
sent word to the governor "not to be angry at his seizing
the salt as he had got none last year and had more than
two thousand men to feed."[1] The Secretary of War had
suggested to Harrison to make Tecumseh and the Prophet
prisoners, but this was never attempted. On June 24,
1811, Harrison sent a lengthy message to them in which
he spoke of his own followers thus: "As soon as they
hear my voice you will see them pouring forth their
swarms of hunting-shirt men as numerous as the mos-
quitoes on the shores of the Wabash. Brothers, take care
of their stings."[2] Tecumseh replied and said among
other things that in eighteen days he would visit Harrison
and that he wished "to wash away all those bad stories
which had been circulated." Some delay occurred but on
July 27th, he appeared at Vincennes accompanied by some
three hundred followers, including twenty or thirty
women and children. To rival this display and to secure
the safety of the people Harrison had the county militia,
composed of about seven hundred fifty men, to display
themselves and remain on guard. Tecumseh stated that
it was not his intention to make war on the United States,
that he would prevent murders on the whites, that he had
united the northern tribes and was now going south to
visit the tribes there and secure their union with those of
the north, and that he would return to the Prophet's town
the following spring and would then visit the President
of the United States and have matters settled between

1. Dillon, 150.
2. Dawson, 180.

them. And that meanwhile he hoped no settlements would be made in the lands newly ceded.

Following this interview, Tecumseh with a band of twenty followers proceeded to the South. Harrison, meanwhile, had been busy in correspondence with the Secretary of War and with Governors Edwards, Howard and Scott.[1] In a letter to Governor Edwards[2] dated July 4, 1811, he urged the necessity of concerted action on the part of Edwards, Howard and himself. He also said that, it being just harvest time, he could not now bear the idea of taking the farmers from their crops. So he tried "to keep up appearances to the Indians while really dependent on Providence for protection * * * "In Indian warfare," he continued, "there is no security but in offensive measures. Bonaparte's army, forming a cordon of posts around our frontiers, would not be sufficient to prevent the ingress of the Indians for the purpose of doing mischief. We must strike them at their towns, capture their women and children and by destroying their corn and eternally harassing them, oblige them to sue for peace."

On July 17th Secretary Eustis wrote Harrison that the 4th Regiment under Colonel Boyd had been ordered to descend the Ohio River from Pittsburgh and to be placed under his command. That letters from Governor Edwards announced several murders and general alarm on the Illinois frontier. That Harrison should consult with Edwards, and that if the Prophet should commence or seriously threaten hostilities, he ought to be attacked, provided the force at Harrison's command was sufficient to

---

1. Edwards of Illinois, Howard of Upper Louisiana (Mo.), Scott of Kentucky.

2. Clark Papers, Ohio Hist. and Phil. Soc., Cincinnati.

insure success. This letter was followed by another three days later, urging extreme caution and every effort to conciliate the Indians and avoid rupture. He said that while the 2d and 4th regiments are to be stationed in Kentucky under Captain Piatt and Colonel Boyd and subject to Harrison's orders if necessary, yet it was highly important that they should be available for other service,[1] and that Harrison should avoid using them if possible. The letter of the 17th seems to have been written by the Secretary without consulting the President, for he said in the letter of the 20th that since writing the former he had been particularly instructed by the President to communicate his earnest desire that peace might be preserved with the Indians, and that to this end every proper means might be adopted. Nothing could be plainer than that President Madison desired no aggressive action at this time. The situation in West Florida was likely to demand all the United States troops.

On the other hand the people of the Territory were driven to distraction. Indians were scouring the country in every direction and occasional murders were occurring. At a meeting of a large number of citizens of Knox county at Vincennes, July 31, just four days after Tecumseh and his three hundred followers had arrived, a set of resolutions[2] was adopted, among which were: "That the safety of the persons and property of this frontier can never be effectually secured, but by breaking up the combination formed by the Shawnee Prophet on the Wabash; That a temporizing policy is not calculated to answer any beneficial purpose with savages, who are only to be controlled by prompt and decisive measures; That we

1. In West Florida.
2. American State Papers, Ind. Affairs 1, 802.

approve highly of the prompt and decisive measures
adopted by the Governor; That the President be requested to take such measures as will free this country
from future apprehensions from the Prophet and his
party." In accordance with these resolutions an address
was sent to the President. This shows that aggressive
action, if not popular with Madison at this time, was so
in the Territory. On August 7th, Harrison wrote Eustis[1]
and suggested moving up the Wabash to the new purchase
about the middle of September. Eustis replied August
22d, but gave no special encouragement for ascending the
Wabash. He said that Colonel Boyd's assistance was authorized under the presumption that the service might be
performed in time for him to ascend the Ohio before
winter and that to facilitate operations, he would be ordered to drop down to Louisville and there await Harrison's orders.

On August 10th Harrison wrote to Governor Edwards[2] that the plan which he had determined to pursue
was more pacific than he thought it ought to be; that he
was determined to take no important step without the
sanction of Governor Howard and himself (Edwards);
that he had written to Howard and also to General Clark,
whom he wished to be admitted into their "cabinet coun-

1. Draper Collection, Harrison Papers

2. Clark Papers.

Note.—In a letter from Harrison to Eustis, August 6, 1811, he says: "Capt.
Z. Taylor has been placed in command at the garrison near this place. To all
the qualities which are esteemed in an amiable man, he appears to unite those
which form a good officer. In the short time he has been in command he has
rendered the garrison defensible. Before his arrival, it resembled anything
but a place of defense."—Draper Collection, Harrison Papers.

    For two of the future presidents of the United States thus to be situated as
Indian fighters together on the frontier seems worthy of notice, and both were
soon to attain distinction. Taylor's brave defense of Ft. Harrison when attacked by the Indians under Tecumseh the following year was only second in
importance to Harrison's achievement at Tippecanoe.

cil." He said he had requested Clark's opinion as to whether the Prophet's party should be dispersed by force if other measures should fail: that he was satisfied that *talking* would have no effect unless backed by the appearance of force. Edwards' advice as to the employment of force was also particularly requested, and Harrison said that if Edwards should be able to join him at Vincennes about the 20th of September, he should be highly gratified; and that he expected General Clark and Governor Howard both about that time. Harrison added that the Secretary of War had given him great latitude and left more to his discretion than he could wish.

Harrison wrote Eustis August 13th[1] that their demands and remonstrances must be supported by an exhibition of force. "It is in vain to threaten unless we show that we are not only willing but able and ready to chastise. Heedless of futurity, it is only by placing the danger before his eyes that a savage is to be controlled. Even the gallant Tecumseh is not insensible to an argument of this kind." * * * * "But let me assure you, sir, that I feel most forcibly the responsibility imposed upon me by the President's directions to preserve peace, if possible, and that recourse to actual hostilities shall be had only when every other means shall have been tried in vain to effect the disbanding of the Prophet's force. Unless this is done, no arrangement that we can make can ensure our tranquility for two months. And it appears to me that the pecuniary interest of the United States is as much concerned in effecting it as are its honor and dignity and the peace and prosperity of the citizens of the frontier. * * * * I shall expect your final directions by the middle of September and whatever they may be, whether

1. Clark Papers.

agreeing with my own opinion or not, they will be punctually and cheerfully obeyed." He concludes by discussing the military authority which he is to have in case it should be necessary to pursue the Indians into Illinois Territory: "From your last letter it appears that the President intended that the principal direction of the military should be with me. Why would it not be proper then that I should receive some special authority for that purpose? * * * * The best understanding exists between Governors Edwards, Howard and myself, and as neither of them has had any military experience, I should have no doubt of receiving any authority that they could give; but by the Ordinance they are precluded from giving any commissions higher than that of Colonel."

On the same day, August 13th, Harrison wrote Governor Edwards,[1] enclosing a copy of the above letter, and telling him if he had any objection to the latter part of it, he begged him to express his thoughts freely. "Be assured," he continued, "that I would be far from desiring any power that would be hurtful to your feelings or to your authority. But such is the nature of military affairs that whoever may *direct* what is to be done, the *execution* must be committed to a single person and his authority over those whom he commands must be sufficient to ensure obedience."

Meanwhile the hostilities and depredations of the Indians increased. They were scouring the settlements and stealing horses, and were replenishing their stores of ammunition copiously from the British stores at Malden.[2] Finally, *September 18th, Secretary Eustis wrote Harrison that a post might be established on the new purchase*

---

1. Clark Papers.
2. State Papers, Indian Affairs I, 801.

on the Wabash if, in his judgment, it was required for the
security of the purchase or the Territories.[1]

But meanwhile Colonel Boyd's troops, about three
hundred strong, had been ordered from Louisville and
had arrived in the Territory early in September. Harrison had been busy collecting his forces and sending them
up the Wabash where they were encamped about sixty-
five miles above Vincennes, and two or three miles above
the present site of Terre Haute, on the east bank of the
Wabash river.[2] Here Harrison joined his army October
6th, and while waiting and wondering what to do next he
had a small wooden fort built to which was given his own
name. While engaged in this work one of his men was
fired at and wounded on the night of October 10th. On
the 12th Eustis's letter of September 18th was received.
This letter together with the atrocity of two days before,
was taken as a warrant for more aggressive action. Re-
enforcing his troops by two of the four companies remaining at Vincennes, and having just completed the fort,
he broke camp at Ft. Harrison, sent a message ahead to
the Prophet demanding that the Indians at his town return to their tribes. The army crossed the Wabash to
avoid the woods and then crossed the Vermillion river,
which marked the boundary line between the last cession
and the Indian lands. Fifty miles further up the Wabash
brought them to the Prophet's town. When they came
near this place some of Harrison's officers favored at-

1. This letter is referred to by Henry Adams in his History of the United
States, Vol. 6, p. 95, as "never published though often referred to, which is not
found in the records of the government." I found the letter among others in
the Department of State. It would naturally be found among the manuscripts
of the War Department archives, but some of this manuscript material has
been lodged in the State Department.

2. The main part of the army left Vincennes, September 26th, and encamped on the future site of Ft. Harrison, October 3d.—Dillon, p. 461.

tack, but Harrison did not feel authorized to go so far until he should first know whether the Indians would disband as he had demanded. This was on November 6th. The army marched to within one hundred and fifty yards of the town, when the Indians, becoming alarmed, called on them to halt and Harrison complied with their wishes. He then asked them to show him a place for encampment, which they did, as it had been agreed to hold the council the following day. Harrison had about 900 men and the Indians, had probably from 600 to 800 effective warriors.[1]   On the following morning, November 7th, soon after four o'clock, Harrison's camp was attacked in the darkness and a hard two hours' fight ensued. The loss to the army, as given in Harrison's official report of November 18th,[2] was: Killed, 37; wounded, since dead, 25; wounded, 126. Total killed and wounded, 188. The bodies of thirty-eight Indians were found on the field; but their total loss is unknown, for they carried off and buried some of their dead.

The Battle of Tippecanoe was fought so many times on paper afterward that there is no need for a lengthy discussion of it here. Todd and Drake, in their Life of Harrison, written in 1840, say that "No battle ever fought in the United States has been more extensively examined or severely criticized than the battle of Tippecanoe."

The three chief subjects of controversy in regard to the battle were: First, Harrison's motives and justification in taking his army into the Indian territory. Secondly, as to whether the attack was really a *surprise* to Harrison and his army. Thirdly, as to whether the militia (Harri-

---

1. The Prophet's town contained about two thousand population, including women and children.—Pirtle's "Battle of Tippecanoe."
2. American State Papers, Indian Affairs 1, 776-779.

son's long time hobby) made a creditable showing in this
battle, especially as compared with the regulars.

As to the first question, Harrison has been charged with
being too eager and aggressive in bringing on the issue
in order that his popularity and fame might be increased,
and to gratify his military ambitions. He knew that a
victory would bring military glory and increase his popularity, and his critics think that he went out of his way
unduly to achieve this object. That he was eager to defeat the Indians seems certain, and this eagerness was
also certainly shared by most of his army; but he had
been advised by both Governors, Edwards and Howard,
to break up the Indian village if they would not disperse.[1] But there seems to have been no intention on Harrison's part to attack the Indians unless they should refuse to remove from their settlement on the Tippecanoe.
In closing a letter of March 26, 1812, to Governor Edwards, Harrison wrote:[2] "A member of Congress who
affects to be a friend of mine wrote to me the other day
that the Secretary of War had submitted to him all our
letters on Indian affairs for the last two years, and he
really could not see that we had any just ground for
undertaking a military expedition against the Prophet,
and that if he had not attacked my troops the affair would
have been a serious one for the President and myself.
I have indeed for some time expected to be called to
Washington to answer for my invasion of the Indian
territory."[3] I can make no better exposition of the situation than to quote further Harrison's words in the same
letter, which apply to the whole Indian question. "But
my friend, you may rely upon it that we have a most

1. Todd & Drake, p. 81.
2. Clark Papers.
3. This expectation was never realized.

difficult part to act. Those who are in safety at a distance and who judge of events after they have happened are strongly disposed to condemn our measures. If we use prompt and energetic measures and thereby avert war, 'Why,' say these gentlemen, 'the Indians who are perfectly pacific are imposed upon and made to hate us by the folly and vindictive disposition of the agents.' If we sit still and do nothing, these very persons would unite with the representatives of the people in declaring us unfit for our stations."

The attack was certainly a surprise although the army was by no means altogether unprepared for it. The Indians had promised on the preceding day a suspension of hostilities until after an interview on the following day. Upon Harrison's request, they then selected the place for his encampment, which was not altogether such as he could wish it, "for" as he himself said, "it afforded great facility to the approach of savages."[1] Harrison's critics of that time charged him with unpardonable stupidity in entering such a trap.[2] By Harrison's direction, the order of encampment was the order of battle. The men slept opposite their posts in the line, with clothes and accouterments on, with arms loaded and bayonets fixed. Only a single line of sentries was purposely posted, because Harrison said that "in Indian warfare, where there is no shock to resist, one rank is nearly as good as two,

1. Harrison's Official Report, State Papers, Indian Affairs I, 776.

2. See especially Marshall's History of Kentucky, Vol. II, for a bitter criticism of Harrison's tactics and policy throughout this campaign. Marshall had lost one of his relatives in this battle, for which he held Harrison responsible.—See Pirtle's Battle of Tippecanoe, Filson Club Publications. For further interesting material on the Tippecanoe campaign, see the "Indiana Quarterly Magazine of History," December, 1906. This contains the account lately brought to light, of Isaac Naylor, who took part in the campaign; also the Tippecanoe Journal, of John Tipton, who participated in the campaign and battle.

and the extension of the line is a matter of first importance. Raw troops also manoeuvre with more facility in
single ranks." Harrison states further that he rose at
4:15 on the morning of November 7th, and that the signal for calling out the men would have been given in two
minutes, when the attack was made. It began on the
left flank. "But a single gun was fired by the sentinels
or by the guard in that direction, which made not the least
resistance, but abandoned their officer and fled into camp,
and the first notice which the troops of that flank had of
the danger was from the yells of the savages within a
short distance of the line." Thus reads Harrison's official
report of the attack, dated at Vincennes eleven days after
the battle.

The origin of the bitter controversy about the militia
arose from two facts: First, that some of the subordi-
nates commanding the regulars—Colonel Boyd and Captain Prescott, in particular—were jealous of Harrison
and his hobby, the militia; and secondly, that in the early
part of the battle some of the militia were forced to retreat from an untenable position. But they soon rallied
and won much credit. This unfortunate repulse was
taken advantage of by some of the Fourth Regiment, who
hinted that the victory was due to the regulars. Harrison, however, wrote in his official report that where merit
was so common it was almost impossible to discriminate.[1]

1. The battlefield of Tippecanoe is right by the west side of the Monon
railway a few miles above LaFayette, Indiana, and an excellent view of it may
be had from the car window in passing. It is surrounded by a high iron fence
and sites are marked by forest trees and monuments. For a map of the field
see Pirtle: The Battle of Tippecanoe, Filson Club Publications; also the "Indiana Quarterly Magazine of History" for December, 1906.

CHAPTER XI.

EFFECTS OF TIPPECANOE AND SUBSEQUENT INDIAN AND MILITARY AFFAIRS.

The immediate effect of the battle of Tippecanoe was to break up the Prophet's town and overthrow his influence. He had told his followers that they would have an easy victory and that they were invulnerable to the bullets of their enemies. But now his teaching had proven false and his followers deserted him. By November 18th Harrison's army had arrived again at Vincennes and though he was severely criticised by some, as I have said, on the whole he was highly praised and was the hero of the time. He had established himself as the military leader of the Northwest. At a meeting of a number of subordinate officers and privates of his army held at Vincennes December 7th, it was resolved unanimously: "That it was owing to the skill and valor of the commander-in-chief, that the victory of Tippecanoe was obtained; That we have the most perfect confidence in him and shall always feel a cheerfulness in serving under him whenever, the exigencies of the country may require it."[1] The legislatures both of Indiana and Kentucky passed resolutions expressing the highest praise and appreciation of his services. The Kentucky legislature resolved that Harrison "behaved like a hero, a patriot and a general and that for his cool, deliberate, skillful and gallant conduct he well deserved the warmest thanks of the nation." A letter to Harrison from Eustis, Secretary of War, dated December 11, 1811, reads: "I congratulate your Excellency on the successful and impor-

---

1. Western Sun.

tant issue of a conflict unparalleled in our history and express to you the great satisfaction derived from the firm and gallant conduct manifested by the troops, both regulars and militia, under circumstances calculated to test the discipline of veterans and the courage of heroes." In his message of December 18th to Congress President Madison said in regard to this battle: "Congress will see with satisfaction the dauntless spirit and fortitude displayed by every description of the troops engaged, as well as the collected firmness which distinguished their commander on an occasion requiring the utmost exertion of valor and discipline."

But despite all these eloquent and appreciative expressions, the peace and quiet on the border was of short duration. Tecumseh soon afterward returned from the south and the Prophet returned to the Tippecanoe. Tecumseh, however, blamed his brother for the battle and said if he had been there it would not have occurred. The Prophet had spoiled Tecumseh's plan by throwing off the mask too soon.[1] Tecumseh sent Harrison a short message informing him of his return and that he was now ready to visit the President and come to an agreement with him. Harrison consented that he might accompany the other Indians[2] but not as their leader. This proposition displeased Tecumseh and the visit was not made.[3] In February still, the Indians seemed peaceful, but in March and April a renewed reign of terror ensued and several cold-blooded murders took place. Tecumseh, however, denied all responsibility for these and said they were committed by Potawatomies and others

1. Letter of Harrison to Eustis, March 4, 1812.
2. Harrison was given authority by letter from Eustis, January 17th, to send the Indians to Washington.
3. North American Review Vol. 73, p. 414.

not under his control. In his letter to Edwards, March 26th, already referred to, Harrison wrote, "The murders on the Mississippi and Illinois rivers are certainly alarming in the highest degree and I can not see how we can avoid a general war."

On April 14, 1812, Harrison wrote Eustis:[1] "It is with great regret that I inform you that the hopes which I had entertained of our being able to avoid a war with the Indians are entirely dissipated. The Prophet and his brother were either altogether insincere in the professions which they made in February or they have been induced to adopt other policies in consequence of the probability of war between the United States and Great Britain. Messrs. Shaw and Wells have, I presume, informed you of the grounds which they have for believing that they are again organizing a force for hostile purposes. * * * * We have, in my opinion, no alternative but war. The propriety of its being undertaken immediately and prosecuted with vigor is an opinion which pervades, I believe, the whole western country. In Kentucky and in this Territory, I know that it does." On April 16th Harrison ordered the militia to be mustered and put in readiness in all the counties. Murders were committed in all parts of the Territory alike and in rapid succession. Harrison wrote Eustis again[2] April 29th, that "The design is to distract and divide our attention and prevent the militia from embodying, and certainly no plan could be more successful than that which they have fallen upon." Again, May 6th, he wrote him:[3] "Most of the citizens in this country (i. e., on White river) have abandoned their farms and taken refuge in such temporary forts as

1. Draper Collection, Harrison Papers.
2. Draper Collection, Harrison Papers.
3. Ibid.

they have been able to construct. Nothing can exhibit more distress than those wretched people crowded together in places almost destitute of every necessary accommodation. Unless something can be done soon to enable the people to return to their farms, I fear that there will be little corn planted this season." But Tecumseh himself was not ready to take up the tomahawk yet, and awaited developments between the United States and England. When this war was declared and he could find such a powerful and now open ally as England, he was not long in resuming hostilities.

During the winter and spring following the battle of Tippecanoe Harrison's attention was too much occupied with Indian affairs to attend to civil administration. In the following summer this was still more the case and he was called to wider and wider fields of military service, and soon lost all official connection with the civil affairs of the Territory. In the spring of 1812 the President assigned Harrison the task of defending the Territories, and two-thirds of the Kentucky quota of militia were subjected to his orders. The other third were destined to support General Hull's expedition, and when the report came of his retreat to Detroit, they were put under marching orders under Brigadier General Payne[1] Meanwhile, on July 9th, Secretary Eustis wrote Harrison[2] that in view of the impending conflict with the Indians, he should keep in touch with Governor Edwards and the Governor of Kentucky and have their co-operation and advice. The Secretary further wrote that "should offensive measures become necessary the command within Indiana Territory will devolve upon you,

1. Autobiographical letter, 1879.
2. Letters in Bureau of Rolls and Library, Dept. of State. See also letter of Harrison to Edwards written from Jeffersonville, August 17.—Clark Papers.

and with Governor Edwards' consent, that also in Illinois." Nine days later, July 18th, the Secretary wrote Harrison, authorizing him to raise and organize 1,500 volunteers for the war with England, and suggesting that when this should be done a commission of Brigadier-General should be given him as their commander. Before receiving this letter, however, Harrison had gone to Cincinnati to visit his family, where he received an express from Governor Scott requesting him to come without delay to Frankfort. Upon arriving at Frankfort Governor Scott informed him that it had been unanimously determined, in a Grand Council composed of Governor-elect Shelby and all the principal citizens then at Frankfort, to request him to take command of the troops then under Payne's command, which were starting for the relief of General Hull. The legal impediment to commanding beyond his own Territory would be overcome, Governor Scott explained, by appointing him a Major-General in the Kentucky militia. Harrison accepted the appointment August 25th and in a few hours was on horseback to overtake the troops. Harrison afterward wrote:[1] "I look upon this to be the most honorable appointment I have ever received—a great State, already conspicuous for the talents of her sons, placing a person belonging to another government in the command of her troops for a difficult and dangerous expedition, to the prejudice of her own generals, some of whom were experienced officers in the Revolutionary War. It was the more grateful to my feelings because I had been blamed by some of the Federal papers for the affair of Tippecanoe, in which Kentucky had suffered the loss of two of her distinguished citizens. In the army now subjected to my

---

1. Autobiographical letter, 1839

command, there were a vast number of that description; among others, two members of Congress, one of them in the ranks."

While on this expedition, on September 2d, near Piqua, Ohio, he was overtaken by an express from the War Department appointing him Brigadier-General in the United States army and assigning him to the command of the troops of Indiana and Illinois Territories.[1] On the 24th of September he received a letter from Secretary Eustis saying that in taking the command on the frontier he had anticipated the wishes of the President and a few days later he received the formal appointment, dated September 17th, to the command of the whole army of the Northwest.[2] In the letter of appointment Secretary Eustis wrote: "You will command such means as may be practicable—exercise your own discretion, and act in all cases according to your own judgment."

From this time Harrison's entire attention was confined to the war, and Secretary Gibson acted as Governor of Indiana Territory until the appointment in the following May of Thomas Posey.

CHAPTER XII.

HARRISON'S REMUNERATION—THE LETTERS OF "DECIUS" AND OTHER ACCUSATIONS AND VINDICATIONS.

The Federal pay-roll for the territorial officials of Indiana in 1802 was $2,000 for the Governor, $750 for the Secretary and $800 for each of the three Judges.[3] But by Act of Congress, approved March 3, 1807, all terri-

---

1. Todd & Drake's Sketches of Harrison.
2. Todd & Drake's Sketches of Harrison.
3. Amer. State Papers, Misc. I, p. 306.

torial judges were allowed $1,200 per annum, and by Act of December 15, 1807, territorial Secretaries were given salaries of $1,000. In writing to President Jefferson,[1] June 18, 1805, Harrison suggests the propriety of making a small addition to his salary as Superintendent of Indian Affairs, saying that he received for his services in this department $800 per annum, which was considerably, less than any of the agents were allowed. "I have never received a single sixpence," he says, "for issuing licenses to trade with the Indians—a practice which gave to my predecessor at least $1,000 per annum." He also refers to his predecessors in Louisiana Territory as receiving the $25 fee allowed under that government for issuing licenses: but even of this, Harrison had declined to avail himself. In a letter from Jefferson to Harrison, dated January 16, 1806,[2] he says: "I have earnestly inculcated the necessity of raising the salaries of the territorial Governors and Judges, and it will be attempted this session, but with what success is very doubtful." We find no law of this session increasing his salary, but after receiving his third commission in 1806 Harrison wrote Jefferson,[3] July 5, "The emoluments of my office afford me a decent support and will, I hope, from henceforth enable me to lay up a small fund for the education of my children."[4]

---

1. State Department Archives.

2. State Department Archives

3. Ibid.

4. Harrison continues in this letter: "I have found, however, that my nursery fills much faster than my strong box, and if our future progress in this way is as great as it has been, and our government should adopt the Roman policy of bestowing rewards on those who contribute most to the population of the country, I do not despair of obtaining the highest premium." We may note in this connection that of the ten children born to W. H. and Mrs. Harrison, five were born while he was Governor of Indiana.—See Harrison family tree by C. P. Keith; published by Lippincott (1893).

In his autobiographical letter of 1839. Harrison said that he was allowed in addition to his pay as Governor, $6 per day and expenses while acting as Commissioner, and that he could assume that character whenever he thought proper. That he was almost constantly acting under it, but as it was difficult to separate the duties of Commissioner from those ordinarily performed by him as Superintendent, he charged in the former character only for the time actually employed in a specific negotiation. All the compensation he received during the whole time he held the commission, he says, did not exceed $3,000, and perhaps not $2,000. His charge for one important treaty was $44. He adds: "I followed the fashion of those times in this course. The systematic plunder of the treasury by the public officers was not then understood."

The public servant has ever been, and will always continue to be criticized, and from this tonic of course Harrison could not escape. Repeatedly he was the victim of bitter attack, but in every case, so far as we know, he was vindicated. Of these cases we shall refer to the three chief ones. The first and most vehement of these attacks was in the summer and autumn of 1805 and consisted of a series of letters written by Isaac Darneille under the pseudonyms of Decius and Philo Decius. These letters were published at the time in a Louisville paper, "The Farmer's Library," edited by Joshua Vail. Later, December 10, 1805. they were collected and published in a pamphlet at Louisville for the author. The letters were dated and addressed as follows: May 10, 1805, to the members of the Indiana Territorial Legislature; August 1, 1805, to the same; October 10, 1805. Congratulatory Address to the Hon. Benjamin Park, Esq., Delegate to

Congress from Indiana Territory; October 15, 1805, letter to Harrison; December 1, 1805, Eleven "Charges against Harrison addressed to James Madison, Secretary of the United States, to be by him laid before the President and the Senate."

The first letter to the Legislature complains that the people were led into the second grade of government "by a whimsical and capricious executive;" warns them of the importance of having 'a good representative in Congress and against the influence of the executive in choosing him. "Decius" recommends Thomas T. Davis for representative to Congress, and says, "You wish to encourage emigration to your country. This is not the interest nor the wish of the Governor. His government and salary will become precarious as population increases." The second letter says that when a change of administration had taken place in the general government the tenure of Harrison's commission had rendered his government precarious, and petitions were circulated in the fall of 1802 addressed to the President and praying for Harrison's reappointment as Governor. The third letter, the "Congratulatory Address," to Benjamin Park, is more bitter and is full of sarcasm. It refers to Park as the sycophant of Harrison and advises him in conclusion: "Cease, viper, for you bite against a file." The fourth letter, which is addressed to Harrison, says: "From the firmest Federalist you wheeled about like the cock on a steeple and declared yourself a Republican.[1] To gain favor you have dealt out commissions. For the sake of popularity you even commissioned three persons who had been indicted for horse-stealing a few years before.[2] * * *

1. In answer to this charge, the reader is referred to the testimony of Jacob Burnett already given, pp. 186-187.

2. These were persons named Whiteside living in St. Clair county.

You refused to confirm grants of land to those who had not voted for you, although their claims were good, the same as those of your friends, which you granted. * * * You withheld confirmation of titles to those in the western counties till you had secured their petitions for your re-appointment, thus using their lack of land titles as a lever to secure their votes. * * * The *primum mobile* of your conduct is your salary. To every other consideration you are perfectly indifferent.~ * * * * In order to effect the destruction of political opponents, you stooped from the station of a Governor to the low drudgery of fabrication, calumny, tale-bearing and defamation." The fifth and last of these letters, addressed to Madison, set forth, as we have seen, eleven charges against Harrison. These are largely a repetition of those already made, but with more detail. The first states that Harrison had shown notorious partiality and had unjustly discriminated against "Decius" himself by refusing his claim to a land title while granting claims to others under precisely similar circumstances. Another charge was that Harrison had interfered in a lawsuit for the emancipation of two negroes and induced them to bind themselves to him for eleven years, while before in a similar suit the negroes had been discharged. Decius argued that either the negroes were entitled to freedom or they were not, so that Harrison was infringing either, upon the rights of the negroes or of those who owned them.[1] Again he was charged with neglect of duty in Louisiana, in not appointing militia officers and thus leaving the districts without organized militia to protect them against the savages.

---

1. See also Record General Court, September term, 1801.

Such was the gist of the charges in the Letters of "Decius." The next note I find upon the subject is in a letter from Harrison to Jefferson[1] dated July 5, 1806. "I have taken the liberty to enclose herewith a paragraph from the 'Farmers' Library,' the vehicle of the abuse which a certain Isaac Darneille has poured upon me for many months past, under the signature of Decius, and which I believe was forwarded to you subscribed with his own name. This recantation was not extorted by the dread of powder and ball or steel—arguments which I have long declined the use of in private quarrels, but from the dread of the indignation of twelve of the citizens of Kentucky who were about to decide upon the merits of his accusations." Though the writer did not find this recantation, he found something almost as convincing, published in the "Palladium," a Frankfort (Ky.) paper of that day, under date of August 14, 1806. It is a statement signed by J. Vail, and reads as follows: "Having waited on Mr. Isaac Darneille, the author of the letters of Decius and Philo Decius, and finding him altogether incompetent to support the charges contained in said letters, I conceive it due to Governor Harrison's public as well as private character to express my disbelief of every insinuation contained in said letters against him; and thus publicly inform him of the author's name. Although I have no hesitation in expressing the above opinion of the charges which Mr. Darneille has exhibited against Governor Harrison, I nevertheless conceive that his public acts (and those of every other officer in the government) are proper subjects for public investigation so long as

1. State Department Archives.

truth is adhered to; but when that is wantonly departed from, the author should be held up to public detestation."[1]

I suppose that this J. Vail was Joshua Vail, the editor of the "Farmers' Library" in which the letters of Decius had been published. Decius had evidently received no favors from Harrison and felt sore. But the radical and abusive expressions at the close of his letter to Harrison are self-condemning.

In the summer of 1807 Dr. McKee wrote a series of attacks in the columns of the Western Sun on the fraudulent dealings of the land agents. He signed his article, "A Friend to the Commissioners," and at first expressly excepted Harrison from the charge. But finally he made some sweeping statements which included Harrison by implication. The charge was that rival companies or parties, to one of which Harrison belonged, would buy each other off from bidding on lands which they both desired. This brought forth a public reply from Harrison in the Western Sun of September 19th in which he cleared himself absolutely of any wrong doing, and this article was followed by the testimony of witnesses that McKee himself had admitted in their presence that Harrison had done no wrong. This was Harrison's first participation in a newspaper controversy.

The third and last attack on Harrison which I shall mention occurred in the spring of 1811. The report was circulated that Harrison had cheated the Indians out of their lands and was thus responsible for all the ill will of

1. The writer found the files of the "Palladium" and the incomplete files of the "Farmer's Library" in the library of Col. R. T. Durrett, Louisville, Ky.; while the brochure containing the letters of Decius was found in the Library of Congress. The small and incomplete file of the "Farmer's Library" preserved by Col. Durrett seems to be the only one in existence; and it does not contain the paragraph of recantation referred to by Harrison.

the Indians toward the whites, etc.[1] Harrison offered
$100 for the name of the originator of the report, and
upon learning that it was William McIntosh, he brought
suit against him for slander. The case was tried in the
General Court at Vincennes, April 11, 1811.[2]   Of the
three judges, Parks was a special friend of Harrison, and
Vanderburg a special friend of McIntosh, and so they declined to sit, which left Waller Taylor as sole judge. The
jury found McIntosh guilty and Harrison was awarded
$4,000 damages.   Harrison afterward returned about
two-thirds of this sum to McIntosh and distributed the
remainder among orphans of soldiers of the war of
1812.[3] In writing of this case to Secretary Eustis April
23d, 1811, Harrison said: "No defendant in such a case
was ever allowed so much latitude as he was by my particular direction to my attorneys. He was allowed to
bring forward testimony wholly irrelevant to the case. In
fact, every part of my conduct and administration for ten
years was scrutinized. After twenty-five witnesses were
examined, the rascally calumniator begged for mercy and
his counsel labored only for a mitigation of damages."

In conclusion, perhaps it is not too much to say, with
J. P. Dunn,[4] that "No man in public life ever had so
many serious charges preferred against his honesty and
came forth from his trials so fully vindicated by his
judges and by the people as did William Henry Harrison."

1. Letter of Harrison to Eustis, April 23, 1811, Draper Collection.
2. Court Records.
3. Dawson, p. 176. Dillon, p. 455.
4. Dunn's Indiana, p. 414.

NOTES.

1. Founding of Jeffersonville.—Harrison wrote to Jefferson August 6, 1802, (State Department Archives): "When I had the honor to see you in Philadelphia in the spring of 1800, you were pleased to recommend to me a plan for a town which you supposed would exempt its inhabitants in a great degree from pestilences." * * * * A town has been laid out with each alternate square to remain vacant forever (excepting one range of squares upon the river) and I have taken the liberty to call it Jeffersonville. * * * * It is my ardent wish that the town may become worthy of the name it bears and that the humane and benevolent views which dictated the plan may be realized." In a letter from Jefferson to Harrison February 27, 1803, (Jefferson's Works) the president explains more fully his sanitary and aesthetic ideas on this subject. But in another letter from Harrison to Jefferson, October 29, 1803, (State Department Archives) he writes that "The streets of Jeffersonville were made to pass diagonally through the squares and not parallel with them, as I knew to be your intention. But the proprietor was so parsimonious that he would not suffer it to be laid out in that manner." We may add that the plan of leaving alternate squares vacant has also been ignored.

2. The "Indiana Gazette" and "Western Sun."—Elihu Stout, the government printer for the territory, came from Kentucky to Vincennes, and on July 4, 1804, issued the first number of the "Indiana Gazette." After about eighteen months, his establishment was burned and none of the Gazettes have been preserved. [1 copy for April 12, 1806, is found in Vol. 4 of Western Sun at Indiana State Library—Editor]. He resumed the work July 4, 1807, entitling his paper the "Western Sun," with "Truth its guide; Liberty its object." This publication was continued about forty years. The only complete files of it which were preserved were those of its editor and these have been secured by the State Library at Indianapolis. It was a weekly paper containing four pages about 12x18 inches. As it was the only publication in the territory under Harrison and is the only place where the journals of the legislature have been published, it is an invaluable source of information.

3. The Salt Springs.—One of the most important industries of the territory arose from the Salt Springs near the mouth of the Wabash. In the spring of 1802 the Secretary of War, by the direction of Jefferson, advised Harrison to lease these springs. Harrison opposed leasing because it would afford only a small allowance to each tribe and thus provoke discontent. He urged buying them outright, along with a surrounding tract, and this was accordingly done. Harrison wrote Jefferson October 29, 1803, (State Department Archives) that the plan thus adopted and the prospect of securing salt at the reduced price of fifty cents a bushel had "diffused a general joy amongst the citizens of this territory and the states of Kentucky and Tennessee." In the "Western Sun" of April 22, 1809, the agent of the springs writes: "Next week the works will make at least 2,000 bushels of salt, with a prospect of increasing the quantity."

4. Census of 1810.—This census gave the territory a population of 24,520. Also thirty-three grist mills, fourteen saw mills, three horse mills, eighteen tanneries, twenty-eight distilleries, three powder mills, 1,256 looms, 1,350 spinning wheels. Value of manufactures for 1810 about $200,000, largely home made fabrics of cotton, wool, hemp and flax. The population of Cincinnati at this time was 2,223; Louisville, 1,353. In writing of Illinois in 1810, Davidson and Stuve, in their History of Illinois (p. 240) say: "Nine-tenths of the territory was a howling wilderness over which red savages held dominion and roamed at will, outnumbering the whites at least three to one." But up on Lake Michigan in 1804 Fort Dearborn had been erected, the germ of the future city of Chicago.

5. Duelling.—This evil was often threatened and occasionally practiced in Indiana Territory under Harrison. The "Western Sun" contains considerable literature on the subject. An example will illustrate the popular view of the subject. Just after the election of 1809 Waller Taylor wrote Thomas Randolph as follows: "I expect you will have passed through the list of your enemies in asking them over the Wabash to partake of your company and the amusement you wish to afford them. I make no doubt they will decline your invitation, although it may be couched in the most polite and ceremonious style. If they do, you will have acquitted yourself agreeable to the rules of modern etiquette, and can then be at liberty to act toward them in whatever way may best suit your honor." In one instance, at least, Mr. Randolph followed Mr. Taylor's suggestion, for it was soon after this that he wrote Dr. Elias McNamee as follows: "I hope a polite invitation to meet me on the other side of the river Wabash in the Illinois Territory will be accepted." It will be recalled that Taylor and Randolph were candidates for Congress and were leading lights in the territory. This particular invitation, however, was not accepted. Harrison's attitude on the subject in the war of 1812, is shown in an article written by him in 1838 (Clark Papers) in which he says that when he took command of the Northwestern army, he used all his authority and influence to prevent it; that the soldiers of the Northwest Territory had been much in the habit of it, but that there never was a duel fought by any of his men after he assumed the command, nor so far as he knew, a challenge given.

6. Intellectual Life at Vincennes.—At the time of the organization of the territory the population of Vincennes were mostly French and half-breed creoles who were unable to read or write. But with the establishment of the seat of government there and the influx of American settlers, conditions began to improve. A large number of able lawyers made the Vincennes Bar unusually strong. In 1806 the young men organized a dramatic (See Sol Smith's "Theatrical Management, etc., pp. 20-21) society, known as the "Thespian Society," which gave frequent entertainments and theatrical plays. It flourished through the territorial period and long afterward. In 1807 a Medical Society was organized, which also continued with vigor till long after statehood. Its membership embraced the physicians and surgeons of the army stationed there. In 1808 the Vincennes Library was founded, and contained from three thousand to four thou-

sand volumes almost from the first. Governor Harrison is said to
have contributed many volumes to it. In this year also the "Vincennes Historical and Antiquarian Society" was organized. On
February 22, 1839, Judge John Law delivered before this society his
great lecture on the Early Settlement of Vincennes. In 1800 the
first Bible Society was organized and led by Benjamin Parke. In
1800 also was organized the "Vincennes Society for the Encouragement of Agriculture and the Useful Arts." This society was especially helpful and was the forerunner of the State Board of Agriculture Incorporated in 1852. In the fall of 1809, only a few months
after its organization, it distributed premiums at the fair amount-
ing to $400. Sheep husbandry and the cultivation of hemp and the
manufacture of cloths were much encouraged in this way. The
mail was brought on horseback from Louisville and Kaskaskia once
a week and returned. (These facts have been gleaned from the
"Western Sun" and from W. H. Venable's "Beginnings of Literary
Culture in the Ohio Valley," the chapter on Indiana by H. S. Cau-
thorn of Vincennes).

INDIANA HISTORICAL SOCIETY PUBLICATIONS

VOLUME IV NUMBER 4

MAKING A CAPITAL IN THE WILDERNESS

BY

DANIEL WAIT HOWE

INDIANAPOLIS

Edward J. Hecker, Printer and Publisher

1908

PREFATORY

The first printed history of Indianapolis was prepared by Ignatius Brown, now deceased, and was published as part of Howard's City Directory for 1857. It was subsequently carefully revised and published as part of Logan's City Directory for 1868. Mr. Brown was formerly a lawyer and afterward a real estate abstractor, and his familiarity with the city's history and records and his accuracy were universally conceded. His history was prepared with great care and after many consultations with old settlers, in order to settle questions about which there was dispute or doubt, and it is the basis of all the subsequent histories of the city and of Marion county.

Mr. Brown retained a copy of his history, containing many annotations made by him, which is now in the possession of his son, Lynn C. Brown, to whom I am indebted for the privilege of examining it while preparing this paper.

I am also indebted to Mr. John H. Holliday for the privilege of making extracts from General John Tipton's Journal, now in his possession, and to Mr. William A. Ketcham for the privilege of making extracts from the journal of his mother, Mrs. Jane M. Ketcham, widow of the late John L. Ketcham, and daughter of Samuel Merrill, Treasurer of State at the time of the removal of the capital from Corydon to Indianapolis.

(301)

MAKING A CAPITAL IN THE WILDERNESS

The act of Congress providing for the admission of the State of Indiana into the Union was approved April 18, 1816. Its conditions were accepted by a convention of the people of the territory at Corydon June 29, 1816,[1] and this was followed by a congressional joint resolution passed December 11, 1816, for the admission of the State. The act of Congress provided: "That four sections of land be, and the same are, hereby granted to the said State, for the purpose of fixing their seat of government thereon, which four sections shall under the direction of the Legislature of said State, be located at any time in such township and range as the Legislature aforesaid may select, on such lands as may hereafter be acquired by the United States, from the Indian tribes within the said territory; *Provided*: That such location shall be made prior to the public sale of the lands of the United States, surrounding such location."

At the time of the admission of the State it contained a population estimated at near 70,000. Thirteen counties had been organized and provided with offices and machinery for civil government. These were all in the southern part of the State, except a tier on the east side, the northernmost of which was Randolph county. The seat of government was then at Corydon.

The Indians were still in possession of the remainder of the State. Treaties had been made with various In-

[1] R. S. 1824, p. 33.

(303)

dian tribes by which they had ceded to the United States portions of the territory in central Indiana, and on October 3, 1818, a treaty with the Delawares was made at St. Marys, Ohio, by which they relinquished their title to the vast tract thereafter known as the New Purchase. The treaty provided that the Indians should retain possession for three years. On the 6th of the same month the Miamis ceded their rights in the same territory, excepting only the portions included in a few small reservations.

The General Assembly, by an act passed January 22, 1820,[1] created out of the newly acquired territory two counties—Delaware and Wabash—but these were not then provided with a county organization. Out of them were subsequently carved about twenty-seven new counties.

The tract known as the New Purchase was of irregular shape. Supposing the State to be divided from east to west into three parts, it included nearly all the central, and part of the north third, and was estimated to contain about 13,000 square miles, or 8,500,000 acres—a little over one-third of the area of the State.[2] Through it ran the Wabash, the east and west forks of White river, and other tributaries of the Wabash.

The mound builders had once inhabited the country and had left traces of their occupation in Madison, Hamilton and other counties included in the New Purchase. They had been succeeded by the Indians.

Of the Indians who lived or roamed in Indiana prior to the middle of the seventeenth century, little is known beyond traditions that vanish into the shadows of the past.

---

[1] Acts 1819-'20, p. 95.
[2] A map showing its location will be found in the Indiana Legislative Manual for 1903, p. 440.

From the middle to the close of the seventeenth century we catch occasional glimpses, chiefly in the writings of the French missionaries, agents, traders and explorers, of the restless and roving Indian tribes of the northwest, continually being pushed forward in their migrations by some mighty force behind them like that which impelled the Goths and Vandals in their invasions of the Roman Empire. These tribes were perpetually carrying on wars with one another or with enemies more remote, like the fierce Iroquois in the east or the fiercer Sioux in the northwest—wars in which sometimes whole tribes were exterminated or absorbed in other tribes and their very names became lost in oblivion.

By the year 1718 the Miamis, after a series of migrations extending over a period of a century or more, occupied or claimed nearly all the territory now included in Indiana, except the north portion, then occupied by the Pottawattomies, and a portion in the southern part of the State. This was the portion separated by the Ohio river from the region designated by the Indians, long before it was known to the white men, as the dark and bloody ground, a region mostly traversed by the Indians only when on the war-path and in which no red man ventured to build his wigwam.

The Miamis had become a great confederation, including four principal tribes—the Twightwees, the Weas or Ouiatanons, the Eel Rivers and the Piankashaws,—the most powerful of the Indian confederations in the northwest and fully able, after getting arms and ammunition, to resist the aggressions of their traditional enemies, the Iroquois, who, until near the close of the seventeenth century, had long waged unceasing and relentless warfare on the tribes between them and the Mississippi.

"According to the best traditional authorities, the do-

minion of the Miami Confederacy extended, for a long
period of time, over that part of the State of Ohio which
lies west of the Scioto river, over the whole of Indiana,
over the southern part of Michigan, and over that part
of the State of Illinois which lies southeast of the Fox
river and the river Illinois. The Miamis, proper, whose
old national name was Twightwees, formed the eastern
and most powerful branch of this confederacy. They
have preserved no tradition of their migrations as a tribe
from one country to another. * * * Neither the
names nor the numbers of the several kindred tribes of
the ancient Miami Confederacy can now be stated with
accuracy. * * * In the early part of the eighteenth
century, and perhaps for a long period before that time,
the Miamis had villages at various suitable places within the boundaries of their large territory. Some of these
villages were on the banks of the Scioto, a few were situated in the country about the headwaters of the great
Miami, some stood on the banks of the river Maumee,
others on the St. Joseph, and many were founded on the
banks of the Wabash and on some of the principal tributaries of that river.'" "In 1765 the Miami Nation or Confederacy was composed of four tribes whose total number of warriors was estimated at one thousand and fifty
men. Of this number, there were two hundred and fifty
Twightwees, three hundred Weas or Ouiatanons, three
hundred Piankashaws and two hundred Shockeys. The
principal villages of the Twightwees were situated on the
headwaters of the Maumee river, at or near the site of the
town of Fort Wayne. The larger Wea villages were
found near the banks of the Wabash in the vicinity of
Ouiatanon and the Shockeys and Piankashaws lived on

'Dillon's "The National Decline of the Miami Indians," Indiana
Historical Society Publications, vol. I, pp. 122, 123.

the banks of the Vermillion river and on the river Wabash, between Vincennes and Ouiatanon. At different periods branches of the Pottawattomies, Shawnees, Delawares and Kickapoos were permitted to enter and reside at various places within the boundary of the large territory which was claimed by the Miamis."[1]

Great changes occurred in the Indian population of the territory now included in Ohio and Indiana between 1750 and the close of the century, especially after the treaty of Greenville in 1795. By that time many of the Indian tribes had lost large numbers by war and disease and some had been nearly exterminated.

After the treaty at Greenville in 1795, most of the Indians in Ohio sought homes elsewhere, large numbers of the Delawares and Shawnees and a portion of the Wyandotts or Hurons going to the territory now included in Indiana. Portions of these and other tribes had migrated to this region before the treaty at Greenville, but the dates of their first coming can not be definitely fixed. At the time of the acquisition of the New Purchase, in 1818, it is said that the Indian tribes then inhabiting Indiana were the "Mascoutins, Piankashaws, Kickapoos, Delawares, Miamis, Shawnees, Weas, Ouiatanons, Eel Rivers, Hurons and Pottawattomies."[2] Of these the Pottawattomies were most numerous. They had five villages on the Elkhart branch of the St. Joseph, and several other villages in the northern part of the State. Most of the other tribes resided at various points in the New Purchase. The Miamis and their branches and allies, the Weas or Ouiatanons, the Eel Rivers and the Piankashaws, had villages on the upper Wabash and

---

[1]*Id.*, p. 133.

[2]Brown's "Western Gazeteer and Emigrant's Directory," pp. 71-73, published at Auburn, N. Y., in 1817.

its tributaries. One of these was at Fort Wayne; another on the Mississinewa near Peru; another on Eel river near Logansport; another on the Wea Plains near Lafayette, and another near Terre Haute. The Delawares lived on the upper branches of White river, the village of Anderson, their chief, being within the limits of what is now Madison county. The Shawnees lived on the banks of the Wabash and the Tippecanoe. Their village, known as the Prophet's town, was on the west bank of the Wabash, a short distance below the mouth of the Tippecanoe. Some of the Kickapoos resided on the west side of the Wabash above the Tippecanoe. The Hurons or Wyandotts had a small village a short distance southeast of Ouiatanon and part of the Winnebagoes had a village a few miles east of the Prophet's town.[1]

It has been supposed that the entire Indian population of Indiana in 1819 did not exceed 7,000 or 8,000.[2] These

---

[1]See Brown's "Western Gazeteer," 71-3; Beckwith's "The Illinois and Indiana Indians," in Fergus's Historical Series, No. 27, pp. 112-113.

[2]Morse's Geography, 7th ed., published in 1819, p. 608. In the first annual report of the Bureau of Ethnology, p. 249, will be found a map by C. C. Royse, showing the cessions of land in Indiana by Indian tribes to the United States, with references to the dates of the treaties pursuant to which the cessions were made. This is reprinted in Smith's History of Indiana, vol. I, pp. 232-9. In Col. Croghan's Journal, reprinted in Butler's History of Kentucky, 2d ed., pp. 470-1, is given a list of Indian tribes in 1765 between the State of New York and the Mississippi. The Indiana Geological Reports, vol. XII. p. 42, contains a map prepared by Daniel Hough, giving the Indian names of the various water courses in Indiana. See also General William Henry Harrison's "Aborigines of the Ohio Valley," reprinted in Fergus's Historical Series, No. 26; Hiram W. Beckwith's "The Illinois and Indiana Indians," in Fergus's Historical Series, No. 27; John B. Dillon's "The National Decline of the Miami Indians," Indiana Historical Society Publications, vol. I, p. 119; Roosevelt's "Winning of the West," vol. I, chap. IV, on "The Algonquins of the Northwest." From these authorities some general idea may be acquired of the Indian tribes inhabiting the State, but no exact information of either their numbers or the boundaries of the territories claimed by them.

were but the remnants of the great Miami Confederacy and of other once powerful Indian tribes whose warriors were famous in all the Indian wars in the northwest in the eighteenth and nineteenth centuries, in the wars between England and France, in Lord Dunmore's war, in the battles with Harmar and St. Clair—warriors never completely subdued by the white men until they were vanquished by General Anthony Wayne, the greatest of all the generals who ever fought against them. Conspicuous among them was Little Turtle, chief of the Miamis, the leader of the allied Indians in the repulse of Harmar and in the disastrous defeat of St. Clair. He was born in the present limits of Indiana, and was buried at Fort Wayne in 1812. He ranks with King Phillip and Pontiac as among the foremost of all the North American Indians who ever fought against the whites. As a military chieftain he ranks even higher than King Phillip or Pontiac, for neither Phillip nor Pontiac ever achieved such victories as those of Little Turtle over Harmar and St. Clair.

It was at Tippecanoe, within the limits of the territory afterward known as the New Purchase, that the last great battle was fought in the northwest in which the Indians under Tecumseh sought to oppose the invasion by the whites of the land in which they and their ancestors had for so long had their homes and their hunting grounds.

Prior to the surrender of Canada by the French, one of their routes in going from Canada to Louisiana was across the Great Lakes, thence up the Maumee, thence by a short portage to the headwaters of the Wabash, thence down the Wabash to the Ohio, thence down the Ohio to the Mississippi, and thence down the Mississippi to Louisiana. They had established posts at Fort Wayne,

Ouiatanon, a place on the Wabash near the present site of Lafayette, and at Vincennes. These posts had passed from the French to Great Britain and from Great Britain to the United States. Fort Harrison had also been erected by the United States in what is now Vigo county. Except as above stated, there were no white settlements in all this vast region. Few white men had ever penetrated it except when it was invaded by armed parties on warlike expeditions.

It was a region of wonderful resources. It has been stated that what scientists term high-grade trees grew in greater variety and profusion in the Ohio Valley than in any other part of North America. Nowhere in the Ohio Valley was there such a magnificent growth of hardwood trees as there was in Indiana, and particularly in the New Purchase.[1]

---

[1]According to Mr. John P. Brown, secretary of the Indiana Forestry Association in a paper read before the Indiana State Board of Commerce, February 8, 1900, "Twenty-eight thousand square miles covered with oak, walnut, hickory, ash, maple, poplar and other valuable woods was our inheritance. Nowhere upon the American continent did there exist a body of timber superior to that nurtured by the soils of Indiana and covering four-fifths of her area." In the same paper Mr. Brown predicts that "the nineteenth century will almost measure the termination of Indiana's forest wealth," and adduces melancholy proof of the rapid destruction of our magnificent forests, supposed fifty years ago to be practically inexhaustible. "The result of a century's clearing is apparent; almost the entire body of this vast forest has disappeared and eighty-two per cent. of the lumber now used in our manufactories is brought from other States."

In a letter bearing date November 29, 1905, Professor Stanley Coulter, of Purdue University, says: "Many of the most valuable hardwood timbers reached their maximum development both as to size and numbers within the limits of the State. No later than 1880 Indiana was sixth in rank in lumber production. The most valuable timber areas were in the southwestern counties along the lower stretches of the Wabash river—though splendid forests of white oaks, walnuts, yellow poplar and ash stretched eastward to the Whitewater valley in the southeastern counties. Even yet it is not unusual in the East to see in lumber advertisements 'Indiana oak,' which is always listed at a higher

Deer, turkeys, pigeons and other wild game were abundant in the New Purchase. The streams swarmed with fish. The soil was of unsurpassed fertility. Nearly everything planted in it seemed to grow as if by magic. That it was an ideal home for the red men is proved by the numbers that inhabited it and the tenacity with which they clung to it.

As yet in all this region solitude reigned almost supreme. No sound of axe was heard in the forests. The surface of the rivers was ruffled only by an occasional Indian canoe. Dotted along the streams were a few straggling Indian villages, and here and there were a few patches of corn. All else was an unbroken wilderness in which wild beasts roamed at will. All nature seemed to await the talismanic touch that was to usher in the coming civilization, to transform the haunts of savage beasts and savage men into peaceful habitations, to draw from the ground its inexhaustible riches, to replace the forests and swamps with beautiful fields and landscapes, to make heard in this vast stillness the hum of industry.

As soon as the making of the treaty for the New Purchase had become generally known, the hardy and adventurous frontiersmen, especially those nearest to the newly acquired territory, began to make preparations to acquire homes within its boundaries, without waiting for the expiration of the time allowed the Indians in which to remove. In later years they would have been called "squatters," and still later "sooners."

---

price than other grades. I have seen advertisements of furniture factories in the East, which state 'nothing but Indiana wood used in our furniture.' Some fifty species of woods of high economic value are still of sufficient number and broad enough distribution to be a valuable asset. It would be difficult to exaggerate the past wealth of the forests of the State; it would be impossible to exaggerate the criminal carelessness which has reduced this wealth so fearfully."

There was no way of getting to this region by water except by the route the early French had traveled, or else by going down the Ohio to the mouth of the Wabash and then up the latter river and its tributaries. There was no way of reaching it by land except by following the Indian trails or cutting a trace through the wilderness.

The earliest white settlers of the New Purchase came principally from the settlements in the older parts of the State along the Whitewater and from the States of Ohio and Kentucky. Those coming from points south of the Ohio river came over old Indian traces, chiefly by one that crossed the Ohio at Louisville and that had existed from time immemorial.[1] Those from the eastern States generally embarked at some point on the Allegheny in river crafts of various kinds, designated according to the nomenclature of that period as "keel-boats," "flat boats," "arks," "broad horns" and "Kentuck boats," floated down the Allegheny to the Ohio, thence down the Ohio to Cincinnati, and then traveled by land to some point on the Whitewater and thence to the New Purchase.[2]

The completion in 1818 of the National Road from Cumberland, Maryland, to Wheeling, on the Ohio river, opened another route and gave a strong impetus to the already great tide of immigration pouring into the western country. With its numerous movers' caravans, interspersed with great Conestoga wagons and stage coaches, it was for many years the most noted road in the country. The road was completed in 1833 to Columbus, Ohio, but it did not reach Indiana until several years afterward.

Prior to the date of the treaty for the New Purchase, William Conner, an Indian trader, had settled at a Dela-

---

[1] See Cockrum, "Pioneer History of Indiana," pp. 156-7.

[2] Dr. Philip Mason in his autobiography gives a full account of such a trip from Olean, a village on the Allegheny in Cattaraugus county, New York.

ware village on White river about four miles south of
the present site of Noblesville in Hamilton county, but
no attempt had been made to establish a permanent white
settlement there.   In the fall of 1818, Jacob Whetzell, a
brother of the noted Indian fighter Lewis, and his son
Cyrus, with the consent of Anderson, chief of the Delawares, cut a trace, long known as Whetzell's trace, from
the Whitewater river in Franklin county to the bluffs
of White river, and camped at a point near the present
site of Waverly in Morgan county.   In the spring of 1819
he made a settlement there, said to have been the first
permanent white settlement in the New Purchase.

In the spring of 1819 or 1820 George Pogue reached
the present site of Indianapolis and built a cabin there.
Mr. Brown says[1] that: "After reaching the river he
turned back and built his cabin on the high ground east
of the creek which now bears his name, close to a large
spring and near the present end of Michigan street."

Little is known of Pogue's early life.   He was a blacksmith and came to Indiana from North Carolina in the
year 1814 and settled first at the blockhouse at William
Wilson's, on the west fork of the Whitewater, six miles
above Brookville in Franklin county; removing in 1816
to Fayette county about five miles southwest of Connersville, and in 1818 to the town of Connersville, where he
remained until he moved to the present site of Indianapolis.   At the time of his death he was about fifty years
old and had a wife and six children.[2]

Nowland describes him[3] as a "large, broad-shouldered

[1]"History of Indianapolis," p. 2.

[2]Reminiscences of Hon. Elijah Hackleman, printed in the
"Rushville Republican" and reprinted in History of Fayette
County, Indiana (published by Warner, Beers & Co., 1885), pp.
194-5; "Indianapolis News," August 5, 1905.

[3]"Sketches," p. 13.

and stout man, with dark hair, eyes and complexion, about fifty years of age, a native of North Carolina. His dress was like that of a 'Pennsylvania Dutchman;' drab overcoat, with many capes, broad brim felt hat. He was a blacksmith, and the first of that trade to enter the New Purchase. To look at the man as we saw him last, one would think he was not afraid to meet a whole camp of Delawares in battle array, which fearlessness, in fact, was most probably the cause of his death."

Pogue left his home in April, 1821, in pursuit of some horses supposed to have been taken by the Indians, by whom it was surmised by his neighbors that he was murdered, as he was never afterward seen or heard of. His name is perpetuated in Pogue's Run—the name of the little stream near which his cabin stood—but he is better known in connection with the controversy of many years' standing, whether he or John McCormick was the first settler of Indianapolis.

John McCormick and his brother James came in the spring of 1820 and built their cabin, a double log house, on the bank of White river just below the mouth of Fall creek. John McCormick kept the first tavern in the place and entertained the commissioners who came to locate the capital.

Mr. Brown claims that Pogue came March 2, 1819, and that he was the first settler, and that John and James McCormick came February 27, 1820;[1] while Mr. Nowland claims that John McCormick built the first house in Indianapolis February 26, 1820, and that Pogue did not come until the following March.[2]

The controversy over the question whether George Pogue or John McCormick built the first house in Indian-

---

[1] "History of Indianapolis," p. 2.
[2] "Sketches," pp. 14-15.

apolis began before the publication of Mr. Brown's History and has continued ever since. It elicited from Mr. Brown a long communication published in the "Indianapolis News" of September 9, 1899, in which he reiterated the statements made by him in his history and, in support of them, marshalled such an array of evidence as seems to leave little room for further doubt.

The Government surveys in the New Purchase were made in 1819 and 1820. On January 11, 1820,[1] the General Assembly passed an act providing: "That George Hunt, of the county of Wayne, John Conner, of the county of Fayette, Stephen Ludlow, of the county of Dearborn, John Gilliland, of the county of Switzerland, Joseph Bartholomew, of the county of Clark, John Tipton, of the county of Harrison, Jesse B. Durham, of the county of Jackson, Frederick Rapp, of the county of Posey, William Prince, of the county of Gibson, and Thomas Emmerson, of the county of Knox, be, and they are hereby, appointed commissioners to select and locate a site for the permanent seat of government of the State of Indiana."

The act further provided that upon notice by proclamation of the Governor, the commissioners should "meet at the house of William Conner on the west fork of White river on a day to be named in the proclamation," and that after having taken an oath for the faithful discharge of their duties they should "proceed to view, select, and locate, among the lands, of the United States, which are unsold, a site which in their opinion, shall be most eligible and advantageous for the permanent seat of government of Indiana, embracing four sections, or as many fractional sections as will amount to four sections." They were also required to appoint a clerk whose duty it was

[1] Acts 1820, p. 18.

to keep a fair record of their proceedings, and that such record should be laid before the next General Assembly, and that the General Assembly should "thereupon proceed to establish a permanent seat of government in and upon the land so selected and located by the commissioners aforesaid."

One of the commissioners, General John Tipton, kept a journal of the proceedings, which is now in the possession of Mr. John H. Holliday.[1]

All the commissioners accepted their appointments and served except William Prince. The commissioners, after viewing several locations, decided on June 7, 1820, upon the present site of Indianapolis as the location for the capital, and a report of their selection was submitted to the next General Assembly.

The proceedings of the commissioners for that day are thus recorded in Tipton's journal:

"Wednesday, 7th, a fine, clear morning. We met at McCormick's, and on my motion the commissioners came to a resolution to select and locate sections numbered 1 and 12, and east and west fractional sections numbered 2, and east fractional section 11, and so much off the east side of west fractional section number 3, to be divided by a north and south line running parallel to the west boundary of said section, as will equal in amount 4 entire sections in T 15 n. of R. 3, E. We left our clerk making out his minutes and our report, and went to camp to dine. Returned after dinner. Our paper being ready, B. D. and myself returned to camp at 4. They went to sleep and me to writing. At 5 we decamped and went over to McCormicks. Our [clerk] having his writing ready the commissioners met and signed there report,

---

[1]This journal has recently been reprinted in the "Indiana Quarterly Magazine of History," vol. I, pp. 9-15; Id., pp. 74-79.

and certified the service of their clerk. At 6:45 the first
boat landed that ever was seen at the seat of government. It was a small ferry flat with a canoe tied alongside, both loaded with the household goods of two families moving to the mouth of Fall creek. They came in a
keel boat as far as they could get it up the river, then un-
loaded the boat and bt [brought] up their goods in the
flat and canoe. I paid for some corn and w [whiskey]
62½."[1]

Judge Franklin Hardin, a well known and highly respected pioneer of Johnson county, once told me of a
tradition that three places were considered by the commissioners appointed to select the site for the State capital. One was the bluff of White river near Waverly in
Morgan county, but to this it was objected that the banks
of the river at that point were too high to allow a convenient boat landing; another site considered was a point
on White river near Glenn's Valley in Marion county.
Here the banks were low enough but the objection to
this point was that there were no small streams sufficient
to run the grist mills. Finally the present site was
chosen because the banks were low enough for a convenient boat landing, and Fall creek and Eagle creek were
deemed sufficient for the grist mills. When I expressed
some surprise at the character of the considerations that
influenced the selection of Indianapolis, particularly that
the navigability of White river and the supposed necessity of a convenient boat landing were considered important factors, the Judge informed me that in 1821 the
general water level was much higher than it was after
the country had been cleared and drained; that White
river then had sufficient water, at least in the spring, to
float flat boats and that in this way a considerable part

---

[1]"Indiana Quarterly Magazine of History," vol. I. pp. 77-78.

of the produce of the country was transported down White river and thence to New Orleans, then the commercial metropolis of the Wabash valley and its tributaries. This accords substantially with the account given by Mr. Robert Duncan.[1]

Strange as all this may seem to modern ears, we must remember that in 1821 canals in this section of the country had not been thought of, or at most only hoped for, and that no man had dreamed of steam railroads, and that White river was then deemed the chief line of commercial communication with the outside world.

The concluding entry in General Tipton's journal is that for June 11, 1821:

"Sunday the 11th—Cloudy, some rain. Set out at ½ p 4. At 15 p 8 stopt at Wilcoxes. Had breakfast, paid $2.00 by me. We set out. Stopt at Major Arganbrites [?] had dinner, etc. Set out and [at] dark got safe home, having been absent 27 days, the compensation allowed us commissioners by the law being $2 for every 25 miles traveling to and from the place where we met, and $2 for each day's service while ingaged in the discharge of our duty, my pay for the trip being $58—not half what I could have made in my office. A very poor compensation.   JOHN TIPTON."[2]

General Tipton's orthography was not quite up to the standard at present recognized in the Indianapolis High School, but we must not judge him by that standard alone. His father, a native of Maryland, had settled in Tennessee, where he was waylaid and murdered by the Indians. In 1807 General Tipton removed to Indiana Territory. As a young ensign he was conspicuous for his

---

[1]"Old Settlers." Indiana Historical Society Publications, vol. II, p. 380.

[2]"Indiana Quarterly Magazine of History." vol. I, pp. 78-79.

bravery at the battle of Tippecanoe, where, after his captain, first and second lieutenants had all been killed, he commanded his company throughout the remainder of the battle. He was a man of decided convictions, clear judgment and sterling honesty, and filled many important offices in the Territory and State, becoming a brigadier-general in the militia, and filling one full term and part of another as United States Senator.

We may infer from the concluding entry in his diary that General Tipton, while deficient in spelling, was equally deficient in the art of "graft," that in modern times has been developed to such a high degree of perfection.

At the time the commissioners determined on the location of the capital, there were about fifteen families on the site selected, including Henry and Samuel Davis, Jeremiah Corbalay, Robert Barnhill, ——— Van Blaricum, Robert Harding and Isaac Wilson. The site selected was covered with a dense growth of oak, elm, poplar, ash, sugar, walnut, hickory, beech, buckeye and other forest trees, with a thick undergrowth of spicewood and prickly ash and pawpaws; alders and leatherwood grew on the banks of the streams. So heavy was the growth of timber that after the trees in Washington street had been felled no way could be found of disposing of them except by burning them, and this required all the following winter.

In the northwest part of the donation was a tract of over one hundred acres on which the heavy timber had been killed by caterpillars or locusts. This was utilized by the settlers for that and ensuing years as a common field. In addition to this common field, each settler cultivated a small vegetable garden in the rear of his cabin. Wild game was abundant and cheap. So late as 1842 "saddles of venison sold at 25 to 50 cents; turkey at 10 and 12 cents, and a bushel of pigeons for 25 cents."[1]

Mr. Brown states[2] that "the selection of the place as the site for the capital had given it a great impetus, and many new families arrived in the summer and fall of 1820 and spring of 1821. Among the new-comers, most of whom came in the spring of 1821, were Morris Morris, Dr. S. G. Mitchell, John and James Givan, Matthias Nowland, James M. Ray, Nathaniel Cox, Thomas Anderson, John Hawkins, Dr. Livingston Dunlap, David Wood, Daniel Yandes, Alexander Ralston, Dr. Isaac Coe, Douglas Maguire and others, and the cabins clustered closely along the river banks, on and near which almost the whole settlement was located."

The next General Assembly, by an act passed January 6, 1821,[3] approved the report of the commissioners made on June 7, 1820, named the capital Indianapolis,[4] and provided: "That sections one and twelve, east and west fractional sections numbered two, east fractional section numbered eleven, and so much of the east part of west fractional section numbered three to be set off by a north and south line as will complete four entire sections, or two thousand five hundred and sixty acres of land in township fifteen north and range three east of the second principal meridian, being the site selected by the commissioners appointed by an act of the General Assembly of this State approved January the eleventh, one thousand eight hundred and twenty, * * * be and the above described land is hereby established as a permanent seat of government of the State of Indiana."

---

[1]Brown's "History of Indianapolis," p. 1.

[2]"History of Indianapolis," p. 2.

[3]Acts 1821, p. 44.

[4]This was done on the suggestion of Jeremiah Sullivan, a representative of Jefferson county.

The act contained further provision for the selection by the General Assembly of three commissioners; that they should meet "at the site above named on the first Monday in April next, or as soon thereafter as they conveniently can, and shall proceed to lay out a town on such part of the land selected and hereby established as the seat of government as they may deem most proper, and on such plan as they may conceive will be advantageous to the State and to the prosperity of said town, having specially in view the health, utility and beauty of the place." They were also direced to employ a skillful surveyor, chainmen and such other assistants as might be found necessary. Provision was also made for two complete copies of the plan of the town, with proper reference and explanatory notes, one copy to be filed with the Secretary of State and the other with the State Agent. The commissioners were also directed to offer at public vendue so many of the lots as they might deem expedient, "reserving unsold every second odd number, commencing with number one," the sale to be duly advertised. The terms of sale prescribed were one-fifth cash to the State Agent and the residue in four equal annual payments. The act also provided for the selection of a State Agent by joint ballot of the General Assembly, who should be commissioned by the Governor, and whose duty it should be to attend the sale of lots and receive the purchase money and give to the purchaser the necessary acquittances and certificates. The act contained further minute provision for the discharge of the duties of the State Agent and accounting by him for the proceeds of the sale, and prescribed that all moneys arising from the sale of lots should "remain in the treasury and constitute a fund for the special purpose of erecting the necessary public buildings of the State."

So valuable were ferry privileges then regarded, and so careful was the General Assembly, that special provision was made in the act "that no person or persons who may purchase any lot or lots in said town adjacent to White river shall thereby be entitled to any right of ferry, but the sole right of ferry at said town or from off the land belonging to the State in this vicinity shall always be and remain vested in the said town, any law or usage to the contrary notwithstanding."

The commissioners selected were Christopher Harrison, James Jones and Samuel P. Booker, and John Carr was elected and commissioned State Agent.

At the appointed time Christopher Harrison was the only commissioner who appeared, but he proceeded to appoint Elias P. Fordham and Alexander Ralston as surveyors, and Benjamin I. Blythe as clerk.[1] To remove doubts subsequently arising as to the validity of the plats and sales made without the concurrence of the other commissioners, they were confirmed by an act of the General Assembly passed November 28, 1821.[2]

The site selected contained 2,560 acres. The ground platted was one mile square. Near the center was a circle around which was a street ninety feet wide; from the corners of blocks adjacent to the circle were four diagonal streets each ninety feet in width; all the streets running east and west and north and south were ninety feet in width except Washington street, which was 120 feet in width. There were eighty-nine blocks, each containing four acres and each being 420 feet square. There were also six fractional squares and three irregular tracts in the Pogue's Run valley. Each block was divided by

---

[1]Ralston was a Scotchman who assisted in the survey of Washington City.

[2]Acts 1821, p. 12.

alleys into four equal parts, and each quarter block was divided into three lots with a frontage of 67½ feet.

There was so much sickness prevailing that after the completion of the plat it was deemed advisable to postpone the sale of lots, and the sale did not take place until October 10, 1821. The sale was had at the house of Matthias Nowland. Thomas Carter acted as auctioneer and James M. Ray as clerk. A great crowd, gathered from nearly every section of the country, attended the sale.

Nowland adds this significant commentary on the honesty of the people:[1] "This sale continued one week, during which time there was not the least disturbance of any kind. Although the woods were filled with moneyed people, there was no robbery or attempt at the same, nor was there the least apprehension of fear. There were no confidence men to prey upon the credulity of the people; although strangers, they looked upon each other as their neighbor and friend. Their money was almost entirely gold and silver, and was left in their leather bags where best they could procure a shelter, and was considered as safe as it now would be in the vaults of our banks."

The highest price paid was $560 for the lot west of Court square on Washington street; the lot west of State square was sold for $500; and the intervening lots on Washington street that have since brought over $4,000 per front foot sold for prices varying between $100 and $300, or from $1.50 to $4.50 per front foot. The prices bid were in those days considered very high; many of the lots were forfeited to the State for non-payment and for several years afterward there was a decline instead of an advance in prices. Nineteen hundred acres of the lots and land remained unsold in 1831, and were subsequently

---

[1] "Sketches," p. 21.

disposed of by order of the General Assembly at a minimum price of $10 per acre.

The State capital had now been located, named and platted, but much yet remained to be done. Until 1821 the territory included in the New Purchase formed part of what was then called Delaware county, but that county was as yet unorganized and came within the jurisdiction of the courts of Fayette and Wayne counties. Marion county had not then been organized. In consequence of the absence of local courts the citizens of Indianapolis were subjected to the great inconvenience of being prosecuted and sued in courts sixty miles or more away.

To remedy this incovenience the General Assembly, by an act passed January 9, 1821,[1] authorized the appointment of two or more justices of the peace for Indianapolis, and in April Governor Jennings appointed John Maxwell. Maxwell resigned in June and was succeeded by John McIlvaine. Quoting from Mr. Brown:[2] "His twelve-foot cabin stood on the northwest corner of Pennsylvania and Michigan streets, where he held court, pipe in mouth, in his cabin door, the jury ranged in front on a fallen tree, and the first constable Corbalay standing guard over the culprits, who nevertheless often escaped through the woods. Calvin Fletcher was then the only lawyer and the last judge in all the knotty cases, the justice privately taking his advice as to their disposal. There was no jail nearer than Connersville, and it being expensive and troublesome to send culprits there in charge of the constable and posse, the plan was adopted of frightening them away. A case of this kind occurred on Christmas, 1821. Four Kentucky boatmen, who had 'whipped their weight in wildcats' on the Kanawha and

---

[1] Acts 1821, p. 99.

[2] "History of Indianapolis," p. 4.

elsewhere, came from the Bluffs to 'Naplis' to have a Christmas spree. It being early, for the citizens were roused before dawn by a great uproar at Daniel Larkins's clapboard grocery, which contained a barrel of whiskey, the four heroes were discovered busily employed in tearing down the grocery. A request to desist produced a volley of oaths, a display of big knives and an advance on the citizens, most of whom found pressing business elsewhere. They were interested, however, in the existence of the grocery, and furthermore such defiance of law and order could not be tolerated. A consultation was held, resulting in the determination to take the rioters at all hazards. James Blake volunteered to grapple the leader, a man of great size and strength, if the rest would take the three others. The attack was made, the party captured and marched under guard through the woods to Justice McIlvaine's cabin, where they were at once tried, heavily fined and ordered to jail at Connersville in default of payment or bail. Payment was out of the question and they could not be taken to Connersville at that season of the year. Ostentatious preparations were made, however, for the trip, the posse was selected for the journey next day, a guard was placed over them." The guard however, had "secret instructions"—doubtless not to exercise undue vigilance—and Mr. Brown records that "during the night the doughty heroes fled to a more congenial clime," no doubt greatly to the relief of the citizens, who had thereby vindicated the majesty of the law, maintained the dignity of Indianapolis, and rid themselves of their unwelcome guests without depleting their little treasury.

There were other inconveniences resulting from the want of local government. When Jeremiah Johnson wanted to get married to Miss Jane Reagan he was compelled to walk to Connersville and back, 120 miles, to get his license. That was not the end of his troubles, for after getting his license he was obliged to wait several weeks for a preacher to come along and tie the marriage knot. It should be noted, however, that there was soon a sufficient number of preachers to supply the home market.[1]

On December 21, 1821, the General Assembly passed an act for the organization of Marion county,[2] providing for the election or appointment of judges and other officers, and appropriating funds for the erection of a two-story brick court-house fifty feet square, to be completed in three years and to be used by the federal, State and county courts, and by the General Assembly for fifty years, or until a state-house should be built.

The first county election was held April 1, 1822. "Nearly half the population," says Mr. Brown,[3] "were candidates for some office and were busily canvassing. Nominating conventions were unknown and each ran on his personal merit." No division seems to have been made on any national or State political issue, but the contest was mainly between the Whitewater settlers, represented by James M. Ray, and the Kentucky settlers, represented by Morris Morris. Mr. Brown adds: "The canvas was thorough and the excitement culminated at the election. Whisky flowed freely. Persons usually sober, excited by

---

[1] It may also be noted that "Jerry," as he was familiarly called, lived to see the first railroad train enter the city, and his exclamation of surprise to one of the by-standers as the locomotive came puffing along graphically expresses his amazement at the rapid advance of civilization: "Good Lord, John, what is this world gwine to come to!"—J. C. Fletcher in "Indianapolis News," June 11, 1879.

[2] Acts 1821, p. 135.

[3] "History of Indianapolis," p. 9.

victory or grieved by defeat, joined in the spree and the whole community got drunk."

Mr. Brown's statement is confirmed by Mr. Fletcher, who says that: "The political issues were entirely geographical and liquid and Whitewater and whiskey carried the day against Kentucky and whiskey."[1] In those days when part of the preachers' salaries was often paid in whiskey, the evils of intemperance were not so fully realized as they are now.

The year 1821 was an eventful one. There was much sickness, and during the late summer and early fall nearly every one in the entire community was prostrated by a species of remittent and intermittent fever, of more malignant type than the ordinary "fever and ague." In consequence of this the cultivation of the common field was neglected and provisions and goods, except such corn as could be bought of the Indians near by, were packed on horses sixty miles from the Whitewater.

Nevertheless, the population continued to increase, and by August, 1821, there were fifty or sixty families in the settlement, and by the end of the year the population had increased to four or five hundred. By February 25, 1822, "forty dwellings and several workshops had been built, a grist and two saw mills were running, and others were being built near town. There were thirteen carpenters, four cabinet makers, eight blacksmiths, four shoemakers, two tailors, one hatter, two tanners, one saddler, one cooper, four bricklayers, one preacher, one teacher, and seven tavern keepers. This list gives, perhaps, half the adult population of the place."[2]

By the year 1822, the little capital had made considerable growth. Schools, churches, a newspaper and a post-

[1]J. C. Fletcher in "Indianapolis News," May 10, 1879.

[2]Brown's "History of Indianapolis," p. 9.

office had been established, business of various kinds was being carried on.

In the "Indianapolis Gazette," the newspaper that had been established there,[1] are these announcements that possess a quaint interest for the citizens of to-day:

"Arrived at this place May 29 (1822) keelboat *Eagle*, 15 tons burthen from Kenhawa [?] Capt. Lindsey—salt, flour, whiskey, dried fruit, tobacco," also "the keel-boat *Boxer*, 133 tons, from Zanesville, Ohio, Capt. Wilson— merchandise and printing material."

Still the settlers labored under great disadvantages. Communication with the outside world was very difficult. The roads, such as they were, in the winter were muddy and it was difficult to travel over them in bad weather, even on horseback, and out of the question to travel over them in wagons. In winter such provisions and merchandise as were needed and could not be produced at home were brought on horseback from the Whitewater, or by boat from the Ohio up the Wabash to White river and thence to Indianapolis. This was a tedious and expensive way. The boats used were called keel-boats and were pulled up by cordelling, that is by tying a rope to a tree and pulling the boat up to it; or by poling, that is by pushing the boat along with poles. The ascent of the Wabash and White river by this method required about six weeks.

Prior to the year 1825 the General Assembly continued to hold its sessions, and the State officers to maintain their offices, at Corydon. This was because the buildings intended to be constructed at Indianapolis for their accommodation had not been completed. In 1824 these buildings were so nearly completed that preparations were made for removal from Corydon to Indian-

---

[1]Established in 1822 by Smith and Bolton.

apolis, and Samuel Merrill, then State Treasurer, was charged with the duty of superintending the removal, which was accomplished in the fall of 1824.

When the time came for moving from Corydon to Indianapolis, all the State's money, records and other movables were loaded into one wagon, the family and household goods of the State Treasurer into another, and the family and household goods of the State Auditor into another, and the little caravan started. "When he came near a small town," says Mrs. Ketcham, "our ambitious teamster would put on all his bells in honor of the Treasurer of State and the State Printer (Auditor), so that every man, woman and child could run to the front to see."

The trip consumed ten days' time. The building designed for the State Treasurer, had not yet been completed, but it was soon ready for occupancy. It was a two-story brick building erected at the southwest corner of Washington and Tennessee streets. On one side was the office of the State Treasurer, and over that was the office of the State Auditor, reached by an outside stairway. On the other side were the rooms designed for the family of the State Treasurer—a parlor, over the parlor a bedroom, and in rear of the parlor a room used as a sitting-room, dining-room and kitchen.

The General Assembly met that winter in the court-house, which was not then finished, the session beginning on the second Monday in January, 1825. The State House was not built until 1835.

By the year 1824 the town had made considerable progress. Some frame and brick houses had been erected of a better class than most of those in the new settlements. Besides the various mechanical trades and other business carried on, the learned professions were also

represented in the new capital. The Methodists and
Presbyterians had churches in Indianapolis at an early
date. It is said that the first Methodist preacher, one
sent by the St. Louis Conference to Indianapolis, lost
his way in the wilderness and had much difficulty in
finding the place.

In this connection special mention should be made of
the early Methodist preachers. That they were not animated
by any hope of pecuniary gain is proved by their pitiful
salaries. They rode immense circuits on horseback, with
nearly all their worldly possessions tucked in a pair of
saddlebags, traveling for hundreds of miles over old
traces and Indian trails, for roads there were none,
through otherwise trackless forests, still infested with
ravenous beasts, swimming swollen streams, braving all
the dangers of the wilderness, the heat of summer, the
malaria of fall, the rigors of winter, inspired only by a
sublime faith that stamps them as at once the humblest
and the foremost of all the pioneer heroes of Indiana.

Some of the Presbyterian preachers had their tribula-
tions also. One of the first, a highly educated man, was
caught in the very act of reading Shakespeare to his wife.
Such an offense was little less reprehensible than that
of a man kissing his wife on Sunday, an offense viewed
with special abhorrence by the New England Puritans.
After such a departure from good morals we need not
be surprised to learn that the unfortunate minister was
viewed with suspicion by the elders, and that not long
afterward he was impeached for heresy and was compelled to quit his charge. He was succeeded by one more
orthodox who preached Calvanism of the genuine quality,
but his sermons, so Mrs. Ketcham tells us, had the singular effect of putting his congregation to sleep, and what
is more singular still, the first to go to sleep was one of

the elders who thought that the preceding preacher was not sufficiently orthodox.

Mrs. Ketcham records in her journal a novel expedient resorted to by the wife of one the elders to rouse the drowsy members: "His wife in the far end of the pew looked to the right and left, far and near, and seeing drowsy ones, passed her bottle of strongest ammonia." Mrs. Ketcham adds that "the people were not used to it" and "the jumps and the instant handing back with the rueful faces" had the effect of setting all the younger members to laughing. One can not avoid instituting a mental comparison between the method adopted by the elder's wife of rousing the drowsy members, and that in vogue among the early New England Puritans, when the tithing man went about admonishing those of the congregation whom he caught napping, of the sin of sleeping by giving them a smart rap on the head with the hard end of his tithing rod, and this, too, though the hour glass had been turned time and again. The question which of the two methods is preferable is a delicate and knotty theological problem, and a discreet layman will wisely refrain from venturing any opinion upon it. When in later years Henry Ward Beecher had charge of the Presbyterian church in Indianapolis he had no trouble in keeping his congregation awake.

A doctor soon appeared. His method of treatment was the one then recognized and approved as "regular." Quoting again from Mrs. Ketcham: "It is no exaggeration to say that his pills were as large as cherries; twenty grains of calomel was a common dose, and antimony till one was sure he was poisoned. He bled equal to any Italian, till his patient fainted away." He bled Mrs. Ketcham once and the mark on her arm remained ever after. A knowledge of the ways of the Indianapolis doctors in early times may enable us the better to appreciate the delicate humor of Nye when he addressed to a convention of doctors assembled in Indianapolis a few years ago the wish "that they might continue *to take life easy*—as heretofore."

One lawyer, Calvin Fletcher, came in 1821. He was, for a time, the sole legal adviser of John McIlvaine, the solitary justice of the peace, who, for a short period, embodied all the visible majesty of the law. It is recorded to Fletcher's credit that he never abused for his own profit the confidence reposed in him by the justice.

The early lawyers of Indiana were men of marked ability, many of whom have left a deep impression upon the history of the State. Like the early Methodist preachers, they rode great circuits, traveling hundreds of miles on horseback through the woods from court to court. Many of them had been educated in Eastern colleges. They had few law books but with these they were thoroughly familiar. They depended far more upon their reasoning powers to apply to new cases their knowledge of elementary principles than do the modern lawyers, many of whom depend too much upon the results of other lawyers' thinking to be found in the books that load the shelves of our immense law libraries.

With all their hardships, the early settlers of Indianapolis fared better in one respect than pioneers in less favored localities, for it seems that they had plenty to eat. Mrs. Ketcham's father was the State Treasurer, and his style of living was probably some better than that of his poorer neighbors. Still it probably was not much different from that of most of the better class of the inhabitants at that time. She says: "Milk was plenty; every lady had her own cow or cows, and they were even milked in Washington street. Butter 6 cts. a pound;

eggs 2 cts. a dozen. So we had griddle cakes, taken from the great round griddle before the great fire. There was no soda; eggs made them light and the baking speedy. Biscuit was kneaded a great deal and baked in a hot skillet quickly. Waffles! I can see the long handled irons thrown into the blazing fire and whirled over so quickly and out and in the same way. Maple syrup was plenty, and wild honey. We had good light bread made of hop yeast. Chickens were almost always broiled. It was considered a great thing to have chickens and new potatoes on the Fourth of July. Currants and cherries grew speedily till then. We had wild strawberries, raspberries and blackberries. In the fall wild grapes for preserves and jelly, and also wild plums. When out in the woods looking for these things, I have been led on by the fragrance of the plum, till walking on the trunk of a huge fallen tree, I put aside with my hands the thicket and the ground was covered with plums of large size and that peculiar beauty of color they have. White sugar was only in the loaf and was 25 cts. a pound, so our preserving was done with New Orleans sugar. We took extra care and they were real good. Maple sugar was also plenty. Great wagon loads of apples were brought from the Ohio river and sold at $1.25 a bushel. How we enjoyed them.

"Wild turkey and game of all kinds abounded. Fish from White river and Fall creek. I have never tasted such fried potatoes as my mother's. * * * These good housekeepers talked of the better ways of doing things and encouraged one another, and thus learned and taught. I remember how good the last roasting ears tasted just before the frost, and as soon as the corn was at all hard, it was grated and made rare mush. The great kettle of lye hominy looked so good on the great kitchen crane and smelled so appetizing as we came home from school. It took the best of white flint corn; then boiling water was poured over the nicest ashes, and when this was settled clear, it was poured on the corn and stood in the corner of the great fireplace till the skin loosened; then it was taken to the well, in a tub, was washed with buckets of water till it was white, and then boiled slowly all day; then eaten in milk or fried as one wished. * * *

"Our smoke-house. Everybody had one. They were full of ham, pickled pork, bacon, dried beef, corned beef, backbones, spare ribs, that were always boiled unless in pot-pie. Bones, sausage, head cheese. How handsome the baked pork looked. We had never heard of its not being healthy nor looked out for a headache after eating it. Our cellars were full of potatoes, turnips, cabbage, cucumber pickles and great jars of preserved fruit. Soon dried fruit grew to be plenty. * * *

"Deer was plenty. Their steaks were broiled and relieved of dryness by being well buttered. Also wild turkeys were so abundant that William Anderson brought down three at one time with his shotgun. The breasts of these were fried."

The inhabitants of Indiana, at the time of its admission into the union, were mostly immigrants from Kentucky and Tennessee, whose ancestors were mainly from Pennsylvania, Virginia and the Carolinas. Those about Vincennes were nearly all French. There was a Swiss settlement in Switzerland county. There were a few immigrants from New York, Pennsylvania and the New England States, but very few foreigners.

The immigration to the New Purchase was chiefly from the older settled portions of the State and from Ohio, but large numbers also came from Kentucky, Vir-

ginia and other Southern States. There were some from
New York, from Vermont, Connecticut and other Eastern States. A considerable number of Quakers came
from Wayne county and from North Carolina. Few
foreigners came, and the population of the New Purchase
was almost wholly American.

The first settlers of the Northwest Territory were
mostly men who had served, or whose fathers had
served, in the Revolutionary War.[1] A very considerable
number of this class settled in Indiana. Very many of
the settlers of the New Purchase were men who had
served in the War of 1812 and in the Indian wars of the
West. They were mostly men of great physical strength,
of strong character, of fearless disposition, and nearly all
were familiar with the hardships and dangers of frontier
life.

A considerable and valuable addition to the immigration to Indiana was of Scotch-Irish descent—most of it
reaching the State by a long and zig-zag route, after the
acquisition of the New Purchase. Large numbers of
Scotch-Irish Presbyterians who left Ulster in Ireland to
avoid the persecutions of the English kings after the
restoration sought refuge in various parts of the American colonies. Much the largest part of them settled in
Pennsylvania.[2] Thence the general course of Scotch-
Irish emigration was to Western Virginia and North
Carolina; from the last two colonies to Tennessee and
Kentucky, and thence to Indiana.

It is not within the scope of this paper to enter into a
minute description of the homes, the social customs and

[1] Burnet's "Notes on the Northwestern Territory," p. 42.

[2] Roosevelt's "Winning of the West," vol. I, chap. V; "The Backwoodsman of the Alleghenies;" Campbell's "History of Virginia,"
p. 424; Hanna's "Scotch-Irish," p. 60.

the daily life of the early settlers of Indianapolis. Their houses were much like those of the early settlers in other portions of the State, and not unlike those in the early settlements of New England. The old chinked log-houses, with clapboard roofs, puncheon floors, stick or catted chimneys, and enormous fireplaces; the outer walls often covered with "coon" skins; the latch-string always out; the wells with their old-fashioned sweeps and the gourds that hung on the curb; the simple furniture and household and farming utensils, mostly made by hand; the house-raisings, the log-rollings, the corn-huskings, the quilting-bees; the varied incidents of daily life—all these are familiar to some still living, and they have been described over and over again in local histories. They recall a vivid picture of pioneer life, of honest manhood, of womanly devotion, of primitive simplicity, of the heroic struggles of the men and women who helped to lay in a wilderness the foundation of a great State—a picture to which each succeeding age lends romantic coloring and dramatic interest.[1]

Most of the early settlers were poor; their houses were rude structures; their clothing was mostly made at home,

---

[1] Elaborate descriptions of early life in Indianapolis will be found in Sulgrove's "History of Indianapolis," Nowland's "Sketches," and the series of papers entitled "Old Settlers," giving the recollections of Mr. Robert Duncan, published in the Indiana Historical Society Publications, vol. II, pp. 377-402. There will also be found a highly interesting description of early life in Indianapolis in the communications of Rev. J. C. Fletcher, son of Calvin Fletcher, contributed to the "Indianapolis News," beginning March 10 and concluding September 19, 1879, giving not only the author's personal recollections, but many extracts from journals kept by his father and mother. A very full and accurate account of the life of the early settlers in other portions of Indiana is given in the autobiography of Dr. Philip Mason, who emigrated from Herkimer county, New York, and settled in 1816 in Fayette county, Indiana. See also Senator David Turple's "Sketches of My Own Times" and Cockrum's "Pioneer History of Indiana."

and their mode of living was plain and simple. There were no marked distinctions based on wealth or rank; the settlers were more or less dependant upon their neighbors, so that each community was a little democracy in which political and social equality were of necessity, if not of choice, the characteristics.

With their limited facilities for education we need not be surprised to find, nor should we count it to their discredit, that they were deficient in literary culture, and even in the rules of spelling. But we shall greatly err if we base our estimate of them upon the rude caricatures depicted in some books of fiction and in some travelers' accounts that attempt to describe them. They were mostly men, from whatever quarter they came, whose ancestors were of the best American blood, courageous, honest, industrious, frugal, hospitable; men who had come to this region to hew out homes in the wilderness; men who fully understood the difficulties and dangers that beset them on every hand and who pursued their purpose undaunted by them.

Senator Turpie's tribute to the early Indiana pioneers is as true as it is beautiful:[1]

"In that primitive age there was an innate honest simplicity of manner, as of thought and action. Fraud, wrong-doing and injustice were denounced as they are at present; they were also discredited, dishonored, and branded with an ostracism more severe than that of Athens. Wealth acquired by such means could not evade, and was unable to conceal, the stigma that attached to the hidden things of dishonesty.

"The moral atmosphere of the time was clear and bracing; it repelled specious pretentions, resisted iniquity

[1]"Sketches," p. 55-6.

and steadily rejected the evil which calls itself good. Moreover, there never has been a people who wrought into the spirit of their public enactments the virtues of their private character more completely than the early settlers of Indiana. We have grown up in the shadow of their achievements; these need not be forgotten in the splendor of our own."

It is not within the scope of this paper to trace the subsequent development of the capital city. For many years it seemed to languish and gave no sign of the wonderful development it has since shown. It suffered like other towns in the State from the collapse of the internal improvement system and the panic of 1837. In 1840 its population was only 2,692. Not until its admirable advantages as a railroad and manufacturing center became apparent did its brilliant future seem to be assured. But railroads were not dreamed of by its founders, and the first one, the old Madison & Indianapolis railroad, did not enter the city until October 1, 1847. Nevertheless, the men who laid the foundations of the city accomplished a great deal. Indeed they builded far better than they knew.

Themistocles, when ridiculed for lack of polite accomplishments, is said to have replied: "True, I never learned how to tune a harp or handle a lute; but I know how to raise a small and inconsiderable city to glory and greatness." The founders of Indianapolis might have said that, though they could not tune a harp or handle a lute, they could found a capital in the wilderness.

INDIANA HISTORICAL SOCIETY PUBLICATIONS

VOLUME IV   NUMBER 5

NAMES

OF

PERSONS ENUMERATED

IN

MARION COUNTY, INDIANA

AT THE

FIFTH CENSUS

EIGHTEEN HUNDRED AND THIRTY

INDIANAPOLIS

Edward J. Hecker, Printer and Publisher

1908

PREFATORY NOTE

A MONG the unpublished documents on file in the Census Bureau at Washington, D. C., pertaining to the census of 1830, are the original returns of the population of Marion County, grouped by families, under the names of the several heads of families. Mr. R. R. Bennett, President of the Washington Legal Aid Society, kindly supervised copying the sheets for the use of the Indiana Historical Society.

This was the first National Census taken after the organization of Marion County.

NAMES OF HEADS OF FAMILIES	FREE WHITE PERSONS (INCLUDING HEADS OF FAMILIES)																									
	MALES													FEMALES												
	Under 5 yrs of age	5 and under 10	10 and under 15	15 and under 20	20 and under 30	30 and under 40	40 and under 50	50 and under 60	60 and under 70	70 and under 80	80 and under 90	90 and under 100	100 and upwards	Under 5 yrs of age	5 and under 10	10 and under 15	15 and under 20	20 and under 30	30 and under 40	40 and under 50	50 and under 60	60 and under 70	70 and under 80	80 and under 90	90 and under 100	100 and upwards
CENTRE TOWNSHIP																										
James B. Ray	1	2	1			1	1							2			1	2	1		1					
James Morrison	1				1		2							1				2								
William Quarles	1	2				1												1								
Jeremiah Johnson	2 3	1			1		1							1 1	1	1	1	1	1							
John Givan					1									1	1	1	1	1	1				1			
Alexander Wylie				1	1	1								3		1		3								
Isaac Kinder																										
Mary Davis														8		2 1	1	1								
Obed Foot			1																							
Alexander F. Morrison														1	1			1								
Glidden True					1	1								1				1								
John McDowell	1			1	1	1	1	1		1				1	1			1	1							
Luke Walpole																	1									
Alfred Harrison					2 1 1	2									2 1	1	1	1								
Harvey Bates		2						1									1	2								
Edward McGuire					1									1			1	1								
Thomas M. Smith																		1								
Alexander Frazier					1													1								
Benjamin I. Blythe		1	1	1	1									1	1	1		2		1						
John Holland																1		1								
William Tichenor						1										1		1		1						
John M. Commingore							1								2	2	1									
Humphrey Griffith															2 1	2 1		2 1	1			1				
Charles Smith																										
Jemison Hawkins	3				1	8		1						2		1	1	2 1	1	1		2				2
Israel Phillips	1	1			1	1	1							1				2								
John Hawkins																										
Henry Porter			1		1																					
Nathaniel Davis					2	2 1								1		2 1	1	2 1								
George Smith														1												
Charles Firestone	1	1			1	1	1							1		1 1		1 1	1							1
James Olliman														1				2								
James Eaton	1														1			1								
George Norwood		2	2		1	1	1	1						2	1			1 2	1	1						2

Name	1	2	3	4	5	6	7	8	9	10	11	12	13	14	15	16	17	18	19	20	21
Benjamin Roberts										1	1					2	1	1	1		
Elizabeth Nowland											1				1	1	3	9		2	
Daniel Yandes		1	1	1	1	1	1		2		1	1	1	3	1		1	1	1	2	1
John Douglass											2		2	2					1	
Douglass Maguire	2	1	2	1	1	1	3				1	1	2	1	1	1	1	1		1	
John Cain	1	1	1	1	1	1					1	1	1	1			1				
Samuel Henderson	1	1	1	1	1					1		1	1		1						
Harvey Gregg	1	1	1	2	1	2			1	1				4	1			1			
Isaac N. Phipps		1		2	1	2	2														
James Smith	1	1	1	1	1																
Nicholas McCarty	1	2	1	1	2			1	2	1	1			1	1	1	2		1	2	2
Fleming T. Luse						1					1						1			1	
Joseph Merrill											1	1					1				
Livingston Dunlap	1	1	1	1	1	2		1				1		2							
Samuel Duke	1	1	1	1					1	1											
Benedict Higdon									1	2											
John Blake	1	1		1	1																
John E. McClure																					
Thomas Donnolan	1	1								2	3	1	2								
James Sulgrove				1		1															
Samuel Scott																					
Charles McDougal		1		1	2							1									
David Mallory	2	1		1		1	1				2	9	1			1					
John Johnson, Sen	1	1									1										
Wilford J. Ungles	1	1						1			2	2									
James Johnson		1	1	1			1				1	1	1	1		2		1			
William W. Wick	1	1	1	1			1				1	2	1	1		1					
Edward Waller													1	2			1				
Cary Smith	1	1				1									1						
Samuel Ray		1	1			1	1		1		1				2	1			1		
John A. Lafond	1	1		1	1								1	1		1					
James Forsee														1							
Arthur St. Clair																					
Thomas Chill																					
John Wilkins	1	1									1	2	1				1				
Hiram Brown	1	1						1			1										
Barney Ball											1										
Sampson Leatherman	2	1	1	2	1								2			1					
James Lester	1	1	1	1	1			1		1											

FREE WHITE PERSONS (INCLUDING HEADS OF FAMILIES)

NAMES OF HEADS OF FAMILIES	Males — Under 5 yrs of age	5 and under 10	10 under 15	15 under 20	20 under 30	30 under 40	40 under 50	50 under 60	60 under 70	70 under 80	80 under 90	90 under 100	100 and upwards	Females — Under 5 yrs of age	5 and under 10	10 under 15	15 under 20	20 under 30	30 under 40	40 under 50	50 under 60	60 under 70	70 under 80	80 under 90	90 under 100	100 and upwards
James P. Drake	2			1		1	1									2		1		1	1	1				
David Buchanan				1		1	1		1					1					1	1		1				
John Vanblaricum	2	1	3				1							1	1			1	1							
Nicholas Swadley	1	1												2	1		1		1							
John Brandon	1		1											1				1	1							
Thomas Garret					1												1	1								
Leah Reagan				1										2				1			1					
William Reagan	1				1													1								
Ann Johnson	3			1	1									2	1		1	1								
James Kettleman	1			2	1	1								1	1				1							
Noah Leverton	1			1	1	1									1				1	1						
Henry Hammel					1	1									1			1	1							
Jacob Loucks		2	1					1						2	1				1			1				
Cornelius Loucks					1	1								3	1				1							
John M. Bay				1	1	1								1				1	1							
Zebulon Chill					1	1									1			1	1							
Andrew Nelson					1	1								1				1	1							
Samuel Eaton	2			1	1	1	1							1				2	1							
Aquellin W. Noe					1		2	1						1	1				1		1					
John Walton					1	1												1	1							
Benjamin Parris	1			1	1	1	1		1					2	1			1		1						
William F. Parris					1	1								1				1	1							
Samuel Morrow					1	1						1		1				1	1							
Simeon Sedwick	1	1		3		2	1		1						1			2		1						
Noah Noble					1	1		1						1	1				1	1		1				
Joshua Stephens	2				2	1	2											2		1						
James Vanblaricum	2		2		1	1	1							2	1	1			1							
Michael Vanblaricum	2		1	3		1	1						1	1	1				1							
Josiah W. Davis	1					1	1											2	1							
Henry P. Coburn				1	1	1	1									1	1	1		1						
James M. Ray					1	1	1								1			1	1							
Nicholas Sheffer																										
Harrod Newland	1						1		1					1				1	1	1			1			
John Peck					1	1													1	1						
Abraham McCord	1	1		1		1								1			1	1	1	1						
Smallwood Noel					1		1							1	1		1	1	1		1	1				

John Newland
Robert Patterson
Isaac Fisher
Pleasant Williams
John Foudray
William Rennick
Thomas Hogland
Samuel Goldsberry
Jesse Coombs
Peter Winciel
George Holland
Archibald Lingenfelter
Uriah Gates
William Lingenfelter
Ebenezer Sharpe
Isaac Coe
Joseph Lafevour
John R. Moreland
Samuel Brown
John Jones
James Parr
Abraham Williams
Jesse Grace
Josiah Grace
James Edgar
Chena Lively
Robert Goudie
William Arnold
Priscilla Myers
Benjamin Drapor
Abner McNabb
John Davis
Joseph Giberson
Joseph Greur
Amos Hanway
Harry Perry
William Barwell
William Garrott
Samuel Chrone
Jacob Landis
Eli C. Bouio
David L. Gregg
James Overall
Robert Davis
Abel Pierce
Earl Pierce
William Davis
John Tucker
John Cook
Mrs. Skinner

FREE WHITE PERSONS (INCLUDING HEADS OF FAMILIES)

NAMES OF HEADS OF FAMILIES	MALES — Under 5 yrs of age	5 and under 10	10 and under 15	15 and under 20	20 and under 30	30 and under 40	40 and under 50	50 and under 60	60 and under 70	70 and under 80	80 and under 90	90 and under 100	100 and upwards	FEMALES — Under 5 yrs of age	5 and under 10	10 and under 15	15 and under 20	20 and under 30	30 and under 40	40 and under 50	50 and under 60	60 and under 70	70 and under 80	80 and under 90	90 and under 100	100 and upwards
John Partridge																										
Joseph Wingate																										
Wilks Reagan																										
Morris Morris																										
Charlotte Knight																										
Francis Baily																										
David Burkhart																										
Moses Frazee																										
Robert Brown																										
Robert Taylor																										
John Reagan																										
William Hooker																										
Elizabeth Paxton																										
Edwin Ray																										
Henry Bradley																										
Alexander W. Russell																										
George W. Gibbs																										
Joseph Childers																										
John W. Redding																										
Mahlon Baty																										
James Taff																										
Archibald Lamaster																										
John Barnell																										
Cass Ann Pogue																										
Zenas Lake																										
Elisha Lake																										
Samuel McCormack																										
James McIlvain																										
Frederick Bailor																										
Adam Brous																										
John Burns																										
Elias C. Baldwin																										
John P. Sharpe																										
William McCole																										
Francis Davis																										
Jarret Davis																										

Shadrach Laquedt
Henry Holston, Jr.
Richard Williams
Rachael Martindale
Henry Holston, Sr
Baswell Landram
George Landram
Alexander Hamilton
Thomas Woolen
Stephen Pitts
Solomon Cook
Charles O'Neal
Thomas O'Neal
James B. McDowel
Thomas Johnson
Thomas McClintock
James Hamilton
Horatio McDowell
William McDowell
John Brown
Jacob Ringer
Peter Brown
Noah Flood
Jeremiah Johnson
William Reagan
John Sutherland
Isaac Stipp
William P. Carpenter
Thomas Lankfort
Joshua Hinosley
Samuel Patten
James Hill
John Parr
Noah Parr
Joseph Trall
Richard Vanlandingham
George Tuffs
John Cloe
John Prewot
Matthias Tyson
Eleanor Bonnel
Joseph Pogue
Enoch Evans
Julius Blackburn
Robert Hannah
James Gordon
David Johnson
John Shueffer
John McFall, Sr
Archibald C. Reid

NAMES OF HEADS OF FAMILIES	FREE WHITE PERSONS (INCLUDING HEADS OF FAMILIES)																									
	MALES													FEMALES												
	Under 5 yrs. of age	5 and under 10	10 and under 15	15 and under 20	20 and under 30	30 and under 40	40 and under 50	50 and under 60	60 and under 70	70 and under 80	80 and under 90	90 and under 100	100 and upwards	Under 5 yrs. of age	5 and under 10	10 and under 15	15 and under 20	20 and under 30	30 and under 40	40 and under 50	50 and under 60	60 and under 70	70 and under 80	80 and under 90	90 and under 100	100 and upwards
Isaac N. Sanders	2			2	3	1		1							1			1				1				
Francis McLaughlin	2 1 1	1 2	1	2		1	1							1 2	1 1	1	1	1 1 1 1	1							
James F. Brady				1	1	1								1		1	1	1								
B. F. Morris				1	1		1	1						1 2 1	1	1 1 1		1	1							
Robert Brinton					1	1	1							2				1	1							
Otis Sprague					1										1											
Harret Parrish														1												
James McFarland			1	1	1	1								1		1	1									
James Goan						1								1 2		1										
Daniel Pattangill					2									1				1								
Daniel Cool					1		1	1						2	1			1		1						
Mary Cool																										
Isaac Johnson	1 2	1		1	1	1	1							1												
Robert F. Lankford	2	1			1	1	1							2		2	1	1	1							
John Bowman														1				1	1							
Aaron Aldridge														1												
Joseph Dare																										
Jeremiah L. Day	1	1	1	1	1	1	1							1		2	1			1						
William Gott	1				1	1								1			1	1		1						
John Groves	2				1	1	1							1			1	1		1						
Preston Lancaster	4		1		1	1	1							1 1	2		1		1							
William McLaughlin		1	2 1		1	1	1				1				2		1	1								
William Wright	1		1	1	1	1	1							1			1	1 1 1	1							
James Hamilton					1	1								1 8 1	2			1	1							
Alexander Bodkin					1	1	1			1																
Otis Hobert	1	1	1	1	1	1		1						1			1		1							
John Hobert	1 2	1	1 1	2	1	1	1							2	2			1 1	1							
John Strong					1	1								1												
John Hearn	3	1	1		1	1								1 1	1			1 1	1		1					1
Richard Coverdill	1		1	2	1	1		2						9	2	2	1				1		1			
Theodore V. Denny	1		1											1				1								
Richard Gott	2	1	2	1	1	1	1							2		2		1	1							
Richard Berry	3				1	1	1			1				1			1		1							1
James McLaughlin	1	1	2	2	1	1	1											1	1							1
William Caufman	2	1			1			1		1				2	2			1		1						
William Bryce	1	1	1	1	1	1	1							1				1	1							

William McLaughlin
William Sanders
Zenas Kimberly
Hugh Campbell
Cornelius Vanhouten
Catharine Smock
David Small
Joseph P. Duvall
Moses Tilly
John McFall, Jr
John Ogle
Andrew Wilson
Noah Sinks
Daniel Sinks
Samuel Snodgrass
Laban Harding
Abraham A. Hall
William Myers
V. P. Campbell
John Pouge
Eliakim Harding
Harrison Harding
Thomas Pouge
Robert Harding
Sarah Wilson
John G. Brown
Benjamin Butler
Benjamin Atherton
Frederick Shoots
Burr F. Dennis
James Robinson
John Thompson

PERRY TOWNSHIP
William H. P. Bristow
Thomas Shelton
John M. Johnson
Samuel L. Johnson
David Mars
Samuel Dabouey
John E. Calls
John Smith
Nicholas Cline
Moses Orm
James Dabney
William Hall
Samuel Smith
Francis Sanders
William Janes
Henry Alcorn

FREE WHITE PERSONS (INCLUDING HEADS OF FAMILIES)

NAMES OF HEADS OF FAMILIES	Males Under 5	5 & under 10	10 & under 15	15 & under 20	20 & under 30	30 & under 40	40 & under 50	50 & under 60	60 & under 70	70 & under 80	80 & under 90	90 & under 100	100 & upwards	Females Under 5	5 & under 10	10 & under 15	15 & under 20	20 & under 30	30 & under 40	40 & under 50	50 & under 60	60 & under 70	70 & under 80	80 & under 90	90 & under 100	100 & upwards
Archibald Bruce	3	1	1		2				1						2			2	1			1				
Thomas Wilson	1						1							1	3	1	1		1							
Samuel Woodfil	1						1							2	1	2										
Zachariah Leamaster				2										1	1				1							
John Ritchie	1			1	2										2			2								
Henry Refuton	3	1		1	1													2								
Hezekiah Smith	1															1	1									
John Smart														1					1							
John Waltz		1					1							1			1		1	1						
Abraham Ellis		2		1	1													1	1		1					
Henrietta McBride																	1			1						
Charles McBride					1									1				1								
Daniel Harris																		1	1							
Elizabeth Wishard							1							1			1		1		1					
Cornelius Hardenbrook	1				1	1												1	1				1			
Joseph Smith									1											1						
James Johnson	1					1									2			1	1							
William Johnson						1		1										1	1							
William McAdoo	1				1	1										1		1	1							
Lawrence DeMott	2	2			2	1										1	1	1	1							
Hampton Bryan						1									2			1	1							
Jacob Turner	1						1											1	1							
Scipio Sedwick			1		1													1	1							
William Myers	2	1		2				1							2	1	1		1			1				
Peyton Bristow	1				1													1	1							
Philip McConnoll			1															1	1							
Joseph Snow	1	1				1									1		1	1	1							
Simon Smock	2	1	1		2	1								2		1		1	1							
John Wright			1															1	1							
Pernell Coverdill	2	1	1		1	1								1		1	1	1	1							
Samuel Arbuckle						1									2		1	1	1							
Thomas Richardson	2	1			1	1								3			1	1	1							
James Braman	1				1	1									1	1		1	1							
James McLaughlin	1					1								1	1		1	1	1							
Daniel Stuck		1											1	2			1	1	1							
Benjamin McFarland					1	1					1			2	1			1	1			1				

Name																																	
Joel Bowling			1					1					2	1					1													
Nancy Silvey		1											1	1				1														
Phannal Graham	3	1												2				1														
Smith McFall					1								3				1															
Primrose Yarbrough	1	1				1							1				1															
Elizabeth Judd	1	2											1				1															
James Hayden													3				1															
Margaret White				1	2											2	2															
John M. Callan	2	1				1											1		1													
Ephraim Arnold	2	1				1								1			1		1													
John Thompson			2	2		1		1									1		1													
William Hughey	1		1			1							1	2	2		1															
William Viney	1				1								1				1															
Samuel Miller			1	1			1						1	2	1	1		1														
William Teith	1	1	1				1						1		1	1		1														
David Fisher	1	1	2			1							1	1	1		1															
William Arnold							1								1	1		1		1												
Susannah Moseley	2				2								1				3		1													
Moses McClain	2				1	1							1				1															
William Alphon	3	1															1															
Benj. L. Crothers	1				1								2				1															
Andrew C. Man	1	1			1								1				1															
William McClain	2	1		2			1							1	1		1															
Edward Lavett	1				1								1				1															
Obediah B. Clark		1				1							2	1			1															
Jacob McClain		1	1			1	1						1	1		1		1														
John McClain	2	1			1								1	1			1															
John Caanfield	1				1								2				1															
William Brinton					1								1				1															
Archelus Clark	2	1				1							1				1															
Barsheba Caanfield			1	1	1											1			1													
Frederick Tysinger			1		1			1									1		1	1												
Lambert Saltor		1			2			1					2				1		1													
William Graham	1	1				1							2				1	1		1												
James Hoagland	1	1		1		1							1	2	1	1		1	1													
Jeremiah Featherstone	2	2	2			1							2	1			1															
John Bruer				1			1						2	1		2		1														
George McClain	2	2	2				1						1				1															
Isaac Bray	1				1								1				1															
Page Rollins					1								3				1															
Peter Smock		1	2	1	1		1						2	1		1	1		1													
Anna Smock			1	1	1												1		1													
Jessie Admire	2	2			1									1	2	2		1														
William Rice	1				1								1				1															
Jacob Smock		2				1							3	1			1															
James P. Caanfield	1				1											1																
Peter Canine	1	1	1			1							1				1															
Jacob Pegge	1					1							1	1			1															
James McClain					1								1			1																
Samuel Brewer	1			1	1								2			1																

NAMES OF HEADS OF FAMILIES	FREE WHITE PERSONS (INCLUDING HEADS OF FAMILIES)																									
	MALES													FEMALES												
	Under 5 yrs. of age	5 and under 10	10 and under 15	15 and under 20	20 and under 30	30 and under 40	40 and under 50	50 and under 60	60 and under 70	70 and under 80	80 and under 90	90 and under 100	100 and upwards	Under 5 yrs. of age	5 and under 10	10 and under 15	15 and under 20	20 and under 30	30 and under 40	40 and under 50	50 and under 60	60 and under 70	70 and under 80	80 and under 90	90 and under 100	100 and upwards
John Tracy	3			1	1		1							1	2		2		1							
John Russell	1	2			1			1						2					1							
Thomas Lewis	1	1			1									1					1							
Henry Brower					1																					
Cornelius Vanarsdell	1	1		1	1	1								1			1	1								
Robert Tumblestone	1	1		2	1									1	2		1	1								
George Tumblestone					1												1	1								
Thomas Carroll					1													1								
Abram Smock	2	2	1	2	2									3	1	2	1		1							
Stephen Hawkins					1										1	1	1	1								
Mary Seburn			1	1	1	1									1	1	1	1		1						
William Evans			1		1	1	1								1	1			1							
Margaret Coffman																										
Alvin Bass	2	2			2									1					2							
Richard Thomas	1	1		1	1													1	1							
Luke Frank			1		1												2	1								
Thomas Bryant			1		1	1		1							1		1									
Henry Wykoff	2	1	1		1			1						1		1	1	1	1							
John M. Jackson	1	1			1									1	1	1		1								
Charles Davis	1		1		1										1	1	1	1								
Samuel True, Jr.	1		2		1									1	2	2	1	1								
Henry Brinton, Jr.		1	1		1			1						1	1	1		1		1						
David McFall			1		1											1		1								
William Farley	1	1	1		1	1								1	1	1	1		1		1					
Jesse Dunn					1	1													1	1						
George Marcus					1														1							
Samuel True, Sr.	1	1		1		1		1						1	1	1			1		1	1				
Abraham Lemaster		1			1									1					1							
Isaac Lemaster	2	2	2		1		1							2	2	1	1		1	2						
Isaac Kelly	2	1	1	1	1									2	1	1			1	1						
Jacob Hill	1	1	1		1	1		1						1	1	1										
Henry D. Bell					1	1					1						1	2								
Pamelia Johnson	2	1	1		1	1								2	2	1	1		1				1			
James Bristow	1	1			1									1	1		1									

DECATUR TOWNSHIP

Athanasius Barnett
Eli Snigrove
Richard Mendenball
John McCreary
James Haworth
Absalom Dallarhide
Frederick Hartsoll
Aaron Wright
William Bowles
Daniel McCreery
James Merrit
Christley Alt
Adam Rasler
Peter Huffman, Sen.
Frederick Price
Parker Keeler
William Kinworthy
Jesse Hawkins
James Epperson
John Leighman
Noah Kelham
Edward Wright
Isaac Reed
Joseph Coner
Charles Merrit
Henry Alt
James Voorhis
Samuel Barlow
Rozin Reagan
Joseph Furnace
John Cook
Josep Allen
Ruben Birclem
John Willson
Henry Fulso
Zadock Jackson
Joseph Mendenhall
Haziel Jessup
Henry Hobbs
James Horton
Adam Ballard
Anna George
Elizabeth Cross
Abel Gibson
Aaron Copnock
Thomas Barnett
William Barnett
Zimri Brown

FREE WHITE PERSONS (INCLUDING HEADS OF FAMILIES)

NAMES OF HEADS OF FAMILIES	MALES													FEMALES												
	Under 5 yrs. of age	5 and under 10	10 and under 15	15 and under 20	20 and under 30	30 and under 40	40 and under 50	50 and under 60	60 and under 70	70 and under 80	80 and under 90	90 and under 100	100 and upwards	Under 5 yrs. of age	5 and under 10	10 and under 15	15 and under 20	20 and under 30	30 and under 40	40 and under 50	50 and under 60	60 and under 70	70 and under 80	80 and under 90	90 and under 100	100 and upwards
Seth Curtis			2			1	1							2			1	1		1						
David Kimes	1													1			1		1							
James Barnett	1													3				1								
Alexander Mendenhall						1								1					1							
Grimes Dryden					1	1								2			1		1							
James Curtis																		1								
Edmund Dallarhide	1	1	1	1			1			1				1		2		1				1				
Ashael Dallarhide	1	2		1		1			1					1	2	1	1	1		1						
Charles Beeler	2	1		1		1								3	2	1		1								
Martin Bush	1					1								1	1			1								
John Clement						1								1				1								
Joseph Beeler														3				1								
John Thompson															1			1	1							
Demas L. McFarland			1			1												1	1							
Benjamin Cuddington						1												1								
Josiah Carson																	1									
Jesse George	2														1											
James Thompson					1	1									1		1	1								
William Hawkins						1								1	1	1		1								
Martha Hawkins																	1			1						
John Kinworthy, Sr.		2						1													1					
John Kinworthy, Jr.					1										1	1	1	1								
Peter Huffman, Jr.																	1									
Uriah Carson				1														1								
Joshua Compton																										
Jesse Jones						1		1				1									1					
Dennis Case	2					1								2												
Jesse Wright	2					1	1							1		1		1								
James Sulgrove, Sr.						1	1									1					1					
John Sulgrove			1			1									1		1	1		1						
James Dryden	1				1		1							1			1		1			1				
David Winkson	1					1			1					1					1				1			
William David			1			1											2						1			
John Rosier	1						1												1							
Jesse Barnett	1	1	1				1			1				2	1	1		1								
John Myers	1					1								2	1	2		1	1			1				

Andrew Roover.
Jacob Sutherland.
Emanuel Glimpse.
James Martin.
John Magee.
John Brown.
David Evans.
Elijah McBride.
Henry Monday, Sr.
Mary Briant.
Henry Myers.
Henry Monday, Jr.
John Monday.
David Knight.
George Haworth.
William James.
Beauchamp Wishard.
Isaac Hoffman.
Winney Dollarhide.

WARREN TOWNSHIP

Nathan Harlen.
Samuel Beeler.
Benjamin Freeman.
William Banks.
David Woods.
Ann Birdwhirtle.
David Wallace.
Henry Brady.
Joel Blackledge.
Edward Hudson.
Josep Clinton.
Andrew Morehous.
John Hall.
Edward Hoizor.
Elias N. Shimer.
William Adams.
Willis G. Atherton.
John Unglos.
William Brady.
Elisha Greer.
James Williams.
John L. Mason.
John McCoy.
Joseph Williams.
John Latham.
Jacob Darluger.
James Doyle.
William Vanlaningham.
Harris Tyner.

FREE WHITE PERSONS (INCLUDING HEADS OF FAMILIES)

NAMES OF HEADS OF FAMILIES	Males — Under 5 yrs. of age	5 and under 10	10 and under 15	15 and under 20	20 and under 30	30 and under 40	40 and under 50	50 and under 60	60 and under 70	70 and under 80	80 and under 90	90 and under 100	100 and upwards	Females — Under 5 yrs. of age	5 and under 10	10 and under 15	15 and under 20	20 and under 30	30 and under 40	40 and under 50	50 and under 60	60 and under 70	70 and under 80	80 and under 90	90 and under 100	100 and upwards
Richard Vanlaningham	2				1									1	1				1							
Nathan Wells	2	2												1					2							
Jacob Cass																										
David Shield	1	1			1	1		1							1		1	1								
John Mcgouree	2	2		1	1			1						1	1	2		1								
Michael Sharrar	1	1			1			1									1									
George Vanlaningham	1				1									1	1		1	1								
Martin Brandon	1	1	1											1				1	1							
Joespah Clark	1	1	1											2	1	1			1	1						
Nelson Hartsock	1	1				1								3				1	1	1						
Caleb Clark	1				1									2		1		1								
John Parker																	1									
Machaga Willson	1	1	1		1									1	1	1	1									
John Willson	1	1	1		1									1		1		1								
John S. Moulton	1	1		1	3			1						1	2				1							
Daniel Devoree	1	1	1		1									1	1	1		1								
Philip Harper	1	1	1		1			1						1			1		1							
Allen Atherton	1			1										1	1		1	1								
Isaac Barrett														2	1		1		1							
Joshua Black	2	1	1					1						2	2	2		1		1						
Jacob Hudson	1	1	1											1		1		1		1						
John Hamilton	2	2	1											1	1	1		1								
Samuel Fuller	2	1	1											1				1								
John Keley															1											
Frederick Horner	2	2	2					1						1		1			1							
James Davis	1	2												1		2				1						
Iseal Green	2	2												1	1	2	1	1								
Obadiah Davis														1				1		1						
Jane Delzell														1		2				1						
James Davis	2		2		1		1							2		1	2	1								
Rufus Jenison	1				2									1				1	1							
James Furgason					2										1											
Robert Hamilton					1			1									1	1	1							
Stephen Brown	2	2	1											2				1								
Abraham Hudson	1		1																							
Thomas Hudson	1		1		1		1								1	1	1	1	1							

Name	1	2	3	4	5	6	7	8	9	10	11	12	13	14	15	16	17	18	19	20	21	22	23	24	25	26	27	28	29	30
John Gillham	2	1					1								1		1		1											
Henry Harper			1	1	1										1	1	2													
Andrew Sharrar			1	1			1												1											
George Sharrar	1	1	1	2	1			1							1			1			1									
Andrew Sharrar, Jr.	1				1													1												
Andrew Vansickle		1	1	1	1		1						2		1	1			1											
John Wright					1								1					1			1									
John Sharrar	1	1	2	2			1						1		1	1	1			1										
David Groves			1	1			1						1	2						1		1							1	
William Coblin	2				1								1																	
Thomas Askins [Askren?]	1	1				1							2	1					1										1	
James P. Hanna	1				1	1							2						1		1									
Rozin Hawkins	1	2	2			1							2							1		1		1						
John Lamb	1	1	1				1						2		1	1	1	2				1								
Philamon Shirley					1								1					1												
Elizabeth Cox					1								2					1												
John Chinn		1	1			1							2	1	2	1			1											
Jacob Coverdill										1					1								1	1						
Richard Gott			2	2			1	1							1															
Henry Bowling	1	2				1	1						1					1	1											
John Jones	1	2	1	1			1						1		2				1											
Jeremiah Kinmen			1	2					1					1	1				1											
Eli Wells	2	1				1							1			1			1											
John Vandermin		2	1				1							2					1											
Aaron Montfort		1			1		1						1					1												
Aron Wells		1	2	2			1								1		1		1											
Solomon Wells			1		1	1		1								1	2		1											
Rural Wells	1				1								1					1												
Nelson Wells	1	2				1								1					1											

WAYNE TOWNSHIP

Name	1	2	3	4	5	6	7	8	9	10	11	12	13	14	15	16	17	18	19	20	21	22	23	24	25	26	27	28	29	30
Luke Strong	1					1							1					1												
Mathew Railsback					1		1						1		1	1		1												
R. J. H. Hanna	1		2			1							1	1		1		1												
John Brown	1				1											1														
Thomas Anderson	2		1			1							1	1				1												
Mathew Brown	3	1		1		1							1	2				1												
Joseph Hanna				1	1			1					1		1					1										
George R. Hanna	1				1								1				2													
J. W. Hanna					1										1															
David Stoops	2		1	2			1						1				3													
Thomas Stoops	2				1												1													
William Logan	1	2	3			1							1		1	1		1												
William Viney			1			1	1						1	2	1	1	1		1											
James Johnson	1	1			1								2				1													
L. B. Noe	1		1		1								3	2			1													
William Williamson	1				1											1	2													
Rachel Martindale	1												1				1		1											
John T. Wilson	1	1			1												1													
Miles Martindale	1	3	1	1		1									2			1												

| | FREE WHITE PERSONS (INCLUDING HEADS OF FAMILIES) | | | | | | | | | | | | | | | | | | | | | | | | | |
| NAMES OF HEADS OF FAMILIES | MALES | | | | | | | | | | | | | FEMALES | | | | | | | | | | | | |
	Under 5 yrs. of age	5 and under 10	10 and under 15	15 and under 20	20 and under 30	30 and under 40	40 and under 50	50 and under 60	60 and under 70	70 and under 80	80 and under 90	90 and under 100	100 and upwards	Under 5 yrs. of age	5 and under 10	10 and under 15	15 and under 20	20 and under 30	30 and under 40	40 and under 50	50 and under 60	60 and under 70	70 and under 80	80 and under 90	90 and under 100	100 and upwards
Enoch Harding	2		1			1	1							1				1	1							
Samuel Harding	2	1	1			1										2		1								
Ephraim Harding	1	2				1									2		1	1								
William Williamson	1		1	1			1							1		1	1	1								
Israel Harding					2										2			1		1						
P. F. Newland				1	1	1								2	1	1		1	1							
Obadiah Harris	4	1												1				1								
James Sloan	1					1	1											1	1							
William Thomas	1		1			1								1			1		1							
Isaac Evans	1				2		2							1				1								
Thomas Lucas																		1								
William Homes									1							2	1	1								
John Baylor	2		1		1	1	1	1						4	2	2		1			1					
John Cosell					1	3	1							2	1			1								
Michael Brown						1		1						2	1			1								
Robert F. Samuel	2	1	1	1		1								2	1	1	1	2								
Jethro Bowie																		1								
Joseph Sharp					2		1							2		2	1									
Barlin Rooks																		1								
Samuel Howard		1			2	1								2	1	1		1			1					
Robert Yancy	1						1							2	1	1	1	2	1		1					
Sarahaner Books								1													1					
Sidney Williams						1			1							1		1			1					
William Gladen	2	1												1												
Isaac Williamson		1	2	1	1	1	1							2		1	1	1	1							
Isaac Harulin														2	2	1		2		1	1					
John Evans	1	1	1	1										1	1	1	1	1	1		1					
John Patterson	1		1			1	1		1										1							
Joseph Griffith	2		1		2													2								
Thomas Martin						1											2	2		1						
Benjamin Petterson		1																1								
Miner Roberts					1		1	1											1							
Isaac Roberts	1		1	1			1							1	1	1		1		1						
Francis McLelland	1			1											2			2								
William Roberts																		2								
Rachel Roots	2	1		1	1	1	1														1					

NAMES OF HEADS OF FAMILIES	MALES													FEMALES												
	Under 5 yrs. of age	5 and under 10	10 and under 15	15 and under 20	20 and under 30	30 and under 40	40 and under 50	50 and under 60	60 and under 70	70 and under 80	80 and under 90	90 and under 100	100 and upwards	Under 5 yrs. of age	5 and under 10	10 and under 15	15 and under 20	20 and under 30	30 and under 40	40 and under 50	50 and under 60	60 and under 70	70 and under 80	80 and under 90	90 and under 100	100 and upwards
Martin Martindale	1				1	1								1	2		1		1			1				
William Dod					2										1					1						
Docus Pugh	2		1												1											
Andrew Roberts	2	3	1			1									1			1								
Robert Smith	2					1								1	1			1								
James Smith	1					1								1	1				1							
Manoah Smith	1					1								1	1			1								
Joel Conrowe														1												
J. J. Corbaley				1		1	1								1	1		1		1						
Robert Speer		2	1	1				1						2	1	2	2		1		1					
James Adams				1		1	1	1						2	2	1		1			1					
Asa B. Strong																		1								
John Barnhill					1									1	1	2		1								
James Ward	2			1		1									2		1	1								
James Frazer								1										1								
David Vanner			1		1	1								1	1	2	1	1	1							
George L. Kennard															1											
G. W. Johnson											1															
H. W. Harber	2	1	1		1	2			1					2	1	2		1		1	1					
Robert Robertson																										
Jordan Wright	1	1	1	1		1	1							1					1							
John Smith	1	1					1							1	1		1									
John Moss	1	1				1				1						2	1									
James Miller		1	1			1								1	2	1		1		1						
Jneck [?] Pugh															1			2								
David Vanblaraun						1								1	1			1		1						
Abraham Coble	2		1																							
John Halm		1					1								1			1								
Elijah Force		2		2		1	1									2		1								
Thomas Force	3	1			1	1					1			1	1			2		1			1			
Godfrey Isaac	2																									
Christian Byerly	1		2	1										1	1					1						
Peter Coppers	8					1	1	1						1	2	1	1	2		1						
Adam Coppers		1			1																					
David Fox		1				1								1	1	1		1		1						
Jesse Isaac	2	1	2		1	1								2		1		1		1						

Benjamin Wright
N. Bell
John Draper
George Avery
Andrew Avery
David West
Joseph Loflin
Joseph West
Isaac Pugh
Thomas Kogge
William Logan
Jonathan Jordan
Elijah Keeler
Polloy Hiner
John Crumpton
William McCan

WASHINGTON TP.
Milton Johnson
William Harden
Thomas Kinson
Siglo McClung
John Shoalids
John St. Clair
Henry Harten
Peter Smith
Elizabeth Thomas
William Evans
Samuel Letters
Hiram Bacon
James Carter
Jonathan Soward
Simon Smith
John Collins
Zachariah Collins
Richard Clark
Catharine Young
Richard Watts
William McIlvain
Samuel Morrow
Louisa Wright
John Nisbet
Ralph Falls
Elijah Dawson
Mary Ann Smith
Abraham Peters
Evan Bullonger
James McIlvain
Daniel Reagan
William D. Rooker

NAMES OF HEADS OF FAMILIES	FREE WHITE PERSONS (INCLUDING HEADS OF FAMILIES)																									
	MALES													FEMALES											
	Under 5 yrs. of age	5 and under 10	10 and under 15	15 and under 20	20 and under 30	30 and under 40	40 and under 50	50 and under 60	60 and under 70	70 and under 80	80 and under 90	90 and under 100	100 and upwards	Under 5 yrs. of age	5 and under 10	10 and under 15	15 and under 20	20 and under 30	30 and under 40	40 and under 50	50 and under 60	60 and under 70	70 and under 80	80 and under 90	90 and under 100	100 and upwards
Zachau Gay	2	1	1					1						1	1				1							
Hezekiah Smith	1					1								1			1									
William McIntosh	1	1	1	2										1		1	1									
James Ellis			1																							
James Ballenger						1								1		1	1									
John Brady	2			2	2										2											
George Boswell					2	1				1								1			1	1				
Andrew Leeper	2	1		2	2					1				1	1			1				1				
John W. Hinesley	1	1	1	2		1				1				1				1	1							
William Duffield						1								1				1								
Jacob Haslian	3	1	1	1		1								3	2	1	1	1	1							
John H. Burroughs					1										1		1	1								
William McCoy			1		1	1										1			1							
Zenas Huffman					1		1								1			1								
Jacob Cile				1		1	1							1	1	1	1	1			1		1			
Edward Wells	1			1	1	1		1		1				1	1	1	1	1	1	1	1					
Samuel Leeper		1	1			1									1											
John McCoy	3	2												1	1	1	1									
Henry L. Brown		1	1			1		1						1			2	1		1						
Edmund Newby			1			1		1						1	2	1	1	1	1							
Daniel McDonald	1	1	1			1		1							1	1		1			1					
John Johnson				2	1											1	2									
James Brown	3	1	1			1								3	2	1		1	1							
Jacob Whiteinger														1												
John G. McIlvain	2	1	1	1	2	1		1		1				1	1	2	2	1	1				1			
Lucy Ann Cruse		1	1			1								1	2	2			1							
Squire Dawson	1	1				1								1	2	1		1		1						
Samuel Sellers	1	1	1		1	2		1									2					1				
Fielding Clark	2			1	1	1		1						1												
William Bacon																										
James Cooke	2				1	1											2									
John Cooke					1		1							1				1					1			
Robert Leeper								1																		
Andrew Leeper						1								1												
Francis Whiteinger			1				1			1				2			2									
Peter Mechal	2					1				1					1	1	1									

David H. Sharp
John Hinsley
Nathan Hemilton
H. G. Hemilton
Thomas Smith
Jacob Ringer
Daniel Bower
Martin Culbertson
John West
William Brunson
Jonathan Brunson
James McCoy
William Orum
Robert Brunson
John Allison
Alexander Mills
Lewis Kimberlin
Willis Alkins
William Ramsey
Joseph Coats
Benjamin Inmana
O. Kimberlin
Daniel Butler
Daniel Wright
John Rougan
Ephraim Elkins
John Harrison
Caleb Harrison
Daniel Smith
Hanna Richerson
Isaac Copper
John Metsker
George Metsker
Henry Whiteinger
William Vinson
Lewis Hoffman
Devis Harrison
Devid Ray
Abraham Booan (?)
Thomas Todd
Nathan Johnson
John Smith
Samuel Harrison
William Hobson
John Ray
John Burns
John Burns, Jr.
Jonathan Ray
William Deford
Samuel Ray

FREE WHITE PERSONS (INCLUDING HEADS OF FAMILIES)

NAMES OF HEADS OF FAMILIES	Males — Under 5 yrs. of age	5 and under 10	10 and under 15	15 and under 20	20 and under 30	30 and under 40	40 and under 50	50 and under 60	60 and under 70	70 and under 80	80 and under 90	90 and under 100	100 and upwards	Females — Under 5 yrs. of age	5 and under 10	10 and under 15	15 and under 20	20 and under 30	30 and under 40	40 and under 50	50 and under 60	60 and under 70	70 and under 80	80 and under 90	90 and under 100	100 and upwards
Jacob Applegate	2		1		1	1								1					1							
Peter E. Blake	1	2					1												1							
John Stephens																			1							
Edmund Newley	1		3		2	1	1							2	1			1	1	1						
Joseph Watts	1		2		1	1	1							2	1	1			1							
Robert Barnhill	1			1	1	1								1					1							
Absalom Cruse	2		1	2	1	1									1		2	1	1							
Daniel Clark		1		1	1									1					1							
Elijah Harding																			1							
Mary Ball		1		1	2	1		1							1		1									
John Jackson	2				1									1					1							
Solomon Jackson					1	1	1							1					1							
James Burnell					1									1												
William Hewitt		1			2	1	1							1				1	1							
Winchoff VanSeekler						1																				
Jacob Roberts	1		1	1		1	1								1	1			1							
Noah Jackson							1			1						2			1							
Cornelius Vanneyuo	1	1			2	1	1							1					1							
Thomas Kooler						1		1											1							
Elias Simpkins						1	1												1							
William Duffield		1					1							1	1				1							
Elias Lemmon			1		1	1									2											
Francis Williamson	1	1				1	1			1				2	1				1	1						
Edward Roberts	2	1		1	1		1							1					1	1						
Sargeant Ransome	1					1	1												1							
Jacob Triggs					1												2		2							
Isaac Stephens					1		1												1							
Jonathan Ingole	1			1			1	1											1	1						
Moses Mills					1	1			1						2				1	1	1					
James M. Long	1	1		1	1		1							2	1			2		1						
Jonathan Masage	1	1			1	1	1							1					1							
Samuel Ray																										
James Porter	1	1		1	1	1	1								2	1	2		1	1						
Nicholas Porter	1	1				1	1								2				1	1						
James Porter	1	1			1	1					1									1						
William Martin					1	1								2					1		1					

Robert Brewer
Elizabeth Earcut
Garret Garrison
Frances Whitinger
James Cansing
Michael Miller
Alexander Nelson
Conrod Collip
Philip Harding
John Mansfield
Mathew Dawson
William McCoy

LAWRENCE TP.
John Essary
John Hutchins
Peter Negley
Jude Reed
William McKinster
George Negley
Benjamin Newhouse
Henry Newhouse
Lewis Brown
John Bowlfader
Joseph Johnston
Daniel Spaise
John McConnell
Jeremiah Blumer
Samuel Plumer
John Shingles
N. C. Plimer
James Hince
John Vanlandingham
Isaac Perkins
Samuel Williams
John Emry
Mathew Day
Elias Riley
James Giles
Jeremiah Vanlandingham
Daniel Shoots
John North
William Gaiber
Stephen Graves
Conrad Ringer
Thomas Woods
Oliver Reavell
David Eller
Andrew Clarke
James North

FREE WHITE PERSONS (INCLUDING HEADS OF FAMILIES)

NAMES OF HEADS OF FAMILIES	MALES													FEMALES												
	Under 5 yrs. of age	5 and under 10	10 under 15	15 and under 20	20 under 30	30 and under 40	40 and under 50	50 and under 60	60 and under 70	70 and under 80	80 under 90	90 and under 100	100 and upwards	Under 5 yrs. of age	5 and under 10	10 under 15	15 and under 20	20 under 30	30 and under 40	40 and under 50	50 and under 60	60 and under 70	70 under 80	80 and under 90	90 under 100	100 and upwards
Adam Eller	1			1	1	1	1							1	1	1	1	1		1						
William Deckson		2			1									2	2											
John Clarke	1					1								1				1	1							
Samuel North	1	2							1					1												
Elizabeth North																1										
Joseph North			1	1						1								1								
John Ballinger		1	1		1	1								1				1								
John Johnson			1	1	1		1							2	2	1	1	1								
Nathan Essary			2		2		1							1	1	1	1		1							
Samuel Morrow			1	1										2	2			1	1							
Henry Harlen			1											1	1		1		1							
Ephraim Morrison					1													1	1							
Peter Castodor					1	1		1						2	1	1	1	1	2							
William McJain		2		2		1									1	1			2							
Alexander McLain		1			1									1				1								
John Brady			1		1	1										1	1		1							
David Ballinger						1								2				1								
Abraham Setters		2	1		1	1		1						1	1	1	1	1			1					
Christen Bever		1	1		1	1								3					1							
Samuel Harrison					1	1								1			1	1								
Fountain Kimberlin		1			1	1	1							2		1		1		1						
Jacob Shankle			1		1	1	1										1	1								
Nancy Moore															1				1							
Joshua Reddick					1	1										1			1							
Elisha Reddick					1	1								1		1			1							
William Reddick		3					1							3		1	1		1							
Alexandria Smith						1											1		1			1				
John Flanagan		1	1		1									1	1		1		1							
Hugh McDonald	3				1	1	1		1					2	1	1	1	1	1							
William Oppear	1	1				1	1							1					1							
John Setters	1		1		1	1	1	1						1		1	1	1	1							
Christopher Setters		2	2		1	1								2				1	1							
James Ballenger						1								1			1		1							
Isaac Ballenger	8	1			1	1								2	1											
Robert Large	1		2	1	1	1	1	1						2	1		1	1	1							
Joseph Culbertson			2	2	1		1	1							1	1	1	1					1			

Alexandria Culbertson
William Christ

FRANKLIN TOWNSHIP

John Bellis
William Bay
Stephen Yager
Garrison Williams
Josiah B. Toon
Simon Adams
William Griffith
James Greer
George Montjoy
Joshua Jackson
John Furgason
William Hines
Benjamin Phillips
Lucy Ann Fray
Daniel Skilley
Jeremiah Burright
Thomas Beley
Jacob Rarrick
William Rector
Jesse Harton
John Stinley
James Amons
William Flint
Isaac Baylor
John Walden
Daniel Smith
Thomas Rows
William Smith
James Smither
Benjamin Kilgore
George Tibbits
Henry Martin
John H. Messinger
John Miller
Peter Carberry
John Kelley
Lewis Smither
James Skeller
John Smither
Joshua Eudaily
Lewis O'Neal
Israel Jennings
Bensin Cornelius
M. D. West
James Freeman
John Perkins

NAMES OF HEADS OF FAMILIES	Males — Under 5 yrs of age	5 and under 10	10 and under 15	15 and under 20	20 and under 30	30 and under 40	40 and under 50	50 and under 60	60 and under 70	70 and under 80	80 and under 90	90 and under 100	100 and upwards	Females — Under 5 yrs of age	5 and under 10	10 and under 15	15 and under 20	20 and under 30	30 and under 40	40 and under 50	50 and under 60	60 and under 70	70 and under 80	80 and under 90	90 and under 100	100 and upwards
Moses Barker					1									2	1				1			1				
Abraham Hendricks	1	1			1									1				1								
James B. Madin	1	2			1	1								2	1			1								
James Pool	2	1	1	1	1									2		1		1								
James McLain					1									1				1								
PIKE TOWNSHIP																										
Abraham Wells	1	2	1	1	1	1			1						1	1	1	1	1							
Thomas Moyer		1	1	1				1						2				1	1		1					
Samuel Hines		1	2	2	1									2	1	1		1								
Joseph Slaton			1	1		1								1				1	1							
Robert Ramsey	1	1		1	1	1									1			1								
William Johnston				2		1										1		1								
Y. P. Hollingsworth		1		1		1								1	1	1		1	1							
Aaron Gullerver	2	1		1	1	1		1						2			1	1								
Stephen Gullerver	1	1		1	1	1	1									1	1	1	1							
Seth Rodebauch					1										1	1		1								
Samuel Rodebauch	2			1	1	1	1							1	1	1		1	1							
David Mogskor					1	1												1								
George Rains						1	1								1			1	1							
David Turner					1			1						2			1	1		1						
Andrew Chilston	3	1	1	1	1	1	1							1	1		1	1			1					
Joseph Clingsmith	2			1							1			2												
Valentine Kenoyer		3	1	1	1	1									1											
Henry Groves	2	2	1	1	1	1	1							2		1		1	1	1						
Daniel Groves	1	1			1	1								1	1			1	1		1					
William Munroe					1			1			1						1	1		1						
Adam Wright				1	1	1										1		1								
George Hollingsworth	1	1		1	1	1	1							1	1			1					1			
Elmer Chilston					1	1												1								
John Reins					1	1								2	1				1							
Leonard West	1	1				1								1		1	1	1								
Jeremiah Wright					1	1	1							1				1								
Lewis Mitchell					1	1								2				1								
Thomas Hume	1	1		1	1	1		1						1	1	1	1	1								
Catharine Jackson														2		1		1	1			1				1

Carter.
?, Jones.
Starkey
l Coonsel.
Brazelton.
rd Hill.
Hamer.
Jackson.
l Heartman.
aun Busenbrush.
Roadman.
3. Harmon.
rd Harmon.
Harmon.
m Harmon.
y Ray
Wilson.
Adams
na Robertson.
Barnhill
as Burns.
Orbor.
rot Starkey.
l Plowman
eth Harrison.
Brazelton.
Babcock.
McCrrody.
m Moares
m Fisher.
Caldwell
am M. Colc.
l Barnhill.
. Delnny.
nes...
C. Jones
Shirtliff
ny Swain.
as B. Jones.
as Shanklin.
as M. Jones.
Cow.
i Lofton.
Mlrvs
. Criss.
3linger.
ol Mitchol.
Free
Hueler.
ol Lakin.

NAMES OF HEADS OF FAMILIES	TOWNSHIP	MALES Under 10 yrs. of age	10 and under 24	24 and under 36	36 and under 55	55 and under 100	100 and upwards	FEMALES Under 10 yrs. of age	10 and under 24	24 and under 36	36 and under 55	55 and under 100	100 and upwards
James Morrison	Centre		1						1				
Luke Walpole	"		1						1	1			
John Hawkins	"												
Samuel Henderson	"												
Livingston Dunlap	"		1					4	1		1		
David Mallory	"		1		1			2	1		1		
Wilford J. Uncles	"								1				
Sampson Leatherman	"												
Henry P. Coburn	"					1			1	1	1		
John R. Moreland	"	2		1				2	1	1	1		
John Jones	"	1	1		1	1							
Chena Lively	"												
Benjamin Draper	"			1				3	1				
Joseph Greer	"												
James Overall	"		1		1	1			1	1	1		
John Tucker	"												
John Partridge	"												
John W. Redding	"		1										
James B. McDowell	"	1	1					1	1				
William McDowell	"		1						1			1	
William Reagan	"		1			1		1	1	1	1		
Eleanor Bennet	"	2	1			2		1	2	1	1	1	
V. P. Campbell	"	1	2									1	
John G. Brown	"		1	1									
Daniel Harris	"												
John Chinn	Perry												
Jacob Coverdill	Warren												

*The colored persons enumerated in this table are not listed under their own names, but under the heads of the white families with whom they lived, for whom they worked or upon whom they were dependent. It may be noted that the Census Bureau provided in the blanks used in making the census spaces for the listing of slaves, but there were no slaves in Marion County.

The whole number of persons within my division, consisting of Centre, Perry and Decatur Townships in Marion Co., Indiana, appears in the foregoing schedule, subscribed by me this fifteenth day of November in the year one thousand eight hundred and thirty.   ALEXANDER F. MORRISON,
Asst. to the Marshal
of the District of Indiana.

We hereby certify that a correct copy of the above schedule, signed by the said Alexander F. Morrison, has been set up at two of the most public places in this Division, open to the inspection of all concerned.
FABIUS M. FINCH,
ISRAEL P. GRIFFITH.

Examined and corrected.
W. A. RIND.

The number of persons within my division, consisting of Washington Township, Wayne Township, Warren Township, Lawrence Township, Franklin Township, and Pike Township, appears in the foregoing schedule, subscribed by me this 25 day Nov. 1830.   JOHN CAIN,
Assistant to the Marshal
of the District of Indiana.

We hereby certify that a correct copy of the above schedule, signed by the said John Cain, has been set up at two of the most public places within the Division opened to the inspection of all concerned.
SAMUEL JENISON,
ELIAS H. LEAHAM.

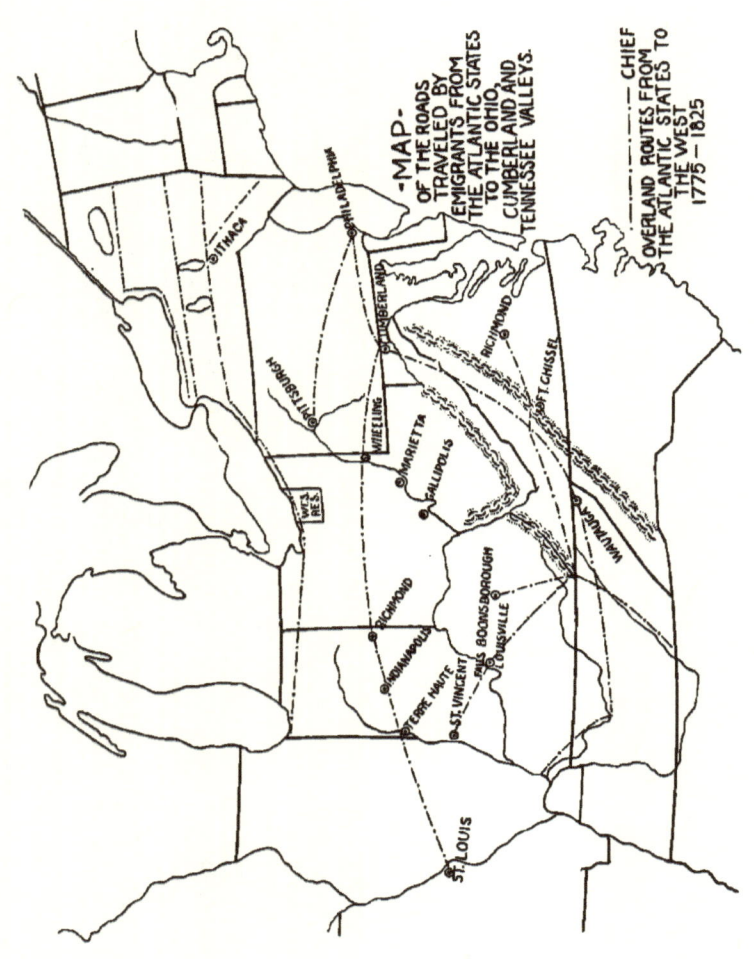

-MAP-
OF THE ROADS
TRAVELED BY
EMIGRANTS FROM
THE ATLANTIC STATES
TO THE OHIO,
CUMBERLAND AND
TENNESSEE VALLEYS.

------ CHIEF
OVERLAND ROUTES FROM
THE ATLANTIC STATES TO
THE WEST
1775 – 1825

INDIANA HISTORICAL SOCIETY PUBLICATIONS
VOLUME IV   NUMBER 6

SOME ELEMENTS

OF

INDIANA'S POPULATION

OR

ROADS WEST AND THEIR
EARLY TRAVELERS

BY

W. E. HENRY

INDIANAPOLIS
Edward J. Hecker, Printer and Publisher
1908

SOME ELEMENTS OF INDIANA'S POPULATION

It would be as delightfully interesting as it is hopelessly difficult to trace out in detail the mixture and commingling of nationalities and hereditary tendencies that make up the present population of Indiana. Behind our complex tastes and tendencies, behind our varied industries, political theories, religious beliefs, and social views and ambitions, a hundred forces from past generations and foreign countries are manifesting their varied influences. Scores of streams have flowed from as many sources and have commingled their waters. Some are clear, crystal and brilliant, others are muddy and turbulent, carrying to this alluvial plain silt from upland and mountain to deposit here, and when our soil shall be analyzed all these sources may be more or less definitely traced. What influences, created and formulated elsewhere, may now be determining our own views would be interesting to know. What the traditions are back of our elements of composition might become the basis for valuable history or interesting fiction.

If we could go to all the older sections of the State and in these to the oldest and most intelligent citizens with a series of quizzes, we should doubtless find in detail whence came those persons and groups of persons who first peopled the present State of Indiana. To go into all these communities to make diligent inquiry as to the ancestral whereabouts of all these people is quite impossible for any one who secures a livelihood by the slow process of earning it. There seem to be no census reports from the State indicating birthplaces of our early comers, except in a few isolated sections.

In a few counties, perhaps, directories were published early enough to give much information of this character for the locality.   \

Some of the county histories give us a small portion of more or less trustworthy information, but few of our counties have been fortunate enough to have such histories written. Some of the histories that have been published are not very reliable, yet it is safe to say no county history has ever been written that is not worth much more than it has cost.

Such of these histories and directories are invaluable so far as they go, but we have too few such aids to the study of our civilization. In the absence of these aids, perhaps the best source of information concerning the streams of population flowing in here is a knowledge of the great highways leading toward and into Indiana from the east and southeast. To know well the sources of all the streams that flowed into this common reservoir is the best method perhaps, of knowing the composition of its contents.

Of all the numerous influences back of us that have molded our composite character, only a few of them can even be hinted at or suggested, none of them fully traced.

Among all the influences upon mankind, perhaps no one power external to man himself has more strongly urged him in his way or out of his way than the geographic conditions around him.

The fact that the great civilizations of the world have grown in the cool temperate zones may not prove anything, but the facts force us to question whether the conditions of life do not largely control, perhaps create or destroy, our energies.

Culture and civilization have grown and must continue to grow where life is neither too easy nor too hard; where a surplus is given to non-essentials of existence—to education and culture.

The Norsemen lived in an unfriendly climate, and much of their soil was unproductive. Both nature and the law of the land drove the sons, except the first born of the family, to the sea, and they became the vikings, the sons of the inlets, the great early navigators, the roamers and travelers of the sea—the dread of all seafaring men and countries. They conquered all the best of France and occupied it; they largely changed the population of the British Isles, and they were the Normans who with William in 1066 overran and modified the whole people and life of England. They came to England to unite with their cousins. The Norse spirit came to America and traveled the trackless woods and prairie —the East as English, and the Mississippi valley as French.

They traveled, explored, settled, fought and conquered the wild life of a new continent, and Boone and Clark and Putnam and Fremont and Carson and Cody are modern Norsemen in a new world. French in the valley, English on the coast, mountains between.

The modern history of the Mississippi valley really begins shortly after the middle of the eighteenth century. Settlements had existed before, but they were the remnants of an old and a foreign civilization; our real modern history began when America began to become America and not merely an outpost of a foreign country.

England had occupied the coast plain to the mountains and France had her chains of forts, her missionaries and her hunters immediately west of the mountains for a hundred years.

For either to cross the ridge meant war, and any one who has read history must see that war was as inevitable at the crossing as the fact of the crossing itself. I can not believe, however, that it was a war of the two nations, but merely a commercial war, as most other wars have been. Subtract commerce, however simple or complicated, and you will obliterate the chief causes of war.

If the hunters had not met, there would probably have been no national collision. The question of monopoly precedes the question of unity. Not only does the French and Indian War fall within this category, but our border wars with the Indians from the Atlantic to the Pacific are all based upon the same principle. The coming of the white man, not because he was white, not merely because he was cruel and frequently devoid of principle, but because his coming interfered with a monopoly upon which the Indian was dependent for his very existence, was always the signal for war. The Indian was a hunter, and civilization makes hunting unprofitable. Indians could live with the French, who were chiefly hunters and explorers, but they could not live with the English, who were settlers who cleared the land and drove away the bison and the bear, the deer and the turkey. Jordan told the whole truth about the Indian when he said, "The Indian required too much land to live on, so we had to kill him."

The British government in 1763 issued a proclamation that no grant of land should be made to the colonists west of the headwaters of those rivers flowing into the Atlantic ocean. This was upon the surface a strange proclamation, but behind it was a good political philosophy. More than one reason has been assigned for this order being promulgated. Was it to secure justice to the Indians, or was it to save to England the commerce of the colonies? They would still be English colonies and English subjects west of the mountains.

But the English statesmen who had read history knew that commerce by primitive methods of transportation could never be carried on over mountain ranges. Neither rivers nor seas, nor deserts even, have prevented commerce, but, before the modern railroad, mountains were a barrier. The British government saw that if colonies were established west of the mountains, an independent and self-sustaining state must grow up and political independence would become not only desirable but a necessity.

The small horses, which we should now call ponies, that were used for pack-horses over mountain roads, each carried an average burden of two hundred pounds. When the National Road was built through western Pennsylvania, men were running pack trains in some instances consisting of as many as five hundred horses. Even at the enormous attendant expense only one hundred thousand pounds of freight could be moved by a five-hundred-horse train, and these trains moved from ten to twenty miles per day.

The commerce of a nation, even of a colony, could not be carried on over a mountain. A colony west of the mountains meant independence. English statesmen certainly saw this possibility, I might almost say, this necessity, and whether or not this fact was the basis of the order not to settle west of the headwaters of the Atlantic rivers, I am inclined to believe it the chief reason.

Regardless, however, of this proclamation or the reason for this command, the eastern population began to move west, and ten years before the Revolutionary war actually began there was a decided looking to the west, although no considerable number of persons actually crossed the mountains. Dr. Walker, of Virginia, as early as 1747 explored the northeast portion of Kentucky and named the Cumberland river after the "Bloody Duke."[1] Walker was not the first white man in Kentucky, but was perhaps the first to leave a journal of his travels.

Of course there were many influences in the last half of the eighteenth century which led men from the Atlantic coast plain to the valley beyond the mountains.

Much of the best land had been taken up, leaving little opportunity, as they thought, for a head of a family to secure a home for himself, so he moved west, where even much better land could be had for little more than the asking. It was the natural overflow of a well-established community.

The spirit of adventure had much to do, for it always exists. There are always men who want to go west wherever they may abide. The Norseman is always with us.

When our progenitors on the Atlantic coast began to look toward homes and conquest beyond the Alleghanies, the greatest impediment in their path was the great blue wall that stood between them and the coveted land. Here geography again asserts itself and deflected the line of travel of even these hardy travelers whose Norse spirit had dared and suffered so much in the century immediately preceding this time. When the tide began to move in western and central Pennsylvania, northern and western Virginia and Maryland, it, rather than attempt "the crossing" directly, moved southwest, down the troughs of the mountains in the lines of least resistance, until in the course of time they

---

[1] So says Mann Butler.

found the breach in the wall.[1] Southwest Virginia and western North Carolina were settled by people largely of the Scotch-Irish stock and Calvinistic faith from Pennsylvania and northern Virginia. In 1769, Daniel Boone, a Scotch-Irishman from the Yadkin, inspired by Walker, found and passed through the Cumberland Gap and blazed out the Wilderness road. No less than seventy thousand people moved through this gap and over this road in fifteen years between 1774 and 1790, and these people became settlers, owners and directors of the life and policies of the great Mississippi valley. A new civilization and an independent self-directing government were established.

The French and Indian War had been fought because English-American hunters had begun to cross the mountains and interfere with the monopoly of the fur trade of the French in the Mississippi valley. Two other wars were yet to be fought, and the principles at issue were carried across the mountains by these same people. For across these mountains and through the Cumberland Gap came love of freedom and self-direction. There came the real Virginian, whose whole economic and social system rested upon slavery; there came also the Scotch-Irish Calvinist from Pennsylvania, via mountain troughs, whose social, economic and religious doctrines had grown in opposition to slavery, for keeping slaves in a cold climate is not economic, and our conscience is largely colored by our economic advantages. Thus we have two reasons why the highlanders of Kentucky and Tennessee were unionists in the Civil War times.

In the original settlement of this highland country

[1] See map facing title page in Imlay's *A Topographical Description of the Western Territory of North America*, London, 1793.

three strains of splendid blood mingled. James Robertson, the Scotch Presbyterian, John Sevier, the French Huguenot, and Evan Shelby, the Welsh Congregationalist, were leaders and types among the pioneers who early settled this region. The fiber and sinew, intellectual and moral as well as physical, possessed by the American Highlanders of to-day they get from these ancestors. Heroic events mark their history. John Sevier, attacking the stronghold at King's Mountain (1780), held by the most experienced British soldiery, and utterly routing them, is the contribution of the Highlanders to the cause of freedom in the Revolutionary War. They were no less heroic and loyal during the War of the Rebellion. Tennessee and Kentucky never went out of the Union by popular vote. The mountains were filled with loyal and patriotic citizens who thwarted the treasonable plans of the inhabitants of the lowlands. These mountain counties put one hundred and forty thousand troops into the loyal army, twenty thousand more than the entire enrollment of New Hampshire, Vermont and Connecticut in the same army. These Highland clans filled their quota in the Union Army from the opening to the close of the War of the Rebellion. They fought beside our bravest and fell beside our best in the battle for human freedom.

Said one traveler: "What impresses one most in riding through the mountains is the vast number of children. A mountaineer pointed to his cabin as I rode beside him on horseback along the winding bridle path some months ago, and said, 'Elder, that is my house over yonder.' I said, 'How many children have you?' He replied, 'Twenty-two; eighteen of them were boys and they were all in the Union army.' This family was somewhat representative."

Let us now turn to the making of roads leading to the west from the Atlantic States.

The logician who first saw the intimate relation existing between the number of maiden ladies and the production of clover seed might, if he had studied western highways, have stated an equally close relationship between modern civilization in the Mississippi valley and the size of a buffalo's hoof. The buffalo, being a large, heavy animal with a comparatively small foot, could not cross low, swampy, marshy lands; being gregarious to a very high degree, he could not continue long in one place, so great herds of many hundreds and sometimes of many thousands ranged together. The best of pasture vanished rapidly before such vast numbers, and frequently long journeys were taken by these herds from one feeding ground to another. Buffalo roads, therefore, were very definitely marked and well beaten in all parts of the continent where they roamed, and that was wherever grass grew and through the timber where native meadows were on opposite sides of the timber.

The small feet of these animals along with their heavy bodies necessitated their roads following the highlands—indeed, the ridges, the water divides—the backbones of various sections of the country. The Indians followed these roads for two reasons—first, because they were as lazy as they dared be and live; second, because they were hungry. It saved labor in making roads and it furnished opportunity to kill a buffalo occasionally by being on the line of trail.

The buffalo and the Indian followed those lines of travel upon which nature drove them by means of the physical needs and economic wants. When the white man came as an explorer, hunter or settler, he followed precisely the same routes for precisely the same reasons, and it is an exceedingly interesting but not at all a strange logic that finally placed all the great highways of commerce and transportation on the lines first laid out by the wild beast. The wild man and these native creatures possessed the same engineering sense but not the same engineering skill that is now exhibited by our great railway systems. The same hand that guided the buffalo still guides the surveyors' instruments—fundamentally an economic interest.

The buffalo avoided the hill and the swamp and therefore took the ridge or the valley.

If you should care to know where the buffaloes built their roads centuries ago, consult your map and find the location of the Cumberland road, the main line of the Pennsylvania, the New York Central and Hudson River, the Baltimore and Ohio, the Chesapeake and Ohio, and the Lake Shore.

The first improvement the white man made in the roads he found was to widen them occasionally, so that his pack-horse in passing through would not injure the pack he carried by contact with the trees on either side. Ultimately these were widened into wagon and stage-coach roads and many were converted into railroads.

I want now to speak of the Wilderness road and its travelers. It was the greatest of its kind and had much to do with Indiana and especially with the southern portion. I do not mean merely the extreme south part, but as far north as Henry county, Hendricks county and Johnson county, and others on this line, which were largely populated by people directly from Kentucky and earlier from Virginia, North Carolina and Pennsylvania.

It might be difficult to indicate just where the Wilderness road began and just where it ceased to be the

Wilderness road, but in brief it is the road that led by way of the Cumberland Gap from the east, northeast and southeast to the west, northwest and southwest of the Cumberland mountains into the valley of the Ohio and Mississippi.

There was one continuous road from Philadelphia by way of Cumberland, Maryland, down the trough of the mountains near what is now the eastern boundary of West Virginia past Fort Chissel to Cumberland Gap, thence to the falls of the Ohio, a distance by that route of eight hundred and twenty-six miles, more than two hundred of which, from Fort Chissel, was without human habitation. When we now think of making a journey on foot with a family through the mountains and forests beset with wild beasts and savage men, we wonder what great hearts, what determined courage, what bold, adventurous spirits our ancestors must have had. even to undertake such a journey. From Richmond, Virginia, a road led nearly due west to Fort Chissel and joined the road leading from all parts of Pennsylvania just described. All these tributaries from east, north and south joined in one great stream at the Cumberland Gap.

A portion of this stream, however, did not come north. It went south into Tennessee, and Nashville was established. Yet not all that came from the east and northeast came through the Gap. That portion that went south into Tennessee and finally up into western Kentucky separated from the main stream at Fort Chissel and followed down the Holston or Nollichuckee rivers again to escape the mountains. They found a pass not far from where Knoxville is now located, following the line of the present railroad from Knoxville to Washington, D. C. A comparatively small portion of the travelers, however, went south of the Cumberland Gap. The main line of travel after passing the Gap turned northwest toward where Boonsborough, Harrodsburg, formerly Harrodstown, and Lexington were afterward located, and toward the falls—later Louisville,—the crossing to Vincennes and St. Louis.

Two conditions led them in this direction. First, it was the road of least resistance. After crossing the Gap the water flows northwest, and the small streams have their source there that later form the Kentucky river. In addition to this natural course, the former travelers in this region had carried east most fabulous stories of the beautiful and fertile grass lands of Kentucky and the great quantities of game available for food. The blue grass region of Kentucky is no modern invention. With its fine natural meadows, its fine supply of running water, its salt licks and its forests, it was the habitat of more game than could be found in the same area almost anywhere else. Buffaloes roamed here in immense herds and deer were relatively as numerous; bear and wild turkey furnished the food for many a hungry traveler and settler. In prehistoric times these same licks were visited by immense numbers of mastodon, who, for sake of keeping the records correct in the absence of a State Geologist or a newspaper, left their bones when they had done with them, and the name "Big Bone Lick" is the written record after printing took the place of living.

Because Kentucky had these great natural resources, the early settlers had great natural enemies in the Indians. Kentucky was for the Indians not so much a home as a hunting ground. In fact, it seems not to have been the abiding place of the tribes, but was a common hunting and therefore a common fighting ground for the tribes from both the north and south, and there were well-beaten paths from the north and south into Kentucky. It is said that the name Kentucky meant dark and bloody ground before the whites came upon the scene. The Indians had questions of monopoly and closed shops to settle for the same purposes and on the same principles as their more civilized followers have, and their methods of settlement were but little more savage. Every Indian was the natural enemy of every white man who settled in Kentucky, and no less than fifteen hundred whites were killed by the Indians in the first few years of Kentucky settlement.

From Kentucky came large numbers of settlers into southern Indiana. Many of their young men came into Indiana and Ohio as soldiers in the early Indian wars down to the close of the War of 1812, and large numbers of these remained north of the Ohio or returned there as settlers. While we may now condemn the fighting instincts of the average Kentuckian, our salvation on several occasions depended almost wholly on his ability in this line.

At first glance it seems rather strange that the Wilderness road should have been used by any except those directly from the southern portion of Virginia and from North Carolina, since the Ohio river was both the natural highway and the shorter route, but, so far as I can find any records, the river did not become the main route of travel, or even a prominent one, until the Ohio Company located its purchase on the Muskingum in 1788. From that time on the river was in general and frequent use not only by the people from New England, Pennsylvania and the East, but as well by those from Maryland and northern Virginia, and many settlers on both sides of the Ohio river used the waterway as a route of travel.

But we must not forget that by the year 1788, when the river came into general use, from fifty to seventy thousand persons had already come overland by the Wilderness road and the Cumberland Gap. So far as I know, up to that period there is no parallel to this great stream of human life pouring over so long, so difficult and so dangerous a road merely to find a more desirable home. Whether the motive assigned for taking the long road rather than the short one is true or an adequate explanation, I can not vouch, yet it is assigned by authoritative historians and to me sounds exceedingly plausible. The motive assigned is that travelers were in greater danger from Indians when traveling upon the river than when traveling overland. The savages could conceal themselves upon the bank of the river at any point and have the traveler absolutely at his mercy with almost no possible means of defense, while that same white traveler in the woods might have been quite a match for the most wily savage. The two in the forest were essentially equals, but one in a boat and the other in the woods made the latter much superior. "A more pitiable sight is not conceivable than a cargo of emigrants on a rude, drifting craft, fifteen feet wide and forty feet long, helpless on the bosom of the Ohio, receiving a murderous fire from the bank."

Mr. Hulbert suggests, in "The Wilderness Road," that even in the forest the traveler was at some disadvantage, in the fact that the buffalo roads that became the white man's road was on the ridge, which made the white more generally visible to his enemy than his enemy was to him. In fact, in the rough country the white traveler was frequently on the sky line of the savage.

Of direct interest to us, beyond their general historic interest, is the fact that these men and women who came through the gap or down the river were the fathers of the early settlers of the south half of Indiana, and the life of the State has been and is still being influenced by all the tendencies that all these people brought with them. There came to us with these people the good stock and the best traditions of the old Virginians, along with some of the worst social views of these same people— exemplified in the strong slavery tendencies and the effort to break down the Ordinance of 1787. Across the Ohio river also came many closely allied to the poor whites of the South, who are as worthless here as they were there, and yet they are the logical product of the social conditions under which their ancestors had lived for several generations, and it is not surprising that they still lower our grade of energy and life.

Along with those with the Southern tendencies came many of the Scotch-Irish Calvinists who had formerly settled in the highlands of Pennsylvania and who had followed down the mountain troughs to Virginia and North Carolina. They were an energetic, sturdy, determined, industrious, religious group of people. They believed in Hades and some of them practiced it.

There were among these also many from Delaware, Maryland and New Jersey, and some from New York and many real New Englanders. In fact, the first real American settlement in the Northwest Territory was a thoroughly Yankee settlement. This was at Marietta, Ohio, under Rufus Putnam, whose name alone tells the whole story.

Marietta was established in 1788, just the year after the Ordinance, and to the New England sentiment and to Putnam himself and to Cutler we owe the best provision of that famous document, the anti-slavery provision.

It was to be the home of the Revolutionary soldier from the New England anti-slavery States.

When I say there were a scattering few New Englanders among all these people who came over these roads to the West, I refer to the group as a whole, but in addition to these isolated cases we must not overlook the fact that there were two considerable reservations where large numbers of New Englanders settled and in such majorities that their characteristics dominated and yet dominate the entire communities.

One of these settlements was Marietta, the earliest made in the State of Ohio. This was organized for and by New England officers of the Revolution to secure to themselves the land and homes that were owing them from the government. In this were Putnam and Cutler, who did much, not only for the settlement, but for Ohio and the entire Northwest Territory.

The other great New England stronghold was Connecticut's Western Reserve of one million five hundred thousand acres in the northeast portion of Ohio, largely settled by Connecticut people. Of this one million five hundred thousand acres, about five hundred thousand were set apart for Connecticut citizens who had lost heavily by fire and other destructive causes in the Revolution. These were called the "fire lands."

Marietta has its college and its historical society. The Western Reserve has its university and its historical society. Even the Firelands in Huron county at Norwalk, Ohio, has its historical society, which has published two quite large volumes.

We see in all these places the New England tendencies of education and preservation. We have in our own State New England settlements, but none so marked as these, for nowhere else were such definite provisions made for them on so large a scale. However, in northern Indiana there are some settlements almost purely New England in composition.

It is doubtless true that a goodly number of the early settlers in the half century covered by this paper came by the overland route which became the National road or the Cumberland road, as it was even more frequently called.

These people settled in the eastern central counties of our own State. They were composed of two characteristic classes of Pennsylvanians, the Pennsylvania Germans and the Pennsylvania Scotch-Irish, and their descendants still occupy the land. Many who came from Uniontown and Brownsville, Pennsylvania, settled in what is now Union county and Brownsville, Indiana.

North of this line of travel, which was about the present line of the Cumberland road, the main lines of travel west were along the lake shore, on essentially the line of the Lake Shore railroad.

This line of travel was followed, not by the people from the States so far considered, but from western New York and the New England States. Across the State of New York from east to west were built as early or earlier than 1809, three turnpikes, all leading essentially from the Hudson river to Lake Erie. These three roads were the New State road, from south of Oneida Lake, from Utica to Ft. Niagara; the Ontario and Genesee turnpike, by Utica and Syracuse, and by the north end of lakes Seneca and Cayuga; the third parallel fifty miles south at the opposite end of these lakes by Ithaca, called the Lake Erie turnpike; and located along the lines are the chief commercial inland cities of New York, Syracuse, Utica, Rochester and Batavia. The main road was the

Genesee, and at the end of that, and because of it, Buffalo grew.

These roads accommodated not only the emigrants from New York State, but also from all the northern portions of the New England States. When New England crossed the Hudson, it crossed at that break in the highlands near Albany. Both north and south of this section are hills and mountains too difficult, which means too expensive, to cross, so the lines of travel, both of animals and men, were in the lines of least resistance and we have the Genesee pike, the Erie canal, and the New York and Hudson River railroads almost parallel and in close proximity.

The builders of transportation lines, whether wagonroads, railroads or canals, have been wise enough first to observe the lines along which men and commerce naturally find outlet.

Over these New York roads there came to the lake a stream of strong, vigorous, healthful people from northern and western New York and from New England, who planted settlements in northern Ohio and then in northern Indiana. Some came directly to Indiana. Many tarried a season in Ohio. These people brought with them their sturdy, vigorous character and manhood and have retained it. Some of these settlers settled down in groups or colonies and gave the names to these groups and towns that had designated the places from which they came. Most of these settlers scattered themselves by ones and twos and leavened the whole section of the country.

Joining these New York and New England groups were sturdy Germans from New York and Pennsylvania, who came almost due west along the line of the Lake

Shore road, and in northern Indiana we have a considerable per cent. of German population.

A large proportion of our population of northern Indiana came directly from Ohio to Indiana, but they had tarried in the Buckeye State but a few years or perhaps a generation or so, and were essentially the Eastern population.

While we are remembering the fact that these turnpikes and wilderness roads and canals and the natural waterways brought thousands of emigrants to the old Northwest Territory and later to the States of that territory, we must remember as well that the Eastern people who expected to remain East, including the government itself, were even more anxious for good roads and artificial waterways—in fact, for any way to transport people and goods—than those who expected to brave the dangers and hardships of savage and wilderness for a home in the then Far West.

In accounting for the anxiety of the Eastern people who were to remain East, we can find much reason in pure commercialism, which is not to be despised, for the East knew enough of the Ohio and Mississippi valleys to know that ultimately a great commerce must flow from these valleys, and that the natural outlet by water, the only method of transportation at that time, was down these two rivers to ocean navigation at New Orleans.

For trade to go its natural course was to place the trade of the continent in the hands of the enemies of the English government and the English colonies while the government was colonial, and the enemies of the American government after the Revolution, for France and Spain controlled New Orleans.

And worse still, to turn the commercial face of these valleys to the west and south must emphasize the natural barrier between the East and West—that is, the mountains—and this meant clearly that two civilizations and two national spirits must grow up where only one was desired.

Especially was this point important when after the Revolution it became apparent that the adhesive power of the colonies was not great enough to endure a severe strain. Washington himself made trips through Maryland and Virginia and what is now West Virginia, personally inspecting the country with the one idea in mind as to what could be done in the lines of transportation that would commercially unite the Ohio valley to the East rather than let its trade follow the natural trade routes south. He advocated the building of a canal across that rough country of West Virginia to unite the waters of the Ohio with the Potomac and the sea. On this same line a turnpike was afterward planned and later was laid the Chesapeake & Ohio railroad.

Later came the Cumberland road, which was the chief band that held the East and the West together and made them one, and Mr. Hulbert, speaking of this road, says of it that it was the greatest influence "to harmonize and strengthen, if not to save, the Union."

Had our commercial interests in 1860 been South and not East, we should certainly not have taken the stand we did. Had the Civil War come on under such conditions, we can guess that the results would have been different from what they were, if not quite the opposite.

The Wabash and Erie canal was built two-thirds of a century ago to make New York the commercial port for this portion of the country rather than New Orleans, and that canal had its origin years earlier in the demand of the fur traders for a connection between the headwaters of the Wabash and the headwaters of the Maumee—a ditch across the portage a distance of only seven or eight miles, yet the Wabash and Erie canal when finished was more than four hundred miles in length.

CONCLUSION.

This whole story is one of daring and hardship, one that tried souls and bodies both. How men, women and children trudged on foot through wilds in all sorts of weather a journey of from five hundred to eight hundred miles over a rough, mountainous, uninhabited country, is now quite beyond our appreciation. They traveled without priest or apothecary and practically without any protection other than that afforded by gun and ax. These statements are true especially of those who came to Kentucky from Virginia and North Carolina by way of the Wilderness road.

Those who started from the New England States and northern New York were very much better prepared for the journey, especially so at starting. Many of them, however, were but little or no better off on reaching their destination. It is well for us in the midst of luxury to look back occasionally and try to appreciate how we came by it.

I am inclined to believe also that there is no better index to nor explanation of our varied tastes and industries—to our composite character—in the valleys of the Ohio and central Mississippi, than is to be gained by a study of our origins. Is it not also the most fundamental explanation of our balance of temperament and character?

I am sure nothing can bring us to a saner view of the immeasurable blessings we enjoy, even of our extravagance in plenty—even luxury—than the knowledge of the hardships, privations and sufferings that our ancestors endured that we might live, yet I doubt not that what they endured is quite as incomprehensible to us as would be our luxury and extravagance to the minds of those people who trudged across Cumberland Gap in the days of the Revolution.

INDIANA HISTORICAL SOCIETY PUBLICATIONS
VOLUME IV   NUMBER 7

LOCKERBIE'S

ASSESSMENT LIST

OF

INDIANAPOLIS, 1835

ELIZA G. BROWNING

INDIANAPOLIS
Edward J. Hecker, Printer and Publisher
1909

GEORGE LOCKERBIE

In Annan, Dumfriesshire, Scotland, George Murray Lockerbie was born in April, 1771.

The little border town on Solway Frith, in Annandale, is in the southern part of the shire, which was the stronghold of the Stewarts and a hotbed of patriotism. Within a radius of a few miles is Elderslie, where the patriot Wallace first saw the light; east of Lochmaben is the castle which Annandale claims as the birthplace of Robert Bruce; and Thomas Carlyle, who was born at Ecclefechan, a village just out of Annan, describes the town of George Lockerbie's birth, during the first quarter of the last century, as "a fine, bright, self-confident little town;" of the people he writes that they were "an argumentative, clear-headed, contentious set of people, more given to intellectual pursuits than some of their neighbors." Nearby is the village of Lockerbie, and the story is told that in early days, when the laird of the castle fared forth to war, he would shut up his wife and other valued possessions for safe keeping during his absence. "Lock her by," he would order. This happened so often that when the custom of surnames became prevalent, this belligerent old Scot had earned the right to his of Lockerbie.

A recognized characteristic of these Lockerbies is that they have the courage of their convictions and never lack the personal courage to express them. In the town of Lockerbie there still remains the memory of the great "Lockerbie lick," when these people in a battle defeated the Maxwells with great slaughter. From people like these, from such surroundings, where the very air is the essence of patriotism, came George Lockerbie. At the beginning of the last century, he had become a writer of note; his political articles and those protesting against and exposing the outrages of the press gang, published in Glasgow and Edinburgh papers, led to his arrest and imprisonment. Inflammatory writings, calculated to incite Scottish subjects to rebellion, was one count in the indictment against him. His trial followed immediately upon his arrest, and he defended his own case and was acquitted. His friends had swarmed up from Dumfriesshire for the trial, and these with a great crowd of sympathizers surrounded him upon his release and bore him upon their shoulders through the streets of Edinburgh.

This experience decided him to leave the country he loved so well and make a new home in America, where thought and speech and pen were free.

He had married Ann Blacklocke some years before, and with his family came to America in 1809; they lived near Philadelphia, in Germantown, until the close of the War of 1812, when they removed to Lexington, Kentucky.

Mr. Lockerbie had been brought up a Presbyterian of the old Scotch type, but in Lexington he and his family became members of the Episcopal church and remained in that faith, identifying themselves with Christ Church in Indianapolis when that church was organized a few years after they came here to live.

It was during his residence in Lexington that General Lafayette visited Kentucky. May 16, 1825, was the date of his visit to Lexington. Mr. Lockerbie was an enthusiastic Mason, and on the occasion of General Lafayette's attendance at a lodge meeting there. Mr. Lockerbie as presiding officer presented the distinguished visitor with his own apron to wear. This was of white kid, and many years after was presented by Mr. Lockerbie's daughter, Mrs. McOuat, to the Indiana State Museum, where it is still preserved as a relic of historic value.

In Lexington, Mr. Lockerbie had a cotton-gin and a large number of slaves. He was a staunch Democrat, but his liberty-loving soul could not bear the idea of slavery. He freed these slaves, and in 1830, still in search of freedom, came to Indianapolis with his family and son-in-law, Thomas McOuat, who had married Janet Lockerbie in Lexington.

Shortly after taking up his residence in Indianapolis he became actively identified with the official life of this his permanent home. He was assessor in the year 1835. He was town trustee from the first ward during the years 1836 and 1837, and councilman and president of the council from the same ward in 1838 and 1839. During the building of the canal, about 1836 and 1837, the town was filled with a very unruly element, and Mr. Lockerbie was a leader in the law and order movement which became a necessity.

He was prominent in Masonry here, as in Lexington, and in 1835 was elected junior warden of Center Lodge.

His home was at the northeast corner of Alabama and Market streets, a small cottage, two rooms of which faced upon Alabama street; one of these was Mr. Lockerbie's office, and, as was usual in those early days, was simply furnished with table and a few chairs. The floor was sanded, and everything about the house and trim little garden at the back spoke eloquently of the care of the good Scotch housewife within. Mrs. Lockerbie's miniature shows that she adhered to the customs and dress of her native country and wore a blue kirtle, a kerchief around her shoulders, crossed and tied at the back, with a mob cap framing a sweet, merry old face.

Here in this cottage home these two, who were favorites wherever they were, received their many friends and acquaintances of all ages. The young children were in and out of the place continually—the little ones climbing upon Mr. Lockerbie's knee, where he trotted them while he sang to them quaint Scotch folk songs or recited verse after verse of his favorite Burns. To the older children he was a mine of information and an encyclopedia; some of these children came to him with their lessons as regularly as they went to school. The older people came to him, and he numbered a great many young men among those who delighted to visit him—young men like Lew Wallace and John Coburn—and very interesting were the arguments and debates that went on under his roof. On a fly-leaf of the old book containing the Assessment Record—a reproduction of which follows this sketch—is a memorandum referring to an article in the *Democratic Review* of 1844 on the "conduct and character of three men of the time of the French Revolution." Of this article he writes, "It defends Robespierre and Marat, and justly as I believe, from the misrepresentations of the enemies of Freedom and of the just rights of mankind." He was a socialist in the ideal sense of the word—never swerving from the furtherance of the cause of freedom nor from the defence of the rights of man.

The fly-leaves of this old assessors' record are filled with memoranda—items of farm, family and general interest. Here are some of them:

"General Zachary Taylor—Newport Kentucky—the Hero!!!"

"June 8, 1846 Wrote this day—for the first time to my nephew Andrew Thomson, Cleveland, Ohio."

"Monday 21 Sept., 1846. This day Andrew (McOuat) entered on his apprenticeship for the term of four years to C. and J. Cox to learn the trade of a tin-plate worker."

"September 3d 1846. Mrs. Elizabeth Gentle died this morning at half-past four o'clock. Buried at 4 o'clock p. m. same day, in the same lot and the same graveyard with her brother Thomas McOuat."

"Mr. William McOuat died Sep 11, 1841, aged 67 years."

"Mrs. Margaret McOuat wife of William McOuat died January 3d 1853 supposed to be 90 years of age."

"December 28th 1846. Martha went to Mrs. Richmonds school.

"January 11th 1847. Jean went to Mrs. Richmonds school."

The last of these family records is:

"Feb. 22, 1853. This day Miss Jane Gentle became Mrs. Morris Howland by marriage."

On the blank leaves following the assessment record is a daily weather report for eight years—from January 1, 1845, to January 3, 1853. It is headed, "Remarks on the weather," and is kept as follows:

"Jan. 15. 1845. Cloudy and mild. Thunder and lightning and rain at 3 p. m. Evening cloudy and mizzling."

"June 7th 1845. Fair and dry. Afternoon fair and

warm. Evening clear and warm. Great drought. Wind
S."

This record is thus carefully kept until the last page
of the book is reached. Doubtless it was continued in
the same methodical way in another volume during his
remaining years, but has not been preserved. This is
perhaps the earliest known weather report of Indianapolis
now in existence.

In the assessment list Mr. Lockerbie has given more
information than the law required him to furnish. The
law calls for "a full assessment roll of persons, lands,
town lots and chattels, taxable in his district." Mr.
Lockerbie gives a full census, instead of merely a list of
persons subject to poll-tax. His notes as to the occupancy of the several pieces of real estate furnish quite
a complete directory of Indianapolis at the time.

After the death of his wife, Mr. Lockerbie lived with
his daughter, Mrs. McOuat, until his death, June 18, 1856.
Mrs. McOuat's home was near the corner of East and
New York streets. In platting this property as an addition to Indianapolis she named the street north of New
York street—from East to Noble streets—Lockerbie in
honor of her father. James Whitcomb Riley, who lives
in this street, has immortalized it in his beautiful little
poem, "Lockerbie Street"—a fitting tribute to that which
bears the name of a man whose life was practical prose,
but whose heart and soul were full of poetry.

LOCKERBIE'S ASSESSMENT LIST
OF INDIANAPOLIS, 1835

NAMES OF PERSONS ASSESSED	In Lots Number	Square	Value of Lots (Dollars)	Value of Buildings (Dollars)	Value of Personal Property (Dollars)	Tax Dols.	Tax Cents	Males Under 10 years	Males 10 to 21	Males 21 to 45	Males 45 to 00	Males Over 60	Females Under 10 years	Females 10 to 21	Females 21 to 45	Females 45 to 60	Females Over 60	Colored persons of all ages	Total number	
Bare, John ......S. half	10	40	40				10			1				1					2	paid
do.					50		25													paid
Bates, Hervey	4	42	200 }	2500	600	16	87½			1			2	1	2				7	paid
do.	5	42	150 }				75													paid
do.	6	42	200 }																	paid
do.	12	64	2500																	paid
Bates, H. & D.				3500	2000	23	75	1		1				1	1				6	paid
Beck, Samuel (lives on)	12	43			100	10	00		2	1			1	1	1					paid
do. ......one-third N.	7	63	200				50													paid
do. ......one-third N.	8	63	200				50													paid
Brown, Hiram (lives on)	4	44			150		50	3		1		1	1	3	1				10	paid
Bush, George	11	45	500			1	75			2					1					paid
Bacon, Elisha (lives on)		49			50		25			2					1					paid
Bardwell, Seth ....two-thirds W.	3	54	400	500	100	4	25		3	1				2	2				5	paid
do. ....two-thirds W.	6	54	800	250		3	25		5	2					1					paid
Burnett, Thomas							75													paid
Bolton, N. (lives on)	6	55	200		150		75	2		1			1		1				8	paid
do.	1	73	200		150		50													paid
do.	3	73	75			4	18¾													paid
do.	4	73	85			3	21¼													paid
Barnes, John S. (store on)	9	55	125		3500	17	50			1								8	9	paid
Barnes & Maxwell	7	72	3000 }		3000	51	62½	1						1					2	paid
Brown, Basil	2	66	1500 }	5000			30¾				1					1			5	paid
do. ......W. half	13	56	150 }																	paid
do. ......Part of	13	56	1800			4	60													paid
Blake, James.....49½ feet E.	4	56						1	9	30	1		4	1	5	1		8	60	paid

Description	Sq.	Lot	Val. 1	Val. 2	Val. 3	Tax $	cts.	Paid
do. ....58 " E.	4	65	2600	2000		16	25	paid
do.	12	67	1500	300	1500	5	25	paid
Brown & Morrison (store on)	6	56				7	50	paid
Blyth, Benjamin........5½ feet E.	8	59	} 625	800	500	8	06¼	paid
do.	9	59	400			1	00	paid
do.	10	59	250				63½	paid
do.	11	62	600	300		3	00	paid
do.	4	59		100			50	paid
Blyth & McCarty, owns building on	10	61	} 150	160	5000	26	87½	paid
do.	7	61					50	paid
do.	8	61	100			2	67½	paid
do.	9	61	450	250	100	2	25	paid
do.	12	62	150	200		2	37½	paid
Blyth, Samuel	3	02	350	300	50		25	paid
Bennet, Morris ....E. half	11	60	700			1	75	paid
do. ....W. half	12	60	400		50	1	00	paid
do. ....E. half	5	63		150	50	1	00	paid
Buchannan, Thomas (lives on)	6	60	300				25	
Barnett, Abm	3	69	700	300		1	75	
do.	1	63	400			1	00	
Burrows, John (lives on)						1	00	
Burnham, John (lives on)	8	63		150			25	
do. 1-6 of 7 & 1-6 of	8	64	300				25	
do. (Building on)							75	
Buchannan, John	8	64					75	
Benbow, Edward (lives on)	0	05	3000	300	50		25	
Blackford, Isaac	3	68	700			8	50	paid
do.	5	68	600			1	75	paid
do.	1	06			3600	17	50	paid
Blyth, Samuel & Co.	9	66	300	200	75	1	75	paid
Bradley & Ungles	5	73	100			1	25	paid
Bradley, Henry	6	73	160	300	200	3	00	paid
do.	9	73	100				37½	paid
do.	10	73	250				09½	paid
do.	6	74	300				75	paid

In Lots Number	Square	NAMES OF PERSONS ASSESSED	Value of Lots (Dollars)	Value of Buildings (Dollars)	Value of Personal Property (Dollars)	TAX Dols.	TAX Cents	M Under 10	M 10-21	M 21-45	M 45-60	M Over 60	F Under 10	F 10-21	F 21-45	F 45-60	F Over 60	Colored persons of all ages	Total number	Paid
6	72	Bowlins heirs, David Fisher	200				50													
1	74	Brown, Miram (John Givan, agent)	300				75													
2	74	do.	200				50													
1	75	Baptist Church	700			5	87½													paid
8	76	Boyd, John H.	400	800		3	12½													paid
12	28	Baldwin, Sam'l (colored man)	150	275	150		75	1		3			2	1	1				8	paid
4	68	Brandon, Armstrong	700			1	87½													paid
10	69	Brown, Peter	150				37½													paid
5	51	Beach	100	75			62½													
3	30	Cobert	60				15													
	38	Coburn, Henry P., owns the whole of	1200			7	00	1	2				1	1	1				8	paid
11	27	do. or a piece	75																	
	41	Coe, Isaac, owns the whole of	1000			2	50													paid
12	45	do.	500																	paid
13	45	do.	500			11	25													paid
14	45	do.	500																	paid
10	72	do.	120																	paid
11	72	do.	120	1000	500			1	1	1			1	1		1			5	paid
9	51	Claypool, Newton	275				30													paid
2	54	do.	350				25													paid
4	54	do.	500				68¾													paid
12	59	Claypool, Jacob	500				87½		1		1		1							paid
5	54	Cropper, Mordecai....5½ feet W.	500	500	200	3	75			1					1		1		2	paid
6	54	do. ....½ E.				1	25													paid
4	55	Covington's heirs	200			4	75				1									paid
5	65	Crowder, John (colored man)		500	20	1	95 10											2	2	paid

Cain, John	8	55	2000	250	900	10 75	...	...	...	...	...	...	...	...	...	...	...	...	paid
do.	5	75	500																paid
do.	6	75	600	1300	500	11 75	2	...	1	...	...	1	...	2	...	...	...	6	paid
Cox, Jacob	3	56	......	......	150	75	1	...	...	...	...	...	1	1	...	...	...	6	paid
Cox, C. & J. (Tin factory)	3	66	......	......	250	1 25	...	...	...	...	...	...	...	...	...	...	...	...	paid
Conner, William	7	57	2500	2000	......	16 25	...	...	...	...	...	...	...	...	...	...	...	...	paid
Court house Square	...	58	5500	10900	......	80 75	...	...	...	...	...	...	...	...	...	...	...	...	paid
Campbell, William	...	...	......	......	......	......	...	...	1	...	...	...	...	1	...	...	...	2	
Chamberlin, Barney (lives on)	7	60	......	......	25	12⅓	1	...	1	...	...	...	1	...	...	...	...	3	paid
Cogswell (J. Wilkins, agent)..W. ½	10	60	175	75	......	87½	...	...	...	...	...	...	...	...	...	...	...	...	paid
Cutler, Jacob	8	52	300	......	......	75	...	...	...	...	...	...	...	...	...	...	...	...	
Cotton. E. ½	10	60	150	......	......	37½	...	...	...	...	...	...	...	...	...	...	...	...	
do. W. ½	11	60	150	......	......	37½	...	...	...	...	...	...	...	...	...	...	...	...	
Carson, John. E. ½	12	60	175	70	30	87½	...	...	...	...	...	...	...	...	...	...	...	...	paid
Campbell, Charles (lives on)	1	63	......	......	100	50	1	...	1	...	...	...	...	1	...	...	...	3	paid
Collins, Jeremiah	1	66	3000	1800	300	18 00	...	...	...	...	...	...	...	...	...	...	...	...	p.50c
Cox, Nathan	5	70	250																paid
do. E. half	6	70	125	350	100	3 28¾	...	1	1	...	...	2	1	1	...	...	...	6	paid
Crawford, Thomas. W. half	5	70	125																paid
do.	6	70	300	700	200	5 56¼	...	...	2	...	...	...	2	1	...	...	2	7	paid
Chinn, Thomas	6	77	......	300	60	1 80	4	...	1	...	1	...	1	1	...	...	...	8	paid
Dysinger, Sullivan (lives on)	...	21	......	......	30	15	1	...	1	...	...	1	1	...	...	...	...	4	paid
Dawson	11	28	100	......	......	25	...	...	...	...	...	...	...	...	...	...	...	...	paid
Douglas, John	7	30	100	200	......	1 25	...	...	...	...	...	...	...	...	...	...	...	...	paid
do.	8	30	50	......	......	12½	...	...	...	...	...	...	...	...	...	...	...	...	paid
do.	9	30	50	......	......	12½	...	...	...	...	...	...	...	...	...	...	...	...	paid
do.	10	32	85	......	......	21¼	...	...	...	...	...	...	...	...	...	...	...	...	paid
do.	11	32	60	......	......	15	...	...	...	...	...	...	...	...	...	...	...	...	paid
do.	12	32	125	......	......	31¼	...	...	...	...	...	...	...	...	...	...	...	...	paid
do.	1	45	600	800	200	6 50	3	2	1	2	...	2	1	2	...	...	...	13	paid
Day, Peter (lives on)	7	30	......	......	50	25	1	3	1	1	...	2	2	1	...	...	...	11	
Dysinger, Frederick (lives on)	8	33	......	......	20	10	...	...	...	1	...	1	...	...	1	...	...	3	paid
Dillon	9	33	150	......	......	37½	...	...	...	...	...	...	...	...	...	...	...	...	
Dennelin, Thomas (lives on)	4	44	......	......	50	25	2	1	1	...	...	...	...	1	...	...	...	5	paid
do. (shop on)	11	64	......	......	150	75	...	...	...	...	...	...	...	...	...	...	...	...	paid
Dunn & Harris. 30 ft E.	6	46	100	400	......	2 25	...	...	...	...	...	...	...	...	...	...	...	...	paid

NAMES OF PERSONS ASSESSED	No.	Sq.	Value of Lots	Value of Buildings	Value of Personal Prop.	Dols.	Cents	M Under 10	M 10 to 21	M 21 to 45	M 45 to 60	M Over 60	F Under 10	F 10 to 21	F 21 to 45	F 45 to 60	F Over 60	Colored persons	Total number	
Dunn, Francis (lives on)	3	47			70		35	1		1				1					3	paid
Davis, James (lives on)	4	49	300		100		50		1		1			2		1			5	paid
Davy, David	5	40	300				75													
do.	5	40	200				50		1							1				
Dewey, Charles .... W. two-thirds	7	54				6	25													
do. .... W. two-thirds	8	54	2500																	
do. .... W. two-thirds	5	54																		
Davis, Edward (lives on)	3	55	2000		125	9	62½	1		1			1		1				3	paid
Davis, Nathan	9	55	2000	700	100	9	00			1				1					5	paid
Douglas & McGuire (printing office)	10	55			1200	6	00													paid
Depew (shoe store on)	1	56			600	3	00	1		1			1		1				11	paid
do.					100		30												3	
Drum, James (lives on)	4	62	500		60		10													
Davy, Mrs. (lives on)	4	63			20	1	00		1				1		1				4	
Drearth or Dearth (D. Yandis, agent)	4	47	2000			5	00			6					3					
do.	6	66	400			1	00		1	1				1	1				6	
Daily, D. W.	4	69	400	1000	2 50	7	75													paid
Dunlap, Livingston	5	64	300			1	00			1				1						paid
do.	1	64	400				07½													paid
do.	2	64	30				10													paid
do.	4	77	40				10													paid
do.	3	77	40				10													paid
no.	4	77	40																	paid
do.	3	77				1	50													paid
Eaton, James	3	47	300	150	125		62½	3	2	1			3	1	1				9	paid
Emison, Benjamin (lives on)	6	54																		paid

Name	No.	Val	Val	Val	Val	Tax										Paid
Edgar, James .... 37 ft. E.	7	78	600	600	300	6 75	2		1		1		2		6	paid
do.	1	56	1500	500	600	6 95									2	paid
Eagon & Campbell (Hat store on)....	1	56			100	3 00									29	paid
Ekle, Jonathan....	3	61	325	600	1200	2 93¾			1			6	1		2	paid
Elder, J....	3	63			75	6 00	1	1	1			1			10	paid
Ellick, Mrs. (lives on)....	9	66			30	37½										paid
Evans, William (lives on)....	6	69			15										9	paid
do. ....N. half	11	71														paid
do. ....N. half	81	71	{100													paid
Farcee, James (lives on)....	12	71		75	50	25	3		1	1		1	1			paid
do. Pd by Jno. D. Thorp	9	37	70			25										paid
do. " " "	11	23	100			17½										paid
Fisher (colored woman)....	12	23	60			25	2		1		1		1			paid
Fearnley, John (lives on)....	1	30			50	15	3	2	2			2	1			paid
do.	2	63	75			25	1	1	1			1				paid
Folsome, Peter....	2	32	200	75	50	18¼	1		1	1		1		1	4	paid
Fletcher & Bradley....	7	33	300			1 12										paid
do.	1	36	300			2 37										paid
do.	2	36	200			2 37										paid
do. (store on)....	3	36	250	100	2200	11 00	1		1		1		1			paid
Foster, John	4	65	200	600	735	8 05	2		2	1	1	2	1		7	paid
Foudray, John	5	37	350	500	175	4 25	1	1	1	2		1	1		9	paid
do. ....N. half	6	37	350			25										paid
do. ....S. third	7	37	100			12½										paid
Fletcher, Calvin......the whole of	9	37	50	100		3 00			3							paid
do.	10	39	1000	50		55										paid
do.	1	42	120			18¼										paid
do.	2	42	75			25	1	1	1		1	1	1		12	paid
do.	3	42	100			12½										paid
Foley....	12	42	250	400	500	5 12½			1		1		1			paid
Foster, E. K. (watch shop)....	9	44	600	250	100	3 25	1		1						3	paid
Ferguson, John....	3	56			200	1 00	2		1	1		2	1	1		paid
Foltz, Frederick (lives on)....					50	25			1		1		1		6	paid
Fisher, Davis....(6-72-200)....	6	57			150	75		1		1					3	paid
Frazee, Moses & Co. (store on)....	2	65														paid
					3500	17 50										paid

NAMES OF PERSONS ASSESSED	In Lots Number	In Lots Square	Value of Lots Dollars	Value of Buildings Dollars	Value of Personal Property Dollars	TAX Dols.	TAX Cents	Males Under 10 years	Males 10 to 21	Males 21 to 45	Males 45 to 60	Males Over 60	Females Under 10 years	Females 10 to 21	Females 21 to 45	Females 45 to 60	Females Over 60	Coloured persons of all ages	Total number	
Fisher, Ezra	8	68	150	350	125	1	75	1		1			1		1				4	paid
Foote's heirs	7	27	150				37½													paid
do.	8	27	100				25													paid
do.	9	27	190				30													paid
do.	1	43	250				62½													paid
(H. Newland lease renter)	3	43	350	125		1	50													paid
do.	4	43	500	200		2	25													paid
do.	1	46	350				87½													paid
do.	2	46	300				75													paid
do.	3	46	300				75													paid
do.	10	57																		paid
W. two-thirds	10	57	1200			5	00													paid
Foote, Mrs. (lives on)	10	57		400	100		50													paid
Fletcher, Calvin (agent for)	11	51	275				68¾		1	5			2	1	2				11	paid
do.	9	52	260				62½													paid
do.	1	23	400			1	00													paid
Goldsberry, Samuel	2	23	75				18¾	2	1	5			2	2	1				13	paid
do.	3	23	75				18¾													paid
do.	4	23	50				12½													paid
do.	5	23	50				12½													paid
do.	6	23	60				15													paid
do.	3	23	75				18¾													paid
do.	10	23	250				62½													paid
do.	4	44	300				25													paid
Gapin	8	34	250	800	100	5	25													paid
Gates, Uriah	5	44	350	160		1	62½													paid
Greggs heirs	11	46	400	150		1	00													paid

Name																	paid
Gibson, Wayland	8	51	250			62½										6	paid
do.	10	52	900	450		50							1				paid
Griffith, Humphrey	6	55	1800	450	75	75	6		2								paid
do. .... E. half	3	50	1500			37½	6										paid
Grazur, Do. (Frazure)	1	09	500	500		25	1										paid
Givan, James	2	57	500	250	2000	50	3										paid
do.	11	57	1500	500		00	15										paid
do.	8	60	300			25	3										paid
do.	2	02	300			75											paid
Givan, John	4	57	400	350		00	1	1	1		1	1	1			9	paid
do. .... B. half	9	64	200			37½	2	4			1	1				7	paid
do. (store on)	12	57			500	50	15										paid
Givan & Foudray					3000	00								3			paid
Gill, Phillip (lives on)	1	62	210		20	10											paid
Grover, Charles	3	52	80			50							1				paid
Holland, John W.	3	24		300	100	20	2	1		1	1					2	paid
do.	5	36	225			56½											paid
Higdon, Benodict	4	24	90	175		22½	1			1	1						paid
Haines	5	32	75			03½											paid
Heloy, Robert (lives on)	3	33			40	20			1		1	1				4	paid
Holliday, Wm. Rev.	7	24	250	500	500	62½	5		2		1	1				2	paid
do.	8	24	200			50											paid
do.	9	24	200			50					1						paid
Handy, Thomas	5	33	250	350		50	1									10	paid
Hoogland, Thomas		36			100	50					1	1		1		6	paid
Hill, James (lives on)	10	42			30	15	2			4	1	1	1			4	paid
Henkle, M. M.	11	42	300	500	300	75	1				1	1					paid
do. (Book store)			200			50											paid
do. (Book binding)						50								1			paid
Hoops, Abner (lives on)	1	43		350	1700	75					1	1				9	paid
Harlan, Elizabeth (lives on)	4	44			150	15	2		2	2	1					3	paid
Harlin, George (Turner's shop)	6	66			30	40	1		1	1	1						paid
Harris, Isaac (lives on)	6	46		500	70	35											paid
Hogan, James L. (lives on)	5	46			50	25			1	3	1	1				3	paid
do. (store on)	11	64			75	37½											paid
					250	25	1									11	paid

| NAMES OF PERSONS ASSESSED | In Lots | | Value of Lots | Value of Buildings | Value of Personal Property | Tax | | NUMBER OF INHABITANTS | | | | | | | | | | | |
	Number	Square	Dollars	Dollars	Dollars	Dols.	Cents	MALES Under 10 years	10 to 21	21 to 45	45 to 60	Over 60	FEMALES Under 10 years	10 to 21	21 to 45	45 to 60	Over 60	Colored persons of all ages	Total number of all ages	
Hanson, Sarah	10	46	500	800		5	25			1				1					2	paid
Hodges, James (lives on)	1	47					15													paid
Hammond, Rezen	6	49	250		30		69½													
Hardin, John	11	49	175				43¾													
do.	12	49	200				50													
Helm, John B	2	52	150				37½													
do.	2	66	2500			6	25													
do.	9	67	350				87½													
do. E. half of	10	67	800			2	00													
Harris, William (lives on)	13	55			125		62½			1					1			1	3	
Home, John (lives on)	1	56			30		15			1				1	1					
Harry, Edwin (Coffee room on)	10	57			100		50													
Hall, Jonathan (lives on)	12	57			20		10			1			2		1					
Henry John (J. M. Ray, agent)	6	63	1000	150	400	3	25		2	1				1	1	1			8	paid
Holland, J. & G. W. (store on)	12	63	3000	6000	2000	2	00			1										paid
Henderson, Samuel	3	65	350			47	50	4	5	22	1		3		8	1		6	50	paid
do.	8	65	400				87½													paid
do.	8	65	600																	paid
Hill, Arthur	9	65	150			1	00													paid
Holmes, William	2	66	150	700	50	5	25			2	1			2				1	11	paid
do.	8	68	175				37½													paid
do.	9	69	200				37½													paid
Holmes, John	3	72	250				43¾													paid
Harrison, Christopher S.	6	51	40				50													paid
Hopkins, James	4	52					62½													paid
Jones, John (lives on)	8	77					10	1	2	2		1	1	1	1		1	1	5	paid

Name						$	c.	Notes	
Johnson, James	7	31	100				25		paid
do.	8	31	50				12½		paid
do.	8	44	500	1000		6	25		paid
do.	7	32	150				37½		paid
do.	6	57	500	1500		8	75		paid
Jamison, John	5	27	125				31¼		paid
do.	10	35	225				56¼		paid
do.	11	35	900				50	paid by	paid
do.	12	35	300	500	500	6	75	McGuire 1 Depew & Francis 1	paid
co. (agent for)	9	46	300				25		paid
do. ......centre third of	14	46	500		100	2	00	paid by 1 2	paid
do.	5	66	300		100	1	00		paid
Jamison, John & Co. (Hat store)	5	77	200	3000	3000	15	00	7	paid
Israel, John	1	40				1	18¾	J. paid by 3 Jamison & Wilkins	paid
do. (lives on)	6	59	75	70			35	1 2	paid
Johnson & Pratt	10	43	400	500		3	50		paid
Johnson, Thomas B	7	44	500	500		1	75	3 1 $10 00	paid
do. ......E. half	11	64	700	600	1800	4	75	7	paid
Jackson, W. N. (store on)	9	55				9	00	1 1 3 1	paid
Johnson, Jeremiah	3	57				1	00		paid
do.	12	57	400	500		7	00		paid
Johnson, Aaron W......7 feet of	1	68	1800						paid
do. ......E. 13 feet of	2	63	180	705		3	96½		paid
do. ......S. third of	7	63	200	don't	own		50		paid
do. ......S. third of	8	63	200	don't	own		50		paid
Judah, Sam'l (John Givan, agent)	4	61	700	300		3	25		paid
do.	7	64	400			1	00		paid
do.	8	64	1000	400 by S. C.		4	00		paid
John, William (shop on)	6	68	700		Stevens		87½		paid
Jenison, Samuel (office on)	6	68			25		12½		paid
Johnson & Emison...29½ ft. E. of	12	63			10		05		paid
Jenison, John (book bindery on)	6	64	1300	1200	1500	16	75		paid
do.	5	65			100		50		paid
do.	3	66	200	100		1	00		paid
do.	7	74	200				25		paid
	8	74	100						paid

NAMES OF PERSONS ASSESSED	Number (In Lots)	Square	Value of Lots (Dollars)	Value of Buildings (Dollars)	Value of Personal Property (Dollars)	TAX Dols.	TAX Cents	Males Under 10 years	Males 10 to 21	Males 21 to 45	Males 45 to 60	Males Over 60	Females Under 10 years	Females 10 to 21	Females 21 to 45	Females 45 to 60	Females Over 60	Colored persons of all ages	Total number	paid
Jenison, John	9	74	150		40		37½		1	2	1							1	6	paid
Jenison, Rufus (lives on)	1	50					20				1							1	1	paid
Isabella (colored woman)	2	50																1		paid
Kelly, Ephriam, or some person	3	50	150				37½							1						paid
do.	1	27	75				18¾													paid
do.	2	27	175				43¾													paid
Kilgore, Jesse	11	46	150		100		37½					1		4	1	1			10	paid
do.	11	46	100		75		25							1		1			5	paid
Kemper, Joel (lives on)	14	54					50				1			1		1				paid
Kemper, John " "	11	54					37½	2		1							2			paid
Kintner, Jacob (C. Scudder, agent)	12	60	300		150		75		3						2				13	paid
do.	1		400		25	1	00	3	1					2					2	paid
Kettleman, James	7	63	200	250		2	50	3		3	1		1		1	1			12	paid
Kirk, Timothy	8	63	{200				12½		1	1				3				6	paid
do. one-sixth	10	64													2				7	paid
do. one-sixth	11	64	1000	500	600	8	00		2	1	1		4	1						paid
Kinder, Isaac	11	66	700	200		2	75		1				1		3	1	1		7	paid
Kellum, Mrs. (T. B. Johnson, agent) W. ½	11						12½				1				2					paid
Kelly, William (lives on)	4	28	180	80	25	1	05		3		1		1	1		1			7	paid
Lemaster, Arch	2	28	120		40		30													paid
Lefavour, Joseph	4	28	300	200		2	50		1		1		1		1				9	paid
do.	9	45	400			1	00		1	1			2	1	1				2	paid
do.	10	45	500		150	2	25													paid
Lingenfetter, William ..68 ft.	11	56	150	100	100			1	1		1	1	1	1	1				9	paid
do.	5	28	60				37½	1	1		1		1		1					paid
Leaverum, Sampson (col. man)	9	31		10	20		30			3								2	2	paid

Name			Value				Paid
Luse, M. W. (Ohio)	6	31	150	250		37½	paid
Lockerbie, George	9	42	350		75	2 50	paid
do.	4	40	60			15	paid
do.	5	40	40			10	paid
do.	6	40	40			10	paid
do.	7	40	150			37½	paid
do.	8	40	100			25	paid
do.	9	40	120			30	paid
Lingenfeller, Arch	6	44	500	75	50	1 87½	paid
Lashley & Foltz (carriage shop)	4	57			350	1 75	paid
Little, John	5	61	325			81¼	paid
do.	6	61	325			81¼	paid
do. .... E. half	1	61	500	1000	200	7 25	paid
do.	2	62	500	80		1 09½	paid
do.	7	60	250			37½	paid
do.	4	60	500	100		1 75	paid
Lewis, Hiram (lives on)	12	63	300		20	12 10	paid
Lee, Sarah	1	68	1500	1200	600	75	paid
Luse, Fleming T.	2	64	300			75	paid
do.	5	64	50			12½	paid
do.	6	76	50			19½	paid
Landis, Jacob (store on)	4	76			1200	6 00	paid
do.	2	65	500	300	150	3 50	paid
Lively, Chinney (col. woman)	12	75	700	550	200	5 50	paid
Landis, Jack (colored man)	9	66	175	20	10	58¾	paid
Lewis, Isiah S. (lives on)	6	08			50	25	paid
Landis, Philip	10	74	150			37½	paid
do.	11	74	100			25	paid
do.	12	74	250			62½	paid
do.	4	75	500	700	200	5 75	paid
Moyer, Jacob, (Wm. Smith, agent)	2	44	Value	charged to		W. Smith	paid
More, Cam (lives on)	3	27	"	"		"	paid
Morrow, John	8	28	100	20	30	25	paid
do. .... S. half	9	28	35			08¾	paid
Morrow, Col.	6	30	125	100		81¼	paid

NAMES OF PERSONS ASSESSED	In Lots No.	In Lots Square	Value of Lots (Dollars)	Value of Buildings (Dollars)	Value of Personal Property (Dollars)	TAX Dols.	TAX Cents	Males Under 10	Males 10 to 21	Males 21 to 45	Males 45 to 60	Males Over 60	Females Under 10	Females 10 to 21	Females 21 to 45	Females 45 to 60	Females Over 60	Colored persons of all ages	Total number	paid
Myers, William (lives on)	6	92			40		20													paid
Martz	5	33	175				43¾	1		1			2		1				5	
Mitchell, Robert (lives on)					50		25			1	1		3	3	2	1			13	paid
Musgrove	7	55	2000	75	20		47¼	2	1	1			1		1				6	paid
Morrison & Bolton	11	55		500	1200	13	50													
Methodist Church	12	51	900	1100																
do. .... E. two-thirds						7	75												8	
Mothershead, John L.	4	35	250		150		62½			2	1			3	1	1				
do.	5	35	200				50								1					
do.	6	35	400			1	00												7	
Moreland, Rachell	11	36	250										3	2	1					
do.	12	36	300	550	50	4	87½													
do.	2	49	250				50													
do.	3	49	200				62½												10	
Moorhouse, Nathan ...... N. half	10	46	40	70			70			1			2	1	1					
Merril, Joseph (H. P. Coburn, agent)	14	56	300				75													
do.	14	55	500			1	50													
Morrison, A. F.	5	62	600	250	150	2	50			1			3	2	1	1				
do.	5	56	500	600		5	25													
More, J. M. & Co. (Store on)	10	56	500		6000	30	00													
Morrison, William	10				300	1	75		1	1			1	1	1	1		1	6	paid
do. .... (lives on)	9	64				1	50													
Maine, Mrs. or David (lives on)	12	57			70		35	1	1	1	1		1	1	1			1	5	paid
May, Enoch (lives on)		57			15		07½	1	1	2	1		2	2	2	1			5	paid
Mattingly, Richard (lives on)	5	58			150		75	2	1	1	1		1	1	1	1			6	paid
Miller, Jacob (lives on)	5	59			75		87½	2	2	3			1	1	1	1			8	paid

Name	Lot	Value	Value	Value	Tax	Paid
Montague & Buchannan...W. 54 ft.	61	240	50	50	1 10	paid
Montgomery, Alex.....(one-fourth)	62	100	60	80	85	paid
Morris, Oliver (lives on)	63			30	15	
Morgan, Joseph	73	300			75	
Morley, William (lives on)	63	500	120	500	2 50	paid
Mallory, David (colored man)	65			30	2 00	paid
Morrison, James (lives on)	67	200	200	300	1 50	paid
Mifflin, Obed (colored man)	72	200		30	1 65	paid
do.	72	150			37½	paid
More, John	72	150	100	70	37½	paid
do.	72	175			28¾	paid
do.	72	100			25	paid
McCord, Hannah	72	120			30	paid
McDonald, Hugh	24	85	20	60	61½	paid
McCormick (name uncertain)	24	150	150	100	1 69½	paid
do.	26	200			50	paid
do.	26	150			37½	paid
McCormick, John	26	200			50	paid
do.	34	350			87½	paid
McMahan, John	34	200			50	paid
do.	31	60			15	paid
do.	31	60			15	paid
do.	31	50			12½	paid
McGuire, Douglas........E. Half	47	500	750	250	6 25	paid
do.	47	400			1 00	paid
do.	35	350			50	paid
do.	35	250			68½	paid
do.	35	225			56½	paid
McGuire, Douglas	47	175			43¾	paid
McGuire & Wiley	47	100			25	paid
McGuire, Edmond	37	175	350	100	2 68¾	paid
McGuire & Francis (tailor shop)	37				25	paid
McKennon, Rev.	65	260	150	50	1 37½	paid
do.........S. half	37	100			25	paid
McCarty, Abner (lives on)	42		375	375	1 87½	paid

In Lots No.	Square	Names of Persons Assessed	Value of Lots (Dols.)	Value of Buildings (Dols.)	Value of Personal Property (Dols.)	Tax Dols.	Tax Cents	M Under 10	M 10 to 21	M 21 to 45	M 45 to 60	M Over 60	F Under 10	F 10 to 21	F 21 to 45	F 45 to 60	F Over 60	Colored persons	Total number	Paid
7	42	McOuat, Thomas	200	100		1	00													paid
11	67	do. .... E. third	1000	1000		2	50													paid
10	67	do.	500			6	25													paid
12	52	McMahan, John (lives on)			75		37½	2	4				1	1	1				10	paid
4	56	McCluer & Davis (drug store on)		1000	1000	5	00													paid
1	65	McCarty, Nicholas	3000			7	50													paid
2	65	do.	2500	5800	300	36	75	1	1	2			2	1	1				8	paid
7	65	do.	450			1	12½													paid
8	75	do.	200				50													paid
9	75	do.	150				37½													paid
10	75	do.	250				62½													paid
11	75	do.	300				75													paid
12	75	do.	200				50													paid
	56	do. .... part of 12 & 13	250				62½													paid
2	57	McCarty & Williams (store)	150	200	6000	1	37½												5	paid
9	57	McClure, Samuel (lives on)			50	30	00	1	1		1		3	3	1				10	paid
2	30	McCarty & Fletcher, E.⅓-p. by C. F.	700				95	1	1	1			2	2					5	paid
2	60	McDaniel, Moses	50	100	20	1	37½													paid
4	60	McClure, Andrew (lives on)		20	75		32½	1	1	1			1	2						paid
8	60	McLaughlin (agent for)	125	40			37½													paid
1	63	McFarland, Mrs. (lives on)			30		51¼					1					1			paid
6	63	McDowell, William .... E. 60½ ft.	700	200			15			1			1		1				3	On e-half paid
11	64	McDowall, John (lives on)		100	100	2	75			1		1			1				3	paid
1	67	McClure & Wheat (shop on)		150	150		50	1	1	1				2						paid
		McChesney, Jeremiah (factory on)		100	100		75		1	1							.37½		3	paid

Name												
McChesney, Jeremiah	4	67	350	75	30	1	30			1	1	1	4	paid
McChesney, Jacob	3	67					25	1	1		1	1	2	paid
McMahan, John .... (Salem)	10	76	300				75						paid
do. .... the whole of	11	76	300	50			75						paid
Noel, Vance		21	750			2	12½						paid
Nisbet	8	26	200				50						paid
do.	9	26	200				50						paid
do.	2	37	250		40		62½						paid
Neil, Elizabeth	3	32	85	50	40		66½	1	1	1	1	3	paid
Newland, Herod	3	43				1	20		1	1	1	4	paid
Newland, Robert C.	12	46	300				75						paid
do.	13	46	300				75						paid
	1	52	900				50						paid
Noble, N.	1	54	500	500	200	4	75	1	1	1	1	9	paid
Norwood, George	5	55	500	400		6	00	3					paid
do.	11	73	2000				50						paid
do. (McCarty)	1	61	200			1	50	1		1			paid
Nooe, Acquilla	1	61	350	500			90	1	1	4	1	9	paid
do. ...... E. 12½ ft.	2	65	60	1000	75	3	90	1	24				paid
Nowland, Elizabeth ...... W. 29½ ft	5	65	1300		700	11	75	3		5	34	paid
Nelson, Andrew & Co.	1	76	250	780	1500	12	40	1					paid
do.	2	76	150		100		50						paid
Nelson, And'w	10	30	50				25	2	2	1	2	8	paid
Overhaul, James (colored man)	11	30	45				11¼						paid
do.	12	30	50				12½						paid
do.	8	64			100	1	75	1	2	1	1	5	paid
Oliman, James (lives on)	8	33	150	250			67½						paid
do.	7	69	200	60			50						paid
do.		22					25			2			paid
Prizor, Abm. (lives on)	4	30	65		50		16¼	1	1		1	6	paid
Perry, Harry (colored man)	5	30	60	30			15						paid
do.	1	49	300		200	1	90				11	11	paid
do.	10	50	100				25						paid
do.	11	50	50				12½						paid
do.	12	50	75				18¾						paid
Patterson, Samuel	10	33	125	30			46¼						paid

NAMES OF PERSONS ASSESSED	In Lots Number	In Lots Square	Value of Lots (Dollars)	Value of Buildings (Dollars)	Value of Personal Property (Dollars)	TAX Dols.	TAX Cents	MALES Under 10 years	MALES 10 to 21	MALES 21 to 45	MALES 45 to 60	MALES Over 60	FEMALES Under 10 years	FEMALES 10 to 21	FEMALES 21 to 45	FEMALES 45 to 60	FEMALES Over 60	Colored persons of all ages	Total number	
Petit, Sanford (lives on)	10	43			40		20		1	1			2		1				4	paid
Pratt, Joseph (lives on)	8	44			50		25			1			1		1				4	paid
Presbyterian Church	2	45	650																	paid
do.	3	45	250	1200		7	62½													paid
Phipps, J. N.	5	45	400				62½													paid
do.	6	45	300	800	300	1	00		1	1			5	1	1				8	paid
do.	7	45	300	1000		6	25													paid
do.	8	45	1200		1500		75													paid
do. ......W. third	5	56		3000	6000	8	00													paid
do. (store)	10	55				7	50													paid
Porter, Henry ...E. 42 feet	12	55	2000			50	00		2	2			1		2		1		8	paid
do. ......W. third	1	47	100	70			60		1	1			2		1				8	paid
do. (personal property)	2	47			250	1	25													paid
Parr, James	7	54	350	100	100	1	87½	2		1			1						5	paid
do. (agent for) ...E. third of	8	54	300				75			1					2					
Patterson, Samuel ...E. third	9	54	1000																	
do. ......E. third	5	56																		
do. ...Center third	10	26		600	250	6	75													
do.	11	26	1000	1000		7	50													
do.	12	26	175				43¾													
do.			150				37½													
Phillips, Israel	2	55	175				43¾													
do.	1	55	500	700	147	5	49½	5		1			1		1				8	
do.	1	56	350				87½													
Palmer, N. B. (lives on) ...W. 37 feet	1	68	1500	450	400	6	00	4		2			1	3	1				11	paid
						2	00													

Name																			paid
Paxton, Elizabeth.........Part of	6	56	1000	1500	150	10 75				3	1			1			5		paid
Peck, John (lives on)					60	30				1				1			5		paid
Pulliam (store on)	4	65			1700	8 50					2	3		2			6		paid
Porter & Yandis (store on)		65			3500	17 50													paid
Porter, Edward					200	1 00		1									6		paid
Porter, George	3	66	2000	900		9 50				1		1		1			7		paid
Quarrels, William (lives on)	3	64			250	1 25				1		1		4		2			paid
Reynolds, William (lives on)	10	24			150	75													paid
do. N. two-thirds	10	37	100			75													paid
do.	11	37	125			75													paid
Riley, William (lives on)	9	31				31¼		2	1		1			1	2	4	4		paid
Rooker, Sam'l S.	3	34	200	150	15	07½		1			1			1			9		paid
do. (shop on)	6	54			100	1 05									2				paid
Record, Mrs.	12	40			100	50													paid
Roop, John (lives on)	8	42	100		150	50											8		paid
Roberts, Benjamin	5	46	300	200		25				1	1	3		1	2				paid
Rooter, H.	13	55	450	250		75													paid
Roop, Jacob (lives on)	1	57			100	2 37½				1	1	2		1		2	6		paid
Russell, A. W. (store)					3500	17 50				1		3		2		1	8		paid
do.	3	75	500	800	200	6 25						2		1		2	6		paid
Reed, A. W. (lives on)	9	57			50	25													paid
Ray, James M.	8	56	1000	1300	400	11 00	1	1		1	1			1	1	1	8		paid
do. part of 12 &	13	56																	paid
do.	6	59	350	300	300	2 37½													paid
do.	1	67	1000			2 50													paid
do.	3	67	300			75													paid
do.	10	77	30			07½													paid
do.	11	77	30			07½													paid
do.	12	77	30			07½													paid
Ray, James B.........W. 54 feet	2	63	500	4300		29 00				2	1	2		2	2	2	9		paid
do.	3	63	700																paid
do.	9	63	250																paid
do.	10	63	250	300		4 12½													paid
do.	11	63	250																paid
do.	12	63	300																paid

NAMES OF PERSONS ASSESSED	In Lots Number	In Lots Square	Value of Lots Dollars	Value of Buildings Dollars	Value of Personal Property Dollars	Tax Dols.	Tax Cents	M Under 10	M 10 to 21	M 21 to 45	M 45 to 60	M Over 60	F Under 10	F 10 to 21	F 21 to 45	F 45 to 60	F Over 60	Colored persons of all ages	Total number	
Ray, William (lives on)	6	59			125		62½	1		1			1		2				5	paid
Reeder, Thomas (lives on)	7	60			20		10													paid
Reagan, Wilkes (office on)	11	64	600		400	2	00												5	paid
Roll, Isaac H. ......E. third	5	66	300	200	450	4	75			1					1					paid
do. ......W. third	8	67	600	450		2	25							2					5	paid
Ramsay, John	7	66	400	250	300	4	25			1			2							paid
do.	11	68	200	300		2	50	1	2	2			1							paid
Ruieer, George ......(Wilkins)	3	74	250				50													
Rennick, Henrietta	1	51	200				62½	2		1			2							
Robb, Robert	2	51	100				50	1		2			1							
do.	3	51	150				25													
Scudder & Hanneman	7	23	100	351	1000	5	37½												3	paid
Smith, Andrew	8	23	75				00			1					1					paid
do.	2	43	200				25													paid
do.	1	24	100	100	100	1	18¾								1					paid
do.	12	24	200				50	1	1	1	1		1		1				7	paid
Sharp, Ebenezer	4	36	250	200	200		95													paid
do.	7	49	250			2	19½	1	1	1	1		1	2						paid
do.	8	49	175				62½													paid
do.	9	49	250				43¾													paid
Senior, Josiah	3	27	125				69¼	1		1			1							paid
do.	10	27	100				31¼													paid
Smith, Abner B. (state)	12	27	40				25													paid
do.	6	28	225				10													paid
							56¼													paid

Name	No.	No.	Value	Value	Value	Tax									Paid
Sutcliff, Johns (dec'd administrator)	4					37½									paid
Scudder, Caleb .... whole of	27		150			2 00									paid
do. .... W. half	29		800												paid
do.	47	8	600	1000	500	9 00	12			1	2	2			paid
do.	47	9	250												paid
Scott (colored man)	47	12	125			62½									paid
do.	31	1	50			31¼									paid
Searle (lives on)	31	2				12½									paid
Smithers, Willis	32	6	200	300	50	25	5			1	1				paid
Sulgrove, Joseph	33	2	200	100	70	2 35	3		1	1		3			paid
Smithers, John	34	4	250	600	75	1 31½				1					paid
do.	34	5	350		100	4 12½	6			1		3		1	paid
do. .... E. 62 ft.	34	3	1000			87½									paid
do.	54	6	250			2 50							1		paid
Schofield	35	5			180	62½	5	1	1	1	2	3		1	paid
Stipp, Dr. (lives on)	36	3			25	90	9		1	1	1	1		2	paid
Springsteel, John	40	5	75	100		81½		1		1					paid
Smith, James B.	42	11	200	500		3 00									paid
do. .... (lives on)	63	8													
Smith, William	43	2	250	500	100	4 50	5		1	1	1	2			paid
do.	63	12	300	150	300	1 50	5		1	1	1	1			paid
do. .... W. 28 feet	56	12	1200	300		4 50									
do. .... (agent for)	44	4	200		200	50									
Smith, Butler K.	44	2	300	200	50	2 75	7	1	1	2	1			1	paid
Spencer, Daniel (lives on)	44	1				25	5			1				2	paid
Sheets, William	44	8	350			13 37½		1						1	paid
do.	44	11	400	1800	500	2 37½	6		4	4		1		4	paid
Sharp, Thomas	44	12	350	300		2 00									paid
Shearer, Ludwick, sen'r.	45	4	350	200	50	75	3	1		1			1		paid
Shearer, Ludwick, Jun.	47	5	300			50									paid
Sheffer, John.	47	4	300			15									paid
Sberman, Frederick (lives on)	49	6	200	600	30	25									paid
Sloan, Andrew	51	10			100	75	2			1		1		1	paid
Smith, Oliver H.	51	5	300			25	10	1	2	1	1		2	1	paid
do.	52	12	300			75				1					paid
Sanders, William ...... W. 28 ft.	52	5	500	800	250	1 25	7			1	1	2			paid
do. .... W. half	55	6	1000			7 75									paid
	67	10	350			87½									paid

NAMES OF PERSONS ASSESSED	In Lots Number	In Lots Square	Value of Lots (Dollars)	Value of Buildings (Dollars)	Value of Personal Property (Dollars)	Tax Dols.	Tax Cents	Males Under 10 years	Males 10 to 21	Males 21 to 45	Males 45 to 60	Males Over 60	Females Under 10 years	Females 10 to 21	Females 21 to 45	Females 45 to 60	Females Over 60	Colored persons of all ages	Total number	
Smith, Abner B.	7	70	150				37½													paid
do.	8	70	100				25													paid
do.	9	70	100				95													paid
Sanders & Mothershead	5	56	1000	1000	600	3	00													paid
Smith, Wilkins & Co......E. third	7	56	600	1000	3000	22	50													paid
St. Clair, Arthur....part of 12 and	13	56	100	200		6	50													paid
do.	1	57	100			1	25	1		1					2				4	paid
Stacy, William (lives on)	5	57	400	200	75		37½	1		1				2	1				6	paid
Strange, Ruth	9	57	600	150	100	2	50													paid
Smith, Thomas.........W. third	7	59	} 1250	500	150	2	25		1	1			2		1	1			3	paid
do.	8	59			50	6	37½													paid
do.........W. 62 feet	11	64			100		25			1				1	1				5	paid
Smith, Hugh (lives on)	12	57					30			1					1					paid
do. (leather store)	4	59	200				50													paid
Sangster, W. J. (store on)	5	59	200	75			50												1	paid
Silvers, Samuel	9	60	175	200	20		87½		3	1			1	1	1	1	1			paid
do.	5	60	100				47½													paid
Sibard, David.........E. half	6	60	150				25												8	paid
do.	6	60		200	35	1	37½	1	1	1			1	1	1					
do.	7	60					17½													
Shinn, Isiah (lives on)	12	75	75			1	17½	1	1	1			1	1	1				3	paid
Stewart, Thomas (lives on)	1	62			40		20	1	1	1			1						3	paid
Spencer.......W. half quarter	5	63	250	300			18¾													
Stevens, Joshua........W. half	9	64	700	700		2	12½													paid
Slayback, Dr.........N. half	7	68	200	paid		5	25													paid
Stevens, Judge (Vevay)							60													paid

Name						Tax			paid by John			Crandeln	n		paid
Stapp, Gen'l	10	68	200	700		4 00		3	1	1		1	1	7	paid
Sulgrove, James	5	74	200	600	100	4 00			1	1			1		paid
Stevens heirs (C. Fletcher, agt.)	9	76	400	30		1 15									paid
Scott, Mary Ann, Dec'd (Merril, agt.)	7	52	400			1 00									paid
Thorp, John	9	28	50			12½									paid
do.	8	29	60			15									paid
do.	10	26	250		150	67½									paid
Taylor, Robert	1	22	350	150	150	75	1	1	1	1		1	1	6	paid
Tucker, John (colored man)	2	34	300	50		87½									paid
do.	2	34	300			75									paid
Tracy		35	200		60	75		3			3	1	1		paid
Temperly, Mathew (lives on)	4	45				50	1							6	paid
Taylor, Roht., jun. (lives in country)	2	48	175	250	125	43¼		2	3	2		2		6	paid
Tomlinson, Mrs. (lives on)	14	55		25	30	62½	2	3				2		3	paid
Truslow, John						15								4	paid
Thornton heirs (C. Fletcher, agent)	1	57	500	150	30	2 00		1	1		1	1	1		paid
Tucker, William ...... W. half	9	60	150	50	30	77½	1	1	1			1			paid
Thomas, Benjamin (lives on)		60			30	10									paid
True, Gliddon (owns building on)					50	15	1	1		1		1		3	paid
True, Chancey (lives on)	6	63			50	25									paid
Tucker, Robert	11	69	150		50	37½									paid
Unthank & Sulgrove (saddlery)	10	65		200	800	4 00	1	2	2	2		2		7	paid
Unthank, W. S. (lives on)	10	24	200	250	125	62½									paid
Underhill, Robert	9	57	600	25		1 75									paid
Underhill & Wood ...... center third						1 02½									paid
Ungles, W. J., his parts of 12 & 13, including part of 11			150	500	200	4 12½	4	2	2	1	2	1	2	6	paid
Vickon, Carson	4	56	650	500		2 83¼		1		1	2	1	1	7	paid
Vandegraff	11	32	85	225	200	1 75									paid
do.	12	33	} 300	100		50	1	1							paid
Varner, James (lives on)	3	33			100	2 75	1	2			3	1 (Varner)	(Vandegraff)		paid
Vanblaricum, John	10	36	500	300	100	5 50	1		1		2				paid
Vanblaricum, James	10	65	500	500	300	2 25	1		1					6	paid
do.	11	66	600	200		62½								7	paid
do.	4	74	250			1 02½		1					1		paid
do. (agent for)	3	55	250	80		1 02½	4		1			3		12	paid

NAMES OF PERSONS ASSESSED	In Lots Number	Square	Value of Lots (Dollars)	Value of Buildings (Dollars)	Value of Personal Property (Dollars)	Tax Dols.	Tax Cents	Males Under 10 years	Males 10 to 21	Males 21 to 45	Males 45 to 60	Males Over 60	Females Under 10 years	Females 10 to 21	Females 21 to 45	Females 45 to 60	Females Over 60	Colored persons of all ages	Total number	
Vanblaricum, Mary Ann	7	73	100	125	60		25	2		1			2		1				6	paid
Weaver, Thomas M	2	24	75	100		1	11¼													paid
Wallace, Henry S	1	32	150				87½	1		1			1		1	1			4	paid
Work, Joseph (lives on)		33			50		25													paid
Wiseman, Jacob	6	24	150				37½													paid
do.	11	52	150				37½													paid
do.	12	52	200				50											7	7	paid
White, Troy (colored man)		27			50		25													paid
Walchins, John L	6	27	200		50		50	1		1			1	1					3	paid
do. (lives on)	4	44			150		75	1	2	1	1		1	1	2				8	paid
Woollen, Lenard	6	33	300	300	100	2	75													paid
do. ......N. half	9	28	35				08¾													paid
do.	10	28	60				15													paid
West, Thomas	10	31	60				15											5	5	paid
do.	11	31	50		110		12½			1			1		1					paid
do.	12	31	75	100		1	23¾													paid
Woollen & Bardwell	4	33	250	150	100	1	12½		2	1			1		2			4	4	paid
Woollen, Milton	9	34		300	100		50	2		3					2	1		5	5	paid
Woollen, John M	11	34	250			2	62½													paid
do.	12	34	350		50		87½													paid
Willard, A. G.	1	35	300	25	700	1	12½	1		1				1	1			3	3	paid
do. (store on)	9	55				3	50													paid
Wiley, Alex	3	37	175	75	40		18¾												5	paid
Wilson, John J	3	40	50	75	30		90	2	1	1					1				6	paid
Wood, William	40	40	60		30		67½	1		1			1	1	1				6	paid
Ward, Avery (lives on)	7	44					15			1				1	1					paid

Name						Value	Value	Value	Assessment	paid
Wilson, John (paid 20 cents)	53	5			1 1	2 1		40	20	paid
Wright, Wm. D. (lives on)	55				1 1	1		30	15	paid
Watchins & Smith (shop)								40	20	
Webb (watch store)								300	50	paid
Wiley, Alex. (shop)								50	25	
Ward, Thomas (lives on)								50	25	
Walpole, Luke	57	2	2000	1200	3000	26 00				
Wilkins & Yandis	57	8								
do.	62	7								
do.	62	8								
do.	62	9	500	1200	4000	27 25				
do.	62	10								
Wilkins, John	64	3	500	150	400	2 00				
Williams, David	65	12	600		150	75				
Watts, Judge, heirs	66	4	2000	500	250	1 50				
White, Dennis J	66	8	300			1 00				
Wilson, Abram	67	7	400			8 75				
William, John	67	6	800	50	60	75				
do.	70	1	300			1 00				
Wernwag, William	70	2	250	800	100	2 55				
do.	70	3	250			5 75				
do.	70	10	100			12½				
do.	70	11	100			62½				
do.	70	12	150			25				
do.	71	1	150			25				
Wernwag & Young	71	2	100	} 1775		37½				
do.	71	3	100							
do.	73	2	100			8 87½				
do.	73	8	200			12½				
Waltz, Frederick	69	3				25				
Wilson, Joseph										
Winchell, Peter (lives on)	71	11			100	50				paid
do. ....S. half	71	12	} 65			21½				
do. ....S. half										
Wilson, Lazarus B	69	5	300			75				paid
do.	69	6	300			75				paid
do.	29	7	225			56¼				paid

NAMES OF PERSONS ASSESSED	In Lots Number	Square	Value of Lots (Dollars)	Value of Buildings (Dollars)	Value of Personal Property (Dollars)	TAX Dols.	TAX Cents	Males Under 10 years	Males 10 to 21	Males 21 to 45	Males 45 to 60	Males Over 60	Females Under 10 years	Females 10 to 21	Females 21 to 45	Females 45 to 60	Females Over 60	Colored persons of all ages	Total number	paid
Weimer, Ithemer	4	51	150				37½													paid
Wilson, David (John Givan, agt.)	3	76	200				50													paid
do.	6	76	50				12½													paid
Winburn, William (colored man)	7	75																4	4	paid
Young, John	4	26	200	1800	200	11	75	3		2			3	1	2				11	paid
do.	5	26	200																	
do.	6	26	300																	
Young, John L.	4	71	100	495	300	4	74½	1	2		1			1	1				6	
do.	5	71	100				18¾													
do.	6	71	150				12½													
do.	7	71	75				12½													
do.	8	71	50				12½													
do.	9	71	50																	
do.	10	71	50																	
John, Sarah W. ... 80 feet	6	46	400	300	50	2	75		1	1				2		1			5	
Yates, Benjamin (lives on)	1	32			75		37½												4	
Yandis, Daniel ... 11½ feet W.	4	65	900	1000	400	9	25					Paid		Ro op	by Roop				11	paid
... 8½ feet E.	5	65	350				87½													paid
do.	6	36	350				87½													paid
do.	10	36	300				75													paid
do.	6	77	40				10													paid
do.	7	77	40				10													paid
do.	8	77																		paid

PROPERTY NOT ASSESSED.

	INLOT	
	No.	Square
Hospital square......................................		22
Academy or college square.............		25
Treasury lot and building............................	1	68
State House square...................................		53
State of Indiana........Lots 1-3-4-5-6-7-8-9-10-11 &̈12		48
do. ....4-5, 6-7-8 & 9		43
do. .... 4-5-6-7-8 & 9		50
do. ....7 & 8		46
do.	10	54

TOTAL VALUATION.

Value of lots...	$231,356
Value of buildings.....................................	136,745
Value of personal property............................	127,647
Total amount......................................	$495,748
Proprietor unknown, lot 11, square 51....................	250
Proprietor unknown, lot 12, square 72..................	150
	$496,148

Whole amount of tax assessed...................		$1898
Deduct tax on Blythe & McCarty tanyard, as by order of Board..............................	$25 00	
Do. cr. Andrew Nelson & Co., do.	7 50	
Do. cr. Wilkins & Yandis, do.	20 00	52
		$1845

Copy of Order of the Board of Trustees of 1st May 1835—"Ordered that the tax assessed on stock in tan yards vats be remitted, and that the order be entered on the assessor's book."

Attest: J. MORRISON, *Clerk.*

NUMBER OF INHABITANTS

	Males	Females	Colored Persons
Under ten years....................	248	267	
Ten to twenty-one years.............	192	184	
Twenty-one to forty-five years.......	372	255	
Forty-five to sixty years............	37	29	
Over sixty years....................	10	8	
	859	743	81

I, George Lockerbie, assessor for the Town of Indianapolis, for the year 1835, do hereby certify that the foregoing 34 pages contain a true assessment and valuation of all the in-lots in said town, together with a true valuation of all houses, buildings or tenements thereon, and of all shops, offices and out-houses connected or contiguous thereto and which are liable to be consumed or injured by fire: Also an assessment and valuation of the personal effects, goods, wares and merchandise in all such buildings, houses, shops, tenements and out-houses, situate on such lots, of a perishable nature, and which might be consumed or injured by fire—together with an enumeration of the inhabitants in said town,—taken by me in pursuance of an ordinance of the President & Trustees of said town, approved and ordained 18th February 1835, entitled "An ordinance to raise a revenue in the town of Indianapolis for the year 1835."

GEORGE LOCKERBIE.

Filed by George Lockerbie, assessor of said Town for the year 1835, and returned to me the 18th day of April A. D. 1835.   JAMES MORRISON,
Clerk of the Board of Trustees
of the Town of Indianapolis.

The State of Indiana
and President and Trustees of
the Town of Indianapolis

To the Marshall of said Town, Greeting:

You are hereby directed and commanded to collect the taxes charged in the annexed and foregoing assessment roll, by demanding payment at the usual or best known place of residence of the several persons charged, or from the persons charged at any other place, or by distress and sale of the goods and chattels of such persons, respectively: and that you pay over the monies by you collected by virtue of this precept as directed by an ordinance of the said President and Trustees of said Town, ordained and established the 22d day of April A. D. 1835, entitled "An ordinance for the collection of the Revenue of the Town of Indianapolis, and for other purposes: and that you make return thereof to the Clerk of said board of Trustees on or before the first day of August next.   Dated Indianapolis, May A. D. 1835.

A. F. MORRISON,
President of the Board.

Attest: JAMES MORRISON,
Clerk of the Board of Trustees.

INDIANA HISTORICAL SOCIETY PUBLICATIONS
VOLUME IV   NUMBER 8

THE

SCOTCH-IRISH PRESBYTERIANS

IN

MONROE COUNTY, INDIANA

A Paper Read before the Monroe County Historical Society
November and December, 1908

BY

JAMES ALBERT WOODBURN

Professor of American History, Indiana University

INDIANAPOLIS
Edward J. Hecker, Printer and Publisher
1910

A WORD OF INTRODUCTION

This paper, as its title page indicates, was prepared for the Monroe County (Indiana) Historical Society, and was read before that society in the fall of 1908. Some friends encouraged its publication, and, with some additions, it is now published by the courtesy of the Indiana Historical Society. A considerable part of the paper deals in general with the people called "Scotch-Irish" and their migrations, and with the ecclesiastical origins and tenets of those Irish Presbyterians who are distinguished by their exclusive use of the Bible Psalms in public and private worship. These parts of the paper do not bear especially on Indiana life, since they deal with subjects of general history and describe a class of people that go to make up the population of many other States as well as that of Indiana. But the life and character of these people go to make up a part of Indiana history, and it is therefore believed that a publication of the State Historical Society may properly deal with them.

Other parts of the paper deal chiefly with matters of local county interest, but since they describe religious bodies that have societies of their kith and kin in other parts of the State, whose antecedents, traits, customs, influence and religious ways are all similar to those of the people here treated of, the author ventures to hope that the subject matter of his paper may prove of more than local county interest.

The psalm-singing Presbyterians have established settlements and have influenced their respective communities in various parts of the State, notably in Rush, Decatur, Gibson, Jefferson and White counties, while many of them, as members of the Presbyterian Church of North America, are scattered generally throughout our population. Their part in the life and progress of the State has not been an unworthy one, and I trust that the "Scotch-Irish Presbyterians" in other parts of Indiana who may chance to read this essay may be able to recognize the portraiture that I have here attempted to draw.

JAMES A. WOODBURN.

Indiana University,
  Bloomington, Indiana.
    November 1, 1909.

BIBLIOGRAPHY

I have used the following material in the preparation of this essay:

Report of the Council of the American Antiquarian Society, 1895. Samuel S. Green's Essay on the Scotch-Irish in America, and the discussion by Thomas Hamilton Murray.

Warner, Thomas, Brochure on Communion Tokens, 1888.

Barrie, J. M., "Auld Licht Idylls."

Hanna, "The Scotch-Irish in America," 2 vols.

Lecky, W. E. H., "History of England in the Eighteenth Century."

Bishop Burnett, "History of My Own Times."

"The United Presbyterian Fathers."

Fleming, John, "A Testimony for an Universal Church," Edinburgh, 1826.

"The Re-Exhibition of the Testimony: A Connected View of the Principles of the Secession Church of Scotland," Glasgow, 1779.

Lathan, Robert, "A History of the Hopewell Church, Chester County, South Carolina, with Biographical Sketches of Its Pastors."

"Napthali, or the Wrestlings of the Church of Scotland."

Proceedings of the Scotch-Irish Congress, 1889, 1890, 1891.

Glasgow, W. M., "History of the Reformed Presbyterian Church in America," 1888.

Roosevelt, Theodore, "Winning of the West."

Turner, Frederick J., "Rise of the New West."

"The McMillans, 1750-1907: A Record of the Descendants of Hugh McMillan and Jane Harvey from Scotland Through Ireland to America," by Rev. James Henry Cooper.

Session Record Books of the "Union Congregation," of Bloomington, of the Associate Reformed Church. I have also used several copies of the "Evangelical Repository," an early journal of the Associate Reformed Church in America.

SCOTCH-IRISH PRESBYTERIANS IN MONROE COUNTY, INDIANA

I.

It is not the purpose of this paper to deal with the whole of Presbyterianism in Monroe county, but rather with the psalm-singing Presbyterians of Bloomington and the immediate vicinity. In the first place, I shall leave out of consideration the Cumberland Presbyterians, who, in the earlier days, formed small congregations in Harrodsburg and Ellettsville. They are now reunited with the larger branch of the Presbyterian Church, and, as they were mostly Arminian rather than Calvinistic in faith and practice, they do not naturally fall within the view of this paper.

The period with which I propose to deal was one of Presbyterian divisions, and when one contemplates the number and extent of these divisions he sees the necessity for a still further limitation of this subject. Within the memory of many men now living, almost within my own memory, there were not fewer than six distinct and rival Presbyterian churches in Bloomington, viz.,—the "Old School" and the "New School" Presbyterian Church; the "Old Side" and the "New Side" Covenanter, or Reformed Presbyterian, Church,—sometimes called the "Old Light" and the "New Light"; the "Associate Presbyterians," called "Seceders"; and the "Associate Reformed Presbyterians." This array of Presbyterian sects is confusing and discouraging to start with, but happily time has reduced these six divided bodies to three; and since Old Father Time is still at work, we are not without hope of still better things to come in the way of reunion. "Old School" and "New School" were merged into one by the Presbyterian reunion in 1870; Associate and Associate Reformed Presbyterians have merged into United Presbyterians, into whose fold, also, have been gathered, for the most part, the former members of the New Side Covenanter Church; while the "Old Side Covenanters," or the Reformed Presbyterian Church, on South Walnut street, is the only one of these early and divisive sects that has not been influenced by the spirit of union. These three surviving and still dissevered Presbyterian bodies were once designated in a facetious way by President David Starr Jordan, of Indiana University, at a time when the regular Presbyterian congregation here was somewhat discordant, as "Reformed Presbyterians, United Presbyterians, and Presbyterians that are neither united nor reformed." The largest and most important of these three branches of Presbyterianism, viz., the regular Presbyterian church, I shall also eliminate from consideration in this paper, and confine myself to those religious bodies in this community who are distinguished by their exclusive use of the Bible Psalms in public worship. These are perhaps more distinctly Scotch-Irish than most of their brethren of the Presbyterian church of North America, while the history and characteristics of these psalm-singing bodies afford a theme quite ample enough for treatment in a single paper.

WHO ARE THE SCOTCH-IRISH?

It may be well to speak first of that element in the American population known as the Scotch-Irish. There are those who object to the use of this term. They claim that the word is unknown in Ireland, and that it has been assumed only to distinguish Irishmen of one faith from those of another; that the Irish Presbyterians, who early came to America from the North of Ireland, called themselves Irish or Irishmen; and that while some of their great-great-grandfathers had come from Scotland, their children had lived in Ireland long enough to become sons of the soil, and were, therefore, true sons of Erin. That is, they are simply Irish and nothing more.

These critics very plausibly claim as Irish all who are born on Irish soil of Irish parents, and their immediate descendants, regardless of creed or of the place from which their ancestors may have come. An Episcopalian voicing this feeling once said: "I notice that so long as an Irishman goes to the Roman Catholic Church he is spoken of as Irish, but should he change his creed and go to the Baptist or Presbyterian church he is immediately referred to as Scotch-Irish."

In reference to this criticism it should, of course, be recognized that all Ulstermen are not of Scotch descent, and that Scotch-Irish is not at all synonymous with Protestant Irish. Thousands of Protestant Irish are of English descent with no Scotch blood in their veins. Some are of Huguenot extraction; that is, they are French-Irish, while other bloods, such as the Welsh, German, Dutch and Dane, are also mixed in the Protestant element of North Ireland.

I think it would be altogether proper to designate the people with whom this paper deals as Irish Presbyterians. They were called that when they first came to America from Ireland. But it is also quite proper, in order to indicate more fully and more distinctly what kind of people they were and whence they came, to call them Scotch-Irish, merely because the fathers were Scotch before the children were Irish. As we may to-day properly distinguish Americans of German blood or of Irish blood as

German- or Irish-Americans, so we may very properly distinguish the Irish of Scotch blood. Those who call themselves Scotch-Irish do not use the term in any invidious sense (or ought not to do so), or as a palliative description of a people who are merely Irish, but who adopt a prefix as a means of escape from Irish relationship. No one need ever apologize for being an Irishman. There are too many worthy thousands proud of the blood to enable any one to be ashamed of it. There are some of those, at least, who call themselves Scotch-Irish who are quite willing to know, and to have it known, that their fathers and mothers were Irish; but they deem it no offense in outlining their ancestral tree, to state that these fathers and mothers were the kind of Irish that were made out of Scotch. They do not claim that this is any better brand of Irish than any other, but only that this is their brand; and they know of no reason why they should not make it known. They were the people who moved from the Lowlands of Scotland to the North of Ireland; then, after a hundred years, more or less, they migrated from Ireland to America. That is, they were Teutonic, not Celtic, in their racial descent, and it seems to me only reasonable to assert, in view of these well-known ethnic distinctions, that the term Scotch-Irish is too well rooted in the ethnology of the American people to permit of its being discarded, denied or annulled.

The Scotch-Irish in America, then, may be defined as the Irish of Scotch descent, who came to this country chiefly from the North of Ireland. They were Protestants in religion and Scotch in blood. One may very properly write of them in their three homes, just as the English historian, Freeman, has written of the English people in their three homes—in Germany, in Old England and in New. The Scotch-Irish have lived in Scotland, Ireland

and America, and their migrations are an interesting and by no means an unimportant phase of human history.

"For some years after the Revolution of 1688," says Mr. Lecky, "a steady stream of Scotch Presbyterians had poured into Ireland, attracted by the cheapness of the farms and by new openings in trade." The last of the seventeenth century saw the last of this migration. In 1715 it was estimated that 50,000 Scotch families had settled in Ulster since the Revolution of 1688.[1]

Why did these Scotch, now to be known as Scotch-Irish, leave Ulster for America? No doubt, chiefly for the same reason that their forefathers had come to Ulster: they came in search of better homes. That emigration from Ulster to America is one of the most striking features of Irish-American history. For about fifty years this migration continued, from about 1715 to 1775. In 1728 it is estimated that about 4,200 men, women and children had been shipped in three years. In consequence of the famine of 1740, and for several years following that year, twelve thousand emigrants annually left Ulster for the American plantations. In the three years, from 1770 to 1773, the emigration from Ulster is estimated at thirty thousand. Of these ten thousand were weavers, and it is known as a fact in the story of this Irish migration that when the linen trade was low the passenger trade was high. In a little over forty years, from 1725 to 1768, from three thousand to six thousand came annually, or two hundred thousand Protestants in all. That is, about one-third of the Protestant population of Ireland came to America in this period.

For this movement in population there were three principal causes—commercial restrictions, exorbitant rents, religious persecutions.

---

[1] Lecky's "England in the Eighteenth Century," Vol. II, p. 260.

Many of the Presbyterian ministers and their people in Ireland had come from Scotland after the Restoration to escape religious restrictions at home. They had been subject to arrest for attending their own religious meetings in violation of the conventicle act; for not going to church; for refusing the oath; and in many instances they were fined, imprisoned or whipped through the streets. "Many were undone by it," says Bishop Burnet, in his "History of My Own Times," "and went over to the Scots in Ulster, where they were received and had all manner of liberty as to their way of religion."

But, as we have indicated, they were soon destined to be followed by religious penalties and strife. On account of these religious restrictions, as well as from economic reasons, Ireland was in a wretched state. About 1715 land leases in North Ireland began to expire. Rents were doubled and trebled and rack-renting had become an unbearable practice.

In 1698, very soon after the English revolution, the Irish woolen manufacturers were suppressed, for the sake of the English. No Irish woolens could be exported. Later acts forbade the Irish to export their wool to any country save England, in order that the English manufacturers might have cheap wool.

The religious penal laws of that time were directed against the Roman Catholics; but all Protestants who did not conform to the Church of England were persecuted.

THE SACRAMENTAL TEST ACT OF 1704.

The Sacramental Test Act, an act which was said to have fashioned the history of Ireland for seventy years (from 1700 to 1770), compelled all serving in any capacity under the government, holding any office, civil or military, or receiving any pay or salary from the Crown, practicing before the courts, those acting in town councils, teaching or performing the marriage ceremony,—all were required to take the communion according to the Church of England. This act emptied the councils of Ulster towns. By an act of 1691 a Presbyterian minister in Ireland was liable to three months' imprisonment for delivering a sermon and to $500 in fines for celebrating the Lord's Supper.

Agriculture was in a miserable condition. There was little commerce, as trade was repressed by government. There were no manufactures, save the slowly growing linen industry of Ulster. The people were suffering under civil and political disabilities. As a consequence of all this, there followed for nearly three-quarters of a century, as I have indicated, a constant drain of the Protestant population of the North of Ireland. There was nothing to induce the active-minded men of the North to remain, and they left in crowds, going away with their wives and children never to return. Ministers and people left together. They came to a new land, and here they founded their homes, built their churches, established their communities, and again set up their religion and the altars of their faith.

These Protestant Irish came to America in two principal streams, the larger landing in Philadelphia and Newcastle, Delaware, near the mouth of the Delaware river; the smaller going to Charleston, S. C. They settled in large numbers in western Pennsylvania. The population of that State is made up historically, as is well known, of three principal factors,—the English Quakers in the east, the Pennsylvania Dutch in the middle portion, and the Scotch-Irish in the western section of the State. From Pennsylvania the Scotch-Irish went south in great numbers, along the foothills and valleys of western Virginia. After Braddock's defeat at the opening of the French and Indian war, 1755, the frontier settlements of Pennsylvania were not so safe from the attacks and depredations of hostile Indians, and the movement south, both of the fresh immigrants and the frontiersmen, was accelerated. These people made their abodes and settlements in the Cumberland valley in Maryland south from Lancaster, Pennsylvania, in the Shenandoah valley in Virginia, and along the foothills and valleys on their way farther southward, until they met their brethren coming northward from Charleston in the back country of the Carolinas. In this Piedmont region, away from tide-water and east of the mountains, they became the principal factor of the population as they are to this day. They were the earliest pioneers to cross the mountains, following Boone into Kentucky and Robertson into Tennessee, and they were among the hardy founders of these young commonwealths in the West. The Calhouns, the Jacksons, the Hemphills, the Houstons, the Craigs, the Maxwells, the Blairs, and the Johnstons of the frontier South were of this Irish stock.

These Scotch-Irish settlers were the frontiersmen of our history. They were stationed on the outposts of civilization and they became, as Mr. Roosevelt says, "A shield of sinewy men thrust in between the people of the seaboard and the red warriors of the wilderness."[1] I quote again from Mr. Roosevelt in his "Winning of the West": "Full credit," he says, "has been awarded the Round Head and the Cavalier for their leadership in our history; nor have we been blind to the deeds of the Hollander and the Huguenot; but it is doubtful if we have wholly realized the importance of the part played by that

---

[1] "Winning of the West."

stern and virile people, the Irish, whose preachers taught the creed of Knox and Calvin. These Irish representatives of the Covenanters were in the West almost what the Puritans were in the North and more than the Cavaliers were in the South. * * * That these Irish Presbyterians were a bold and hardy race is proved by their pushing at once past the settled regions and plunging into the wilderness as the leaders of the white advance. They were the first and last set of immigrants to do this; all others have merely followed in the wake of their predecessors. They were fitter to be Americans from the start. They were kinsfolk of the Covenanters. They claimed it as a religious duty to interpret their own Bible and held it to be a divine right to elect their own clergy. For generations their whole ecclesiastical system had been fundamentally democratic."[1]

Mr. Roosevelt here emphasizes two facts of importance concerning the migration and local history of this people.

1. The western portions of Virginia and the Carolinas were peopled by an entirely different stock from that of the tide-water region.

2. Except for the few who came by way of Charleston the immigrants of this stock were mostly from the North, from their great breeding ground in western Pennsylvania.

This is in harmony with the recital of Ramsay, the historian of South Carolina, who speaks of a thousand immigrants coming in a single year from Pennsylvania and Virginia, driving their horses, cattle and hogs before them, and who were assigned places in the western woods of the South Carolina Province.

This also harmonizes with what I know of the immigration of my own Scotch-Irish ancestors to this country.

---

[1] "Winning of the West," pp. 8, 9, 10.

My great-grandfather, James Woodburn, left to his family a little piece of his personal history which he called his "Peregrinations." It tells whence and where and when he "peregrinated," in journeying from the Old World to the New. This little document tells that he was born in County Derry, Ireland, in 1748; that he left his home for America in 1767; landed at Newcastle, at the mouth of the Delaware; stopped a while in Pennsylvania; went to South Carolina; returned to Ireland and was married, and again came to South Carolina, settling in Orangeburg District and later on Rocky creek, Chester county, among others of his Covenanter faith.

Here, in South Carolina, was one of these Scotch-Irish settlements to which the Scotch-Irish Presbyterians of this county are ancestrally related. In the southeastern part of what is now Chester county, South Carolina, on the waters of Little Rocky creek, about fifteen miles southeast of the town of Chester, and only a few miles from the Fairfield county line—here, a hundred years ago, was one of the most numerous settlements of Irish Presbyterians in America. They were not United Presbyterians in those days—in the latter part of the eighteenth and the first of the nineteenth century. They were, on the contrary, much divided, and their divisions existed over what we to-day would consider the most fruitless, not to say trifling, subjects of controversy. Some were "Associate Presbyterians," some were "Reformed Presbyterians," some were "Burghers" and some were "Anti-Burghers." But they were all strict, strait-laced, rigid, stiff-backed, blue Presbyterians. Each little body believed it held to the only original faith once delivered to the saints, and in long, argumentative, doctrinal sermons their ministers opposed one another with a tenacity and a zeal greater than they, or their flock of the elect, could ever hope to show in combatting the world, the flesh and the devil. This rigid, ecclesiastical stock had come, as we have seen, from Scotland to Ireland, and from Ireland to Pennsylvania and Carolina. Another migration was to bring a company of these people, whose history we are attempting to record, from South Carolina to Indiana.

II.

In the story of westward expansion in America the forty years from 1820 to 1860 was marked by a wonderful movement of population to the Northwest. In this period Indiana twice quadrupled her population, rising from 147,000 to 1,350,000, while Illinois in less time twice quadrupled her population, rising from 55,000 souls in 1820 to 1,700,000 in 1860, while Ohio rose from 580,000 to 2,340,000. This movement of population is one of the prime factors in American history. Within the years to which I refer, 1820 to 1860, more than a million people came to the Northwest from the slave States of the South, and among these were two notable religious societies that came in considerable numbers to Indiana—the Quakers from North Carolina, and the Scotch-Irish from South Carolina. A group of the Scotch-Irish Presbyterians came to Monroe county from another source, but were of identical stock. I refer to some families that came from western Pennsylvania and eastern Ohio about 1855, the time at which Rev. John Bryan came to Bloomington as the minister of the Associate Church. These included the families of John Robinson, David Hunter, Harvey Phillips, Dr. G. W. Bryan, Mrs. John Cherry (Miss Crabb), and doubtless others. But the bulk of the people in these Scotch-Irish Presbyterian churches that were established in this county were from South Carolina, as an inspection of the tombstones in the graveyards in the west part of town and two miles southeast of Bloomington will clearly demonstrate.

These people, like the Quakers, were strongly anti-slavery in sentiment. No doubt many of them were moved in this last migration by a desire to get away from the institution of slavery, and to secure the advantages of free soil for themselves and their children. For it was true that some of these religious societies, even in the slave States, refused to admit slave-holders to their communion. I have been told, also, in answer to inquiries addressed to children of the first comers, that their fathers did not like nullification, and they wished to get away from the tyranny of that majority that was bringing their State into dangerous collision with the Federal Union.[1]

---

[1] Evidence of the anti-nullification spirit among the Scotch-Irish in the upland region of South Carolina is found in some letters written by Mr. Samuel MacCalla from Chester county, South Carolina, to Mr. Dorrance Woodburn, in Indiana, from 1831 to 1834. Mr. MacCalla sent to his friend a hand-bill, which, as he said, "gives a correct idea of our views and determinations." "I could not," he continued, "get a copy of the military act. We have a committee of vigilance for each company and a central committee for the regiment. They meet weekly and monthly. The Union Convention meets next Monday at Greenville. If the *Nullies* don't go back we will fight. If they once begin it, it will be short and bloody. You won't hear of it until it will be over. I command the Rifle Company, and, you may depend, we will clean the coasts of our enemies. We have not only the best rifles but the best marksmen in the State. We have been training two years, and they can blow the ball of an otter's eye out at his other end. You may communicate this information to your friends and you and them lay your heads together to put in Clay or a man of his politics for President. I am sick and tired of this wicked old savage now in office."

As this letter was written on March 20, 1834, some time after Jackson's decisive work against nullification, it would appear that the attitude of the "Old Hero" was not properly appreciated by this Unionist of South Carolina.

In an earlier letter, under the date of November 19, 1831, Mr. MacCalla speaks of slavery and the Southhampton Insurrection as follows:

"The panic on the guilty slave holders was not trifling. I heard of some that took their guns and blankets and concealed themselves in deep gullies in the night to avoid danger, and some stories is too ridiculous to tell or be believed; but the scripture was verified where it says, 'the wicked flee when no man pursueth.' "

"These commotions has a terrible tendency to make more people want to get

However these things may be, it is also doubtless true that the chief motive in this migration was the same as in the other two—it came from economic pressure, from a desire to improve their material condition, and to find better homes.

Their coming to the West was a part of the great westward movement of that era. One of the causes of this movement, as we know, was the financial panic of 1819, and the hard times that followed. The debtor farmer had to sell, and, together with the man out of work, he sought to find a new home where land was cheap and where he could again start out to better his

away from such hard service, for the whole military in some places performed patrol duty for five days and nights in succession. The negroes were treated with severity and they all knew that the whites were in great terror. You will, no doubt, hear a great deal about this business. Folks here are getting more and more anxious to leave this State of sin and misery. Money is harder to get here than you ever knew it and the price of labor is lower than in Indiana. Heavy debts and ruin to many families, I fear, will be the consequence of the present depressed state of business."

Mr. MacCalla reports that some farms sold in his neighborhood in 1831 for $3.25 per acre, some for $5.25, while he sold his own land in 1834 for $6 per acre. The Harbison farm, in Chester county, sold, about that time, for $8 per acre. It was some time before Mr. MacCalla was able to sell his land, as he desired to follow his kith and kin in his household of faith, who had been moving in families and neighborhoods to Indiana, Ohio and Illinois. His neighbors had ceased to be of his kind, and he described them as "singular and outlandish people." In the year of his departure for Indiana he writes in a critical and depressed spirit of the decline of his State and community: "The church is all gone down the hill," he says. "'Our clergy are a set of dull conceited hashes, who fash their brains in college classes, they gang in stirks and come out asses.' Plain truth to speak. They know how to make a bow, play the flute, shake you by the hand, or argue metaphysics, but knows no more about the bible than the Emperor Nicholas knows about the rights of man.

"The State is still worse, for we were harangued last year about liberty, free trade, and such stuff. Now there is a bold attempt on the very fundamentals of equal rights. The State authorities claim a right to exact an oath of primary allegiance to the State and to vacate all commissions at their pleasure. We are to be made slaves for no offense on our part because we can not swallow an alligator tail first."

In 1834 Mr. MacCalla, with a family of ten children, joined the South Carolina colony in Indiana. He lived to be more than ninety years of age. He had four sons who fought against nullification and secession in the war for the Union, and better soldiers never enlisted for their country's cause.

fortune. It was not altogether the conscience of the
Quaker and the Scotch-Irishman that brought these
people from the Carolinas to Indiana. Cotton, no doubt,
played as large a part as conscience, as a motive power.
The price of that great Southern staple was steadily de-
clining. In 1816 the average price of Carolina upland
cotton was 30 cents; in 1820 it was 17 cents; in 1824 it
had fallen to 14¾ cents, while in 1827 middling uplands
had reached the low figure of 9 cents.[1] It was then that
the leaders in South Carolina and the larger owners of
slaves in the tide-water region, resorted to the device of
nullification and threatened the country with civil war
in defense of what they considered their economic interests; while the little farmers found it desirable, if not
necessary, to sell their land and move. It was from this
middle class in the South, not yet pressed to the sad lot
of the poor and landless whites, that this migration of
which we write came from the Carolinas to Indiana.

Cotton culture could be most economically conducted
by the plantation system. This system involved large
farms, or plantations, on which one overseer could direct the work of many hands, since among the slaves
the old men, the women and the children could be employed in cotton-picking. The low price of cotton was
bringing the less desirable uplands into more intensive
cultivation, or under the plantation management, and the
small farmers in the back country could not compete with
large land-holders. The Scotch-Irish of this region in the
Carolinas were small land-holders; they had their forty,
eighty, or, perhaps, one hundred and sixty acres, and they,
as a rule, had but few slaves; most of them had no slaves
at all. The richer land-holders, the plantation masters,
who could afford to add field to field, were ready to buy

---

[1] Frederick J. Turner, "Rise of the New West," p. 325.

out the little farmers; new lands in the Northwest were
being offered for sale at cheap government prices on easy
terms, and there began a movement, a steady tide of
movers with their covered wagons, like the famous Con-
estogas, and their horses, cattle and household effects, to
the new lands of the Indiana and the Illinois country.
They came up the east side of the Blue Ridge, through
Cumberland Gap and Kentucky, crossing the Ohio below
Cincinnati. The Scotch-Irish coming out of South Carolina made settlements near Bloomington, Princeton and
Madison, Indiana; Xenia, Ohio; Sparta, Monmouth and
Paxton, Illinois, and they were scattered through many
other neighborhoods of the Northwest.

Religion is recognized as being one of the principal
factors in forming the character of a people. It may
therefore be desirable, in order to understand the character of the people of whom we speak, to go somewhat
into the ecclesiastical history of these small Presbyterian
bodies. Let us take up first the Reformed Presbyterians,
the oldest Presbyterian body in Monroe county.

THE REFORMED PRESBYTERIANS, OR COVENANTERS.

Originally the Covenanters comprised the greater portion of the Scotch Presbyterians of the sixteenth and
seventeenth centuries, who bound themselves together
by a solemn promise called a covenant, by which they
agreed to establish and maintain the Presbyterian doctrine and policy as the sole religion of the country, to
the exclusion both of Prelacy and Popery. As Abraham
covenanted with God, by which Israel became God's
chosen people, so now, the Jew having broken the covenant by rejecting the Christ, God was ready to offer a
new covenant of grace to all who, by the strength of that
grace, would vow to be his people and perform the du-

ties which he has enjoined upon them in his word. In
this covenant promise God says: "I will be to them a
God and they shall be to me a people." To accept this
offer and to promise to be a faithful and loyal people is to
covenant with God. The act may be personal—an act
of the individual at God's altar; it may be social—an act
of the congregation in public worship; it may be national—an act of the nation by its representatives in
solemn assembly. There were special occasions on which
the covenant was to be entered into by a formal and
solemn deed. As the Jewish nation did at Horeb, so the
Scottish nation did at Grayfriars. "All that the Lord
hath spoken we will do, to the end that the Lord might
establish them a people unto himself." Joshua, as God's
appointed leader, made a covenant with the people in
which they declared, "The Lord our God will we serve
and his voice will we obey," and Joshua committed the
covenant to writing.

On this Old Testament idea of a covenant between
God and man, Scotch Presbyterianism was founded.
John Knox, in the early days of the Scotch reformation, brought the idea from Calvin, and Zwingli and Knox
laid the foundations for the covenants in the Presbyterian
standards. The National Covenant was first sworn to
by the King and the national representatives in 1580. It
was renewed in 1638, and the "Solemn League and Covenant" was proclaimed for Scotland by the English Parliament in 1643—the only condition on which the Scotch
would consent to join the English Puritans to fight
Charles I.

By the revolution settlement of 1688, after a hundred
years of struggle, the Cameronian Convenanters triumphed. By that settlement Episcopacy was established
for England and Ireland, but Presbyterianism for Scot-

land. The settlement was a kind of mutual compromise
between the state and church, made for the purpose of
avoiding a destructive collision. The Reformed Presbyterians of to-day are a remnant—a "saving remnant," it
may be—who refused to accept the revolution settlement of 1688. They would not compromise or recognize
any form of state supremacy. They held to their principles and boldly censured the Presbyterian Church of
Scotland, which now became the state church, for want
of faithfulness and zeal, more especially because in the
revolution settlement no direct recognition had been
made of the National Covenants and of the reformation.
The settlement contained "Erastian elements," as their
theologians would put it, in recognizing royal supremacy
over the church, against which true Covenanters had long
struggled, and against which, also, they had just passed
through a period of persecution and martyrdom.[1]

This Covenanter remnant would recognize no settlement that established a connection between church and
state, or that allowed the civil magistrate to usurp over
the church an authority that was inconsistent with her
independence and with the leadership of Christ. Christ
was the head of the church, not James II, nor William
III, nor any other potentate under heaven. Their preachers held their places, and their assemblies and synods
sat in council and authority, not by the favor of a king
or by the confirmation of a bishop, but as the representatives and by the free election of the people. These men
were republicans in church and state. Their Calvinism
had led them to adopt a church policy that provided for
absolute self-government in little parish republics, elect-

---

[1] Erastianism involves the doctrine of state supremacy in ecclesiastical causes,
though this doctrine is by no means due to Erastus (1524-1583), whose writings
really condemned it.

ing their own pastors and ruling elders under universal suffrage, free from any hierarchy, as well as from any civil interference or control.

These ideas in church government led to similar republican ideas as to the control of the state and the basis of its authority.

The zealous Cameronians in 1680 had taken the ground in what is known as the "Sanquhar Declaration," that when a sovereign violates his solemn engagements with his subjects and becomes a tyrant, the people are released from their allegiance, and are no longer bound to support and defend him. They were ready to act upon Hooker's and Locke's philosophy of self-government. The abettors of this doctrine were accused of treason and adjudged worthy of death, but in the revolution of 1688 the entire British nation virtually endorsed the position by the coronation of William and Mary, and the same principle of the right to resist a perverse government was involved in the American revolution, and lies at the foundation of the American republic.

For sixteen years these dissenting Covenanters, who refused to join the Established Church of Scotland at its settlement in 1688, were without a ministry. They organized themselves into praying societies, and in 1706 the Rev. John McMillan came to them from the Established Church, having been deposed for asserting the rigid principles of the Covenanters.

In 1743 the Rev. Mr. Nairn became identified with these Covenanters, and these two ministers, McMillan and Nairn, with a few ruling elders, constituted the Reformed Presbytery. From this little Presbytery, taking its rise and form in 1743, the Reformed Presbyterians in Scotland, Ireland and America received their ministry. In 1752 Rev. Mr. Cuthbertson came to America from the

Reformed Presbytery of Scotland. He was soon joined
by the Rev. Mr. Lind and Rev. Mr. Dobbin, from the Reformed Presbytery of Ireland, and in 1774 these three
ministers formed a presbytery, and the Reformed Presbyterian Church of North America became a distinct
ecclesiastical body. Born from the spirit of resistance to
state control over the church, it has long since ceased to
have cause for separate existence on that score; but it
has since announced another cause for which it justifies
its separate organization in America. Of this I shall
speak later.

THE UNITED PRESBYTERIANS.

In ecclesiastical history the United Presbyterian
Church has its origin in essentially the same principles
and causes that distinguish the Reformed Presbyterians.
The ancestors of this church did not stay out of the
Presbyterian Church of Scotland at the settlement in
1688, but they soon came out, chiefly upon the issue of
opposition to state and civil control. This secession from
the Church of Scotland occurred in 1733, when four ministers of the Scottish Church were expelled from their
charges, and were suspended from all connection with
the church by action of the general assembly. The
four ministers were Ebenezer Erskine, William Wilson,
Alex. Moncrief and James Fisher. The occasion of the
action was the preaching of a sermon by Erskine before
the Synod of Perth and Sterling, in which he protested
against certain abuses. Erskine was condemned by the
synod to suffer censure for his bold arraignment of the
church. He protested and appealed to the assembly.
Erskine, and the three ministers who stood by him were
then cut off "from the office of the holy ministry, each
being prohibited from exercising this office within this

church for all time to come." They were thus deprived of their churches and their emoluments, but they were not deprived of the sympathy and support of their people.

A few words may be in order to set forth the merits of this controversy.

Erskine and the men who stood with him in leading this secession belonged to what may be called the extreme Puritan party in the Church of Scotland. While living within the church they earnestly desired that the church should be independent of the state; they believed that the settlement of 1688 was not Erastian, and that the church under that settlement need not abandon its fundamental principles, but should have the courage to assert its own intrinsic powers. It was through the influence of such men, no doubt, that the "Seasonable Admonition" was published in 1698, to vindicate the conduct of the church from the accusations brought against it by the protesting Covenanters, and to prove that there was no just reason for these people to continue in a state of separation from the established church. This "Admonition" asserted: "We do believe and own that Jesus Christ is the only head and king of his church; and that he hath instituted in his church officers and ordinances, order and government, and not left it to the will of man, magistrate or church to alter at their pleasure." This asserted ecclesiastical leadership for Christ and his church and gave notice that civil magistrates should keep their hands off from its control. But within a quarter of a century those in the church, to whom this principle was most dear, were grieved and offended at the conditions and practices which they found growing up within the church.

They bewailed the laxity of the standards in doctrine, in worship, in government and discipline, and they deemed it their duty to speak out, like true watchmen upon the walls of Jerusalem, against the errors and corruptions that prevailed. These corruptions they held to be certain Arian and Arminian errors that had been taught in one of their theological seminaries where their youth were trained for the holy ministry; that conversion, regeneration and serious godliness had been treated with ridicule; that "certain nurseries of worldliness and wickedness, viz., the diversions of the stage, night assemblies and balls, have prevailed in the principal city of the nation and elsewhere"; and in the face of this spiritual decay the national assembly have not sanctified a fast nor called a solemn assembly; but instead prelatic curates were admitted to the church on the easiest terms, and were allowed to hold their livings, while faithful and zealous Presbyterians, like the Covenanters and Mr. McMillan, were disregarded and deposed; and men were thrust upon the ministry by patronage and intrusion, who were unacceptable and unfit to edify and rule the flock of God.

The grounds of the secession, therefore, may be summarized as follows:

1. Suffrance of error within the church without adequate censure.

The secession fathers seemed to be vigorous heresy-hunters in their time. As Barrie says, "They could swoop down on a heretic like an eagle on carrion."

2. The neglect or relaxation of discipline.

They were Puritans who wished the church courts to arraign and try and discipline, or excommunicate, the erring brothers, and especially those who did not believe soundly.

3. Restraint of ministerial freedom in opposing corruption and mal-administration.

They would cry aloud and spare not, and they were offended with the prevailing party in the church for rebuking and restraining their crying.

4. The crowning wrong of all was the infringement on the right of the Christian people to choose and settle their own ministers—by the practice of patronage and intrusion.

All these grounds of secession, save one, relate to a difference that always exists within every church, i. e., the difference between rigid, or orthodox and strict, religious life upon the one hand, and the disposition to laxity, liberality and worldliness upon the other. If such a difference is a cause of secession it is a cause that is always present, the reforming Puritan party always alleging corruption and spiritual decay, as a justification for its withdrawal. On that cause every seceding church soon confronts another secession within her own pale.

But the chief historic cause on which the secession schism in the Church of Scotland really came to pass in 1733, and on which it is to be justified, was found in the abuse of patronage and intrusion.

The Presbyterian Church had held from its beginning as a fundamental principle, that congregations had a right to choose their own ministers. The practice of patronage and intrusion involved the settlement of pastors over churches by the influence, if not by the order, of some wealthy nobleman to whom the church living was a source of revenue; or by civil magistrates who might thereby strengthen their political power over the church, its officers and members. An abuse like that strikes at the fundamental freedom of the church. The church had always protested against this abuse, and it had been legally renounced, if not denounced, by the authorities of the state in the revolution of 1688. But in

1712 an act was passed by the British Parliament for the restoration of patronage in Scotland. The act was not only contrary to the constitution of the Presbyterian Church and to the revolution settlement of 1688, but it was contrary to the rights guaranteed by the act of union of 1707, by which Scotland and England came under the same parliamentary control. It was agreed at the union that the constitution of the Scottish Church should not be impaired. The kirk session was a branch of that constitution, and the effort to take from the ruling elders, chosen by the people, the final authority in the kirk, was an unconstitutional violence and usurpation that called for resistance.

The design of this attempt to restore lay patronage in Anne's time is apparent. It was to separate the ministers of the kirk from the people. The people could not be supposed to be so attached to, or influenced by, a minister who held his living by the gift of some great man or of some magistrate, as they would by one who was chosen by their own free voices. Patronage would make the ministers more dependant upon the nobility and the gentry, among whom episcopacy predominated, and thus, in time, Presbyterianism would be undermined; and it was believed that this effort to restore patronage represented a concealed purpose of forcing episcopacy upon Presbyterian Scotland.

In 1725 an instance arose of the operation of patronage and intrusion. A vacancy occurred in Aberdeen. The magistrates and town council, who, as heritors, had a right along with the session, to propose a person to the congregation for their approbation and call, thought proper to avail themselves of the patronage act and appoint absolutely, without regard to the wish of the congregation. The synod disapproved and the magistrates appealed to the assembly. The assembly directed that a new call should be moderated and that the wishes of heads of families should be ascertained. When the call took place one hundred and thirty-nine heads of families voted for the person proposed by the town council; three hundred and seven against him. The commission of the assembly, to whom the call was reported, sustained it. This was reported to the general assembly, which disapproved of the commission's proceeding in settling the intended minister over Aberdeen, but refusd to rescind the settlement. The deed was done. The thief that had climbed in by some other way than the door of the sheepfold had been caught with the goods upon him, but nothing could be done about it; and this thief, or hireling, had to be accepted as the shepherd of the flock.

This was the first instance on record since the revolution of a minister's being forced upon a congregation against the consent of its people. But more flagrant abuses followed, cases soon appearing in which ministers were intruded upon congregations who opposed their settlement over them by votes of twelve to one. The ministers were named by *heritors*—i. e., magistrates, councilmen, landlords—who were not even required to reside in the parish. They might be Jacobites, and therefore sworn enemies to the constitution of the realm; they might be infidels, and therefore sworn enemies to the faith; they might outnumber the elders, and therefore the spectacle might be presented of a band of men forcing a presentee upon a parish in the face at once of a remonstrating eldership and a protesting people. Clearly, it was the intention to break up all connection between the people and their ministers, and to bind the church at the feet of the secular power.

It was this tendency and purpose that Erskine and his

little handful of secession colleagues resisted. Their cause is a cause that is now won, against an abuse that now has no defenders. We may have a more vivid idea of the cause for which these men stood if we imagine the proposal being made and executed to-day, that the city council of an Indiana city of the fourth class, like Bloomington, should determine who should be pastors of our city churches. His honor, the mayor, and the common council may appoint the city marshal and his vigilant policemen, but if it were proposed to allow these city magistrates to name and settle the ministers over the city, we can hardly imagine the commotion and the mass meetings that would result. It would then be the duty of all good men to seek to turn church government right side up, by turning city and state upside down.

This may seem like an exaggerated or fantastic analogy, but it represents in a homely way the wrong to the church, that was to be resisted. It was resistance to this wrong that led Erskine and his colleagues to take upon themselves the responsibility of a secession. Whether their cause could have been won within the church without schism may be an open question, but the rightfulness of their cause is not an open question within any realm of Presbyterianism that I know of to-day—certainly not within American Presbyterianism. Essentially the same battle was fought by the Free Church of Scotland, which caused another division in 1843, and now the United Presbyterian Church of Scotland and the Free Church of Scotland have joined together into the United Free Church, both together standing on the platform of the secession of 1733. Together they make up probably 75 per cent. of Scottish Presbyterians, and the Old Church of Scotland, from which these once severed but now mutually united branches sprang, is ready to concede the principle which gave them life.

III.

The men who led the secession of 1733 in Scotland formed themselves into a presbytery. In this seceding body the United Presbyterian Church finds its origin. These seceders organized at Garney's Bridge and called themselves the "Associate Presbytery." It issued a "Testimony," after the manner of the times, and by 1747 the presbytery embraced forty-five congregations.

In this year (1747) the Burgher and the Anti-Burgher difference arose. The burgesses of Edinburgh, Glasgow and Perth were required to take an oath agreeing to maintain "the true religion presently professed within this realm." Some said this alluded to the established church, which they had forsworn, and that it was therefore unlawful to take the oath. Others said that it referred only to the recognized Protestant religion and was meant merely to protect the burgesses (city council) from what they called "Paptists," and that the oath might be taken by true "Seceders." Consequently there was a division in the secession church into "Burghers" and "Anti-Burghers," those who were willing to take the oath and qualify as burghers and those who refused. The Associate Synod were the Burghers. The General Associate Synod were the Anti-Burghers. The Anti-Burghers separated from their brethren and passed sentence of excommunication and suspension against their fellow-ministers and fellow-Christians merely because the latter refused to exclude from the communion those who had taken this burgess's oath. The Burghers were ready to proscribe the Roman Catholics and prevent their holding civil office, and they were therefore only a little less proscriptive and intolerant than the more schmismatic Anti-Burghers. It was merely a matter of degree.

These two denominations of Associate Presbyterians,

the Burghers and the Anti-Burghers, grew together side by side for seventy years. Their ministers and members had no ecclesiastical fellowship with one another. In fact, the controversy between them became so bitter and their spirit of contention was so pronounced that the ministers and members of these little kindred but contentious sects seemed more tolerant toward Christian bodies more widely separated from them in origin and creed than they were toward one another. Rev. Peter McMillan, a flaming, argumentative Anti-Burgher in South Carolina, full of the prejudice and violence of his party in the latter part of the eighteenth century, asserted that he would rather commune with the devil in hell than with a Rev. Mr. Clark, a pious and devoted pioneer preacher among the Associate Presbyterians in America at that time. But it turned out that Mr. McMillan met and heard Mr. Clark, and at his first "occasional hearing" he was converted and joined the Associate Presbyterian Church.[1]

As illustrating further the hair-splitting contentions and divisive spirit of these Scotch people, it may be mentioned that near the opening of the nineteenth century each of these bodies, Burghers and Anti-Burghers, was divided again over the matter of the civil magistrates'

---

[1] These Irish Presbyterian ministers, while orthodox to the marrow, were not always up to modern standards in their morality. This Rev. Peter McMillan, who became a pastor at Due West, South Carolina, was censured for dishonesty in money matters, for drunkenness and profanity. Rev. Mr. Dickson was a kindred spirit in his love for the bottle. McMillan was continued in the ministry. His lapses from morality did not trouble him nor his presbytery very much, but he soon became so conscientious that he had to resign from the presbytery in protest "against the apostacies of the synod from the faith and practices of the Scotch church in the days of its purity." The purity of the church, like the good old days, was always in the distant past; the present was always corrupt in its beliefs and forms of worship. Personal practice was another matter. Mr. Martin, the only Reformed Presbyterian minister left in America after the union of 1782, was suspended for drunkenness, or "silenced for intemperate habits," as the record expresses it, as was also Rev. James McGarragh, lately arrived from Ireland (1795). —*Glasgow's Reformed Presbyterian Church, p. 77.*

province in religion, a small minority of each branch going off, each claiming to be the "original." This was the result of the "Old Light" controversy. And these divisions and contentions continued to exist long years after the causes that gave rise to them, and in America, too, where the conditions were such that the causes of division never could have existed. All this seems like a dreary record of controversy, representing hardly more than opinionated obstinacy; for there probably never was a more fruitless controversy than that about the burgess oath among any society of professed Christians upon the earth. No wonder that Thomas Campbell and his greater son, Alexander Campbell, who were brought up in these Scotch seceder churches, were discouraged and disgusted with church divisions. With the younger men of Christian meekness and spiritual vision there was sure to be a reaction and a swing of the pendulum toward union and away from divisive contention. But whether these founders of another sect pursued the wisest course for the promotion of church union is an open question.[1]

We have noticed the early beginnings of two of these Scotch Presbyterian bodies—the Reformed Presbyterians, called the Covenanters, and the Associate Presbyterians, sometimes called the Church of the Secession or the "Seceders." The majority of the Irish Presbyterians of these churches who settled in Rocky Creek and Fishing Creek in Chester District, South Carolina, were from County Derry, County Down and County Antrim, Ireland. Some had been members of a covenanter church in Ballymoney, Ireland, and some of a church near Colerain, in County Derry. One of the

---

[1] By 1820 the Burgher and Anti-Burgher breach was healed by the formation of a united Secession Church, with 262 churches, 139 being Burgher, 123 Anti-Burgher.

early preachers from Ireland, Rev. Matthew Lynn, came
to South Carolina for the purpose of uniting these two
divided branches of Scottish Presbyterians, the Associate
Presbyterians and the Reformed Presbyterians, and in
1782 a union was brought about between these two
bodies and the united body became known as the Associate Reformed Presbyterians. But by this union the
"Seceders" (Associates) and Covenanters (Reformed
Presbyterians) did not disappear, because, as is usually
the case in such attempts at union, a minority in each
church refused to go into the union. So instead of two
churches becoming one, two churches became three, and
we now had the "Associate Presbyterians," the "Reformed Presbyterians" and the "Associate Reformed
Presbyterians." Of course, the latter body was much the
larger, and the minorities that stayed out of the union
were quite weak. A respectable number of the Sepa-
ratist Covenanters organized churches or scattered societies of their own in different parts of York and Chester counties in South Carolina and in other scattered settlements, and in 1798 they reorganized their presbytery.

IV.

We come now to consider the character of these Irish
Presbyterian societies in this community.

The Reformed Presbyterians were the first to organize. The Bloomington congregation was organized
by the Western Presbytery, October 10, 1821. Rev.
James Faris was pastor from November 22, 1827, until
May 20, 1855. Mr. Faris came from South Carolina, as
did the greater part of these Covenanters. He tried, but
failed, to get the legislature of South Carolina to pass a
law allowing benevolent slaveholders to free their slaves.
He had been a teacher in the academy at Pendleton,

South Carolina, of which John C. Calhoun and other congressmen were patrons.

The first Covenanter settlement in Bloomington was made in March, 1820, and was led by John Thomas Moore. The society increased by immigration from the South. At the organization in 1821 there were eight members, John Moore and Isaac Faris being made elders. The society was disorganized in 1823 by the death of John Moore, but in 1825 it was again organized, and Thomas Moore and James Blair were made ruling elders. There were now twenty members. In 1830 David Smith and Dorrance B. Woodburn were added to the session.

Mr. Faris preached in the early days in a small log church, or schoolhouse, in the yard of the old McQuiston homestead on West Tenth street, property now owned by the Indianapolis Southern Railway.

In the fall and winter of 1830 and 1831 a considerable colony of Scotch-Irish Presbyterians came to Monroe county from the Rocky Creek neighborhood, Chester District, South Carolina, the Tates, Woodburns and Fees being among the number. One Covenanter congregation left South Carolina in a body, following their pastor, Rev. Hugh McMillan, to Greene county, Ohio, near Xenia. Others left South Carolina at about the same time, some going to Princeton, Indiana; some to Sparta and Paxton, Illinois; while a goodly colony came to Bloomington.

In 1833 the Reformed Presbyterian Church in North America was divided into what is known as the New Side and Old Side branches. The split occurred on the question of civil duties. The New Side portion of the church believed that voting, sitting on juries, holding office and supporting the government were not inconsistent with the word of God or their Christian obligations; that while the constitution of the United States was not all that was to be desired, it was not infidel nor atheistic, and that the government of the land was worthy of honor and support. It appears that the general synod of the church was changing the former standards in proposing to allow the members of the church to recognize the government in this light and to take part in civil affairs. Mr. Faris, and, presumably, the majority of the session and congregation in Bloomington, would not stand for this action of the synod. Then those of the congregation here who were in sympathy with the new doctrine and who wished to stand by the synod, organized the New Side branch of the church.[1] I copy from the manuscript of the clerk at this meeting for New Side organization in 1834:

"At a late meeting of the Reformed Congregation of Presbyterians, near Bloomington, it appeared that the Rev. Mr. Faris and others did consider themselves not bound to the General Synod for having (as they considered) departed from her former principles on the head of civil government, whereupon a meeting of those in favor of the transactions of the General Synod was held at the meeting-house on Thursday, the twenty-first of August, 1834, to consider what was their duty and how they ought to act in this day of perplexity and doubt. Heads of families present, viz., James Blair, D. B. Woodburn, James Hemphill, Thomas Fullerton, James Bratney and Peter Keeny.

"James Hemphill was chosen chairman and D. B. Woodburn clerk, and the following resolutions adopted, viz.:

---

[1] Rev. Mr. Faris, who remained with the Old Side Convenanter Church, died in 1855 and was succeeded as pastor by Rev. David Shaw, who continued in this field for thirty-six years. I am indebted for the facts connected with this organization to Rev. Renwick Steele, of the Reformed Presbyterian Church, of Bloomington.

"1.   That we adhere to the doctrines of the Reformed Synod of North America, as laid down in the Westminster Confession of Faith and practice, and to the testimony of said church, as being agreeable to and founded on the word of God.

"2.   That we consider the actings of the Bloomington session in suspending from the privileges of the church, and citing to appear before their court, elders and others on account of voting and sitting as jurors, inconsistent with the above standards, also a usurpation of power not delegated to them by synod, being no infringement on any known judicial act of our church on record.

"3.   That we consider ourselves in all due subordination bound in the Lord to the Reformed Synod, which last met in Dr. Wylie's church, Philedalphia, and was moderated by the Rev. Hugh McMillan.

"4.   That we consider ourselves a vacant society in the bounds of the Western Presbytery, under the direction of the General Synod.

"5.   That a copy of the above resolutions be sent to the Rev. H. McMillan with a general request————that he will pay them a visit if practicable.————[Manuscript destroyed here.]

"Adjourned to meet at this place the twentieth of September at 12 o'clock.

"James K. Hemphill, Chairman.
"D. B. Woodburn, Clerk."[1]

Mr. James Blair was appointed delegate "to represent their case in presbytery and seek supplies"; and James K. Hemphill, "to correspond with Rev. H. McMillan, to see whether a stated supply could be obtained of a part of his time." They hoped that Mr. McMillan

---

[1] These two men were the grandfathers of the writer. This record was copied in 1883, since which time the record book has been lost.

would come here from Xenia, Ohio, once a month or oftener, to minister to them—which illustrates how few and widely scattered were the seeds of this small household of faith.

At this organization in 1834 there were four elders— James Blair, James K. Hemphill, Dorrance B. Woodburn and James Bratney. The small flock was sheperdless for four years. Still they maintained their organization, meeting from house to house as a religious "Society." The record always refers to the congregation as the "Society." In 1838 they numbered forty members, and in that year they obtained the pastoral services of Rev. T. A. Wylie, who had come to Bloomington in 1837 as one of the professors in the university.[1] Professor Wylie belonged to this branch of the Covenanter Church and he preached for this small congregation in Bloomington until 1869, excepting the years 1852 to 1854, when he was a teacher in Miami University. Rev. Mr. Wylie's first sermon was delivered in the house of Mr. James Blair, a log farmhouse then fully a half mile from the edge of town on the Ellettsville road. Usually, when there was no preaching, the "Society," as the prayer-meeting was called, was held at the homes of the mem-

---

[1] Professor Theophilus Adam Wylie was born in Philadelphia, October 8, 1810; graduated from the University of Pennsylvania in 1830. In 1837 he came to Indiana University as professor of natural philosophy and chemistry, occupying ten days in travel from Philadelphia to Bloomington. With the exception of two years, 1852-1854, during which he held a professorship in Miami University, Oxford, Ohio, he served Indiana University continuously for forty-nine years. He was a versatile scholar and a virile teacher, capable of teaching any of the courses offered in the college curriculum in the early days, and he was occasionally called upon to exercise his varied attainments. He was a personal friend of his fellow-churchman, the distinguished philanthropist, Hon. George H. Stuart, of Philadelphia. In addition to his University teaching, Dr. Wylie preached regularly to this little congregation of Reformed Presbyterians. He died June 11, 1895, and is buried in Rose Hill Cemetery, Bloomington. The widow of Dr. Wylie, who came to Bloomington as a bride in 1837, still survives, at the advanced age of ninety-seven.

bers, frequently at Mr. James K. Hemphill's, who then lived opposite the court-house on College avenue. For public preaching the Reformed Presbyterian Church building was used, the one on the McQuiston property, a log building twenty by fifteen feet.

Professor Wylie's services to the church were largely in the nature of a generous offering, without hope of material reward. His salary, if he may be said to have had a salary, came in the form of donations, through "donation parties," gotten up occasionally by members of the congregation as a pastor's benefit. Perhaps during the later years of his pastorate as much as $200 a year was paid him in cash donations.

The number of communicants in this little congregation on September 26, 1858, twenty years after its organization, was only fifty-eight, while there were only one hundred all told in the congregation, and this, presumably, counted the children and adherents of the church families. The congregation, following the advice of Professor Wylie, consented to its dissolution in 1869, most of its members joining the United Presbyterian Church, though several of them joined the First Presbyterian Church, whose house of worship was then on the east side of the court-house square on Walnut street.

There had been a rupture in the little body, a church quarrel of some kind. They had been invited to join with the United Presbyterians a few years before, but had refused to do so. "The church often prayed," as Professor Wylie said, "that God would heal the divisions of Zion"; but "when the opportunity was offered to heal one small division, and when no one could tell what the differences were, they refused to unite." A quarrel among themselves put an end to their schism and forced their members into a larger union—and again God had made the wrath of man to praise him.

From its organization to its dissolution this New Side Reformed Presbyterian Church contained only one hundred and thirty-eight members. Its later house of worship was at the present site of the United Presbyterian Church. Its frame building later came into possession of the colored Methodist Episcopal Church and is still standing, with an added wing, on North Grant street.

Here are some of the families making up this branch of Reformed Presbyterians: The Alexanders, Blairs, Bratneys, Craigs, Dinsmores, Farises, Fullertons, Glenns, Hemphills, Keenys, McKinleys, McQuistons, Moores, Russells, Smalls, Stormonts, Semples, Tates, Woodburns and Wylies.

THE ASSOCIATE PRESBYTERIANS OR SECEDERS.

The Associate congregation ("Seceders"), another branch that helped to make up the United Presbyterian Church of Bloomington, was organized in the fall of 1834, by the Rev. James Templeton. Two years later, on November 16, 1836, it was organized by Rev. James M. Henderson, with twenty-four members. Four of these were elders—Samuel Wylie, Andrew Roddy, Robert Gourley and John McKissock. Other names appearing in the organizing list are the Browns, Cassles, Harrows, Martins, Neills and Roddys. These people first worshiped in a small log church four miles southeast of Bloomington, but about 1839 they built a neat frame church on East Second street, near the south end of Dunn street, a building which has since been remodeled as a dwelling house.

For three years this congregation was without a pastor, receiving supplies from the presbytery. In 1839 Rev. I. N. Lawhead became their pastor and continued to labor among them in that capacity until 1843. From

1843 to 1855 they were again without a pastor, being ministered to by only occasional supplies. In January, 1855, Rev. John Bryan, the father of President William Lowe Bryan, of Indiana University, and of President Enoch Albert Bryan, of Washington State College, came to the congregation as stated supply. Mr. Bryan received a call to the pastorate and was installed in September of the same year.

The grandfather of Rev. John Bryan came to the United States from Ireland about 1750. In 1777 he was living on the Brandywine creek near the site of the battle of Brandywine. There is a family tradition that General Washington ate dinner in his house on the day before that battle, and that British soldiers carried away the family dinner the next day. The father of Rev. John Bryan, whose name also was John, settled in Beaver county, western Pennsylvania, after the Revolution. There the subject of our notice was born in 1811. He was educated in Jefferson College, Cannonsburg, Pennsylvania, and in the Theological Seminary at Cannonsburg. His first pastorate was in Jefferson, Ohio. He was pastor of the Associate Church in Bloomington from 1855 until 1861, when he resigned with a view to promoting a union of his congregation with the Associate Reformed congregation. The whole number of members received into the Associate or Seceder congregation, from its organization to its union with the larger body in 1864, was about 163, eight of whom were elders. The church building in which Mr. Bryan preached, having been turned into a residence, was bought by E. A. Bryan about 1879, and was used by the Bryans as a family residence for a number of years. There the mother and father died, Mrs. Bryan in 1880, Mr. Bryan in 1887.

Some of the families of this branch of the church are the Bains, Boyds, Browns, Bryans, Calhouns, Crabbs, Fullertons (quite numerous), Gourleys, Hammills, Harrows (Harrahs?), Henrys, Hunters, Kelseys (numerous), Lathans, Marshalls, Martins, Morrisons, McKissocks, Neills, Phillipses, Roddys, Robinsons, Services (numerous), Storys and Wylies.

V.

THE ASSOCIATE REFORMED PRESBYTERIANS.

The principal arm of the present United Presbyterian Church was the Union congregation of the Associate Reformed Church. The congregation was named "Union" after the Union congregation in Chester District, South Carolina, in which many of its members had been baptized, and from which they had come to Monroe county. Many of them had been under the pastoral care of the Rev. John Hemphill, a notable minister of long service among these people in Carolina.

In the Session Record Book of the Associate Reformed Church of Bloomington, the first entry is for September 7, 1833, and is as follows:

"The congregation was organized by the Rev. John Reynolds. The session was organized by Mr. Reynolds as moderator, aided by Mr. Henry from Decatur county, Indiana.

"Mr. William Fee, being elected, was ordained as elder and took his seat as a member of the court.

"The following persons were received as members of the church at this time on certificate:

"William Fee and his wife, Elizabeth; David Cherry and Sarah his wife; Martha Cherry and her daughter, Molly Cherry; James Millen and Hannah, his wife; Widow Harrow.

"The following were received on personal examination: William Curry, George Johnston, Rachel and Margaret Fee, Ebenezer V. Elliot."

This made fourteen in all, to constitute the first organization. Mr. Fee was the first and for a while the only elder of the congregation, and has been called the "Father of the United Presbyterian Church" in this community. He was born in County Antrim, Ireland, in 1786, but when he was four years old his father, Robert Fee, migrated with his family to Chester county, South Carolina. Here in 1810 William Fee married Elizabeth Ferguson Orr, a native of Chester county, of the Scotch-Irish stock. In 1830 William Fee sold his land in Chester county and with his father and brother-in-law, William Tate, left for the Northwest. When they left South Carolina they had not decided whether they would seek new homes in the Illinois country, or in the Indiana, and when the party came to the parting of the ways they left the matter for decision to one of the horses, which turned into the road leading to Indiana. They arrived in Bloomington on December 31, 1830—in the dead of winter—and for their first night they were taken into the home of Mr. Dorrance B. Woodburn, who had come from South Carolina but a few months before. The whole company that night, counting Mr. Woodburn's family of twelve, numbered forty adults and children. Presumably they must have slept twelve or fourteen in a room, and mostly on the floor. People lived the simple life in those days, and their hospitality was simplicity itself. Guests did not have their dinners in courses nor their bedrooms in suites; they lived in log cabins, and they climbed by a common ladder to the lofts, sleeping in small bedrooms whose furniture consisted chiefly of beds.

On May 10, 1834, Andrew Bonar (or Bonner) was

added to the session. At the same time the following were received into the church on certificate: William Millen and Elizabeth, his wife; John Wier and his wife; William Bonner[1] and his daughter, Margaret; John C. Harbison and wife, Samuel Wier and wife, William M. Millen and wife, Archibald Wilson and wife, S. C. Millen, Margaret Millen and John Millen. John Fee and Eli Millen were received on examination.

On the fourth Saturday of May, 1835, the following were received on certificate: James Richey, Mathew Harbison and his wife, Jane Harbison; James Douglas and wife; Jennet Hemphill and Robert and Andrew, her sons; Mary Moffett, Jane McCaw, John McCaw and wife, Samuel Strong and wife, Samuel Harbison and wife, Barbara Millen, Robert Harbison and wife, Jennet Strong, Thomas Bonner and wife and Sarah McCaw.

On examination, Mrs. Westbrook; Polly, Sarah and Nancy Cherry; Elizabeth Curry, William Millen, Jr., and Robert Strong were admitted. This made thirty accessions at this spring communion (1835), showing that another colony had arrived in the fall of 1834 from South Carolina.

In the fall of 1835 the session was "constituted" (called to order and presided over) by the Rev. Hugh Parks, and on December 1, 1835, the Rev. William Turner was settled as pastor over Union congregation, being ordained and installed in said congregation on June 16, 1836. The migration from South Carolina was still going on as is indicated by the fact that in the spring of 1836 Mr. Turner and the session received into the communion of the church the following members:

On examination: Jane Strong, John Glenn, Samuel

---

[1] These three men were received as ruling elders, having been ordained elsewhere.

Millen, Jonathan Archer (by baptism) and Elizabeth Fee.

On certificate: Robert Harbison and wife, Jane; Rosanna Harbison, Esther Harbison, Samuel Harbison, Jr., Maxwell Wilson and Martha, his wife; James Glenn and Agnes, his wife; Elizabeth, Margaret and Mary Ann Glenn; James Miller and Letitia, his wife; Jennet Brown, widow; John, Margaret and Thomas Brown; Julia Ann Turner, Alexander Henry and Jenny, his wife; Daniel T. Shaw, David Meek and Nancy, his wife.

There were, thus, thirty-one accessions at this time; the moving from the South was pretty steady.

On the same date (June, 1836) it is recorded that David ——— appeared before session and "confessed himself to have been guilty of the sin of intoxication, pledged himself to abstain from the use of ardent spirits; was rebuked before the session, and it was ordered that the proceeding be published to the congregation."

The following are the principal families in this branch of the Scotch-Irish Presbyterians—the Associate Reformed body: Archers, Allens, Alexanders, Baxters, Bonners, Browns, Calhouns, Campbells, Cathcarts, Cherrys, Cirgins, Collins, Crabbs, Craigs, Creas, Currys, Dicksons, Douglass's, Farringtons, Fees, Fullertons, Galloways, Gettys, Gibsons, Gillespys, Gordans, Glenns, Grahams, Harbisons, Hemphills, Henrys, Hendersons, Hunters, Jamisons, Johnstons, Junkins, Kerrs, Meeks, Millens, Millers, Moffatts, McCaws, McKissocks, McMichaels, Orrs, Reeds, Rocks, Semples, Smiths, Strongs, Swearingens, Turners, Weirs, Westbrooks and Wilsons.[1]

---

[1] The United States Government has recently published a reprint of the census of 1790, which gives the names of heads of families in the original thirteen States at that time. From the volume devoted to South Carolina, I have taken a few names that are familiar in this neighborhood, to illustrate the source of the migration of these families. The following taken chiefly from Chester District,

THE UNITED PRESBYTERIANS.

These two churches, the Associate Reformed and the Associate, united in the country at large in 1858, forming the United Presbyterian Church, and in 1908 that church celebrated its semi-centennial. But the two congregations here did not unite until 1864. However, in the fall of 1858 they agreed to a joint communion. The differences between them had at last been reconciled—differences that had all been reduced to only one of any significance, namely that one branch, as some one said, sang the Psalms of David, while the other sang David's Psalms. The fact is, all differences that ever existed had disappeared nearly a hundred years before, and there never had been any difference between these churches during their existence in America. So persistent is Scotch persistence!

The record for August 18, 1858, relates that the first Sabbath (of September) be the day for a joint communion; that "the preceding Thursday be observed as a day of preparation; and that we have preaching on Saturday and Monday." It was moved and seconded that the "session of both churches stand together while the tokens are being distributed, that Mr. Bryan distribute first to his congregation, then Mr. Turner to his." The joint meeting was to be held in the Associate Reformed church. It was moved that a collection be taken up to defray the expenses of the communion, and that the surplus be sent to the church at Philadelphia; and that the two congregations meet together for worship in the afternoon of Communion Sabbath.

South Carolina, were the ancestral "heads of families" now represented in this and other Indiana communities: Alexander, Blair, Boyd, Campbell, Cherry, Collins, Cowen, Curry, Douglass, Farris, Gordon, Grimes. Harbison, Hemphill, Hudleson, Johnston, Kilpatrick, Kirkpatrick, Lathan, Logan, MacCalla, McDill, McQuiston, Miller, More, Nesbit, Reed, Robbison, Robertson, Service, Turner, Weer, Wilson, Woodburn.

It appears that from 1858 to 1864 these two bodies went under the name of First and Second United Presbyterian Churches. But on May 7, 1864, it is recorded that "the First and Second United Presbyterian congregations of Bloomington, Indiana, having previous to this date held a meeting to consult on the propriety of uniting in one congregation, and asking presbytery to confirm the same, and as presbytery did at its late meeting held at Princeton, Indiana, on the twenty-seventh of April, 1864, unite the above named congregations in one, the sessions of those above named congregations met on the above date, May 7, 1864, and was constituted by prayer by the pastor, Rev. William Turner." M. Wilson, James L. Roddy and Chrissy Jane Hunter (Mrs. Ben. Smith) were received at this time on examination. From this time on the two bodies were one.

CHARACTERISTICS OF SCOTCH-IRISH CHURCHES.

Enough has been said of the early organization and membership of these congregations. I shall speak now of some of their characteristics, ideas and practices.

In the first place, they were strong in their attendance upon the sanctuary. One of them, as Barrie says, was "equal to a dozen ordinary church-goers." With them being at church on the Lord's day was one of the first duties of the Christian. And he must be in his own church and not be listening to the loose and uncertain teaching of another denomination. The Seceders especially were intolerant of this sin of "occasional hearing," i. e., attending upon the services of some other church. A member was liable to be haled before the session for that offense.[1] If a member were absent from church,

---

[1] A Seceder minister, who was belated one Saturday night in finding the home of Mr. Robert Gourley, a Seceder elder, was entertained over night at the home of Mr. James Blair, who was a Covenanter. The minister and Mr. Blair engaged

which would be invariably noticed, it would be supposed
that he was sick, and if he were absent again without
some such obvious excuse, the session would be likely to
inquire into the cause. They did not have evening services, being widely separated and distant from the house
of worship, as a rule; but they had two services on the
Sabbath day, with a brief intermission between. This
kept them at church from ten o'clock in the morning until
nearly four in the afternoon, with a half hour for rest
and luncheon and a little neighborhood gossip in the
churchyard, between the services.

One of the customs among these people, practiced
much more seriously in those days than in these, was the
practice of pastoral visiting and catechising. There were
stated times for these family visits, and the coming of
the minister was something of a solemn event in the
family. It was prepared for, the house was swept and
garnished, the children were called in from their work
or play and were washed and dressed; the old and the
young sat in solemn order to receive the minister and
to undergo the ordeal of his inspection and catechising.
All were expected to show that they had read the Bible,
and that they were well up on the questions of the Westminster Shorter Catechism. The minister was looked
upon with great respect, if not with awe. He was, likely,
the only educated man in their society, and he was the
authorized and ordained expounder of the Word, though
if he had not a "thus saith the Lord" for his message,

---

in a controversy on the sin of "occasional hearing," and Mr. Blair was led to say
that since the minister so insisted upon his doctrine, he, Mr. Blair, and his family
would not be able to go to hear him preach on the Sabbath, as they had hoped to
do, if it were a sin for a man to hear any preacher not of his own denomination.
The preacher probably thought that Seceder preaching would do a Covenanter
no harm, but was well convinced that Convenanter preaching should be avoided
by all Seceders.

he would be certain to hear from his laymen who were dangerously well read in the Bible, if in nothing else. The minister was expected to take full pastoral charge of the congregation. He was bound not to neglect, from fear of giving offense, this duty of visiting and catechising. The pastor and the ruling elders were under obligations to watch over and promote the spiritual improvement of the flock. Catechising was a necessary part of this duty. The pastor was careful to inspect the state of his flock, acquaint himself with the disposition and conduct of every member seeking rightly to "divide the word of truth." He was to visit from house to house, not merely as a friend, but as one who watches for their souls, and to see how they were attending to the duties of personal and family religion. At the time of this family visit the pastor would hold a family service, exhorting and praying with and for the members of the home, and it was expected, even required, that in every household family worship should be maintained—the form of family service almost uniformly consisting of the singing of a psalm, scripture reading and prayer. In this exercise of family worship the Scotch Presbyterians were generally stricter than most religious bodies. There is a maxim, "Like priest, like people." No doubt a visiting pastor makes a church-going people, and in that religious society among whom there is a family altar in every home, the services of the public sanctuary will be the more honored and promoted.

These Scotch-Irish Presbyterians stood for strict and close communion, and they usually built the bars around their communion table strong and high. The doors of the church were always open, and whosover would might come; but if an erring sinner or an Arminian heretic came, he had to go through a pretty rigid examination for admission, and it may almost be said that it was easier to be put out of one of these Presbyterian churches than it was to get in. An unsympathetic outsider may somewhat reasonably have said: "If you join that church you must swallow election and predestination and particular redemption; you must believe in the damnation of infants; you must sing the old psalms, and nothing else; you must not commune anywhere but in your own church; you must, before you can join, commit to memory the whole of the Confession of Faith, a book as big as the Bible; you must keep up family worship and make your children go to church, and you yourself must see to it that you are not of the class for whom the old Scotch-Irish minister prayed—the ungodly sick, 'who are aye seek on Sabbath but aye weel on Monday.' You must go to church or the session would know the reason why."

It was not quite so bad as all this, but as a rule the bars were not let down very much.

In South Carolina a story is told of some Irish Seceders lately come to America, who presented themselves to a Reformed Presbyterian Church for membership. One strict old elder in the session suggested that to admit them on certificate from the Seceder Church without the proper examination would be to "let down the bars." One old lady among the applicants, irritated at the suggestion, because she thought the bars of the Seceders were as high and strong and as respectable as any need be, jumped to her feet and exclaimed, "We dinna ask ye to let doon the bars; come oot!" And with that she started out of the session house followed by the others, and they went over and joined the nearby Associate Reformed church—a union of the Seceders and the Reformed Presbyterians.

VI.

CHURCH DISCIPLINE AMONG THE SCOTCH-IRISH PRESBY-TERIANS—SABBATH-KEEPING—TOKENS.

It was necessary, of course, to be admitted to the church before one could go to the communion table. Christians of all other denominations were barred. The communion was generally observed only twice a year. To these people in those days all Sabbaths were solemn, but the communion Sabbath was more solemn. It was a day of special sanctity. It was to be approached only after proper preparation and searching of hearts. The preceding Sabbath was the preparation Sabbath, and the Friday and Saturday before communion day were preparation days, to be observed with religious solemnity, and this made three Sabbaths hand running within a week, and oftentimes the Thursday before these preparation days was made a fast day, and the Monday following the communion Sabbath was given over to preaching and the closing services; so that communion season in fall and spring occupied almost a week in religious services. I remember those fast days and preparation days, but about the only solace that children had out of them was the pleasure that came from being kept out of school. The great bulk of their service consisted of preaching. They were long on preaching, and their sermons were largely doctrinal and argumentative, and often from an hour to two hours long. And it may be said that their preachers were more inclined to resort to the Old Testament rather than the New for their texts. It was a church that was largely influenced by Judaism— almost as much as by Christianity. The law of the Jew was to them almost as strong as the law of Christ.

On the Saturday before the communion the tokens

were distributed. The minister came down from the high pulpit, or two elders stood by the pulpit, and, as the members passed by, each was given a "token," a small rectangular piece of lead bearing the initials of the congregation. If one could not go to the Saturday preparatory service to get his token, some friend, or relative, must ask for it for him. The token was given to distinguish those who were entitled to come to the communion. It was something like a ticket of admission, and was kept by the recipient with great care, the good grandmothers generally tying theirs in the corners of their handkerchiefs. I remember my own grandmother once on the morning of communion Sabbath, hunting and rummaging with great anxiety for her lost communion token, and the fact that it was found in her Sunday cloves-box showed that it had been guarded with due concern. To lose the token would have caused pain and sorrow, as, if it were lost, with it, it was supposed, would be lost also the right to go to the communion table. Perhaps the session would have had to pass upon the application for another token.

A few words may be in place about the historical origin of these tokens. They were used among the Covenanters of Scotland as early as 1635. A rubric, or rule, of the church of Scotland of that year says: "So many as intend to be partakers of the Holy Communion shall receive these tokens from the minister the night before." They were used in Glasgow as early as 1638. Spaulding, a writer on the church life of Scotland, says: "Within the said church the assembly thereafter sits down; the church doors are strictly guarded by the toun; none had entrance but he who had ane token of lead, declaring he was ane Covenanter." The custom descended from these early times in Scotland, from a period of religious rivalry

and persecution, when the people came great distances to
the communion and were largely strangers to one another, and when it was deemed necessary to guard their
church services from the presence of spies ready to report
them to the government, or from other hostile intruders.

Whatever the original cause may have been, the use
of the token lingered for generations, even for centuries
after the first occasion for them had passed away—and
they came then to be used for another purpose: for dis-
tinguishing the elect, or, as one may say, of separating
the sheep from the goats.[1]

On communion morning an assisting minister was always present. There was an explanation of the psalm—
a discourse long enough for a sermon—designed to enable the people to understand what they were going to
sing. The psalm was sung, of course, without instrumental music, without even so much as a tuning-fork,

---

[1] A pamphlet on "Communion Tokens" was published in 1888 by Mr. Thomas
Warner, of Cohocton, N. Y., who became interested in this branch of numismatics.
Mr. Warner was able to collect, and in this pamphlet he describes with illustrations, more than two hundred sacramental tokens, with date of use. Four kinds
of tokens used in Bloomington, Monroe county, Indiana, are described. One a
plain oblong piece of lead with the letters A. R. P. C. (Associate Reformed Presbyterian Church); another a plain square piece of copper, with the letters To for
token; another a plain square piece of brass, with the letter B. for Bloomington;
another, an oblong piece of lead with the letters B. C. (Bloomington Congregation) on one side and R. P. (Reformed Presbyterian) on the other. So far as I
have been able to learn, all the churches that the Scotch-Irish Presbyterians planted in America used these tokens.

As the tokens were constantly being lost, one by one, it came to pass in the
course of time in the United Presbyterian church in this community that there
were not enough tokens to go around among the communicants. The result was
that the elders having collected the tokens from those who had come to the communion table redistributed these to others who were yet to come. Such a situation revealed how useless, not to say absurd, the practice was. However, some
irresponsible person found a use for the tokens of one of the other churches of
Bloomington. The tokens of this congregation disappeared about the time the
slot machines came into use, having been stolen by some one who had discovered that they would do the work of the nickel in the slot. Most of these tokens
were found a short time after in one of these machines, but after such desecration
they were not again used for sacramental purposes. It was with the advent of
such modern contrivances and practices that the ancient tokens went out of use.

the song being started by some one appointed to "raise
the tune." Then came a long sermon, seldom under an
hour. Then after an interval of ten or twenty minutes,
or at times without an interval, the members entitled to
commune were invited to come to the table. A table
reached in front of the church from one side to the other,
spread with white linen, with the communion elements
on a side table at the head. There were benches for seats
at the table. There were two aisles in the church, and
the people came up one aisle to fill the table and went
down the other as they left it. When the table was full,
the pastor, standing at the head of the table, with an
elder seated on either side, gave an address, "debarring,"
or "fencing" the table as it was called—a kind of warning against unworthy communing. Then, about to partake of the sacred emblems, they would sing in solemn
praise another psalm, perhaps two verses from the One
Hundred and Thirty-ninth Psalm:

> "Lord, thou hast searched me and hast known
> My rising up and lying down,
> And from afar thy searching eye
> Beholds my thoughts that secret lie.
>
> "Search me, O God, my heart discern,
> Try me, my very heart to learn;
> See if in evil paths I stray,
> And guide me in th' eternal way."

The scripture passage authorizing this commemorative
service was read, the commandments were recited, sin
and wrong-doing were brought to mind, a prayer was
offered, and the pastor broke a long piece of unleavened
bread, giving half to each of two elders sitting at the pastor's right and left, and these elders broke off a small bit

and passed the rest down the table. The wine was served in turn, other elders passing behind the communicants, supplying more bread and wine as needed. The wine was not started till all at table had partaken of the bread, and while the people were in solemn contemplation the pastor, or the assisting minister, made some remarks to direct the thoughts of the people in proper channels to suitable themes.

A service at table lasted fifteen or twenty minutes, and then the communicants were invited to arise and give place to others. As these went and others came they sang again, perhaps verses of the One Hundred and Sixteenth Psalm:

> "What fit return, Lord, can I make
>   For all thy gifts on me bestowed?
> The cup of blessing I will take
>   And call upon the name of God.

> "Before God's people I'll appear,
>   And pay my vows there with delight;
> The death of saints to God is dear,
>   Most precious in Jehovah's sight.

> "With sacrifice of thanks I'll go,
>   And on Jehovah's name will call;
> Will pay to God the vows I owe
>   In presence of his people all."

As the long metre version of a psalm was not carried at a galloping gait in those days, about two stanzas were enough for the filling of the next table.

Another similar service followed of nearly equal length, and then the table was filled a third time, and as many times again as were necessary to enable all to be served.

I remember after the three branches of the United Presbyterian Church had come together in 1869, at the present site of their church, after the Rev. W. P. McNary had become the pastor of the congregation, in order to accommodate the more than three hundred members of the church, six or seven tables were necessary, and the service of communion Sabbath beginning at 10:30 in the morning lasted until 2:30 in the afternoon. This was in comparatively recent times, when very long sermons had gone out of vogue. In earlier times a communion Sabbath meant practically a whole day devoted to the service. The members of the church were largely country people, and the shades of night were falling fast when the farmer members got home from the communion service to their work of necessity and mercy—the milking of the cows and the feeding of the stock.

Within my early memory a modern innovation crept into the order of the communion service. If only a few members were left over in filling the last table, they were allowed to take the communion in the vacant pews at the front of the church. The new minister, Mr. McNary, connived at this overlapping at each table, if he did not encourage it. It was permitted to grow till only four tables were served, then three, then two, and finally the real table at which the people sat has been taken away and all the congregation are served in their pews—with individual communion cups. It is written, "Your old men shall dream dreams," but the fathers of the church would never have dreamed of a change like that.

When going up and sitting down at the table was abandoned, some good souls were offended. Their fathers and mothers had so communed, and they had no memory of, or experience with, other forms. The Scotch-Irish were naturally and extremely conservative, and to them changes came hard. When a new version of the Psalms was introduced, only forty years ago, and when the use of the tokens was abandoned, two good sisters left the church in great displeasure. They would not consent to the lowering of the standard, and they proposed to stand strictly and bravely for the faith as their fathers had bequeathed it to them.

J. M. Barrie's picture in his "Auld Licht Idylls" of how Miss Tibbie McQuatty almost split the Old Side Covenanter Church in Scotland over "run line," will be recognized as true to life by those who knew Tibbie's kith and kin in America. Lining out the psalm was never held to be a fundamental article of faith and practice by any of these churches here, so far as I know. But when the frivolous and flighty innovation of reading the psalm all it once and singing it forthwith—when this worldly practice was substituted in the New Side Covenanter Church in Bloomington, instead of the old and revered custom of "lining out," the congregation lost two of its members, almost 5 per cent. of its membership. Two good members, Mr. and Mrs. Fullerton, sought membership in the Associate Reformed Church, where they could still hear the psalms lined out. There were always some who balked at innovation, no matter what. The good pair, the Fullertons, said they were leaving their old church on this account, because the good wife could not read, and therefore after the change she was not able to worship God in "psalms, hymns and spiritual songs." But I have a lurking notion that their principles were offended—that is, their conservative disposition and their dislike and suspicion of change. Often it was only this disposition of mind that they called their principles.

VII.

CHURCH TRIALS.

These psalm-singing Presbyterians believed that the church was responsible for the conduct of its members, and that church discipline was the principal means by which the members were to be kept within the straight and narrow way. This belief they practiced much more strictly in their day than their descendants do in this day. Hour upon hour was spent in church courts, year by year, trying offenders and turning them over to the moderator of the session (the minister) for public admonition and rebuke before the whole congregation. The congregation claimed the right to know how the session dealt with the offender who had violated the laws of God and the church.

One of the chief offenses, the one that called for the most frequent trials, was the violation of the Sabbath. With these people the Fourth Commandment, "Remember the Sabbath day to keep it holy," was coordinate with all the rest. "Thou shalt not steal," "Thou shalt not kill," "Thou shalt not bear false witness," bore no more directly nor forcibly upon their consciences and conduct than did the command to keep the Sabbath day in holiness and awe. Indeed, it seemed that they selected the Fourth Commandment as one of peculiar favor, to be guarded by jealous and special care. Their Sunday law was the law of the Hebrew Sabbath. On that day no work was to be done, save the works of mercy and necessity. The people were not to give themselves over to their own wills, nor to follow after any worldly pleasures. But the whole day was to be spent in religious devotion and solemn worship, in the sanctuary or in the home. Public worship occupied a large part of the day, and then came the Bible reading, or the catechism, around the fireside, or a lesson from some religious work, with solemn admonition from parents to children. The day was so holy that the word *Sunday* itself was looked upon as an immoral and irreligious word, an ungodly intrusion from heathenism. A story is told of a young minister in Scotland, who on a beautiful Sunday morning greeted one of his elders with cheerful smile and joyous remark that it was an unusually lovely day. "It is," said the good old elder, "but is this a day to be talking of days?" The rebuke was intended to remind the bold young minister of the ever-present burden of keeping the Sabbath solemn and holy.

All possible work for the Sabbath was attended to on Saturday. The wood and kindling were all laid by for the Sabbath fires; the shoes were blackened and the Sabbath apparel arranged, and everything was done to make it possible to keep the Sabbath as a day of complete rest from secular toil. Sabbath cooking was reduced to a minimum. Two meals on the Sabbath day was the universal custom, and one of these was usually cold, eaten as a bite in the recess between the long sermons at the meeting-house, or at home after four or five hours of sermons and services in the sanctuary. If in the evening the children were hungry, they could be allowed to "cut a pie" or have a cold piece of bread and brown sugar, or more likely of rye bread and sorghum molasses. It was a day not for hilarity and feasting, but for abstinence and solemnity, and they were taught to believe that God's wrath was certain to descend upon the man or the people who forsook or desecrated his holy day.

MADDEN IRWIN.

A local story is told of a pious old Scotch-Irish Covenanter by the name of Irwin, who had a son by the name of Madden. Madden Irwin will be remembered by some

now living. It was early in July. By some mistake or
lapse of memory, or by the rapid passage of time, or from
lack of almanac or calendar, the Irwin family had lost run
of the days of the week. It was the holy Sabbath, but the
family were ignorant of that awful fact. Thinking it was
Saturday, the old man had sent his son into the field
bright and early in the morning to finish gathering in the
golden harvest. Some Covenanter brethren and neighbors, as they were driving by on their way to church, were
astonished at the sight of the harvest hand in the field
with sickle and scythe, as on an ordinary secular day.
They stopped at the house and with due solemnity asked
to know the meaning of this unheard-of desecration.
When the truth had been revealed to the old man that it
was indeed the Sabbath day, and the terrible thought
came to him that his son stood exposed in the open field
to the punishment due to the wicked violator of God's
law, he was stricken with horror. He rushed from the
house toward the harvest field, waving his arms fran-
tically and shouting, "Madden! Madden! flay to the
house, flay to the house, Madden, flay from the wrath of
God!"

This story is one of the neighborhood traditions, but
there are others in the records of the church which are as
instructive if not as amusing. Under date of April 17,
1839, I find this entry in the session records of the Associate Reformed Church:

"At this time the session took up the case of John Fee,
who appeared before the Session on the charge, *fama
clamosa,* of Sabbath-breaking, by travelling on that day.
On being interrogated he acknowledged he did travel on
that day referred to by the Court, and that under similar
circumstances he had done so before. The circumstances
referred to as the reason why he travelled on the partic-

ular day, known to the Court by report, were that he left
his wife unwell when he started to Cincinnati, and that
he had been detained from home some four or five days
longer than he expected.   One member of the Court, Mr.
William Fee, stated that by him the accused had heard,
previous to the Sabbath of his arrival home, that his wife
was better, but that one of his children [was sick] yet
not dangerous.

"The similar circumstances under which he said he
travelled on the Sabbath before appeared to be, from his
own statement, that when his business was closed in the
city where he traded, he was always anxious to get home,
and considered that he could keep the Sabbath as well on
his way home as in a tavern where there was rough company, and thus did the accused object to the relevancy of
the charge.

"The Session, however, after considering his objections, decided that the charge was relevant, and on the
confession of the accused to the fact, or facts with which
he was charged, the Session pronounced him guilty and
gave judgment to censure him by admonition before the
Session, the decision to be publicly read to the Congregation.   The accused refused to acknowledge that he had
done wrong under the circumstances, and the Session
gave him to the 27th of the same month to consider the
same matter.

"The Session then took up the case of Joseph Henderson, who by order of the Session was requested to appear
before them.   He appeared.   The charge preferred, on
fama clamosa, was Sabbath-breaking, in driving hogs to
market on that day.   He was interrogated as to the
affair, and stated in substance that it was his calculation
to start the wagon Monday, and that his Partner came to
him Friday evening and stated that the hogs were out of

corn; that one of the wagons employed to haul corn for them had failed to do it, and that he had not been able to procure another and that they must start on the next morning, Saturday. They started, and he stated further that on Sabbath morning, considering the pen in which the hogs were unsafe, some of them having actually got out, they started and did drive on the Sabbath, stating at the same time that he knew it to be wrong, but could not see how he could avoid it. The Session then decided that the charge was relevant, admitting that the circumstances of the case was in some degree Palliating, yet they deemed that sufficient exertion had not been made to avoid the breaking of the Sabbath.

"The accused having acknowledged the fact of which he was charged, professed sorrow for it and promised to be more circumspect in future, was admonished and the Moderator directed to read the decision to the Congregation.

"The Session then took up the case of Thomas Mc-Calla, who appeared, being requested by the Moderator according to the direction of the Session. He was accused, on *fama clamosa*, of Sabbath-breaking by travelling on the Sabbath. The charge was found relevant, and on being interrogated as to the facts he stated substantially that he had done so and usually did so when from home. Session then decided to censure by admonition, requiring the decision to be read to the Congregation. On his refusing to submit to any censure or make any acknowledgment, Session gave him to the 27th inst. to consider the matter."

Evidently John Fee and Thomas McCalla were a little recalcitrant. When the 27th of April came, the time set for their repentance, the session again took up their cases. Fee acknowledged his fault and was admonished and re-

stored to good standing in the church. Thomas McCalla
did not appear at this meeting, thereupon he was by private resolution of the court suspended.

A year later, April 25, 1840, the case of Mr. McCalla
again came up. He appeared before the session, confessed his fault, promised amendment, was admonished
before the session, which was publicly intimated to the
congregation, and was restored to privilege.

For the long trial and suspension from the church and
public rebuke his offense had been that he had traveled
on the Sabbath, not by the noisy and desecrating railway
trains, for there were none in those days, but likely by
stage coach or steamboat, though it is more likely that it
was by horseback, or by his own conveyance, through the
country side.

On April 6, 1842, the session had up the case of James
Glenn, "who," as the record says, "had drove his waggon
or permitted it to be drove on the Sabbath day." He appeared and gave his reasons for driving, which were
sustained as "pretty good." The session thought fit,
however, "to admonish him to be more circumspect in
future and to avoid the appearance of evil."

Jonathan Archer was tried for "driving his waggon on
the Sabbath, in going to and from the South last fall."
He was admonished and restored to good standing.

Samuel Kirk and William Hunter were tried, who,
from report, had traveled on the Sabbath. They appeared and stated their reasons for so doing. The session sustained their reasons under their circumstances,
but thought they did wrong in starting from home with
the company they did. They were admonished to be
"more careful in future with regard to the company they
engaged to travel with."

On September 23, 1843, the case of Robert Graham was

taken up, "who, according to his own confession, drove his waggon on the Sabbath day last spring as he was coming from the river." He was admonished.

On February 29, 1844, Samuel Harbison, "who, from his own confession, drove his hogs to market on the Sabbath," submitted to censure and was publicly rebuked.

On March 8, 1844, the case of John Millen came up, "who, from his own confession, drove his hogs to market on the Sabbath day in company with others who rather had control over him." He submitted to censure, was admonished and restored.

In 1844 (March 2) Joseph Henderson and John Fee appeared and "gave a statement of having drove hogs on the Sabbath toward market, for no other reason than because they could not get good accommodations, and feared a break up in the roads; and in the second instance, Mr. Henderson stated in substance that he drove a second drove on the Sabbath because he had made an engagement at a certain price, and he found if he did not drive he would lose his engagement."

"Mr. Fee having confessed his fault and given evidence of penitence, was rebuked by the Session in the name of the Lord Jesus, and restored to his privileges. But Mr. Henderson, being interrogated refused to acknowledge that he had done wrong, and even to promise that he would [not] do so again under similar circumstances, was suspended from the enjoyment of his privileges in the church until he confess his fault and give evidence of penitence."

Such was the character of the trials in the old session house of the Associate Reformed Presbyterian Church in this county. Though Sabbath-breaking took the lead in cases of discipline, there were many cases of other kinds, all going to show that the session had a due sense of responsibility and oversight for the flock, and were trying to do their duty in saving them from evil ways, and saving the church from scandal.

One member was arraigned and rebuked for profane swearing. Another is reproved in mixed English for having married his niece, and "for living with her as man and wife." The session, after mature deliberation, resolved that he could "not be received into the church in his present situation."

In April, 1854, the case of John Moffet came up, it being reported that he had not given in a correct account list of his taxable property. "On examination it appeared, as Mr. Moffet had already acknowledged, that it was a mistake inadvertently made. The session, therefore, concluded for Mr. Moffet's sake to make public the conclusion to which the session came."

At the same meeting the session was officially informed that some of the young people of the congregation had been engaged in dancing. The session having reason to believe the report, concluded that on Saturday previous to the communion the moderator should give information generally to the congregation, that "such practices can not be tolerated in future."

As I have said, the members of the congregation were expected to come to church, and if they did not the session wanted to know why. On April 15, 1856, on motion made by Mr. William Curry, Mr. Peter Johnston was appointed to visit Mr. Thomas Gourley and inquire why he does not attend church more punctually. Four days later Mr. Johnston reported that he had seen Mr. Thomas Gourley and that his excuse for not attending church more regularly was satisfactory. As to what the satisfactory reasons were our curiosity is not satisfied. Alexander Weir and wife were also visited to learn why they did not come to church.

The case of David Junkin was unique. Reports were out on him as to his having feloniously taken some small articles from Mr. Howe's store. He appeared before the session. No witness appeared to testify, but on being interrogated Mr. Junkin stated in substance that he did take a piece of tobacco out of Mr. Howe's store, but that he had done so before in the presence of Mr. Howe, and that he had allowed him to do so, but he acknowledged that he did wrong in going behind the counter and taking it when Mr. Howe was not present, and in the presence of another person.

Probably if this other "busy-body" had not been present this comparatively innocent and unintentional felony would never have appeared upon the record. But the case may perhaps be used to illustrate the fact that the tale-bearer and the scandal-monger were also within the pale of the kirk, or it may illustrate the fact that the members of the church knew quite well that there was another court besides the civil court to which they might expect to be held to pretty strict account for their walk and conversation. The session thought best to admonish Mr. Junkin to be more circumspect in the future, and they agreed to give public intimation of the case.

THE GRAHAM CASE—GOSSIP AND SLANDER.

Another unique case of discipline, and from the nature of the circumstances, one of the most troublesome of all, was a slander case. Robert had married Polina, and Robert's mother and his brother Andrew were accused by Polina's father of saying some hard things about her. This caused Andrew and his mother to complain to the session of unchristian treatment. They accused Polina's father of slander for saying that they (Andrew and his mother) were trying to ruin Polina's character. The identical words which the father was accused of using were these: "You, Mrs. H., are the very woman that broke covenant between man and wife and have been doing it." Andrew and his mother were asked if they were guilty of talking about Polina, and they said, "No." Then Mr. G. was asked if he was prepared to make any acknowledgments, and he said, "No." The parties were informed that they should stay back from the approaching communion, and the whole matter was laid over for future consideration. (May 2, 1844.) It was later decided that Mr. R. G. should be rebuked and that public announcement thereof be made to the congregation. He appealed to the presbytery against this decision. The presbytery sustained the session, with this difference, that he be "admonished instead of rebuked." Mr. G. appeared and was admonished. Polina being rebuked for imprudent conduct, appealed to the presbytery, but when the presbytery sustained the session, Polina appeared and submitted to censure. (October 22, 1844.) Polina's father was not satisfied with this disposition of the case. He was evidently one of the contentious kind with a hankering after church litigation. Nearly two years later, January 21, 1846, we find a bill of charges preferred against him by the Union Session:

"1. He has neglected to attend upon the preaching of the word since October 22, 1844, with the exception of a very few days, and that generally [when] some other person officiated besides the regular pastor of the congregation, nor has he since that time partaken of the Lord's supper, though it has been dispensed semi-annually since that time.

"2. He has neglected and virtually refused to pay his subscription of eight dollars for the support of the gospel in Union Congregation, for 1844.

"3. It is reported that some time last fall, or this winter, he drove his wagon coming from market on the Sabbath day.

"Done by order of the session,

"JOHN MOFFET, *Clerk*."

"Mr. G. being interrogated as to the truth of the charge, admitted it, and being called upon to give his reasons for neglect of ordinances as set forth in the first charge, and being asked why he thus acted, replied that he felt aggrieved at the action of the session in his daughter's, and in his own case also, which had been before the session; and one occasion of his grief was that the session insisted on and did ask witnesses living in the very neighborhood of her defamers how her character stood. And another grievance was the spirit manifested in both cases not to let us exculpate ourselves from the charges tabled against us."

Under the second charge Mr. G. answered that if his case was not adjusted he would lay in a claim against the moderator of some $2.50 or $3.00, which he once paid to Mr. Boyce when a subscription was got up to assist him in finishing his studies; also a claim of $5.00 which he says he paid to Mr. Moffet shortly after he came to this place to help the congregation out of debt.

"The session having considered the reasons given by Mr. G. in his defense, and also the testimony of Mr. John D. Whiseand in regard to Mr. G.'s answer to the first charge, as insufficient, because—first, they do not know that the question put by the session and objected to by Mr. G. was an improper one, and even admitting it to have been so, it was not the ground of her suspension, and Mr. G. should remember that it is human to err but Divine to forgive. And because, secondly, we regard Mr. G. as making an unreasonable excuse for his conduct when he says a spirit was manifested not to let him and his daughter exculpate themselves. This we think unreasonable when it is remembered that the session spent twelve or fourteen days on these two cases, and Mr. G. had their action reviewed by a higher court; and as it respects the charge made as an offset to his subscription, the session think it is a thing almost unheard of for men to expect any pecuniary reward for what they have voluntarily given for charitable purposes.

"As to his travelling on the Sabbath, they are of the opinion his situation was somewhat critical and a kind of necessity drove him to it, and that should he acknowledge before the session his sorrow for the occurrence they would forgive him this offense.

"The session do therefore resolve as in their judgment the only means of removing the offense, that Mr. R. C. G. be and [he] hereby [is] suspended from the enjoyment of sealing ordinances in this church till such time as he shall give signs of Repentance or Reformation, and that whenever he shall do this by returning to his Duty in the church and confessing his faults in these Respects we feel Disposed to Reverse this Decision, and to Treat him as a Brother."

Such were the church problems in the country congregation in this vicinity seventy years ago. Days and weeks of trouble and trial because of some neighborhood gossip about a frisky lass, or because Polina G.'s mother-in-law was not fond of her.

DRINKING AND DRUNKENNESS.

There are many cases of another kind—a kind that will serve to illustrate the progress of the temperance reform in this community and in the country at large. Respectable men imbibed strong drink in those days more than

they do now.   The Irish were strong drinkers, and what
they drank was not the comparatively innocent beer or
"near-beer" of our day, but good, strong Scotch-Irish
whiskey.   It may have been corn-juice or apple jack, but
whatever it was it had *spirits* in it.   In still earlier days
it not infrequently happened that some of their ministers
were incapacitated by this habit.[1]   In this community, in
the times of which we write, sixty or seventy years ago,
drunkenness was a grievous sin among the elect of the
Irish Presbyterian faith.   With this lapse from morals
the minister and the session frequently had to deal.   If
any one doubts that the influence of the church was a
positive force in restraining men from their evil ways, let
him read the record of the church courts.   The church
was the moral leader, the guide of the people.   Reform
began with the house of God, and in the days of which we
speak the ministers themselves were setting an example
of abstinence and were preaching the sound doctrine of
righteousness, temperance and judgment to come.

But the temperance reform seemed to come hard with
the Irish Presbyterians.   In Mr. Bryan's congregation of
the Seceder Church in Ohio there was an old Irish elder
by the name of Galbreath, who was quite fond of his
cups.   He would frequently come to the meeting of the
session half tipsy—or tipsy-full—or in such voluble condition as would lead him to contribute more than his
share of talk to the deliberations of the session.   Mr.
Bryan preached repeatedly and boldly against the sin of
intemperate drinking, and his sermons bore so obviously
and directly on the case of the offending elder that the
old man took his pastor to task for calling public attention to his habit.   "Well," said Mr. Bryan, "what objection have you to my doctrine?"   "It's na your doctrine I

---

[1] See page 467.

object to; it's the application of it," replied the elder. At any rate, the elder, though himself past hope in fondness for his cups, was willing that the youth of the congregation should be taught these lessons in abstinence.

In Mr. Turner's church (the Associate Reformed) the following entry appears under date of March 12, 1840:

"Session took up the case of James Glenn who had taken too much spirits at Fairport about Christmas. He appeared, confessed, was admonished and restored."

Under April 27, 1841, "John Doe appeared before the session, confessed he had been guilty of the sins of intoxication and quarrelling in Bloomington, professed repentance, was rebuked before the session and ordered to be published to the congregation."

I shall not mention further names, as that would be to mention the ancestral names of people now highly respected and honored in this community. One other case will serve to illustrate the moral problem with which the session was dealing.

April 17, 1839, "the Session took up the case of R. S., who had for six months or so before [been] suspended by a private resolution of the session, from the enjoyment of sealing ordinances for the sin and scandal [of] drunkenness, and some evidence being offered that a reformation had taken [place] in the conduct of this individual, and being willing if consistent with their duty to encourage him, after he had appeared before them, confessed his guilt, professed penitence and solemnly promised that he would not again taste intoxicating liquors except prescribed to him for medicine in case of Bodily Infirmity, and been by the moderator rebuked in the name of the Head of the church before the session to be publicly read to the congregation, he was by them restored again to the privileges of the church."

We may smile at these cases of trial and discipline, and we may in some instances consider them as petty and mean. But who can doubt, as he considers the times and ways in which these men lived, that the minister and the session exercised a strong influence for goodness, righteousness and sobriety among their people? No doubt their lives were narrow in many ways, but there was among them the true light that lighteth every man, and they were being gradually lifted and led to larger and nobler lives. And who will say that the church gains power as it loses its disciplinary authority over the lives and conduct of its members?

VIII.

THE SCOTCH-IRISH PRESBYTERIANS AND POLITICS.

One branch of these Irish Presbyterians, the "Old Side" Covenanters, was prohibited by their church from voting or holding office, and these did not belong to any party nor take part in politics. As a rule the members conformed to this church law. Also, as a rule, in the days when slavery was the dominant issue before the country, the members of the Covenanter Church were in intense sympathy with the party that was most committed and pronounced for the anti-slavery cause. They were also strong Union men during the war. Some of the Covenanters have been known to shout and march in parade for the party cause on Saturday, but they would refuse to vote for the cause on the following Tuesday. They were usually Republicans in sympathy and disposition, in the days when that party was distinctly an anti-slavery and Union party.

ANTI-SLAVERY DECLARATION.

The Reformed Presbyterian Church of North America was one of the few small churches, and one of the earliest, openly to condemn the institution of slavery. Their Testimony (the announcement of what they believed), published in 1806 and republished in 1848, specifically condemned the following as errors to be opposed:

"That it is lawful for civil rulers to authorize the purchase and sale of any part of the human family as slaves.

"That a Constitution of government which deprives unoffending men of liberty and property, is a moral institution to be recognized as God's ordinance."

These errors they consistently and constantly opposed, and they not only refused to admit slave-holders to their communion, but they refused also to fellowship with those whose opinions were favorable to slave-holding. They were as much concerned about men's doctrine as they were about their conduct.

To illustrate the early opposition to slavery on the part of these Reformed Presbyterians in the South, the following resolutions are copied from an old manuscript which was sent by Rev. Hugh McMillan, the pastor of one of the churches in Chester county, South Carolina, to Mr. Dorrance Woodburn, teacher, in 1825. The paper is as follows:

"For the better application of the principles of the Reformed Church respecting slavery; and for the preservation of the character of the church from the evil contagion thereof, the Southern Presbytery have adopted the following resolutions:

"1.   First, that slavery as its exists in the United States is immoral; and that it is, under all circumstances, prohibited by the principles and practices of this church.

"2.   Second, that no application for membership to any

session under the direction of Presbytery by persons possessing slaves shall hereafter be attended to till the connection betwixt such persons and slavery be righteously dissolved.

"3. Third, that no wife of a slave-holding husband shall hereafter be admitted to the communion of the church, except by a public renunciation of the principles and practices of slavery and the session admitting her having previously consulted the Presbytery as to the propriety and expediency of such admission.

"4. Fourth, that all members of the church having persons of color at their disposal be required forthwith to petition the Legislature of the State for the liberty of emancipation and to become their guardians, if necessary.

"5. Fifth, that all members of the church having persons of color at their disposal, and not obtaining from the State the liberty of emancipation, be required to act toward such persons of color as freedmen, and to give them a lawful compensation for their services according to justice and equity.

"6. Sixth, that all members of the church having under their care persons of color in a state of minority, be required to act toward them and to raise them in all respects as white minors, according to the laws of christianity.

"7. Seventh, that the removal of persons of color from the United States to Liberia in Africa, or to the Republic of Hayti, is approved of by the Presbytery, and the same is hereby earnestly recommended to the persons of color and to those who have the direction thereof within the church.

"8. Eighth, that a committee of three or more persons be appointed within each congregation under the direction of Presbytery whose business it shall be to carry the above resolutions into effect, and to give, from time to time, to the Presbytery faithfull reports of their proceedings.

"Done at Little R. C. [Rocky Creek] Meeting House, May 4th, 1825."

The Rev. Mr. McMillan accompanies the resolutions with a letter to Mr. Woodburn as follows:

"Sir: As I am informed you are appointed by the Moderator of the Southern Presbytery Chairman of the above Committee, I herewith transmit you a copy of the resolutions adopted by the Presbytery. I hope the Committee will feel the importance of the work committed to them and with sufficient energy see the resolutions executed. Should this fail the church will truly appear in the eyes of all beholders contemptible, and in the eyes of the church's Head highly criminal for knowing their Master's will and doing it not. There is present need of at least two of them being speedily executed at I. Creek. I request that the committee, or a competent member go up with me when I next go and relieve the church either from causeless reproach or lay ground for the church, in a regular way, to exclude from her fellowship those who should not be in it. I am to be at Poplar Spring on the first Sabbath of July. You and some of the other members, I hope, will make it to suit them to go."

If any church, North or South, took a bolder or more outspoken stand on slavery in those early years, it has not come to the knowledge of the writer. These resolutions were passed six years before Garrison founded his *Liberator*, and a year before the Rev. John Rankin, a forerunner of Garrison, wrote his famous anti-slavery letters from Ohio to his brother in Virginia. Rev. Mr. McMillan, like the Rev. Mr. Faris, probably soon became discouraged with the progress of the anti-slavery cause in

South Carolina, since within a few years he, with almost his entire congregation, left Carolina and settled in Greene county, Ohio. Hardly a decade had gone by after these resolutions were passed until Senator Preston, of South Carolina, the colleague of John C. Calhoun in the United States Senate, declared from his seat in that body that "if an abolitionist came within the borders of South Carolina and we can catch him, we will try him, and, notwithstanding all the interference of all the governments of the earth, including this Federal Government, *we will hang him.*" By that time South Carolina had driven most of her abolitionists from her borders, but they continued to be abolitionists in the Northwest, and some of the South Carolina Covenanters who moved from that State to Indiana were among the anti-slavery forces who cast their votes for "free soil, free speech, free labor, free men," and later for Fremont, during the great anti-slavery struggle.

The Associate Reformed Presbyterians, while they did not in the South excommunicate slave-holders and those who apologized for slavery, yet their testimony condemned slavery as an evil, and their influence as a church was pronounced and positive against it. In most Northern communities their attitude on slavery was essentially the same as that of the Reformed Presbyterians. With many of their people in the South, as with thousands of other Christian men, slave-holding appeared in the light of a necessity, or a duty. They had the responsibility of caring for the helpless blacks, or guiding and providing for them, and they believed that to set them free would result only in adding to their hardships and suffering and destitution. Some set their slaves free and brought them to the North; others continued to provide for their slaves through life. In 1825 the Associate Reformed Synod of the West published a "Warning Against Hopkinsian and Other Allied Errors." Later they added Testimonies on slavery, evil-speaking, Sabbath-breaking and other evils. All these Acts and Testimonies were collected by the Synod of the West in a small volume in 1830, which contains much religious information. On slavery they said, in substance: "The man who holds slaves, not from necessity, nor from a sense of duty, but from choice and for the profit of it, should be excluded from Christian privileges. We can not see how a man who holds his brother in bondage *from choice*, and for filthy lucre's sake, especially after he has had instruction and admonition, can be a Christian. We *know* that he can not and insist that he be excluded. Men who would hold Christian slaves in servitude for lucre's sake,—with such men, God judging us, we shall never have fellow-ship."

It will be seen that these Scotch-Irish Presbyterians stand well alongside the Quakers of their common Southland as pioneers in the movement for the abolition of American slavery.

AN ANTI-SLAVERY CHURCH AND A PRO-SLAVERY BELIEVER.

This anti-slavery spirit and the political and party discussions that grew out of it had two notable illustrations in the history of the Bloomington congregation.

Under March 26, 1846, the session records reveal the following:

"Hugh Marlin and his [wife] presented [their certificates] but was not received on account of their views on slavery."

A week later (April 4, 1846), "Mr. Hugh Marlin and wife, having satisfied the session with regard to slavery, was received into the church."

There is a proverbial Scotchman who is reported to have said that he was open to conviction, but, by jing! he would just like to see the man who could convince him! And it was no doubt a Scotch-Irish Presbyterian who prayed devoutly that he might be set right because, the Lord knows, if he ever gets wrong heaven and earth can't change him.

It is not likely that Mr. Marlin's examination before the session did much toward changing his opinion on the subject of slavery. Be that as it may, five years later his case and his opinions were again before the session. Under date of September 21, 1851, we read:

"Mr. Hugh Marlin having been dealt with privately by a committee of Session, and whereas he by request appeared before the Session and denied that slavery in the United States was a moral evil, and whereas the Session understood Mr. Marlin when he united with the church to admit slavery to be a moral evil, therefore, resolved that he be suspended for the time from sealing ordinances, and that the case be referred to Presbytery for advice."

This was unanimously adopted. Then the session turned about and reconsidered the resolution and gave Mr. Marlin liberty to enjoy his privileges.

Whether the case was carried to the presbytery or whether some members of the church continued to press upon the session the matter of Mr. Marlin's opinion on slavery, the record does not state, and I am not informed. But six months later, under date of April 27, 1852, the following entry appears:

"Whereas Mr. Marlin having been requested to attend, made his appearance, and having been interrogated upon the subject of slavery, the following preamble and resolution were adopted: Whereas Mr. Marlin was understood, when he united with the church, to assent to the act of Synod on the subject of slavery, but it has since appeared that he does not regard slavery as it exists in the United States to be a moral evil, agreeing at the same time that the institution is abused and that the abuses are moral evils, but maintaining that the institution as it exists in the United States is not unscriptural; and whereas, we have used means repeatedly to convince Mr. Marlin of his error but without effect, whereas, we regard his reason as nullifying the act of Synod and calculated to grieve the hearts of the godly, and destroy the edification of the church, therefore, resolved that he be and he hereby is suspended from the enjoyment of sealing ordinances till such time as he shall give evidence of a change of sentiment on this subject."   ·

HUGH MARLIN.

So Mr. Marlin was put out of the church, not for holding slaves—he had never owned a slave—but for holding opinions on slavery that he would not keep to himself, and which the majority of his church had condemned.

It seemed difficult for the Scotch Presbyterian mind to distinguish between conduct and opinion. Their church was a church with a *creed*. What men believed, in politics or religion, was made the basis of judgment and of the action of church courts. No one who remembers Mr. Marlin, as many of us do, would ever question his integrity of purpose, the uprightness of his character, or the true piety and godliness of his life. He was a kind neighbor and a liberal giver to all good causes. The trouble was with his opinions. He was otherwise-minded. His mental makeup merely accentuated a characteristic trait of his Scotch-Irish stock. That is, he was *opinionated*, and his opinions did not depend upon his being in the majority. He lived and died in a hopeless minority. But his opinions were his own. He did his own thinking, and he had the courage of his convictions. He was essentially a protestant, a non-conformist and a dissenter. He was a sincere democrat and an extreme individualist. It was difficult for him to agree for any length of time with any considerable body of his fellow-men. He joined the Presbyterian church, but many years later, when the congregation here substituted the unfermented for the fermented juice of the grape for wine in the communion service, Mr. Marlin protested. He denounced the innovation as unsound and unscriptural, and being determined to stand for the truth, as he saw it, he left the church and wrote a pamphlet upon the subject of the communion wine, in defense of what he considered the faith of the fathers.

THE SCOTCH-IRISH AND THE CIVIL WAR—A SOUTHERN SYMPATHIZER.

At the time of Mr. Marlin's trial before the session of the Associate Reformed Church for his opinions on slavery, John Moffet was the clerk of the session. The clerk himself was destined, a few years later, to face the same court on charges relating to his political opinions. Moffet was from the South. He had friends and relatives there, and when the war came on his Southern sympathies were strong. He was not a supporter of the war for the Union, or of Mr. Lincoln's administration. He was what might be called a mean kind of "copperhead." But from what I can learn of John Moffet by inquiry among those who remember him, he seems to have been a good man. He was upright in his life, a good neighbor, faithful to his obligations. He was one of the earliest elders of the church, and was for a number of years the clerk of its session. He sustained the church by his means. But, like most of these Scotch-Irish, he had opinions, and it happened that on the subject of the war his opinions were quite different from those of the rest of the congregation. It appears that he had no appreciation of the idea that language was given to man to conceal his thought. He could not keep silent even in the one language that he knew, and he held in contempt the "rascally virtue" of prudence that would prompt him to keep still when the prevailing opinion of his friends and brethren would be offended by his utterances. Mr. Moffet talked. Perhaps he talked too much. In Civil War times, as we all know, political discussions were warm, and there was a disposition among Union men and Republicans to denounce the Democrats who opposed the war as "copperheads," "secessionists" and "rebels." Mr. Moffet, like Mr. Marlin, was classed among the "copperhead" group. His talk in favor of the South and in opposition to the war policy of Mr. Lincoln no doubt greatly grieved and offended his friends, neighbors and churchmen.

A Civil War veteran, still living, who was then, as he is now, a member of the United Presbyterian Church in Bloomington, was engaged in raising a company for the war. He was to be commissioned as captain of his company. Naturally, the young captain was anxious that the young men among the families of the church should enlist for the war. It came to his ears that Mrs. Moffet had said at a quilting party in the neighborhood that, if the boys enlisted, she hoped "their bones would be left to bleach on Southern soil." This was too much. The young captain went to Uncle Johnnie Moffet about the matter, who disclaimed the utterance for himself, but if the disclaimer was accepted it was still believed that the remark expressed his sentiments.

The regiment was raised and the boys went to war, but after a few years the young captain was compelled on account of wounds and sickness to return to his home. At the communion service in the old church in the early spring of 1865, he stayed back from the communion table, and of course it was the duty of the pastor, Father Turner, to inquire the reason why. When he came on his pastoral visit to the young soldier, to learn the reason for this disregard of the church ordinances, the captain said that he had been "fighting rebels in the South for three years and he did not propose to sit down at communion with one at home."

There were others in the church and neighborhood who felt as this young captain did. Among these was James Gordon, an ardent Unionist, who lived southeast of town. Under April 11, 1865, in the last month of the war, the following "lible," or complaint, was presented by Mr. James Gordon against Mr. John Moffet, in the words following:[1]

"To the Session of the United Presbyterian Congregation in Monroe County, Indiana: The undersigned, a mamber of the above Congregation, feeling deeply grieved at the corse of Mr. John Moffet, a member and elder of said Congregation, in upholding and supporting by his influence and vote a political party and platform whose principles and designs are in oposition to the doctrines and testimony of our church in refference to human slavery and in opposition to our government, a government lawfully constituted and administered, and [which]

---

[1] The complaint is copied as the record presents it with all its imperfections.

demands and therefore rightfully shares and claims the
support of all its citizens who are bound by the laws of
God to Support and Sustain it—the undersigned knowing
also ingury is being done to the church and a reproach
cast upon it by the said course of the said Moffett and I
at the same time disclaiming all feelings of anger and
malice and solicitous only for the good of the church and
the honour of religion and having taken the steps laid
down in the new Testament for the removal of offences[1];
having done all this without effect would hereby ask that
you will take such steps as may seem right and proper for
the removal of this scandle and the vindication of the
honour of religion and purity of the church.

"JAMES GORDON."

"Mr. Moffett professed his willingness to go into trial,
though not notified beforehand as required by the discipline. It was then decided by a vote of the session that
the charges were *relivent*. Mr. Moffett was then interrogated as to the facts in the case and he admitted substantially that he had acted as charged, but did not consider
his conduct censurable. In reply to some statement by
the Moderator with a view to reconcile Mr. Moffett, he
declared himself opposed both to slavery and secession.
When further interrogated he refused to make confession
for the past or to make any promise how he would vote
in the future, and being interogated by a member of session as to his view of the Democratic platform adopted at
Chicago, Mr. Moffett expressed it as his belief that its
principles and doctrines were correct,—whereupon with-

---

[1] Matthew 18:15-18: "If thy brother sin against thee, go, show him his fault
between thee and him alone. If he hear thee not, take with thee one or two more,
that at the mouth of two witnesses or three every word may be established. And
if he refuses to hear them, tell it unto the church; and if he refuses to hear the
church also, let him be unto thee as the Gentile and the publican."

out further testimony by a vote of the session he was deprived of his office for the time being as a ruling elder."[1]

Presumably, Mr. Moffet was the only Democratic voter
in the church in that year. That was the year when it
was supposed the Union was at stake, and that its preservation depended upon the reelection of Lincoln. But,
evidently, in the county at large outside of his church,
Mr. Moffet had a good deal of company in his voting,
and if all the people who voted with him were "rebel
Democrats" the county was not very loyal, for in that
notable election the county voted against the reelection
of Lincoln (for General McClellan) by eight majority.
In 1862 the Democrats had carried the county by three
hundred and twelve majority.[2]

I have not considered it my function in the preparation of this paper to vindicate the Scotch-Irish Presbyterians against the attacks of their critics, to eulogize
them, or to enter upon an apology of their beliefs and
their ways. I have not sought to make them out, as the
custom often is with those who write of their own, as the
"salt of the earth" and "the best people in the world."
When one writes of his own kith and kin he may, indeed,
be permitted to indulge in a natural amount of self-glori-

---

[1] Church records.

[2] In 1864 Oliver P. Morton had four majority in Monroe county over Joseph E.
McDonald for Governor. In 1860 Lincoln received more votes in the county than
all the other three candidates put together. Breckinridge, Southern Democrat,
had 395; Douglas, Northern Democrat, 716; Bell, Constitutional Unionist, had 64
making a total vote for the three of 1175. Lincoln, Republican, had 1198. This
gave Lincoln a plurality of 482 over Douglas, his nearest opponent, and a majority
of twenty-three over all. This illustrates how Lincoln came to be elected in 1860,
by a division among his opponents; and the Democrat majority of 312 in 1862 illustrates the general reaction against Lincoln's administration during the first two
years of the war.

In 1840 Monroe county had a population of 10,140; in 1850 she had 11,280, a gain of
1140 in ten years.

fication. But I have sought to avoid partiality and praise, and perhaps my purpose to reveal these people as they were has not been fairly fulfilled, since what I have written has, for the most part, held up their homelier ways, their exceptional characters, their cruder habits, their peculiarities and oddities. I have felt that these oddities and peculiarities were typical; if they were not, it has been out of place to mention them. I may have exaggerated their faults. But I should feel like a recreant child of their race if I did not appreciate their virtues, their courage, devotion, piety, self-sacrifice, and the ways in which, by all their religious thoughts and lives, they sought to exalt both the justice and the grace of God. It is not necessary that my pen should attempt the portrayal of their virtues. Many of us still living have reason to remember what constant and unselfish neighborliness was manifested in the lives of such men as Alexander Henry, Samuel MacCalla, David Hunter, Harvey Phillips, William Wylie, John Blair, and many others that might be named. To all—not only to those of their own household of faith, but to all who were in sickness or in need—these men and their kindred Scotch-Irish were ever constant helpers and friends. And we who have seen the Tibbie McQuattys and the Martha McCaws at the sickbed, "when the hard look had gone from their eyes," and there was nothing but tenderness and sympathy in all their ways, will not care to smile at their oddities nor disparage their virtues.

I would claim only for these Scotch-Irish Presbyterians that they were good, plain, common people. They were good citizens and they played an honorable part in the frontier life of this community. Like all religious societies, they contained a mixture—there were tares among the wheat. There were among them both the good and the bad. There were individuals and traits that were petty and mean and unlovely, and there were among them men and women who were noble, faithful, generous, inspiring—calculated to instill and cultivate those qualities in children that make for abiding righteousness and character. It was not easy for them to conform to the ways of large masses of men. They were natural seceders, come-outers. "Come ye out from among them and be ye separate"—this text seems to have served for them like a second golden rule; and while we may not accept all their applications of this text, yet we may concede that the side of the truth which they have emphasized, or their view of the truth, has, in many ways, had an influence for good. They were not yielding and soft and flabby and uncertain in their Christianity. Their idea of a Christian was one who *believed*, and who was ready to stand up with grit and backbone to fight for his faith. Emotional religion begotten of the excitement of the camp-meeting revival, which soon wilted in the humdrum of life, or when the sun got hot,—this was not their kind.

They were as ready to fight for their country as for their creed.

On the Roll of Honor of the Grand Army of the Republic, among the "Boys in Blue" of Monroe county, who stood on the firing line for their country while she was passing through her dark hour of trial by battle and blood, I think it may safely be said that these Scotch-Irish Presbyterians furnished their full quota. It is doubtful whether better soldiers ever went to war. I only need to mention the names of Captain Allen, Captain Wylie, Captain McCalla, and his brothers, the Mc-

Dermott boys (who were killed at Chickamauga), the Pattons, the Smiths, the Wilsons, Kilpatrick, Harbison, Alexander, Gordon, Weir, Hanna, Harrah and Strong—and there were many others—to indicate that they had within them the stuff of which good soldiers were made.

And I think it may also, with due modesty, be said that while these Scotch-Irish have shown characteristics that were sinewy and gritty, unbending and hard, yet when their sense of God's justice and truth was once fairly blended with a conviction of His love and grace, there were produced among them some of the gentlest, most serviceable and most unselfish spirits that ever found a home within the church universal.

INDIANA HISTORICAL SOCIETY PUBLICATIONS
VOLUME IV   NUMBER 9

INDIANAPOLIS AND THE CIVIL WAR

BY

JOHN H. HOLLIDAY

INDIANAPOLIS
Edward J. Hecker, Printer and Publisher
1911

INDIANAPOLIS AND THE CIVIL WAR

CHAPTER I.

The Settlement and Its Life.

Whoever may have been the first settler of this place, he came in March, 1820, but it was more than a year later that the town was laid out and the squatters had the opportunity to buy lots. It was named in no chance fashion, but, by an edict of the Legislature, when the location was fixed, was christened Indianapolis, the City of Indiana. It was fortunate in its name, unique, dignified, prophetic. It was fortunate in being started for a city, and not being allowed to straggle up from the woods along the cowpaths and short cuts. It was also fortunate in its designer, a Scotch engineer who knew much about cities, and who made the lots large and the streets wide, the place attractive with the central circle and the convenient diverging avenues. His was the genius that, in this day of enlarged vision, would make "the City Beautiful."

Fortunate above all things was the town in the people who made it. They came from all parts of the older States, many drifting through the earlier settlements of Ohio, Kentucky and southeastern Indiana, before they found lodgment here. The Middle and Southern States furnished the larger part; the number from New England was not great, but it was choice. The attraction was that of a new country being opened, which has always been fascinating to Americans; a settlement that was to be the capital of a State and therefore had a fixed status and a certainty of attaining some importance. Many of them had some means, enough to buy farms and lots on payments or to use as capital in business. All came to better their condition. In those days land was the chief thing to accumulate. It would always furnish a living. The prudent's man's ambition was to get a farm for each of his children, and those who had land elsewhere sold it in order that they might buy a larger quantity at the low government price.

Probably few of these people dreamed of accumulating wealth. The opportunity was small. There was no transportation that would create much commerce, though it was expected that at some time the streams would be available for that purpose. The community was cast upon its own resources, and the land must provide the living. Of course there were traders and tradesmen, lawyers and doctors, but the backbone was agriculture. The settlers averaged well. They were all of American stock, filled with the American spirit of energy and progression, optimistic and determined. The moral tone was good. It was not long until a Sunday-school was started, followed by a church, and then another and another. Two newspapers were established, the advocates of the two political parties and of the new capital. Education was valued and the best available provisions made for it. Among the settlers were men who would have been noted in any community, and these natural leaders gave a tone and trend to the young settlement that was fostered and grew with the years, the impress of which is felt to this day and is likely to abide for a long time. They gave the town a character, for communities have character as well as individuals, that it has never gotten away from, though there have been retrogressions as population increased and changed.

It were invidious, perhaps, to single out any from this noble list of benefactors, but no mention of the town would be complete without giving the names of four men who were the most active in putting it upon the stable foundation of religion and morality. These were Dr. Isaac Coe, James Blake, James M. Ray and Calvin Fletcher. They were all diligent in business, but they were public-spirited, and always had time to give to help their neighbors or the public in general. Dr. Coe was more noticeable for the influence he had upon Blake and Ray, and possibly Fletcher. He it was who started the Sunday-school and church and brought these men into both. James Blake was the leader of the community, and a born-leader he was. Large and brawny, full of enthusiasm and never-flagging energy, he it was who presided over every public meeting for fifty years and was the head of every public movement that looked to the well-being of the people, whether spiritual or material. He it was who was the marshal of every parade and procession, who led the Sunday-school children every Fourth of July that they might have a lesson in patriotism, and who kept up the annual observance of the anniversary of founding Sabbath schools in Indianapolis till he died. He it was who looked after the poor as president of the Benevolent Society, and who never had a thought for himself if some one needed help. During the war he gave his whole time to the cause. Scarcely a regiment left the city that he did not go with them to the train to say farewell, and never did one return, no matter how small the fragment, that he was not there to welcome it home. He was the "Grand Old Man of Indianapolis," and if ever a man deserved a statue to perpetuate the memory of his virtues and his usefulness, it was James Blake.

The others were only second to him in that they were cast in different molds. Mr. Ray was a man of delicate physique and handsome face. He was an accurate, painstaking business man, of large ability as a financier, quiet, unassuming, yet persistent and gifted with rare good judgment. Where Mr. Blake was president he was usually secretary, and his patient methods and work often gained the success that the more aggressive leader might have failed to secure. Mr. Fletcher was a fitting complement. He was a clear-headed and able lawyer and banker, a man of sound views and fine sense, not so methodical as Mr. Ray, perhaps, and not so impulsive as Mr. Blake, with more humor and possibly more originality than the others. Both his qualities and his character commanded respect. Where a vice-president or treasurer was needed, he filled the place. There should be statues of these men as well as of Mr. Blake, to tell the future generations who were the most influential in making Indianapolis what it has been and is. All of these lived to see results that they scarcely anticipated when they came here in 1821. Mr. Fletcher died in 1866 at the age of sixty-eight, Mr. Blake in 1870 at the age of eighty-four, and Mr. Ray in 1881 at the age of eighty-one. There were others, as I have said, who were valuable cooperators and to whom a debt of gratitude is due, but these were facile princeps.

The town thus started went on its way and met the usual experiences of towns, ups and downs, but making progress steadily. In 1824 it was estimated that five hundred persons were living on "the donation," as the grant of four sections of land was called. Out of this was carved a mile square and platted into lots, the whole bounded by North, South, East and West streets. The rest was divided into larger tracts, called out-lots. From the sale of lots the Courthouse, State House and other public buildings were built, and the sum realized in the long run was $125,000. In 1827 a canvass was taken and 1066 inhabitants were counted. In 1830 an estimate of about 1500 was made. In 1840 the Government census showed 2692; in 1850, 8091, and in 1860, 18,611. The first railroad came in 1847 and since that time the growth has been rapid.

In attempting a brief sketch of the war as seen in Indianapolis and affecting its history, it is necessary to show what the town was before that period. Younger people often profess amusement when older ones date or locate events as before or since the war. They do not understand how that great conflict made a sharp cleavage through all the lines of life, distinctly separating one period from another; how it brought about radical and far-reaching changes in all conditions. To them it may be a period of some interest, just as the Revolutionary War was to their parents, but they do not comprehend the revolution in manners, habits and circumstances caused by the great struggle. It has always been my regret that I was not born three or four years sooner, in order that I might have entered more fully into the life and actions of each period and have arrived at an age where greater knowledge and experience would have brought clearer insight. I would then have been better qualified to paint a picture of the life of the town during the '50's, but as it is I must give the impressions of a boy, modified or confirmed to some extent by the recollections of others. Let it be understood that I write as an artist must paint—as I saw it.

It was a great place to be born in and a good place to live in, after thirty or more years had passed over its head. It seems now almost ideal. Its people were homogeneous, holding and striving for high standards and exhibiting the best traits engendered in a simple democracy. It was a place that encouraged the virtues of faith, hope, courage, kindliness and patriotism; that brought up boys and girls to real manhood and womanhood. The fiery ordeal of the war and the terrible sacrifices the people were called upon to make, demonstrated the power of its environment, and many lives of fullness and goodness have borne testimony to the value of the examples and training of their youth.

To begin with, life was simple as compared with what we now have. The community was small, but, while the rule in small places is still toward simplicity, it is influenced by the thoughts and customs of large cities, which did not obtain fifty years ago, for there were but few such cities. The great increase of wealth, fashion and luxury affects even our villages now, while in that day New York and Boston seemed as far apart from Indiana as London or St. Petersburgh. Here the life was simple, because it was the life of a new country in which wealth was small and the opportunities for its acquisition limited. Simplicity was a necessity. The community was largely self-dependent still, although it had developed from the pioneer stage in which it had to produce everything for itself except a few unusual articles. Thirty years had improved conditions very much, houses were better, more comforts were obtainable, markets had been opened and there was more money to buy with. But the spirit and habits of the early days remained in great measure, unaffected by improved conditions. The population was not so large as to crush the neighborly feeling, the democratic idea that one man was as good as another provided he behaved himself. There was little disposition to flaunt wealth when it existed, but people clung to the old standards, the old manners and the old friends. Wealth had nothing to do with social position. It was

an accident; the worth of the man and the woman was
the test of merit. The woman who "kept a girl," in the
phrase of the day, had no call to look down upon her
neighbors who did not, for these were in the great majority. The tastes of the community frowned down any
attempt at ostentation, and even the family which first
ventured upon the use of a two-horse carriage or barouche
gained nothing in the esteem of their friends from that
appendage. The majority of the people owned their own
houses, with more or less ground, in which there was
usually a garden and fruit trees that contributed to the
family living, assisted often by the ownership of a cow,
a pig and chickens. A thousand dollars a year was a
large salary or income. One of our prominent citizens
tells how he overheard some well-to-do business men
talking about the salary of the president of the State
Bank, $1500, and characterizing it as "princely," and one
of the boys of his class, sixteen or seventeen years old,
said "no wonder his boys can have their boots blacked
for them." Hundreds of families lived well and educated
their children, sometimes sending them to college, where
the income was not nearly $1000. As late as 1861 the
bookkeeper of the Journal, a thoroughly competent man,
had a salary of $500 a year and supported a family of
five or six persons and maintained a respectable position.
This was true of many families, and can be explained in
comparison with our ideas of living by the fact that their
extraneous wants were few. Food, shelter, clothing,
taxes, something for the church and sometimes for the
doctor, being provided, there was little else to call for
money. People did not travel except in rare emergencies,
many never. Such things as vacations were unknown.
There were no street-cars or daily sodas, no matinees,
indeed few amusements of any kind, no lunching down

town, no clubs and dues, no secret societies except the
Masons and Odd Fellows, no array of charities with their
insistent needs, no costly entertaining, no many things
we have now clamorously calling for the dimes and dollars. Then, too, the necessities of life were cheap as a
rule, meat, bread, vegetables, fuel. Wood was universally used except in stores and schoolhouses, where
coal from Clay county was generally burned after 1853
or 1854. Clothing was probably not so cheap, but nearly
all clothes were made at home or by women, and the
chief cost was for the material.

The houses were well furnished with substantial things,
but there was a notable lack of ornaments and bric-a-brac.
A whatnot with some seashells and daguerreotypes on it,
a center table with a family Bible and a lamp on it, an
occasional candelabra with glass pendants, some artificial
flowers and a plaster cast, a vase or two perhaps, a half-
dozen haircloth chairs, a sofa and an occasional piano,
constituted the array of a well-furnished parlor, which
was a sacred place not to be opened every day to ordinary
persons. People did not live in their parlors, but in the
"sitting room," which sometimes was the dining room as
well, and (let it be whispered low), there were some
ostensibly reputable people who even ate in the kitchen.
There were no bathrooms or toilet facilities. The first
plumber came here in 1853 to work on the Bates House,
but it was not till five or six years later that a bathroom
was installed in a residence, that of Mr. Vajen on South
Meridian street. There were no waterworks; water had
to be pumped for such use and heated on a stove. Daily
baths were unknown in practice and in theory regarded
as the luxury of an effete people, while cleanliness was
preserved by a weekly bath in a washtub. Only the
houses of the very richest were lighted by gas, which

was also used in the larger churches and stores. The ordinary light was from candles and lard oil lamps, followed by camphene, an explosive distillation from turpentine that made a beautiful light but was dangerous to use. This was succeeded in 1856 or '57 by coal oil—not petroleum, but an oil distilled from coal, which was driven out by the discovery and utilization of petroleum in the early years of the war. The houses were poorly warmed as a rule. Furnaces were known, but were not common. Despite the abundance of wood, most people heated only the living rooms, fires being made in bedrooms only for visitors, sick or old people, while the halls were always left in natural frigidity. Carriages, buggies and spring wagons were not uncommon, but the man of the house or his boys took care of the horse. A "hired man" was a curiosity.

Necessarily, the making of the living was the chief thing. There were not many who could live on accumulated wealth. It was a working community, and the work was often hard and the hours long. Stores were opened by six o'clock generally, sometimes before. Mr. Vajen tells of opening his hardware store never later than five o'clock, and as a rule none closed before nine. Factories and mechanics began work at seven and quit at six, with an hour's intermission at noon. Doctors, lawyers and public officials were at work early, and the banks ran from eight to four. Everybody ate dinner at noon and shuddered at the idea of kings and noblemen eating dinner after dark. Dinner as a function was unknown. Supper was the great social manifestation of hospitality. Dinner was just for the family eating, except sometimes on a Sunday there was leisure to entertain a passing guest. But supper was the meal to invite one's friends to. It was then that the tables groaned with the good things the housewife could provide. Fried chicken, quails, oysters, ducks, ham, cheese, tongue, jellies, preserves, pickles, custards, cakes and even pies enriched the larder, with tea and coffee as beverages. Ice cream was unknown except as bought and eaten in the ice cream saloons or parlors and at church festivals, and its purchase was a sort of a wild dissipation on summer nights to be eagerly anticipated and joyfully remembered.

The church social was a great event. Sometimes the gatherings took place at the church, but usually at a private house. It was under the auspices of the sewing society. The ladies met in the afternoon and sewed for some worthy cause. In the evening the men came and the young people, and a substantial supper, not "mere refreshments," was served, provided by the hostess. Every two or three weeks in the winter season was the rule in some churches, but it was not confined to that season, though not held so often in others. The church festival was more uncommon and entirely different. That was a commercial enterprise for the benefit of the church itself. The refreshments were partly contributed, partly bought, as when the entertainment was called an oyster supper and an admission fee charged. Sometimes this was large enough to include the supper, and sometimes it did not, which was not favorably regarded by some of the attendants. Sometimes articles of fancy work were for sale, and always there was ice cream as an extra at "ten cents a saucer." In some churches there were "donation parties," where a body of friends would swoop down upon the home of the pastor and present gifts, and eat the supper they had brought with them. This function was the source of mirth to the humorist of the day, as were also church festivals and oyster suppers. It was said that the guests frequently ate up the presents of food they brought, that the minister was always the poorer, and that a donation party was as bad as a fire. This was an exaggeration, for usually the occasion abounded in good fellowship, kindly remembrance and real benefit, and enriched the social life of the organization.

CHAPTER II.

RELIGION AND POLITICS.

Next to making a living, the two most engrossing and vital things in Indianapolis before the war were religion and politics. It was a day of serious things. The light and trifling manner in which many people view the affairs and influences of life now was not in favor then. The town had been under the influence of earnest people from its start, people who worked and suffered and to whom life was no merry jest. To them religion was a solemn matter, and even those who cared little for it or made no professions were bound to respect it. The whole tone of the place was religious. There were numerous churches of various sects, but probably no place in the country ever had less of the bitter, sectarian feeling that existed widely and that we wonder at now. The churches here, with few exceptions, were friendly. The ministers and members fellowshipped and united in movements for the common good, just as they do now. The Sabbath school parade on the Fourth of July, the event of that day for over thirty years, was evidence of this, possibly a contributing cause. The Episcopalians and Catholics were the exceptions, the latter naturally enough, for the bitterness of the reformation was still in evidence against papacy, and almost every preacher felt bound to launch a thunderbolt against Rome, "that terrible menace to the Republic," at least once a year. It was natural then that the Catholics should assume the historic attitude of the church against "heretics," but the Episcopalians had no such reason for exclusiveness. In the famous celebrations of the Fourth the Catholic children actually joined once or twice, but the Episcopalians never, and thereby their children missed a lot of fun and a good lesson in toleration.

The thought of the day was altogether orthodox, and orthodox on the lines laid down two hundred years before. The preaching to a considerable degree was still doctrinal if not dogmatic. There was a fixity of opinion. There were no doubts of the fundamental truths of Christianity, no suspicion even that the Bible as a whole was not inspired in the fullest sense. Moreover, criticism was undreamed of in the church, though of course the opinions of Voltaire and Paine and Volney were known, and these were regarded as fearful examples of depravity of whose punishment there could be no doubt. Few disbelieved in hell, as an actual place of unspeakable and inconceivable torture of lost souls, and a depiction of its awful realities and the danger of the sinner who neglected or refused to be reconciled to God, was a fruitful theme for many agonizing sermons, especially at "times of revival." There has been as great a change in the past forty years in the attitude of people toward religion as in any other line of thought, and while the old truths may be as true as ever, they are viewed from another point and often present a different appearance. The pendulum has swung away, and different doctrines or different aspects of doctrines are emphasized now than were then. Religion has lost much of its somberness, its harshness has been smoothed down, its more pleasing features are accentuated, and it makes its most powerful plea for the Christian life through love and aspiration for the good, and not by words of fear or the hope of reward. It no longer differentiates or intimates a severance of this life from the life to come. It is one indivisible whole.

Religion was a main factor in the life of Indianapolis, and that not only as governing the moral conduct of the

people but their social relations. Church-going was
proper, reputable and fashionable, whether people were
members or not. It was a custom that must be observed
by all who wished to stand well with their neighbors.
One's chief friends and associates were usually in the
church attended, and almost the first question about new-
comers was, "What church will they go to?" Particular
churches were often chosen because of their attractive-
ness in this respect. Of course, the social life was not
confined to any one church for most people. There was
another and possibly larger circle outside, made up from
other churches, but one's own church was the center of
the whole fabric.

The ministers, too, were more influential then than
now, but no abler or wiser, though Indianapolis had some
preachers of marked ability in that period. The church
was more of an intellectual force then. Books and periodicals were comparatively few. The minister was
usually better educated than his flock, and he spoke with
more intellectual authority. To-day his hearers are more
nearly on a plane with him, and his utterances are judged
more freely. The democratic spirit tending often toward
lack of reverence is nowhere more apparent than in this.
From this and other causes is due the passing of the
church discipline. It is obsolete. There is a looseness
in the ties, a feeling of independence that will not brook
admonition and is indifferent to the bell, book and candle.
In that day discipline was a powerful thing. Business
differences were brought before church tribunals. Members were dealt with for breaches of rules and faithless-
ness to their vows as well as for sinfulness, and the penalties of suspension or expulsion were dreaded. They
brought disgrace and shame, as well as spiritual suffering.
Whether the change has been beneficial or not, time will

tell. There is a strong reason to believe that this relaxation of bonds has caused deterioration in Christian life.

Under the conditions, there was necessarily a strict observance of Sunday, both in home life and business. Among the more rigid the line was closely drawn between secular and Sunday pursuits. Reading was confined to certain channels, riding and visiting were tabooed, even walking for the walk's sake was not regarded favorably. On Sundays the business establishments were shut, except possibly some of the saloons that kept a back door unlocked. The people went to church morning and night, and many to Sunday-school besides. The latter was always held in the afternoon. Almost every principal church had a bell to call the worshipers together. Those who did not go to church remained at home, and the streets were almost deserted except for the church-goers.

The attitude of the church toward amusements was pronounced and is now regarded as severe. Theater-going, dancing and card-playing were prohibited, and many thought them as evil as drunkenness. Circuses were an abomination of wickedness, although there was a modification for the menagerie, which was considered as useful and educative. In 1859 a principal charity, the orphan asylum, was tendered a benefit by the manager of the Metropolitan theater. A part of the board was anxious to accept, but another part was horrified at the idea of taking "tainted money." A fierce contest ensued with general discussion, both private and public, but in the end the benefit was declined. A large number of the "rising generation" therefore grew up ignorant of cards and dancing, though some attained more or less knowledge in ways they did not advertise in the newspapers and sometimes became the subjects of ecclesiastical discipline.

Boys may have had as good times in other places as

in Indianapolis, but none better. The town was large enough to have advantages over smaller ones or villages, but not large enough to forbid contact with the country and rural life. There were plenty of good swimming holes in the river and canal, in Fall creek and Pogue's run. There were equally good places for fishing. The town was surrounded by woods that afforded plenty of opportunities for hunting rabbits, squirrels and birds. There were visits of wild pigeons, making sport easy and delightful. The woods, too, were full of nut-bearing trees, from which a winter's supply could be had, pawpaws, berries, haws, etc. In the winter there was ice on the streams, and, as few streets were improved, there were many ponds all over the town where boys could slide and skate. It was not until during the war that girls took to skating. There were so many vacant lots and commons that there never was a loss for a playground at the proper seasons. Nowadays one must go for miles to meet most of these things, and some are impossible to get at all, while the streets are the playgrounds. As fond memory recalls those events and scenes of boyhood days, it seems to have been "just the best" place to have grown up in.

Probably there was as much regard for fashion in those days as now, but boys are not expected to notice such things. The headgear and dresses of the day look very queer now in old pictures, though well enough then, crinoline or hoops, for instance, arraying the form divine until it looked like a balloon. It seems to me that colors were worn more and were more striking, but that may be a fancy, or a difference in fabrics. Then calicoes, delaines, muslins and prints of various sorts were in great favor, with leghorn straw hats gaily beribboned. There were no uniforms except those of the military companies, which must seem strange to this generation accustomed to the liveries of policemen, railway employes, letter carriers, coachmen and porters. Some of the old fashions prevailed with both sexes. Some oldish men clung to the blue swallow-tail coat with brass buttons and buff vests, usually accompanied by a gold- or silver-headed cane. Tall silk hats or "plugs" were in every-day use; no derby or other stiff one was known. The only alternative was a soft hat or a straw in summer. A few ruffled shirts survived, and the gentleman done up in this fashion was a pretty sight. In winter men wore shawls almost altogether, though occasionally an old-fashioned cloak appeared. Some disposed to be more stylish wore a fur collar, and the furs of the women were long, reaching around the shoulders and to within eighteen inches of the ground. Every boy and man wore boots in the winter. I mean what are called long boots now, and which passed out of use here over thirty years ago when the streets had been paved and cleaned, so that there was no use for them. In the earlier times, however, there was deep snow sometimes, and almost always depths of mud to be waded through so that their use was necessary. Consequent upon them was the bootjack, an implement as necessary to a house as a frying-pan, but whose use none of the moderns could guess now. Shawls, too, were worn almost universally by the women. They were of all grades and price, from the serviceable woolens to the costly crepes and Indias.

Manners were more formal in those days. This was reflected among the young people. Unless they were cousins, boys of twelve or over always addressed the girls as miss and in reply were called mister. There was no such familiarity as to-day, when young people of all ages call each other by their first names after they have been acquainted a month or even less. Neither did the young fellows take the girls' arm when walking. The young lady was then set upon a pedestal, now she is on a level.

The second great interest in Indianapolis life was politics, and to many it was the most absorbing one. Public life offered prizes in that day of limited opportunity and scarce money, and beyond the pecuniary reward was the distinction achieved. Candidates were perhaps more numerous then than now. The community was pretty equally divided. The majority of the leading people were Whigs and Republicans, but a very considerable minority were Democrats, and the contests were sharp and close with varying results. Politics was the great subject for talk and was broached on all occasions. There was intense partisan feeling and much bitterness evolved. Men of one stripe would believe anything of men on the other side. The Democrats having opposed prohibition—"Old Sumptuary" even then was a household term"—were denounced by their adversaries as a party of whisky-drinkers, and the charge was believed by the makers. When the slavery question became prominent, the Democrats denounced the opposition as "nigger lovers" and Black Republicans, a name clung to until after the war. Everything of a political nature was fought for and over. A race for constable or councilman was contested as if it were the Presidency itself. Wherever a chance for spoils came it was seized greedily. The Democrats were in power at the time of the Mexican War and apparently used all their power for party benefit, keeping the Whigs out as much as possible. When the Republicans got on top they played much the same game. Party advantage was always looked after and party discipline was very strict and well enforced. This led to a faith in parties that was almost absolute, and blinded men's eyes to the truth. It created such a conceit that men considered their parties infallible, their welfare more important than that of the government itself. Indeed, myriads of Democrats believed that their party alone was fit to manage the government, and this partisan belief later led them into opposition to the war and sympathy with the South. There was more or less corruption in the elections, chiefly in crude methods of repeating and cheating in the returns, but this was done in party enthusiasm with the motto "fight the devil with fire," and, whether better or worse, was not on the sordid basis of buying and selling votes. "Anything to beat the enemy" was another motto, and all sorts of trickery, cheap debate and withering denunciation was indulged in on any and every occasion.

There was, however, one good thing in politics then. Men hated to be taxed. Money came hardly, and representatives and officials were held to strict accountability for expenditures. Economy was universally demanded and the tax-payers were a force to be reckoned with. Once in a long while you now see a card in the paper, signed "Tax-payer," condemning extravagance somewhere or somehow. This belated wanderer crying to a generation of which two-thirds are not tax-payers and gladly vote other people's money away, is a survival of that period and does not know that he is as extinct as the great auk. But once he was a "live wire," and the politicians feared and courted him, and his words had weight. Possibly in some far distant future, when taxation has ground the people down and their eyes are opened, the tax-payer again may have something to say.

The culmination of the political battles came in 1860, when the Democracy was divided and the Republicans

triumphed over all. The vote in Indiana is worth remembering:

Lincoln	139,033
Douglas	115,509
Breckenridge	12,295
Bell	5,306

Breckenridge was the candidate of the extreme Southern wing, but, notwithstanding his small vote, it was
that faction that later on became the representative Democratic party, the tail that wagged the dog.

The newspapers of the day were political organs
mainly. Judged by the present standards, they did not
know news when they saw it. Their columns were filled
with political disquisitions, discussions and speeches.
Politics, politics without end. Outside of the advertisements the insight they give into the life of the day
is very meager, and the reader would think that only one
thing engrossed the attention of the people. Their tone
was coarse, boastful and provincial, exhibiting the character that Dickens broadly caricatured in Colonel Diver,
editor of the "New York Rowdy Journal," and Jefferson
Brick, his war correspondent, who made the courts of
Europe tremble. The tone was that of a new country,
self-centered, proud of its achievements and avid of
recognition, lacking perspective and culture.

In 1860 Indianapolis showed a population of over
18,000 and considered itself quite a city. It was making
way fast. Dreams were being realized. Beyond the
lines of the mile square dwellings had extended in almost
every direction, though probably 80 per cent. lived between those boundaries. The lots were still large and
many unbuilt on. There were whole squares even with
no houses or only one on them. Washington street

embraced practically all the business district, though
there were some manifestations about the old Madison
and Union depots. There were but six drug stores and
less than a half-dozen wholesalers. Many people still
lived on Washington street. There were some four-
story buildings, chiefly the hotels, of which the Bates and
Palmer houses were the principal ones. The streets as
a rule were unimproved or coated with gravel which
was taken from pits dug in the streets themselves.
Washington street for some part was bowldered, the
only permanent improvement known or available. Its
sidewalks were bricked, as were parts of some other principal streets, but usually the sidewalks were simply
gravelled. In consequence, mud abounded after any wet
or thawing weather. Only the streets about the center
were lighted. Residences were numerous south of Washington street in what has long since been a business district, and some of the best in the city were among them.
The most really citified property of the municipality was
the steam fire department, which had become a paid one
the year before, and which was the pride of the town as
well as a vast improvement upon the old volunteer one.
Meetings were still announced to take place at early
candle lighting, and ten o'clock found the town wrapped
in silence. The theater was an exception, but even that
began at 7:30.

Business had increased greatly in the decade and establishments had multiplied. Rents had mounted. In 1851
Mr. Vajen started a hardware store where the Saks building is now, and paid the highest rent known for a room
on Washington street, $400 per year. In ten years it
was worth $1000 probably. In 1860 the Branch Bank
of the State paid $1200 a year for the Yohn corner on
Meridian street. Probably there was not a foot of

ground worth $250. The people were more hopeful and energetic than ever before. The town was the largest and most important in the State, a great railroad center, and its future seemed assured along the lines laid down. Such, in brief, was the old town when the tocsin of war sounded and brought in a new era.

CHAPTER III.

The First Year of the Struggle.

The election of Lincoln had been preceded by threats of secession, but these met with utter incredulity. They were considered as ante-election bluffs. Every one believed the South would accept the situation after a little blustering. The Republicans were not abolitionists. Their contention was that slavery should not be extended, and the far-seeing ones who agreed with Lincoln, that the government could not exist half slave and half free, were few indeed in comparison with the mass who were contented to let slavery keep what it had. The Republicans had condemned Brown's raid the year before, and they had no sympathy with Garrison, Phillips and abolitionists generally. In these later days it has been claimed in many obituary notices that their subjects were original abolitionists. If they had been, the South would have been correct in the charge that the Republican party was an abolition party, but the fact is that most of the abolitionists were made such by the necessities of the war. Wendell Phillips was egged in Cincinnati in 1862 for an abolition speech. After the election the "fire-eaters," as they were called. proceeded to carry their threats into speedy operation. South Carolina seceded, followed by other States. The national forts and property were seized when possible, and the administration offered no hindrances if it did not abet the movement. Even when the Confederacy was organized and the country was rushing on to war, the Northern people believed it would be averted and did nothing but talk and agree to certain peace conferences that might hit upon a compromise.

Still, there was some war talk in Indianapolis that winter. One faction of the Republican party, headed by Governor Morton, spoke for coercion, another, led by the Journal, thought it unnecessary and was almost ready for "peace at any price." On January 7th, 1861, the Zouave Guards, a recently organized military company, offered its services to the Governor in case of war. On the 22d the flag was publicly raised on the State House dome after a procession of the military and fire department in the presence of a vast concourse; a salute was fired and Caroline Richings, a popular actress, sang "The Star-Spangled Banner" and aroused great enthusiasm. February 12th Mr. Lincoln came on his way to Washington, the first President-elect to visit here, and that was one of the great days of the town. What he said was not much, but it inspired confidence that there would be no yielding without a struggle. He was inaugurated, but the rush of office-seekers almost obscured the condition of the country and the rising Confederacy.

Within two months, April 12th, the blow fell with the attack on Ft. Sumter. Sentiment crystallized in a flash. War had come unprovoked. The flag had been fired on and humiliated by defeat. There was but one voice—sustain the government and put down the rebellion. The 13th day of April was another great day in Indianapolis, the greatest it had yet seen; and probably it has never been surpassed in the intense interest, anxiety and enthusiasm exhibited. Never were its people so aroused. It was Saturday. Business was practically forgotten; the streets were crowded; the newspaper neighborhoods were thronged; a deep solemnity was over all as they waited to hear the news, or discussed in low tones the crisis that was upon them. In the afternoon dodgers were issued calling for a public meeting at the Court-house at seven o'clock. Before the time the little room was packed. Ebenezer Dumont, a Democrat who had been an officer in the Mexican war, was made chairman, and immediately a motion was made to adjourn to the Metropolitan theater. The crowd, constantly augmenting, hurried down Washington street to the theater, which was soon filled to overflowing. Then Masonic Hall, across the street, was opened and filled, with hundreds standing in the streets. The meetings were full of the war spirit. Governor Morton and others spoke. Patriotic resolutions were adopted declaring in favor of armed resistance. Major Gordon announced that he would organize a flying artillery company, for which Governor Morton had already secured six guns, and forty-five men enrolled their names for the war. At the close the surrender of Ft. Sumter was announced, and the meetings dispersed in deep gloom but with firm purpose.

Sunday was little observed in the usual way. There was no demonstration of excitement but great seriousness, for hundreds were pondering over the future and their possible part in it. The Journal published an extra with an account of the meetings Saturday night. The next day recruiting offices were opened, the military companies volunteered in large part; volunteers were offered from many other places; and on Wednesday, the 17th, the first troops went into Camp Morton, then the new fair grounds, covering the site of Morton Place. Then they poured in by thousands from town and country, some with flags, some with fife and drums or brass band; the streets were alive with them. It is beyond my power to give any adequate idea of those days with the hurry and bustle, the innumerable details of the swift preparations, the deepening feeling and the continued excitement.

The Journal of the 16th reports it in a way as follows: "There is but one feeling in Indiana. We are no longer Republicans or Democrats. Never did party names lose their significance so rapidly or completely as since the news of Saturday. Parties are forgotten and only our common danger is remembered. Here and there inveterate sympathizers with Southern institutions and feelings scowl and curse the mighty tempest of patriotism they dare not encounter; but they are few, as pitiful in strength as in spirit. Even the Sentinel now avows its devotion to the stars and stripes, and gives us some cause to modify if not recall the harsh censures we expressed yesterday. Our streets are blazing with national flags. Huge banners wave from the tops of houses and hundreds of flags flutter in windows and along the walks. The drum and fife are sounding the whole day long at Military Hall, where volunteers are pouring in to record their names and enter the service of their country; and crowds are gathered constantly around the doors of Colonel Dumont's station, where he is enlisting volunteers for a regiment of picked men. Though the news of the fight has as yet only reached towns along the lines of railroads, and no official or other notice has been published that the service of volunteers would be needed, two thousand men, regularly organized and ready to start at the word, have already been tendered to Governor Morton, and more than twenty thousand are forming with eager haste to be in time for acceptance. By the time the news can be thoroughly circulated through the State that men are needed, there will be more than fifty thousand officered and ready. In the full spirit of the times Governor Morton has sunk party distinctions, and yesterday appointed to the important post of Adjutant General of the State, Captain Lewis Wallace, of Montgomery county, a prominent Democrat and widely known for his military zeal and skill. Lewis H. Sands, of Putnam, another Democrat devoted to his country, has been appointed colonel. There will be no more Republicans or Democrats hereafter till the country is at peace."

A vain prediction was this. The Sentinel, though for the moment cowed into half-hearted approval of the war, soon reverted to the denunciation of the administration, and the battles of opposing politics were as many and as fierce as those of the armies before the country was at peace.

There had been a lull in military spirit after the Mexican War, and Indianapolis had no permanent company for a decade. The City Guards were organized in 1852, with Governor Wallace as captain, and the Mechanic Rifles in 1853, but both soon went to pieces. A visit of the St. Louis Guards to the city in 1856 aroused the dormant sentiment, and the National Guards were organized, with General W. J. Elliott as captain. They were uniformed in blue, with caps bearing white plumes. Some dissensions arose, and in 1857 General Elliott organized the City Greys, who wore grey uniforms and bear-skin shakos. These were the only permanent companies until 1860, when a visit from Lew Wallace's Montgomery Guards, who were Zouaves, and drilled by drum beat, wakened new ambitions. The Independent Zouaves were then organized, on the same basis, with Francis A. Shoup as captain; and these three Indianapolis companies, with the Montgomery Guards and two Terre Haute companies, held a State encampment at the fair grounds (Military Park) the week beginning September 19th. In October, 1860, the Zouave Guards were organized, with John Fahnestock as captain. They were gorgeous, in blue jackets with gold lace, baggy scarlet trousers to the knee, orange leggings and shirts, white belts, and rimless scarlet caps with tassels. They also made the record of being the first company to tender services to the Governor for any duty that might arise.[1]

These four companies went out in the Eleventh regiment in the three months' service. The Greys were Co. A, with R. S. Foster, captain; George Butler, first lieutenant, and Joseph H. Livesey, second lieutenant. The Zouave Guards were Co. B, with John Fahnestock, captain; Orin S. Fahnestock, first lieutenant, and Daniel B. Culley, second lieutenant. The Independent Zouaves were Co. E, with Dewitt C. Rugg, captain; Henry Tindall, first lieutenant, and Nicholas Ruckle, second lieutenant. The National Guards were Co. K, with William Darnall, captain; John McLaughlin, first lieutenant, and William Dawson, second lieutenant. There was one other Indianapolis company in the Eleventh, Co. H, which was organized in the spring of 1861, with W. J. H. Robinson, captain; Fred Knefler, first lieutenant, and Wallace Foster, second lieutenant. The Eleventh was a Zouave regiment, but with very mild uniforms of a greyish cloth resembling blue jeans, not made very full, and with very little color in the trimmings.

The Independent Zouaves went out a trifle warmer than the others. Their original captain, Francis A. Shoup, was a West Pointer who had served in the artillery in the regular army, and held the rank of second lieutenant when he resigned on January 10th, 1860, and located at Indianapolis. He was a good-looking fellow, quite talented, and a fine drill-master. The boys esteemed him highly, and at a company meeting in the

---

[1] Journal, January 8, 1861.

winter of 1860-'61, at which patriotic speeches were made by several, including Shoup, they presented him a pair of revolvers with holsters and trappings, being under the impression that the officers would ride, in the event of war. That night he went South, and it was soon rumored that he had gone to stay. There was a meeting of the company, and Volney T. Malott was delegated to correspond with him and learn his intentions. Shoup, who was then visiting Captain Hood—later General Hood—at Charleston, promptly replied that he had decided to cast his fortunes with the South in the event of war. The meeting at which this answer was read was an occasion for "thoughts that breathe and words that burn." The idea that a native Hoosier, educated by the government and sent to West Point, from Wayne county at that, should go over to the South, was simply appalling. However, there was nothing in the papers about it except mention that Shoup had resigned, and Lieutenant Dewitt C. Rugg had been elected captain in his place.[1]

Shoup fared very well with his Southern friends. He was a major in 1861, commanding three batteries of artillery, and was made brigadier-general April 11th, 1863. He was in command of the artillery at Mobile, chief of artillery of Johnston's army in the Dalton campaign, and chief of staff under General Hood at Atlanta. When Vicksburg was captured, he was commanding a Louisiana brigade there, under Pemberton. Just after the capitulation, a private of the Eleventh Indiana saw a gorgeously attired Confederate officer approaching our lines on horseback, and recognized Shoup. With a yell of, "Get off that horse, Frank Shoup, you — — —!" he

---

[1] *Journal*, January 30, 1861.

made for a stand of arms near by, but was stopped by
an officer before anything serious occurred. In reply to
the officer's question as to what he wanted, Shoup explained that he understood that the Eleventh Indiana
was in his front, and he had come out to see some of his
old friends. "Well," replied the officer, "you have seen
a specimen of what the Eleventh Indiana thinks of you.
You had better get back to your quarters at once; and
I would advise you to dispose of those side-arms at your
earliest convenience." Shoup was paroled, with Pemberton and others, and a few weeks later the Confederate
exchange agent announced them as "exchanged," authorizing an equal exchange of paroled Union men; they
then resumed their service. After the war Shoup entered the ministry of the Episcopal Church.

Human nature soon adjusts itself to extraordinary
conditions. The town settled down and resumed its
life, with the great new interest of the war. The six
regiments that were called for to serve three months
were quickly filled to overflowing. The Eleventh was
the pride of Indianapolis. This was the Zouave regiment, organized and commanded by Lew Wallace, into
which went the four militia companies of Indianapolis
and one other. It not only wore the Zouave uniform,
and had guns with sword bayonets, but the drill was the
Zouave system, introduced into this country from France
by Colonel Ellsworth of Chicago. It was a picturesque
body, and its colonel was a picturesque figure. Who
that witnessed it can ever forget how, when the regiment was gathered in the State House yard to receive a
stand of colors from the ladies of Indiana, he made the
men kneel and with uplifted hands swear to remember
Buena Vista and the stigma put upon Indiana valor on
that field by Jefferson Davis? What hopes animated

and followed these departing troops! How hearts were sorely tried and bereft as their boys marched away to face the unknown and perilous future! For they were but boys in the main, as we realize now, but they were men in purpose, and courage, and deeds.

Six regiments of State troops were called for by the Governor and these were soon filled and accepted by the general government for twelve months and three years. The whole State was awake. Governor Morton called a special session of the Legislature to provide means for the war. The ladies met and formed an aid society, composed of branches from each ward, to make shirts and other garments and havelocks, a head protection modeled on the sunbonnet and borrowed from the British Indian army—an article in great request at first, but it was never liked by the soldiers, and soon disappeared from public mention. The Journal issued an extra every afternoon. The City Council voted $10,000 for the soldiers' families. Some railroads offered to carry troops free. Banks gave money. Gifts were showered on soldiers. There was eagerness to get into the service before the war could be finished. A man ninety-two years old enlisted; another shaved his beard and dyed his hair to pass muster. Home guards were organized in the wards, among them the Silver Grays, composed of men above military age, captained by James Blake, seventy years young, and with Caleb Scudder as president.

Illustrative of journalism was this item in the Journal on April 23d: "Erratum. In Mr. Hyde's sermon as printed in our extra of yesterday there were two misprints which every intelligent reader corrected for himself. In the first sentence Kingdom of Israel should read Kingdom of Saul; and in the seventh paragraph peaceable resistance should read forcible resistance."

The Legislature met on the 24th and all was amity.
It organized by a unanimous election of officers, the
only instance in the State's history, probably, and then
adjourned to visit Camp Morton and hear Stephen A.
Douglas speak, which he did not; but he did speak that
night from the Bates House veranda, of which no mention was made by the papers, when he again took his
stand on the side of the Union and in support of the
administration, an act of inestimable value to the cause.
Within a few days he was dead.

The Eleventh was sent to Evansville to quell possible
disturbances on the border, but the remaining regiments
were reviewed by General McClellan, Governors Yates
of Illinois, Dennison of Ohio, and Morton and Senator
Trumbull on May 24th, on the commons northwest of
Military Park, then Camp Sullivan. Three regiments
were in full uniform, one had everything but hats, and
one had nothing military, but all made a gallant appearance. It was the first time that Indianapolis had seen so
many soldiers together and it was witnessed with great
enthusiasm. It was the first of many such displays.
The work of equipping these men was necessarily slow.
It took time to make uniforms, and longer time to procure arms and ammunition, much of which was imported. It may be of interest to know what the uniforms
cost. Two regiments were clothed in cadet satinet, cost-
ing $7.90 each, one in jeans at $6.50 and another at $7.50;
the fifth of gray satinet at $6.75 and the Zouaves at $10
each. Flannel shirts cost $1.40, hats $1.25, and shoes
$1.15. While waiting, the troops were drilled constantly,
but it was not until June 19th that the last of the three
months' regiments left for the seat of war. After this
more regiments were called for, recruited and mustered,
with two or three independent cavalry companies and a

number of artillery companies, and later full cavalry regiments. A number of these never came here, but some passed through or camped here for a few days. There was a German regiment, an Irish regiment formed and a second projected, a railroad regiment, a mechanics' regiment, and a preachers' regiment, the field officers and captains of which were to be ministers, a scheme not fully carried out. Altogether fifty-eight regiments were authorized during 1861, although about half a dozen were never completed. Besides these many Indianians had gone into the regular army and into outside companies that recruited here, until the State authorities put a stop to it. It was a tremendous achievement to raise an army of over fifty thousand men in less than nine months. Indianapolis contributed a number of companies to various regiments; and in almost every regiment there was some representative of the town. It was also true that many citizens of other places came here and enlisted.

A very important event was the return of three months' troops in August. They had not had much war. as war appeared later; but they had done all that was in their power to do, and had borne themselves gallantly. Each regiment received an ovation of salutes, speeches, feasting at the west market-house, and a heartfelt welcome. Each man was a hero, and nothing was too good for him. All these regiments reorganized for three years. Many of the men became officers in the new regiments, many new men were recruited, and before sixty days they were off to the war again.

The raising and drilling of troops was no more important than equipping them, for there was difficulty in obtaining arms, ammunition or accoutrements. On February 1st, 1861, the State's supply of arms in possession of the State's quartermaster were "505 muskets, worthless and incapable of being repaired; 54 flint lock Yager rifles, which could be altered at $2 each to percussion locks; 40 serviceable muskets in the hands of military companies at Indianapolis, which could be returned at once; 80 muskets with accoutrements in store; 13 artillery musketoons; 75 holster pistols; 26 Sharpe's rifles; 20 Colt's navy pistols; 2 boxes of cavalry sabres; 1 box powder flasks; 3 boxes accoutrements."[1]

There were also estimated to be 600 muskets in fair condition, distributed among 15 militia companies in the State. The State was entitled to 488 muskets from the national government on its 1861 quota, and Governor Morton took in place of them a 6-pounder cannon and 350 minie rifles with bayonets. On April 27th Calvin Fletcher was commissioned to learn what could be obtained from manufactories of arms in the United States, and later Miles J. Fletcher was sent on the same mission, but they found practically nothing available. On May 30th Robert Dale Owen was commissioned to purchase arms to the extent of 6000 rifles and 1000 carbines in this country or in Europe, and this order was from time to time enlarged. To the close of his service on February 6th, 1863, he purchased 30,000 Enfield rifles, 2731 carbines, 751 revolvers, and 797 sabres, at a cost of $752,-694.75; besides expending $3905 for cavalry equipments, $50,407 for blankets, and $84,829 for overcoats. His total bill for services and expenses for twenty months employed in this service was $3452.[2]

Ammunition was almost impossible to obtain, and Morton, who balked at no obstacle, determined to try making it. Captain Herman Sturm, who had learned the business in Europe, was put in charge of the ex-

1 Terrell's Report, Vol. I, p. 428.
2 Terrell, Vol. I, pp. 433-5.

periment in rented quarters on the square south of the
State House, with a blacksmith's forge for melting lead,
a room for making cartridges, and a detail of men from
the Eleventh regiment to do the work. The work was a
success, and our first troops were furnished with ammunition from this source. The work was started on April
27th; and a month later Governor Morton ordered the construction of buildings for the work on the square north
of the State House—now the north half of the State
House grounds. On June 15th the Journal reported the
buildings about completed. On the north side of the
enclosure was a small brick building with furnaces for
melting lead, and room for eight men to work at mold-
ing bullets, as well as benches for swedging and perfect-
ing the bullets. Adjoining this was a room for filling
shells and preparing fuses. On the east and west sides
of the enclosure were frame buildings for making
cartridges and storing ammunition. There were soon
about one hundred women and girls employed in making
cartridges, and the institution grew steadily. In October, 1861, Secretary of War Cameron and General
Thomas visited this arsenal and inspected the work. They
recommended its continuance; and it not only supplied
most of the Indiana troops but very largely others. The
transactions of the arsenal to its close on April 18th,
1864, amounted to $788,838.45, and the State made a clear
profit from its operation of $77,457.32. As high as seven
hundred persons were employed in it at one time. In
the winter of 1861, the furniture factory of John Ott, on
West Washington street, was rented for the work, and
canister-shot and signal lights were added to the
products. In 1862, partly for safety and partly for economy, the arsenal was moved about a mile and a half
east of the State House on Washington street. In 1863

the United States purchased the tract now known as the Winona Technical Institute grounds, and began the erection of an arsenal there.

In all this time the town was feeling an acceleration of blood in every vein. Military careers opened up to many; other service to some; and business opportunities to those who remained. Money was more plentiful than ever before, and population was increasing. Even politics was not forgotten. Candidates at the election of city officers on May 3d had been nominated before the war began. A few days later "C. A. R.," in a communication to the Journal, advises that "the Republican candidates should resign in favor of a patriotic ticket or a new party," "embracing all its country's friends." "Let us all unite now and forget party till the war is over." Sound advice, that if heeded and followed up would have been of untold value, but the selfish desire for office was too great and the election was held on party lines with Republican success. Soon after two new wards were organized, but the councilmen were Democrats and they were kept out of office by the Republican majority until their terms were almost out. Such peanut politics bore bitter fruit in increasing partisan hostility. The Sentinel, though professing extreme loyalty, soon began a course of censorious criticism and opposition to the State and Federal administration that grew fiercer as the war progressed, and was terribly effective for harm to the national cause. Possibly a different attitude on the part of the Republicans might have prevented this, or at least modified it. Later in the summer the Democrats offered to withdraw their candidates for county and township officers and unite with the Republicans on a union ticket, but the offer was treated with contempt and another opportunity for conciliation lost.

Here are some interesting facts from the papers covering several months: A self-appointed vigilance committee was formed, and as early as May 4th began stopping the passage of arms to the South. There was a good deal of talk about disciplining "Secessionists." On May 3d the Journal said: "Spot Him—That Secessionist who was chased out of Lewisville, Indiana, a few days since, who had been corresponding from that place with Southern traitors, was seen in our city yesterday. He should be attended to. Later—At a citizens' meeting he was ordered to leave instanter." It was about this time that a mob called on some well-known Democrats and made them take the oath of allegiance. It is interesting to note that among the first to advertise for recruits was H. H. Dodd. His company of "Marion Dragoons" was never formed, and later he became the head of the Sons of Liberty. Within three months men began to be discharged from service for disability; officers resigned, some under compulsion; and on November 15th deserters are first mentioned, mainly from one regiment that had lost 150 men by disease in four months—a horrible commentary on the lack of camp sanitation and care of men. Regiments scarcely got to the field before they sent back recruiting officers to fill depleted ranks. An entertainment given in the fall by the Sons of Malta, exhibiting the burlesque ritual of that order, netted $682 for soldiers' families. The city marshal gave notice that he would take up all hogs that did not have rings in their noses; and every man that planted a shade tree was commended by the papers. October 10th Governor Morton appealed to the women to furnish blankets, socks, gloves, mittens, woolen shirts and drawers, and on November 23d it was announced that tons had been received and that nothing more was wanted, except gloves and mittens. This indicates something of what the women did. But for their sacrifices and support, the war would not have succeeded. They were useful in a hundred ways and at all times. In November the Ladies' Patriotic Association was organized, with Mrs. Morton as president, and glorious work it did.

In this same month the Journal says: "Two men refusing to take the oath mustering them into the U. S. service, were yesterday drummed out of one of the camps near the city. One side of their heads was shaved, bundles of straw tied to their backs, they were moved on double quick time in front of the line to the lively tune styled the Rogue's March." A notable reception was given to ex-Governor Wright on his return from Prussia. He had been the great Democratic leader of the Douglas wing, as opposed to Jesse D. Bright; but from that time forward was an ardent Union man for whom his former party had no use. It is noted that fall that many riotous acts were being committed in saloons and evil resorts by soldiers. Much more of this is heard later on.

Indianapolis might be called the birthplace of machine guns. On November 7th a Mr. Hatch, of Springfield, Ohio, exhibited a model of a breech-loading cannon, made like a revolver, with percussion caps, and firing twenty-five shots per minute. It is noted that Dr. Richard J. Gatling, the inventor of the wheat-drill and other things, was present at the trial, and later he produced the celebrated "Gatling gun," exhibiting it first on May 30th, 1862. The postoffice was moved on the 18th of November from South Meridian street to the new Federal building at Pennsylvania and Market streets. A national loan was offered, interest, 7.3%, for popular subscription, which realized after several weeks $31,235; Humphrey Griffith, the largest subscriber, taking $3000.

A review was held November 21st of 1000 cavalry, 4000 infantry and two batteries. The theater went on steadily at the Metropolitan with such actors as Felix Vincent and Marian Maccarthy, Sallie St. Clair, Adah Isaacs Menken, C. W. Couldock, J. Wilkes Booth, with a daily change of bill. Prices, reduced, were 75 cents for a gentleman and lady to the dress circle, each additional lady 25 cents. Those to the pit, or parquet as now known, and the gallery were not given. The Sentinel continued its nagging opposition. It had much to say about "niggers." Witness the following: "The Rev. Dr. Weaver. This divine, late pastor of the African church opposite the Terre Haute depot, arrived in the city a day or two ago, and, we noticed, was very cordially greeted on the street by Mr. Barton D. Jones, of the Journal, the nigger's hand being grasped warmly by the latter."

The progress of the war was not smooth in 1861. The principal battle fought, Bull Run, was a defeat, and plunged the North into gloom; but it had a valuable result in demonstrating that the war was not to be an easy task, and convincing the people of the need of thorough preparation and larger effort. In West Virginia and Missouri the Union troops met with decided success, but the conflicts were small. In October, November and December an advance was made into Kentucky with gratifying results, but no serious fighting took place. This is not the place in which to follow the general course of the war, the aim being to allude only to incidents that directly affected Indianapolis, or to those great events that stirred it as well as the whole country to either gloom or rejoicing.

CHAPTER IV.

Rapidly Moving Events.

The next year, 1862, was filled with big military events, great campaigns and huge battles, with varying fortunes, but as a rule the Federal troops were successful in the West and the Confederates in the East. The story of the year can best be given in a running recital covering all matters of interest, rather than in a consecutive narrative.

Gold had gone to a slight premium in August or September, that had run by January to a point of alarm, and a number of Eastern banks had suspended specie payments with the almost certainty that all would have to do so. Hugh McCulloch, president of the Bank of the State of Indiana, that had not suspended during the panic of '57, wrote a card to the Journal early in January in which he said: "Under no conceivable circumstances will the Bank of the State of Indiana suspend specie payments." By the last of February nearly all the branches had voted to make redemptions in legal tender notes instead of gold. Another instance of Horace Greeley's wisdom when he said "it is hard enough to tell the truth about what has been, without trying to tell what is going to be."[1]

---

[1] The bank did not suspend specie payments officially until after the Supreme Court had decided, at the May term, 1862, that it could legally do so. Its charter required the redemption of its notes "in gold or silver," but the court said: "The true interpretation of the section must be that the bank shall not refuse to redeem her bills in what Congress shall constitutionally make legal tender money. The bank can not be compelled to receive treasury notes from the citizen, in one hand, and pay to the citizen gold and silver in the other. Under this construction of the charter, the act of Congress in question does not impair its obligation regarded as a contract." (Reynolds vs. The Bank, 18 Ind., p. 467.)

The Indianapolis Horticultural Society was one of the institutions of the town. It met bi-weekly, and, as gardens were plentiful, had a good membership in which professional gentlemen were prominent. Apparently it never suspended meetings but kept right along during the whole war, discussing topics of importance. It is interesting to see that the subject in January was shade-trees; and that the silver leaf poplar was decided to be a business tree, suitable for Washington street. Complaints were made of the Circle that it was used for beating carpets and littered with straw, probably the refuse of beds or straw ticks. It had a dilapidated fence around it, but University Square, which was used by the 19th Regulars as a drill ground, had none, and the esthetic ideas of some of our aspiring citizens began to be offended.

On January 8th there was a grand review of all the troops, but singularly the Sentinel did not mention it. A public meeting to eulogize Douglas, seven months dead, was held. Robert Heller, illusionist, composer and pianist, gave an entertainment; Bayard Taylor lectured; Charles Bass played Falstaff, and Annette Ince Jennie Deans. The Underhill Block, being three-quarters of the square on which Shortridge High School stands, was platted into lots and offered for sale at $45 per foot on Pennsylvania street, except the northwest corner, which was $46.50. The southwestern quarter was occupied by the Baptist Female Seminary. The Delaware street lots were offered at $35 for inside ones, $37.50 for the northern and $45 for the southern corners. The next month a lot 30 feet front centrally located within two and a half squares of Odd Fellows' Hall was advertised at $25 per foot. A Sentinel editorial February 6th gives the Democratic opposition in a nutshell: "He who loves abolitionism hates the Constitution and the Union. There is no friend of that pernicious heresy but who is for the vigorous prosecution of the war, provided it is for the emancipation of the negro, but not to preserve the Constitution and maintain the Union as framed by the patriots of the Revolution."

The donations of clothing and bedding for the troops were so great that Quartermaster General Vajen had to advertise for applications for them from regiments, and this seemed to be unsuccessful; so, late in March they were turned over to the Sanitary Commission. This was an organization formed to look after the health and comfort of the soldiers in the field. It was a national society with a branch in each State. The one in Indiana was established in January, and of course James Blake was president and James M. Ray, secretary. There was also a Christian Commission later, on the same basis. It furnished material comforts as well as religious literature and evangelistic laborers. When the emancipated slaves became numerous, the Freedmen's Aid Society was also organized on the same plan, to look after their needs. These various societies collected large sums of money and quantities of supplies, and were of great usefulness. Indiana, however, became noted for the care taken of its soldiers. This was Governor Morton's work, and embraced not only the meeting of sudden demands after a battle, when he would secure surgeons and nurses with medicines and supplies as quickly as they could be transported, but also an unremitting attention to their health and comfort. When possible, the sick and wounded were brought home or to hospitals in the North, at Evansville and Madison for instance, where large ones had been built. Permanent agents were maintained in cities near the front and others visited troops in the field. It was the duty of some of these to receive the soldiers' money, when desired, and bring it safely home to their families. The system was executed carefully and Indiana gained the reputation of looking after its men more thoroughly than any other State, the credit for which was due to Governor Morton, who was justly named "The Soldiers' Friend."

In February the realization of what war was came near. Ft. Donaldson had been taken with many thousand prisoners. On the 22d and 23d, 2398 of them arrived here, all from Kentucky, Tennessee and Mississippi regiments. They were taken to Camp Morton and in a few days the number increased to 4000. From that time on Camp Morton was a prison. This great victory gave rise to high hopes. It was freely asserted that the backbone of the rebellion was broken. The weather was severe and the prisoners were thinly clad, and many became sick. The town rallied to their aid. Hospitals were improvised, one in the old Athenæum building at Maryland and Meridian streets, another in the old postoffice building in South Meridian, and in other places. The ladies turned out as nurses, and the best possible care was given them, as much as if they had been Union men. Humanity knew no distinction, at least not much—for it was asserted that certain Democratic ladies who had never been known to help before were very active at this time. The arrival of the prisoners created great interest. The Journal advised that "no rudeness be allowed or taunting expressions. Let us do as we would be done by." Later it reported the conduct of the people was perfectly exemplary. One young man was said to be so anxious to "see the Secesh" that he followed them to Camp Morton, and getting mixed with them was taken in and held as one till the next morning. The Sentinel called them "Secession prisoners," never rebels. A public subscription for the wounded Federals reached $5400 in three days. On February 28th men were urged to joint a new battery as it was probably the last one that would be organized in the State.

The price for the daily paper then was 12½ cents a week. There were no Sunday issues. All holidays were observed and there was no issue the next day. Train service was bad. The time to Chicago was eight hours and considered fast. News came slowly. It took ten days to find out that Pittsburg Landing was not a great victory. The Journal published many letters from regiments and was beginning to discover what news was. After the Battle of Shiloh, Berry Sulgrove, the editor of the Journal, paid a visit to the front there, and on the 29th of April wrote, among other things, this paragraph, which has more than passing interest: "Of General Grant I heard much and little to his credit. The army may know nothing of the real guilt of the late sacrifice and the real cause of the confusion that was left to arrange itself in a storm of bullets and fire, but they believe that Grant is at fault. No respect is felt for him and no confidence felt in him. I heard nobody attempt to exculpate him, and his conduct was the one topic of discussion around camp fires during my stay."

The Sentinel manifested some concern about public morals that savored more of a desire to carp and sneer than of sincere regret, for instance the following: "The Holy Sabbath—There is no Sabbath now. This is a time of war. It pains us, as indeed it must pain every other Christian gentleman, to see such open desecration of the holy day, although we suppose it is absolutely necessary now. Yesterday throughout our streets, soldiers were marching and countermarching continually. The drum and fife everywhere were heard. Companies and battalions with glittering bayonets and flaunting flags paraded under the Good God's glorious sun which He Himself with His own hand placed in the firmament all for His own honor and glory and not all for man's. President Lincoln's administration must be sustained, if we do smash the sacred day, which as innocent little boys we were taught to reverence, all to pieces. This might just as well be understood at once in heaven as it is on earth."

Real estate began to show activity. March 14th the Maxwell property (now the Fitzgerald), three lots and a good brick house, at the northeast corner of Meridian and St. Clair streets, was sold for $9000 and considered a good sale, as showing that real estate had not depreciated much on account of the war. Vacant ground within one and a half squares of the Circle was offered at $60 per foot in 50 and 100 foot lots. The papers began to talk of contemplated buildings and probable large improvements. In April John C. New bought Nos. 10 and 12 East Washington street of S. A. Fletcher, Sr., for $25,000, with the buildings that are still there. The Stewart corner at Vermont and New Jersey streets sold for $45 a foot. The council ordered some street improvements, mainly down town, which meant between Maryland and Ohio streets. The houses were renumbered to make room for more. What was 102 North Alabama street, for example, became No. 242. The low Courthouse grounds were filled up in June and so much building was done that the supply of brick ran out in the summer. On June 25th the Sentinel said: "Business in the city is brisk. Houses are not to be had. The war so far has added to our population and the business of our city." The police were first uniformed in July. Before that the only mark of their business was a silver star. The coat was dark blue with brass buttons, the trousers a light blue with a small cord along the seam, and the caps were blue, a palpable imitation of army uniforms.

At this time we catch the last effort to enforce the fugitive slave law. Two Kentuckians found a runaway slave here, who agreed to return with them to Kentucky. Friends intervened and he was taken to a lawyer's office, where he escaped or walked off. Prosecutor Fishback arrested the men on a charge of kidnapping. They were brought before Judge Perkins of the Supreme Court on a writ of habeas corpus, who released them as having done nothing contrary to law, saying that while the fugitive slave law existed it must be enforced, no matter how repugnant it might be to the people of this Nation.

On July 7th Governor Morton issued a proclamation under the President's call for 300,000 more men. Recruiting had practically ceased for some time. A dangerous apathy was growing. He urged every man "to put aside his business and come to the rescue of his country," adding, "And to the women of Indiana, let me especially appeal. * * * Emulate the virtues of the Roman mothers; urge your husbands and brothers to the field. Your influence is all-pervading and powerful. And to the lovely maiden let me say, beware of that lover who, full of health and vigor, lingers at home in inglorious ease when his country calls him to arms." In spite of this appeal enlistments were few. On Saturday, July 12th, a "grand rally" to promote them was held. Governor Morton presided and spoke, as did Colonel Dumont, William Wallace and Benjamin Harrison, the latter emphasizing his call by saying he would go himself. Money and land to be sold for money was offered by citizens to those who would volunteer in the 70th regiment, the one assigned to this district, and the meeting adjourned until Tuesday. On Monday Mr. Harrison was commissioned a second lieutenant and empowered to raise a company, which was the method used. The City Council voted to pay ten dollars per man to the first fifty and to make no more street improvements this year except those that were actually necessary for the safety of the city. The County Commissioners voted $10 each to the first five hundred men. This stimulated the work and the response was such that the camp of the regiment was established on the 22d. It was in that month that the Soldiers' Home was constructed. So many soldiers were continually passing through the city or remaining for a short time, both in bodies and individually, and for whom camps were not suitable, that it was absolutely necessary to provide a place for them. It was located on West street, south of Maryland, where there was open ground and a fine grove. Mr. George Merritt was the superintendent. At first it accommodated one hundred, but was enlarged from time to time until it could care for many more. All re-enlisting or returning regiments were fed there, and a hospital with forty beds was established. The maintenance came from the allowance for rations of the soldiers and the home more than paid its way. Somewhat later a house was rented near the depot that was used for the same purpose by the wives and children of soldiers who had to remain overnight. The provost guard had its headquarters at the home and several hundred men were in a permanent camp there for many months.

Recruiting became quite active, but it was greatly accelerated by the President's call on August 4th for 300,-

ooo more men, to be taken by draft. Men fairly fell over each other to get into the army, rather than stand the draft, and what was considered the disgrace of being drawn. The regiments filled at once for both calls, and the scenes of the fall before were re-enacted all over the State, in this, the second great enlistment period of the war. The State's quota of the 300,000 was 21,250. In the end it was filled without the draft. In August, Kentucky was invaded in great force and our troops driven back. All available forces were sent forward at once, often unequipped and all green. Many battles were fought, both East and West, and for weeks the Journal was filled with lists of casualties at Richmond, Perryville, Iuka, Corinth, Manassas and Antietam. A list of deaths of Indiana soldiers in hospitals had long before become an almost daily publication. Many prisoners were released in August, five hundred taking the oath of allegiance at one time, but the most being exchanged.

In the last half of 1862 the more interesting facts noted are as follows: There was such a dearth of change, all silver having disappeared by reason of the premium, that various merchants issued tickets for 5, 10 and 25 cents, payable in goods. The government then issued fractional currency, or "shinplasters" as it was called, in denominations from 3 to 50 cents, and these remained in circulation for years. They were counterfeited extensively even down to the ten-cent ones, but were a necessary nuisance. By this time taxes had been levied on almost everything, it seemed, but they were to be more and higher before the end. There were stamp duties, income tax, business licenses, taxes on manufactures, etc. Besides this was the tariff law, designated "an act increasing temporarily the duties on imports and for other purposes," and which filled six or seven columns of the Journal's smallest type. It was considered a terrible taxation on business and a prominent merchant said, "If that tax is levied it will make me disloyal." But that "temporary tariff" would be considered a light affair now. Shipments to Europe of Pennsylvania rock oil or petroleum to the extent of several million gallons during the first six months of 1862 caused the Journal to say: "This for a trade that is in its infancy is a large business." An event of more than usual interest was the resignation in July of Rev. Horace Stringfellow, rector of Christ Church. He was a Southern man and his sympathies were ill-concealed. Soon after the war began he was waited upon by a committee and firmly requested to pray for the administration, which he had not done before, and from time to time there were reports that he would leave. It was currently reported that his resignation was not voluntary, and that he was given a certain number of days in which to get out of town; but this was untrue, according to the statement of one of his warm friends, a lady still living here, who could not have been mistaken. He left because the situation had become unpleasant to him. He made his way to Virginia and remained there until the war was over. Frequent Union meetings were held to keep up the spirit. "In all directions new buildings are going up, convincing proof of the prosperity of the place." The custom of ringing the fire bells when a member of the department died was inaugurated and only dropped in recent years. When the man who carried the mails between the postoffice and the depot was buried, the postoffice was closed for two hours. Nothing less than the President's death would do that now. While the draft was pending men leaving the county or State had to get passes from the military authorities. The Ladies' Protective Association reported that 10,858 articles, clothing, bedding, lint, bandages, compresses, etc., had been made since October, 1861. The State Fair was held that year at the old Military grounds, but did not prove very attractive.

October 1st there was the finest review yet seen, ten thousand men of all branches of service engaging in a sham battle afterward. Christ Church was dedicated November 21st, though finished some years before. It had been planned to cost $15,000, but ran much over. Deserters began to be very numerous and rewards were offered for their arrest, eighty-six from the 51st being missing. Crime had become so prevalent, and disorder of all sorts, that the streets were not safe. A permanent provost guard was established, that patrolled the streets, watched the Union Station and other places. Somewhat later guards were placed on every train when in the station and no soldier could enter unless he had a pass. Annoyances to citizens occurred sometimes and people began to realize what military rule meant. The Council was petitioned to remove Foot's dairy on Michigan street west of Pennsylvania, and referred the request with instructions to report an ordinance forbidding dairies in the city limits. Apparently this never was done. Thanksgiving day there was another review. There were then twelve thousand men in the various camps, probably the largest number at any one time. D. J. Callinan's store, next to Fletcher's bank, was robbed of $8000 worth of goods, the record haul to that date. The court of inquiry into the conduct of General Buell began here. The owners of prominent newspapers met here and organized the Western Associated Press. Horses for the army cost $94 each for a lot of three thousand. The largest taxpayers in the county were Calvin Fletcher, assessed for

$137,155; S. A. Fletcher, $132,824; N. McCarty's heirs, $132,670; James M. Ray, $135,772. The Schnull Bros. bought the Baptist Church lot, southwest corner of Meridian and Maryland streets (the building had burned), 55x94½ feet, for $5000, also the Hasselman house adjoining (built by Mr. Vajen), for $13,700. The house and lot on West Maryland on the west side of the alley back of these properties sold for $5400, the lot being 67½ feet front by 195 deep, and the house a good two-story one of ten or twelve rooms.

The Journal was an ardent admirer of General Wallace. He had been ordered to take the field in General Grant's department of Corinth, but General Grant immediately ordered him back to Cincinnati, whereupon the Journal said on November 13th: "General Grant has been living a good while on whiskey and the reputation he made without any effort of his own at Ft. Donelson, and if he has taken on himself to defy his superiors and flout his equals, he has about exhausted the patience that has factitious honors entitle him to."

Probably few know that on account of the scarcity of cotton, an effort was made to encourage its growth in the North. The government advertised that it would furnish free seed and instruction and appointed agents who travelled through the country to persuade farmers to plant it, making all sorts of plausible statements. So far as newspaper accounts show nobody took it up seriously. Captain Oglesbey raised some in his yard, which caused the Journal to make the following extraordinary statement that probably could not be verified: "Cotton was once grown in considerable quantities in this place. When Calvin Fletcher came here (that was in 1821) there was a large field of cotton full grown on Pennsylvania street, a little south of where the Blind Asylum now stands."[1]

The general condition of the country as well as the depreciation in the value of the currency had by now vastly increased the cost of living. Prices had risen to unheard of figures and the question of living had become a very serious matter to the most of the people. Business men who were making more money than ever before might stand it, but there were scores and hundreds whose means had not increased much or were fixed. On these fell a burden that could not be lightened and they were forced to economies that often amounted to privation. Hundreds had to abandon tea and coffee and use parched rye or wheat as a substitute, and to exist on as little as possible. This was one of the uncounted sacrifices of the war. The high prices of the last few years, though bad enough, bear no comparison. On November 29th, 1862, Governor Morton sent a communication to Senators and Representatives in Congress urging increased pay for the soldiers on the ground that the cost of living had vastly increased and the price of labor as well. He embodied in this a comparison of prices in August, 1861, and November 21st, 1862, showing an increased cost in percentage as follows: Brown muslins, 190; bleached muslins, 175; American prints, 95; blue checks, 100; hickory checks, 100; canton flannel, 150; drillings, 170; cassinetts, 100; jeans, 100; boots, 33; shoes, 56; brown sugar, 62; Rio coffee, 150; tea, 50; rice, 25; molasses, 40; flour, 44; salt, 180; meal, 75; fish, 33; potatoes, 130; candles, 50; wood, 100.

---

[1] The Journal's statement is broader than the evidence, but Rev. J. C. Fletcher gives his father as authority for the assertion that James McIlvain raised a patch of cotton, in 1821, on Pennsylvania street where the Second Presbyterian Church now stands. (News, April 12, 1879.) It was used for candle wicking.

"It will be entirely safe," said he, "to say that the cost of living on the most economical scale throughout the Northern States has increased at least 75 per cent. within the last fifteen months, and prices are still advancing. Thus $8.00 per month in August, 1861, would have been a better compensation and gone farther in maintaining a family than $13.00 per month in November, 1862. Soldiers are paid in treasury notes at par and as these notes have depreciated thirty per cent. as shown by the price of gold, their pay from this fact alone is substantially reduced to $9.00 per month." This appeal bore no fruit and the soldier's pay was unchanged. Think what penury it meant to thousands of families whose breadwinners earned so little, or perhaps were cut off entirely. We hear much of late years of the fortitude of the Southern people under privation, but it seems to be unknown or forgotten that distress was widely spread in the North, in spite of more favorable conditions.

The October election had been carried by the Democrats, who claimed to stand for constitutional liberty, the freedom of opinion, of speech and of the press, which had been trodden under foot. In reality they were opposed to the war. The vote was a surprise, showing a majority of 9391, with seven out of eleven Congressmen and both houses of the Legislature by good majorities. The Democrats claimed that the election here was unfair, and probably they were right, as any soldier who chose to could vote without question. The total vote of this State was 246,163, a decrease of 25,980 over 1860. Counting out the natural increase of 20,000, this showed a decrease of about 45,000. The Republicans claimed frauds in numerous counties and probably they were right, too, as there were extraordinary gains in some whose population had not increased, and many had gone

to the war.   Soldiers in the field were not entitled
to vote.   Only three counties increased Republican
majorities, two on account of Democratic splits, and
Marion, but fifty-seven counties gave a larger Democratic vote than in 1860.   Undoubtedly there was a reaction against the war; the repeated assertions of "abolition war" had been confirmed to many by the announcement of speedy emancipation.   Many people were not
educated to the point of seeing its necessity as a war
measure and were full of the old prejudices and dislike
of the negro and the "Black Republicans," who now
openly confessed to be hated abolitionists; they voted the
old way.   Even in the army, there was considerable of
this sentiment, and it took time to correct it.   It is likely,
however, that many who voted the ticket had no idea
that the party when once in power would proceed to the
lengths that it did.

I close the year with an anecdote of Lincoln that seems
to have been lost sight of: A gentleman, after pouring
out his vials of wrath upon a prominent officer, was surprised to hear the President quietly remark: "Now you
are just the man I have been looking for.   I want you to
give me your advice and tell me if you were in my place
and had learned all you've been telling and didn't believe
a word of it, what would you do?"

CHAPTER V.

THE BITTERNESS AND MAGNITUDE OF CONFLICT.

The war during 1863 was a gigantic struggle marked by great battles with varying fortunes. McClellan was succeeded after Antietam by Burnside, who lost the terrible battle of Fredericksburg in December. Grant's operations against Vicksburg that month were met by defeat, and Rosencrans's battle of Stone River was practically a drawn one. Hooker succeeded Burnside and was whipped at Chancellorsville in May. Meade succeeded him, and Lee broke for the North to be whipped back at Gettysburg in July. Rosencrans moved to Chattanooga and lost the battle of Chickamauga. In November the disaster was retrieved by Lookout Mountain and Mission Ridge. On the whole, the advantage was with the North, but Richmond's capture seemed as far off as ever. At home the war came nearer in a form of actual peril for a few days during the Morgan raid, days that were full of excitement and apprehension to the town.

The Legislature held its session during the winter and the majority tried to obstruct Governor Morton in every way that it could. Daily the opposition of that faction became more violent and pronounced, and while that is another story, it is well to know what the Sentinel said about President Lincoln's emancipation proclamation in January. "The policy of the party now in power is developed. It is the abolition of slavery. It is the subjugation of the slave States—the destruction of the white race, where slavery exists, by servile insurrections. It is to make one-half the country a howling wilderness and to elevate to the status of citizenship a worthless and improvident race. The two races cannot live upon terms of equality. The attempt will result in the extermination of one of them. The Administration has deliberately chosen to invite such a contest and aid the negroes in the destruction of the white race. The present condition of public affairs is partly attributable to the folly, fanaticism and imbecility of the party in power. The sectional difficulties of the country would have been amicably adjusted, but the Republican leaders refused all overtures to that end. They preferred war to peace—they chose war rather than union, and what is the result of their policy? An united South, willing to make any sacrifice, warring to secure their independence, and a divided North. * * * If this act of usurpation passes unrebuked, then we may bid farewell to constitutional liberty. The constitutional guarantees of personal rights and personal liberty will not be worth the parchment upon which they are written."

Notable incidents are as follows: Caleb B. Smith was appointed Judge of the United States District Court. Emerson lectured to a small audience, subject not given. Butternuts were worn as jewelry and caused numerous outbursts. Real estate went higher. W. C. Holmes paid $4,000 for the lot where Judge Martindale lives, 429 North Meridian street. A room on West Washington street, No. 9, where Bobbs-Merrill Company are, sold for $450 per foot, and the lot where Sommers's store is, 11-13 East Washington street, went at the same price to Robert Browning. The Farmers' Hotel, northeast corner of Illinois and Georgia streets, now the Stubbins Hotel, sold for $14,500 in specie, gold being worth 160. No. 15 West Washington street sold for $9050 to J. A. Heidlinger. In March gold dropped to 38 and for some time fluctuated between that and 58. There began to be much speculation in that article, with a wide range of prices. The sale of arms was forbidden. Dr. Bullard declined to meet Dr. J. F. Johnston, the dentist, in consultation because he was a Secessionist and a subscriber to the Sentinel. Crime was rife and liquor dealers were forbidden to sell to soldiers, but apparently did not obey. Laborers got $1.50 per day and carpenters and masons $2.50, and were scarce at that.

In two years the City Hospital, so called, though maintained by the Government, Dr. Kitchen in charge, had treated 6114 cases, 847 of which were prisoners of war, 277 of whom died. At the city election in May the Democrats withdrew thir ticket on the ground that the election would be unfair, and only fourteen Democratic votes were cast for councilmen in nine wards. Revenue stamps were sold at a discount of 2 per cent. on $50, 3 per cent. on $100 and 4 per cent. on $500 worth. A full company of negroes was enlisted for the 54th Massachusetts Regiment. In May the famous "Battle of Pogue's Run" occurred, and 1500 pistols were taken from delegates to a Democratic convention by soldiers who searched the outgoing trains, in addition to which many were thrown into Pogue's run, as the trains passed along it. W. S. Hubbard paid $10,626 for four acres of ground on North Meridian street, just above Eleventh street and running through to Illinois.

The first military execution took place on March 27th, Robert Gray being the victim. He was a Parke or Clay county school teacher who enlisted in the 71st, and a few days later was captured at Richmond, Kentucky. Thinking he could escape military service, he took the oath of allegiance to the Confederacy. General Carrington said he became a spy for them in Indiana, but the newspapers make no mention of that charge. He was convicted of treason and the sentence approved after several months' delay. The execution took place in the rear of Burnside Barracks, between Eighteenth and Nineteenth streets. He was quite cool, and made a confession that he had acted wrongly through a desire to get out of the service.

On July 7th the town turned itself loose in rejoicing over Vicksburg and Gettysburg. There were fireworks, bonfires and speeches. The next day word came that Morgan had crossed the Ohio, heading for Indianapolis, and the scene shifted. His purpose was said to be the capture of the city, the release and arming of the rebel prisoners, the destruction of the railroads, and the bringing of the horrors of war to the State. The excitement was indescribable. The bells rang alarms and a great crowd gathered at the Bates House. Governor Morton read the dispatches and urged the people to fill up companies in every ward, meeting places being designated. The next morning Governor Morton issued a proclamation asking business houses to close at 3 p. m., and calling on every able-bodied citizen to bring whatever arms he had and muster. Almost instantly the City Regiment was organized with one or more companies from every ward to the number of twelve. Eight additional companies were also mustered in the city. Morgan moved more rapidly than the news about him and there was much ignorance and uncertainty. The City Regiment drilled on University Square, and the signaling for its assembling was the fire alarm bell. This rang several times but each time it was found the exigency was not great and the men were dismissed. The railroads and telegraph lines were taken possession of by the military and public use was excluded. Louisville sent $1,500,000 of specie north for safety, and the Indianapolis banks did the same with theirs. Morgan had crossed at Brandenburg, Kentucky, and moved north to Paoli, thence east through Salem and North Vernon, but his course was uncertain for several days during which time the armed populace of the State poured into Indianapolis to the extent of 60,000. By Monday, the 13th, more troops had arrived than could be used. All saloons were closed and business almost suspended. On Sunday afternoon the bell was sounded and in forty-five minutes all the troops in the city were in line. Five regiments slept in the State House yard that night. During this time many troops had been sent to the supposed field of action, but none came in contact with the enemy. None of the city companies left town, though twice they were marched to the trains and then ordered back. On the 14th it was announced with authority that Morgan had passed into Ohio and the raid was over so far as Indiana was concerned. Then came the natural revulsion of feeling and there was much joking over the events of the week; and, as usual, what was so threatening before was lightly spoken of. Even to this day some men will smile when they say they are veterans of the Morgan Raid, but no one who went through it would care to repeat the experience. An unusual accident took place on the 13th, when the 12th Michigan Battery, then located here, was ordered away. As it came dashing down Indiana avenue from the camp in the northwest part of the town, ammunition in a caisson exploded, killing three soldiers. a boy with two horses, and breaking all the glass within some distance. Disorder almost ceased during the excitement, and be it remembered the saloons were closed.

That month Kingan & Co. located here and began building a mammoth packing house and flour mill. Dwellings were reported scarce and not a single business room to be had. The list of income-tax payers for 1862 was published. Only two exceeded $10,000—Calvin

Fletcher and J. A. Crossland. In August gold fell to 26, and in September the first mention of a bathroom in a contemplated house was made. Agitation for street-cars began. The Crown Hill Cemetery corporation was organized and bought Martin Williams's fruit and nursery farm. Fish and game were abundant and a wild turkey weighing twenty-seven pounds was said to have been shot in the vicinity of Broad Ripple. The Young Men's Library Association was organized. On October 22, two thousand prisoners were in Camp Morton. Judge Roache bought the fine Bishop Ames residence on North Pennsylvania street, now No. 1029, with four acres of ground for $20,000. In May a day of fasting and prayer was proclaimed by the President, and on August 6 a day of thanksgiving for the recent victories. Both were well observed.

Prices continued to soar. At the first of the year the newspapers had advanced their price to 15 cents a week. Paper had risen from 8 and 9 cents to 16 cents per pound, besides which an excise tax was put on advertisements. The Journal had prospered with other business. It was crowded with advertising so much that it had to enlarge twice, and its circulation grew so that it had to buy a faster press twice, in three years. The Sentinel shared little of the prosperity, such was the antagonism to it. Before the war ceased the prices of both papers was 25 cents per week, or double the original. The Ladies' Fair in October netted $7000 from the raffling of various donated articles alone. Bishop Upfold, Episcopalian, condemned the use of flowers in churches, and declared that he would not visit or officiate in any church on Easter Sunday where a floral display was attempted.

The year 1864 opened with the cold New Year's day,

probably the coldest day on record the world over. The day before was warm and rainy, temperature above 60. By three o'clock the next morning it had dropped to 28 degrees by the then thermometers. A great social event, the house warming of John M. Lord's new residence on the southeast corner of North and Pennsylvania streets, took place on the 31st. Many of the guests were lightly clad, and it is a story to this day how they suffered in getting home. The suffering in the camps everywhere, north and south, was terrific, and many persons were frozen to death. Gold closed December 31st at 52 and reached 75 in April. Wheat in New York was worth from $1.44 to $1.61 and corn $1.30. The churches were reported as prospering. Protracted meetings were held in several, with some additions. A daily prayer meeting was maintained at the Soldiers' Home under the auspices of the Indianapolis Branch of the United States Christian Association. The Scottish Rite of Masons was established. Judge Caleb B. Smith died. Butchers began to agitate for stockyards.

Military funerals were quite common, and the circumstances of death were sometimes grievous beyond description. Adjutant Marshall Hayden was wounded at the attack on Vicksburg and captured in December, 1862. For months his parents lived in hope under the belief that he had been taken prisoner merely, when he had died in a few days. After that was known, his body could not be secured for months more, and in February he was buried here, having been dead thirteen months. The town was becoming used to horrors. Every day corpses were transported through; the express companies left them on the pavements over night, and the Union Depot authorities refused to allow them to remain there more than an hour. Death was so common as to cause little comment. A Pennsylvania officer stopped over here and was found dead on the street, murdered. His father came soon to investigate and after a few days went away with no success, but complaining that he got no sympathy or aid and that the people seemed so inured to murder and death that they were indifferent. This was an exaggeration, but there was some foundation for it.

In February a draft for 500,000 men was ordered. The portions of regiments that had veteranized or reenlisted for three years more began to return on furlough and were publicly received and feasted. The Chamber of Commerce, or Merchants' Exchange, was organized and gave daily market reports, an evidence of business progress. A great change was made in the theater. What was known as the pit or parquet, which was always occupied by men, was opened to ladies and called "orchestra chairs." These sold for fifty cents, except about fifty that brought seventy-five cents. The general admission was raised to fifty cents. Many of the leading stars performed and the houses were packed nightly. A great union meeting was held February 22d, with a parade of troops and speeches, Andrew Johnson of Tennessee being the star. Two arches were built on Washington street, one at Pennsylvania, the other at Illinois. Within these two squares there was a "scarlet fever" of flags. The Journal said the city never before "was so gallantly and profusely illustrated with our national colors." "At night," it goes on to say, "an illumination burst out along the streets that borrowed little splendor from the bonfires below. The Journal's office was also brilliantly alight, and was probably the finest sight that any single building made. From floor to roof and from the roof to the upper lights of the tower it glittered with a splendor that might have recalled to travelers in Europe the great illumination of St. Peter's. In the lower windows blazed every admissible row of candles, while along the Circle street and Meridian street sides with their profuseness of window service, lights flamed and sparkled upon rows of Union flags that glowed almost as brilliantly as during the day in their new radiance." "At one time there were six bonfires going on Washington street." This showed a proper self appreciation, but as the lights were candles and probably not more than sixteen could be placed in a window, the modern sceptic will scoff at the brilliancy and be reminded of "Little Pedlington."

The street railroad system was begun that spring on a charter given to some New York people, who associated some home people with them. The first line was built on Illinois street from the depot to Washington, thence to West, thence to the Military grounds, and opened on the first week of the State and Sanitary Fairs in October. It was finished that year on North Illinois street to St. Clair. On May 3d it was said that 1400 pieces of real estate had changed hands since January 1st. John Morris sold his lot on the southwest corner of Meridian and Georgia streets, 99x205 feet, for $200 per foot. The First Presbyterian Church bought 125 feet of the Daniel Yandes home, at Pennsylvania and New York streets for $22,000, and property across the street was valued at $80 per foot—now held at $1250 or $1500. The Second Presbyterian Church on the Circle was offered for $14,000. Joseph E. McDonald bought 32 feet on North Pennsylvania street next Wood & Foudray's livery stable for $375 per foot, and E. S. Alvord refused $30,000 for his house and lot on which the Newton Claypool block now stands. Forty thousand dollars was offered for the old Athenæum or Gymnasium building at the northwest corner of Meridian and Maryland streets. The First National Bank, opened in the December before, was the only incorporated one here except the Branch Bank of the State. Horse board was not less than $5.00 per week. The retail grocers combined to sell for cash only, as wholesalers had agreed to credit no one. The school enumeration was 11,907, a gain in one year of 5044. Baled hay was worth $29 per ton, and the government was paying $156 for horses. Marion county had thus far spent $120,900 for bounties and relief of soldiers. The Chamber of Commerce reported sales of goods in one year $15,298,000, manufactures $5,069,000, provisions $776,524, total business $23,026,524. It enumerated among the industries two woolen factories, one saw, one hub and spoke, two agricultural implement, several flouring mills, six foundries and machine shops, two harness and two cooper shops, one rolling-mill making 10,000 tons of rails, furniture factories, bakeries, confectioners, three railroad shops and packing houses. Elsewhere it was told that there were seven hundred liquor sellers in the city.

The City Regiment had maintained an organization since the Morgan Raid. In April it was believed that the coming summer would end the war and Governor Morton proposed that certain States should furnish 100,000 men for one hundred days who would guard the transportation lines and release that many seasoned troops for active operations at the front, which was adopted and a call made. On April 26 the City Regiment was called to meet that afternoon to decide whether it should tender its services for that period. Few appeared, however. An enthusiastic war meeting was held at Masonic Hall and every known influence to fill the call was brought to bear. Employers paid the salary of clerks who would go. Additional bounties were offered, young ladies volunteered to take the places of clerks while they were gone and in due time the regiment was filled, together with others from the State. Six and a half companies of the City Regiment were from Indianapolis, the remainder from adjoining counties. Probably this regiment was the best beloved of all that the town was interested in. The greatest pride and admiration was lavished on the 11th, for that was the first-born. Next to that probably came the 70th and then the 79th, though the 26th and 33d were highly esteemed. But the City, or 132d, was the youngest born, the Benjamin, and the town's affection was lavished on it. Many of its members were really boys and many were older men, who were prominent and gave up much in order to help in the emergency. It was raised, too, by hard work, and the zeal and enthusiasm of the war seemed to culminate in the effort. It could not vie with the others in point of service, for its life was short and its field narrow, but it did the work laid out for it, and who could do more? The Journal said that more people gathered to see it go than any other.

In May, with gold at 70, beef sirloin was worth 20 cents; veal 15 and 20, mutton 15, pork 12 and 15, eggs 18, chickens $3.00 and $3.25 per dozen, potatoes $1.50, butter 40 cents, canned tomatoes 25 cents, turnips 60 cents and wood $7.50 a cord—unheard of prices. On May 17th a meeting of ladies was held at Masonic Hall and addressed by Hon. Albert G. Porter, who asserted that the country was being ruined by buying for gold $500,000,000 worth of foreign products annually and reducing the value of greenbacks. A platform was adopted as follows: "To promote economy, to show our sympathy with the great hardships and sufferings of our brave soldiers and to aid the finances of the Government, we the undersigned ladies pledge ourselves not to purchase during the war any imported article of dress or house furnishing. We also pledge ourselves to lay aside during the war silk and other expensive dresses and mantillas, all laces, velvets and jewels, and appear as soon as practicable only in clothes of American manufacture." The merchants were not pleased with this action and although some 800 or 1000 signers were procured, exceptions began to be called for and the whole movement seems to have died "a-bornin'."

Gold soared that summer, getting way over 200, where it stayed until the fall elections and victories caused a reduction below that figure. Its highest price as noted here was 280. The University Square was improved by a public subscription of $2100. The first street-car arrived in August "with cushioned seats affording ample room for sixteen passengers." A Sanitary fair was projected and later held successfully in conjunction with the State Fair. On June 1st Crown Hill Cemetery was dedicated, Judge Albert S. White being the orator. The first interment took place on the second—Mrs. Lucy Ann Seaton, of Paducah, Kentucky.

As anticipated, there was fearful fighting all along the line with Union gains. Politics warmed up, and just before the October election came the sensational and effective expose of the Sons of Liberty or Knights of the Golden Circle that had much to do with Democratic defeat, but which can not be described here, though an interesting chapter in city history. On the 18th of October the Sentinel prophesied as follows: "If Mr. Lincoln is reelected the man is not now living who will see peace and prosperity in the Union. It is certain that future generations will never see that result if the radical policy prevails. It is hopeless of good." Within six months it welcomed the advent of peace. The theater that fall introduced reserved seats, to be held until the end of the first act. Bandmann, Laura Keene, Lawrence Barrett and others played. A tabernacle for union meetings was built on the Washington street front of the Courthouse square. It was afterward turned into an amusement hall and was not torn down until 1866. The assessments for the income tax were published officially in order to encourage informers. Bounty jumpers were paraded through the streets tied by ropes and preceded by a huge negro ringing a bell, and then sent to punishment. Live hogs were worth 14 cents. An era of oil speculation began that lasted a year or two and cost much money. Numerous companies were formed to bore for oil in Ohio, Indiana, West Virginia and Kentucky. D. M. Boyd sold twenty-one feet on the east side of Meridian just below Maryland street to Murphy and Holliday for $347 per foot. Up to January 31st there had been 1307 rebel prisoners buried in Greenlawn Cemetery.

The year should not close without reporting this from the Journal, though occurring in August. It was written in the style of Berry Sulgrove that pervaded the Journal, though scarcely by him. Colonel James Blake's old bay horse and low-seated old rockaway had been stolen; after recounting the incident it then says: "The miscreant who would steal Colonel Blake's buggy from the Circle fence while the Colonel is presiding over a Union meeting, would sneak into heaven and steal the supper of the Angel Gabriel." About New Years it was reported that some friends had presented the good old man with a new vehicle.

The New Year 1865 opened with confident expectation that the war would soon end. Another draft was
ordered and many citizens still living were among the
chosen, but by great effort and expenditure of money
the quota was filled. The last regiment, including the
156th, a half regiment, were raised for one year. The
Journal declared that "Rebel prayers were a mockery
to the Almighty." The Governor's mansion was sold
for $42,500. The era of combination among grocers, ice
dealers, etc., began. An opera house and Masonic Tem-
ple were projected; also waterworks, with a stand-pipe
on Shortridge High School site—said to be the highest
point in the city. Grant moved to the finish. Richmond fell on April 3d. Lee surrendered on the 9th.
The news was received at 11 p. m., but the town rose
and, as the expression was, "whooped it up" all night.
"Indianapolis never before was so thoroughly demented,"
said the Journal. Gold dropped from 191 to 144. Governor Morton appointed the 20th as a day of thanksgiv-
ing, but changed it to "a day of mourning, humiliation
and prayer," when on the 15th news came of the assas-
sination of President Lincoln. That day is described
as "the most exciting one ever known in Indianapolis."
The whole town was in mourning garb and all business
suspended. Even the sun refused to shine. But time
forbids the recital of that awful and never-to-be-for-
gotten experience, followed by the protracted mourning
and the funeral march from Washington to Springfield,
during which the body of the martyred President rested
in the State House for eighteen hours of the gloomiest
Sunday ever known, and was viewed by thousands of
weeping mourners. That is a story to itself. It was the
last of the five greatest days of the struggle: Lincoln's
visit, the day Sumter fell, the opening of the Morgan

Raid, the fall of Richmond and this one. May their like never be seen again.

The incidents of the closing up must be passed over lightly. Troops were soon discharged and sent home. All were publicly welcomed as they deserved, and, while most came within a few months, it was more than a year before the last Indiana soldiers were discharged. The great armies vanished into private life as easily as they came from it, and all apprehensions of trouble were groundless.

Indianapolis kept on her course of material progress that year. Prices continued high, building increased, rents were at unheard of figures, $5000 being paid for one single room by the First National Bank the southeast corner of Washington and Meridian streets. More banks and insurance companies were organized, railroads were projected, a steamboat built on the river, real estate boomed, and expansion was everywhere. In July there were thirty-four wholesale houses running, with five more to open up as soon as buildings could be finished. The largest income-tax payers were: Calvin Fletcher, $31,043; S. A. Fletcher, $30,960; Thomas H. Sharpe, $27,847, and Oliver Tousey, $28,530. Washington street property between Meridian and Illinois streets sold at $800 per foot. The lot at the southeast corner of Meridian and Maryland, 25x130, was sold for $400 per foot. In February, 1909, with a building on it, it brought $60,000. Grant and Sherman visited the city and had rousing receptions. Baseball was started. The last rebel left Camp Morton June 12th. A public bathhouse was erected. On July 25th, Sherman's wagon train, twenty-eight miles long, en route from Washington to Louisville, passed through, and that fall witnessed the closing of the Soldiers' Home, the Ladies' Home and all the camps.

A crop of oats was cut from University Square, probably the only cereal ever raised there, having been sown as a cover for getting grass established there. A government military hospital was ordered, and the selection of a site developed great hostility from every locality suggested, but the close of the war caused the abandonment of the proposition and gave widespread relief. In November the Blake orchard, a tract lying between Tennessee and Mississippi streets, extending from the alley below Walnut to St. Clair street, was sold at auction, realizing an average price of $70 per foot, and attracting "the biggest crowd ever at a real estate sale in Indianapolis."

The cost of the war to the town may be conceived by a brief statement of some of the taxation. For the year ending June 30th, 1865, the internal revenue tax on Marion county was $517,742, the income tax $161,861 on a total of $2,618,007. In the year ending May 12th the city's income was $597,831, of which only about $170,000 was from taxes, licenses and fines, the rest was from loans and contributions to the draft fund. The expenses were $854,391, a deficit of $301,707, and $775,000 went for the war fund. The estimated expenses for the next year were $137,000. In addition to this the county had also incurred a war debt. The contribution of life can not be estimated, but it was large, many hundreds. Possibly as many as four thousand men from this town went into the army first and last, and many never returned.

The war was over, but its grim era closed upon a new Indianapolis. The quiet town with its simple life was gone forever and in its place was the bustling city with new ideas, new aspirations, new ways. Much more than half the population were new-comers. As it had changed materially, it had changed in other respects. Its life was different. The war had brought sorrow to many households and broken up many. In four ordinary years there are likely to be many changes, but how much more in those four years of awful havoc and heart-breaking experience. Old friendships and social relations had been severed by death and by estrangement through differing opinions. The alteration in circumstances made a difference, for many large fortunes had been made and many families had been impoverished or had gained nothing. There was more luxurious living and ostentation. The inevitable demoralization of war had to be reckoned with, and both morality and religion were affected. Hundreds of young men had become addicted to intemperance and the general moral tone had been lowered. Extravagance had increased in many things and was driving out the former simplicity. Change was over all.

"The old order changeth." That is the rule of life. Without the war Indianapolis would have changed at some time, but it would have taken a generation for it instead of being hammered out in the white heat of the four years' conflict, and the slow transformation, almost imperceptible, would have been natural. But with all the changes something, yes, much, was left. The impress of the early settlers could not be effaced. The influences that made for civic righteousness, for public spirit, for education, for cleanly living, for kindliness, for general well being and progress, were not destroyed, and they abide with us yet. However feeble their force has seemed at times, at others it has burst out in unrestrained volume, showing that it had not lost its power, and that while material environment may alter, the spirit persists.

INDIANAPOLIS, MARCH, 1909.

INDEX

GENERAL INDEX

INDEX OF NAMES

www.ingramcontent.com/pod-product-compliance
Lightning Source LLC
Chambersburg PA
CBHW021930110726
47901CB00003B/788